ASH WEDNESDAY

A NOVEL

J.R. MABRY

APOCRYPHILE
PRESS

Apocryphile Press
PO Box 255
Hannacroix, NY 12087
www.apocryphilepress.com

Please join our mailing list at
www.apocryphilepress.com/free
We'll keep you up-to-date on all our new releases,
and we'll also send you a FREE BOOK.
Visit us today!

ALSO BY J.R. MABRY

CONTENTS

For Nancy McKay
My friend and colleague of many years.
You inspire me.

PROLOGUE

J ulie Barkley yearned for a good, satisfying occult ritual. She tapped her foot impatiently and glanced at the barn. Light blazed from between the rustic slats that composed its walls, and the sound of merriment carried over the droning chirp of insects and frogs. "Clive, will you hurry it up? We're going to miss the lesser banishing ritual."

Clive Foster had taken off one hiking boot and was feeling around in it with his hand.

"What the fuck are you doing?" Julie asked him. She tugged her jean jacket closed at her throat against the chill as the wind whipped at her red, shoulder-length hair.

"I've got a rock in my shoe."

"Deal with it inside!"

Clive ignored her and pressed his hand even further into the shoe. He looked troubled.

"Can't find the rock?"

"No."

"Just shake it and come on."

Clive hit the bottom of the shoe with his left hand, knocking it out of his grip. It fell to the ground. Julie rolled her eyes. "You have fun with your shoe. I'm going to go in before they lock the doors."

"They lock the doors?" Clive sounded worried.

"Sometimes. That's up to the lodge master."

"Jeez." Clive hastily forced his foot into his shoe, but apparently it wouldn't drop all the way down, as he began to limp with an air of resigned desperation toward the barn.

"If you were just two degrees more annoying, I wouldn't be able to put up with you," Julie said, falling into step beside him. She resisted the urge to limp in sympathy.

They reached the barn just as the hubbub began to quiet. Julie pounded on the door, and a second later, it opened just a crack. One bleary eye stared out at them. "Password?"

"Therion's tits," Julie said.

"93," the owner of the eye said, pulling the door open. "You just made it in under the wire." Julie and Clive scampered inside, and the warden shut the barn door behind them.

"Wow," Julie said. The barn had been decked out like a kabuki theater, with Japanese lanterns hanging from ropes looped over the beams of the old barn. Umbrellas bearing enormous kanji characters were placed at either side of the risers that composed a makeshift stage. The room was filled with revelers, most cradling large red plastic cups that no doubt contained beer, wine, or spirits. Many of the people were wearing kimonos. Julie frowned that she hadn't gotten the memo on the theme of this particular rite. *Not that I have a kimono,* she thought. *Still, it would have been nice to know.*

The lights went out and the rite began. A male figure dressed in an ornate kimono strode onstage toward a Japanese lantern made of blue paper. He turned it off, blanketing the entire barn in darkness. Julie heard the rustle of many feet then, and red paper lanterns were lit and carried onto the stage by others in traditional Japanese dress. A small choir began to chant as the red lamps were carried into a tented section that glowed from within. A seated figure Julie hadn't noticed before lit another blue lamp, then stood, holding a spear. He pounded the spear on the floor with a resounding crack. Then he did it again, and a third time. "Procul, O procul este profani!" His voice carried throughout the barn. Everyone seemed to be holding their breaths. The speaker then brandished his spear and began the banishing ritual of the pentagram.

Julie was not a Thelemite, but she knew Thelemites. Dog Star Oasis was the largest OTO community in California's Central Valley, and she rarely missed an opportunity to see one of the Rites of Eleusis. But she knew the entire population of Dog Star would only account for the actors in the rite. The audience was largely composed of friends from the wider occult community. Some had probably travelled a hundred miles or more to be there.

She was a Wiccan herself. Once upon a time she'd been part of a coven, but that was long ago, in college. Now she was a barely observant solitary practitioner. She looked over at Clive, and his mouth hung open in a way that made him look stupid. She reached up and, placing her crooked index finger beneath his chin, raised it until his mouth closed. He appeared not to notice.

Then, beyond Clive, she saw another face she recognized. "Oy," she said out loud. She shook her head, "What is Jake doing here?" she whispered.

"What?" Clive asked.

Using his chin again, she moved his head to his right until he was staring straight at Jake Hessup. "What is *he* doing here?" she asked again.

Clive's eyes were wide as he turned back to meet Julie's gaze. "What *is* he doing here?" he whispered.

"Nothing good," Julie said.

A burly man who looked like a biker shushed her. She decided the better part of valor would be to heed that instruction. She tried to turn her attention back to the play.

The Mother of Heaven had been invoked, and Julie had to keep herself from giggling at the sight of her. She was being played by a young woman who was not conventionally attractive, her hair piled on top of her head in a lopsided beehive pierced by numerous chopsticks. Her kimono was open, revealing almost impossibly large breasts with areolae the size of a child's hand. Julie had a hard time not staring at them and wondered what it would be like to suckle them. Her jeans began to grow warm, and it suddenly didn't matter that the girl wasn't all that pretty.

"Be it unto your desire!" the Mother of Heaven intoned. Then she picked up a ukulele and began to play "Wake Up, Little Susie" by the Everly Brothers, her breasts bouncing to the beat. A cheer erupted from the crowd; several people raised their cups of beer.

Typical Rite of Eleusis, Julie thought, and smiled, thoroughly enjoying the spectacle. But an ominous feeling intruded on her merriment, and every few moments she found herself glancing over at Jake. *This is not good*, she thought. He wasn't in uniform, thank the goddess, and he was wearing a hoodie that partially covered his wild brown hair that usually stuck out at odd angles—but she knew it was him. She leaned over and whispered to Clive, "I'll be right back." Then she began to edge her way through the crowd toward her partner.

As she approached, she saw his eyes widen in what must have been horrified disbelief at the sight of her. "Julie, what—? What the hell are you doing here?" he stammered.

He was much taller than she, so she frowned up at him. "I was about to ask you the same question."

Someone shushed them. "C'mon," she said, tugging at his sleeve. Together they wound their way through the crowd, out the door of the barn, and into the frigid late winter air.

She could still hear the merriment over the sound of the croaking wildlife. She turned to face Jake and placed her hands on her hips. The top of her red head only came up to his chest, but he took a step back anyway. "What the hell are you doing here, Jake?"

"I asked first," he said. "Are you..." he leaned in, "undercover?"

"What the fuck?" Her eyebrows bunched in disbelief. "Are you high?"

"Certainly not!" His head jerked back. "Just...answer the question, deputy."

"Look who's giving orders, *deputy*." She spat and then turned her face back to him. "I outrank you, and I have seniority."

"It's going to be like that?" he asked.

"Apparently it is," she said.

"No." He crossed his arms and pointed his chin at the moon. "I'm not telling you why I'm here until you tell me why you're here."

Julie rolled her eyes. "All right. All *right*. I'm here because I live in a podunk town with limited live entertainment opportunities. I'm here because, as a solitary witch, I am part of the wider Central Valley occult community. We don't agree on *anything*—we especially don't agree with Thelemites—but that doesn't matter. They're friends and they were gracious enough to invite us. And the Rites are a hoot! Now…why are *you* here?"

"I'm undercover," he said, his voice lowered as if someone might be listening.

"You think so? Dude, you scream 'cop.' How did you even get in there?"

"Uh…" he rubbed at his neck. "I flashed my badge."

"Oh…*good* undercover. You also could have done a little homework that also works." She squinted at him. "And just why are you so ineptly 'undercover'? Who are you spying on, and why?"

"They're Satanists!" Jake whispered.

"What? Who are Satanists?" Julie shook her head in disbelief.

Jake pointed to the barn.

"The *barn* is a Satanist? How would you be able to tell?"

"The people in there," Jake said. She could see color rising in his face, even in the moonlight. "They're all Satanists."

"Uh…okay, I will grant you that there *are* Satanists in there. Exactly two, Arnold and Tony. They're sick fucks and losers besides. They're also harmless. Arnold is wearing the Baphomet t-shirt and the party hat. Tony is staggering drunk."

"What about all the rest of them?" Jake looked like he was about to burst a neck vein.

"The rest of them are not Satanists. Jesus Christ, Jake, where did you get that idea? Look, do you want to know who is in there? I can tell you." She raised one index finger. "The members of Dog Star Oasis—they're the ones on stage. They're Thelemites."

"What's that?"

"Do you even know the meaning of the word 'homework'?" She clucked her tongue at him. "They're members of the religion started by Aleister Crowley—"

"Who is that?"

"Seriously? Jake, I—" She was at a complete loss for words. She closed her eyes and counted to ten. Then she opened them and said, "They are ceremonial magickians. They're harmless…mostly."

Jake's frown became more grave. "Magicians? Like, pulling a rabbit out of a hat?"

"No, you clod-hopping idiot. I—" She put a firm hand on his arm. "Jake, I'm sorry I said that. I like you and I respect you. You're a good cop. You just…you don't belong here."

"I heard there were a bunch of Satanists doing an occult ritual," he said. "I figured they might be, you know, sacrificing babies or something, and I thought that, you know, if I *stopped* them, then Thom—"

"Then Thom might say, 'Good job, Jake'?"

"Uh…yeah."

"And maybe give you a little bit more responsibility?"

"Yeah."

"Jake. I am your crime-fighting partner. I have your back. You believe that, don't you?"

"Sure, but—"

"Do you trust me, Jake? Do you trust me with your life? Because when we hit those streets again tomorrow, I gotta know that you trust me."

"Of course I trust you."

"Okay, then trust me now. There's nothing nefarious going on in there. It's just…a lot of spooky good fun."

"It's weird," Jake said. "I thought they'd be sacrificing babies."

"It *is* weird," Julie admitted. "Weird is kind of the point."

"I didn't expect it to be silly," Jake said.

"Well, silliness is not the point, but irreverence is," Julie explained.

"I don't understand what they're doing," Jake admitted.

"Appreciating the Rites requires an enormous learning curve. It is highly specialized geekery."

"Do you get it?"

"I do."

"And you...*like* this?"

"It will be a lot more fun when I get three shots of whiskey in me," Julie confessed.

"Are these...your people?" Jake asked. "Because they're weird people."

"I'm a solitary witch," Julie explained. "No people are my people. But I'm friendly with these people."

"Are they *good* people?" Jake asked. "Because my mama told me I should only associate with good people."

"If I've learned one thing from my mother, Jake, it's that there *are* no good people. There are only people in various stages of being fucked up. Some less, some more."

"And which are you?"

"I'm medium. Medium fucked up."

"And them?" Jake pointed to the barn.

"All over the map, just like any other gathering of humans."

"I feel like an idiot," Jake said.

"You'd have felt like more of an idiot if you'd taken your service revolver out in the middle of the ritual and tried to arrest everyone in there as a group. Did you notice the bikers? Did you think they were just going to line up and wait for you to put plastic ties on their wrists?"

"I didn't think that far ahead," Jake confessed.

"Well, if you want to get on Thom's good side...you better start."

For a few moments they stood together in the cold moonlight. Julie shivered.

"What's it about?" Jake asked.

"What's what about?" Julie asked.

"That...the play, or ritual or whatever."

"Oh...it's the Rite of Saturn. It's about the great riddle of the universe."

"And what is that? The riddle of the universe?"

"Death," Julie answered. "They go looking for God, but only find a little pile of dust."

"That's...depressing," Jake said.

"Oh, that's not the end. The Master of the Temple is going to shout, 'O melancholy brothers, dark, dark, dark!' and then he commits suicide."

"Not really," Jake's eyes grew wide and his hand went to his service revolver.

Julie reached out and touched his hand. "No, cowboy. Not really. Just...settle."

"That's horrible," Jake said.

"It's...a play. It explores our darkest fears. It's art."

"I guess I don't really *get* art," Jake confessed.

"There's art and then there's art. I think you're the kind of guy who appreciates a good picture of dogs playing cards," Julie said.

Jake smiled. "I *love* that painting."

"See? Different strokes." She reached up and touched his cheek. "Go home, cowboy. This is no place for someone as...well, unbroken as you are."

Jake looked uncertain. "What are you going to do?"

Julie was already walking back toward the barn. "I'm going to drink whiskey and stare at flopping tits. See you in the morning."

Pastor Peg shut the door behind her and hung up her coat with a sigh. She was a short woman, and while she had been slim most of her life, her hips had begun to widen in recent years. Her hair, jet black in her youth, had been salt-and-pepper for some time. As she neared sixty, the salt was beginning to win out. She kept it on the short side, so as to have one less thing to fuss with.

The stained glass windows of her office were dark, keeping out the cold but grudgingly withholding the inspiration and joy they symbolized so gloriously during the day. *They look like my soul,* Peg thought, and shuddered.

It isn't as bad as that, another voice in her head insisted. A brief and silent argument ensued, which was brought to an abrupt end when Peg cried, "Enough!" Then she felt silly speaking to the empty room.

She was about to go through the weird, narrow hallway that led to her parsonage—tea beckoned—but she remembered she'd not seen the mail. She sighed and went back to the door. There, on the floor, was a pile of envelopes and garish grocery store ads the size of newspaper pages. She tossed the junk mail without looking at it and sorted quickly through the letters. Two were utility bills, one was an offer to buy her house for cash—what would she get for a plain meetinghouse sanctuary with water stains on the walls?—and one was from her oncologist.

"Oh, boy," she said. He'd told her to expect it. The test results were on the way. He'd told her the gist of it, and it hadn't been good. Six months. But it had also seemed somehow unreal, like gossip or the gray mist that covered the cornfields in the early morning. But this letter was real. It was solid. It was heavy in her hand.

She wondered if she should call Ted. She should. She would. He would want to know. But she also knew that he was a distraction. She really needed to call Julie.

She made her way over to her desk and, leaning over it, snatched up the letter opener and cut along the top of the envelope. A sheaf of very official-looking papers greeted her. There was a brief cover letter from her doctor—pro forma stuff. But underneath were the real test results. Her hands shook as she tried to interpret each page.

She suddenly felt weak and light-headed. She pulled her chair out and sat heavily. The chair wheezed its complaint. She ignored it.

In her fifty-nine years, she had seen most things that life had on offer—some of them good and wholesome, but a good deal otherwise. It had been a long and circuitous path that had led her to ministry. She had grown to love the cyclic regularity of the church year—Advent, Christmas, Epiphanytide, Lent, and then the long green stretch until the feast of Christ the King. She would see only one more Lent, then —and only one more Easter until her own.

"Oh, Jesus," she said. It had become Real. The shekel had dropped. She let the papers fall to her desk and grabbed a tissue. She held it to her eyes and squeezed them shut.

In her mind's eye, she saw Jesus standing behind her, rubbing her shoulders, kissing her neck. She leaned into him and a sob escaped her lips. Jesus shushed her and held her close, her back to his chest now, his arms pressing her breasts flat against her body. She concentrated on the heat of his breath in her ear until the moment passed. She opened her eyes and seemed to be alone again. She sighed.

"You are a fickle lover, Lord," she said out loud. But her heart knew it wasn't true.

A voice in her head that sounded suspiciously like Ted's chided her. *You need to call Julie. She has a right to know.*

The voice was right. It usually was, damn its squamous hide. She shook her head at the notion that the voice had a hide. *I am going batshit crazy,* she thought.

She picked up the receiver of the landline. She didn't often use it anymore. It seemed a relic of a bygone time. *Just like me,* she thought. Her finger moved to the keypad in the phone's base, but she stopped. She didn't often call Julie—Julie didn't like it when she called—but when she did call, it was on her cell phone. She felt suddenly sad that she didn't know Julie's phone number by heart. *How many numbers do I know by heart anymore?* she wondered. She knew her own. She knew the number she'd had thirty years ago in Berkeley when she had shared a walkup with two other hookers. She remembered the number of her ex-husband, long dead now of the AIDS he'd acquired in prison.

And that was about it. She sighed and fished her cell phone out of the pocket of her sweater.

She called up Julie's number and pressed the big green button.

"This is Deputy Julie Barkley. If you have an emergency, call 911. If you don't have an emergency, leave a message. Boo-ya." There was a beep.

Peg opened her mouth, but nothing came out. The seconds ticked away, and she knew somewhere, somehow, a computer was capturing the deafening silence that filled the room. As quick as lightning, she rehearsed several possible openings. *Julie, this is your mom. Call me. Julie, I need to talk with you. Can you give me a call when you get a chance? Julie, something important has happened. We need to talk.*

There was another beep, and suddenly it was too late. The screen shifted back to a photo of a stained glass window depicting St. Raphael she'd taken in Mexico on the last vacation she'd had…and the last she would ever have, she realized.

She threw the phone on top of the papers. *I'll tell her tomorrow,* she resolved. What more could she do? Julie would not welcome her banging on her door. She seemed ashamed of her pastor mom even under the best of circumstances. And she'd probably interrupt her doing…whatever lesbians do, she supposed. She had long ago relinquished any conscious judgment about her daughter's sexuality. Intellectually, she was in favor of Julie embracing her true identity. But there was an ancient lizard part of her brain that still recoiled at the thought of it. Peg had overcompensated by embracing Julie's queerness with enthusiastic extroversion—which had only served to irritate her daughter more.

She sighed, feeling impossibly sad. She also felt momentarily disoriented. What was there for her now? Oh, yes. Tea. There was tea.

Julie paused just inside the barn to let her eyes adjust. On stage, the Master of the Temple made large, swooping, overdramatic flourishes with the long sleeves of his kimono as he shouted, "There was no crackling in the dry leaves! There was no heart in the black lamb! The sacred python was found dead!" He was a squat, stout man with flaming red hair and an English accent that sounded more affected than real.

"You go, dude," Julie whispered under her breath. "Give it to them straight."

She looked around for Clive but didn't see him in the place they'd been standing. Her brows knit as she searched. She'd like to think that Clive could take care of himself in a friendly crowd such as this…but she knew better. *Clive could turn a paper cut into an international incident,* she thought. She'd known him since high school, and they'd been chummy over the years. But while Julie had moved on in her life, had made something of herself, Clive was still stuck in a perpetual state of late adolescence. She worried about him at the best of times. She worried about him now.

Her training kicked in, and she decided to start at her left and do a sweep of the barn, arcing around the stage to her right. *Deosil,* her witch training said—the theological term for clockwise. It was the direction of binding. She hesitated. *Should I be doing this search widdershins instead?* she wondered. Widdershins was the theological term for counterclockwise, the direction of unbinding. She quickly discerned— was finding Clive a binding or an unbinding activity? *I'm overthinking this,* she told herself. *Trust your instincts. Deosil.* As she walked, her thoughts caught up with her. Of course, finding Clive was an unbinding activity—it was an act of unveiling his location, an act of revelation, it was apocryphilic.

Telling herself to focus, she scanned the crowd. She looked in the corners and against the walls, where wallflowers like Clive tended to gravitate. But she did not see him.

"Alas! There is no god!" The Master of the Temple wailed on stage. All of his kimonoed attendants threw themselves into exaggerated fits of mourning, keening and falling over each other in dramatic swoons.

A voice in Julie's head said, *You're missing the show. Fuck Clive. Grab yourself a beer and relax.* She was sympathetic to this voice. It was a reasonable voice. But it was not the only voice, nor the loudest. She continued her scan. She picked her way through the crowd, aware that she was annoying people, yet she could not stop. She felt protective of Clive in a way that she did not fully comprehend. It was a compulsion, she knew.

She saw lots of folks she recognized. Some of them saw her and waved. She forced a smile and waved back. She even saw a couple of old friends from college—Sandra, Lorraine, and draped over the arm of a tattooed amazon, her old friend Priscilla Niles. She acknowledged them all as she passed, and hoped she'd get a chance to catch up after the rite.

Renewed motion on the stage caught her attention again. As she remembered the rite, the Mother of Heaven was supposed to be back behind the temple veil at this point in the play, but there she was, tits akimbo, playing another song on her ukulele while the Specter of Death rode a unicycle. The crowd was electric, cheering them on, erupting into laughter when the Specter of Death fell on his head.

As religious rituals went, she far preferred these rites to the fusty old services her mother presided over. To be fair, she'd never darkened the door of one of her mother's churches, and didn't intend to. And if she were honest, she had to admit that she found the sabbats of most covens to be drearily rote and empty of authentic feeling. She told herself it was one of the reasons she was a solitary practitioner, but a niggling voice in her head countered that it was because she was a cynical misanthrope. *So be it,* she thought. *The two are not mutually exclusive.*

As she approached the makeshift bar in the back corner of the barn, the hair on her arms bristled. The bartender was not tending to the long line of people waiting impatiently. His back was turned, watching something behind him, his arms hanging helplessly by his sides.

Instinctively, her right hand reached for her service revolver at her belt. But it wasn't there. *Idiot. You're off duty,* she reminded herself. Reaching under her jean jacket, her hand went to her shoulder holster and unbuttoned the catch enabling her to draw her Rossi 352 at a moment's notice.

The bar was really a wooden door set up on two sawhorses, stained with spilled beer and who knew what else. A keg could be seen next to one of the sawhorses; the black snake of its tube was in the bartender's hand. A dozen bottles of wine—reds, whites, and rosés—were scattered over the door's surface. She ignored the glares and walked around the line, past the sawhorses, and stopped next to the bartender. Then she drew her weapon. She cocked it. Even with the ambient noise in the crowd, it was audible.

Stay calm, the voice in her head said as she studied the scene. She had found Clive. His nose was a bloody pulp, and one eye was nearly swollen shut. Arnold Koffer, one of the county's two self-identified Satanists, was sitting on Clive's chest, his balled fist raised in preparation for another blow. Next to him was Tony Boucher—the county's other Satanist—and two other friends that Julie recognized, although she couldn't quite place their names.

They saw her, though, and her gun. Their mischievous smiles melted into frowns of doubt, and then the grim pinch of panic. They caught Arnold's arm before he could do more damage and pointed behind him. She trained her pistol directly at his puffy face as he turned to look at her.

With her left hand she reached into her pocket and pulled out her wallet. She let it fall open to reveal her badge. "Inyo County Deputy Sheriff," she said, raising her voice above the din of the play and the crowd. "Do we have a problem here?"

Arnold's eyes went wide as he saw her gun, then narrowed into a sneer as he recognized her. This was the same fucker who had beat Clive up numerous times in high school, the same asshole who had tried to get into her pants after she had passed out drunk at a party in her senior year. Clive had saved her that night. It was her turn to return the favor.

"Barkley, how the hell are you?"

"Armed and highly skilled. How the hell are you? I'm guessing drunk, dumb as meat, and rancid as a bitch's anal sacks."

Arnold seemed disarmed by this assault, and he merely blinked in response. Laughter broke out behind Julie, however.

"Ooo, burn," one of his friends said to him.

"Shut the fuck up!" Arnold said to his friend.

"Now, Arnold, what I'm going to ask you to do isn't hard. I just want you to stand up and move away from Clive. That goes for your goon squad, too. Hands where I can see them."

Arnold put his hands in the air and rose slowly, not looking directly at Julie.

"Now move away," she prompted, keeping the muzzle of the Rossi trained directly on him. The attackers shuffled to her right, away from her friend. "Now turn around and put your hands on the wall, all of you."

Arnold and his two friends did. She looked at the bartender. If eyes could grin, his were. She appreciated his obvious admiration, but had no time to savor it. "This is a barn. Find me rope. Duct tape will do."

The bartender leaped into action. Replacing her wallet, Julie reached for her cell phone. "Siri, call Jake," she said. She didn't know if Siri would be able to comply, due to the ambient noise, but was relieved to hear her partner's surprised response.

"Julie?"

"You were right. We got some troublesome Satanists. I need three sets of cuffs and a shop for transport. I'm going to keep them in my sights 'til you get here, but don't fucking stop for doughnuts." She hung up and put the phone back in the pocket of her jeans.

"You okay?" she asked Clive.

Clive nodded, but it was clear he was not. His eye was completely swollen shut now and his nose was no longer in the center of his face. "What was that all about?" she asked him.

"They asked me what kind of magick I was doing," Clive said.

"Yeah? And what did you tell them?"

"I told them I was doing Cthulu magick." Clive reached up to touch his nose but recoiled at the pain.

"What the fuck, Clive?" Julie asked. "Why the fuck would you be messing around with that shit?"

Clive looked away from her as if rehearsing his answer, but didn't give one.

"*We* are going to *talk*," she said.

"That's dangerous shit," the person first in line for beer said.

Julie ignored him. "It also has the disadvantage of being fictional. What grimoire are you using, if I might ask?"

"The Simon *Necronomicon*," he admitted.

Hoots of derision erupted from everyone behind her. Julie grimaced. "Dude, that is sooo lame."

Clive seemed to shrink. A voice in her head told her not to kick a man while he was down. "Can you get up?"

"Uh...yeah," he said. But she wasn't at all sure he could. Yet he did. He was unsteady and listed to one side. Blood ran from his nose down to his navel. Suddenly Priscilla was at her elbow.

"Egad, Barkley, can't you stay out of trouble?"

"Not with these wannabe Setians around."

"There's no way the Temple of Set would admit those losers," Priscilla said. "They have standards. 'Fit companions for Set' these asshats are not."

"No argument here. Can you take Clive home and clean him up?"

"Yeah, sure."

"I owe you one," Julie said.

"Fuck that. Now you owe me two," Priscilla said. Julie watched as Priscilla helped Clive limp away.

Arnold began to turn around, but Julie leveled at kick at his kidneys. The side of his face hit the wall of the barn while the patrons behind her roared their approval. "You stay right where you are," Julie said. She ignored how heavy her pistol was becoming. "Or I swear to the goddess the Specter of Death is going to crush your head with his unicycle."

Clive Foster tried to pry his eye open, but winced from the pain. He thought about applying some fresh rubbing alcohol, but the last time he tried, he'd gotten some of it in his eye, and he didn't care to repeat that mistake.

"Fucking loser," he said to his reflection in the mirror. He was not yet thirty, but his cheeks had the sunken look of an old man. His hair was a matted, oily bird's nest fixed to his head at a drunken angle, and his one working eye was an ashen gray pool. He wondered when he had last smiled. He couldn't remember.

It wasn't that he was miserable because of getting beat up. He was miserable all the time. He thought about Julie coming to his rescue and winced again. He wanted her to love him, not pity him. He wanted to make love to her, to show her he was manful, powerful, desirable.

"You're just lame," he said.

And he knew none of that was likely to change. Julie liked girls. She always had. It wasn't personal. It wasn't a rejection of him, but it still felt that way. He didn't resent it, he just hoped that somehow, someday, he would change her mind. But his supply of hope was exhausted.

It occurred to him that the only way to get her attention now was to do something dramatic, something irrevocable, something fatal. It wouldn't mean that they'd end up together—that was a lost cause, and he knew it. But it might mean that she'd be sorry that she had not returned his love. And that felt…good.

He could think of lots of ways he might end his miserable life, but few of them seemed appealing. He sat down at his kitchen table, peered at a pad of yellow legal paper with his one openable eye, and drew up a list of possible methods. Then, one at a time, he imagined what each method would feel like.

He loved the quarry like no other place on earth—it was where his soul felt the most peaceful. But the idea of throwing himself on the rocks in its depths gave him vertigo. Poison seemed like a good option at first, but there were so many unknowns. Nobody tells you how much it might hurt, and he shuddered at the thought of it. Slitting his wrists in the bathtub just felt desperate. No, if he was going to go out, he wanted to do it with a little bit of flair, something a cut above how he had done…well, pretty much everything else in his life. After draining most of a bottle of rum, he had crossed every idea off his list but one.

"Death by magick," he said aloud. And he loved the sound of that. There was mystery in that. There was, perhaps, even some admiration to be had from it, at least from other magickians. And maybe, if he was lucky, from Julie.

He liked to think that he had some talent at magick. He had read voraciously, and he had done a good many magickal workings, but he had to admit to himself that he had always gotten pretty spotty results. Still, he could make this work. He was sure of it.

Killing himself by magickal means would still contain some unknowns, but he hadn't heard of anyone else ever having done it. Just that fact alone recommended it. But that left a lot of decisions yet to be made. Which magickal system would he use? What powers would he call upon? How, exactly, did he want the end to come?

Despite Julie's incredulity the night before, none of the godforms were as close to his heart as the great Cthulu. He didn't need her to remind him that the Great Old One was fictional. But it didn't seem to matter. He had performed all the rituals in the Simon *Necronomicon* —at least all that had been practicable. Nothing had happened, but he had felt the warm glow of communion between the god and himself. It was an unfamiliar feeling—intimacy across vast, harrowing distances. At its core, magick was about mysticism, but this was the first time he had actually felt it. *I will become food for the Great Old One*, he thought, and as he did so, he felt his shoulders relax. It was right and fitting. If he couldn't give himself to Julie, he would give himself to Cthulu.

Yet the Simon *Necronomicon* had no ritual that would summon the Old One to feast upon the flesh of a supplicant. Nor did the Hay *Necronomicon*, nor any of the grimoires promising acquaintance with the Lovecraftian deities. He had collected them all and tried them all. Most were frauds intended to cash in on gullible dabblers—he knew that, but it hadn't stopped him from trying them…just in case. Simon's collection was the best of the lot, but contained nothing that would help him achieve his end. He could simply summon one of the Old Ones and see what would happen…

What had once been a tendril of despair had grown into a thick vine, encircling his neck and threatening to choke him. He was tired. He laid his head on the table and simply allowed himself to stop. For one brief, blessed moment, all the voices in his head shouting about how he was seventeen kinds of shit somehow just shut the fuck up, and in the stillness, the space, the silence, the void, a symbol took shape.

He jerked upright, his sunken eye now suddenly quick, moving back and forth as he seized upon the image. He turned to a blank page on the legal pad and drew the image burning in his brain. A thousand questions shouted themselves, so many that he could not hear himself think. He closed his eyes and tried to find the quiet place again. Gradually the voices faded, as if he were walking away from them into an empty room. And there was another image. He copied it onto the page.

With a great effort of will, he continued to empty his mind of thought, evaluation, and inquiry. As he focused on silence, more images came into being. He recognized none of them. But to his great surprise, he understood them all. He copied each one as it appeared, taking note of the sequence.

At first he thought they were sigils, but the meanings that came with them did not square with any sigils he knew. He tried not to evaluate them, but only to keep an empty space within so that they would keep coming, but wisps of questions still blew through his brain. Were they an alphabet? No, the meanings did not support that either. *They're cryptograms*, he realized, before trying to banish the thought. They were like Chinese characters, older than alphabets, each containing a world of meaning bound to its symbolic form.

And he knew that was right.

He didn't know how long he copied them. He only knew that when he was done, he had filled most of the legal pad with symbols he had never seen before. Then, uncertain that he would be able to recall their meanings, he opened a Mead composition book and began to translate the whole of it into English. Looking at each of the pictograms he had transcribed, he was relieved to find that their meanings flashed into his mind as quickly as he could write them down. After an exhausting couple of hours, he finally set down his pen. His eyes stung. He was tired.

There was banging on the door. "Clive!"

He knew the voice. It was Julie. He shrank in his chair. He did not want her to see him, not like this. Not roiling in shame as he was, his hair matted and his skin reeking as powerfully as he knew it was. He let her pound and yell. "I know you're in there, Clive! Let me in!"

He wanted to let her in, badly. But she had rejected him, just like every other girl he had ever taken a shine to. He didn't know why she insisted on being a friend to him now. She owed him nothing. He opened his mouth to say, "Go away," but he stopped himself. It would only encourage her. Hell, she might shoot off the lock and come in anyway. It would be just like her.

So he kept quiet. Tearing the sheets from the legal pad, he arranged the pages so that all the symbols were visible. *"Mors in Manibus Nostris:* A Rite for the Reification of Death," he read. He didn't know how he could read it, but he could. Each of the symbols had lodged themselves in his brain and didn't seem to be going anywhere.

And it was a ritual. That was clear. He was relieved to see that it was not complex—unlike the Sacred Magick of Abramelin the Mage, this would not take weeks to perform, nor did it involve any ghastly bloodletting. It was simple, clean, and it seemed impossibly old. There were correspondences that did not seem at all intuitive to him, yet he understood even them. There was a structure to the ritual that defied logic, which seemed somehow fitting. But what surprised him most was the godform at the belly of the thing—not Cthulu, but Zushakon. Old Night, the Dark Silent One.

Very well, if Cthulu would not have him, if Yog-Sothoth would not hear him, he would tender his worship to the eldritch god of death. It seemed right, somehow. And he had been rejected enough to know that he ought to take love where he could get it.

PART ONE
THE WIND

Here life has death for neighbor,
And far from eye or ear
Wan waves and wet winds labour,
Weak ships and spirits steer;
They drive adrift, and whither
They wot not who make thither;
But no such winds blow hither,
And no such things grow here.

—*Algernon Charles Swinburne,*
"The Garden of Proserpine"

CHAPTER ONE

A rooster crowed, and as if in response, pink light broke out across Abel Nyland's cornfield. Mia paused at the window over the sink at the sight of it, winding a strand of her hair around her fingertip that was now just a bit too red.

"What?" Abel asked.

"The light," Mia said. "I know it comes every morning, but a part of me is always a little surprised."

Abel huffed. "What worries me is this wind whipping up. When there's wind, there's fire." He took a swig of his coffee and grimaced at the acid taste. Mia was a lovely woman and a good wife, but she couldn't make coffee worth shit. And she had a romantic streak to her that he didn't understand and that often put her at odds with common sense, as he understood it. Abel was not a man who understood beauty. He understood tractors and numbers and the fickleness of a six-inch plank.

Mia was always putting strange things in his food—spices he'd never heard of, and was reasonably certain she hadn't either. He suspected that she bought things at the grocery at random just to torment him, and he didn't understand why the woman couldn't simply let eggs be eggs.

"Abel?"

"Mmmm," he said, flipping over the previous day's paper. Today's paper wouldn't arrive for a couple hours. Abel didn't mind living a day behind the rest of the world. There was a strange comfort in knowing that the world had gotten used to whatever had happened and was still there. Thus, whatever had happened could not have been too bad.

Ginger Beer whined. Abel adjusted his glasses and looked down at her. As soon as he met her eye, her tail started thumping. Glancing up to make sure Mia was still looking elsewhere, Abel fed her a bit of strangely spiced egg from his own fork. The yellow lab scarfed it up noisily with no attempt at deception.

"Abel, what is that?"

"What? What is what?" Abel said, a bit too quickly.

"What is *that?*" she pointed out the window.

He groaned. She wanted him to get up and come to the window. He did not want to get up and go to the window. Yet he knew from previous experience that she was not going to leave him be until he did. Grumbling, he wiped the sour coffee from his mustache on the sleeve of his flannel shirt and rose with a groan. *Might as well get some fresh coffee while I'm up,* he thought, feeling every day of his sixty-seven years as he made his way to the window.

"What is it?" he asked, feeling a pang of Scandinavian guilt that he had just used three words where one would have sufficed.

"Look there, *gubben*, what is that?"

He squinted in the direction she was pointing. He saw the barn, but it looked as it always looked, just darker. So he looked to left of the barn, toward the first field. "I don't see nothing, *gumman.*"

"Open your eyes," she said. "I've looked out this window every morning for forty-five years. That shadow was not there yesterday."

Abel let out an exasperated sigh. Next, she was going to ask him to go out there. Thing was, he knew he would. He saw it all unspool before him, an inevitable progression that was going to take him away from his coffee, his day-old news, and his exotically spiced eggs long before God intended him to budge from his chair. "I'll get my coat," he sighed.

"I'm coming with you," she said.

"Suit yourself," he said, his voice ripe with resignation.

He snatched up his quilted hunting jacket. As soon as he did so, Ginger Beer barked and leaped up, tail wagging in anticipation. "Inside voice," Abel said to her.

He paused and waited for Mia to put on her coat. Then he had to wait for her to check the stove. Then he had to wait for her to trade her slippers for her boots. *I could have had another cup of coffee,* he grumbled inwardly, but he didn't dare say it aloud. Ginger Beer turned tight circles in excited anxiety.

Finally, Mia was ready. Abel snatched up a flashlight next to the door and undid the latch. He held it open for his wife and dog and then followed, the smells of coffee and bacon and dusty couches blown away by the crisp bite of the dawn breeze. His nostrils twitched as he took in the smell of wet earth, manure, and alfalfa, the most enticing scent known to humankind. Abel felt suddenly awake and blessed. The dark, quiet earth seemed charged with a divine power that every farmer worth his salt lived for. He knew some would call that a romantic notion, but in his heart he knew that it was simply the plain fact of it.

He descended the five steps at the end of the porch with an alacrity that surprised even him, then held a hand up to Mia as she approached the stairs. She took it, but as soon as she was down, she withdrew it and put it back in her pocket.

They walked toward the shadow as Ginger Beer ran ahead of them. Abel could see the shadow now, but he wasn't going to say so. He switched on the flashlight and illumined their path.

"Thy word is a lamp unto my feet," she said.

"It's a flashlight," he objected. This was the problem with romantic people. They were always inserting symbols and such that only got in the way of seeing things plain. Mia's fancy irritated him, but in his honest moments, he had to admit that it brought needed ornamentation to his life—like the delicate doilies she put under everything that rested on anything else, like the flower pattern she'd painted near the ceiling of the bathroom all the way around, like the goddam garam masala in his eggs, whatever that was.

They slowed as they neared the field. In a couple of months, the corn would be coming up—Abel's main crop. There shouldn't be anything in his field right now except meticulously plowed rows and writhing segmented worms, as God intended.

But there was something. Ginger Beer had noticed it too. Her ears flattened against her head as she alternated between sniffing and barking.

"Is that a car?" Mia asked. "I've seen these new boxy cars. Ugly things. It could be that."

"Looks more like a shed."

"Someone put a shed in our field in the middle of the night? Who would do that?"

Abel grunted. There was more light now, the pink drawing yellows and reds alongside it, and increasing its potency with every passing second. Abel still shone the flashlight ahead of them. They were a stone's throw away from the thing when he held out his arm to stop her.

Ginger Beer had halted about four feet from the thing and was barking continually. A frown clouded Abel's Scandinavian brow—an expression that was no stranger to his face, but not ordinarily this severe. "Stay here," he said to his wife. He stepped forward toward the thing and was relieved that she obeyed him. He was also a bit surprised, but he let the thought go as soon as it came.

He stopped again, about fifteen feet away from…whatever it was. The light was breaking in grand form over the sky now, bathing the few stratocumulus clouds with brilliant color. Ordinarily, he would no longer have needed the flashlight, but he kept it trained on the object, because he still had no idea what he was seeing.

"Ginger, be quiet! I can't hear myself think!" he shouted. The dog looked uncertain, but came to his side, whining as she kept pace with him. He began to circle the thing, moving to his left.

"Abel! What is it?" Mia called.

He didn't answer. He didn't know. It appeared to be a block of stone, rough but regular, an almost perfect cube. It looked like it might be pink in color, but Abel distrusted the light. Yet every moment the morning grew brighter, and he began to suspect it was the color of adobe brick.

"It looks like a block of...I don't know, not a rock, but..." he trailed off. As he and Ginger Beer continued to circle, he saw that the uniformity of the shape was changing.

He sensed motion behind him and glanced over his shoulder. Mia was no closer to the thing than she had been, but she was circumambulating now as well. He thought of telling her to stay still, but bit his tongue. She was a grown woman, after all. "Abel, are you scared?" she called out.

He didn't answer. He kept the flashlight trained on the object as he walked. He saw a concave opening in it. No, that wasn't quite right. There were huge sections missing from one side of it, jagged indentations, almost digging into the thing like the mouth of a cave. But if it was the mouth of a cave, there was something in that mouth.

Ginger Beer was sniffing furiously around the thing, keeping a distance of about two feet. The flashlight no longer had any effect, so Abel shut it off and slung it on his belt. Then he returned his attention to the object. Suddenly, Mia was beside him, and when she spoke it startled him.

"Abel, what is that?"

He didn't rebuke her. He felt her hand on his arm and he did not refuse it. A part of him was glad of it. He grasped her hand; holding it tightly, they advanced toward what Abel began to think of as "the cube."

Mia stopped and pulled him back. "That's a sculpture."

"What?"

"There's an opening there—"

"I see it."

"—and there's something in the opening."

"I see that too, *gumman*."

"But it's not moving."

"No."

They took another step toward it, then another. Abel began to suspect that she was right. As the light increased, he saw that there was the figure of a man carved into the block. But it was as if the sculpture was not finished, as the man's torso blended into the block at about belt level. Abel blinked. He could make out the details of the belt buckle, in fact, just before it became an amorphous expanse of stone or clay or whatever it was.

But this was not a sculpture of a man in repose. It was a man in pain. His fingers were extended, palms facing Abel, and his face distorted as if pressed against glass. But there was no glass. The man wore a flannel shirt over a t-shirt and a vest over both. More detail than that was hard to gauge, as everything was the same orange/pink color. The man's mouth was open in a silent cry—but whether it was supposed to be expressing agony or surprise, Abel could not tell.

"It's horrible," Mia said, clutching his arm so tight it had begun to tingle. He did not remove her hand, however. Instead, they stepped closer.

He didn't disagree with her assessment. It *was* horrible. It was also confusing. Was the man flying? His arms were spread wide, hands ready for impact with...something. His eyes were wide with what could only be terror.

Abel's own eyes widened. "I know that man."

"What?" Mia asked.

"I know *that man*," Abel repeated. He never repeated himself, not ever. "That there is Troy Swanson."

Peg rose from her seat by the stained glass in her office. Having finished her morning prayer, she tottered over to her desk to check her calendar for the day. *I should have checked it before I prayed,* she chastised herself. *That way I could have invited Jesus to join me for all the meetings I have lined up.* But she knew she had the Lord's ear anytime and didn't waste much energy berating herself over it.

Her shoulders slumped as she saw the first item, underscored in red. CALL JULIE. She sighed. She looked over the other commitments for the day—a visit to Emil Peters, now on oxygen for emphysema; then a quick car trip out to the nursing home in Coleman to visit Faye Garfield. She had dementia, and it was always a toss-up whether Faye would remember her or not. But whether she recognized her was not important. What was important was that Peg brought her, in the metonymous form of her own pastorly person, the presence of her church, the congregation that had held her and loved her and nurtured her for eighty-nine years. It was a sacramental act, and she was herself that sacrament. It didn't matter if Faye recognized it as such or not. It was so. And it was important.

Peg sighed. In the afternoon, she had an appointment to have her hair and nails done. She considered cancelling it and taking the time for a nap instead. *It doesn't bode well that you're daydreaming about your nap at seven in the morning,* she thought. She decided to keep the appointment.

"No use putting this off any further," she said aloud and fished her cell phone out of her pocket.

"Wullo," her daughter's sleepy voice responded after three rings.

"Good morning, sunshine," her mother said.

"God, mother, do you know what time it is?"

"Don't you have to be at work at eight?"

"Yeah, so? Let a girl sleep."

Peg blinked, not following her daughter's logic. When Peg was her age, she would have needed at least two hours to prepare for her day —showering, fixing her hair, applying makeup, eating breakfast. It suddenly occurred to her that her daughter had a very different relationship to her body. Could she really roll out of bed, put on her clothes, and rush out the door in fifteen minutes or less? It seemed implausible.

"Honey, I have something to talk to you about. It's important."

"Are you dying?" her daughter asked.

The question startled her. Peg opened her mouth to say, "Yes," but thought better of it. "Not...right now," she said finally.

"Then it can wait." The phone went dead.

Peg deflated a bit. She had missed her chance. She set the phone down on her desk and stared at it. Should she call back? She hated to think what her daughter might say in her somnolent wrath. *Julie's right,* a voice in her head said. *It can wait. You have six months, after all.*

Peg knew that voice. It was the voice of procrastination and easy outs. It was the voice of temptation, and it was all too easy to give in to it.

She was so lost in thought that when the phone rang, she jumped several inches off the floor. "Jesus fleas!" she swore. She glanced at the phone, hoping against hope it would be Julie, apologizing for her grumpiness, asking her mother what she wanted to talk about.

But it wasn't Julie. The phone flashed "TED" in large block letters.

She picked it up. "Hello, dear," she said.

"Peg, dear, are we still on for tea?" Ted's voice was somewhere in between a Boston and a British accent. If she didn't know him so well, she'd swear it was an affectation. Instead, she knew that it was just Ted.

"I am. Are you?"

"Quite. But I wanted to check because someone—a very cute someone, mind—asked me what I was doing this afternoon."

She marveled at Ted's libido. He was older than she was, but his drive—especially for younger Filipino men—seemed limitless. "Well, Ted, if you'd rather—"

"Posh. I'll tell him I'll meet him for supper. I just wanted to be sure first."

"Thank you, dear, because...well, I have something rather important I need to talk with you about."

"Oh? And you don't want to spill it over the phone?"

"I'd rather not."

"Well, tea *and* intrigue. I feel as if I'm in a cozy mystery. All we need now are scones."

"I won't stop you from bringing them."

"Consider it done. La-ta." He hung up.

"Well, that's something to look forward to," she said to herself. After her hair and nails, Ted. She willed herself to brighten. But she wished he were here now. She would tell him everything, and he would hold her hand and comfort her and tell her all would be well. He would hold her steady with his eye. He would exhort her to avoid the temptation of despair. He would remind her that God cares about her and will not forsake her. She needed to hear all of that desperately.

She thought about going back into prayer and asking Jesus to hold her. But a glance at the clock told her that she didn't have time for such indulgences. Grabbing a tissue, she dabbed at her eyes, straightened her back, and raised her chin. "Time to *pastor*," she said to the empty room. She headed toward her coatrack, toward the door, toward the town she had vowed to shepherd and love.

Milala Caballero put the tiny butane torch to her cigar and puckered her lips, drawing in just enough air to make the end glow. She blew out the smoke with an air of satisfaction, turning her head to bless everything around as she did so.

Milala, a squat young woman in her mid-twenties, was of the South Sierra Miwok people. She had raven black hair gathered into a single braid hanging down her back. Her fingers were stubby; her eyebrows were thick enough to comb. She wore crocs that did not match—one blue, one pink—and that suited her. Every step proclaimed her status as a two-spirit, blessed by the Creator with gender fluidity, and therefore worthy of the world's esteem.

The porch of the Starbucks was deserted, which she thought odd for a morning joint. But it *was* cold, she conceded. She felt the chill, but it was an objective thing, not something within her. The cold had always been a comforting friend to her. She sat in her friend's company and smoked.

"Hi, there!" said a bubbly woman emerging from the stainless-steel door of the Starbucks. She had a ponytail, but her hair was blond and seemed to defy gravity. "I'm Chrissy. Welcome to Starbucks!"

"Chrissy. Of course you are. I guess 'Bambi' was taken?" Milala asked.

Chrissy was holding a wash rag, and her smile was exaggerated. She cocked her head like a confused dog. "I'm so sorry, but I'm afraid there's no smoking on the patio," she said.

"Because…"

"Because it will disturb our other guests." She flashed Milala a smile that seemed almost sincere. But it was clearly a practiced smile, lacking any mirth or warmth.

"I don't see any other guests. Who am I disturbing?" Milala asked. She took an exaggerated drag on her cheroot and blew it in Chrissy's direction. She watched her wince.

"If anyone chooses to sit out here, we want them to feel welcome and not have to worry about smoke."

"So, I should not smoke just *in case* anyone else wants to sit out here?" Milala asked.

"That's right."

Milala nodded, but she did not put out the cigar. "To my people, this is a sacred plant. We don't use it mindlessly. We use it to pray."

"So…you were out here…praying?"

She moved her head back and forth. "I was about to. But it blesses everything it touches. We bless, and then we pray." That was not exactly true, but she didn't expect Miss Hair to know that.

"I see. Well, if Father Mallory wanted to fire up his censor and blast the porch with frankincense, I'm afraid I'd have to tell him the same thing."

Milala raised one eyebrow. That was a worthy comeback. Perhaps she had underestimated Chrissy. She put her feet on the chair across from her and leaned back, cigar still between her teeth, but probably starting to go out, she reckoned.

"Oh, and please—no feet on the furniture," Chrissy said.

Milala did not move. Instead, she narrowed her eyes. She opened her mouth, but Chrissy seemed to be on a roll.

"Also, the porch is for customers only. If you'd like to come in and order a beverage, I would be happy to serve you." She flashed that smile again. It was a pretty smile, Milala had to admit. Those were lips she would not mind tasting—but this was not a woman of substance; she was a woman of air, not of soil. Still, those lips would be good for one night. Yes, she would like to be served by Chrissy. She would like that very much.

"And if I don't order a…beverage?"

"Then I'll have to ask you to take your cigar and your feet and your prayers somewhere else."

Milala nodded again and stood up. If they were naked and she embraced Chrissy, the young woman's pert teats would rest on the top of Milala's head. The idea of kissing her tummy was lovely. "I guess I'll move along then, someplace where a cup of coffee doesn't cost my whole day's budget for food."

"Thank you for coming to Starbucks." That smile again.

"Uh…Chrissy. Could I have your phone number?"

The smile faded quickly—amazingly so. It was replaced by confusion, and then comprehension, and then disgust. "Ew!" she said, and turned on her heel, snapping open the stainless steel door with a yank.

Milala pulled out her lighter again and relit the cigar. She puffed a few times, a final blessing for the *oje-ajnt* shop. Her feet were beginning to feel a little too blessed by the cold, so it was time to walk.

She was wearing a blanket as a scarf, and now she gathered it around herself. Glancing up at the sky, she knew she would not need it for long. The sun would be showing off today, after he got his coffee in him.

She decided to walk to Elmo's where she could get good coffee—strong, bitter, and sour as Creator intended. And only fifty cents to boot for a bottomless cup. She blessed each shop she passed with the smoke of her cigar.

"She was hot."

Milala stopped and looked around. She knew that voice. It was not velcome voice. "Where are you, you tricky son of a bitch?" she asked.

Coyote stepped out from behind a mailbox and showed her his teeth. His gray fur was still bushy from his winter coat. His tail was down, which suggested that he was *not* in a good mood. Nevertheless, he said, "It's a blessed morning, Caballero."

"It was. And then you showed up," she answered.

"Hey, now. That's no way to speak to a deity." He did not look offended, however.

"It's no way to speak to a *respectable* deity," she countered.

"It's no way to speak to your elders or your betters," he insisted.

Milala had no answer for that. "What do you want?"

"I want to walk with you for a stretch."

"So walk. Unless you're going to object to the cigar as well," she said.

"Bless the whole block. *Hiyi,* bless the whole town. I like it."

"Me, too."

"She *was* pretty," Coyote said.

"She was," Milala said. "But she would never make an *ohjant* for me."

"No. Fun, though."

"That's not the Beauty Way," Milala reminded him.

"You've never let that stop you before."

"Hmf. You here for a reason, or you just decide to pick on me today?"

"The wind does not command me, little daughter."

"Then what? Play your trick and be done with me."

"No tricks," Coyote assured her.

"Then what?" Milala repeated. "I'm gonna plant my feet like a black oak until you tell me what you're up to."

"I would rather walk together."

Milala stopped and glared at him.

Coyote sniggered, made a circle, and sat, looking up at her. "That's fine."

Milala let out an exasperated sigh and started walking again. Coyote fell into step beside her, his coat gliding over his haunches like flowing water.

"I have a task for you," he said.

"Is it a request or an order?"

"That depends on whether you choose to defy me, daughter."

"It's an order, then," Milala decided.

"Harmony is being wounded. Someone needs to bring the balance."

"And that someone is me?" Milala asked.

"We would like it to be so."

Milala stopped again and looked down at him. "We?"

Coyote showed her his teeth again. It was an attempt at a human smile, she knew, but it looked terrifying.

"Did Creator send you?" Milala asked.

"Would that make a difference?" Coyote asked.

"I think it would."

Coyote said nothing. Instead he sat, parted one leg, and started to lick at his belly.

"All right then, what is it?" Her voice was still full of something—indignance, distrust, uncertainty—it was a stew. There was also a quaver in it. She could not refuse Creator anything.

"We want you to go south, to the *oje-ajnt* village, Karlstadt. They need one of The People to drum for them."

"Since when?" Milala asked.

"Since the harmony was broken," Coyote answered.

"The harmony was broken a long time ago, big brother."

"Not like this. They need medicine…or they will. Very soon now. You need to drum for them."

"I could do this, I suppose. But I would only consider doing it for Creator, not for you. Is this request from Creator?"

Coyote flashed his teeth at her.

"Tricks," Milala said. "All right. I have given you a hearing. You can go."

"Will you drum?" Coyote asked.

"I'll pray on this. I will stir my kettle."

Coyote licked his lips. "If you stir too long, stew becomes mush." Looking both ways, he dashed across the street and disappeared behind a dumpster.

Julie set down her coffee cup and sighed. On her desk a mountain of paperwork taunted her.

Jake's desk faced hers, the front edge butting up against the front edge of her own. Her stack of paperwork threatened to topple over and slide down from her desk to his. She straightened the stack.

Jake looked up from the file folder he was perusing and gave her a tentative smile. "Morning," he said.

"If you say so," she returned.

"Bad day?" he asked.

"My mother called me at, like, 7am."

Jake blinked. "I love your mom."

"You can have her," Julie said.

"For a pastor, she's pretty cool. I heard her cuss once," Jake said.

Julie narrowed one eye at him, then turned back to the pile on her desk. She pulled her chair out and sat in it like she was dropping a sack of rocks. She pulled the first of the files from the top and snatched up a pen.

This was the one part of the job she truly hated. She loved being out in the town, being on patrol, answering calls, investigating. But in the end, every significant thing that happened required someone to write about it, and all too often that someone was her. She told herself that every job had good parts and bad parts. It didn't help.

"Uh, Julie...in your report about last night—"

Julie jerked upright. "Clive!" she said.

"Uh...yeah, he was part of it, I guess. But—"

"I have to check on Clive." She pulled out her cell phone. Then she hesitated. She thought about how upset she had been when her mom woke her up that morning. Clive fancied himself a ceremonial magickian, and in typical magickal fashion that meant staying up impossibly late and rising after noon. She would not endear herself to her friend if she woke him. Plus, he was injured. She wanted him to heal, and that meant she wanted him to sleep. She put the phone back down.

"I'm turning into my mother," she told Jake.

"You don't look anything like your mother," Jake said.

"No, but I act like her. *Just* like her. I hate it."

Jake cleared his throat. "Um...like I was saying...about last night. Can you...you know...not mention in your report...or to Thom...that I went there...you know...hoping to catch Satanists?"

"Don't want tilting at windmills going into your permanent file, eh, Cowboy?" Julie cocked her head.

"I have no idea what that means, but...I feel embarrassed about it, now." Jake ran his fingers through his hair, glanced up to check that Celia was at her desk by the door and not close enough to hear. Nevertheless, he lowered his voice to a hoarse whisper. "I don't want Thom to think he can't trust me with...you know, important assignments."

"Like single-handedly busting a Central Valley Satanic Sewing Circle?"

"It's not funny." Jake sighed. "Sometimes I look at myself and I just think I'm ridiculous. How could anyone take me seriously? I mean, that time when I asked you out—that was the most humiliating experience of my life. And I've got a whole catalog of fuck-ups."

"Look, Jake, I'm not holding onto that, so you gotta let it go too. And it's not like I was mean to you. I told you that you're a wonderful guy, a *good* guy. You're just not *my* guy. *No* guy is my guy. That's not humiliating, that's just the truth. But you focused on the last thing I said, and not the first things. But those are also true: you are a *good* guy, wonderful even. And you're a competent deputy—"

"Ouch—that's faint praise," he muttered.

"You're green, dude. You'll get better. Look, you don't want to fail upward, do you?"

"What does that mean?"

"It means you don't want to be given more responsibility than you can handle and fuck it up, do you?"

Jake stared at his desk. "I guess not."

"No. You want to be right where you are, solid and dependable and boring—"

"I'm *boring*?" Jake almost wailed.

Julie looked over at Celia. She was looking at them now and scowling.

Julie shushed him. Then, in a lowered voice she said, "I just mean that you shouldn't try anything flashy, like you tried to pull last night. That would have ended in sitcom-style disaster. Just...do what you're doing, but focus on doing it *excellently*. Thom will notice. I promise."

Jake didn't look sure.

"Thom will give you more responsibility when he thinks you're ready. Do you trust Thom?"

"Yeah, of course. He's a great sheriff."

"Yeah? Well, I think so too. But he's also a good judge of character."

"I think he's afraid."

"Afraid? Of what?"

"Of anyone...me or you...getting hurt. I mean, he lost his brother and Emma in the same week. People say...he's gun-shy."

"Thom is *not* gun-shy. I've seen him with a gun."

"That's not what I mean. I mean...he takes all the dangerous calls himself. He's afraid we'll get hurt, just like...you know."

"You know what that sounds like to me? Sour grapes. Thom isn't giving you more responsibility because you're not ready for it, and so you make up some bullshit conspiracy theory to explain it instead of just taking responsibility for your own shit."

"That's not true—"

"It's totally fucking true. Now...get to work."

She turned over another file with a huff. Then she remembered she wasn't finished with the first one, and turned back to it a little sheepishly. She hoped she sounded convincing. Jake was on to something, but she felt protective of Thom. She knew that a part of him was deeply sad, broken even. But Thom had trusted her in this job when other departments had passed on her. She was too small, too weak, too female, too witchy, too weird, too...something. But Thom had seen *her*. He had given her a chance. And she was going to make damn sure Jake gave Thom the benefit of the doubt.

A telephone rang on the other side of the office, and Celia picked it up. A few moments later, she called out. "Hessup! Got a call for you. Missing person."

"Do I need backup?" He glanced at Julie.

She raised an eyebrow, waiting.

"Earl Sjöberg has gone missing again."

Julie snorted. Earl had dementia and had repeatedly "left for work" from the nursing home on Fifth, sometimes clothed, sometimes not. That would mean Jake would most likely be spending the next couple of hours working a grid in his shop until he found him. "Have fun, Cowboy. And Jake?"

"Yeah?"

"Find Earl before he freezes his testicles off. Get the little stuff right. The big stuff will follow."

―――――――

Peg Barkley handed Ted the letter and looked away.

"What's this?" he asked, setting down his peach scone. Every Tuesday at 3pm, the former Father Ted Fitzwilliam came to Peg's office at the First Congregational Church for tea. Usually, they gossiped and teased one another and brainstormed the lectionary readings for the following Sunday. But Peg wasn't feeling particularly jolly.

Cloud cover dimmed the normally bright stained glass, casting an ominous shadow over her office, which only added to her melancholy. And wafting in through the window was the sound of Martin Olafson's New Orleans-style jazz band. They normally rehearsed at the Methodist Church, but every now and then there was a conflict and they used the sanctuary at First Congregational. Peg hated Jazz in pretty much any form. It was an irrational antipathy, she knew, but it had seemed to be the soundtrack to many dark episodes in her life, so it was not a kind of music she chose to listen to. Unfortunately, when Martin and his merry band were storming it up in her own sanctuary, it was hard to escape it. Its strains were melancholy, too, but with a forced cheerfulness on top that struck her as disingenuous.

Peg tried to block it out. She focused on Ted as he examined the envelope. His pencil-thin mustache twitched as he read the return address. He looked up and caught her eye. She realized she had been pacing. She forced herself to sit down. She watched as his slender fingers opened the envelope and extracted the letter. He set the envelope aside as he unfolded the papers within and glanced over them with quick eyes.

He had been the parish priest here when she'd arrived. And then he'd fallen in love. Instead of hiding it, he'd stepped down from the altar and petitioned for laicization. She admired him for that, more than she could say, even if the man he'd fallen for *was* thirty years his junior and had little in common with him other than a devotion to the Blessed Mother. "The heart operates by its own inscrutable logic," she'd told herself when it happened. The townsfolk had not been quite as accepting, but they were coming around. Ted had always been well-liked. He had also always been a bit flamboyant, so his orientation had come as a surprise to few.

He flipped through the other papers in the short stack, folded them again neatly, and replaced them in the envelope. When he looked up at her again, his eyes were brimming. "Oh, my dear. I don't know what half of these test results mean, but I get the gist of it. I'm so, so sorry."

She leaned over, took his hand, and squeezed it. Then she sat back again. She was no longer tempted to pace. Now she wasn't sure if she could fight the gravity.

"What's the treatment?" he asked.

"I don't know, Ted."

"Your doctor didn't discuss treatments?"

"Yes, and I have to give him my answer at our next meeting." She looked at him hopefully. "Will you come with me?"

"Of course, dear."

The narrow stained glass strip that ran from floor to ceiling bathed the office in multicolored glory. She had always loved this office, mostly because of that window, but today it was doing little to cheer her. "If I go through with the chemo, I'll have six months at most. Six months of puking into little bags and feeling like shit until I die. Or...I could refuse treatment and feel fine...until I don't."

"And how long will you have?"

"Four months, give or take."

Ted's face fell, and he blinked against tears already falling on his cheeks. "Oh love," he said and leaned over, covering her like the sky, squeezing her shoulders and touching his ear to her cheek. It was the most awkward hug Peg could remember in ages, but she patted at his hand until he rose up again.

He pulled a bright handkerchief from his breast pocket and blew. His short-cropped gray hair was always perfect, which frustrated her, as her efforts to wrangle her own hair into submission every morning failed as often as they succeeded. He was also painfully thin, while she had put on a little padding at the hips. She realized with a note of dark humor that both problems would soon be solved.

"What?" He noticed. "What's funny?"

"Nothing." She waved him away. "Just...if I do the treatment, I'll lose my hair. If I don't, I'll be as skinny as you."

"So?"

She shook her head. "Never mind. Look, the tea is getting cold."

"Can't have that." The teapot was covered in a knitted cozy that had been bright yellow at one time. Now most of its color was borrowed from the light thrown by the stained glass. Peg poured two cups and offered one to Ted. The jazz band next door in the sanctuary struck up "Tailgate Ramble." She recognized the song immediately, but couldn't remember why.

"I wonder," Ted said, taking up his cup. "Would you rather not know?"

"And just let it surprise me? Wake up dead one morning?" She eyed her scone, sitting on its napkin, but didn't pick it up.

He laughed darkly. "I suppose. The results are like a little window into the future. And not a welcome future."

"No. I can see how getting hit by a truck would be a surprise, but...I can't see how this is much of a surprise. And yet...it doesn't tell me *how* the end will come—what I'll look like, the room I'll be in, how skinny I'll be—"

"My dear, this is a very selfish thing to say," Ted interrupted, "but I don't know how I'm going to carry on without our time together."

"You're right—it's a very selfish thing to say. Selfish...and sweet." She sipped at the tea. It was still warm enough to enjoy. So for a brief moment she let herself enjoy it.

"How do you feel?"

"How do I feel?" Peg asked. "I feel fine. I mean, I feel like a woman in middle age is supposed to feel, I suppose. My joints hurt and my toenails look like potato chips—don't know when that happened. But I feel...normal."

Ted nodded. "But...how do you *feel?*"

"Oh. Emotionally."

"Yes, dear."

She blew on the tea, enjoying the steam tickling her nose. "I don't know yet. I'm still...processing, I suppose."

"Because you're a computer." Ted raised an eyebrow. She loved the way he held his pinky aloft ostentatiously, as if the teacup were caustic to it somehow. "Where do you feel your feelings...in your body?"

"Oh, Ted." She lowered the cup and saucer to her lap. "I can't allow myself to ask questions like that."

"You can't allow yourself not to," he said.

She said nothing. She hated when he was right. But there was work to be done. "I have work," she said.

"Your work is to form parishioners into ministers. So...give them an opportunity to minister to *you.*"

"Ideally, I would agree with you. But...I don't want to give them a reason."

He didn't push it. She knew he understood. He knew what it was like to be at the mercy of public opinion. Peg had not come into her job under the best of circumstances, and there were some among her congregation who did not want anyone to forget it.

"Have you told Julie?" Ted asked.

Peg did not look at him. Instead, she looked at a spot far away as she shook her head slowly back and forth.

"Ah." He set his cup and saucer down. "Why not?"

"I tried, but..." She looked at him and forced a smile. "But turns out I'm telling *you* first. You have to tell *someone* first."

"Alright...and I'm flattered, dear. But Julie deserves to know."

"She does."

"When are you going to tell her?"

She considered getting huffy with her friend, but then sighed instead. "Soon. I guess. When the time is right."

"That sounds a lot like never. You're going to have to tell her *sometime*."

"Yes."

"Why not today?"

"She's working."

"She takes breaks."

"She..." Peg looked away again. "She doesn't want to talk to me. She makes excuses every time I try. I tried to call this morning, but I woke her up and I only ended up making her mad."

"So? Make her mad. She'll forget all about being mad the moment *you actually tell her*." He narrowed one eye at her.

"I hate upsetting her. She takes any excuse to push me away."

"You don't want to upset her, or you don't want to *feel* upset?"

Peg looked at her friend again—a warning look. "Julie and I...it's complicated. You *know* that."

"'It's complicated' is a relationship status, not a reason."

"Well, it's *our* relationship status—Julie and mine's."

"Your grammar makes me wince, dear."

"And pushing me like this makes me..."

"Yes, makes you what?"

She blinked back her own tears now. She didn't know why. She sniffed and focused on her friend's face. She noticed several gray hairs on his neck that he had missed while shaving. They made her love him even more.

It sounded like Martin stopped his band halfway through "As I Lay My Burden Down," but the trombone didn't get the message. It carried on for a couple of measures by itself before trailing off. A moment later, they all launched into it again.

Ted continued, "Peg, dear, every relationship I have ever had was complicated. Messy. Fucked up, even. It's a fallen world, and no one gets out of here without getting bunged up. Your relationship with your daughter is broken. Welcome to the club. It's called being human. Man up and go talk to her."

"Did you just say 'Man up' to me?"

"I did. Fine. Woman up, whatever. Grow a pair of ovaries and go tell your daughter. She deserves to know."

"I suppose she does."

"There's no *supposing* about it. You're going to need her."

"That's a scary thought."

"Swallowing your pride and having to lean on her? Yes. Scary."

"I did everything wrong with her, and she never misses an opportunity to rub it in my face."

"Well, now is your time to turn that around, do something right for a change."

"Why break a streak, though?"

Ted smiled. "There's my girl."

Sheriff Thom Lind paused at the top stair. He was just about to reach for the door handle to the Inyo County Sheriff's office when it occurred to him that his life was on a loop. *I'm stuck in fucking Groundhog Day*, he thought. In a moment, he'd reach for that door handle, just as he had done yesterday and the day before that and the day before that. He sighed, knowing it was inevitable. He reached for it again and stepped into the office.

It was quiet, as usual, the silence punctuated by the occasional pings of cell phones and whining of printers. A phone was ringing, but that was efficiently squelched by Celia, who gave him a wave as she greeted a caller. She picked up a small stack of pink notes and held them aloft in his direction. Like a trained dog, he moved toward her and took them, then shuffled toward his office. In a few minutes, Celia would be finished with her call and would bring him coffee. The coffee would never have enough sugar, so he would open his desk and remedy that.

"Good morning, Emma," he said to the pine box that had pride of place on his bookshelf. Emma said nothing. The flowers he had placed in a crystal vase next to the box were starting to wilt. He pulled his cell phone from his hip pocket and opened the TO DO list app. "Flowers," he typed, then put it back. He sat down with a groan that might have seemed exaggerated for a man in his early forties, but he felt every bit of it. *Just once*, he thought, *I'd like the day to bring…something different.*

"G'mornin' sheriff," Celia said, a steaming cup of coffee in hand. She smiled professionally and set the cup on his desk, as she always did.

"Thank you, Cel," he said, as he always did.

Celia was exactly his age. They'd gone to school together, from kindergarten straight through high school. He'd gone to college, and she'd gotten married. She was smarter than he was, he knew that, but he'd gotten the degree. Now she ran the place, and he was the figurehead. She'd been pretty once, but she wasn't one of those women to whom the years had been kind. Her hips could generously be called impressive, and she embraced a high-school librarian aesthetic, complete with cat eye glasses that hung from a lanyard.

"Drink up. You'll need two of these in you, quick," she said, pointing to the coffee.

"Why? What's up?"

"You haven't looked at the pink slips yet?"

"No. Saving those for *after* my coffee."

"I'll save you the trouble then. They're all from Abel Nyland—"

"*All* of them?"

"All of them."

"Jesus God, help me. What's he want?"

"Someone dumped a piece of public art in his cornfield last night."

"Public art? What does that even mean?"

"Like a big sculpture that you see next to a state building, with a fountain to one side."

"I hate that stuff. I can never figure it out. Have you seen that one in Chicago? Looks like the top of a spaceship melted?"

"No, but I know what you mean. I'll take a bronze bust of Walt Disney any day."

"Now *that's* art," Thom agreed. "Why did someone dump a…is it a sculpture?"

"It is."

"Why did someone dump a sculpture in Abel's field?"

"That appears to be the question of the hour."

"What's it a sculpture of? Or can anyone tell?"

"Ah…I think you'd better go see for yourself. Abel's pretty wound up about it. I suggest you go out and see if you can smooth some feathers."

"Jesus. Who's in?"

"Hessup is out looking for Earl Sjöberg—"

"Again? It's—" He glanced at the clock. "Oh. Yep, time for Earl to leave for work. Damn."

"Third time this month," Celia noted.

Thom frowned. "Think he can handle it? Maybe I better help him—"

Celia held her hand up to stop him. Then she pointed to a chair. "May I?"

Thom's eyebrows rose. This was a departure from the daily script, and he felt a bit lost.

Celia sat. She put her hands in her lap and cocked her head, shaking it sadly as she looked at him.

"Celia, you are looking at me as if I were a wet kitten who's just gotten into mischief."

She ignored that. Instead, she said, "If a younger man isn't being admired by an older man, he's being hurt."

"He is?"

She nodded. "He is."

"Aaaand…the younger man here is Jake?"

"Yes."

"And the older man in question is me, I take it?"

"Yes."

"And you're telling me to *admire* him?"

"I am."

"Doesn't he need to…oh, I don't know…do something *admirable* first?"

"How can he, when you keep his leash so tight that he can't turn around without tripping on it?"

"He trips on his leash?"

"He does."

Thom scowled and looked at his coffee. "Do you think that's really true?"

"I don't think it, boss, I know it."

Thom looked away. He desperately wanted to reach for a square of chocolate, but a voice in his head warned him not to do that in front of Celia. He pursed his lips and rocked back and forth a bit in his chair. "You don't think I should go back him up?"

She narrowed one eye. "It's Earl *Sjöberg*."

"We found him naked as a Christmas goose last time he went missing. He had hypothermia."

She said nothing to this.

"You know, I wasn't there when Roy needed me. Or when Emma needed me—"

Celia cut him off. "You remind me of that every day."

"Nonsense. This is the first time I've ever—"

"You remind me of that every single day when you hover over your deputies as if they're fragile little flowers. You try to be everywhere. You try to be there for everyone. And you can't. Goddam it, Thom, you're going to burn yourself out."

Thom stared at her. *Fuck it,* the voice in his head said. *Have some chocolate.*

He opened the drawer of his desk and took out a bar of Trader Joe's milk chocolate. He broke off a square and looked up at Celia.

"Did you check your sugar level today?" she asked.

He put the square on the desk again. It stared at him. It mocked him. He looked up at Celia again. "Where is Barkley?"

"She's here. Just finished up a phone call with the tribal reps on some trouble out at Big Pine."

"What kind of trouble?"

"Bar brawl, what else?"

"At nine in the morning? Jesus. Well, do they need us?"

"Nope. Tribal deputies have it under control. Just calling in the incident prior to faxing the paperwork—same as usual. But if she does need to go out there, you need to let her *go* out there. Alone. She doesn't need you to babysit."

"She might need backup."

"Because of the dangerous tribal elders?"

He stared at her. "You're making fun of me."

"Boss, I'm only mirroring back to you the ludicrosity of your own position."

"Ludicrosity is a word, is it?"

"Did you understand my meaning?"

"I did."

"Then it has succeeded in doing the one thing a word needs to do."

"I suppose." His eyes flashed back and forth as he thought. "Uh... Barkley knows this art shit, right?"

"Her BA was in Art History at Cal State Bakersfield."

"So of course she's a cop." Thom permitted himself a grin, but it hurt his face. Humor would come easier after the coffee. He took a swig and made a face.

"What's wrong? It's not cold is it?"

"No, no, it's just...strong stuff. I'm guess it's me who's the fragile little flower."

"And *I'm* a rabid tiger."

"Got that right." He gave her a lopsided grin. "Tell Julie she's with me, paying Abel a visit."

"Thom…" Celia looked exasperated.

Thom held his hand up. "I heard you. And I trust Julie to take care of herself a damn sight more than I do Jake. I just…I'm out of my league when it comes to art stuff. It's me who needs the backup here."

"I'll tell her to gear up," Celia said.

"Do that," he agreed. As soon as her back was turned, he popped the square of chocolate into his mouth. He savored it as it began to melt. Then he pulled out the top drawer of his desk and opened a tin that had once contained Altoids, but now housed his surreptitious supply of sugar cubes. He tossed two into his coffee and gave it a swirl.

He glanced through the pink notes, his eyebrows lifting as he saw progressively more urgent tones the further down the stack he went. He tossed them in the waste can by his knee and turned to his computer. Celia had set up two folders in his email client. One was marked "READ" and the other was marked, "REPLY." He opened the "READ" folder and began to truly work on his coffee as he made his way down the list.

All of these Celia had either already acknowledged or sent a stock reply to, under his name, or they were simply for-your-information. Every now and then she'd include a link to a cartoon. This morning there was one from the New Yorker showing an urn on the mantel of a couple's fireplace. The woman was saying, "Your mother still criticizes my housework."

It didn't strike him as very funny, but that was probably because it was a message. He looked up at Emma's pine box and felt his gut tighten. *Maybe I should take her home,* he thought. But the thought of getting through a workday without her seemed unbearable.

His thoughts were interrupted by a tap on his door. Julie Barkley leaned against the doorpost, looking just a little too small and a bit too pretty to be a proper cop.

"Celia said we got a visit to make," she said. "What do we need?"

"Let's get a couple rifles in Old Bill, and the camera."

"Easier to just use my cell phone," she said.

"Suit yourself," he said, getting up.

"What's up?" she asked.

"What's up is I need an expert in Art History."

Julie cocked her head and grinned. "I *told* Mom that would come in handy someday."

Thom knocked back the rest of his coffee. "Well then, today is the day those four years and $40,000 finally pay off."

CHAPTER TWO

The fields rushed by the open window of Old Bill, the sheriff's SUV. Thom didn't look away from the road, but in his peripheral vision he saw the vast patchwork of farmlands that made up the greater part of Karlstadt. Some of the fields had been planted, but most had not, depending on the crop. After spending the greater part of his life in California's Central Valley, he could perceive a great many things invisible to passers-through. By smell alone he could tell you what was growing in a field. The silhouette of a migrant worker would call to mind not simply the family name of the person, but generations of their relatives in Thom's acquaintance, as well as the region of Mexico, Central or South America they hailed from. None of this was conscious. It was simply part of the warp and woof of the sheriff's daily life. It was as reliable as the sun, inevitable as rain, good as the soil.

He glanced over at his deputy. Julie's face was buried in her cell phone. "You're quiet," he said.

"I'm worried about Clive."

"Clive? You mean the Foster kid?"

"Yeah. We went to a play the other night and he got beat up pretty bad."

"Oh yeah, that dustup at the barn on the way to Coleman?"

"That's the one. I haven't heard from him since, and I'm…" She trailed off.

"You're worried," Thom said.

"Yeah. He's my best friend."

"He's weird as a weasel," Thom noted.

"Sure. But he's *my* weasel." Julie put her phone away. "I've left four messages and even more text messages and emails. I think it's time to stop in."

"Does he still live in town?" Thom asked.

"Yeah."

"You want to swing by after?"

"No. It'll keep. I'll stop by after work."

"You're sure?"

"Yeah, thanks. It's probably nothing. He wasn't hurt that bad."

Thom shot her a worried glance, but said nothing more about it. Instead, he cleared his throat and changed the subject. "Uh…if you don't mind me asking…art history?" He scowled and shook his head. "I don't see it."

"Gah!" Julie looked out the window. "It was one of those 'I have to do something with my life and I don't know what' college dilemmas. You know?"

"'Fraid I don't."

"Huh. Well, you're lucky. My mom was pressuring me to major in something 'marketable,' and my teachers were saying, 'Follow your heart, the money will come!', which is crap. I didn't know what to do, so I just picked something."

"What? At random?"

"Pretty much."

"But…were you an artist?"

"Nope."

"Did you, at least, like art?"

She shrugged. "I liked looking at it. I *got* it, I suppose. So I must have some facility for it, because lots of people don't."

Thom grunted. "My idea of art is dogs playing poker."

Julie laughed. "Oh, yeah...that was a series by Cassius Marcellus Coolidge. He painted the first one in 1894, but a cigar company commissioned a series of them, eighteen of them, in fact—although I don't remember whether that includes the original or not. Probably the one you're thinking of was titled 'A Friend in Need,' 1906. It's the most famous."

Thom was silent for a long time, although his eyes were wide.

"Don't look so surprised. I looked it up recently because Jake and I were talking about it."

"You and Jake were talking about a painting?"

"You had to be there."

He finally looked over at his deputy and shook his head. "Still, Barkley, it seems like you know your stuff. Guess I picked me the right partner for the day."

"Well, it hasn't come in handy yet, so here's hoping."

"What does your mom say about you being a sheriff's deputy now?"

"Do you...talk to my mom?" She narrowed one eye at him.

"I'm not a churchgoing man, as you know. Or maybe you don't. But I'm not. Emma was the pious one—"

Julie laughed.

"—but we're friendly when we see each other at Debbie's. Why? Shouldn't we be? Seems polite. I say, 'Pastor Peg,' and she says, 'Sheriff,' and that's about it." He sniffed. "But that doesn't matter. I have great respect for the clergy."

Julie shook her head. "She's just my mom. She slips into her bra one boob at a time."

He looked over at her quickly, narrowing one eye. "What is it between you two, anyway?"

"Old news. Too old," Julie said. She did not look at him, but instead stared out the passenger window at the rows of what would soon be barley rushing by.

"Didn't mean to pry."

"It's alright. My mom's alright. Mostly."

"Do you go to her church?"

"Ew. No. Are you kidding?" She shuddered.

"There's a story there!" he said, eyebrows up.

She stared a bit more. Finally, she looked back at him. "When you come out as gay, it's a journey. You have to accept it about yourself first, and it's hard. It's even harder when you have to stay the course as everyone around you freaks out about it."

"Your mom didn't handle it well, I take it?"

"She does now. Hell, now she's a rainbow-flag-waving enthusiast and president of the local chapter of PFLAG. It's embarrassing. But... she had her own journey. You know. And then there was the breakup with my dad, and then he died. There was just...there was a lot of hurt."

Thom didn't know what PFLAG was, but he let it go.

"Why would someone dump a sculpture in Abel Nyland's field?" Julie asked, obviously changing the subject.

"That is the question. That's where I'm hoping you can help. Maybe there's a clue in its origin, the artist, I don't know. I just know it might be good to have someone who knows their ass from their underwear when it comes to sculpture."

"I was more of a paintings girl, but I get it. And what I don't know, I know how to find out. And I have an old classmate who specializes in sculpture. We stay in touch, mostly through Instagram."

"What's Instagram?"

"You are a hopeless relic of a bygone age, Thom."

"I'll wear that as a badge of honor, I think." He was half teasing her. He had heard of Instagram, of course, but he'd never seen it. He knew it was a computer thing. His skill maxed out at email, however, and he struggled with that.

"Here we are," he said, turning into a driveway that was nearly invisible from the main road. The house was more than a half mile back, and Thom was surrounded on all sides by what would soon be cornfields. He knew the planting schedule, so he knew there was seed in the ground already, and probably, if he looked close enough, he'd detect seedlings, but they were too small to see from his perch in Old Bill.

He pulled in alongside Abel's 4x4 and set the brake. He slipped the key into his pocket and put a beat-up cowboy hat on his head. An old-fashioned sheriff's badge was fixed to the front of the thing. It wasn't real, but it served well enough as a stand-in for the one on his breast pocket.

He waited for Barkley to fall into step behind him and together they ascended the six stairs to the porch of the farmhouse.

Mia opened the door before they got to the top and gave them an awkward wave through the screen door. Ginger Beer barked excitedly behind her. "Ginger, *shush!*" she threw over her shoulder a little too loudly. She turned back to them and gave them a forced smile. "Sheriff. Deputy."

Thom touched the brim of his hat in greeting. Abel came up behind her. Thom noted that they both looked jumpy, maybe even a little spooked. He'd never seen Abel rattled by anything before, and that fact alone worried him. Ginger Beer whined.

"I'm sorry, where are my manners?" Mia asked. "Sheriff, do you want to go right out to the cornfield, or can I offer you some coffee and biscuits first?"

The biscuits sounded better than Thom cared to admit, and he knew just how they'd be—a tiny bit burnt on the bottom, slathered with butter and probably honey. *Focus*, he told himself. "We've got a busy day ahead of us," he lied. "We'd best just go straight out to the cornfield."

She nodded as if hearing the answer she expected, met Abel's eye for the briefest moment, and then turned back inside the house. "Come on, Ginger," she said. Thom saw her grab the dog by her collar and pull her toward the kitchen.

"Whatcha got, Abel?" Thom asked.

"Come and see," Abel said. He opened the screen door and let it slam behind him as he headed for the stairs. Thom and Julie followed. Thom had a hundred questions, but he knew Abel wouldn't take them kindly. Besides, he was a patient man. Abel would start talking, and most of his questions would be addressed in due course, he knew. He edged ahead of Julie, falling into step alongside the farmer.

"Mia seems a mite rattled," he noted.

"She is," Abel conceded. "She's fluttering like a hummingbird. Ginger too."

Thom nodded. "Any theories since you called last?"

"Not a one. See for yourself." He pointed ahead of him. Thom looked up and got his first glimpse of the block. He stopped. It was larger than he expected, a little taller than most men. It was pinkish orange, the color of the tile on the roofs of a lot of southwestern-style houses. It seemed to be perfectly square.

"It's a block."

"I call it 'the cube,'" Abel added. Thom looked back at Julie. Her eyes were wide.

"Look here," Abel said, pointing at the ground. "The thing is heavy —I couldn't rock it, couldn't budge it. What I can't figure out is how whoever got it here...well, got it here. These here are my tire tracks, trying to move this thing, but there aren't any other tracks, not of any kind. And there sure weren't any this morning. You'd need heavy machinery to move something that big into place. A crane maybe, fixed to a tractor."

Thom saw the tracks he was pointing at, yet other than those the planting rows were undisturbed. They'd had rain earlier in the week, too, so the soil was soft. Thom left footprints wherever he stepped. Thom looked at the block, then back toward the road, then at the undisturbed ground in between. His brows knit in concentration. "That don't make sense."

"No. No, it don't, sheriff."

Thom looked at Julie. Her eyes were still large as she studied the ground. When she noticed him looking at her, she shrugged, clearly as baffled as he was.

"Could it have dropped out of the sky?" Thom asked. "Did you hear a chopper?"

"Nope. We've had helicopters around—like that time the convict escaped from Corcoran. I know what they sound like. It would have woken me up, I can tell you that."

"Did it drop from a plane?" Thom looked up at the sky, saw nothing but the sun, and then felt stupid. He looked back down.

"Could be, I suppose. But you'd think we'd hear it hit. It would shake the house, something that heavy falling from 30,000 feet or what have you. There would probably also be a crater. Ain't no crater." Abel shook his head.

"Still, it's the best theory I've got right now," Thom said. "Thought you said it was a sculpture? It just looks like a block of industrial material to me."

"You're looking at the back of it," Abel explained. "Come 'round the other side."

He headed off straight toward the thing. Thom met Julie's eyes and gave her a nod of encouragement. She didn't seem to need it, however, as she stepped past him and made a beeline for the object. He followed quickly. He didn't want it to seem like his deputy was braver than he.

As they came around the corner of the thing, he heard Julie gasp. He circled wide, and slowly the "front" of it was revealed. Thom stopped, blinking, unsure for a moment what he was seeing.

At first, it looked as if someone had shot at the block, and its contents had exploded outward and then frozen in place. But as he looked closer, he saw that the "exploded" material had form. The front of the block had been carved into, with large sections of the block missing, forming a picture—a picture of a man frozen in place, his hands up defensively. It was, he saw, the statue of a man embedded in the block, as if an artist had carved away the front of the block to expose the man's form. The man's cheek was flattened. His midsection was bent at a strange angle, as if the man had been sitting before he had rushed forward to smack into—into what? The statue didn't show that. A soda can beside him seemed to be airborne, connected to the rest of the sculpture by a trail of what looked like liquid carved out of the block.

"You know who that is, right?" Abel asked.

"Who what is?" Thom asked.

"Who *that* is, the man."

It hadn't occurred to Thom that he might recognize the man. He looked closer, unconsciously stepping toward the thing. Thom shook his head.

"Don't you think that looks like Troy Swanson?"

Thom cocked his head. Troy was a trucker who lived in Tracy, but often stopped in Karlstadt for a bite at Debbie's on his regular route. He didn't know the man well, but Abel was right. It did look remarkably like Troy. The man had curly hair that covered most of his ears. Troy's hair was black, while everything on the block was pink, but the shape of the hair and the facial features was near enough. "Yeah, I can see that," Thom conceded. "That could be Troy."

"That *is* Troy, or I'll eat my britches."

Thom watched Julie approach the block. When she was close enough to touch it, she looked over at him, her eyes asking permission. Thom nodded. Slowly, hesitantly, she reached out and touched the block.

Thom wasn't sure what he expected to happen, but he realized he was holding his breath. But nothing happened—she touched it, and then began to feel at it, in different places. Her face was serious, curious. In a moment's time she had transformed from a reliable deputy into a scientist of sorts. Thom found himself strangely eager for her findings.

They weren't long in coming. Still feeling at the block's contours, she said, "I thought it was a bas relief at first, but the cuts are too deep. It's more like *non finito*, an unfinished sculpture." Her features darkened. "But the material is strange." She pulled a small pen knife from her uniform trousers and opened it. This time she looked to Abel for permission. He nodded, and she began to scrape gingerly at the surface of the cube, away from the carved portion. Then she began to scrape at a portion that had been carved. Thom watched her quick eyes dart back and forth, obviously thinking furiously. She closed the pen knife and walked over to where Thom and Abel were standing together.

"It's not stone. It doesn't scratch. I thought perhaps it was a molded epoxy, but I can't shave anything off. I'd love to get a chunk of it over to the lab in Bakersfield, but I can't get so much as a sliver from it."

"Can the lab send someone here?" Abel asked.

Thom removed his hat and ran his fingers through his hair. He replaced the hat. "That's...expensive. I'm not saying no, but I'm not setting up a house call just yet either. Better to take it to them, I'm thinking."

"Well, how're you going to move it?"

"It'll fit on a flatbed truck," Thom said.

"Good luck to you," Abel said. "I put a chain around it and tried to pull it over to the barn. It's in the way of the tractor, where it's at." He pointed at something, but Thom didn't know what he was trying to explain. It didn't matter. Abel didn't want it where it was, that was clear. Not that Thom blamed him. As a work of art, the thing was disturbingly macabre. He could well imagine it at a museum of modern art, but it had no place on a farm.

"No luck, eh?" Thom asked.

"Couldn't budge it. Tried the truck. Then I tried the tractor. Not an inch."

"I don't see any fresh tractor tracks."

"Kept it on the gravel for traction and used the long chain."

Thom felt at the stubble on his chin as he studied the thing. It looked heavy, all right, but could it be *that* heavy? "You've had a busy morning," Thom said offhandedly.

"Only because you took your sweet time, Sheriff."

Thom grunted, but otherwise ignored the remark. Julie's brows were still knit in thought. "You got more?" Thom asked her.

"If it were made of some sort of stone, you'd see where the spoon chisel bites into the surface. No direct sculpture is perfect—you'll always see some evidence of carving. But there's none. Which means it's probably cast—but from what? It's not metal. It's not plastic. It's...I have absolutely no idea what it's made of."

"Should we tell Troy?" Abel asked.

"What?" Thom asked, tearing his eyes away from the thing.

Abel pointed at the man's image, fairly bursting out of the block.

"Troy. Should we tell him about this? I think I'd want to know if I was the subject of a...a work of art. Seems like a violation, to do it without his permission. And it's...it's not flattering. Troy ain't an ugly man, but that there is an ugly, ugly thing."

"Do you know where Troy is, or how to get ahold of him?"

"Nope. Drives for Interstate Foods, though."

Thom nodded. Wouldn't be hard to hunt him down. But the question remained, *should* they?

"That's an ethics question and above my pay grade," Thom said. "Let me give that some thought."

"You do that," Abel said. "But sheriff, as long as this thing is on my land, I want to be kept in the loop."

"That seems fair. Unless we stumble upon something top-secret, which seems unlikely, I'll give you a call if we discover anything."

"And what can you do about removing it?"

Thom shook his head. "I don't know that, Abel. I need some time to think about this, to ask around. I'll let you know. I promise."

Abel nodded, seemingly content with that. Julie took her cell phone out of her pocket and began taking pictures. Thom watched as she circled the thing, getting several shots from each angle. Finally she pocketed the phone and nodded at him.

"Abel, we're going to head back in. You see anything else... strange...or if anything about this changes—"

"Like how?" Abel asked.

"I don't know *how*," Thom confessed. "I don't know how it got here in the first place. It's a mystery, and in my experience, mysteries generally drag other mysteries in tow. I'm not expecting anything, mind, I'm just saying, if something else unexpected happens, call me."

Abel kicked at a clod and nodded, not meeting the sheriff's eyes.

"Oh, and Abel...I'm thinking it's best if no one says anything about this right now."

Abel looked up at him, a questioning look on his face.

Thom put his hands on his hips and surveyed the block for a final time. "It's a curiosity. And folks love curiosities. I'm just saying, if you don't want people driving out here to your farm and treading seedlings, I'd keep quiet about it."

"Uh…yeah. All right." Abel's face looked momentarily alarmed, as if he hadn't thought of that. The last thing Thom needed was Abel calling him to arrest trespassers.

Thom gave Julie a quick nod and began walking back toward the farm house, toward the SUV, toward the road into town.

Becky Travers chopped at the carrot until it was nearly mush. Her eyes were red and her throat was raw. The knife in her hands shook. She dropped it on the cutting board and pressed her palms to her chest, hugging herself. But the moment she did that the tears started coming.

Her eyes snapped open in panic. If Paul saw her crying… She dashed to the refrigerator and pulled out an onion. She began chopping it. The recipe didn't call for it, but that didn't matter. It provided cover, and Paul wouldn't inquire into the minutiae laid out by the cookbook…she hoped.

He could be unpredictable. Her senses always seemed to be on high alert. They needed to be. She let the tears flow freely now, as she felt the sting of the onion's fumes. She concentrated on her breath, willing it to be slow and steady.

Outside, she could hear Paul yelling at their dog, Samson. The big, goofy German Shepherd was eager to please, but like Becky herself, cowered in Paul's presence. She knew the dog loved his master but feared him too. Becky understood that. For a couple of years now, she had felt a kinship with that dog. They were comrades-in-arms, enduring the battlefield that was their home life day in and day out. Sometimes when Paul left the house, Samson would jump up on the couch and try to curl up in her lap. She let him. At those times, he often shook like a chihuahua. She held him tightly until he stopped shaking.

She heard Samson protest—a yelp, then a shriek. Becky winced, closing her eyes and biting her lip. She couldn't hold the knife anymore. She let it fall to the board. She couldn't bottle up the tears anymore, and they gushed out in gasping sobs.

Then her eyes sprung open. She heard the sound of Paul's heavy footsteps on the deck. She rushed to pull herself together. She wiped her nose on her sleeve, then her eyes, then picked up the knife again and began to attack the onion with renewed vigor.

Paul stepped through the kitchen's back door and slammed it behind him. "Fucking dog!" he shouted.

Becky tried to stifle a sniff, terrified that a drop of snot would fall onto the onion paste she had produced, terrified that Paul would notice.

He was a big man. At six-foot-four he towered over her. He had a beer belly that had grown substantially since their wedding day three years ago, and the wavy brown hair on the top of his head was beginning to thin. He had a baby face, which she knew he hated. He wanted people to think he was hard, and he compensated by acting the part. But she alone knew just how much his face belied his true nature—she and Samson, her cellmate.

It was quiet outside, she noticed. Too quiet. Samson was a vocal dog. But she didn't hear anything coming through the open slit of the window.

"Are you crying?" Paul asked, his voice rising with incredulity.

"No, I...I'm cutting onions, see?" She pointed with the knife at the mash on her cutting board.

"Oh."

"My eyes sting like crazy," she said. That was true.

"I'm going to take a shower," Paul announced. He flexed his fingers.

"What's wrong with your hand?"

"Damned dog bit me. Or tried to."

"Samson? I don't believe it."

"Are you calling me a liar?"

She'd fucked up. She knew it the minute she'd said it. "Of course not. It's just...it's not like him. He's a good dog."

"He's a wild fucking animal."

She opened her mouth. She couldn't help herself. "Why, what did you do to him?"

Paul's eyes flared. He raised his fist, but for some reason thought better of it. She still winced involuntarily. Maybe that had been enough to satisfy him, just to see her cower. It was what he wanted anyway, and if he could get it without further injuring his hand, why not? She didn't begrudge him.

She stood in place over her cutting board until she heard the bathroom door slam. She felt it in her feet, felt the bones of the house shudder. Then she breathed a great, heaving sigh of relief. *He'll want to have sex now*, she thought. It was his pattern.

She took off her apron and placed it on top of the cutting board, covering the mashed onion. Her hands still shaking, she opened the back door and stepped out onto the porch. Samson should be leaping at her. She should be telling him to get down. His tail should be pumping at the sight of her. Instead, there was only the wind. She did not like its message.

"Samson?" she called. She held her hand up to shield her eyes from the late winter sun. She surveyed the whole of the back yard. She did not see Sampson. A pool of dread began to gather in her belly. Swallowing the bile that threatened to choke her, she went to the side of the house, where Paul had his worktable and shed.

And then she saw him. He was lying on his side by one of the sawhorses. His eyes were open, staring at heaven. Becky's hand went to her mouth. She knelt by the dog and put her hand on his withers. He was warm. She put her ear by his mouth, but there was no breath. Her jaw began to quiver, and she buried her face in his black fur. Then she sobbed until his fur was wet.

When the sobbing subsided, she sat up again. She noticed how the hair around his neck looked unnatural. Paul liked to strangle things. He loved to strangle her while they were having sex. More than once, she'd had to hide marks on her neck. She hated it, but there was no saying "no" to him. He had trouble getting it up otherwise. But put his fingers around her throat and squeeze? Suddenly he was hard as a rock.

She looked at Samson's eyes again. Had there still been love in them while Paul had taken his life? She knew the answer to that. She tried to close his eyes. She was successful with one, but the other stubbornly kept opening a slit. "I'm so, so sorry, boy," she said to the only other being in the world who knew how she felt.

Now she was alone.

Truly and utterly.

⸻

"Whisky," Milala said. It took some effort to get up onto the barstool, and she did not do it with grace. Once there, however, she snatched at the wisps of her dignity and pulled them taut, straightening her spine.

The barkeep nodded at her—a lanky fellow with a concave belly, flannel shirt, and a chain drooping from his belt to his pocket. He had a mustache that struck Milala as ridiculous, but most facial hair struck her that way—on men, anyway. On women it was just sexy. She patiently watched as he finished what he was doing—a little too deliberately, in her opinion. Then he picked up a tumbler and set it on the bar in front of her.

"Ice?" he asked.

"Do I *look* like I want ice?"

He just shrugged and poured her a couple of fingers.

She knocked it back, savoring the complex swirl of flavors—caramel, smoke, sour mash. She banged the glass on the bar. "Again," she said.

He poured her another, although he looked hesitant about it. She downed this one as well. It did not taste nearly as glorious as the first.

"Again," she said, setting the glass down more gingerly this time.

The man did not pour her another. She looked up at his face and saw that the hesitancy had soured into suspicion. "Can you pay for this?"

"Unless you're gouging for your well drinks, I can pay."

"Let me see." The man set the bottle on the counter behind him and crossed his arms.

Milala narrowed her eyes. "Creator's balls," she swore. She reached into her skirt pocket and pulled out a battered wallet. She placed a twenty on the bar in front of her. "Take it now. Give me change later, if there is any."

She watched the man soften, but he did not move to take the bill. Instead, he brought the bottle out from behind him and poured her another drink. "Injun should beware the firewater," he said.

She knocked it back and smacked her lips. "I give you a new, Injun name. I call you *hyjiksy kukalant,* Fucks Himself with Spoon."

A deadly silence followed. Milala wondered if she had pressed this *oje-ajnt* too far. Then he burst out laughing, and a relieved smile crept onto her own face as well. He turned his back to her and began to empty his dishwasher.

Just then the whisky began to send its numbing tendrils into her brain, and she reveled in the sensation, feeling the tension pour out of her shoulders. It was the best she had felt all day. *Too bad it doesn't last,* she thought. The euphoria dissipated as her mind flashed on the image of coyote, running across the street in front of her.

What did I do to attract his attention? she wondered. Coyote was a powerful spirit, and it did no good to get on the wrong side of him. Indeed, it wasn't good for a body to be noticed by him at all. He wasn't an evil spirit, but only a fool would trust Coyote. It was one of the reasons she had come into the bar—she doubted he would follow her and she needed to get away from him. She needed to think.

She wasn't sure the whisky would help her do that, but she didn't care. In the absence of a girlfriend, the whisky had become a lover of sorts. It was dependable in all the ways a girlfriend wasn't, and trust-worthy in a way that Coyote was not.

Is Creator angry at me? she wondered. She frowned and squirmed on her stool. She had done plenty to piss off her parents. She had done more than her share to anger the tribal elders, but her transgressions were petty things. As a two-spirit, it was almost expected of her. She had medicine; she knew that. The People knew that too, and that was why they gave her a lot of slack.

She was one of Creator's favorites, possessed of an extra helping of spirit, a masculine spirit alongside the feminine spirit proper to her gender. It was this additional spirit that gave her her power. It was also this spirit that got her into fistfights, caused her to say things she later regretted, and made her long to bury her nose between the thighs of *oje-ajnt* women. Not all two-spirits were queer, but her masculine spirit possessed a fierce love of women. There are some who would say that the masculine spirit was not a friend to her, but Milala knew better. It was as much a part of her as the acorn-shaped birthmark on her belly.

"The People say there are five directions, but there are hundreds of ways to run."

Milala closed her eyes and sighed. She turned on her bar stool and faced Coyote. He was lying on the concrete floor, as if he had been there a while. *How long* has *he been there?* she wondered. "What are you doing here?"

"What are *you* doing here?"

"Having a drink."

"It's not yet noon."

"Call it lunch, then."

Coyote pulled back his lips and showed Milala his teeth. It was a terrible, ferocious smile, and she didn't understand what he meant by it.

"I'm not running," she said. Coyote said nothing. It seemed that her own words betrayed her. She might just as well have admitted to it. "Ask someone else to go drum for the *oje-ajnt.*"

"Creator chose you."

"Tell Creator to choose someone else."

"*You* tell Creator to choose someone else." Coyote showed her his teeth again. Milala shuddered.

She turned back to the barkeep. "You let dogs in here?"

He gave her a confused face. "Dogs? Is that symbolic?" He held his hands up, as if she were holding a gun on him. "I got no beef wit Indian folk."

She rolled her eyes and pushed the twenty dollar bill at him. "Keep it," she said. With as much dignity as she could, she descended the bar stool and began to walk toward the door a little too quickly.

Outside, the light was far brighter than was necessary or comfortable. Coyote fell into step beside her. "See? Running."

The whisky was in full effect now, and Milala concentrated on not weaving from one side of the sidewalk to the other. It would not have been so difficult if Coyote had not been watching her.

"Aren't you worried some rancher might see you walking the street and shoot you?" she asked.

Coyote answered quickly. "*Oje-ajnt* can't usually see me. They think there's nothing beneath their feet but concrete. When it gets quiet, they do not hear Earth Mother's heartbeat as you do."

"Just my luck."

Just then Coyote paused and rocked back on his haunches, gathering for a spring. Quicker than she could see, he leaped in front of her, blocking her path. "You cannot outrun me, Daughter."

"You have no right to chase me, Father."

"But I do. You are the bud, tender and new. I am the tree, old as time. You are mine. You will find my hairs on your new clothes. I will piss on the side of every house you sleep in. You cannot outrun me because everywhere you go, I ride on your back."

Milala swallowed. An *oje-ajnt* woman nearly bumped into her. Across the street, a shopkeeper was arguing with someone on his cell phone. Pickups chugged by trailing smoke that did not contain prayers.

"You want me to drum for the *oje-ajnt*."

"*Creator* wants you to drum," Coyote corrected her.

"Where?" Milala asked.

"The Swedish town," Coyote answered.

"Solvang?" Milala asked, her brows bunched in concern. Solvang was a long way.

"That's the city of the Danes."

"Oh. Karlstadt?"

Coyote grinned.

At least Karlstadt was closer. "Why should I go to Karlstadt? And why should I drum for *them*? They don't respect our medicine."

Coyote did not answer. Nor did he move.

"The *oje-ajnt* killed our grandparents and forced our parents into schools to unlearn the Beauty Way. They have only taken from us. Why should I give to them?"

Coyote cocked his head. "You should give because Creator loves the other peoples, even if they are blind and stupid."

"They shit in their tents."

"They do."

"They worship only sky and have no reverence for the ground."

"That is true."

"They have coiled, twisted hearts like rattlesnakes, and they are twice as deadly."

"They are."

"And Creator wants me to bring sacred medicine to them?"

"He does."

"I do not understand Creator."

"No one understands Creator except Creator." Coyote showed her his teeth again. It did not seem so scary this time.

"I'll pray about this," Milala said.

"That is what you said last time…before you started running."

"I am *not* running."

"This is why you drink the whisky. It masks the taste of lie."

Milala took a deep breath. She did not think Coyote would be so persistent. "What if I say no?"

"You would say 'no' to Creator? Next you will say 'no' to life. And what then?" He paused and waited for her answer. When she gave none, he gestured at her with his snout. "Then you will be *oje-ajnt*," he said.

Milala shuddered. "I will pray on this." She stepped past Coyote. To her great relief, he did not trot after her.

Peg opened the door to Debbie's and held it as Terry Shaloub exited, arms full of newspapers. He called a thank-you over his shoulder and Peg walked inside. The roar of the lunch crowd filled her ears, a familiar and welcome sound. Motion caught her eye. As she looked to her left she saw Allison Williams waving at her.

Apart from Ted, Allison was her closest friend in Karlstadt—despite the fact that she was barely older than her daughter. Allison was one of the few African American residents of the mostly Swedish town; her exuberant spirit lit up every room she was in. She ran an arts-and-crafts shop on Main Street that had the only working commercial kiln for fifty miles.

Quickly, Peg took off her windbreaker and hung it on the large silver coat rack near the door. Then she slid into the booth across from Allison.

Debbie's was like a second home to her. She didn't mind that the upholstery was a bit shabby and the lace curtains had begun to yellow —that reminded her of home too. She'd heard that, at one time, long before she had come to Karlstadt, the waitresses used to wear white uniforms. Now, of course, they wore jeans and t-shirts, but a vestige remained: a forest green apron with "Debbie's" scrawled in white across its bosom.

Tali was wearing one as she breezed in and began pouring coffee. "Afternoon, ladies. Do you need a menu, or are you ordering by memory?"

"I'll look at your menu again when you proofread it," Allison said.

"Typos steal your appetite, I guess?" Tali gave Allison a mock grimace. She was a skinny kid with a streak of green in her dark hair and a tiny silver ring through one nostril.

"I'll have the special," Allison said.

"I'll have the usual," Peg said. "No need to mess with perfection."

Tali flashed Peg a genuine smile and twirled away.

Peg savored the nutty perfume of the coffee. "I always feel like I'm in good hands with Tali."

Allison narrowed one eye at her. "She's pretty, in a Miss Crack Whore 1990 kind of way."

"Stop it," Peg hunkered down and lowered her voice. "That is *not* the kind of thing you say in public, even if it were true. And it isn't. She's a lovely girl."

In answer, Allison added sugar to her coffee and stirred. Allison had been the first person Peg had met in Karlstadt. She dressed in a way that reminded Peg of Stevie Nicks or a Renaissance Faire enthusiast. A bit of a new-age princess, Allison was more woo-woo than Peg was comfortable with sometimes, but that was just one of the things that made her friend unique and interesting. She was younger than Peg by about twenty years, but she didn't feel the age difference. Allison seemed to have an old soul.

"How has your morning gone, Pastor?" Allison asked.

Peg thought about that a minute. She was about to say, "Fine," but her throat began to swell. She looked away.

Allison noticed and put down the spoon. She reached a hand across the table and put it on top of one of Peg's. "Oh. My dear. What is it? Or can't you say?"

Clergy confidentiality was something Peg took very seriously, and sometimes she simply had to stop a conversation when it got near an invisible line that often took practice to discern. "No, I can say. I just —" Peg's eyes began to shine. Allison squeezed her hand.

Peg took the letter from her pocket and gave it to Allison. She watched her friend's face as it went through the range of expressions Ted's had. Without a word, but with tight, grim lips, Allison folded the letter, put it back in the envelope, and handed it back to her. When she met her eyes, she could see there all the love and pain and sorrow she had expected. "Oh, Peg. That's…" And just like that, Allison, who was never at a loss for words, suddenly was.

Peg felt a burning feeling on the side of her face, as if she were being watched. She looked to her right and then she saw it. Rachel Lindstrom was crossing the room, staring straight at her. Her eyes were not kind. She was glowering. Halfway across, she changed course and headed straight for them.

"Incoming," Allison said, grabbing a menu from the rack and holding it up in front of her face, upside down.

"Ladies," Rachel said. Peg marveled that she was able to look down on them and still manage to have her nose in the air at the same time. "Is this how good Christian women spend their time, gossiping and idling?"

"Rachel, how could you possibly know what we were talking about? And since when is getting lunch *idling*?"

Allison put the menu down and turned to her. "And there's only one Christian here. I'm a crystal-wearing, woman-loving, orisha-praising, tree-hugging dirt worshipper, myself." She smiled.

Rachel felt at her chest, at exactly the spot where her bra formed a V. "Mind the company you keep, Pastor," she said, and turned away.

"What's that about?" Peg wondered aloud as she watched Rachel stride off.

"She's got a bee in her bonnet."

"About what?"

"About how you spend your time. I heard her at Pete's a couple days ago."

Pete didn't run the only hair salon in Karlstadt, but it was the best.

"What was she saying?" Peg wanted to know.

"She thinks you're paid too much and you do too little."

"And how could she possibly know what I do with my time?"

Allison shrugged. "She doesn't. She can't."

Peg shook her head. "Just because most people only see us leading worship on Sunday morning, they think that's all we do. If she only knew."

"You could invite her on a ride-along."

"Well, except for the confidentiality," Peg said.

"Oh. Right," Allison agreed.

"Besides, it's none of her goddam business what I do with my time. She's not even a parishioner."

"She ran the Methodist pastor out last year."

"Could be she's one of those clergy-killers," Peg suggested.

"No doubt about it. She convinced the Methodist bishop that Jeff Sarks was a freeloader. Maybe she's coming after you now."

"Good thing Congregationalists don't have bishops."

"I'd still be careful."

"She doesn't even know me."

"That can be rectified," Allison said.

"I'd be afraid of giving her ammunition."

"There is that," Allison agreed. She put her hand on Peg's arm again. "Hey. Thank you for showing me the letter. Did you tell Julie?"

"Do you *think* I told Julie?"

"No, I don't. But you should."

"Ted took me to task for that already. Don't you start in."

"You don't need to tap-dance around that girl. Just sit her down and have a heart-to-heart."

"It's just not that simple." Peg sighed.

"Except that it is, girl," Allison said. She pointed at Peg with her spoon. "You know what your problem is?"

"Is there only one?" Peg raised an eyebrow hopefully.

"You're a perfectionist," Allison said.

"I'm not!" Peg objected.

"You are. You're such a perfectionist that you can't forgive yourself for not being 'the perfect parent,' whatever that looks like. Yeah, you screwed up. Who hasn't? You learned. You did better the next time. That's how life works. It's how it's *supposed* to work. It's like Adam and Eve—if they hadn't fucked up, none of this beauty would have happened." She waved her hand around the coffeeshop, ending her swoop at the yellowed lace curtains.

"O *felix culpa*," Peg said.

"Wait—who's Felix Culpa?" Allison's eyebrows bunched in confusion. "I don't know any Felix Culpa."

Tali swept in and in a single motion presented them with steaming plates. "More coffee?" she asked. But she could clearly see that their cups were full, so Tali spun away.

Allison leaned in and allowed the steam from her chipped beef on toast to waft over her.

"You can't eat like that every day," Peg said. "You'll get big as a house."

"I think you're projecting," Allison said.

"What? I'm strictly a soup and salad girl."

"And I've worn a size three since high school," Allison said.

"No need to gloat."

Once more Peg had a strange feeling. She looked quickly to her right and expected to lock angry eyes with Rachel Lindstrom again. But she wasn't there. Instead, she found someone else looking at her. Phil Prugh's face brightened when she saw him—a bit too bright. He raised a coffee cup in her direction, as if making a toast.

She nodded politely at him.

"You're blushing," Allison said. She looked to her left, trying to figure out why. "Why are you blushing?"

Peg sniffed and looked back to the table. She found her spoon and began to stir the soup. Lentil, with dark green wisps of kale in it.

"Don't look," Peg said. "But I think Phil Prugh was flirting with me just now."

"Phil Prugh? Eww." Allison made a face.

"What's wrong with Phil Prugh?"

"He has a comb-over."

"And I'm getting hippy...and old," Peg protested. "He's a very sweet man."

"Huh. I've never thought of that before," Allison said. "But you see there? Someone is sweet on you. There's still a lot to live for."

Peg dropped her spoon. It clattered to the floor.

"Don't get it," Allison said. "Take another." She got up and snatched one off of a table Tali had just set.

"Did Tali see you do that?"

"Who cares if she did?"

Peg put her face in her hands and breathed.

"Oh, my dear." Allison reached across the table and squeezed Peg's elbow. "You're...there's a *lot* going on."

Peg didn't need to answer. *Get hold of yourself,* she thought. *Be a big girl.* She did not need Rachel Lindstrom to see her cry.

"Do you know what you need?" Allison asked.

"Don't you dare tell me I need to get laid," Peg said.

"Now that you mention it, but…no. You need to do *art*."

"That's your answer to everything."

"That *is* the answer to everything. You're just not listening."

Peg took a very deep breath and let it out slowly. She was grateful for the calming rush of oxygen. With focused control, she picked up the new spoon and once more gave her attention to the soup.

"Come by the studio. Punch some clay. You'll be surprised at how much better it will make you feel."

"I have no talent for art. I've told you that before."

"Nonsense. I have heard you preach. Your sermons are works of art. And I'm not just saying that. You *are* an artist, Peg. You just haven't admitted it to yourself."

Peg's shoulders rounded. "I've never thought of sermon-writing as art. I'll…I'll have to think about that."

"Come over this afternoon. Just for half an hour. See if you can carve the contours of the gospel out of a block of clay."

The idea seemed strangely appealing. "Maybe. What if Rachel sees me going into your den of bohemian iniquity?"

"I'll drape a hundred scarves around her neck and inform her that if she wants to bitch about you, she can only do it through interpretive dance."

Peg barked a laugh and then coughed. "Oh. I'm sorry. Oh. That went down the wrong pipe. Don't make me laugh when I eat, dear."

"Sorry about that. Are you all right?"

"I am. Whoo!" She reached for her water glass.

"Seriously. Come and work some clay. Think of it as a form of prayer."

Thom placed a small clutch of flowers by Emma's urn. He had gathered them from the parking lot where they were growing wild—the first glimmers of spring. He heard the clearing of a feminine throat. He looked away from the bookcase quickly. "Barkley, what you got?"

Julie looked uncomfortable, as if she knew she'd interrupted something personal and sacred. "I just sorted and printed the photos."

"I'll be right there."

Julie flashed him a sad smile and left the door.

Thom opened his desk drawer and helped himself to exactly one square of dark chocolate. He closed his eyes and entered a completely chocolate world. Then he swallowed, straightened his uniform, and went out into the squad room.

Celia was on the phone as usual. She met his eyes, but then looked away, raising her voice to interrupt someone who probably didn't like what she was saying. Celia was his bulldog, and one of her great joys in life was running interference for him. He felt a brief wave of gratitude for her.

He walked over to Barkley and Hessup's desks. Hessup had hair that reminded Thom of the band A Flock of Seagulls from his youth. The front was stiff as a surfboard and pointed up diagonally over his right eyebrow. What Thom thought extra strange was that he'd seen Jake Hessup in the morning before he'd applied any product to his hair and it looked exactly the same, although softer. He sometimes had the urge to take an electric clipper to his entire head, but he was a disciplined man and didn't let on. He also knew that, deep in his heart, he envied the young man such an extroverted thatch. Such would never come again for Thom, outside of a wig.

Barkley and Hessup were arguing, but that was normal. They stopped as Thom approached. "Let's see them photos," Thom said.

Julie began to hang them on a white board with little bits of tape she'd cut beforehand. Thom could see a row of little tape pieces hanging off the steel tray of the board. With quick hands she put the assortment of photos in place.

"This is what was up at Nyland's?" Jake asked, frowning at the photos. "What the hell is it?"

"It's a cube, tall as you are," Thom answered. "With a sculpture cut into one side."

Jake moved toward the white board as if drawn magnetically. "That's just…fucking weird."

"Language!" Celia called from across the room, covering the mouthpiece of her phone.

"It is," Thom agreed.

A few moments later, the white board was full. There were still bits of tape left. Thom would not admonish Julie for the waste.

The three of them stood in a semi-circle and studied the photos. "Any movement on what it's made of?" Thom asked.

Julie didn't look away from the photos when she answered. "I called an old professor of mine. I described it. Without a sample, though, he couldn't tell me anything."

"Damn."

"There aren't many natural stones it could be," Julie continued, "but I'd have been able to get a shaving from most of them. I'll assemble a list of possible materials. It'll be a short list."

"Well, then, there's the possibility that it's not natural," Thom said.

"You mean…*super*natural?" Jake asked, cocking an eyebrow.

"Tuesday ain't your day to be dim, Jake," Thom said, still looking at the photos. "I mean it could be man-made. Some kind of plastic, maybe even metal—"

"It wasn't metal," Julie opined.

"I'm not ruling anything out."

Jake looked down. "Is there a crime here?"

"What?" Julie asked.

"I'm just asking. So this…cube…shows up in Nyland's field. So what? Is anyone hurt? Is anyone dead? Have any laws been broken? Why are we giving this our time?"

Julie opened her mouth, and it looked like she was about to blast him, so Thom spoke first. "Someone put it in Nyland's field without permission. That's trespassing for a start."

"Yeah, alright." Jake sounded mildly defeated.

"Besides, deputy, it's a mystery. We're kind of in the mystery business."

"Funny, that's what my mom says about her business," Julie said.

"Different kind of mystery." Thom nodded slowly.

"Maybe," Julie said. Thom had no idea what she meant by that, but he let it go.

"So, we're treating this as a trespassing case?" Jake asked. It wasn't really a repeat of what the young man had just heard, it was a good question. It was a question about procedure and would determine their next steps.

"No. We're going to treat it as vandalism," Thom said, stroking his chin. Out of the corner of his eye, he saw the surprised reactions of both deputies. He enjoyed that. He felt little joy these days, so he was glad to take it where he could get it.

"Vandalism?" Jake asked.

"It's presence in the cornfield did damage to the upcoming crop—"

"A tiny corner of a row—"

"It's also artwork, like graffiti, obviously intended to shock and upset people," Thom continued.

Julie was nodding her head. She was getting it. "It's defacing property," she said.

"It is," Thom agreed. It was a tactical ploy. Trespassing cases generally required a trespasser to get rolling. A vandalism case only needed damaged property to properly open a case.

"This is a prank," Jake said.

"At the very least," Thom said—not disagreeing, but not embracing the notion. "What if it's more than that?"

"Like what?" Jake asked.

"There *is* another victim," Thom pointed out, "besides the Nylands, I mean."

"Who?" Jake asked.

"That's who," Thom stepped in and pointed at the man in the sculpture, frozen in screaming agony.

Julie stepped up and, picking up a red dry-erase marker, wrote "Troy Swanson" over the picture Thom had indicated. She added a question mark after the name.

"Nah, that's Troy Swanson, all right. Looks even more like him in this photo here," Thom said, pointing.

Julie erased the question mark.

"Intimidation?" Jake asked.

Thom grinned at his deputy. He tapped the side of his nose.

"But why?" Jake asked.

"That's the question," Thom said. "Let's find the answer."

"Abel..." Mia stuck her head in the door hesitantly.

Abel was sitting in his workshop, staring at the dismantled engine on his workbench. But he wasn't actually working on it, or he didn't seem to be. He was just staring.

She went down the two concrete steps and came up behind him, slipping one hand around him, placing it on his heart.

"What?" he said, not unkindly.

"How are you, *gubben*?" she asked.

"Wha—? I'm just fine," he said, holding an engine part up to the light.

"No, I mean *really*," she insisted.

"Woman, I have absolutely no idea what you're on about," he set the piece down and grabbed his bottle of WD-40. He shook it.

Mia reached over and snatched the bottle out of his hand. "Goddam it, *gubben*, I just want to know how you *feel!*"

Abel turned to face his wife, his brows furrowed with irritation. He took the bottle of lubricant back from her and set it down on his workbench a bit too firmly. "*Gumman*, what has gotten into you? Who —who have you been listening to?"

"Listening to?" Mia blinked. "I don't—"

"It's that Doctor Cici on the radio, isn't it?" Abel pointed at her with a Philips screwdriver. He turned back to his engine. "Thirty years and you've never asked me how I 'feel.' Don't see why I should try to figure that out *now*."

Mia took a step back and looked at her feet. Abel sprayed the thread of a screw and tried to insert it. It still gave some resistance, but after a bit of pressure, it finally sank into its groove.

Mia cleared her throat. "The sheriff…did he…what did he say?"

"He doesn't know any more than we do. He said he has some leads to run. I think that translates into 'Don't know shit about it.' Same goes for his deputy—whatshername, the pastor's daughter."

"Julie?"

"Yeah."

Mia didn't know what to say. "I…Abel, I keep thinking about it. I can't get that man out of my head."

Abel turned to face her again. "Ordinarily, that's the kind of statement might make a man jealous."

Was that a wisp of a smile on his grizzled lips? She blushed. Abel reached out and pulled her close to him. He was on his stool, so he rested his head on her bosom, and she cradled it in her arms. They rocked back and forth for a few minutes.

"I want to…I want to go out to see it again, Abel." She held her breath.

Gently, he pushed her back from him and looked up at her face. "You do? Why?"

"I don't know. I just…" But she didn't have an end to that sentence, so she let it hang.

"I don't think it's a good idea, *gumman*." He shook his head. "I've been thinking…it's probably some college kids from UC Bakersfield playing a prank. It's…I don't know, maybe it's the new version of tipping cows."

"So?" She wanted to say more. She wanted to say, "If it's just a prank, what harm would it do for me to go look at it again?" but she didn't want to push him or anger him. And he was already on edge. No, caution was needed.

"But what if it's not that?" Abel asked. "What if it's like that cube from the Superman movie, landed in our field from outer space, emitting some kind of dangerous radiation that we can't feel until it's too late?"

She knit her eyebrows together. "Why Abel Nyland, where did you pick up an imagination?"

"It was an impulse buy at Costco." Abel actually smiled.

"I'm serious, Abel."

"So am I, *gumman.* Steer clear of it, at least until we know what it is. Besides, something like that…could give you nightmares."

She nodded, kissed the top of his bald head, and turned back into the house. The old man was right; she already suspected the thing would give her nightmares. But that was why she wanted to see it in the full light of day—she was hoping it might seem less horrible than the half-shadowed image that had invaded her brain and wouldn't leave.

But Abel had said 'no,' and they were a God-fearing house. Christ was the head of the man, man was the head of the woman, as Jesus and St. Paul had intended. Abel had spoken, and that was the end of it. She sighed.

She sometimes wondered if Jesus and St. Paul were friends of women at all. She knew Jesus had had women friends—there was Mary of Bethany, sitting at his feet while Martha banged away in the kitchen. But she wasn't so sure about St. Paul. She suspected he thought women were only good for two things: making him supper and tempting him to fornicate. She secretly thanked the Father that St. Paul was not her savior.

She felt suddenly tired. It was mid-afternoon; she should turn to dinner preparations. But for some reason, she couldn't muster the will to start. The phone rang, a shrill sound so loud that it made her teeth knock together. Abel had rigged up a second set of bells so that he could hear it in the field. It didn't work—he couldn't hear it past the barn, or she suspected he couldn't. And besides, he'd never made it back before whoever it was had hung up. But the chief utility of the new ringer was giving her fright.

"Hello?" she said as she picked up the receiver from its cradle on the wall. The cord was so long it formed a yellowed snake pit on the floor.

"Mia, this is Rachel—"

Rachel Lindstrom was a couple years younger than she and could talk the paint off the walls. But she was also the closest thing Mia had to a friend these days. "Hello, Ra—"

"Don't talk, just listen. You know that Congo pastor? The one from *Berkeley*?"

"Sure. I mean, I don't know her, but I know who she is."

"You want to know what I hear? I hear she's freeloading. She's living high on the hog over there, getting full-time pay and working half-time hours."

"Where did you hear that from?"

"You know...around. I hear things. And from her own church members, mind you."

"Rachel, isn't that exactly what you said about Pastor Mills a couple years ago?" Mia asked.

"I don't remember. Was it?"

"Almost exactly. You can't tell me you don't remember that. You made a big stink."

"Ah, well, things fade with time."

"Rachel, you're not even a member of the Congo church. What business is it of yours?"

"It's not my business when friends and neighbors are being fleeced?"

Mia sighed. "I guess it is, but—"

"So, I've been following her, you know, a bit...I'm compiling a report on her suspicious activities."

"Suspicious activities? What on earth?"

"Well, she *is* from Berkeley, so she's probably a communist, or a socialist at the very least. Scratch one, you find the other, so I hear."

"That's nonsense," Mia declared.

"She's got a lesbian daughter."

"That pretty young deputy?" Mia asked. "How did I not know that?"

Mia felt herself relax as she fell into the gossip. Suddenly, the tension of the day melted away and she got lost in the delicious world of Other People's Troubles. Then she was unceremoniously yanked back into her own when Rachel said, "Heard the Sheriff was out at your place."

"How did you know that?"

"Rachel knows all."

Mia blinked. Rachel very nearly did. Mia coiled the phone cord around her finger and glanced quickly back and forth between the hallway leading to Abel's workshop and the kitchen.

"Mia, why was the sheriff out at your place today?"

Mia caught her breath and held it. She looked at the hallway. There was no motion. She knew that if she kept her voice down, Abel would not hear her. She turned away from the hallway and bunched the cord around her hand, squeezing it, enjoying the pressure.

"Rachel, I'm going to tell you something, but you've got to promise me you won't tell another living soul. Can you promise me that?"

"Of course, dear! Tell Rachel all about it."

"All right, then. Are you sitting down?"

CHAPTER THREE

Abel woke to the sound of barking. He groaned and turned over. The barking continued. He put his pillow over his face and mashed it over his ears. He knew that would do no good, but it seemed like the thing to do. He reached for his glasses and looked at the glowing LED of the clock. His alarm would go off in exactly ten minutes. It wasn't worth mumbling over.

He was just getting his suspenders up when Mia sat up and rubbed at her eyes. "Is that Ginger Beer?"

"Sounds like her. And she's the only dog for three miles around."

"That isn't like her."

"No, it isn't. I'm gonna see what's got her dander up."

"I'll get coffee started," Mia said, drawing back the bedclothes.

Abel handed her her robe.

"Thank you, *gubben*," she said.

Abel grunted and headed for the stairs. He flipped on the light and took them quickly, the sound of Ginger Beer's barking increasing in urgency. At the landing, he put on his boots, then his coat. He opened a chest that lived to the left of the door and took out a flashlight. He checked it. Then he reached up above the door and lifted his 12-gauge from its cradle. He cracked it and confirmed that there were two live shells, one in each of the chambers. Reaching into the chest again, he clutched at a handful of shells and put them in his pocket.

Turning on the flashlight, he opened the door.

"Abel," Mia called.

He looked back to see her halfway down the stairs. The light above her made her hair look like a corona of flame around her darkened face. She glided over the floor to him on silent cat feet and planted a kiss on his cheek. "You want me to come with you?"

"No. I'll have Ginger. She'll come get you if anything happens."

"Now I *really* want to come with you," Mia frowned.

"Stay. Ten-to-one she's treed a possum."

"All right. I'll work on breakfast."

"Fix the venison sausage this morning, will you?"

"Is today a special occasion?" Mia gave him a half-smile.

"Compensation for gettin' up early."

"Any excuse you want to use is good for me." She kissed him again and turned toward the kitchen with a yawn.

He wanted coffee. But more than he wanted coffee, he wanted the barking to stop. He opened the door and went out into the brisk air of morning. He was just beginning to see orange streaks of light on the horizon. He barely touched the porch steps as he headed toward the barn. He followed Ginger Beer's barking as well as he could. His boots crunched the gravel of the drive and he smelled the chthonic odors of dirt and manure, overshadowed by the crisp scent of dew.

Ginger Beer's barking grew louder as Abel passed the barn. He corrected his course once beyond it, having realized that the big building had distorted his sense of where the dog actually was. But there was nothing between him and Ginger now, and he began to jog as he entered the field, careful not to trip over the rows. He was doubly careful in that he had already planted this section and didn't want to disturb the seed.

"Ginger! Ginger Beer!" he shouted.

The barking stopped. A couple of moments later, he heard panting and the sound of Ginger running toward him. The dog leaped at him, and he swatted her down. "Stop that. You know better than that." But the fiery retriever was clearly overexcited. "All right, girl. Whatever it is, take me to it." Ginger seemed to understand, because she lit out in the direction from which she'd come. After a few pounces she stopped and looked back at him, clearly eager for him to hurry up.

He tried not to disappoint her. No longer jogging, he set himself a quick-walking pace. They continued in that manner for a while, with Ginger running ahead and then waiting for him. The sky had turned fourteen shades of beautiful as they progressed, with tendrils of red, pink, orange, and purple snaking into the dark of dawn and threatening to unseat it. Slowly the flashlight became obsolete. Abel looked up at where Ginger Beer was waiting, nearly vibrating with excitement, and that's when he saw them.

Just beyond the red dog were the shadows of two cubes. "Oh, Jesus," Abel swore. Ginger ran toward the cubes, but Abel whistled and she bounced back. "Keep clear of them, honey-dog," he said, as if she could understand him. Strangely, she seemed to understand just fine. Although still overly excited, she kept a bit of distance from them.

They were dark and looming, reminding Abel of photos of Scotland he'd seen in the National Geographic. Enormous blocks of stone had been placed in open fields back in caveman times, or at least that's what he'd been able to glean from the article. *Standing Stones*, he recalled the name for them. He'd thought they were eerie at the time, mystical even. But he didn't know what to think of these.

There was enough light now to see that they were the same color as the cube yesterday. They also seemed to be exactly the same shape and size. He trained the flashlight on one of them, and saw that, yes, one side was carved. He circled around until he saw that the other had a carved side, too. "Troy, whatever you did to piss someone off, I am glad I am not you," he said out loud. But as he grew closer, he saw that the carvings were different. They weren't of Troy at all. They were—

"Holy Jesus."

Ginger Beer was leaping around, barking wildly. "Ginger! That's enough. No! No!" he shouted. The dog didn't stop leaping, but she did stop barking, replacing it with a worried whine. That was easier to bear, and it was possible for Abel to think. He shone the flashlight on the nearest of the sculptures and saw the figure of a man frozen in the midst of what looked like flames. He knew the man—not Troy, but Bill Arenson, the butcher at the supermarket, plain as day. Bill, who always slipped Mia an extra beef rib or a femur for Ginger Beer. He shook his head as he stared at the frozen-still flames.

For some reason, Abel started whistling. It was tuneless, and he wasn't conscious of it. Ginger Beer's ears pricked up at the sound of it. Abel began to circle around to get a good look at the other statue. And then he stopped, the whistling cut off, the only sound the fading chirping of crickets.

"Jesus," he said, as he stared at a statue of his wife.

"Sheriff?" Celia called.

Thom looked up from the stack of paperwork he was working through.

"Abel Nyland to see you."

"Here?"

"Yep. He's sitting next to my desk. Looks distraught."

"I didn't think Abel had a setting for 'distraught.' All right, send him in. I'm going cross-eyed anyway." He rubbed at his eyes and yawned as Celia headed back to her desk. A few moments later, Abel Nyland paused at the threshold of his office, fumbling at the brim of his hat.

"Abel," Thom stood up, leaned over, and offered Abel his hand. "Come in, come in. Not much room, but have a seat."

Abel's face was ashen. And his eyes were, what? Both watery and nervous, he decided. "What is it?" Thom asked.

Abel looked at the door. Thom got up and closed it.

"No one can hear us," he said. "This is just between us."

"Whoever done this…" Abel began. "Done it again."

Thom cocked his head. "What do you mean?"

"I found two more cubes out there. This morning. Further out."

"Now there's *three* cubes?" Thom asked. Abel nodded. Thom whistled. "Are they the same?"

"Yes…and no. They seem to be the same size, made of the same material. And they all have…people in them, but…these are different people."

"Different people? Who?"

"Bill Arenson—"

"The butcher down at the Safeway?"

Abel nodded. "And the other is…Mia."

Thom blinked. "Mia. Your *wife* Mia?" Mia was a common Swedish name, and Karlstadt had more than its share of them.

"Yes."

"And can you describe the…statues?"

"They both involve fire. Bill seems to be burning to death."

"Oh my god, that's horrible."

Abel nodded. "And Mia…she's lying in a bathtub, naked. It looks like there's fire all around her, too. Her eyes are open under the water. She doesn't look older than she is now."

A wave of vertigo threatened to unseat Thom. He held on to his desk for ballast. "Now we're seeing a pattern," he said.

Abel nodded. "Whoever is making these is imagining how people might die."

Thom nodded, his mind racing. He tapped absently at the top of his desk. He looked up at Emma's urn. He felt a knot tighten in his stomach. At that moment, he desperately wanted a square of chocolate. He told himself to wait until Abel was out of his office.

"Where is Mia now?"

"She's in the truck. I…made up some excuse to get her into town. I didn't want her wandering out…and I didn't want her to overhear me on the phone."

Thom opened his mouth to say something like, *You know, Abel, you could get a cell phone,* but he didn't. "So she hasn't seen it?"

"Nope. Ginger Beer woke us up this morning, barking at the things. But I told her it was a possum. I couldn't…she's emotional."

Thom nodded. "You can't babysit her every moment, Abel."

Abel sat back and sighed. It was the sound of a man who felt defeated already. "I know it. I just…"

"I get it. Okay, I need to update my deputies. We're following some leads now. But we'll need to come out there and see these, photograph them, you know… I'm not going to lie to your wife, Abel. So between now and when we get out there, you'll need to break it to her."

Abel nodded, but he didn't meet Thom's eyes.

"Okay, thanks for coming out, Abel. We'll be out soon. Probably within the hour."

"You gotta arrest these people, Thom. These things could…upset people."

"I think they already have. It's a prank, Abel. Don't let them win."

Abel held his eye. He gave a quick nod of assent, then stood up and offered Thom his hand. Thom shook it. "I'll see you at the farm, Sheriff."

Abel left the room and Thom stared at the top of his desk. He quickly opened the drawer and withdrew two squares of chocolate. He closed his eyes and sucked on them until they were no more than nubs. Then he rose and went into the squad room. "Barkley, Hessup, we've had a development in the Nyland Farm case."

Julie and Jake looked at each other across their desks and rose to face the sheriff. Thom briefly related the news, watching their faces carefully. Julie's eyebrows rose in an expression of wonder and excitement, while Jake's darkened into a glower.

"Poor Mia. Boss, this is turning into an expensive prank," Julie offered.

"Well, we don't know what that stuff is, so I don't know about the expense exactly, but it certainly is elaborate. But here's the macabre part—they all seem to show people at the moment they're dying."

"It's intimidation," Jake said. "Harassment."

"Maybe," Thom said. "We'll need to establish motive to prove that."

"We'll need a perp first," Julie said.

"Where are you on the materials, Barkley?"

"I have a call in to an old classmate, now professor of Geology at UC Bakersfield."

"Well, the sooner you can talk to him—"

"Her."

"...okay, to her then, the better. Abel's pretty shook."

"Abel brings up a sensitive question, boss," Julie said.

"What's that?"

"Who do we tell and when?" Thom mulled that over, as Julie continued, "I mean, we got three statues. Abel has to tell Mia sometime—it's cowardly not to—but what about Bill and Troy? Do they have a right to know? Do we have an obligation to tell them?"

Thom scratched at his head. "I'm gonna have to think about that."

"And what if word gets out?" Julie continued. "People are going to want to see for themselves. Do we stop them?"

"It's Abel's property—him and Mia's. They get to say who goes on their land."

"Then you need to ask them about this before...well, before a flood of curiosity-seekers starts heading out there. You know it's going to happen. People talk."

Thom nodded "You're right. Okay then, here's the policy. We don't volunteer any information, but if someone asks us a direct question, we don't deny it either. We don't comment on ongoing cases. Clear?"

The deputies nodded.

"I'm thinking we also need someone out in that field. I'll call the State Troopers, see if they can send over some help."

"What about us?" Julie asked.

"What about you?" Thom asked.

"We can take shifts in that field."

Thom looked from one of his deputies to the other. He opened his mouth to say something, but Julie interrupted. "Thom...Sheriff... we're not kids. We've both had way more training than we need to... to guard a fucking cornfield—"

"Language!" Celia called from across the room.

Thom looked down and shuffled his feet. "I, uh—" His mind raced.

He trusted his deputies, but he didn't trust himself to keep them safe. He just didn't know how to say that. "Fair enough. I'm still going to call for some support, but...in the meantime, Jake, I want you out in that field."

Jake nodded, completely rigid from the tension in the room. "I'm supposed to...just stand around in the field?"

"No, not just stand around. I want you to *guard* those things, all three of them," Thom said, his voice soft. "Don't let anyone near them. They got there, somehow. Someone put them there. I want you to report *anything* suspicious. I'll have someone to relieve you by 8 o'clock. Maybe Barkley, maybe myself, maybe one of the Troopers."

Julie started to protest, but Thom shot her a glance and she bit her lip.

Jake nodded. "Okay."

"I'm going to go out and have a look around, so I want you to follow me up in your Jeep. Mind, not a word to anyone about this. I want to solve this before people get curious. More than that, I want to catch them in the act."

Melinda Wulfson waved to her parents from behind the screen door. Then she shut the door against the chill and curled up on the couch. She punched the button on the remote and the television flared to life. She was glad when her parents left the house, left her alone. She could act the way she wanted then. She could eat what she wanted. She could watch what she wanted. *I can dress the way I want,* a voice in her head said, but that voice frightened her and she tamped it down.

She began flipping through the channels, but stopped when she saw a girl who seemed odd in a way that she couldn't quite put her finger on. She was not much older than Melinda's fifteen years. She had a severity to her cheek bones that made her look masculine. The girl seemed to radiate an androgyny so profound that Mel found it difficult to look away. Then she noticed the girl had an Adam's apple, and she sat up straight as a telephone pole.

"She's like me," she said aloud. "Only...opposite." The parade the sentence did not occur to her. It was clear in her own mind what she meant—as clear and sharp as cut diamond.

"I realized no one was going to save me from being in the wrong body," the odd girl said, tossing back her feathery strawberry blonde hair. "No fairy godmother was going to swoop down and make me into a girl. No help was coming. The only person who could help me was me. And that's when I really understood it, you know. Things don't just happen. They happen because someone makes a decision to *make* them happen. So..." The girl smiled then, and it was like sun breaking through a field of dark clouds. Melinda felt something in her chest melt. "...so I decided to be my own hero. I decided to make it happen. And *that* day was the best day in my entire life."

Melinda realized she was standing up. The scene on the television had cut to something else, but she didn't really notice. The girl was gone. And it didn't matter. Melinda looked up at the ceiling, in the direction of her room. As if in a dream, she ascended the stairs and hovered in her doorway.

Her room was a mishmash and a mess. A part of her deflated. But then she stepped into it and turned around slowly, looking at every-thing on the walls. There were pink curtains that her mother had made ten years ago to match the pink canopy on her bed. For the first time she noticed there were spiderwebs strung between the canopy and the ceiling. She wondered at this for a moment. Then she decided to do something about it. She jumped up on her bed and tore the canopy down, wiping away the spiderwebs with the balled up cloth. Then she aimed the ball of cloth at the empty clothes hamper under her window and threw. It went right in. She smiled at this and, leaping off the bed, grabbed her chair from its normal place by the desk and put it by the window. Climbing up, she tore down the curtains as well, placing these, too, in the basket.

She then began to go through her clothes. She had always been a tomboy, so she had plenty of jeans and t-shirts. Most of these she kept, but she did toss the jeans with flowers embroidered on the pock-ets. It just wasn't her anymore. It never had been.

She had tried. She had tried with everything in her to please her mother. She had done the tea parties. She had played with Barbies. And for a while, it had been fine. But she had always preferred trucks, even though she never had the courage to ask for them. When they went to her cousin Craig's house, she had played with his trucks, and no one had stopped her. They had only remarked at how well the two children were playing together, even though one of them was a girl and the other a boy.

She was too old for trucks now. Her passion was drawing. Her desk was full of art supplies, and her sketchpad full of buildings. She didn't know why she liked drawing buildings, but she did. They were strong. They had bones. They stood up against the elements and kept people safe. They stood for things.

By the time she had finished going through her closet, the hamper was overflowing. It was a mountain of clothes—frilly clothes that she had always secretly hated. "I don't have to wear them anymore," she said out loud, and she paused to feel the effect of her words in her body. It settled and became solid—just like a building. She breathed deep and felt power surge into her belly.

She cleaned her room then. She tossed onto the pile of clothes anything that no longer spoke to her. She tore posters of boy bands from the walls, along with a fantasy scene with unicorns. She threw them onto the pile. She made her bed, but something didn't seem right. Even though the canopy was gone, the bedposts still made it seem a bit girly. She saw that the bedposts had a seam. About halfway up, the top part screwed into the lower part. She unscrewed the top parts. It looked a bit odd, the bedposts chopped off midway, but at least it didn't look girly. She tossed the posts onto the pile and watched them roll down to the floor. She smiled at that. In a few moments, she'd take that pile down to the garbage can and burn it. The thought of it made her smile even more broadly.

Going into the bathroom, she stood up on the toilet and reached for the top shelf of the vanity just over the sink. She almost lost her balance but caught the vanity just in time. Willing herself to be steadier, she opened the vanity and took out the electric razor her father used on his hair once a week. She didn't bother to check the comb setting—she liked her father's hair and knew the setting would be perfect for her, too.

Jumping down, she plugged the razor in and felt it leap to life in her fist, like an electric eel threatening to squirm out of her grasp. She smiled at the novelty of it and looked at herself in the mirror. She had a round face, with dark hair that fell just below her shoulders. "Good-bye, Melinda," she said. Then she held the electric razor up to her head and watched as curl after long curl fell, leaving fallow tracks across her head.

"I'm off to the store, *gumman*," Abel called through the bathroom door. "Need anything?"

"Just a minute," Mia called, drying her hands quickly and incompletely. She finished the job on her apron. She pulled open the door and watched him jerk back a bit. "Sorry," she said, with a slight smile.

He followed her into the kitchen, where she pulled a list off the refrigerator and added a couple of items to it. She set down her pen and handed him the list. "I like the Greek yogurt nowadays," she said.

"Greek," he repeated. "I remember when yogurt was just yogurt."

"Thank you, *gubben*."

"What do you have going this afternoon?" he asked.

She cocked her head at him. In the whole of their married life, he had not asked her such a question. He had never asked her, "How was your day?" or "What do you hope for?" either. That was the stuff of romance novels, not day-to-day marriage to a farmer—or at least *this* farmer. "Well, if you must know, I have beans soaking. I plan to clear another four-foot-square space in the attic. And while you're out there preparing to feed the nation, I've got a vegetable garden to plant. And that's all on top of my regular chores for the day. Why?"

"I thought…I don't know…maybe you could come with me."

"I came with you this morning, Abel," she said. "I have work to do, same as you."

"True enough," Abel said.

"Abel, what's going on?"

His face revealed nothing, but there was a hesitance in his movements. Something *was* going on. She frowned.

"Just...rattled."

"I can see that. About what? Is it those danged cubes?" His eyes widened, and she saw a spark of fear in them. "*Gubben*, what are you afraid of?" She waited for the denial, as Abel had never admitted to being afraid of anything, not ever. But the denial did not come. She placed her hand on his chest. "You'd better get going."

He nodded. He looked out the window toward the fields, toward the one visible block. He looked back at her. "Just...promise me you'll keep to the house."

"And just how am I going to work on my garden *inside* the house? And why am I to be a prisoner in my own home?" He was beginning to scare her a little.

Abel fidgeted with his shirt. "Uh...I, uh...I better go."

And then he was gone. Mia's brows furrowed. It seemed to her that her husband really did not want her to leave the house, yet explaining it would somehow make everything worse, and he did not know how to resolve the situation. Her husband was as impassive a blank slate as many men she knew, but she knew how to read him, and read him well.

She waited until she heard the truck pull away. She checked on her beans until the sound of the motor faded into the distance. Then she counted to a hundred. Then she put on her hat and sweater.

Ginger Beer met her at the door with excited leaps and sloppy kisses. She pushed her away impatiently. She was a good dog, but Mia did not care for demonstrative dogs any more than she did demonstrative men. "Love me from over there," she told her, and Ginger ran down the porch steps ahead of her. When she reached the ground, she turned to make sure Abel was really gone. She felt momentarily guilty, as she was not in the habit of acting against his wishes. But her curiosity had grown more urgent than her sense of guilt.

Abel had told her about two new cubes, but he wouldn't say much about them. Just the appearance of them was unsettling; she shared in that discomfort. But there was something else, something she couldn't quite figure out. She expected him to radiate irritation, as indeed he had ever since the first cube had appeared. What she didn't expect was fear.

And it was this that propelled her into the fields. She rounded the corner of the barn, and for the first time she caught a glimpse of the new cubes. Her eyebrows rose. They looked just like the other cube. She held her hand over her eyes to block the sun, but that accomplished no more than the brim of her hat had already done. She started toward them, careful not to disturb any of Abel's planting. Ginger Beer ran circles around her, not nearly so careful.

As she approached the first of the blocks, she gasped. A man was engulfed in flames, his mouth open in a scream of protest and agony— a man who had just sold her three pounds of venison sausage the day before. "Bill. O my lord, Bill," she breathed. She shook her head. She liked Bill. He had always struck her as a stand-up kind of fellow—a deacon at his church, she recalled. And here he was, standing there like a character out of Dante's inferno, writhing in the flames of Hell.

She shuddered and looked toward the other cube. If it also had a figure carved into it, as the other cubes did, she was on the far side of it. She rounded the edge of the cube and gasped.

She stared at herself. It took her a moment to figure out what she was seeing; her arms and legs appeared to be coming directly out of the rock. And then the perspective clicked in her head, and she understood completely. It was as if she was on the ceiling, staring down at herself lying in the bathtub. Her limbs emerged from a flat expanse of pink stone, and she realized that this represented the water in the tub. Her arms and legs weren't stepping out of an expanse of rock—she wasn't walking through a wall, like Jesus stepping into the upper room to surprise the disciples shortly after his resurrection. No, her arm was simply coming up out of the water, along with two embarrassingly gnarled kneecaps and two breasts that had always seemed inadequate to her.

The carved eyes stared straight out—straight into her own. They were wide—too wide, as if she were comically surprised. But the tension on her face was anything but comic. She puzzled over what the strange expression could mean. And then she realized what it reminded her of. She remembered her little brother, when they were kids, shoving a fork into the power outlet. His eyes had looked like that—exactly like that. She hugged her sweater closer to her lean frame, stretching over her too-small breasts. "Oh, *gubben*," she said. Suddenly, her husband's actions did not seem strange.

She turned away then and began to wander back in the direction of the house. She needed to talk to someone, but it wouldn't be Abel. So who? *Rachel*, she thought. *I can talk to Rachel.* She did not pay much attention to where she stepped. All she could see was the shocked expression of her own dead eyes.

Bill Arenson slapped the bell on the top of the glass counter over the choice cuts of beef. "Number Twenty-two, twenty-two!"

Rachel Lindstrom waved a scrap of paper at him and stepped forward.

"Good day, Rachel," Bill said affably. "What can I get for you?" He noticed there was a strand of viscera clinging to the side of his hand. Unobtrusively, he tried to brush it off on his white apron. It continued to cling.

"Morning, Bill." Rachel smiled at him, her eyes moving back and forth slyly. He narrowed his eyes at her. She was a monstrous gossip. Depending on how you looked at it, she was either a public nuisance or an expert in her field. Bill was inclined to be wary.

Rachel leaned on the glass counter. "I'll take two pounds of pork chops and some pork loin—just one fat one, please. And some lamb for stew."

"Two pounds again?" Bill asked.

"If you'd be so kind," Rachel said. She wasn't an old woman, he noted; she just seemed like it. Her shoulders hunched over as if she suffered from some spinal condition; her once-black hair had gone gray and she'd had the good sense to let it. Her hands were beginning to curl in a way he'd seen in people with advanced arthritis, although she didn't seem to be in pain. Bill wondered if somehow talking about other people's pain made her own more bearable.

He bundled up the stew meat first—mostly because it was oldest and he wanted to get it out of the store. He then began weighing out the pork chops.

"Have you heard about what they've found up at the Nyland Farm?" Rachel asked. She raised one eyebrow.

"No," Bill said. "What did they find?"

Rachel looked behind her at the half dozen others milling about holding their numbers. She turned back and whispered over the glass counter, leaning on it a bit too heavily for Bill's comfort. "They say there's a sculpture there—a sculpture of *you*."

Bill's hand froze halfway to the scale and he scowled. "A sculpture of me?"

"That's what they say."

"Who is *they*?" Bill narrowed one eye.

"You know," Rachel's lip curled in a smile. "The ladies."

"The *ladies* say there's a sculpture of me up at the Nyland Farm?"

Rachel nodded.

"Rachel, have you…you know, been drinking mimosas for breakfast or something?"

"Oh, pshaw, Bill, you know better than that." She waved him away playfully.

He *didn't* know better than that. Rachel was acting very strange indeed.

"Why on earth would someone make a sculpture of me? It's just not a thing that happens." He glanced at the other customers and forced himself to package up the loin. He weighed it quickly and pressed the price tag on with his thumb.

"I don't know that," Rachel said. "I only know that it's there."

He handed her her packages and she put them in her arm basket and began to shuffle away. Before she got three steps, however, she looked back at him and winked.

Peg listed off her morning in her head. She had Lenten liturgies to prepare. Plus, it was going to be a heavy visiting day. She needed to stop by the convalescent hospital to check up on Leah Oswald, whose hip was healing from surgery. Then she had two visits to elderly parishioners, Norma and Simon, who unfortunately were in different nursing facilities as far apart as one could get and still be in the same small town. And then there was something else, but she couldn't remember what it was. *I'll check the day planner when I get to Norma's place*, she thought.

There will be a day—soon—when you won't be able to walk all morning, a voice in her head informed her. "Then I best make use of these legs while I can still walk," she answered it. Her left arm ached as she thought it. She rubbed at her arm, readjusted her handbag, and tried to think of something else.

The clinic was four more blocks. Karlstadt wasn't a large town, but her morning's route had her crisscrossing its area in the most ineffi- cient manner possible. *Better planning could have helped with this*, she scolded herself. "Yes, but think of the steps!" Julie had suggested one of those gadgets people wore to keep track of their steps. Peg had thought about getting one, but gadgets—even computers—just frus- trated her. *I'll take pen and paper any day*, she was fond of saying, and she said it to herself now.

Julie. Both Ted and Allison had gone there almost immediately after she'd told them about her diagnosis. "Have you told Julie?" The question echoed in her mind as she paused at the stoplight between Lingonberry and Main. Just across the street she could see Betty's Scandinavian Boutique, one of two of the town's Nordic curio shops, filled with overpriced Norwegian preserves, Danish clothes, and Swedish Dala horses. In fact, there was a bright blue Dala horse painted on the side of the building. It was normally a Christmas orna- ment, but that didn't matter. In Karlstadt, you could buy Dala horses year 'round.

The light changed and Peg walked across, past Betty's and toward the park, where she could see the white top of the gazebo already. "What *is* the best way to tell Julie?" she mumbled aloud. She desperately wished she had a better relationship with her only child. Peg had been a stupid girl, falling for Gene, and an even stupider young mother, putting up with his flirtations—and worse. When she finally wised up and dumped his unfaithful ass, she found herself in San Jose with a child and no means of support. It was a difficult time, and Julie had been whisked out of a comfortable and relatively stable home into Dorothy's Place, a women's homeless shelter run by the Catholic Workers. The rift between her and her daughter had begun then, and every new crisis had only served to drive a deeper wedge between them.

There were many times she thought she should just apologize for leaving Gene, but in her heart, she knew she wasn't sorry. Leaving him had been the right thing to do. She couldn't apologize for marrying him in the first place—it would be the same as saying that Julie herself had been a mistake. She could say that she was sorry it had been so disruptive for Julie—but that sounded an awful lot like saying, "I'm sorry my actions upset you," which wasn't a proper apology at all. Yet she was sorry. Deeply, painfully, sorrowfully sorry. She just wasn't able to put into words exactly what for. "I'm sorry that so much hurt has come between us," she said out loud, and a knot in her chest loosened. She longed to say that to her daughter, but it wasn't easy having tender conversations with Julie. The young woman impatiently shut down any talk that smacked of being...well, anything substantial, really.

She sighed. *In a few months, it won't matter,* the voice in her head said. And the pain in her left arm returned.

The slide of a trombone brought her back to reality. She stopped suddenly, causing Mack Harmon walking behind her to nearly crash into her. She apologized and then looked toward the park. "Egad," she said, her shoulders deflating. There, in the gazebo, was Martin Olofsen and his octogenarian New Orleans Jazz Band. He raised his hands, conducting, and when he lowered them the band started playing a raucous, maniacally cheery tune. *That man is the bane of my existence*, she thought. It did seem that wherever she went, she could hardly escape him. She sighed and resolved to make the best of it. He would *not* drive her out of the park.

It occurred to her that she was winded. She headed for the bench under the shade of the enormous black oak that brooded over the park with a latticework of branches, each branch thin and vulnerable, but together creating something so formidable that even the fierce Central Valley sun could not threaten it.

It was only then that she noticed the other people about—people who did not seem annoyed by the music, oddly. She loved to watch people. She loved to guess what propelled them—in their lives as well as on that particular morning. The problem with a small town is that you usually knew the former, and often you knew the latter as well. She froze as she saw Rachel Lindstrom. The spiteful woman was on the other side of Lingonberry, but Peg could see her looking straight at her. The woman pointed to her own eyes, then pointed at Peg. *I'm watching you*, she was saying. Peg did not doubt it for a second.

"Jesus help me," she prayed aloud and forced herself to look away.

She was startled by a voice just behind her. "Mind if I sit with you a moment?"

She knew the voice. She inhaled sharply and dropped her handbag, spilling its contents all over the dusty ground. Peg flushed, wondering if Rachel Lindstrom was witnessing—and no doubt enjoying—her embarrassment, but she was disciplined enough not to look up to see.

"Oh dear, let me help you with that," Philip Prugh said, running on his spindly legs after a couple of pieces of paper that had taken flight. "Here you are," he said, returning them with a bit more panting that he probably wanted her to witness. She had scooped most of her personal detritus back into her handbag, along with a good bit of dust. She held the bag open for him and nodded toward it. He dropped the papers in. Then he knelt and picked up something she hadn't seen, tucked behind one of the bench's wrought-iron legs.

"What's this?" He held up a small brown vial.

"Oh, would you put that in here too, please?" She held the bag open again.

He was clearly curious and shook the vial. "Pastor, you're not dealing drugs out of the back of the parsonage, are you?"

"There are some who would be very pleased to hear such a thing, but no," Peg informed him. "That's oil, blessed by the Episcopal bishop. I get one every year from Charley, the rector of St. Michael's in Bakersfield. It's for anointing the sick."

"Oh." He dropped the vial in. "That's…I never…it's a strange…"

"Every occupation has its miscellany, Phil."

"I suppose it does." He smiled at her. "Do you mind if I…well, sit a spell?"

"Oh, of course, I was just catching my breath—"

"With you, I mean."

"Oh. Well. All right. I have a busy morning. But I did need a bit of a rest. I'd be glad of the company for a few minutes."

"That's good enough for me." He sat down next to her. Then, strangely, he leaned into her. "I think you're cute as a button."

Peg blinked. It was such an odd thing to hear. Phil Prugh was a widower—a cheerful fellow, in her experience. A Lutheran, as many were in Karlstadt. But she had never thought of him as being on the prowl. A thought pricked at her mind. Could he have dementia? It was hard to tell when it was in the early stages. But it was common for folks suffering from it to make inappropriate statements.

"I hope you don't think that too forward." He glanced up at her eyes, a little shyly.

But then again, most dementia patients aren't self-conscious about what they say, she thought. And suddenly, she didn't know what to think. Disarmed, all she was left with was the pain returning to her left arm and Phil's admission of affection. And she didn't know what to do with either one.

Martin Olafsen was tapping at his music stand for attention. Peg gave him a poisonous glance before the band broke into a giddy version of "Mary Don't You Weep."

Peg turned her attention back to Phil. "Why, Mr. Prugh, that's…it's very sweet of you. I think you're…" What was she going to say? She did think him attractive, and his face was kindly. He was in every way

a man of moderation, so far as she knew. He was well liked and generally well-respected in the community. He had owned a machinery
rental place about ten miles from town, closer to Eaglesberg, until
he'd sold it and retired. He was a man completely free of scandal,
which was not something Peg could say about herself. Wisps of thin
gray hair rose from his otherwise bald scalp in a way that seemed to
defy gravity. His eyes were merry. And suddenly, she could see it. The
puzzle pieces of their lives aligned. But did she want to put them
together? She would need to think about that. And pray about it too,
no doubt. Jesus always had the most surprising opinions about things,
not to mention people. "I think you're a very sweet man," she said
after what seemed like an eternity, but was actually, she knew, only a
few seconds.

He smiled at this, as if grateful for a small gift. "Do you use that oil
often?"

"Oh, yes. Several times a week. But it's like the oil in that story of
Elisha and the widow of Zarephath—I somehow never run out of it."

"'Go and sell the oil and pay your debt,'" Phil quoted.

She turned and looked at him, more seriously this time.
"Lutherans don't have a reputation for biblical literacy these days."

"Oh, but back in the day we were fierce, we were." He winked
at her.

She felt a warm feeling filling her abdomen. It might have been
bile, but she knew better.

"Um, Pastor...may I call you Peg?"

"Of course. That's my name!" Peg laughed.

"Peg, then, can I...may I...that is to say—"

"Don't go shy on me now, Phil, Mr. Cute-as-a Button. I'm going to
remember that."

He laughed, a bit embarrassed. "Quite right. But, um, would you
do me the honor of letting me buy you dinner sometime?"

"Well, Mr. Prugh, I can't promise that anything will come of it, but
I can't see how dinner will do anyone any harm."

"Lovely!" he said with a bright, relieved face. "How about Friday
then?"

"Why not?" She smiled at him. *It's a good thing I'm sitting down, because I'm not used to these chemicals*, she thought to herself.

He rose and bowed toward her. "Till Friday then. Seven o'clock at the Prickly Sow?"

So, it was to be ribs. That was fine with her. "Let's make it six, please. I fall asleep early and I'd hate to pitch face-first into my coleslaw on a first date."

His smile was so broad she felt giddy at the sight of it. "Until then," he said.

The afternoon crawled by. No matter how busy it got, Bill couldn't shake the image of Rachel Lindstrom winking at him. He tried to simply dismiss what she'd said as idle gossip—because indeed, that was her stock-in-trade. But whenever his diligence flagged, he saw her face again, her wink. All afternoon he wracked his brain, trying to think of artists he knew that might be interested in him as a subject. And while he could think of a couple of painters, he couldn't think of a single sculptor. When his shift ended at three o'clock, he barely said a word to the evening crew. He'd done everything he was supposed to do, but he knew he was distracted. He'd had to really concentrate to make sure everything got done, and properly. As soon as he'd scrubbed his hands and forearms for the last time, he punched out and headed for his pickup.

He started it up and then sat as it idled. *Where am I going?* he asked himself. He should go home. He was halfway through remodeling the half-bath and there was a lot that needed doing. But he knew that if he didn't go to the Nyland farm, it would eat at him all night. Pulling out of the Safeway parking lot, he turned left toward the farm rather than right toward town.

For the whole of the trip, he found his stomach knotting up. He hadn't even seen this alleged sculpture and he already felt violated. He told himself to relax. He told himself that there was no reason to think that it was actually of him—whatever *it* was. Rachel Lindstrom was a notoriously unreliable source of news. He knew that. He clung to it.

He remembered back to a time when Rachel had been attractive to him. In high school she had been a bright, cheery girl with a shocking mane of black hair and a bitter sense of humor. He smiled at the memory of her. He had actually considered asking her out once, but something had prevented it—he didn't remember what. He worked at the memory, trying to prise it open as he drove, but he never got at it. Eventually he let it go. She had married Art Lindstrom, and Bill had married Luisah. Luisah had died nine years ago. And Art had run off with a younger woman he met at Debbie's over pie. He felt a pang of sympathy for Rachel as he remembered that. Not enough to excuse her for an incontinent tongue, but enough for the knot in his stomach to unspool a bit.

Reaching the Nyland farm, he pulled up the long drive and went slow, as the unpaved gravel road was bumpy and unpredictable. He was surprised to see someone walking down the middle of the road toward him, blocking his way. He was even more surprised to see that it was a deputy sheriff.

He slowed to a stop and rolled down his window. "Jake," he said.

Jake Hessup looked troubled. "Bill...what are you doing here?"

That was a good question. He opened his mouth to say, "I hear there's a sculpture of me," but that sounded stupid, now that he thought about it. It was so unlikely as to be ludicrous.

Jake leaned his arm across the top of the truck's passenger window, checking out the interior. *As cops do*, Bill thought. He elected not to let it annoy him. He cleared his throat. He decided to go the confessional route. "There's a bit of gossip in town, Jake. I don't know what to make of it. But the fact that you're here...well, it means *something* is going on. And if that something involves me in any way, I think I have a right to know about it." There. That hadn't sounded stupid at all. He relaxed a bit.

Jake's eyebrows knotted. Bill could see his eyes darting quickly from side to side. The kid was thinking, and thinking hard. There was *something*, Bill realized.

"Does Abel or Mia know you're here?" Jake asked. "Are they expecting you, I mean?"

"Not that I'm aware of. Isn't it okay to pull up to their house and say 'howdy'?"

"Is that what you're doing? Pulling up to say, 'howdy'?"

Bill didn't answer that. They both knew it wasn't. Bill shook his head. "Look, Jake, I'm not here to start trouble. I'm not here to trespass. I'm here because Rachel Lindstrom can't keep her mouth shut."

That made Jake laugh. "I'm sorry, Bill. I get it."

The kid was all right, really. Bill had always thought so. But it was also clear that he didn't have a clue what to do at the moment.

"Look, if you need to check with Abel, or with Thom, that's okay by me. I can wait."

Jake blinked. Something shifted in the young man, something Bill didn't understand.

"No, it's…" Jake looked up the road, toward the Nyland place. "You're right. This involves you, and you have a right to see it."

"Okay."

"Okay, then. Ah…mind if I get in?"

"Not at all," Bill said, surprised. He hit the button on his arm rest and heard the locks snap up.

The deputy climbed inside. Bill looked over at the young man and gave him a nod. It occurred to him that Jake was just a kid—a kid with a gun.

This didn't strike Bill as odd. He'd had guns when he was a kid. When he was Jake's age, he'd had about twelve of them—rifles, shotguns, pistols, as well as the prize in his collection at the time, a Browning M1917 machine gun from the Second World War, adapted from full automation to a semi-automatic, of course. Bill always followed the law. "What kind of service weapon do you carry?" he asked, pulling onto the gravel road.

Jake seemed taken aback by the question. "Uh…Smith & Wesson Model 10 snub-nosed revolver. Take a right, up there."

"Thanks. Model 10, I've got one of those," Bill said, nodding. "Good sidearm."

"Hell of a kick," Jake said. "I always come back from the range with a sore arm."

Bill laughed. "You hunt?"

"Oh…" Jake blew air threw his cheeks. "My dad and I used to, once upon a time. He's passed on, so—"

"Sorry," Bill said, making the right.

"Go down about 500 yards, then pull over."

"Is that it?" Bill pointed.

"Yep."

"There's two of them."

"There's another one closer to the house. That was the first one."

Bill slowed the truck to a stop. "Who are the other ones of?"

"The first one is—we think—Troy Swanson."

"I don't know him."

"He doesn't live in town," Jake answered. "He's a trucker, stops in at Debbie's every week on his usual route. I haven't met him, either."

"Huh. And the other one?"

Jake met his eyes. "Mia. Nyland."

Bill nodded. "So those two there are of me and Mrs. Nyland?"

"Yep."

"Well, I reckon—" Bill stopped. "Jake, do I want to see this?"

"If I were you? No. But then again, if I were you, I wouldn't be able to stop myself."

Bill nodded. "That about sums it up. Well, let's get it over with." He opened his door and swung his legs to the dirt.

He started walking toward the cubes, with Jake falling into step beside him. He walked toward the nearest of the cubes.

"Uh…that's of Mia," Jake offered.

"That's okay. Figure I'll work my way up," Bill said.

"Okay."

"It's just a block," Bill said.

"You have to go around it," Jake said.

Bill moved clockwise around the cube, and gasped when the hidden side came into view. "This is…pornographic."

Jake put his hands on his hips. "I don't know about that. There's nothing erotic about it, you know? She's just...naked. And, you know, she's old."

Bill shot him a glare. "She's *my* age, deputy. And she's a damn fine-looking woman."

"Oh." Jake seemed to shrink a bit. "Sorry."

"What is she...where is she?" Bill cocked his head, first one way, then the other.

"Yeah, it's a little disorienting," Jake seemed eager to get past his uncomfortable misstep. "We finally figured out that she's in the bathtub. It's like we're on the ceiling looking down at her."

Bill nodded. The weightlessness of her hair suddenly made sense. "And these?"

"Flames, near as we can tell."

"Huh." Bill's eyes widened with alarm. He looked over at Jake. "This is...disturbing."

Jake nodded. "It is."

"Are they all...disturbing?"

"Uh...yeah."

"Cheee-rist, deputy."

"Pretty much."

"So mine is disturbing, too?"

Jake didn't look at him. He nodded though.

"Well, alright then. Let's do this."

He pried himself away from the sculpture of Mia and walked to his own cube, then began to circumambulate it. Out of the corner of his eye, he saw the indentation start, but he intentionally averted his eyes until he was square on and able to take it all in. He planted his legs and took a deep, long breath. He looked up.

Like the other, the figure had been carved into the cube by a process of displacement. Whatever material it was made of had been scooped out artfully to form the sculpture in its interior. Nearly the whole of one side had been scooped out. Peering into the cavity, he saw a figure that was unmistakably himself. *I need a haircut.* The absurdity of the thought struck him, and he almost laughed—but he didn't. He was holding a rifle—a rifle he did not own. He squinted at it and realized what it was—a TNW Aeor Survival Rifle. He'd been lusting after one of those for ages, but couldn't quite justify the price tag, especially since he had no shortage of survival rifles already.

He seemed to be caught in motion, looking over his shoulder, as if gazing at his past. Bill shifted to his right to see if he could get a glimpse of what the figure was looking at, but whatever it was seemed to be further back than the cube went. But what was strange was that the entire scene seemed to be wreathed in roiling tentacles. Bill cocked his head. *Oh. They're flames. Like Mia's*, he thought. He was surrounded by flames.

He cleared his throat. "Did the...the Troy guy...was he surrounded by flames, too?"

"Uh...no. He was...well, forcefully impacting a windshield. You know, from the inside."

"Like a car crash?" Bill asked.

"Well, he's a truck driver. So whatever he hit...it was big."

Bill nodded. "So, all of these are of people...when they die?"

"So far," Jake said.

"What do you mean, 'so far'?"

"Well, the Troy cube appeared yesterday. Just the one. And then this morning, these two showed up."

"So tomorrow, there might be more?"

"It's...who knows?" Jake took off his cowboy hat and scratched at his hair.

"Who knows about this?" Bill asked.

"Well, obviously Rachel Lindstrom does, so that means—"

"Everybody does. Shit." Bill spat on the cornfield. Then he pulled out his phone. "Do you mind if I snap a picture?"

"No. I mean..." Jake looked uncertain. "Uh...go ahead."

"Thanks." Bill snapped a couple of pictures from slightly different angles. He thought about taking a few pictures of Mia's cube as well, but then thought better of it. *A woman is entitled to her privacy*, he thought. "Do you have any idea who made this, or who put it here?"

"Nope. We've got an open investigation now."

"In other words, ask Thom."

Jake nodded.

"What's going to happen to this?" Bill asked.

Jake shrugged. "No idea."

Bill nodded. He felt the breeze on his neck, and his hands felt cold. *I'm alive,* he thought. *No matter what this is, I'm alive.* "Okay, deputy," he said out loud. "I've seen enough."

CHAPTER FOUR

Deena Knolls poured a cup of coffee from the pot behind the counter of Jim's Hunting and Fishing Emporium. The Emporium itself was about four hundred square feet of dilapidated outbuildings that had, over the years, been connected by makeshift hallways, covered with corrugated aluminum, and held together with plywood and quarter-inch screws. Deena managed the Emporium, which meant she usually occupied the office behind the shop itself. The shop had been in her family for two generations, and she could never step into the place without half expecting to see her father, now long deceased. Sometimes she fancied she caught a whiff of her grandfather's aftershave, usually over by the barrel filled with coffee grounds and nightcrawlers.

"Mornin' mayor," Sy said, coming through the front door with an armful of boxes containing empty shotgun shells for hunters who liked to make their own ammo.

"Mornin' Sy. Tell me this coffee isn't left over from last night."

"Nope. I forgot to turn off the coffee burner last night, and when I got here this morning it had boiled down to sludge. Had to swish some salt around in the pot to clean it out."

"That explained why the coffee is salty. Rinse it better next time."

"Check that, boss."

Sy was her brother's son. He was never going to set the world on fire with his wit or ambition, but he was affable and responsible enough...usually. Sy's head was going bald early in life, and he compensated by growing the kind of beard ZZ Top had made famous back when she was in college. Whenever the young man put on sunglasses, it made her smile as she remembered watching the band's videos back when she was young and careless and often very, very high.

Those days were behind her now, as she had enveloped herself in marriage, then law, then the family business, and most recently, being mayor of the fine hamlet of Karlstadt. She had shed a husband along the way, but she'd come to see that as dead weight—a coat she no longer needed to carry around. Her real love was work, and always had been.

She'd been pretty once. She fancied that under the right light, and in hunting clothes, she still might be. Her brown hair had begun to gray, and there was the faintest suggestion of a wattle forming under her neck. She hated it.

She carried her cup of coffee up the three short stairs into the clap-trap hallway, went four feet, then down another three stairs into her windowless office. The walls were adorned by a poster of a music festival the town had put on the past summer. It had been a bust. It turned out that the town's octogenarian string quartet, a high school heavy metal band, and Martin Olofson's New Orleans Jazz Band had combined to create a program designed to appeal to many but ended up pleasing none. She had hoped it would showcase the diversity of musical talent in the tiny town, but it was months before she stopped fielding complaints.

She sighed and realized she should take the damn poster down, as every time she saw it she got depressed. *Later*, she thought.

The phone rang. She set her cup down and picked up the yellowed handset. It smelled like coffee. "Jim's Hunting and Fishing Emporium —and Mayor's Office," she said.

"Is this Mayor Knolls?" came a man's voice.

"It is. Who is this?"

"Uh…that's not really important. I—"

"The hell it isn't. You want to talk to me, you tell me who you are."

"Well, I—"

Deena hung up. She sat down and glowered at the mess of paperwork before her. She glanced at her laptop. No doubt an untold mountain of emails awaited her. She decided to tackle the papers first. As quickly as she could, she sorted them into piles, the largest of which she thought of as 'papers which really, really ought to be read.'

The phone rang again. She picked it up. "Jim's Hunting and Fishing Emporium—and Mayor's Office. Deena Knolls here."

"It's rude to hang up on people."

"Not anonymous people, it isn't. Actual people have names, and only actual people get their feelings hurt. You got an owie, you gotta name. You don't gotta name, I don't give a shit."

"Oh all right, goddam it. My name is Miles Pointer."

"Miles Pointer?" Deena asked. "That sounds familiar. Why is your name familiar? Do you live in Karlstadt? I know everyone in Karlstadt, but I don't know you."

"No, I live in Coleman. I—"

"Then what the fuck kind of business do you have with me?"

"I represent the Central Valley Klan and Philan—Philan—"

"You can't even say it, can you?" Deena rolled her eyes. She took a sip of her coffee and instantly regretted it. It was still too hot and now she'd burned her lip. Damn it. She hadn't been in a great mood before. Now she was in a not-great mood with a burned lip. One of the fluorescent lights overhead buzzed. "What do you want, Miles Pointer from the Central Valley Klan and Philanthropic Society?"

"Uh…did you get our permit application?"

"That's where I remember your name from! That damned application. Let me see, what did I do with that? Oh, yeah, it's in the crapper. I wiped my ass with it three weeks ago."

"You—wait, you what?"

"I wiped my ass with it. You want to stage a Klan march through the streets of Karlstadt. That's a 'no' without even needing to rub two neurons together."

"But Karlstadt has a great Nordic, European history, and we want to celebrate it."

"Great! You can bake a cake and you and your albino buddies can gather in your studio apartment to drink mead, sing songs of the fatherland, and jerk each other off in grateful praise of blessed whiteness. And you can do all of that from the comfort of your home in Coleman. Application denied." She hung up.

She turned to the short stack of things that needed filing and suddenly wished she had a secretary. Then she thought better of it. Not only could she not afford a secretary, she knew she would only abuse the poor soul, and that wasn't fair to anyone. Best to damn well do it herself and spare the world a measure of pain.

The phone rang again. She picked it up. "Jim's Hunting and Fishing Emporium—and Mayor's Office. If this is that KKK asshole again, our business is finished."

"Mayor, you have no idea who you are dealing with. I advise you to treat the Klan with the respect it—"

She hung up. She'd succeeded in filing two receipts when the phone rang again. She picked it up. "I know exactly who I'm dealing with, and I'm ordering you to keep your bedsheets and philanthropic asses out of this town."

"Um…Mayor?"

It wasn't the voice she'd expected to hear. "Oh. Sorry. Is that you, Thom?"

"Uh…yeah. Anything I can help you with?"

"No, no. Everything under control." She laughed, a bit nervously. If there was one man in town with the power to fluster her, it was Thom Lind.

"Okay, if you're sure. Uh, mayor, I'm just calling with a bit of a heads-up. We've got a situation you ought to know about. No one is in danger, not that I know of. Think of it as a nuisance crime, if anything."

"All right. What's going on?"

"It's about the Nyland farm…"

———

"Margaret Barkley?" The nurse stood in the doorway, clipboard in hand, looking over the waiting room.

"That's me," Peg said, standing up. She looked down at Ted. "Will you be all right out here?"

"Dear, I'm alright anywhere." He reached up and grasped her hand. "Do you want me to come in with you?"

Peg hesitated. "I…would you mind, terribly?"

"Of course not," Ted said, getting up. He set the magazine he had been flipping through aside.

"You're a dear," Peg said.

"Keep that to yourself. I have a crusty reputation to uphold," Ted warned.

She dropped his hand and began to walk toward the nurse. "He's family," she lied, pointing to Ted. The nurse nodded, apparently accepting this. Peg looked back at Ted and gave him an encouraging smile, but it wasn't a pure smile. It was sullied by anxiety, and at the moment, she didn't care that it showed. In fact, she wanted Ted to know she was nervous. If she had to feel such things, she didn't want to feel them alone.

The nurse led them not to an examining room as Peg had expected, but to a small consulting room, a large table occupying most of the space. Peg looked at Ted uncertainly. Ted shrugged and followed her inside.

"Please have a seat. The doctor will be with you in just a moment."

Peg sat down at the side of the table she thought the nurse had indicated. Ted sat beside her. On the opposite wall, Peg saw light-boards affixed to the wall. She knew they were for displaying x-rays. It was then she realized they were in the right place. The doctor didn't need to examine her. He'd already done that—prodded and probed and scanned. And she already knew the result. Now she simply had a decision to make. The taut muscle of her gut twisted.

"Can you believe it's almost Lent?" Ted asked.

"No," Peg said. "How can that be?"

"Take a sharp left after Epiphany, drive for a month, and it will be on your right, hiding under a shroud."

"I've been agonizing about it. There's so much to do," Peg said.

"You haven't planned your liturgies yet?" Ted asked.

"I...it's on my to-do list."

"No respect for the liturgical year. Congos," Ted tsked.

"It's not that, it's...there's been a lot..." Peg was making excuses, but she couldn't help herself.

"I have an Anglican friend who calls the first stretch of ordinary time 'Epiphanytide,'" Ted noted.

"I like that," Peg smiled. "It has a delightful feel to it."

Ted sniffed. "One does not go about making up liturgical seasons willy-nilly."

"One doesn't, I suppose, but it sounds like your Anglican friend does," Peg noted.

"He also calls the time between the Feast of St. Francis and the Feast of Christ the King 'Remembrancetide' and has declared the liturgical color to be orange."

"I love that!" Peg said.

"I figured you would." Ted cringed. "Remind me never, ever to introduce the two of you. You'll start cooking up Protestant Feast days."

"Do you mean like Reformation Sunday, to commemorate Martin Luther nailing his 95 theses to the door of the castle church in Wittenberg?"

"That is precisely the kind of thing I mean."

"Well, you're too late. It's already a thing—October 31."

"I'm alarmed and appalled," Ted confessed.

"Really? Because you look bored."

Ted opened his mouth to reply, but just then the door opened and the doctor walked in. Peg felt the urge to stand out of respect, but willed herself to stay in her seat. The doctor did not seem to mind.

Doctor Keller was about Peg's own age, and fortunate enough to still have his hair, although it was now an attractive salt-and-pepper. His left hand sported a gold wedding ring, Peg noted, and internally kicked herself for noticing such things.

He nodded his greeting and sat down across from them, placing a manila folder adorned with multicolored filing stripes on the table.

"Peg, how are you?" He gave her a compassionate smile. But before she could answer, he turned to Ted. "And who's this? Your boyfriend?"

Ted recoiled. "Please. I wouldn't do the bone dance with this saucy cow." He turned to Peg. "I hate that I can't smoke in here."

She slapped at his arm. Ted hadn't smoked in years and was just being difficult, she knew, but she also knew he was doing it for her, so her protest was more playful than anything else.

The doctor seemed to take it as such and returned his attention to her. "How are you feeling?" This time he paused for an answer.

"I feel just fine," she said. "If I didn't know I was sick, I wouldn't have a clue."

Dr. Keller gave her a grim smile and nodded. "Well, thank God for small favors, eh?"

"I suppose so," Peg said.

"You received our letter," the doctor said, "and I don't have news beyond that. But I think you should probably look at this." He pulled what looked like a transparent x-ray cell from the folder in front of him and stood. He flipped on one of the light boxes, and with a practiced flip of the wrist, secured the cell along its top. "That there is your right kidney. As you can see, it's perfectly fine."

"I see a tangled mass of shadows," Ted said.

"Oh. Sorry," Keller said. He pulled a pen from his pocket and pointed at a round shadow with its tip. "This here is Peg's right kidney. It looks exactly like it should. But over here—" he pointed to a larger mass with blurrier edges. "That is Peg's left kidney, and it's shot through with the cancer."

"Can't you just take out the affected kidney?" Ted asked.

"We could, and that is my recommendation," the doctor said. "But..." He pulled out another cell and put it into a different light box.

"We caught this too late for such an easy fix. You see this here?" He pointed again with the pen. "The cancer has spread to her lymph nodes, and from there to almost every organ. We can't take them all out."

Peg's eyes went wide at the thought. "No," she said.

"No," Doctor Keller agreed. "What we can do is take out the kidney, as I said, and then do aggressive chemo."

"Will that cure her?" Ted asked.

Keller shook his head sadly. "No, but it will buy her some time."

"How much time?" Ted asked, his voice rising with alarm.

"It's hard to say. Two, maybe three months."

"So let me make sure I'm hearing this right," Peg said. "If I do nothing, I have about six months left."

"Maybe," the doctor said.

"Okay, but if I have a painful surgery and chemo that will make me sick every day, I might have eight months?"

Keller nodded. "Give or take. Yes."

"That doesn't seem like much of a choice at all," Peg said. Her gaze drifted off into space. A moment or two later, she focused on the doctor again. "So...what can I expect...as the cancer progresses?"

"There is good news there. It is not nearly as painful as some other forms of cancer. You'll probably get a fever that will come and go. You'll experience some night sweats...and that will get worse as the cancer progresses. You'll probably lose some weight. And eventually you'll feel a pain in your side that just won't go away." He gave her a pained but compassionate smile. "Don't worry...we'll make sure you're comfortable at all times."

"That means good drugs," Ted said.

Peg nodded, but felt disconnected from what was going on around her. Time seemed to be slowing down, and the light emitting from the fluorescents seemed unnaturally bright.

The doctor cleared his throat. "I'd like to prep you for surgery—"

"I don't think so," Peg said.

"What?" Keller's eyebrows shot up. He looked stunned.

"I said, I don't think so," Peg repeated. "I mean, an extra two months just isn't worth being sick as a dog for this whole time, or spending one of those precious months in bed recovering from surgery. Who needs that?"

"Well...I think you do." Doctor Keller looked concerned.

"But it is my decision, isn't it?" Peg asked.

"Well, yes," the doctor said.

Peg nodded. She looked down at her hands. They had been her friends her whole life, and now they had begun to prune up on her. She could depend on nothing, she realized. Then she remembered Jesus. Her shoulders relaxed.

"Doctor, I am a Christian," she said.

"That does not surprise me," he smiled. "You *are* a pastor."

"And I believe in the resurrection of the dead," Peg continued. "When Jesus comes to give me a hand up on the last day, I want to meet him with both of my kidneys, even if it means he has to fix one of them up."

The doctor blinked at her. He opened his mouth, but before he could say anything, Peg said, "Don't worry, Doctor Keller. You've done your duty. You gave me my choice. I choose to live what's left of my life in such a way that I can dance until I can't."

Ted looked over his shoulder at her. "I didn't know you danced, dear."

"I don't, but...maybe we could take a class."

Ted sniffed. "I wouldn't do that for just anyone."

"You're sure about this?" Dr. Keller asked. He took the cells down and replaced them in the folder.

Peg nodded. "I hate hospitals, and I don't want to spend what time I have left feeling like shit. I want to spend it at home. And I want to work until I can't. All I ask is that, when there's pain, we can manage it."

Dr. Keller nodded. "We can do that."

Peg placed her hand on Ted's arm. "So that's done," she said.

"Do you really want to go dancing?" Ted asked.

"Right now, I want a piece of carrot cake and a nap," Peg said. "In that order."

Becky paused at her front door. She looked around for signs of Paul, signs of trouble, but the street seemed quiet, oblivious to the dark storm that perpetually hovered over their house. She sighed, moved her shopping bags to her other arm, and tried the door. It was open. She went in.

She half expected Samson to run to her, tail pumping, eyes shining his excitement. But the quiet that actually met her seemed oppressive. She walked straight through the living room to the kitchen and set the bags down on the table. Mid-afternoon sun shone through the curtains, informing her that she needed to get dinner started, and quickly.

She stiffened as she heard movement behind her. She whirled. Paul was framed in the doorway of the hall that led to the bedrooms. He slumped against it in the way he did only when he was drunk—very drunk. "Where were you?" he asked. It might have been an innocent inquiry, but there was an edge to it that was one part condescension and two parts suspicion.

"Shopping," she said, giving him a fake, bright smile. "With Mildred and Heather. Tuesday and Jane had a church thing." *Thank God for my friends,* she thought. *I would go bat-fucking crazy without them.*

"Ugh," he grunted. "Suppose I call Mildred and Heather, just to check?"

"Suppose you'll interrupt them fixing supper, then," she said. "Like I'm about to do now, if you'll get out of the kitchen." She tried to make it sound light, like playful teasing. She held her breath to see if it would work.

He screwed one eye nearly shut as he examined her. "I think you're lying to me."

She put her hands on her hips and gave a little laugh. "Paul! Why would you think such a thing?"

"I think you've been fucking Johnny Pepper-thingy."

Johnny Pepperidge was their car mechanic. He was about their own age, and Becky would agree with most folks that he was handsome. But Johnny had a girlfriend, she knew. In truth, the idea of having an affair with Johnny had never even occurred to her. It wasn't an unpleasant fantasy, and she filed it away for future daydreaming, but she quickly returned her attention to the present moment. "That's ridiculous," she said, turning away from him. She grabbed her apron and pulled the string over her head.

She turned toward the refrigerator when she felt a violent jerk backwards. Paul had grabbed the apron before she could finish tying the bottom up and hauled back on it with force. The string cut into her windpipe and she lost her balance, falling to the floor. He continued to haul on the apron, dragging her toward the doorway. Her fingers clutched at the string at her throat, but she could find no space to dig them in.

A moment later, the pressure of the string was replaced by the larger, warmer, firmer pressure of her husband's hands. This feeling she knew well. She hated this feeling more than any other.

For a brief moment, the pressure relented, but she saw that he was only finding better purchase. He scrambled from behind her to in front of her. *Of course,* she thought, *he wants to see my face—my fear, my submission, maybe my death…*

She kicked, trying to find a foothold, but only succeeded in propelling the kitchen table backwards. Crashing sounds filled her ears as her shopping bags fell to the floor, spilling their contents— groceries, a box containing a new nightgown for her, a new frying pan to replace the one now leaving Teflon flakes in their food.

She waited, hoping Paul would let up, but he didn't. Panic rose in her gut as her brain began to scream for oxygen. Flailing with her arms, her fist closed around the lip of the new frying pan. Without thinking, she lashed out with the pan, aiming for his head. It connected, but her grip was not good and it fell out of her grasp.

It had done its job, however, and Paul's hands released her as they went to his own head. He rocked back on his heels as she sprang up, not wasting a single second. She leaped over him, through the doorway into the living room. She grasped the doorknob, her heart pounding in her throat as she jerked it open and ran outside. She almost ran into Jeff Amory, their mailman, who was walking up the path to their door. His eyes widened and he stumbled, trying to avoid hitting her. She stopped in front of him and panted. She knew her hair was wild—and her eyes too, probably.

"Becky, what's wrong?" he asked.

She turned and looked back at the house in time to see Paul jerk the door open. But before he could rush out, he saw Jeff and stopped short.

"Afternoon, Paul," Jeff said, as if it were a perfectly ordinary day. The problem was, she realized, that it was. It was just an ordinary day for Jeff the mailman and for them. The thought made her feel sick inside.

She turned away from Paul, facing Jeff so that only he could see her lips moving. "Help me," she whispered.

Jeff cocked his head, glanced up at Paul, then back at Becky. "I have the rest of the street to deliver," he said. "It's a lovely day. Would you like to walk with me?"

"Yes," she said, a little too desperately.

"Uh, here's your mail, then," Jeff said, handing a small bundle to her. "Do you mind carrying that?"

"No," she said.

"All right then," he smiled. It was a sad smile, and she knew that he understood then. "Well, let's walk, shall we?"

Milala jumped the last, long step from the bus to the ground. She smoothed out her skirt, looked up at the sun, and squinted. It was beginning its slow descent, which meant The People would be gathering soon. The dancing would begin at twilight. She could already smell the savory aroma of fry bread on the breeze, or she thought she could. She swung the leather straps of her bag over her shoulder and lit the stub of a cigar she'd been sucking on for most of the trip. Releasing the smoke in measured puffs, she blessed everything she passed.

The dance was being held at the Tuolomne County Fairgrounds that year, which had been the cause of much heated discussion. A couple of tribes were boycotting, since it was not on tribal land. Other tribes argued that no land belonged to anyone but Creator, so it did not matter. None of this surprised Milala. The People were good at many things, but they truly excelled at bickering among themselves. She did not care whose ground they danced on, so long as they danced. They were there to dance the planting, to dance the seeds into germinating, to dance fecundity into being.

Milala scowled to see a battered picnic table barring the entrance to the fairgrounds. Tony Martinez was seated at the table, wearing his broad-brimmed black hat with the rounded crown, a long pheasant feather stuck in the tan hatband. Tony had played football in college. He was the size of two ordinary People—both tall and hefty. Milala guessed no one would try to get by him unless he wanted them to. No one else seemed to be outraged at the fact that there was, for some reason, a checkpoint through which The People had to go, even if that checkpoint was someone as respected and loved as Tony Martinez. So she waited in line, buoyed by the carnival atmosphere and the cheery laughter of those in line ahead of her.

It took about ten minutes before she was standing in front of Tony. "Tony," she said in greeting.

Tony looked up from the clipboard he was studying. There were sixteen clipboards on the table. She had counted them while the last person was standing in front of him. There was one for each tribe, and she could see lines through some of the names, with new names scrawled in Tony's blue chicken-scratch.

Recognizing her, Tony leaned back and set the clipboard aside. "Caballero," he said, "Milala."

"Miwok," she said, pointing at the correct clipboard.

He ignored the clipboard. "You shouldn't be here."

She scowled at him. "What?" She cast the nub of her cigar into the dirt. "What do you mean, Martinez?" It was a question meant to draw him out, for she knew exactly what he meant.

Resting his elbows on the picnic table, he steepled his fingers in front of his nose. Tony was gregarious, generous. But now his normally kind face was hard. "For a couple of reasons, cousin. First, you'll want to drum. Miwok don't drum."

That was true. Traditionally, her tribe used rattles or clappersticks. But gatherings such as this one had, over time, led to the exchange of practices among the tribes. "Bear gave me my drum. Who is Tony Martinez to argue with Bear?"

"Maybe so, but The People don't let women drum."

There it was, the real reason. She narrowed her eyes at him. "Bear gave the drum to me. He has given it to other *ohant* in the past."

He shrugged. "That may be so. Who am I to say? But that doesn't mean The People have let them drum in ceremony."

That was also true. The women who tried often ended up being shamed. It was the chief reason she was on the outs with the tribal leadership. Milala felt uncertain. To cover for it, she reached into the pocket of her skirt and pulled out a new cigar. She bit the end off it and spit it out. She felt Tony's eyes on her as she lit it.

"Are you finished?" he asked.

"What if I promise that I will not try to drum?" she asked.

"I would say that I do not trust you, cousin."

The tobacco calmed her almost instantly. She silently blessed Creator for the gift of it.

"Besides," Tony continued, "there's another reason."

She put her hands on her hips. "And just what is that? I am Miwok. I am one of The People. You have no right to keep me from dancing."

"I don't, no. But *he* does." Tony pointed behind her. Slowly, Milala turned around. Her shoulders deflated as she saw Coyote, sitting off to the side of the road, leaning back against a chain-link fence, trying to bite at his withers, but not quite able to reach them. As soon as her eyes were upon him, he stopped, looked at her, and showed her his teeth. Then he went back to trying to scratch whatever itch was pestering him.

"That's a coyote," Milala said.

"Don't play stupid. That's not *a* coyote, *yta-ant*, and you know it. That's our Father."

"You know you can't trust Coyote. He leads The People on twisty paths."

"Yeah, but his twisty paths lead to wisdom. And *he* says I shouldn't let *you* dance."

"Because?"

"I asked him that, because…heh…I'm on your side." Tony pointed his blue pen at her. "All The People should dance, or Spring might falter and fall back into winter."

Milala nodded. "And what did he say?"

"He said Creator told you to go somewhere else."

"And where is that?"

Tony shrugged. "He didn't tell me that." Tony leaned over and whispered, "But from the look on your face, little sister, I think you know."

Milala wanted to punch something. But it would not be wise to punch Tony. It would also not be wise to try to punch Coyote. But she would show him the roughness of her tongue. "I want to dance anyway," she said, "to make me holy for the trip."

"Nice try, *yta-ant*," Tony chuckled. "Take it up with Father." He pointed at Coyote.

Milala's eyes flicked back and forth and she looked beyond Tony Martinez, assessing the likelihood that she could get past him.

"Ah-ah-ah!" He shook his finger at her. "Don't even think about it, Caballero. I am quicker on my feet than you think. I was running back for the Bakersfield Roadrunners."

Milala rolled her eyes. "Fifty pounds ago."

"I'm still faster than you. Now go, you have held up The People for too long already."

Milala was aware of the line behind her. "I'll be back," she said.

Tony closed his eyes in a display of exaggerated patience and shook his head slowly. "Not this spring, little sister. Next!"

A woman pushed Milala aside and began speaking to Tony. She named her tribe and gave her family name, but Milala had stopped listening. Feeling tired, like a little girl who had just been scolded, she reluctantly walked to where Coyote was still trying to reach a spot on his withers. When he noticed Milala, he said, "Help me with this, daughter."

Milala reached for the spot on his withers just above where he was able to bite and gave it a long, deep scratching. A moan of pleasure escaped his black lips, and his gray muzzle pulled back in a ferocious grin. "Yes, yes, yes—" One of his hind legs began twitching, as if it might start scratching too. "That's it." Coyote was sprawled in an undignified manner, showing his belly to Brother Sun and all who cared to look. He righted himself and smacked his lips. "Thank you, Daughter."

"You told Tony Martinez to turn me away? Why?"

"Yes. You should not be here. Creator has sent you to the white people. Where is your drum?"

"In my bag."

"Good. Then you have all you need."

"I don't *want* to drum for the *oje-ajnt*. I want to dance with The People. This is where I belong, not throwing scraps to the dogs."

"Great Spirit has laid *hacahime* on you, a burden. When you have done it, *then* you can dance." He sneezed and licked his black lips. "We don't always get to do what we want, daughter. You are acting like a spoiled *oje-ajnt* girl. You act like you do not respect your elders."

Milala's cigar nearly dropped from her mouth. She took it between her thumb and forefinger and let it hang by her side. She looked at her boots. "That was not a kind thing to say."

"Creator is always kind. But he does not suffer insolence, Daughter."

"And you?"

He narrowed his eyes at her. "It is only Creator's kindness that keeps me from rending your liver from your body." His tongue licked at the tip of his nose. "Warm, wet, tasty liver."

Milala took a step back and swallowed hard. She turned on her heel and walked back to the bus stop.

"Where shall I say you are going, Daughter?" Coyote called after her. "What shall I tell Creator? Where are you taking your delicious liver?"

Milala did not answer. She lit her cigar again and ground her teeth into it as she stormed away from the god as quickly as she could without running.

After burning his clothes, Mel Wulfson felt an elation in his body that he'd never felt before. He kept going back to the mirror to see his haircut—a half-inch buzz uniformly framing his head. He choked back tears at the sight of himself. As he stared at the masculine face staring back at him, the flannel shirt hanging open over a t-shirt covering his bound bosoms, his faded jeans, he felt...right—for the first time in his life. He breathed deep and wiped the water from his eyes. He looked at his hands.

I need something to do, he thought. It was chilly in the house, and he realized he was cold. "I'll build a fire in the fireplace," he thought. He went downstairs and knelt by the fireplace, but discovered there was no wood. *Even better,* he thought. *I'll chop some wood. I won't be cold after that.*

He grabbed the ax from the garage and set to work on some of the felled wood his dad had dragged behind the garage. There was enough to get them through the rest of the winter and spring, but it needed chopping. He felt energy surging through his muscles, strangely quick-ened by his new state.

It wasn't as if he'd never contemplated becoming a boy. Indeed, it was some years ago that he realized that, deep down, he *was* a boy. But there was an inertia to the way a person lived, and it was difficult to jump the track. It was especially difficult when one's parents were dead set against it.

Mel frowned as he brought the ax head down onto a particularly stubborn log. He'd gotten the angle wrong and it had nearly bounced out of his grip. He focused, tried to remember what his father had told him, and started again with smaller cuts. It would take longer, but it would still get the job done.

He realized that, much like the wood, he'd been chipping away at the problem of his body for some time. He had been ready, he just hadn't realized he was ready. But he had certainly felt the pressure building, the pressure that would not—could not—be denied forever. It was the pressure of integrity, of inner-outer congruence. It was the pressure of truth longing to assert itself.

Mel was sweating. He rarely sweat. It felt good. He sensed the congruence again, the manliness of it. For the first time, he did not feel a need to apologize for his sweat. It was appropriate, both to his activity and his gender. He was also pleasingly warm.

His mind flashed to the girl on the television, the trans girl. *The trans girl.* His lips formed the words as he brought his ax down again and again on a large, gnarled branch. The words "trans boy" flashed through his mind, but they didn't feel right somehow. The words "trans man" flashed through, and he felt his muscles relax. The next strike severed the branch just where he'd intended. Would he always need the "trans"? He didn't know. He decided that for now it didn't matter. He didn't mind it at the moment. It pointed to a process, a journey—a journey he'd hoped to take for what seemed a very long time. A journey he had set out on today.

He heard the crunch of tires on gravel and looked up. His parents were returning in their wood-paneled Buick Roadmaster. Mel felt his heart skip a beat, then begin to race. He wiped the sweat from his brow and leaned on his ax as the car rolled to a stop.

His mother was the first out of the car, a stricken look on her face. "My god, Melinda! What have you done to your hair?"

Mel didn't answer, but by some instinctive impulse he didn't understand, he imagined that a part of him had put down roots, was burrowing deep into the soil, drawing nourishment and courage from it. He smiled, but there was a sadness to the smile. "Hi, Mom."

"What have you done?!" his mother repeated, shaking her head.

Mel knew she was only a hair's breadth from screaming at him. He felt his anxiety traveling down his solid legs into the earth. He drew up courage. His father had gotten out of the car and was absently holding a shopping bag by its plastic handles. He cocked his head as he took in Mel's transformation. "I'm sorry," Mel said to them both. "I know this is going to be hard for you. I don't want you to feel hurt, but you probably will. Melinda is dead. She's...she's been dying for a while. And today she passed away. It was sudden, and there wasn't any pain."

He gave them an encouraging smile. His mother's mouth gaped in utter incomprehension. "I burned her things." He pointed to the metal barrel they typically used to burn trash. "Don't worry, Dad. I was careful."

His father cocked his head to an even more acute angle. Mel set the ax aside. Incredibly, when he moved his feet, he did not feel the resistance of the roots he'd put down. Instead, he moved easily, almost gliding toward his parents. He went first to his father and put out his hand. "My name is Mel, and I'm pleased to meet you. I am your son."

Absently, his father took his hand and shook it, a bemused look twisting his face.

He turned now to his mother and drew in a large breath. "Mother, please call me Mel. I will now be your son." He stuck out his hand, but his mother only looked at it as if it were covered in filth. "You are a wicked, evil child. I want you to stop this nonsense right now! You look ridiculous. After supper, you'll put on a stocking cap and we'll go get you a wig to wear until your hair grows back in." Then she pushed past him into the house.

Julie leaned into Thom's doorway. "Heading out, boss. Gonna take the jeep."

"Going?" Thom looked up, chocolate halfway to his mouth.

She smiled at that. "Nowhere dangerous, just meeting with that expert I was telling you about."

"Going far?"

"Delano."

"What's so special about Delano?"

"Halfway to Bakersfield. The expert's an old friend from the UC there."

He nodded. "All right. Don't bring it back empty. And come straight back—I don't want to be out 'til all hours looking for you."

She narrowed her eyes. "We got radios, you know."

"Will you get going already?"

She gave the doorframe two thumps and headed out, waving at Celia as she passed the threshold. Reaching for the keys in her pocket, she crossed the gravel parking lot and swung herself into the cab of the truck.

She'd promised Thom she'd come right back, but she hadn't promised she'd go straight out to Delano. She checked her watch. Assuming there weren't any capsized big rigs on the 5, she had a little time to spare. Careful to stay under the speed limit, she rolled through the downtown and pulled into a parking place near the theater. It wouldn't be open for another hour, but the day shift would be there already. Hopefully that would include Clive.

With a gesture, she invoked the blessing of the triple goddess and climbed down from the cab. She straightened her uniform and walked past the ticket booth, pulling open the door. It was unlocked, she was glad to find. She wasn't in the habit of visiting Clive at work, but she certainly knew the theater well enough—it was the only movie house in town.

A young woman frowned at her. She sported a spiked collar, far too much eyeliner, and hair so unnaturally black it seemed to absorb all surrounding light. "We're not open for an hour."

"Do I look like I'm here for pleasure?" Julie asked. "I'm here to talk to Clive."

"Clive's not here."

"Where is he?"

The girl shrugged.

"Then I guess I'm here to talk to Floyd."

"He's in the office." She turned back to stocking the concessions.

"Thanks." Julie crossed the lobby and knocked on the door with a simple brass plaque that read, "Office."

"What?" came a muffled voice.

Julie pushed the door open. Floyd was at his desk. He was a short, round, hirsute man, the kind that sweat profusely even in winter. A lock of long dark hair was carefully combed to hide a prominent bald spot. His eyes widened when he saw her. "Officer! What a surprise. Is anything wrong?"

"Uh...lots, as it turns out," Julie said, giving him a professional smile. She held the door open and leaned in the frame, but didn't enter. "But one thing at a time. Right now I'm looking for Clive."

He shook his head. "Haven't seen him all week. Had to ask Benji to pull double shifts to cover."

Julie winced. "Sorry to hear that."

Floyd shrugged. "Benji's not complaining. I think he's grateful for the overtime. But *I'm* not happy about it at all. I didn't budget for no goddam overtime. Goddam labor laws."

Julie ignored that bait. "Do you know where he is?"

"Nope. Called several times, straight to voicemail. No one's seen him. Seems to have fallen off the face of the earth." Just then he seemed to notice there was a bong on his desk. He feigned being casual as he placed it under his desk, out of sight.

"You know that's legal now. You don't need to hide it from me."

"Old habits." He squirmed in his chair. "Haven't gone by his apartment, but I have his address—"

She held her hand up. "I know where it is. He's not opening the door."

"Is he home?"

"I don't know."

"Uh...do you think you should check?"

"Maybe. I'll talk to the sheriff about it. In the meantime, if you catch wind of him, call the station and leave me a message?"

"Will do."

"I mean it, Floyd. You hear of him or see him, you gotta let me know."

Floyd cocked his head. "This isn't police business, is it?"

"No. Not yet. I'm…I'm worried about him."

"Should I be worried too?" he asked

"I don't know. Are you a friend?"

"Not really. He's a pain in the ass."

"Then don't worry. I'll let you know what I find."

Floyd nodded, and Julie let the door shut. She felt numb and anxious as she made her way back out to the truck. She drove through the town at a modest pace, but floored it when she cleared the tracks. A mile later, she was turning onto the on-ramp to the 99. She checked her watch again, scowled, and accelerated, going a bit more than the speed limit to compensate. She'd misjudged the time, but that wasn't unusual. She had a knack for that, always aiming for how long something *should* take, rather than for how long it actually did.

She chewed on her lip as she thought about Clive. Short, grim movies played out in her mind, starring herself as she busted down the door to his apartment, only to find him dead, staring up at the ceiling with hollow, sightless eyes. She shuddered and made a warding motion in the air against such an eventuality.

She drove the way everyone did in the Central Valley—with as little attention to the actual road as possible. It was, after all, the single most uninteresting freeway in the contiguous United States. You didn't drive it for fun, you drove to get through it—mile after mile of asphalt, crops, billboards, the overwhelming odor of cow shit, and absolutely nothing else. Like most folks, she entered a fugue state once she passed the speed limit and didn't reemerge until her blinker miraculously engaged, pointing the way to the offramp.

As soon as she hit the surface streets, she put her phone in the cradle and checked her maps app. She followed its bright blue lines until she pulled into the parking lot of the Arby's. Someone waved. She recognized the outline of Priscilla Niles sitting at one of the outdoor tables, a to-go bag next to her. "Right on time, damn her," Julie said out loud.

A couple minutes later, she jogged over to her friend. "Prissy, I'm so sorry."

"Hey, this is you we're talking about," Priscilla said, as if that said it all. She stood up and held her arms out. As if to a magnet, Julie was drawn directly to her, and they shared a quick embrace. Releasing her, Julie gave her friend a look-over. Priscilla was as thin as celery, with skin nearly as translucent. She was a goth chick that had matured into a goth woman. She was dressed smartly, but if it wasn't black or lace, she wasn't wearing it. She embodied an archetype that Morticia Adams had only aspired to. "Sit. Eat," Priscilla said, her impossibly long fingers opening the Arby's bag. "I have to get back to teach a class at 2pm. Can't believe I let you talk me into this."

"But I'm glad you did," Julie said, with real warmth in her smile.

"Ha!" Priscilla laughed and pointed at a pentagram ring on Julie's right hand. "I've still got mine too. I can't believe you still wear it."

"Yeah, I've thought of putting it in a box, but...it reminds me of who I am. Whose I am, I suppose."

Priscilla grunted. "I don't know. For me Wicca was kind of a starter religion."

Julie shook her head at this. "You can keep all that dark arts stuff."

"That's where the real power is."

"Uh-huh. Clive would agree with you on that. I can't believe he was experimenting with Cthulu magick."

"That's not dark arts, honey, that's delusional arts."

"Word." Julie sighed, then changed the subject. "Hey, it was great to see you at the Rite of Saturn the other night."

"Was that a hoot or what?" Priscilla asked. "I had a hangover for days."

"You were drunk? But you drove Clive home!"

"I handle my liquor a hell of a lot better than you do, Barkley. How *is* Clive, anyway?"

A cloud passed over Julie's face. "I wish I knew. He wasn't at work today, and he's not answering my phone calls or emails or texts."

Priscilla pointed a long fingernail adorned with black nail polish at her. "That's some serious shame, right there. He can't face you."

"Maybe—"

"No maybe about it. You're a girl, and you rushed in and saved him. The male ego does not easily recover from a blow like that."

Julie felt her shoulders deflate a bit. "You...you could be right."

"When am I *ever* wrong?" Priscilla winked at her and laid their sandwiches out.

"BBQ beef?" Julie inquired.

"I know what you like," Priscilla said.

"Yes you do," Julie said, blushing a bit. They'd been lovers for a brief time in college. Julie trusted they would always have that bond that old lovers who still love one another do.

"Got yourself a mystery," Priscilla broke the ice. She needed to, Julie reminded herself. Their time was short.

"Yep. We've got three six-foot-square blocks of unknown origin in a cornfield, and no clue what they're made of."

"Pinkish-orange, you said? Harder than granite?" Priscilla took a bite off her turkey sandwich, set it down, and daintily wiped her hands on a paper napkin.

"I couldn't even get a scraping to bring you."

"It would have been better if you could have."

"Sorry." Julie's shoulders deflated.

"Did it look like this?" Priscilla fished a plastic baggie out of her pocket and threw it on the table.

It landed with a heavier clanking sound than Julie was prepared for. She picked up the baggie, struck by how unnaturally heavy it seemed. Even if the contents had been stone, it would not have weighed half as much.

"Is it...dangerous in any way?"

"Nope. Open it. Won't hurt you. Nothing hurts *you*."

Julie let that one slide. She prised open the baggie and withdrew a single bit of what looked like pink rock, about the size of a large man's thumb. She didn't recognize the striations along the stone, but she knew the color instantly.

"That's it. That's the…stone, rock, epoxy, whatever it is. That's it."

"You're sure?"

"Not a doubt in my mind," Julie said. She gingerly placed the artifact on top of the baggie so that it wouldn't blow away. The artifact wasn't going anywhere, no matter how hard the wind might blow.

"I was afraid of that," Priscilla said, reaching for a French fry.

"Why?" Julie asked, unable to take her eyes from the thing.

"Because it isn't from around here," Priscilla said.

"Define 'here,'" Julie countered.

"I mean this plane of existence."

"That sounds a little woo-woo," Julie said.

"This from Miss 'I'm-a-witch-watch-me-roar,' 2009."

"You've seen me in some embarrassing moments."

"Including that time you were wearing nothing but your training bra hugging the toilet seat and bringing back up $200 in fine spirits."

"They were much more enjoyable going down, I'll concede that. I'll also concede that you know me far too well to ever speak to you again, if I was smart."

"You're just lucky I'm not the crazy, *vindictive* kind of bitch."

"I reckon I am. So, where's it from?" She pointed to the artifact. "If it's not from here, where's it from?"

"I don't know that," Priscilla said. "I only know how it got here."

"Don't toy with me, you prick-tease," Julie said. "How did it get here?"

Julie looked around, as if checking to make sure they wouldn't be heard. "You've heard about the Simon *Necronomicon*, yes?"

"Yeah, it's a fraud."

"No, it isn't. I mean, yes it is, but the source rituals work."

"Explain. The *Necronomicon* is fictional. Everyone knows that."

"It's true that Simon packaged a grimoire to appeal to Lovecraft fans—you know, *ooooo*, the *Necronomicon*. That's all fake. But Simon pulled several of the rituals from a much older work called the *Fenestram in Infernum*—"

"I don't know that one."

"Good. Keep it that way. Little shits who use it have no idea what they're doing."

"So what does it have to do with that?" Julie pointed at the artifact with a French fry.

"That is what some numbnuts junior at the UC brought through one night, experimenting with the rituals in the *Fenestram in Infernum*."

"This is—what? What are you saying?" Julie asked.

"*Fenestram in Infernum* means 'Window into Hell.' This is from there, wherever *there* is."

"Your saying this bit of…whatever it is…was magically transported from…from where?"

Priscilla shrugged. "Beats me."

Julie took out her phone and snapped several pictures of the artifact from different angles. "Do you know how many magnitudes of flaming shit this is going to go down in if I try to tell my boss about it?"

"Not a sentence I'd care to parse, girlfriend, but I don't care what you tell your boss. Why does he need to know?"

"Because it's why I'm here. It's a clue. I can't not read him in."

"Suit yourself." She picked up the artifact, put it back in its baggie and put it in her pocket.

"You're not going to let me take that?"

"It's an alien rock, and the only one of its kind in the UC collection —or on earth for that matter, at least that we know of. Until now, if your theory is correct."

"How did you break it?"

"I didn't break it. It was surgically removed."

Julie's brows bunched. "From where?"

"From the inside of said asshole's thigh, where it materialized."

"Let me get this straight. You're saying that some wannabe magickian at UC Bakersfield was stupidly performing a ritual by himself one night, and as a result of the magickal operation, this piece of alien flotsam materialized inside the meat of his leg?"

"All correct, except for the 'by himself' part. There was a confederate—even stupider, if that's possible."

Priscilla had always had a high regard for magick, but was less enamored of magickians. It was a position Julie felt a lot of sympathy with. Julie stared at the table, trying to comprehend the revelation.

"Look," Priscilla said, "you don't have to like it. Hell, you *shouldn't* like it. But this material is not native to this planet, maybe even to this universe. I'm a geologist. I've studied every kind of rock there is, and I can usually tell you a rock's entire history just from looking at it. But this," she held up the baggie, "is not part of our history. It's from somewhere else. And if you're right, and those cubes of yours are made of the same stuff? They're not part of our history, either."

CHAPTER FIVE

The morning brought rain, so by the time Thom reached the steps of the station, his boots were already caked with mud. He scraped them on the first of the cement steps, enough so that until he might get by with only a warning glance from Celia.

Inside, he took off his coat and hung it near the door on one of the pegs set into the wall. It was already heavy with rain. The Valley didn't see a lot of rain, and it was always welcome, so he could hardly complain about it. "Celia," he said.

"Boss," she replied. "Can I see you?"

"Oh," he said, lips pursed. That didn't sound good. He looked around quickly and saw Barkley at her desk, on the phone, not looking happy. Across from her, Jake looked like he was doing paperwork while mindlessly twirling a toothpick with his tongue.

Thom went to his office and shut the door behind him. "G'morning, Emma," he said, blowing a kiss in the direction of her urn. Then he sat down at his desk and waited for his notes and his coffee. He didn't wait long. Celia knocked once, then let herself in, putting the coffee on Thom's desk near his elbow. Then she placed a short stack of pink "while-you-were-out" notes next to it.

Thom looked down at his coffee. He desperately needed the coffee, but he couldn't drink it as it was, and he didn't want Celia to see him put sugar into it. The dilemma must have shown on his face, because a moment later Celia said, "Oh, go ahead. I won't say anything. Do what you need to do."

Thom shrank into his shoulders a bit, but he opened his desk drawer just the same and took out two cubes of sugar. Then two more. He stirred them with the dirty spoon he kept in the drawer. He pretended not to notice Celia rolling her eyes. "What's up?" he asked, finally taking a sip.

"Abel called, left a voice mail at 6am."

"Don't tell me there's more of them goddam things?"

Celia nodded. "Four more, spread out across his fields willy-nilly. All showing different people."

"Christ." Thom rubbed his cheek. "You know, whoever is doing this, it's turning into an expensive little prank. Those blocks cannot be cheap to make."

Celia shrugged. "There's more. Abel knew them all—the people in the cubes. Janet Ringweather, Clem Odinswood, Matt Cooper, and Imelda Johansen. Strange thing is, sometimes they're older than they are now, a lot older—in the sculpture."

"And the sculptures—are they violent?"

"Some are, some aren't. But they could all be...you know, a death."

"Won't hurt to say the word, Celia."

"No, Sheriff."

"Is that all?"

"I wish it were. See those slips? Mostly people who called because they heard about the cubes. People are getting curious, Thom. Tongues are wagging. If we're not careful—"

"If we're not careful, people will start trespassing, and Abel will not be happy about it."

"That's what I was thinking."

"Let's see if we can avoid that, shall we?"

"I'm going to leave that up to you. Pay special attention to Bill Arenson. Jake says he's been out to see his, and he's a bit spooked by it."

"That it?"

"Call Abel first," she instructed. "He's…upset."

"Let me guess, Mia saw her cube."

Celia nodded, her lips pursed sideways.

Thom sighed. "And?"

"Holed up in their bedroom. She won't come out, won't let Abel in."

"Where'd he sleep?"

"Uh…he didn't say."

Thom sighed. "All right. I'll call him. Is *that* it? Or do you have any more bad news waiting in the wings?"

"That's it. I'll keep you abreast." She gave him a professional nod and let herself out. He rose and followed her into the squad room. He loomed over Barkley's desk, waiting for her to finish her call. Jake looked up at him with what looked like a bit of trepidation. Thom nodded. Jake lowered his eyes and returned to his paperwork. A few moments later, Julie put the phone back into its cradle and looked up at him.

"Boss?"

"Abel's got four more cubes—all known townspeople. The gossip mill has caught word of it too. I want to know what you've got."

Jake cleared his throat. "I stood out there all day yesterday with the spooky things and got nothing but a sunburn on my neck to show for it. Other than Bill Arenson, I didn't see a soul, not even Mrs. Nyland."

"I heard about Bill," Thom said. "As for Mia, I figure she beat you out there, saw her cube, and then holed up."

"Holed up?" Julie asked.

"Won't come out of her bedroom."

"Oh. Poor woman."

"But no trespassers, no curiosity-seekers, no clues that I could see," Jake continued. "Just a bunch of creepy statues."

"And what are you doing here now?" Thom asked.

"It's not yet nine—how early do you want me out there? And for how long? It's raining!"

"I want you out there now, before Abel gets himself into trouble. And I don't know how long. Barkley, what do you got?"

Julie's eyes went wide. She looked over at Jake, then back at Thom. "Uh...can we speak...in private, boss?"

Thom scowled but nodded, waving her toward his office.

"There something going on I don't know about?" Jake called after them.

"Trust that that is always the case," Thom called back over his shoulder.

Once inside his office, Thom motioned her toward the only other chair in the tiny space. Julie had a manila folder in her hand, but didn't sit. Instead, she took a chocolate bar out of her breast pocket and set it on his desk. Without even glancing at it, he placed it in his top drawer and closed it again. "What's so sensitive you couldn't say it in front of the kid?" Jake was a little older than Julie, Thom knew, but he didn't *seem* older.

"I've identified the material...the material the cubes are made of," she said.

Thom's eyebrows leaped up at the news. "Oh? What is it?"

"We don't know."

"You just said—"

Julie held her hand up. "What I mean is, we've matched it to... other material. My friend Priscilla Niles is a geologist at the UC. She had a sample of the same stuff. She sent a spectrographic analysis over." She placed the manila folder on his desk. "You can see for yourself."

"What's it made of?"

"Nothing native to this planet."

"What??"

"The analysis matches no known elements."

"That's not possible."

"It is if it isn't from here...from this planet, I mean. Or maybe this universe."

"Now you're just talking nonsense."

She pointed to the analysis. He scanned it. He didn't understand a word of it. He closed the folder again. "So how did it get here?"

"You're not going to like this," she said.

"Try me."

"Uh...magick."

"Magic."

"Uh...yeah."

"Deputy, what in Hell's waiting room are you talking about?"

Julie sat. "Boss, before I signed on at the academy, I was a student at UC Bakersfield."

"Yep. You graduated with honors. What's your point?"

"I was a pretty messed-up kid back then. That's when I discovered magick—"

"Oh yeah. I did magic tricks when I was a kid. I can still do a card trick or two. It's good clean fun."

"That's...not what I'm talking about. That's stage magic. I'm talking about the real thing. Ceremonial magick. Magick with a 'k' at the end of it."

"Real thing? I don't follow."

"Thom, I'm a witch."

Thom's eyes widened. "You are?"

"Lot of people are. It's not unusual, not anymore. We do spells. It's part of our religion."

"It is?" He blinked.

"I became a witch when I was a teenager. Mostly to freak out my mom. It worked. But witchcraft is...it's nature magick. It's focused on healing, on getting in tune with the natural rhythms of the earth."

"It is?"

"But when I got to college, I met people who were...they were not witches. They were...they were into scarier shit. I mean, everyone in the occult community—"

"There's an occult *community*?"

"Everyone knows each other—even people who practice kinds of magick you don't or don't even approve of. Witches, ceremonial magickians, even Satanists—"

"Satanists?" Thom felt his pulse surge. He opened his desk drawer and broke off a bit of chocolate. He put part of it in his mouth, but he didn't taste it.

"We all know each other, but our practices are very different."

"You lost me at Satanist. Are you a Satanist?"

"Thom, you're not listening to me."

"Oh, I'm listening all right."

"I am *not* a Satanist. I'm a witch. Witches don't believe in Satan. We—hoo boy," she cradled her head for a moment. "Okay." She grabbed a bunch of pens out of the old coffee cup where they lived. She put them in three piles. "Look, here you have Catholics," she pointed at one pile, "and here you have Methodists," she pointed at another, "and here you have Congos, like my mom." She pointed at the last pile of pens.

"Okay," Thom said, looking at the three piles of pens.

"Catholics and Methodists and Congregationalists. They're all part of a larger, overarching religion, but they're not the same."

"No, not to ask them."

"Right. So, okay, different tradition now. In the same way you have witches," she pointed to the first pile, "and you have ceremonial magickians," she pointed at the second pile, "and you have Satanists," she pointed to the third pile. "They're all part of the larger occult community, but they have very different beliefs and practices."

Thom nodded. "So you're *not* a Satanist?"

"No."

"That's a relief."

Julie rolled her eyes. "Are you even listening to me?"

"I am. I'm following. Three different sub-categories of religiously flaky people."

Julie seemed to let that slide. "All three groups do magick. But some magick is...well, darker than others. Think of witchcraft as white magick—good magick. Think of Satanism as black magick, because...well, that's what it is. They summon demons and bend them to their will."

"They do?"

"And then there's the ceremonial magickians in the middle, and their magick is...well, it's kind of gray."

"When you say 'gray,' you mean morally ambiguous," Thom said, not really a question.

"Yes, exactly."

"And this is a real thing, not playing."

"It's a real thing."

"Shit, this is Karlstadt, not Berkeley. There aren't witches around every corner here."

"Well, actually..." Julie let the sentence trail off.

Thom rubbed at his chin. "So...you do magick?"

"Yes, and lots of other people do too."

"And it's not card tricks?"

"No."

"Then what is it?"

Julie froze, apparently not sure what or how much to say. "Thom, it's complicated. We have tables of correspondences—"

"Come again?"

She sighed. "Nature has certain...unseen connections within it—like energetic resonances."

"It does?"

"Witches and magickians make maps of these correspondences, and we activate them in order to effect change in the world."

"And how do you do that?"

"Through focused intention and ritual."

"I'm getting the picture this rabbit hole goes a lot deeper than I want to go."

"That's probably accurate," she said.

"And you...*like* this kind of thing?"

"Like? It's religion. It's the way things *are*."

Thom's eyes narrowed. "What does this have to do with Abel's cubes?"

"As I said, the material they're made of isn't from this universe. It was brought here through magick."

"Your...rituals and focused intention."

"Yes...not mine, but...someone's."

"And it's not some kind of rock?"

"None that we have here—not on earth, anyway."

"So, who is responsible for bringing this...alien stuff...from God-knows-where and puttin' it in Abel's cornfield?"

"That's the question. But at least I know where to start asking."

"Okay. You do that. But...let's just keep it between us."

"What about the reports?"

Thom nodded. "Let me think about that. Reports don't have to be submitted until a case is closed, so let's see where it takes us before we figure out how to spin it."

Julie nodded. "Thank you for...believing me."

"To be honest, deputy, I'm not sure I do believe you. I believe *you* believe it, though, and that's enough for now."

Julie kept nodding, a sad shadow passing over her features.

Just then Celia burst into the door. "Sheriff, come quick. Shots fired out at the Nyland farm."

Milala wanted to light her cigar, but she knew better. The ticket counter at the Greyhound station was indoors, and the *oje-ajnt* were very particular about where you could and could not smoke. She mashed the end of the cigar between her teeth until she wasn't sure she'd be able to light it again without some minor surgery to it.

Her quick black eyes scanned the station but saw no trace of Coyote. Perhaps the god did not like to appear where there were so many people? Or perhaps where there were so many *oje-ajnt* people? That felt right in her bones, and she made a mental note of it.

Milala shifted her bag to her other shoulder and willed herself to relax. The one person in line in front of her stepped to the ticket agent's window, and Milala stopped at the line painted on the floor. She wondered at the arbitrariness of the *oje-ajnt* and their lines— county lines, city limits, where to stand, and even when noon was to be counted. All of them were fictional, residing nowhere except on maps, clock faces, and in the *oje-ajnts'* imaginations.

"Next!" Milala's head jerked up. She saw the previous customer moving away from the ticket agent's window. She stepped up, barely able to see over the counter. "One ticket to Merced, please," she said.

"That'll be $12.45," the woman behind the glass said. Her voice was thin and tinny from the speaker just over Milala's head. The woman's eyes looked bored. It was clear that a little native woman was not a novelty for her.

Milala reached for her bag and fished in it for her wallet. She didn't feel it. "Uh, just a minute," she said, feeling at the bag with both hands now. She started to panic. She looked behind her and noted several *oje-ajnt* in line, one of them glancing at his watch and looking nervous. Quickly, she dumped the contents of her bag onto the floor at her feet. Half a donut, three pens, a small plastic bag with vitamins and aspirin, five tampons, two wadded tissues, and a dog-eared lesbian romance novel clattered to the floor. She felt at the empty bag with both hands again. No wallet.

Her eyes were wide now, and her breathing came in short gasps. She had some change, but it was less than half the amount she'd need for the ticket. "Uh...I'll have to stand in line again," she said, and scurried to scoop up her detritus to make way for the person behind her. As she scrambled out of the way, her mind raced. Where had her wallet gone? What would she do without any money? Or identification? Or credit cards? She may not like the *oje-ajnt* world much, but she still had to navigate it. How had she—

"Coyote," she said. She removed the cigar from her mouth and spat. She saw a security guard narrow his eyes at her. She quickly knelt and cleaned up the spittle with one of her used tissues. She looked around and realized both the security guards were watching her. "Shit," she breathed. "I *hate* being profiled." She positioned the straps of her bag over one shoulder and headed for the door.

There was a bench just outside the door, about twelve feet away. The sky was heavy and it was just starting to rain, but the bench was under an awning, at a place where buses routinely pulled up. She sat on it and continued to chew at the cigar. A white-crowned sparrow lit on the seat next to her, taking her in with quick, jerky motions.

"You can't get away from him," the sparrow said.

Milala frowned at the sparrow. Was this an unusually verbal sparrow, or was it White-Crowned Sparrow, the spirit of all white-crowned sparrows, speaking to her? White-crowned sparrows did not usually speak, and she realized the honor she had been given.

"He cannot make me do something I don't want to do," Milala told her.

"How can you refuse Creator? He has been so gracious to you."

"I'm not refusing Creator! I refuse Coyote. Besides, what do you know of it?" That sounded testier than she had intended.

"Lie!" the sparrow chirped.

It *was* a lie, the sparrow was right. She looked down again and caught the little bird's eye. For a long moment, they just stared at one another.

"What are you afraid of?" the bird asked.

"Me? I'm not afraid of anything," Milala answered.

"What is it you refuse to give?"

"I don't refuse to give anything. Everything is a gift from Creator. What can I own?"

"Then what is it you cannot forgive?" the sparrow pressed.

Milala blinked and looked away. She felt heat rise to her neck. She shooed the sparrow away, and it took off with a panicked fluttering of wings. Bile rose up in the back of Milala's throat. She instantly regretted frightening the bird spirit. It had only spoken truth to her. The People honored the truth. For a few terrible moments, she felt unworthy to be counted among The People.

The buses were lined up in formation at the boarding curb, each of them with an electronic sign in the front window announcing their destinations. She knew she wanted the bus to San Bernardino, as it stopped in Barstow. She watched people climbing aboard. Others were handing their bags to a uniformed young man. He looked like he was still in high school, and he took the bags without looking too closely at their owners, positioning them in the luggage hold beneath the bus.

Suddenly, a man started shouting, and every head swiveled toward the sound. Milala looked too. A man was holding the wilted body of an old woman awkwardly, and it seemed to her that the woman had collapsed and the man had just barely succeeded in catching her before she hit the asphalt. He was calling for help. Several people leaped toward the old woman, including the young man stowing baggage.

Without thinking about it, Milala walked calmly to the San Bernardino bus, unslung her bag, and walked the few steps to the baggage hold. Without looking around, as that might attract attention, she simply stepped into the hold and took refuge behind a large suitcase. She quickly moved a few smaller items, stacking them to create a further visual barrier between herself and the door. She was a short woman, and while she had rarely thanked Creator for that, it was a fact worthy of blessing in the moment. She peeked around the large suitcase and found herself staring straight into the eye of a little boy, one hand held up, clutching the hand of his mother. Milala blinked. The boy blinked. Then the hold door closed, and Milala was swallowed up by darkness.

Julie didn't need to consult her GPS. She knew exactly where she was going. *Lux Revelare* was the oldest, funkiest, most revered occult bookstore in the Valley. It was in Bakersfield, of course, which meant that most of her morning was spent driving in the rain, but that didn't bother her. What bothered her more was the idea of revisiting the place. Certainly, the atmosphere of the shop had always been ripe with dust and mold and spirits of questionable intent. But it was also thick with the ghosts of her past, and it was these she feared most.

She didn't need to drive fast, which was good, because the Central Valley got little rain, and when it did the oil slicks could be deadly. But she hardly noticed the passage of time as she drove, as her mind kept going relentlessly back to Clive. Where on earth could he be? Was he angry at her? Or just ashamed, as Priscilla opined? *Maybe both*, she thought. Or perhaps he was hurt. She resolved that, no matter how busy she was, she would go to his apartment, even if it was late. She'd knock on his door. Hell, she'd shoot out the lock if she had to. The idea made her smile. She wouldn't, of course, but she relished the raw, satisfying emotion of the fantasy.

She remembered that the bookstore opened at 11am, sometimes later. Occultists are notoriously late risers, by and large. It was 11:15 when she cracked the door of the place, momentarily startled by the tinkling of a bell overhead as the door swung inward. She'd forgotten about that, yet the bell brought back even more memories as its ringing faded. She leaned her umbrella by the door.

In truth, it hadn't occurred to her until she was halfway to the city that the store might be closed after all this time. Online booksellers had rendered such little shops redundant. Yet she did not bother to call. A part of her knew it was still here. She could smell it.

Now, standing amidst the dim stacks, the pine bookshelves painted black, stacks of books nearly obscuring the window, the buzzing fluorescent lights above, the air electric with acidic paper and profane secrets, it was as if the last five years of her life had never happened. She had perused these shelves with sisters from her coven, giggling children, all of them. And she had not been able to keep her hands off Jill.

She swallowed and reached out to brush the leather spines of a set of Cornelius Agrippa—

"Julie Barkley?"

She looked up, straight into the eyes of someone she had never expected to see again. "Hi...Ben." The name came back to her quickly, but not quite quick enough. "It's been a long time."

Benjamin Azor seemed smaller than she remembered him. He had always seemed ageless, and he still did. But the creases around his eyes were deeper. He wore coke-bottle glasses, almost comically thick. He was so thin his body was concave; his shoulders were not even, sloping dramatically to the right. When she first met him, she thought he was a hunchback, but observing him after many visits, she gradually realized that he suffered a mild paralysis on his right side. He walked with a shuffle and did most things with his left hand. It occurred to her now that he might have had a stroke once upon a time. But she had never known him well enough to ask him about it. If she were honest, she'd admit that she'd never really cared enough to ask. He was the guy who worked at the bookstore; he'd never been more than that to her.

Ben raised one of the boards forming the counter, swinging it up on its hinges as he shuffled out. The board stood straight up as if giving the middle finger to the world. That was *Lux Revelare* in a nutshell, she realized. Ben held his hands out unevenly, as if to say, "Behold!"

"Look at you! Look at that uniform! I almost didn't recognize you." He stopped just shy of her and looked up at her through his impossibly thick glasses. They wildly distorted his eyes, making them appear as giant, subaquatic creatures—leviathan and his mate, roiling in an amorous frenzy across the bridge of his nose.

"How are you, Ben?" Julie asked.

"Oh, you know, about the same. Asthma, palsy, hedonism—the usual constellation of maladies magickians are prone to."

She forced a smile. "You look well," she lied. She looked around the place. Had there always been cobwebs in the corners? Probably. "I'm glad to see you're still here."

"Well, the big A isn't making things easy for us." He took off his glasses and fished a handkerchief from his hip pocket. Without them his eyes looked like the rounded backs of tiny beetles. He polished them absently as he talked. "The trick is to diversify, to become indispensable. The big A can sell books, but can they offer classes on occult philosophy? Can they rent people an operable temple? Can they offer elixirs and potions made to order?" He pointed behind the counter, where she saw row upon row of wooden boxes, exactly like the drawers she'd seen for herbs in Chinese pharmacies.

He put his glasses back on and cocked his head. "To best the beast, you have to be beastier."

"You're the beastiest, Ben," Julie said, more lightheartedly than she felt.

"What can I get for you?" Ben asked. "As I recall, you were part of a Wiccan coven at the UC. Are you still in the craft?"

"I am, but I'm mostly a solitary practitioner."

"I'm sure you've got Cunningham—"

Julie issued something like a raspberry. "Please. Cunningham. The training wheels are off, Ben."

"No offense intended. It's hard to know where people are on their journeys just by looking."

"None taken, not really. In fact, Ben, I'm not looking for a book. Well, I am, just not for myself."

"Oh? A gift?"

"Not exactly. I'm here because I'm...well, it's official business." She pointed to her badge.

Through his mammoth lenses, she saw the capybara of his eyebrows sit up on their haunches.

"Satanic ritual murder?" His voice sounded a bit too much like a little boy on Christmas morning. Julie shuddered.

"No, nothing that dramatic...although, dramatic enough, I suppose. But no, no one's dead. It's not a murder investigation. It's more...more like vandalism, I suppose."

"Occult vandalism. Is someone spray-painting sigils? I heard something like that took down the East Bay. Nasty business..."

"No, nothing like that."

"What then?"

"Have you sold a copy of the *Fenestram in Infernum* anytime in the past year or so?"

Ben recoiled as if she'd slapped him. "Uh...no. Not...as such."

"So, that's a yes."

"You did say you were too advanced for Cunningham, but...Jesus."

"Let's get back to that yes," Julie insisted.

"That's Cthulu magick," Ben said. "And not the play stuff."

"Right. Someone's playing with it and people are going to get hurt...emotionally, I suppose, they already are."

"There wouldn't be the....I don't know....the Reification of Death, would there?" Ben asked.

"You see there? I knew I came to the right place." Julie smiled.

"Oh gods. Sheesh. I told him to be careful."

"Told who?"

"Some guy. He wasn't a magickian."

"How do you know?"

"Please. It's like gaydar. I can smell a magickian from fifty paces."

"That's because magickians don't bathe."

"Unfortunately true," Ben conceded. "Um...has there been an actual crime?"

"Don't worry, you're not a suspect," Julie said. "We've got...reifications appearing in a farmer's field."

"How many?" Ben asked.

"Seven, so far."

"That makes sense. They usually come in prime numbers," Ben muttered, looking away, as if trying to remember something.

"They do?"

"Usually."

"So you've seen this kind of thing before?" Julie asked.

"They're pink, aren't they? Orangy-pink?"

"You *have* seen this before." Julie put her hands on her hips.

"It's the Reification of Death ritual from the *Fenestram*, no question."

"How can you possibly sell something that dangerous?" Julie asked.

Instead of answering immediately, Ben shuffled back to the counter, went behind it and lowered the board again. Safely behind his barrier, Ben leaned on it, resting on his elbows, and said in a low, conspiratorial voice. "What do you think magick is about?"

Julie stopped. It was such an odd question. It was the kind of question she'd need a long car ride to tease apart. So she turned it around. "What do *you* think magick is about?" she asked.

"It's about power. It's always about power. A guy feels weak, powerless, impotent to stand against the pretty people and the rich people and the faceless corporations." He waved his left hand about, as if conjuring enemies from the aether. "The kind of power they have is out of his reach and always will be. He doesn't have the intellect or the money or the connections or the time to amass it like they do—"

"Or the work ethic?" Julie added.

He ignored her amendment. "—so they turn to magick. If power isn't earned, it can be stolen. It can just be *taken*."

Julie was fascinated by his explication. "Magick is stealing power?"

"What else could it be?" Ben asked.

"Wiccans always say it's about shaping the power that's latent in nature."

"Pah. Wicca. Yeah, I'm not talking about Little Becky Granola with her easy-bake-oven cakes of light. I'm talking about summoning demons, or in this case...the Great Old Ones."

"Who are, strictly speaking, fictional."

Ben shrugged. It looked weird, since only the left half of his body could shrug. "Hey, the magick works. It's making contact with *something*."

"I'm going to need the name of the person you sold it to."

"I'm sure that's true, but I don't think I'm obligated to give it to you."

Julie scowled and unconsciously placed her right hand on the holster of her service revolver. "Oh? And why is that?"

"Our customers have an expectation of discretion."

"I'm not asking for a list of your customers, Ben. I'm asking you to tell me who you sold one book to."

"You're a county deputy sheriff. And judging from the patch on your arm, we're not in your county. You don't have any jurisdiction here."

That was true. Technically, Julie shouldn't be here without part-nering up with a representative of the Kern County sheriff's office. "I'm investigating, not making an arrest. And you know, we *do* talk to each other." She hadn't talked to anyone from Kern County, but he didn't need to know that.

His enormous eyes wavered behind his glasses. She imagined he was sizing her up, sussing out her level of nerve. She knew she had the power to surprise him on that score, but she didn't need to prove it. She leaned on the counter and sighed, her shoulders relaxing. "Look, Ben, I'm not here to arrest anyone. I'm just here to stop this thing before someone gets hurt. Surely, you want that too."

Ben said nothing. His brows were bunched, but Julie couldn't divine what that meant. She continued, "I'm not trying to invade anyone's privacy. I'm not here to make trouble for you. I'm here because I *get* this world—and of all the deputies in this entire state, I'm probably the only one who knows just how badly we need your help."

She looked him in the eye and held it. His eyes loomed and soared behind his enormous lenses to such a degree that Julie felt nauseated. She clenched her jaw and forced herself to hold his eyes.

He nodded then, and looked away. "Wait here," he said. She watched as he shuffled off toward the back room. He went through a door to what she had always assumed was the office, but returned quickly, a little moleskin book in his left hand.

He set the book on the counter. "He paid cash, so I don't have a credit card number to give you."

"Damn," Julie said. "That would have been helpful. How much did he pay, just for grins?"

He consulted the book. "Seven thousand dollars."

Julie whistled. "That's a lot for a book."

"Eh...it is and it isn't. I've seen books go for a lot more. Especially grimoires."

"What magician could afford seven thousand dollars?"

"Precious few...except for rich dabblers."

"Was this guy a rich dabbler?"

"No. He was in some redneck gang."

Julie drew back. "Really?"

Ben nodded. "Really. White guy. Skinhead. Got some Klan tattoos on his fingers."

"What in the world would a guy like that..." Julie let her words trail off.

"I don't know. Gangs are always trying to get an edge over other gangs, I imagine," Ben mused. "Why not a magickal edge?"

"They must have a magickian on the payroll then. I mean, it's not just something you pick up."

"Well, people try. That's how people fry their chakra systems."

"True enough. Okay, how can I find this gangbanger?"

"Right next to the Klan tatt was a sigil."

"This just gets more interesting," Julie said. "Can you draw it for me?"

"Don't need to. It's from the *Clavicula Salomonis Regis*, the *Lesser Key of Solomon*. It's the sigil for Duunel."

"That's the name of a demon, I take it?"

"Yeah. Not a very powerful demon, but...influential."

"I still want you to draw it. I don't have a copy of the *Lesser Key*, and no reason to pick one up. We Becky Granolas don't do demons."

"Okay, okay. But under protest. You can't draw a sigil without drawing attention."

"I believe that," Julie said. "Do a warding. Hell, do a Lesser Banishing Ritual. Do what you need to do."

"One more thing. He left this phone number. I was supposed to call when I found it—the book."

"That's more like it," Julie said. "Write that down too, please."

Ben shook his head. "Promise me this guy will never know I gave this to you."

"I promise. And Ben," she caught his eye. "You're doing the right thing."

He didn't look so sure. "This guy could snap me in half as easy as look at me," Ben said. "You know, I'm not into magick because I'm strong or anything. I'm into it because I'm not."

———————

Thom saw the new cubes before he ever left Route 128. He pulled up the long drive to the Nyland house a bit faster than was prudent in the rain. Along the way he finished off the half-a-Hershey's bar that had been living in his ashtray. He'd only meant to take a square, but before he knew what was happening, he'd eaten it all.

He sucked the chocolate off his fingers just as he was setting the brake.

Everything seemed quiet, and the quiet precipitation only added to that effect. He relished that, even as he knew in his heart that the peace he felt wasn't trustworthy. He got out and put his beat-up cowboy hat on his head. Looking around, he saw Jake's truck alongside Abel's, a stone's throw from the tractor. He heard barking, and a moment later Ginger Beer burst into view, heading straight for him. He turned his hip to the dog as the yellow lab tried to jump up on him. "Nope! You just stay on the ground, as God intended. Now where's your master?"

Ginger Beer did not oblige, but instead sniffed at his trouser legs, oblivious to the rain. Continuing to look around, Thom noted that the barn door had been slid back on its track. He headed for it, the lab on his heels.

He'd never known Abel to be a hasty or reckless man. He had a shotgun, but every farm needed one. There were foxes, wolves, coyotes, and occasionally human threats, and a farm could feel a long way from help. But even a man as rock-solid as Abel Nyland was bound to be a bit jumpy being targeted by vandals, pranksters...whatever and whoever they were. Thom felt sorry for him. It was a familiar feeling. He encountered a lot of victims in his work, and few of them deserved the pain and stress that were visited upon them. No one had ever told him that empathy was part of the job description, but the job had taught him that.

He slipped through the cracked barn door and blinked, willing his eyes to adjust more quickly.

"Boss!" He heard Jake's voice. He moved toward it. Too slowly, he began to understand what he was seeing. Jake and Abel were seated on bales of hay. Abel was sitting up too straight, and his hands were behind his back. A shotgun leaned against one wall. Jake looked... what? Angry? Concerned? Jake only had one emotion that Thom knew of—anxious uncertainty—so he was unfamiliar with the emotions his deputy was currently displaying. Ginger Beer went straight to her master, who ignored her.

Thom shook the water off his hat and looked down on both of the men. "Abel. Jake. Bring me up to speed on what just happened."

"I'm not the criminal here!" Abel shouted.

"Abel, are you cuffed?" Thom leaned over, trying to see Abel's hands.

"Yes, he's cuffed—" Jake began.

"Jake, take off Abel's cuffs." Thom ran his fingers through his hair.

"But—"

"Do it now, deputy."

Jake scowled at Abel, who turned to show the deputy his hands. Jake shook his head as he selected the right key and removed the cuffs. Jake put them back in the holster at his belt while Abel rubbed at his wrists.

"That's the first thing that's made sense today, Sheriff," Abel said. "Thank you."

Thom nodded. He rolled another hay bale over so that he could sit on it facing the other two men. He put his hat to one side. Ginger Beer came to him and stuck her nose into the hollow between the bale and his crotch. He stroked the fur on her neck.

"What happened here? You start, Abel."

Jake scowled even harder.

"Your deputy was supposed to keep trespassers off my land."

Jake's eyes widened and he looked like he'd been slapped. "This is *not* my fault!"

"Easy, Jake. You'll get your turn. Abel?"

"It was the Beeson kids, the teenagers. Just standing in the field, gawking at the...at *them*."

Thom nodded. The Beesons had a lot of kids, none of them terribly civilized even by country standards. Thom could never remember seeing them but that he suspected they were up to no good. He had little trouble understanding Abel's contempt.

"What were they doing?"

"Taking pictures with their phones," Abel said.

"And did they?"

"Only from a distance. I got off a good shot before Dudley Do-Right grabbed my shotgun and put the cuffs on me."

Thom nodded. Jake's face was growing red. The kid looked like he was about to blow a gasket. Thom found he was enjoying that. He knew how badly the deputy wanted to leap in, set the record straight. He made him wait for it.

"Where's Mia?"

"Up at the house."

"How is she doing?"

Abel looked at his boots. "She won't come out of our bedroom. She's holed up in there."

"How long?"

"Ever since...ever since she saw...you know. It."

Thom nodded. "She's rattled."

"Hell yes, she's rattled. I just wish she'd...I wish she'd talk to me."

Thom couldn't stop the curl of a smile turning up one side of his mouth. "Those are not words you are accustomed to uttering, Abel."

Abel looked confused, then thoughtful. Thom stroked Ginger Beer's head and let it pass. He finally turned to his deputy. It was cruel to stretch it out further. "Jake?"

"I was in the field near the Arenson cube—"

"Is that how we're talking about them now?" Thom leaned back on his bale. "I'm not sure I like that. But we can figure out *how* to talk about them later, I suppose. Go on."

"I didn't see the trespassers, as they were on the other side of the barn," Jake explained. "Hell, I can't be everywhere at once. The cubes are pretty spread out. Anyway, the Beesons were looking at the...well, the new arrivals." Thom nodded. Jake continued, "That's when I heard the shotgun blast. I ran toward the sound, toward the barn. Once I was on the East side of it, I saw Abel with his 12-gauge taking a bead. I ordered him to stand down, and when he didn't, I removed the firearm from his possession and restrained him. Then I ran toward the kids."

"Any damage?"

Jake nodded. "Scored Dale Beeson good in the shoulder. I called for a bus. Took him to Mercy in Bakersfield. They're going to be working all day to get the buckshot out."

Thom nodded. "That it?"

"That's it," Jake said.

"Abel, instead of just shooting, why didn't you alert Deputy Hessup of the trespassers so that he could deal with them properly?"

"They were trespassing on my land!"

"It's why I put him here, Abel."

Abel looked away. Thom stood up and adjusted his belt. He picked up his hat and waved at his deputy. Jake rose and followed him to the barn door. They slipped out, but didn't lose sight of the farmer.

Jake lowered his voice. "You want me to arrest him, boss?"

"No, I don't want you to arrest him."

"But boss—"

"Jake, you've lived most of your life here. Have you ever known Abel Nyland to be a public menace?"

"No, but—"

"This isn't like him. He's upset. Someone—God knows why—is pranking him and it's got him and Mia rattled something fierce. I don't blame them a bit."

"But that still doesn't—"

"Look, I'll have a chat with the Beeson twins. If they want to press charges, we'll see. But until then, let's just hold on to Abel's weapons for a bit. Don't process them, just…throw them in your trunk until things settle down. Abel's not to blame here, he's just…he's in rough shape."

Jake didn't look happy. "What now?"

"After you secure his firearms, I want you back out in that field."

"Boss—"

"Just do it. The Beeson kids were taking pictures, which means they're probably posting them to their social media machines. It's not just gossip now. Word is out. There'll be more. Next time stop them *before* Abel does them bodily harm."

"What are you going to do?"

Thom nodded toward the house. "I'm gonna check on Mia." He stepped back into the barn. "Abel? I'd like to talk to your wife."

Abel pushed past the sheriff and glared at Jake. "C'mon, then." Ginger Beer leaped at him playfully as he strode toward the house, but the farmer ignored her.

Thom pointed to the field. Jake's brow furrowed. "It's raining."

"That's why God made hats and coats. Get yours." Then Thom followed Abel up to the house. As they climbed the steps, Thom put a hand on Abel's elbow. Abel paused. "You shot a kid today, Abel. Maybe you think it isn't that serious, but it is." Abel moved toward the door, but more slowly. He didn't meet Thom's eye. "If the kid has complications, or God forbid, dies, it's going to be worse for you."

"Kid was trespassing."

"Which warrants a call to my office, not an armed response. The kid was unarmed. The only thing he was shooting was pictures."

The door was open, but Abel didn't enter. He hovered at the threshold. He turned to face Thom. "How...how bad is it?"

"Depends on if the kid wants to press charges. If'n he does, you could be looking at a couple of years."

"You don't really think—"

"I think you'll need a good lawyer. Your lack of a record and community standing will go a long way. But I can't promise you won't serve, Abel. I just want you to really hear me, without Jake here, cause he's got under your skin now. But he did the right thing, and you've got to let that go. And..." He took off his hat and rubbed at his head. "...you've got to be extra careful now. This has to be a fluke. We're going to take your guns, and you're going to let us. And you're going to get them back on the other side of all this. But you didn't do yourself any favors today. I'm just giving it to you straight, because I respect you."

"I appreciate that, Sheriff."

"Tell me about Mia."

Abel entered finally, and Thom followed after. Abel pointed up the stairs. "She's in the bedroom. Got the door locked."

"She say anything?"

"Not really. But I've never been much of a talker. Maybe I don't know the right questions." He met Thom's eye. Thom saw the concern in it, maybe even a bit of fear. He reached out and clapped Abel on the shoulder.

"Okay if I go on up?"

Abel nodded and led Thom up the stairs. At the top, Abel went past the bathroom, turned toward the bedroom, and knocked. "*Gumman?* The sheriff is here."

Abel waited, but there was no response. He met the sheriff's eyes, then looked away. He was about to say something, but then thought better of it and stopped. His eyes moved back and forth, thinking. Finally, he said, "*Gumman,* tell me how you feel."

At first there was no response. Abel sighed. But then a weak voice came from behind the door. "You've never asked me how I feel before."

"Well, I'm asking now. I'm..." Abel seemed at a loss for words, and he fidgeted in place. "I'm worried about you, *gumman.*"

He waited, but she didn't say anything else. He cleared his throat. "Sheriff Thom Lind is here. He'd like a word with you."

Abel moved away from the door and gave Thom a nod. "She's alive."

Thom briefly put a hand on his shoulder and then moved to stand by the door. "Mia, this is Sheriff Lind. Can you come to the door, please? You don't need to open it, you just need to talk to me. If you don't, I'll break it down and come in. That's not a threat, that's just the way it is. I don't want to do any damage to your home, so just come to the door...please."

He heard motion then. A moment later, he heard a tentative voice through the door. "Thom?"

"How are you, Mia?"

She didn't answer that. Thom cleared his throat. "Uh...Abel shot one of the Beeson kids. He's in no little bit of trouble. He's going to need you."

"He shot someone?"

"He did."

"Are they okay?"

"Don't know yet. I reckon he's in surgery now."

"Which one?"

"What?"

"Which Beeson kid?"

"Abel says it was Dale," Thom said, a little too loudly.

"That's terrible," Mia almost moaned.

"It…well, we'll see. You should pray that it's not too bad for the kid."

"I will."

"Mia, why won't you come out?"

A long silence passed. Finally, though, Mia said. "I'm going to die. Soon."

"What? How do you figure?"

"I saw it in the cube."

"The only thing that cube showed anybody is what Mia Nyland looks like when she takes a bath."

"No. It shows me what I look like…dead."

"Mia, I don't really think—"

"No, Thom. I know. *I know*. Okay? And I'm not old when it happens."

"Mia, whoever is making these blocks—or cubes or whatever—they're just trying to get a rise out of you. It's nothing but nonsense. If you hole up like this, it means they win. Don't give them what they want, Mia."

"Are they watching?" Mia asked.

Thom scowled. Involuntarily, he looked up, wondering if, indeed, there were any bugs, any hidden cameras, anything that might convey to the perpetrators news of their success. But that was the stuff of conspiracy theories. He shook his head to clear it of the ridiculous notion. "No, Mia, they're not watching. I just… Look, Mia, whoever is doing this, the only reason I can think of for doing it is…well, just to upset you. No one is dead. Troy's not dead, Bill Arenson isn't dead. You're not dead. Janet, Clem, Matt, and Ari, they're all fine. This is just a big hoax."

"Are you sure?"

"Am I sure about what?"

"That they're all still...alive?"

"Well, I'm usually among the first to hear, if it were otherwise. And I have not heard. But...if it will make you feel better, I'll have Celia call them up to check. How's that?"

She didn't respond.

"Mia, whoever did this, they wanted to spook you. And they did. But you don't have to give them a win so easily. Those cubes don't mean nothin'."

He stood there for several minutes, listening. Mia was silent. Then, to his great surprise, the doorknob turned, and the door opened slowly. Mia leaned against the doorframe, her eyes puffy and her face gaunt and hollow-looking. Her hand was shaking as she lifted it and pointed toward the bathroom. "I want...can you...put police tape over the door?"

"Police tape?" Thom scowled. "You want me to put police tape over the door of your bathroom?"

"Yes. A big 'X' over the door, so no one will go in or out."

"Mia, your bathroom is not a crime scene."

"No, I know." Her eyes flickered with a crazed light Thom did not recognize. "But I don't want it to become one."

Thom's brows knit together as he looked over at Abel. "It's okay with me, Sheriff. We can use the shower downstairs. And we got two other toilets in the house."

Thom nodded. He looked back at Mia. He knew her fear was irrational, but he doubted that attempting to reason with her would get him anywhere. He nodded. "All right. That's...prudent. It's not a crime scene...yet. Let's make sure it stays that way."

Troy Swanson hated his life. He hated the I-5 corridor and his regular route from Sacramento to San Bernardino. One of the ways he made it bearable was finding little bright spots to look forward to at every stop. He could drive two hours at a clip without blinking, but he didn't want to do more—it wasn't good for him and he knew himself. Any more and he'd start to get sleepy. After several years driving for the Pacific Stevedore company he found that his days consisted of driving from one oasis to another. He lived for his breaks, for the twenty to thirty minutes he spent out of his rig every couple of hours. And hands down, one of his favorite oases was Debbie's.

The supper crowd was just starting to assemble when he stepped through the door and waved at Tali. He expected her to acknowledge him with a smile and a flip of her chin, sending him toward a table or maybe even a booth on a slow day. But she didn't do that. Instead, she froze; the look on her face was hard to read. She looked...what? Guilty? Ashamed? He cocked his head and wondered what dark secret Tali might possibly know that she might have betrayed him with. Other than the fact that he tipped her a little extra for a second scoop of spumoni on his apple pie, he had no clue what it might be.

But now he saw that she wasn't the only one staring at him. The whole place had gone quiet, and every eye in the room was on him. His mind raced. *Do I have bed hair?* he wondered. *Do I have coke dust beneath my nostrils?* He involuntarily felt at his upper lip. *Am I trailing toilet paper from my shoe?* But he hadn't visited the toilet yet—that was going to be his next stop after finding a table. "What?" he finally said out loud to the whole room. "What are you staring at?" It was an unregulated outburst—he was sure he would regret it. But he was not a man with a long fuse, and he was beginning to get spooked.

"As you were!" Tali shouted. That seemed to break the spell. People looked away from him and glanced at one another guiltily. A few eyes glanced back at him. He wasn't sure, but it seemed like they were looking at him with pity—a strange, unfamiliar, and uncomfortable emotion for him.

"Gus, I'm going to take my break," Tali shouted over the serving counter.

"What, *now*?" Gus called back.

Troy saw Tali's head jerk in his own direction and caught a brief glimpse of Gus' eyes over a steaming plate of corned beef hash waiting to be served.

"Oh," he saw Gus' lips form the sound, but didn't hear it.

Tali pulled a cup of coffee and walked toward him, that same strange look of pity in her eyes. "Troy, do you mind if I take my break with you?" Without waiting for his response, she pointed at a booth. "Have a seat."

He really did need to visit the rest room, but he didn't argue with her. If there was one thing he was good at, it was managing a swollen bladder. As he sat, he said, "Am I in the Twilight Zone? What's going on?"

"No one's talked to you yet?" Tali asked.

"No," Troy said.

"How time-sensitive is your cargo today?" she asked.

"I'm a trucker, not running guns up the Congo on the African Queen. We don't say 'cargo,'" he said.

"I'm sorry I don't have the right words. I don't know how to say this to you. I didn't rehearse." For the first time he could remember, Tali looked lost.

"Tali, what's going on?" he asked again.

"I'm going to make your sandwich to go," she said. "And then I'm going to get someone to run you up to the Nyland farm."

Troy blinked. "I don't even know where that is. I've got a schedule. What?—" But he couldn't formulate the question.

She put a hand on his arm. "There's...there's just something you need to see."

———

Milala was running. She was running toward a cliff, the wide expanse of the Pacific bobbing before her. Suddenly her way was blocked by a barking dog. The dog was gold in color, its tail was wagging, yet it was insistent. It would let her get no closer to the cliff. She tried to go around it, but the dog moved to block her path again. She turned and ran the other way, but the dog was faster, circling to her right, blocking her way again. She realized the dog was steering her, forcing her to go a certain direction. She stopped and the dog stopped. The dog's tail wagged again.

It was just a great game as far as the dog was concerned, but Milala began to feel desperate. She realized she was out of options. She could confront the dog, if the dog would let her, or she could go the way the dog was trying to force her. She turned and looked in that direction. A footpath wound down a mountain, but as she watched, flowers sprouted all along its length. She thought about how lovely it would feel beneath her feet, and she began to take off her boots. A blinding light occluded all else in the meadow, then, as if the sun had just gone nova—

Milala blinked. She still felt the gentle rumble of the engines beneath her—a relaxing, primordial feeling, as if she were once more in the womb or in the belly of a great beast, feeling the rush of blood and its heart beating in rhythm all around her. They whined as they slowed down, and eventually the bus lurched to a stop. The door clanked and hissed as it opened, flexing its hydraulic assembly. Searing light intruded into the hold—painful and jagged, rudely breaking the mood of her neotenous rapture. Indistinct shapes loomed, like walking trees. As Milala squinted, the forms gradually resolved into shapes identifiable as people.

"Where?" A man's voice asked. He sounded uncertain, like a man who was at the end of his patience.

"There." A child's voice. A tiny tree—a bush, really—pointed at her.

The larger shape wove around in space, then swore under his breath. He did not bother to apologize to the boy. "All right, whoever you are, I want you to come out of there right now."

As her vision improved, Milala saw that it was the bus driver speaking, and he seemed to be addressing *her*. More people were crowding around now, and they were all looking directly at her. The bus driver swore again and began to pace. "Don't let her leave," he said, and stepped away from the opening.

"Where would she go?" a woman's voice asked. Perhaps the child's mother?

Milala couldn't tell. She was waking up, but a dull ache behind her eyes began to assert itself. She was having a very hard time struggling to consciousness; it reminded her of times she had woken up sick. *I need to get out*, she thought, not because she was being told to, but because something was wrong. She forced herself up onto one elbow and rolled off the bulky, modular, yet comfortable bed of luggage she had been lying on.

She raised one leg to exit the luggage hold. Hands reached for her to steady her, hands that seemed unattached to human bodies, hands that seemed to come out of nowhere. She stood then, a little shakily. Then she vomited.

A firmer set of hands held her by her shoulders, and she saw a middle-aged *oje-ajnt* woman supporting her, steering her away from the bus. Her mind flashed on the dog in her dream, steering her away from the cliffs, toward the Beauty Way—and she let herself be steered.

The sun was not only far too bright, she realized, it was too hot as well. *Hadn't it been raining?* she wondered. But the rain had stopped. Milala could see nothing but blacktop and brush, extending before her into seeming infinity. The ground was stony and the rain had left it slightly red. The sky was a deep blue adorned by clumps of dark clouds, pressing down upon her like a pillow held over her face, smothering her.

"Where are we?" Milala asked the *oje-ajnt* woman.

"I don't know. We've been on the road for a couple of hours," the woman said, a compassionate tone coloring her voice.

She could hear a man's voice talking in the distance. It was the bus driver, she realized, speaking into his cell phone. But she couldn't make out what he was saying. A few minutes later, someone pressed a cool bottle of water into her hands. She twisted the cap off and drank greedily. As soon as the water washed over her throat, she felt nauseated again. But this time she did not throw up.

A man was approaching along with his uniform—the bus driver. He placed his hands on his hips. "You do know that stowing away is against the law, don't you?"

"Um..." she said, but couldn't manage more than that.

"Do you have a headache?" he asked. "Feel sick?"

She nodded.

"Diesel poisoning," he said. "The luggage hold gets a lot of blow-back from the engines. You're lucky to be alive."

"Um..." Milala responded. It was a very different "um" than the first—a confirmation of fact.

"You're going to make us late," the driver said. "Because we can't leave until the sheriff gets here."

"Sheriff?" Milala's heavy eyes widened a bit.

"He's on his way," the driver said.

"Just...let me ride with you the rest of the way," Milala pointed to the bus.

"No ma'am. Regulations are clear. I'm to call law enforcement and wait until they arrive. Besides, you probably need medical attention."

"No..." Milala thought. She could barely afford the clinic on the reservation, how could she possibly pay an *oje-ajnt* doctor? It was a crazy idea. She began to look around, she needed to find a way out. But like the dog in her dream, every avenue of escape seemed blocked to her. A distant siren heralded the imminent arrival of the sheriff, or an ambulance—she couldn't tell which just yet. The pain in her head was getting worse as the anesthetizing effects of the diesel were wearing off and she was able to feel the full effects of the poisoning.

She heard the sound of laughter then, and the surreality of her experience reasserted itself. She felt like she needed to lie down, but her head was spinning. And the laughter got louder. Biting her lip, she forced her eyes open and searched the roadside for the laugher. She found him. "Coyote," she snarled.

Just then the phone rang. Peg was momentarily startled. She picked up the phone. "First Congregational Church of Karlstadt. Jesus loves you and so do we."

"Pastor Peg?"

She recognized the voice, but it took a second or two to connect it to a face. "Imelda?"

"I...Peg, do you know about the...the cubes?" Imelda sounded upset.

"Cubes?" Peg asked.

"They...they're in a cornfield, out at the Nyland place."

"There are cubes in a cornfield at Nyland's farm?" Peg said, trying to make sense of it.

"Yes...and one of them...so I hear...is mine. I..." She began to cry.

Peg's eyes moved back and forth quickly. "Imelda, I have no idea—"

"Will you go with me?" Imelda interrupted her. "To the cornfield?"

"Will I go with you to a cornfield to see a cube that is somehow yours?" Peg asked. "Um...when?"

"Now?"

Peg cleared her throat. "It's a little late in the day," she said. "I'm afraid it would be dark by the time we got there. Or raining again. Why don't we go first thing in the morning?"

She waited for the sniffling to stop. Then Imelda said, "Okay."

"I'll pick you up at nine," Peg offered.

"Okay," Imelda said.

"Will you be all right until then, or do you want me to come over now, just to be with you?" Peg asked. *Please say no, please say no,* the voice in her head pleaded.

"No, I'll be all right until morning."

Peg breathed a silent sigh of relief. "Are you sure?"

"Yes."

"All right then, love. I'll see you on the bright side of nine."

———

"Dog, what are you whining about?" Abel snapped.

Ginger Beer's ears flattened and she hung her head.

Abel took a deep breath. "I'm sorry, girl. I'm just..." Was he really apologizing to a dog? *Yes, and it's right that I do,* he thought. He was on edge, and poor Ginger didn't deserve to be snapped at. He shook his head to clear it and began to look around for some clue as to what was causing her to make so much noise. It wasn't like her.

He wandered into the kitchen and his eyes lit upon her water bowl —it was empty. He brought it to the sink and noted Ginger's pumping tail as he began to fill it. *At least there's one mystery solved,* he thought, setting the bowl down and getting out of the way as the dog lapped at the water eagerly.

He climbed the stairs and stopped as soon as the police tape over the bathroom became visible. He glanced over at his bedroom door— the shut door, the locked door, the door behind which his wife was... what? What could she possibly be doing? The voice in his head said *cowering,* and he didn't rebuke it. It seemed true enough.

A moment later, Ginger Beer was at his heels again, ready for whatever adventure might await them. Absently, he reached down and scratched her ears.

A knock at the door interrupted him. Ginger Beer barked and leaped away. With one final glance at the barrier between his wife and himself, Abel descended the last of the stairs and opened the door.

He started when he saw who it was. "Afternoon, Troy." Troy Swanson nodded, holding a baseball cap by the brim. Brown hair fell nearly to his shoulders, and his nose bulged in mid-arc, as if it had been broken one too many times.

"Mr. Nyland."

"You can call me Abel."

Troy nodded, but the friendly offer didn't unseat the troubled look on his face.

"You drive the rig all the way out here?" Abel asked.

"No. It's in town. I caught a ride."

"Ah. Well...I reckon you're here to see *it.*"

Troy looked away but nodded. "I'm not exactly sure what *it* is, but...yes."

"I knew this moment would come. I knew it from the very first morning." He didn't expect Troy to know what that meant, but the trucker didn't ask. "C'mon, then." He grabbed his hat and held the door for Ginger Beer, who darted out and began to sniff and snort at

Troy's crotch. Troy pushed her nose away, not unkindly, and followed Abel down the stairs. Abel waved at Jake out in the cornfield. The deputy waved back. Abel understood that he'd been watching the house ever since Troy had been dropped off. He gave another "all is well" wave and saw Jake turn back to his vigil.

"This way," Abel said, pointing in the direction of the first cube.

"What is that?" Troy asked as they drew near to it. It was clear how large it was, and of course they were coming up behind it. Abel waited until Troy was standing next to him, close enough to the cube to reach out and touch it.

"You ready for this?" Abel asked.

Troy's eyebrows were bunched in curiosity and alarm. He nodded.

Abel waved him on, leading to the left around the edge of the cube. Once around the corner, Abel stepped back and clasped his hands behind his back, waiting. He watched Troy closely as the trucker rounded the corner and caught his first glimpse of himself.

The immediacy of the sculpture still impressed Abel. It captured Troy so perfectly—his long hair floating weightlessly, seeming to defy gravity, his cheek flattened against a pane of glass unseen but suggested by the artist. There was pain and surprise and helpless abandon on that face, frozen in a tangle of emotions.

A similar tangle was unspooling on the real Troy's face as well. His eyes were wide as he took in the details. He stepped back toward Abel, apparently to get the full context of the thing. When his eyes finally broke away and looked at Abel, there was fire in them.

"Who did this?" Troy demanded. "Who...did *this*?" He pointed at the cube.

"We don't know. The sheriff is investigating."

"I want to sue," Troy said.

"Gotta know *who* to sue to file suit," Abel said.

"It isn't right," Troy said.

"No," Abel agreed. "There is nothing *right* about this."

Troy's nostrils twitched, and a vein in his forehead turned purple. Abel feared the young man would have a stroke on the spot. "If you leave your number, I'll keep you informed on our progress," Abel said. "I promise."

Troy ignored him. He didn't get closer to the sculpture, but nor could he look away. "Is this it?"

"There are others...lots of 'em. Fourteen of them, so far. But—"

"I want to see them," Troy snapped.

"This is the only one that shows you," Abel finished his sentence.

"Oh," Troy said. That seemed to calm him a bit. "Are the others...?"

"Violent?" Abel guessed. Troy nodded. Abel continued, "Not all. But they're all...or they could be...they sure *look* like...they're all dying. Or dead."

Troy shook his head slowly. "What kind of sick motherfucker...?"

"That is the question," Abel said.

"What am I supposed to do with this?" Troy asked.

Abel didn't understand the question. What *was* there to do? But then Abel remembered how helpless he had felt when the sheriff had asked him to stay put and leave the investigation to the authorities. Abel had wanted to leap into it himself. He had wanted to *do* something. Every impulse in him wanted to *fix it* somehow.

But there was nothing to fix. And Abel needed to let the police do the policing. The only thing he *could* do was to be patient. In some moments, even that felt like too much.

"You need a minute?" Abel asked Troy.

"Do you mind?" Troy asked.

"Not at all. C'mon, Ginger girl. Let's give the man some privacy." He gave Troy a smile that was more of a polite grimace than anything else, then turned back toward the house.

Ginger Beer barked and leaped after him, but she kept throwing a glance over her shoulder at the trucker as they walked. Abel looked at his watch and wondered if Mia would emerge from her isolation soon to start supper. On the one hand, he wasn't very hungry. His stomach was knotted with worry; he wondered if he *could* eat, even if Mia fixed her best. Hell yes, he'd eat twice if it would give her a reason to come out of hiding.

Something out of place caught his attention, and he stopped. A portion of the 9-gauge wire fencing near the farmhouse had come loose. He whistled at Ginger Beer to alert her to his change of course and he walked over to look at it. He'd need a hammer and probably two or three fresh tacks. *Or I could just use the staple gun,* he thought. It was a quicker fix, but not quite as permanent.

He turned back toward the barn to get the staple gun when he heard the first of the sledgehammer blows. He stopped and cocked his head to listen. He scanned the farm, trying to figure out where it was coming from, but he couldn't see anything. But he heard it again and again.

Ginger Beer flew past him in the direction of the sound, and within moments he found himself running after her, directly toward the place he had left Troy. As he drew near, the sound of the hammer blows became louder. As he came around the backside of the cube, he saw Troy, sledgehammer high over his right shoulder, taking aim before bringing the hammer down onto the statue of himself.

Abel recognized the sledgehammer—it was his own. As soon as his back was turned, Troy must have run to the barn looking for something to bash the block with. That must have been what Ginger Beer had been so riled about.

Abel stepped back to give Troy room to do whatever it was Troy needed to do. Again and again the hammer came down on the statue cut into the cube. Abel saw how the trucker took aim at the most fragile and unsupported aspects of the sculpture. If it had been made of stone, even granite, the sledgehammer would have made quick work of those sections. But whatever the cube was made of, it held, kicking the hammer back from the force of its impact. Again and again Troy attacked the statue. But nothing broke, nothing gave, nothing fell away.

Abel felt a resigned calm come over him as he watched. He had already tried this. He had used different tools, his attack wasn't as aggressive as Troy's, but the result was the same: the statue seemed to be completely unharmed.

"They got no right!" Troy shouted in between blows.

Abel didn't disagree with the trucker, but he didn't feel the need to say anything. He started to walk back toward the trucker.

Troy made one final blow, this time to the head of the statue, as if trying to knock the flattened cheek right off of himself. But the hammer shot away from the impact, just as it had every time before. Troy threw the hammer, balled his fists and bellowed his rage. He moved toward the cube, swinging his fists, apparently attempting to do with his bare hands what the hammer had failed to do.

Abel stepped in and caught Troy's elbow. "That's enough, son."

He could see Troy trembling. He felt the young man's sweat as he pulled his hand back. The breeze made his fingertips feel cold. The chill rippled through his body.

He steered Troy away, toward the farmhouse. He didn't have a plan for what he would do once they got there. Maybe Troy would just sit in the kitchen and stare, thinking about what he'd just seen. Maybe the kid would have dinner with them. Maybe he and Mia would talk about how it felt to be the objects of such a cruel prank—but he doubted that. And it didn't matter. The important thing was to get Troy away…just away.

But before they reached the farmhouse, Jake intercepted them with a wave of his hat. Abel called for Troy to hold up, and the two men waited as Jake caught up to them. The young deputy pulled off his hat and ran his fingers through sweaty hair. He put the hat back on. "More people coming. Just thought you'd like to know."

"More people? Who?"

"Can't tell yet—but I counted four cars."

"Together?" Abel's eyebrows rose.

"I don't think so, but who knows?"

Abel looked up and saw a cloud of dust, no doubt kicked up by the first of those cars coming down the dirt road straight toward them. "What can they want?"

"I don't know that either. Reckon we're about to find out. But Abel, promise me…no shooting, okay?"

PART TWO
THE FIRE

And now at last authentic word I bring,
Witnessed by every dead and living thing;
Good tidings of great joy for you, for all:
There is no God: no Fiend with names divine
Made us and tortures us; if we must pine,
It is to satiate no Beings gall.

—Aliester Crowley,
The Rite of Saturn, Pt IV

CHAPTER SIX

Peg was bleary as she pulled her twenty-year-old Honda Civic to a stop in front of Imelda's house. She'd not slept well. She had tossed and turned for several hours before she finally got up and mixed a shot of rum into a cup of hot milk. That had done the trick, but too late. She yawned, keenly aware of exactly how much sleep she needed to feel like a human being. She reached for the door handle, but then spotted movement. Imelda's door opened, and the woman emerged, bundled for winter.

Peg looked up at the sky—the rain had gone. And although mornings in the Central Valley could be nippy, they started to warm early on. Peg imagined that the outer layers of Imelda's clothes would be lying on her back seat on the way back.

That's okay, Peg thought. *She's dressing protectively.* Imelda was wearing a large sun hat, a sweater, a light jacket, a scarf, and sunglasses. Peg flashed her lights at her, and Imelda began to totter toward the Civic. Peg thought of Imelda as older than herself, but upon reflection, she realized that they were probably around the same age. She wondered at the plasticity of age—how different people could make different ages seem older or younger than they actually were. Peg felt like a young fifty-five. Imelda seemed to her an old fifty-five.

And it seemed to Peg there was about a twenty-year difference between young fifty-five and old fifty-five, and the calendar had very little to do with it.

Imelda was a parishioner, which normally meant that she was not a person that Peg could socialize with. Clergy boundaries were fuzzy and sometimes hard to navigate, but Peg did her best. She tried to keep her intimate friends outside the parish, while at the same time being friendly with those inside it. But she could never be anything but a pastor to those inside it. *Thank God for Ted and Allison,* she thought, and suddenly felt very lonely.

The image of Phil Prugh flashed through her mind, and she smiled to herself. Maybe she need not be lonely. *We'll see,* she thought, making a mental note about chickens and hatching. Imelda yanked open the door and stuffed herself into the little car.

"How are you, Imelda dear?" Peg asked.

"I didn't get much sleep," Imelda answered. "And my nose itches."

Peg was expecting that. She had never had a conversation with Imelda in which the itchiness of her nose did not arise as a subject, at least in passing. It was a good sign, Peg decided, a sign of normalcy.

"Put your seat belt on, please," Peg said, nodding toward the opposite side of the car.

"Oh. Yes." Imelda scrambled for it, and after a few frantic moments, clicked it into place with a sigh.

Peg smiled patiently, then pulled the Civic onto the road. "Now," Peg said. "Tell me what we're going to see and why."

"Well, I haven't seen it myself," Imelda began. "But I heard from Betty MacIntyre who heard it from Teri Shoemaker who heard from Rachel Lindstrom who heard it from Mia herself."

Peg didn't take her eyes off the road, but she frowned anyway. "Mia?"

"Mia Nyland. It's her farm, her and her husband's."

"Mia Nyland. Yes? So what did you hear...through this game of telephone...from Mia?"

Imelda rubbed at her nose. "I heard that there are man-sized sculptures appearing in their cornfield—in the form of cubes. Lots of them. And they're all of people, mostly people we know."

Peg wasn't sure she understood. "Do you mean the sculptures depict people we know?"

"Yes, that's it. There's one of Mia herself. In the bathtub."

"One of the…cubes…is also a sculpture…depicting Mia Nyland in the bathtub?" Peg clarified.

"Yes."

Peg nodded, although her face betrayed only confusion. Imelda seemed not to notice. She continued, "But the others are of other people. I heard…one was of me. So…I feel like I need to see it. I just… didn't want to see it alone."

Peg felt lost. She knew where she was on the road, just not in the conversation. "What are the people doing in the…sculptures?"

Imelda looked away. Her hand went to her mouth, her elbow propped against the passenger-side window. A tiny squeak emitted from her throat. Peg looked over at her, a crease of concern darkening her brow. "Imelda? Are you crying?"

Imelda sniffed. "They're dying."

"What? Who's dying?"

"The people. In the sculptures."

"The people in the sculptures are dying? You mean in real life? Because everyone is dying in real life," she reasoned. "Or do you mean, the subject of the statues is their death?" The conversation was getting more surreal, and Peg wondered just how much of a thread of reason she might still be able to pull at. She decided to let it go and change the subject. "What have you been working on?"

It was a very open-ended question. One of the things Peg admired about Imelda is that the woman always had projects going, most of which enriched the community in one way or another. At most times Imelda was an unstoppable fountain of industry.

"I was working on a quilt for the volunteer firefighters. I was making a panel for each of the firemen who had died, all the way back to the beginning of the town. I just…"

Peg glanced over at her, then back to the road. "Just what, dear?"

"It's too close. Right now. It's too much the same."

"The same as what?" Peg asked.

Imelda said nothing, although she looked like she might cry again. Peg sighed—and then hoped it was not too audible. "Where do I turn?"

"Up here," Imelda said, pointing. Peg knew the general direction, but was trusting Imelda to guide her. Fortunately, it seemed she was up to the task. Peg turned into a long drive leading past what seemed like a mile or more of cornfield. Eventually, they pulled up near a lovely white farmhouse. Peg set the brake and grabbed her hat.

"There they are," Imelda was out of the car already, facing one of the cornfields.

Peg adjusted her wide-brimmed straw sun hat, decorated with a fuchsia band, and went to stand beside her. "There who are, dear?" she asked.

Imelda just pointed. Peg followed the direction of her arm...and then she saw it. It was, in fact, a six-foot-tall cube, salmon colored. "Well, I'll be," Peg breathed.

A screen door slammed, a dog barked, and suddenly a yellow lab was bounding toward them, barking gleefully. A man in his mid-sixties came out of the farmhouse. Glowering, he stomped down the steps and headed straight for them. "And here we go," Peg said, turning toward him. The dog reached her first, barks surrendering to furious wagging. Absently, Peg gave the dog's head a pat, but as the man approached, she suddenly wished she'd worn her clerical collar. She didn't usually wear it, unless she was visiting the hospital, but there were times when it came in handy.

"Can I help you?" the man asked.

"Good morning," Peg said. "I don't think we've been formally introduced. I'm Pastor Peg Barkley from First Congregational Church, in town. And this is one of our parishioners, Imelda Konig."

The man stopped stomping, and as if he'd suddenly hit a thicker patch of air, slowed down. His face changed, too, from angry to concerned. "Oh. Uh, pastor. Imelda. I'm Abel Nyland. This is my farm." He headed for Peg first and shook her hand. Imelda was still facing the cornfield, away from Abel.

"We're so sorry to intrude, Mr. Nyland," Peg said. "We should have called."

"Well, you probably should have," Abel agreed, although without a hint of blame in his tone. "But you're here. And I reckon you're here… for her." He pointed to Imelda with his chin.

"Yes," Peg said. "She asked me to come. Said something about a sculpture…of her. Could that be right?" She watched his eyes, and had trouble reading what she saw. He looked like he had not slept for a couple of days. He looked harried, like a man who had been in the middle of a panic attack mere moments ago but had been interrupted.

He stood shoulder-to-shoulder with Imelda, gazing out at the cornfield. To Peg's great surprise, he put his arm around her shoulder, giving her an awkward squeeze. She had seen the like before; it was simply out of place, and it took her a moment to make the connection. Then she got it—it was as if he were comforting her at a funeral. Peg had seen it many times before—more than she could count. *Something strange and big is happening here,* a voice inside her head told her. *Pay attention.* Inwardly, she reached for Jesus' hand. This time she found it. She closed her eyes for a moment and breathed a sigh of relief.

"Seven more appeared this morning," Abel said. "Can't see most of them from here—they're spread out across the farm, and we've got a little more than four hundred acres. Imelda, yours is a bit of a hike. I can drive you, if you don't mind squeezing into the truck." He pointed at an enormous pickup. Even if all three of them were as heavy as Imelda, no one would be "squeezing" into a rig that spacious.

Peg was about to say that she could use the exercise, but one glance at Imelda and she bit her tongue. Tears were streaming down the woman's face. Abel's hand was still cradling her shoulder. Peg went to stand on her other side. "Imelda, dear, what's wrong?"

"I want to see it…and I don't want to see it."

Abel was nodding almost imperceptibly. "Mia has one, just there, beyond the barn." He pointed with his chin again. Peg squinted in the direction of the barn but didn't see any cubes in that direction. She reckoned the barn blocked them from her immediate view. "She just had to look. I told her to stay in the house, but…"

Peg's brow furrowed. "And how is…Mia?" she asked. Karlstadt was a small town, but she still did not know everyone, especially if they did not come to her church.

"Holed up in the bedroom most of the time," Abel said. "Sheriff came and got her to come out, and she does, but…she goes back in once her chores are done. Don't know what she does in there. She doesn't seem to want to talk about it, and that's not like her."

Peg could see the man was worried about his wife. A prickly feeling of dread made the hair on the back of her neck assume the orans position.

"C'mon," Abel said. "We'll drive out there, and along the way you can decide if you want to see it."

He released her shoulder and gave a whistle. Around the side of the barn came a man wearing a tan uniform. It took Peg a moment to realize it was Jake, a man who worked with her daughter. The dog ran out toward him, barked once, then ran back to them. A minute later, Jake was within earshot.

"Pastor," he said, lifting his hat an inch away from his scalp and nodding to her. He replaced the hat. "Imelda. What are…oh." He glanced at Abel. "I told you this was going to happen."

"And you were right," Abel admitted.

Peg's mind raced to fill in the blanks, but there were still too many missing pieces.

"There's going to be more," Jake said. "And we can't shoot them."

"Who's shooting who?" Peg asked, her voice rising in indignation.

Neither of the men spoke, which she found mildly infuriating. Her left eye began to twitch.

"Get in the truck," Abel said, apparently to the women. Peg's twitch increased in severity. Abel moved toward Jake and the two began to converse in tones too low for Peg to hear. She watched Jake's hands go to his belt, resting them there as if it were a handrail, the way lawmen often do. Peg's twitch developed into a full-blown tic.

"Fuck this," Peg said to no one in particular, and stepped up to the two men, inserting herself into their conversation. "Gentlemen, I am not a child. Treat me like one, and you will not like the shitstorm that results."

Both men's eyes widened. They blinked. They looked at each other. They looked at Peg. Peg continued, "By all means, converse; but Imelda and I are standing right here. We are adults. You will include us in your conversation. You will also offer Imelda an apology for your lapse in propriety."

The men looked over at Imelda, who was looking out at the one visible cube, wringing her hands. Jake cleared his throat. "Uh…of course, Pastor. Miss Imelda, I'm sorry for not…including you."

Imelda did not seem to hear. Her flowered dress answered with a quiet whipping sound from the wind.

"Thank you, Jake." Peg smiled.

"Of course. Now I know where Julie gets…" he trailed off.

"Gets what?" Peg raised one eyebrow.

Jake cleared his throat again. "Girl has balls of steel. Pardon my French, Pastor."

"I will take that as a compliment," Peg smiled. She turned back to Abel. "Now I suggest we all get in the truck and take Imelda to see… whatever it is."

"Well, that's just what we were saying, Pastor," Jake said, his voice becoming low again.

"She's not a fucking child," Peg reminded him again, her voice rising in direct proportion to his softer tone.

"No ma'am," Jake said. "Sorry again, Miss Imelda." The deputy adjusted his hat nervously. He looked back to Peg and said in a voice that was a bit louder than normal conversation, "It's…disturbing. They all are. We're concerned, that's all."

"How disturbing is disturbing?" Peg asked. "I mean, how disturbing can it be?"

The men looked at each other again.

"Well, c'mon then," Abel said, turning toward the truck. Ginger Beer barked and leaped at the new game, running toward the truck, reaching it and running back—a relay race with one runner.

⸥did not protest this time, and as she climbed up into the cab of the truck, she scolded herself silently for her temper. She was feeling more irritable than normal. The reasonable part of her brain understood—she was tired, and there was the fact that she was dying. A little self-compassion was called for, but she found it a rare substance to locate at present.

She offered Imelda a hand, and the rattled woman climbed onto the seat beside her. To her left, Abel released the emergency brake. Turning to look out the window behind her, Peg saw that Ginger Beer had jumped into the back, ears flat and tail wagging.

"Is Jake coming?" Peg asked.

"Nah. He's standing guard by the cubes closest to the road, trying to warn trespassers off so they don't get shot."

She noticed the passive mood. "Get shot by whom, Mr. Nyland?"

He didn't answer. He drove the truck onto a gravel road that seemingly ran nowhere. The only thing Peg could see all around her were plowed fields. Little wisps of green poked out of the ground, wisps that she knew would soon be looming, vibrant stalks of corn, covering the landscape like a blanket of lush green. Everything in her body longed for that verdancy, that veriditas, especially the part that was sick.

"How are you doing, dear?" she asked Imelda.

Imelda's mouth twitched in the effort to give her a smile, but it was a weak attempt. She fumbled with the strings of her handbag and stared at the dashboard. Peg wanted to say something about how country air seems to render perfectly intelligent people temporarily inarticulate, but she bit her tongue. She was still a city girl to them. She didn't need to open her mouth and confirm it.

They weren't able to drive very fast on the gravel, and it seemed to be taking longer to reach their destination than she'd expected. But then suddenly, the truck slowed to a halt and Abel set the brake. He pointed. Three of the pinkish cubes peeked out of the distance at them, partially obscured by the gentle rolling of the field.

"Still thinking we could've walked?" Abel asked.

"No indeed," Peg said. "Thank you for driving us. We would never have found it on our own."

"I wouldn't've let you," Abel said. He could have said it meanly, but he didn't. He opened the door and got out. She nudged Imelda. "C'mon, dear. This is what we've come for."

Imelda nodded and opened the door. As soon as they were on the ground, Abel began to walk toward one of the cubes. Ginger Beer jumped out of the back and sniffed around, tail wagging. She trotted after her master. "This here is Miss Imelda's," Abel threw over his shoulder.

A feeling pulled at Peg's gut. It was a familiar feeling. Peg tried to discern what it was. It took a few moments, but she located it. A couple of times, she had needed to accompany people to the morgue to identify a body. For some reason, it felt exactly like that.

They paused in front of a cube. It appeared perfectly square. It looked like it might be made from concrete, or some kind of rock.

"Isn't it supposed to be a sculpture?" Peg asked.

"That part always seems to be facing away from you," Abel said. "Can't figure it, myself. Over here."

Abel led them around the cube, and Peg's eyes widened as she saw that the far side was not the same as the others. It was concave, sculpted, the meat of the block carved out to form an image within the cube. And the face of that image was Imelda's.

She looked much the same—except she was the pink color of the cube. Her hair seemed to be the same length and style. She seemed the same age as the Imelda before her. Her eyes seemed unnaturally large, and her mouth was open in a silent scream. Her dress was over-large, like a muumuu, shapelessly covering her form, ending just below her knees. Peg could see varicose veins wind their way over her bloated calves, like rivers during the snow melt at Yosemite.

But dominating the statue were two gaping slashes—one at her neck, the other tearing open not only her dress, but also the meat of her belly, exposing her intestines and fibrous viscera.

Peg found that she could not move. Nor could she look away from the cube. It was, somehow, beautiful and terrible at once. Peg could see that it was not photo-realistic—her hair was represented with sculpted angles, not individual fibers. Yet it was not abstract. It was a person. It was Imelda. And she was dead.

As if an unseen hand let go of her, Peg found she could look away again. "Imelda, dear, I don't think—" she said, turning toward the woman. But Imelda had already seen. Peg watched her as she tottered toward the cube. Her mouth was open in a prolonged, "Noooo." Her eyes were wide and already wet. She stumbled. Peg leaped to catch her elbow, but Imelda did not fall. Her legs were shaking and Peg was afraid they would give way.

"Sit down," she ordered. "Imelda, sit."

But Imelda did not sit. She hovered, wavered, listed. Ginger Beer sniffed the periphery of the cube, fascinated with a whole other range of novel sensory input unavailable to the humans.

Imelda's face seemed like a frozen mask of anguish, as immobile as the material of the cube, unable to look away. She reached one hand out toward it, frail and shaking. She took a step, and then another. And then she touched it. She began with her own nose, then her hair. Finally, trembling, she touched the flayed skin of her neck, traced the contours of the gaping wound, the sharp edges of the cut. She made whimpering animal noises. Ginger Beer's ears pricked up at the sound of it, and she began to whine in sympathy.

Peg shook her own head in an attempt to clear it. Instinctively, she stepped forward, coming up behind Imelda. She wrapped her arms around the woman's formidable chest. She squeezed, then with great effort steered her away to face the pickup. As soon as the cube was out of Imelda's line of sight, the woman began to howl and she collapsed to the ground, her legs finally losing their solidity. Peg accompanied her to the dirt, using the mass of her own body to affect a more controlled fall. They landed awkwardly, but without injury, with Imelda partially sitting on Peg's lap, still held in the pastor's embrace. She howled again. Ginger Beer joined in, filling the air with an anguished duet. Peg squeezed and shushed her until the howling subsided. The shaking, however, continued.

"I'm going to die," Imelda choked.

"It's not a prophesy, Imelda." Peg spoke the voice of reason, which was forcefully asserting itself in her own thoughts. "It's art...it's nasty, cruel art that should never have been made...it's an invasion of your privacy...it's horrible and it's not true...I want you to hear me, Imelda...it's not true...that statue did not happen...it will not happen...someone is playing a trick, it's a hoax, it's..." The words had been coming in an unbroken string, but they suddenly stopped.

Abel Nyland spat. He removed the hat from his head, ran a hand through his hair and replaced it. There was a look on his face that was something in between rage and distaste and embarrassment. Peg looked up at him. "I'm sorry, Mr. Nyland. I'm sorry this is happening to you. I'm sorry it's happening to you, too, Imelda. I had no idea. This is...it's..." But just what it was she could not find words for.

For a good many minutes, none of them moved. A slight breeze belied the awfulness of the moment, whispering the promise of Spring and new rain and the grace of seedlings budding to life just beneath them and out of sight. Peg smelled the holiness of the soil and the intrusive bite of chemical fertilizer. She smelled a hint of lavender in Imelda's hair along with a hint of her body odor. She felt the squishiness of Imelda's flesh pressed against the yielding solidity of her own. She rocked the woman gently. The world was silent.

"Let's get you home, dear," Peg said at last.

Ellen set a plate of pancakes in front of her husband, and another in front of her child. Jorge was reading the newspaper, his face impassive as stone as he flipped from one page to another. Every now and then he took a sip of his coffee and returned his attention to the page.

Melinda, also, did not look at her. At dinner the previous evening, Ellen had screamed at them both. She knew it was wrong to be so angry, and her outburst had frightened even her a little bit. She wondered if perhaps her daughter was not the only one in the family who was unhinged. She certainly felt like she was teetering on the brink of it.

Ellen grabbed a plate for herself and sat in her chair, with Melinda on her left and her husband on her right. Jorge did not acknowledge her presence, but only turned the page.

In some ways it was a very ordinary morning. Jorge was lost in the paper and Melinda was sulking. So what else was new? Only the fact that Melinda was insisting that she was a boy. Ellen shook her head at the ridiculousness of it.

"Melinda, please hand me the jam," she said.

Her daughter ignored her. She stared at her food, moving a bit of bacon back and forth across the plate with her butter knife.

"Melinda Ann! Don't you dare ignore me!"

She only used her daughter's middle name when she was in trouble, but Melinda did not budge. She blinked but did not look up. She did not move to pass the jam.

Ellen felt rage rise up within her. Her stomach began to shiver. "Melinda Ann! You look at me this instant!"

Melinda stared at her plate, unmoving.

Ellen realized that her grip on her fork was so tight her fist was turning white. She willed her hand to relax.

"Mel, hand that jam to your mother, would you please?" Jorge said, without looking up from his paper.

"Of course, Daddy," Melinda said. She didn't smile, but she instantly picked up the jar of jam and placed it within her mother's reach.

Ellen looked at her husband, but his face was unreadable. She looked back at her daughter, who had resumed staring at her plate, but she detected just the hint of a smile. That ignited her ire even more. "Stop this, both of you!"

Jorge turned the page, punching the paper in the middle of the fold so that it would lay correctly on his crossed leg.

Ellen's mouth worked, and she blinked back tears. She counted to ten, then did it again backwards, until she felt the knot in her stomach begin to unwind. Gathering the shreds of her dignity, she turned to Melinda again.

"Melinda, I want to know how things are going at school. Are you being…teased? Or bullied?" It was unthinkable that she was not, and that broke Ellen's heart. Children were without mercy, after all, and why her daughter would choose to be the target of their cruelty was beyond her.

Melinda stared at her plate and did not acknowledge her mother.

Jorge didn't look up from his paper but cleared his throat. "Mel, answer your mother."

Melinda looked down at her plate. "It's going just fine."

"That doesn't tell me anything!" Ellen complained.

"Can you say a little more about that? Your mother likes to hear talking."

Ellen scowled at her husband, but Melinda answered him in a bored, sulking tone. "I have a geography test today…and in math we're starting linear equations."

"That sounds…downright impractical." Jorge did not look up from his paper.

"Yeah…kids are complaining about it. But…I think I want to be an architect, and actually those kinds of equations are probably things I'm going to be using every day."

"Not going to take over the farm?"

Melinda blinked.

"Jorge, what are you talking about?" Ellen exclaimed. "Taking over the farm? She's a girl!"

They both ignored her. Melinda answered, "I don't think so, Daddy. I don't think that's my calling."

"Calling?" Ellen asked, her brow knitting together in confusion. Where did her daughter get these odd ideas? School, no doubt. From those radical, democrat, lesbian teachers.

"Anyone bullying you?" Jorge asked.

"There was one kid, Cal," Melinda answered.

"Cal Davidson?" Jorge asked.

"Yeah. He started picking on me, calling me a transexual."

"Isn't that what you are? Or want to be, I mean?" Jorge put his paper down and met his child's eye.

"I don't think I know what that word means. I'm trans*gendered*. The other word sounds...mean."

Jorge nodded. "I'm not sure I know what it means either. What are you going to do about Cal?"

"I punched him in the throat," Melinda said. "I was aiming for his chin, but I missed."

Ellen dropped her fork and gasped.

"Did you now?" Jorge asked. A smile tugged at the edge of his lip. "And what happened then?"

"He staggered backwards, so I followed him and hit him in the stomach. He doubled over and I kicked him in the nuts."

"Melinda! Language!" Ellen shouted. Absently, she picked up her fork again.

Jorge chuckled and turned back to his newspaper. "Have you had any trouble from Cal since then?"

"Not a word," Melinda said. "Not from him or anyone."

Jorge nodded. "You want to start boxing lessons, down at the gym in Coleman?"

"Absolutely not!" Ellen protested.

"You bet!" Melinda said, her face widening into a grin.

"Young lady, you will do no such thing!" Ellen pronounced.

"I'll call over and see when the next class starts," Jorge said.

"You have to stop this," Ellen pleaded with her husband. He ignored her. Exasperated, she turned to her daughter again. "Melinda, I forbid you to carry this craziness on for another instant."

To her great surprise, Melinda looked up at her and said, "The only crazy person here is you."

Ellen's fist flashed out before she could let go of the fork. She intended to slap her daughter, but instead scored five neat rows of gore into her daughter's face with the tines of the fork. Melinda screamed and clutched at her face. She stood up, knocking her chair backwards as she howled.

Ellen looked at the fork, still in her hand. She looked at her husband, who had leaped out of his own chair and covered Melinda's head in his arms. His eyes met his wife's, and there was a bitterness in them she'd never beheld before. "Get out," he said. "You let me handle this. But you…just get out of this house. You're not fit to be here."

———

Mayor Deena Knolls was up to her elbows in nightcrawlers. Sy had called in sick this morning, so it was left to her to mind the shop as well as keep the town of Karlstadt on an even keel. What had complicated her morning was a complaint from a local fisherman that there had been bloodworms mixed in with the nightcrawlers he'd bought from them last night. She'd told him that was impossible, but after hanging up, she felt an anxiety in her gut that wouldn't let her alone.

Pulling up the hinged section of the counter, she walked over to the barrel of night crawlers and lifted the lid. The powerful stench of fermented coffee grounds blasted her. She moved some of the grounds around until she found a nightcrawler. Then she felt a sting. Jerking her arm back, she saw a drop of blood on the end of her finger.

"Goddam it," she said. She returned to the counter, pulled on a pair of thick rubber gloves and grabbed a plastic container made from the bottom half of a milk jug. Then she returned to the barrel and began to scoop the grounds into the container with one gloved hand. After a couple of scoops, she began to sort through the grounds with the finger of her free hand. "Nightcrawler, nightcrawler, nightcrawler…bloodworm. Fuck." She pulled the small, fiery red, wriggling offender out of the coffee. "Goddam it."

She tossed the contents of the jug back into the barrel, pulled the gloves off and went straight to the telephone. She'd never heard of a bait distributor mixing up their worms before, yet here it was. She was gathering steam for a fight, but she forced herself to be calm. "Honey, not vinegar," she warned herself—not that it would do any good, she knew. She dialed and waited.

"Bait Boys," the voice on the other side answered.

"Gabe, this is Deena."

"Oh shit."

"'Oh shit' is right. I'm guessing I don't need to tell you what this is about."

"Uh…does it involve bloodworms?"

"And I've got the bleeding finger to prove it."

"Shit, I'm sorry, Deena. I guess you've had complaints."

"Only one so far, but you can bet your boots I'll get a whole slew of them later, when the twenty or so fishermen that bought night-crawlers from me this morning get back. Plus, I'm gonna get a whole lot more when I don't have any *Lumbricus terrestris* to sell tomorrow."

"Jeez, I'm sorry, Deena. We've got a new guy, who…oh, never mind. That's a reason, but it's not an excuse." He sighed. "How can I make it up to you?"

"I'm going to properly label this barrel and discount it. Hopefully, I can move some of the stock to fishermen who need both and don't mind doing their own sorting. But I want replacement stock ASAP, and I don't want to be charged for it."

"Of course, Deena. I'll have Gus make a special trip…as soon as he's done with…you know, all the other special trips."

"So, today?"

"Yeah. Somehow. Today."

"You call me if you're going to be late, you hear?"

"Yes, ma'am."

She hung up. She felt good about herself. She had not lost her cool. Most of that was due to Gabe's eager contrition, she knew, and she was grateful for it. If other people were similarly compliant, she realized, she wouldn't need to be a bitch so often.

The bell rang and her head snapped up. A fake smile rushed to her face as she greeted her customer. It fell away as she realized it wasn't a customer. She knew her customers, and she knew how they were dressed. This man was in a suit, holding a documents pouch. That was never good news.

"The fuck do you want?" she asked.

"Are you Deena Knolls, mayor of Karlstadt?"

Her shoulders fell. *Oh. So that's what this is,* she thought. "Yes," she said, her voice registering her defeat.

The man took an envelope out of his pouch. He handed it to her. "You have been served." Without another word, he turned on his heel and left.

"Good lord, what now?" Deena asked as she tore open the envelope. She unfolded the papers and scanned them. "Coleman Klan and Philanthropic Society," she said out loud as her eyes flitted over the complaint. "Oh, bless your hearts," she said, her voice filled with sarcasm. She remembered back to the conversation she'd had with the Klan's representative. Then she laughed. "You just can't take 'no' for an answer, can you?"

With some relief Thom pulled into the parking lot of the Central Valley Marksman, the local gun range. Reaching behind the seat, he pulled out a black tactical bag and slung it over his shoulder. He was glad the rain had stopped. It had been a cold, bitter rain, and he felt it painfully in his bones.

He didn't really have time for the gun range, but he made time. His mind had begun to circle obsessively, picking at the mystery surrounding the cubes, and he needed to clear it. Entering the cinderblock building, he nodded to Carl at the front desk.

"Sheriff," Carl waved to him. "Got a new AK-101, if you want to give it a go."

It was a kind offer, and ordinarily Thom might have taken him up on it. "Nah, I don't have that much time, and I got a lot of guns to get through."

"Business not pleasure this time?"

"Eh." Thom shrugged and gave him a half-smile. "Bit of both, I guess."

"Well, ain't no one here but us old goats. You take your pick of lanes."

"I'm partial to five," Thom said.

"Five it is. You want targets, or you got your own?"

"Yeah, I'll take a stack, if you don't mind."

"On the house, today only. Paying on account?"

"Yeah, bill it to the county. Like I said, I got a lot of guns to get through."

"You okay on ammo?"

Thom shook his head. If Carl wasn't trying to sell him ammo, he was trying to upsell him on ammo. He steeled himself against the pitch. "I got everything I need."

"You sure? Because I got some new .22 shells with a Teflon coating like I've never seen—"

"Got everything I need, Carl, thanks."

"Well, you let me know. Got a round on the house if you want to give 'em a try."

"I'll remember that." He tipped his hat and carried his bag to lane five.

Stepping up to the small shelf that separated the shooter from the firing lane, he carefully drew his weapons from the bag and laid them out in an orderly fashion. There were two service Glocks, to which he quickly added a third from his side holster. He removed the Smith & Wesson Model 10 snub-nosed revolver from his boot holster and placed it alongside the others. Then he pulled out the Barret MRAD from the bag and assembled it. It was a sharpshooter rifle—originally intended for sniper work—and it hadn't been shot in over six months. Guns were meant to be shot, and if they weren't they became dangerous liabilities. Thom made sure that each gun in the office armory got a good workout every six months or less to keep them in good condition. He remembered his father telling him that a sharp hatchet was a useful tool and a dull one a dangerous weapon—it was the same with guns.

He started with the Model 10 and mused—it was one of the most popular handguns in the world. It was certainly a favorite of cops. In fact, he didn't know a law enforcement officer who didn't have one. He routinely gave them as gifts to recruits. He'd bought one for Jake only last year.

He pulled on the goggles, spun the cylinder, and loaded the chambers. Then he put the gun down again and fixed one of the targets to the line. Pulling on the parallel cord, he ran the target to the back wall, and picked up the snub-nose again. Taking aim, he fired three shots as quickly as he could squeeze them off. Two were in the bullseye, one was about half an inch wide. Thom nodded. It was not a bad start.

He caught movement out of the side of his eye and looked over his right shoulder. He recognized Bill Arenson and set his pistol down. Bill was setting up in lane seven. Jake had told him Bill had visited the Nyland place. Thom studied him. Bill's eyes were red, as if he'd been having an allergy attack, or had been rubbing at them, or even crying —it was impossible to tell which. The man's jaw was set in a grim resolve that betrayed little. He set his bag down, but then thought better of its placement and put it somewhere else. Then he changed it again. Then he looked around, apparently aware that he was being watched. Thom beat him to the punch. "Hey, Bill," he called across the lanes.

It was poor shooting range etiquette, but there were only the two of them, so Thom allowed himself the transgression.

"Thom," Bill nodded at him.

As Thom watched, Bill softened. Thom wondered at that. When he didn't know he was being watched, Bill was edgy and nervous. But once he knew Thom was there, the man affected a nonchalant calm. Thom narrowed his eyes. "Whatcha shootin'?"

Bill fidgeted. Finally, though, the man looked up and smiled. "Oh, just keeping some of these rifles current."

"Same here. What rifles you got tonight?" Thom pressed.

"I got two semi-automatics—got a Colt AR-15 and a USAS-12—"

"That's a shotgun, isn't it?"

"Yeah," Bill broke out into a genuine-looking smile. "It's my baby."

"Good deal," Thom said. "Safe shooting."

"You, too."

Thom turned back to his lane and finished the rounds in his revolver. As he pulled on the cord to reel his target in, he tried to watch Bill in his peripheral vision. Something was off. He didn't know what, but he knew it was something. In his gut, he knew there had to be. If Thom had seen one of those cubes with a sculpture of himself in it, he'd be rattled, that was certain. He considered going over and talking to Bill about it, straight out in the open.

He sighed. It was none of his business. Here the man was, minding his own affairs, working off his aggression and fear in a healthy way. *Best leave him alone,* Thom thought.

He pulled on the parallel cord again to set a new target in place, then loaded a fresh clip into his Glock. This was his standard sidearm and it was always a pleasure to shoot. He squeezed off three quick shots and grinned. Bullseye, every one of them.

Milala stopped by the mural of the Dala horse and looked it up and down. Horses weren't cobalt blue, in her experience, and she frowned at the painting. The Dala horse was much taller than she was, but so were real horses, so she could hardly fault it for that. But there was something about its festive ornamentation that unsettled her. She suspected there was much more to the story than she knew. "Everything has a story," she said aloud. "It's what the world is made of." It was her father's voice she heard, though, and they were his words, although she didn't remember what had happened that made him say them.

The sheriff had let her off with a slap on the wrist and dropped her at the nearest hospital, where she had slept on a gurney waiting for them to see her. Discharged shortly after sunup, Milala still felt sick. She was also broke and completely out of ideas. So she conceded defeat. As if Coyote had planned it, the South Inyo Hospital was not far from Karlstadt. She could have walked the rest of the way, but it would have been a very long day of walking. She had hitched a ride instead.

She forced her eyes to look away from the fantastical Dala horse and walked further down the street. She saw a park, with a gazebo and a long, durable swing set. There were benches there too, in the shade of a mighty oak, and she was sorely tempted to rest, perhaps even to nap. But she knew from hard-won experience that little towns like this did not take kindly to napping Indians. She forced herself to move along and doubled back to the Main Street.

Like many small towns in the Central Valley, there wasn't much to it. The business district was composed of two streets, about four blocks in length, lined on both sides with exactly the sort of businesses you'd expect. She passed the barber shop, and two doors down, the beauty salon. There was a grocer with produce on the sidewalk, kept cool by mist from a series of hoses just over Milala's head. They felt good and she hovered by the eggplant as long as she dared, soaking up both the water and the coolness. But as soon as the grocer started to shoot her glances, she adjusted the strap of her bag and moved on.

Doubling back again, she passed the Dala horse painting once more. Bitten with renewed curiosity, she decided to go into the store. The faded sign over the door said, "Betty's Scandinavian Boutique." Pushing open the door, she blinked until her eyes adjusted. She wondered at the statues of reindeer, T-shirts sporting the names of sports teams she had never heard of, snow globes depicting places she had never seen, and dusty grocery items that listed their prices in Kronor—yellow stickie tags gave the price in dollars. She scrunched her face at a jar of lingonberry jam. *What in the world are lingonberries?* she wondered. It was tempting to buy a jar, but it cost half again the amount she had in change. A jar of jam near the reservation was a dollar fifty. This jar of jam was over ten dollars. She carefully placed it back and, trying to avoid the suspicious glances of the shopkeeper, stepped back out onto the street.

Coyote was waiting near the door. "How was your trip?" he asked.

"Very funny," she said, refusing to look at him. She turned right, to continue exploring the part of the street she had not yet seen. Coyote fell into step beside her.

"You could be more grateful. I provided curbside service," Coyote said.

"Like hell you did. I had to hitch a ride the rest of the way here."

"You are just like the *oje-ajnt* children. Ungrateful."

Milala bristled at the insult. "So, this is the place? I'm supposed to drum for these *oje-ajnt?*"

"This is the place you've been avoiding, yes."

"It's not so bad," Milala said. And it wasn't. As small towns in her part of the world went, it had a whimsical streak that she kind of enjoyed. She couldn't shake the image of the Dala horse.

"But stop and sniff," Coyote said. As soon as they'd finished crossing the street he sat and lifted his nose to the wind. He closed his eyes, and she watched his nose twitch. "Go on."

Milala sighed and lowered her bag to the ground. She closed her eyes as well, concentrating on her nose. She sniffed and began to catalog the complex bouquet of aromas. Foremost, she smelled tar— the sun was baking the blacktop and making it soft. Next, she smelled the far-off stink of manure—cows, mostly. The third layer was savory —a bakery perhaps, or a diner. *Pie,* she decided. It was the smell of fresh-baked pie.

"Beneath the tar, beneath the shit, beneath the pie," Coyote said. "What do you smell?"

Milala's eyes snapped open. "Mold," she said.

"Yes," Coyote agree. "But what kind?"

There were healthy molds and unhealthy molds. There was mold that healed you and mold that made you sick. And then there was mold that Creator made, and mold that he didn't. "This isn't the kind of mold you can see."

"No. This is the mold that creeps into the bones of a house unseen." Coyote's eyes were open now, but his nose was still twitching. "And makes it collapse."

"Where did it come from?" Milala asked.

"That is a good question, Daughter. Someone brought it here... from somewhere else. It does not belong here. If we don't bring medicine, it will infect everyone here. The People will die."

"You mean *these people* will die. They aren't *cins,* they aren't The People."

"To Creator, all people are *cins*. All people are The People."

"All people are *not* The People." Milala scowled. "These people

have no nose." She could have added that they had no sense, either—
or any concept of justice or mercy or compassion or kinship with the
earth—but it didn't seem necessary.

"If you can't see that they smell like you do, then perhaps you are
in danger of losing your nose, too."

"My nose is just fine," Milala insisted.

Coyote shrugged.

"Okay, I'm here," Milala said, putting her hands on her hips and
facing Coyote. "Now what?"

"At the proper time, you will drum. You will bring the medicine, so
that The People will live."

"*These* people," Milala clarified, although she did not say it as a
question.

"These people."

"I have no love for them," Milala admitted.

"Not even the cute girls with perky teats?" Coyote grinned.

Milala scowled.

"You have no love for them, fine," Coyote said. "But Creator does."

Milala sighed.

"You know this would be easier if you did not fight me every step
of the way," Coyote pointed out. "You might find joy in obeying
Creator, instead of...whatever you're doing now."

"Creator might ask me to do something that made more sense."

"Creator sits higher than you and can see farther."

"Creator ought to be a bit more selective about who he loves,"
Milala said.

"But if he were, would he have chosen you?" Coyote flashed her
one of those smiles that looked suspiciously like a threat involving
fangs.

She narrowed one eye at him and turned away. "I smell it now,"
she said. "The mold."

"It did not come from here," Coyote said. "It was brought
through...from somewhere else."

"Who would do such a thing?" Milala asked. "Who would bring
something from where it belongs to a place where it doesn't?"

"We both know the answer to that," Coyote said.

"*Oje-ajnt*," Milala said. "If they have no sense, why does Creator smile on them?"

"Who can understand Creator?" Coyote asked.

Milala did not answer. She certainly did not understand Creator. Her nostrils twitched. "It is wrong."

"It *is* wrong," Coyote agreed.

"I'm hungry," Milala said.

"Then I suggest you follow the scent of pie," Coyote said.

Peg's face fell as the call went to voicemail.

"Julie, it's me. Uh…I need to talk to you about something. Can you give me a call when you can? Thanks, honey. Bye."

Peg put the cell phone back in her bag and sighed. She'd been so close. A part of her was annoyed, but the reasonable part of her reminded the unreasonable part that Julie was a deputy sheriff and it was the middle of her workday. But it had been hard to work up the courage to make the call. She wasn't sure she'd be able to do it again.

Her tummy rumbled and she realized it was almost time for lunch. She had one arm into her windbreaker when a knock came at the door.

First Church wasn't large enough to have a parish secretary. There was no one to schedule visits or field phone calls or answer the door—no one but Peg herself. She sighed, realizing the bowl of soup she'd been envisioning was going to be a little farther off than she thought.

She was surprised to see Ellen Wulfson on the porch, clutching a scarf to her chin against the wind. "Come in, dear," Peg said, throwing the door wide.

As Ellen entered, Peg felt the prick of curiosity. Ellen and her family had been parishioners when Peg had first arrived but, except for Christmas and Easter, they had stopped attending shortly after. That was normal for a new pastor—not every pastor clicks with every parishioner—and Peg had not taken it personally. Or she had tried not to.

"You look cold," Peg said. "Can I make you some tea?"

"That would be…very nice," Ellen said.

"Have a seat, and I'll be right with you." Peg pointed toward one of the very cozy chairs in her office. Ellen sat in the one Peg thought of as "Ted's chair."

"I'm glad the rain has stopped," Ellen said, sitting tentatively on the edge of the seat.

"I'm not sure your husband would agree," Peg said, pushing the button down on the electric kettle. "Although, I swear, if anyone but God was responsible for making water fall from the sky, they'd get arrested." Peg smiled. "Perhaps Jorge enjoys the day off, though?"

"No. He just puts on his raincoat and goes to it. He doesn't let it slow him down one bit."

"No, I reckon not," Peg said.

"I'm sorry I didn't make an appointment. Is this…is it a good time?"

"It's the perfect time, because we're both here," Peg answered. She poured water from the kettle into two cups, added teabags, and placed them on the tray next to the honey pot. Then she carried the tray to the small table near Ted's chair. She handed a mug to Ellen. "Honey?"

"No. It's fine as it is."

Peg nodded but placed a spoonful of honey into her own mug and stirred it. Then she took her seat. "Ellen, it is so good to see you," Peg lied. "What's on your heart?"

Ellen looked away, and already Peg could see tears welling up in her eyes.

Peg took a deep breath. She didn't mind waiting. Silence was her friend. She closed her eyes and imagined her left hand holding Jesus'. Jesus squeezed her hand. She squeezed back. She opened her eyes again and gave Ellen an encouraging smile.

"It's Melinda."

"Ah, yes." The last time Peg remembered seeing Melinda in church, the child had been no more than twelve or thirteen, and it was not so long ago. "What's going on with her?"

"She's pretending she's a boy. She wants everyone to call her Mel, including us."

Peg nodded.

"And now she's asking us for hormones."

"Hormones?"

"She keeps talking about 'transitioning.' I don't know who is filling her head with such nonsense."

"How is Jorge taking it?"

"He..." Ellen looked away before she resumed her sentence. "...he hit her."

"Hit her?" Peg recoiled in her seat. "That doesn't sound like Jorge."

"It was her fault, of course," Ellen continued. "She made him so... so *mad*. She wants us to call her 'he' and 'him.' Jorge finally just couldn't take it anymore. He hit her across the face...with a fork. It was a nasty...there were cuts."

"Oh my god, Ellen," Peg's hand went to her mouth. "I'm so sorry. Did you try to stop him?"

"No! She had it coming, didn't she? I probably would have hit her myself if he hadn't..." Ellen collapsed into sobs. "Where are these kids getting this stuff? How can I talk reason to her? Pastor, I don't know what to do. She's turning our life upside down. She's turning into this defiant little...monster. I want my sweet baby girl back...and she's gone." Her shoulders shook.

Peg reached over and snagged a box of tissues. She put it in front of Ellen. "Here, dear."

Ellen nodded gratefully and snatched at a tissue. She blew her nose, then pinched the space between her eyes, still holding the wadded tissue. Peg let a full minute of silence pass, waiting for the wave of emotion to fully roll through. When Ellen sniffed and sat up a bit straighter, Peg said, "She isn't your sweet baby girl anymore."

Ellen frowned and looked at the pastor. Obviously, that was not what she wanted to hear. Peg took a deep breath. "And she's right on schedule. She's, what, fourteen?"

Ellen nodded.

"That was exactly the age that Julie became…someone else. It's no fun, but it just means they're growing up. They have to figure out who they are. And they have to figure out who they are *apart from you*."

"My girl is *not* a lesbian." There was poison in her voice, but Peg reminded herself that Ellen had probably said it with more poison than she'd intended. But she still heard the unspoken "Unlike *your* daughter." Peg squeezed Jesus' hand. He squeezed back. She took another deep breath and held it.

"Maybe not, but that's not the point. She's…a teenager now. She's got to show how she's different from you. Sometimes that will be in dramatic ways that will be painful. Sometimes, that will be her intention, and sometimes it won't be. As painful as this is, Ellen…it's normal."

"It's not normal for her to cut her hair like a boy and start wearing workboots."

"Every kid does it differently, but every kid has to do it."

Ellen scowled. "Are we talking about two different things?"

Peg smiled. "I think we are. There are two issues here. One is Melinda's need to individuate—"

"What does that mean?"

"It means becoming her own person. It's an instinctual drive. Every child goes through it as a teenager—"

"I never did. I was a good girl. I don't deserve this."

"Well…we can talk about that some other time. But…focusing on *Melinda* right now…I'm just saying that kids have to find out who they are by finding out who they're not. They play dress up, to see if the clothes fit. If they don't, they take them off and put on something else. It's…this is normal. It hurts, but it's normal."

"You're saying that dressing like a boy is just a…a what? A phase? She'll realize it isn't really her and move on?"

"Maybe. And maybe not. But I…I can only tell you about me." She set her mug down. It was too hot anyway, and she really didn't need to burn her lip today. "One day Julie just announced that she liked girls instead of boys. I told her to stop being silly. And then she started to change. She became…dark…angry…surly…sarcastic. She became a truly terrible person. I can't believe I'm saying this out loud, but...I hated her...who she was turning into. And I fought it. And the more I fought it, the further away from me she ran. Until..." Peg felt her throat swell up. She reached for a tissue herself. She waited for her breath to slow. "I'm still waiting to get my little girl back. But she's not coming back. And the woman she's turned into...I want to love her, but she won't let me."

Peg sniffed and met Ellen's eye. "But this isn't about me and Julie. I guess I'm saying that the further you dig your heels in, the farther and faster she'll run away from you. And there will be a time when you'll regret the things you say now. I feel like I can say that with... well, with some confidence, some authority."

She picked up her mug again and blew on it. "I know you don't want to hear this, Ellen, but you did come to me today, so here it is. Until she says otherwise, you don't have a daughter anymore, you have a son. And if you don't love him, you'll lose him. Maybe forever. You can be his best friend or you can be his bitterest enemy—you get to choose. But you need to choose now, or it will be too late."

She did not say, *Maybe it already is*, but she thought it. *Okay Jesus, I've completely fucked this up. Time for you to swoop in and fix it.* Peg relaxed a bit. Nothing was quite as comforting as prayer.

Ellen blew into another tissue. "But it's *unnatural*. God cannot approve of this...of her."

"Of *him*," Peg corrected her. "And I don't think God's approval is what she's...*he's* concerned about. I don't think it's something he *needs* to be concerned about. This isn't really about God. It's about you deciding whether or not you really love your child, or whether you only love some fairy-tale notion of who you think your child *should* be."

Ellen blinked. Peg wondered if she'd gotten too cerebral. A Berkeley education did her no favors at times. She squeezed Jesus' hand. Jesus squeezed back. And as she watched Ellen's face, she saw that no, the woman had been tracking with her after all.

"You've...you've given me a lot to think about, Pastor."

"That's why they pay me the big money."

Ellen looked confused.

Peg waved the joke away. "I'm glad you came. It took a lot of courage. Would you like to pray together?"

Ellen shifted in her chair and seemed to rear back a bit. "No... that's okay."

Peg smiled. "Well, listen, you come talk to me anytime."

"Will you talk to Melinda?"

"With Mel, you mean? Of course. But only if you want me to support him."

Ellen stood up, looking more disturbed than when she'd first entered. Peg rose, went to the door, and handed her her scarf. Wordlessly, Ellen put it on. She opened the door and paused. "Um...thank you." It almost sounded like a question. After another moment's hesitation, she shut the door.

Ministry is like riding a toboggan in a blinding snowstorm, Peg thought. *You have no idea what's coming, and there are no brakes on the thing.* "Thank you, Jesus," Peg said. And then her thoughts turned to soup.

Becky spread a blanket next to the mound of earth in the back yard. It was the place she'd buried Samson. She'd done it while Paul was at work and had just barely finished the job when he came home. He'd given her a thrashing for not having his dinner ready. Involuntarily, her hand went to the scrape on her cheek. It still smarted.

She didn't know why she was there, not really. She knew that Samson was not there. Just a few feet from her, a corpse was decomposing. There was nothing romantic about it. It was macabre, when she thought of it like that. But when she didn't think of it like that, it was a place she felt close to him, the only other living soul who knew the geography of her private hell.

She reached out her hand and touched the soil. There were already tiny green tendrils of weeds beginning to sprout on the mound. Without thinking, she began to pluck them out. Then she hesitated.

Who was she to curb life? *I'm not like him,* she thought. *I refuse to be like him.* She stopped pulling the weeds.

A bellow wafted over the chilly breeze, and she winced. She touched a spot on her dress, just to reassure herself. She felt the hard protruding outlines. She felt her pulse quicken. She thought maybe she would feel safer, but she was wrong. It felt more dangerous.

It wouldn't do for Paul to find her here. He would harangue her for being sentimental, and lazy as well. She touched the mound of earth. "I'll come see you again soon, boy." Then she got up and dusted off the seat of her jeans. She smoothed her apron, then turned back toward the house.

When she got back to the kitchen, Paul began yelling. She took a deep breath and tried to hold on to her center.

"When did you become a thief?" he asked her. He pressed his face close into hers, and she could smell the beer on his breath.

"What are you talking about?" she asked. "How am I a thief?"

"I looked at our bank statement today." He held up his phone. "On the app." His eyes flashed triumph. He looked like he had just caught her with her hand in the cash register. He was *glad.*

She refused to play. She crossed her arms. "Paul, I have no idea what you're talking about."

"Yesterday," he shouted, his face suddenly becoming very red, "there was $5,000 in that account. Today there is only $3,500. Where did that $1500 go? Huh? Fifteen hundred-fucking dollars, bitch! Where did it go? What did you do with it?" He reached for her hair, but she darted back toward the kitchen door just in time.

"Paul! Stop it. Calm down long enough to talk to me, okay?"

"Don't you fucking tell me to calm down!"

"I did *not* take that money. I wrote a check. It's the end of the first quarter. It's property taxes. If I didn't pay that money by Friday, we'd get a penalty from the state. Is that what you want?"

"Nice try," he said.

"I can show you the checkbook—" she headed for the little hutch where she kept the checkbook. But he reached for her hair again. This time he succeeded. She cried out in pain as he jerked her head sideways and then up. Her scalp burned.

She flailed out and succeeded in smashing her palm onto his nose with sufficient force to hear an audible crunch. "Bitch!" he bellowed. He let go of her hair and clutched at his nose.

Hands shaking, she reached into the pocket of her apron and pulled out the revolver. It was loaded. She had made sure of that. She hadn't shot it before, but the man at the store had showed her how. She'd practiced a few times without any bullets in the chamber.

Her scalp felt like it was on fire as she gripped the pistol in both hands and pointed it at her husband. The whole gun shook. She squeezed her grip harder, willing the shaking to stop. It didn't.

"What the fuck, Beck?" he said.

"I will shower with this gun. I will sleep with this gun. I will eat fucking breakfast with this gun. And if you ever—ever!—touch me again, I will empty it into your guts. Do you understand me?"

Incredibly, his face turned an even deeper red. He shrank a bit and it seemed to her that he was gathering himself to spring at her. In her mind's eye, she saw him lunge at her, grab the gun from her, and use its heft to beat her face into hamburger.

With her thumb, she drew back the hammer. The click reverberated throughout the kitchen, far louder than she had expected it to be. She knew she didn't need to pull it back—it would happen automatically if she squeezed the trigger. She had done it for effect.

It seemed to work. She watched him hesitate. His tiny eyes—too small for the size of his head—moved back and forth quickly. He was thinking, she could see that. He was looking for an option. But eventually his shoulders relaxed. "Okay." He held his palms toward her, fingers spread. "Okay, Beck. Just...lower the gun."

"Don't you dare touch me again. And I mean *ever*."

"Okay. I get it. I...Jesus, woman. Calm down."

She laughed then. It seemed like such a ludicrous thing to say. *He* was telling *her* to calm down? She laughed harder. He looked confused. "Get out of my sight," she said.

Milala had followed the scent of pie and found it. She spent all that she had left on a slice and a cup of coffee. It had been delicious— cherry, with a scoop of vanilla ice cream on top of it. Full and flush with sugar, she stumbled out of the bakery and smacked her lips with pleasure as she took in the midafternoon sun. Her eyes drooped, and she felt a desperate need to lie down. She swung her bag over her shoulder and crossed the street toward the park.

The little white gazebo came into view after a couple of minutes' walk, a giant willow providing shade. She'd been cautious about lying down on one of the benches earlier, but another voice inside her head argued that there was nothing wrong with lying on the grass. After all, she'd seen *oje-ajnt* women napping on the grass in the shade before—it was a thing that was done. And perhaps people would not look close enough to notice she was one of The People. Thus rationalized, she set her bag down in the willow's shade and settled down onto a soft, grassy patch.

For a few blissful moments, she watched dappled sunlight peek through the willow's branches. She heard the songs of her bird cousins and was able to identify most of them without even thinking about it. Then her eyelids grew heavy, and she allowed the grass to buoy her into sleep.

She slept hard, without dreaming. When she woke, the sun had begun its slow descent. She felt at her head and sat up. She had a slight headache that might have been because of the sugar in the pie, or perhaps it was due to the angle of her neck as she was sleeping. She rubbed at the back of her head, trying to work the pain out.

She reached for her bag but felt only grass. She frowned and looked down, surprised that the bag had gone so far from her fingers that she couldn't find it by touch. But the bag was not there. Milala saw nothing around her but grass. Her breath caught and she reminded herself not to panic. She stood up and looked all around her—but there was no bag. She widened the area of her search, but there was no bag.

"Shit," she breathed.

She felt suddenly naked without her bag, and now she felt violated as well. Who had taken her bag? and why? She thought of asking the bird cousins, but she saw none now. She thought of sending out a call to Coyote, but she didn't want to give him the satisfaction.

She sniffed and realized her only pack of tissues had been in her bag. She stood up and waited for the dizziness to pass, then she turned back toward the street. She debated where she should go or what she should do. Ordinarily, she would give the police a wide berth, but when she saw the county sheriff's office, it felt right to walk toward it. After all, someone had stolen her only possessions. Crime should be reported.

She climbed the three steps to a little porch, tugged the door open, and went inside. She was met with a blast of warm air that felt lovely. She seemed to be alone.

The implications of this delighted her. Was it possible that the staff had gone home already? Had someone simply forgotten to lock the door? Might she sleep indoors tonight on this comfy industrial carpet? What foodstuffs might she find in the break room? But her fantasies were interrupted by the arrival of a single woman, much older than she, with a turned-up nose and cat's-eye glasses hanging from a lanyard, resting just atop her bosoms. "Can I help you?" the woman asked.

"Yes, I—"

"We're very busy," the woman said.

Milala looked around at the empty station. *Who is the "we"?* she wondered. And how busy could this woman be? She looked like she was ready to lock the place up for the night and go home to a dinner of boiled cabbage.

"I'd like to report a crime," Milala said.

The woman looked momentarily uncomfortable. "Well, our—" She looked around, then looked back at Milala. She sighed. "Just…sit there. I can fill out a report, I suppose. The sheriff and our deputies are…indisposed right now."

"Oh," Milala said. "All of them?"

es, I'm afraid so. The night shift starts in an hour or so, but they ll have their hands full…" The woman trailed off, her quick eyes betraying that she felt she'd said too much. Milala decided to like this woman. "My name is Celia," the woman said, indicating a chair near a small desk. "Have a seat."

Milala sat. The woman opened a desk drawer and withdrew a form. Then she snatched a pen out of a coffee cup. "What is your name?"

"Milala Caballero."

"You look like one of The People," Celia said.

"D'you think?" Milala quipped. But she sensed that she did not need to be sarcastic with this woman. She was trying to help her, after all. She softened. "My people are Miwok, South Sierra."

"You're a little afield, aren't you? We got mostly Yakuts and Tubatulabal in these parts."

It was true—her reservation was more than a hundred miles away. She shrugged. "I guess."

"What's the crime?"

"I was lying down in the park after…lunch," she began.

"Were you sleeping? Because it's illegal to sleep in the park."

Milala blinked. If she said "yes," she would be admitting to a crime, albeit probably not a serious one. But there might be a fine associated with it, and she had no money for a hotel room, let alone a fine. But if she said "no," how could she explain the fact that someone had snuck off with her bag without her noticing? Neither option seemed like a good one. She stumbled into a middle way. "Uh…I'm not sure. I closed my eyes for a few minutes. It felt good to be out of the sun."

Celia frowned, meeting her eye, but then looked back down at the form and scrawled something on it. "I'm still not hearing a crime," she said.

"My bag. When I wo—when I opened my eyes," she corrected herself, "my bag was gone."

"What kind of bag?"

"Just a small duffel, with a strap. Canvas. Dyed yellow."

Celia wrote furiously as she talked. "And what was in your bag?"

"A small pack of Kleenex," Milala started, "my wallet, three pieces of candy, an eagle feather, a small pack of tobacco, four cigars, a box of matches, and…my drum."

"Wait, I can't write that fast. Can you give me the list again?"

She did, but this time she didn't hesitate when mentioning her drum.

"Your drum?" Celia asked when she got to the end of the list.

"Yes. You know…" she mimed holding the drum in one hand by its crosspieces and using her other hand to strike it with the padded mallet.

"A drum…like a Native American drum used in ceremony?" Celia asked.

"Yes." She wanted to mention that the drum had been blessed by Old Mike Cornfeather of the Northern Pomo People, but decided against it. She wouldn't know Old Mike, and if she looked him up, it would not help her any—not with his record.

"Any…valuables?"

"My wallet isn't valuable?" Milala scowled.

"Was there any money in it?" Celia asked.

"Well…no," Milala conceded.

"Any credit cards?" Celia asked.

"No."

"Any gift cards?"

"No."

"So…no valuables."

"My drum is valuable," Milala said, "to me."

"But not much resale value, I'm going to guess," Celia said. "Sounds like your thief might have got the raw end of the deal."

Milala's eyes narrowed. She could tell Celia was making a joke. She did not think it was funny.

"What's your cell number?" Celia asked. "You know, just in case it turns up?"

"I don't have a phone," Milala said.

"So, if your bag turns up, how should we get in touch with you?" Celia asked.

...lala didn't know the answer to that. She sighed. She rose. "Thank you for your time," she said.

Just then it struck her that Celia actually looked sad.

"Where are you staying, dear?" Celia asked.

Milala didn't answer. "I'll...come by again tomorrow," she said, and headed for the door.

Julie stepped down out of her Jeep and headed up the sidewalk to Clive's apartment. It had taken her too long to get there, and she cursed the constant demands of her job that always seemed to take priority. *I should have come last night,* she thought. But she had been bone tired. She had called again...to no answer.

She knocked on the door. It was quiet as a graveyard. She sensed no movement inside...indeed, she sensed no one *was* inside. She tried the doorknob. It was locked. She rattled it, pushing and pulling from slightly different angles, but it was solid. For a few fleeting moments, she considered breaking it down. *I would get in such a shitstorm of trouble if I did that,* she thought. She sighed. *Work the system,* she told herself. *Trust the system.*

The system said that the next step was to ask the manager. She went to the mailboxes and scoured them for a hint. She brightened up when one of the labels did indeed say "manager." "Ebert Taylor." She said the name aloud to fix it in her mind. "12b."

She began to circumambulate the apartment building, looking for 12b. She went the wrong direction at first, but eventually found it. She knocked firmly on the door. This time, she *did* sense movement within, and was relieved when the door opened a crack.

Inside was a man in his late 30s, head shaved except for some extraordinarily bushy eyebrows. He had one lazy eye. He was dressed in sweatpants and a t-shirt. "Officer?" His eyebrows rose as he took her in.

"Are you Mr. Taylor?" she asked, trying to appear professional.

"Yes?"

"Are you the manager of this apartment building?"

"This and two others. They're nearby. What can I...they aren't dealing the oxy again, are they?"

Julie's spine straightened instantly. "Um...*who* is dealing oxy?"

"Never mind. I got no evidence. Keeping my mouth shut."

Julie raised one eyebrow. "Uh-huh. Listen, Mr. Taylor, no one has heard from Clive Foster for over a week. I'm...well, I'm wondering if you could let me in to look at his apartment."

"Are you a relative?" Taylor asked, squinting one eye—not the lazy one.

"No. I'm...he's my best friend, though."

"Ah, so this is not official police business?"

"No...not yet."

"Well, people got a right to their privacy. When you got a warrant...come talk to me." He started to shut the door.

She jammed her foot into the gap. "Mr. Taylor, when was the last time *you* saw him?"

"Couple weeks. Last time he paid rent."

"Aren't you worried?"

"I don't get paid enough to worry about things like that."

"He could be dead in there; he could be stinking up the place." It pained her even to say it, but she could see the effect on him. She watched him weighing her words, his eyes moving back and forth quickly. He was wavering. She tried to press it home. "If he is dead and you catch it early, cleanup is going to be so much easier. Easier to rent the place, too."

Few people were clamoring to rent in the Central Valley. She removed her foot and assumed a more solid stance.

"Warrant," he said, and slammed the door.

"Damn," she said to herself. Once more she briefly considered going back to Clive's apartment and breaking the door down, but now that she'd talked to Taylor, she knew she'd be in real shit with the boss if she tried something like that. Could she *break* in? As she walked away from Taylor's apartment, she studied the building. Clive's apartment was on the ground floor, and there were windows.

She looked around to see if anyone was watching—and saw no one. She craned her neck to see if she could see Taylor's apartment—she couldn't. She abruptly turned and headed for Clive's windows.

The apartments faced an interior courtyard, leaving the rear entrances for these apartments facing the street. But as she got closer, she saw that the windows were higher than she remembered. *Of course, at the front door, you go up two steps,* she thought. She stuffed her hands into her trouser pockets as she looked up at the windows— tantalizingly close, but still beyond her reach.

"Damn," she said, and turned back toward her Jeep. *I could come back, bring a ladder, get into one of those windows,* she mused. She nodded to herself. It was a possibility...but one that would have to wait until a more opportune moment—preferably a darker one, as well.

As she got into her Jeep, she pulled the scrap of paper on which she'd written the phone number Ben had given her from her pocket. That was her next move. She felt the rightness of it in her bones. A part of her screamed at the prospect of leaving Clive's disappearance for another time. She didn't have enough to file a missing person's report, and she had actual duties to perform. She decided to have a talk with Thom about it. If anyone would know what she could and should do, it would be him.

She realized that others might seek out her mother's counsel. That seemed absurd to her. Her mother knew nothing about the law, and even less about investigation. Peg was a preacher, which meant she had a Master's degree in patriarchal bullshit, and was of limited use to anyone, especially to Julie.

No, there was only one thing before her now, and it was whoever belonged to this number. Opening her shop laptop, she accessed the reverse directory and entered the number. An address appeared—in Coleman, about a half hour drive. The number was registered to an Otto Mercer. She memorized the address and fed it into her GPS. A map resolved on the screen, showing her the route. She pushed the button for "overview" and scanned the map. She saw enough to get her to the right neighborhood without listening to the annoying thing tell her how to do every little turn. She'd consult it again when she got close. She eased up on the brake and punched the gas on the Jeep.

A tiny part of her brain worried about confronting a skinhead alone, and she wondered if she ought to call in some backup. The problem was that both Thom and Jake were busy elsewhere. She could call someone from the night crew—maybe Skinner? He owed her one. But ultimately she decided against it. After failing at Clive's, she was feeling an internal pressure to accomplish something, and calling him in would only delay her. He'd need to shower, or run an errand first, or finish his goddam dinner. It would be something, she was sure, and she didn't want to deal with it.

It took forty-five minutes to drive to the address, much of it over freeway that cut through mile after mind-numbing mile of farmland. Once more, she entered a kind of fugue state, only emerging a split second before missing her off-ramp. The Jeep lurched and veered, but kept its wheels as she steered off and braked to a roll at the stop sign. *I need a plan,* she thought. But no plan emerged. A feeling of dread descended on her, ominous yet somehow distant. A warning.

She made a sign in the air to ward against evil and said a silent prayer to the Mother. She had no idea whether her prayers did a damn thing, but it seemed to be the thing to do in the moment. *How different from Mom*, she thought, remembering how her skin crawled whenever Peg talked about Jesus as if he weren't dead and in the dirt somewhere for more than two thousand years.

The fact was, she didn't know what to make of her mother's religion. As a child, she didn't know her mother had a religious bone in her body. Life had been an endless string of nocturnal battle scenes that usually involved booze, tears, and bruises in some combination. Even after her father went to prison, there had been an endless string of boyfriends with similar results. If she had met her then-mother now, she'd dismiss her as trailer-trash, and a part of her would blame her for the situation she was in. Why didn't she get rid of that pugilistic motherfucker who threatened her child? Why didn't she get off the drugs? Why didn't she go to school and make something of herself?

"She did," Julie said aloud. And the sound of her own voice swam in the air, echoing and somehow distant. Julie blinked and let the Jeep roll to a stop at the side of the road. Her mother had done all those things. She had cleaned herself up. She had shed those abusive boyfriends. She had gone to school, even grad school. She had become someone worthy of admiration and respect. She had been trailer trash once upon a time, but *now* she was a respected pastor.

Maybe not respectable, as some would consider it—this was Peg she was thinking about, after all. She would always be quirky and come at everything sideways—but nevertheless, she was a pastor in good standing in a major denomination. She had a paycheck. She had a job.

Julie blinked back a tear and felt the bile rise up in her throat. It was anger—she recognized that. But for the first time, she didn't know who to direct that anger at. Peg had always been the target, but that wasn't clear now. Her anger dissipated a bit, not having anything to latch onto. *This anger is mine,* she thought. *This is my problem. It isn't Peg's, and it's not fair to keep putting it on her.*

Julie watched the black clouds in the distance, troubling the otherwise blue sky. *You have a right to your anger,* a voice in her head told her. It wasn't Peg's voice. Perhaps it was the voice of the Goddess? Or perhaps it was just a voice of reason. *You had a terrible childhood. And that was Peg's fault. But she made heroic efforts to get herself—and you—out of that life. And she succeeded. How long do you intend to punish her? And are you punishing her for being a screwed up kid or a responsible adult? Because you need to get that straight.*

She didn't know the answer to that. She supposed she was angry at Peg for not protecting her from the trauma when she was young. That was all right. But Peg *had* turned it around and had done her best to keep her safe from that kind of life. And she had succeeded. But she had succeeded just as Julie became a teenager, and ever since, all Julie could muster for her was contempt. And in that moment, watching the clouds ride the wind into the distance, for the very first time she felt a twinge of remorse.

Focus, the voice in Julie's head said. It was a different voice. This was the voice of duty. Julie shook her head and steered the Jeep back onto the pavement. She punched at her map app, and with one eye on the road, studied the route with the other. With one hand, she fixed it into a frame that held it at eye level, freeing up her hands. A soothing woman's voice told her where to turn, and she let it guide her to the destination. "The skinhead's lair," she said under her breath as she rolled to the curb.

She opened the door and was just about to swing her legs to the pavement, when a couple of unsettling realizations occurred to her. First, that someone needed to know where she was. The second was that she was, in fact, a one-hundred-and-twenty-pound female, and the man she was about to confront was bound to be twice her weight and size. "I need a big gun," she said. But all she had was her service weapon. It would have to do. She snagged the transceiver from its hook and pushed the button. "Karlstadt, this is Adam three—code four, over."

A moment later, she heard Celia's voice. "Three, code four, go ahead."

"Code eleven to 4493 Sweetwater Circle, Coleman. About to engage suspect, over."

"Confirm 4493 Sweetwater Circle, Coleman."

"Affirmative, Karlstadt."

"Do you require backup, three?" Celia asked.

"Negative, Karlstadt. Can you run a quick check on an Otto Mercer?"

"Copy that, three. Stand by."

While she waited, Julie removed the tablet from its cradle under the radio and activated its touchscreen. She flipped through a couple pages until she had navigated to the proper screen. A moment later, it populated, and she found herself looking at her suspect. It was a mug shot, which did not surprise her, about four years old. Mercer had a black eye and a swollen lip. Julie pursed her lips as she scanned his priors—a laundry list of petty crime and near-misses. This guy was bad news who'd caught some lucky breaks.

"Not this noche," Julie said under her breath. She scrolled to the bottom of the file, to check for outstanding warrants. There were two.

"Hot damn," she said. "Payday."

"Thanks, Karlstadt. I'll be thirteen with the suspect before dinner time." Thirteen meant she'd be back at the station.

"Sure you don't need an eight?" Celia asked. An eight was backup.

Ordinarily, she would. But she knew that Thom and Jake had their hands full with the Nyland farm. "Negative, Karlstadt. I'll take it from here. If you don't hear from me in forty-five, send in the cavalry."

"Copy that, three. Advise caution."

"Copy that, Karlstadt. Three out."

A part of her brain was screaming that this was a bad idea. She climbed out of the Jeep and shut the door. She unsnapped her holster and rested her hand on her service revolver as she strode to the house. It was light blue in color, with paint cracked and peeling from the sun. The house could generously be called a fixer-upper. Two wheel-less cars rested on blocks in the front yard, adorned by dead grass poking out of the dirt.

She kept her hand floating just above her weapon as she gave a commanding rap on the door. A moment later, the door swung open, and Otto Mercer threw what seemed to be the second half of a joke over his shoulder. He froze when he saw her, his eyes widening in what looked like momentary panic.

She counted to three as she watched him settle into the fact that there was a cop at the door. His eyes then moved back and forth quickly, scanning the sidewalk and street behind her. Finally, with a forced air of calm, his eyes settled on her. He was tall and seemed impossibly thin. It seemed to Julie that if the wind caught him wrong, he'd snap. His fingers were shaking, and his face twitched repeatedly. "Officer?"

"Are you Otto Mercer?"

He narrowed his eyes. She had caught him off guard, but now he was adjusting. "Who wants to know?"

"Inyo County Sheriff's Office," she pointed to her badge.

"You here to bring me in?" he asked.

"Who is it?" a voice from within called.

"Cops," Mercer called over his shoulder.

"Shit," the person behind him said, then went completely silent.

"That depends," Julie answered his question. "Do you plan to run? Because if you run, then yes. We're in the middle of fucking nowhere. I will get in my Jeep and I will run you the fuck down."

The man blinked. The side of his nose twitched. "And if I don't run?"

"Then I just have some questions for you. Might not even be *about* you." Julie watched his face for some sign of his intentions. She could see him thinking fast. "We're in the middle of an investigation, and we think you might have some valuable information. You help us, and we might be able to help you."

"With what?" Mercer asked.

"With those outstanding warrants," she said.

"I know how this works," he said with a snarl. "You can't just wave your hand and make them go away."

An interesting choice of words for a magickian, Julie thought. He didn't look like a magickian, though. He looked like white trash—the kind of guy who lived on a steady diet of axle grease, potato chips, and cheap beer. "No, but we can recommend leniency."

"Not good enough," Mercer said.

Did he actually just spit on the floor of his own house? She shook her head. "You haven't got a lot of options."

"You here by yourself?" he asked.

"Backup is on the way," she lied. "Do you mind if I come in?"

His eyes widened in fear. He caught it and moderated his reaction, but she'd seen it just the same.

"I mind," he said.

"Then do you mind stepping out here so we can talk—privately?" she asked.

He looked behind him, and with an apparent wariness she did not yet understand, he walked out onto the porch. She was about to make a joke about the deleterious effect of sunlight on magickians, but she decided against tipping her hand too quickly.

Once outside, she was able to see the full extent of his trembling. *Meth addict,* she thought, *and I caught him in full mid-tweak.* "You cooking?" she asked.

She didn't think it was possible for a man to look more nervous than Mercer already was, but he managed it.

"Nah-no, why would you think that? You'd smell it if we were."

That was true. They weren't cooking meth...at least they weren't cooking it *here*.

"I could search the place though," she said. "Wonder what I'd find?"

Now the man looked like he was about to vibrate through the slats of the porch. She enjoyed rattling him. But if she kept it up, it would soon prove counterproductive. Julie held her hand up. "Relax. I'm not here to serve a search warrant. I'm just here to ask some questions."

"Okay," Mercer said.

In the sunlight, the sores on his neck and arms came to life and danced on his skin like the spots of leopards. Inwardly, she shuddered at the thought of the kind of life the man must have descended into. She glanced behind him into the house, looking for a sign of whomever else was within, but she saw nothing. *Well, at least he has friends,* she thought. She flashed on the memory of Peg telling her, "Friends are a blessing," when she was very young and no one would play with her because she was the poor new girl who lived in a mobile home. She didn't remember why her mother had said that, just that it wasn't particularly helpful. She assumed her mother had gotten better at giving advice like that, being a pastor and all, but she hadn't really given Peg any opportunity to demonstrate that skill.

She cleared her throat and leaned in toward Mercer, her voice little more than a whisper. "I hear you've got a copy of *Fenestram in Infernum.* Any chance you'd let me take a look at it?"

Mercer reared back and looked her up and down, as if seeing her for the first time. He started to speak, but suddenly seemed to be rendered inarticulate. After a string of nonsense, the man scratched his head. There were sores there too, she saw. "You're...really not here to bust me?"

She shook her head. "I'm really not. I'm investigating some… occult phenomena, shall we say. There are some…manifestations that lead me to believe that the *Fenestram* is involved. I know you have a copy—"

"An' how do you know that?"

"I'm *investigating*—"

"It was that little crippled Jew at the Lux, wasn't it?" He looked up and away from her. He balled his trembling hands into fists, and she noted for the first time the tattoos on each of his fingers, just above the first knuckles. And one of those tattoos was the sigil of Duunel. "I'll fucking cut him."

"I'll…pretend I didn't hear that, and Ben had no choice—I threatened him." That wasn't true, of course, but Mercer didn't need to know that. "So you'd better hope nothing happens to Ben, or I'll be here asking even more uncomfortable questions."

"Goddam Jew snitch."

"Let's focus, shall we?" Julie asked. "Do you have a copy of the *Fenestram* on the premises?"

"It's not stolen," he said. "I paid top dollar for that book."

"I'm not accusing you of stealing anything," Julie said, using her most reassuring voice. "I just want to see the book. If you would be so kind."

"You want to see the book?" Mercer looked wary.

"I do. Maybe snap a few pictures with my phone. Then I'll leave you in peace to…do whatever it was you were doing."

"Do you…*know* what we were doing?" He met her eyes and there was a new kind of fear in them.

Julie's brow darkened. "No…should I?"

Mercer's eyes moved back and forth again, a little too quickly, even for a tweaker. She watched his eyes flicker toward somewhere behind her. Then she saw him smile. Then she felt the blow to the back of her head. Then she saw and felt…nothing.

CHAPTER SEVEN

Peg yawned. The late afternoon grogginess had usually passed by this time, but not today. She wondered if she dared lay down for a brief nap before supper. It sometimes interfered with her sleep if she napped too late. She was weighing the pros and cons when the phone rang.

"So much for that," she said as she reached for her cell phone.

"Pastor?" came the voice. She knew that voice.

"Alec?" Alec Marlowe was the chair of her church council—he was essentially her boss. Peg scowled. A call from Alec was unusual, and it usually meant bad news. She steadied herself for whatever was coming next.

"I hope you are having a good day," he said.

Because it's about to get very bad, the voice in her head continued. She didn't dislike Alec, but he was a sour, humorless man at the best of times. When delivering bad news, he was a bit like an automaton, and she couldn't decide whether that was good or bad. In person, he could be gruff and unyielding. That had sometimes worked in her favor, when the church needed a bulldog. But she hated being on the other side of the leash.

"It was long, and I'm tired," she confessed. "What's up?" No need to beat around the bush.

That seemed to suit Alec just fine. "There are some issues we need to discuss."

"Issues? Plural?"

"Yes. I wonder when I might be able to make an appointment to meet."

"As in, face to face?"

"Yes."

"This *is* serious," Peg breathed.

"Well, it's not fitness review serious. We're not getting the Association involved...yet. I thought perhaps we might be able to handle it in-house."

"That...sounds good to me. Alec, you've got me concerned."

"How about tomorrow morning, nine o'clock?"

"Sure, I'll be working on my sermon, but I can push pause whenever you get here." She feigned a smile, even though he could not see it.

"That'll be fine. See you then." He hung up.

Peg stood staring at her cell phone. *There's nothing worse that knowing you're in trouble and not knowing why,* she thought. It was cruel.

She knew Alec didn't think of himself as cruel, just business-like and efficient. He made no attempt to be pastoral. And why should he? She was the pastor. It was his job to run the church, and that he did with dispassionate efficiency that she usually appreciated.

She willed herself to relax. *Whatever it is, it can't be that bad. They're not taking it to the judicatory,* she told herself. She instantly knew what she needed to do. She needed to take this to Jesus, to let him hold her. Maybe she needed a good cry. Jesus would hold her while she did that too.

She lit a candle and settled into her regular chair—the chair that had, over the past several years, morphed to perfectly fit her shape. She closed her eyes and vividly imagined standing at the door of Jesus' woodworking shop. She knocked on the door, anticipating an exuberant welcome.

But a knock came at her own door instead. "Christ in a cracker," she said, snapping her eyes open. "What now?" She had been so close to comfort, so close to the healing balm of Jesus' presence, the tender touch of his hands, his spicy smell, those full, dark lips…

She sighed and stood up. Wearily, she crossed to the door and opened it a crack. Outside she spied Bren Helvig. Peg forced a smile and opened the door wide. "Bren, what a surprise! Come in, my dear. Can I get you some tea?"

Bren flashed her a brief, inauthentic smile of her own and made a beeline for a chair. It happened to be Peg's chair, probably still warm, but she said nothing. Instead, she simply made the internal adjustment, picked up a clean cup, swapped her own cup for the clean one, and put it close to Bren's hand.

"It's not especially hot, I fear," Peg said. "I hope that's all right."

"I don't really drink tea," Bren said.

"Don't say that too loud," Peg said. "Around here that might be mistaken for blasphemy."

Bren's forehead bunched in confusion.

"Never mind. A poor joke. Tea is one of my great passions in life. Is that sad? I don't know. Everyone needs something, or several somethings, I think. Surely you are passionate about some trivial things, aren't you?"

Bren said nothing. She hugged herself and looked at her feet.

Peg frowned. She was getting nowhere with her small talk. She filled her own cup, put it on Ted's coaster, and sat in her chair. "What's troubling you, Bren?" she asked.

Bren was a short, dark-haired woman in her middle twenties, or so it seemed to Peg, and she'd been at the church for a couple of years. She had always struck her as a serious person, perhaps overly so. Peg had never found a joke that could crack her.

Peg had done enough spiritual counseling in her life to know that waiting in silence was the best strategy for drawing someone out on spiritual matters. *Just be a calm, non-anxious presence,* she reminded herself. Some days that was easier than others.

"Ash Wednesday is coming soon," Bren said.

"Yes indeed. Coming like a freight train and bringing Le Holy Week and Easter with it." Peg was tempted to launch . description of how much work that was all going to be, but she bit her tongue. Whatever this was about, it was not likely to involve the busy season for pastors.

"I don't like Ash Wednesday," she said.

"Oh? Whyever not?"

Bren narrowed her eyes at her, as if wondering whether the pastor was stupid or something. Peg gave her a patient smile and waited for a verbal response. When the silence was on the verge of being painful, Bren spat out, "Really?"

"Really, dear. I have no idea what you mean. Why don't you like Ash Wednesday?"

"I guess it's the service I don't like."

"Ah, not the day itself then. The calendar will be relieved."

Bren darkened. Peg chastened herself for the attempt at humor. She did an internal adjustment, trying to match Bren's level of sobriety. "What about the service don't you like?"

"I don't like it when you put the ashes on."

Peg nodded. "Because they're messy?"

"No! It's what you say."

"Oh. 'Remember O woman that you are dust, and to dust you shall return.' Is that what you mean?"

"Yes. It's very negative."

Kettle, meet black, Peg thought. But she said, "Say more."

"You don't think that's negative?" Bren asked.

"I don't, actually," Peg said. "I think it's honest."

"I think it's oppressive. Abusive, even."

Peg's eyebrows shot up. "Abusive? How in the world—?" A note of indignance shot out of her, and Peg clamped down on it before any more damage could be done. She awkwardly forced a kindly look onto her face.

"I can't believe you're so clueless," Bren said. She sniffed.

Don't take offense, Peg reminded herself. *Just be curious.* "Well, perhaps I am clueless about this. Pretend I'm a child. Tell me why it's abusive."

"People don't like to be reminded that they're going to die. It's traumatizing. You can't just go around traumatizing people. It's toxic religion. No wonder people don't go to church anymore."

Peg didn't disagree with much of that, so she nodded. "I can see how that's true about a lot of things we've—the church, I mean—that we've done wrong. I just don't see how it applies to this particular ritual. I mean...you *will* die. We all will."

"But it's mean to say so."

"Is it?" Peg felt a bit confounded. In her imagination, she reached out for Jesus' hand, found it, squeezed it. She felt the squeeze come back. She relaxed. She wasn't alone in this. Jesus was here to do the heavy lifting. She smiled, her face full of compassion. "Bren, dear, life is hard. I don't think this faith would be much good to us if it didn't face the truth of that. If it didn't address it, it would just be a way to help us *avoid* the hard things. My colleagues have a phrase for that— spiritual bypass. That's when your spirituality is so much about sweetness and light that it serves as an escape from the difficulties you face. That's not religion, that's anaesthesia. Following Jesus doesn't mean following him into a fairyland where there's no suffering or hardship. It means that we're not alone in our suffering or hardship...or even our dying. And it also promises that dying isn't the end. Ash Wednesday is just the first sentence. That paragraph ends with the Resurrection."

"No, now you're justifying abuse. The end doesn't justify the means."

Peg sat back and took a deep breath. She suddenly remembered the time Bren had come before the church council to petition them to require trigger warnings on sermons that might contain difficult themes. Peg had never been so grateful to Alec Marlowe than she had been that day. He had declared the request nonsense. What sermon didn't have difficult themes? Sermons—and the scriptures they were based on—were all about difficult themes. Alec had protected her that day. Perhaps he was protecting her now? She returned her attention to

the present moment and reminded herself to have compas
Bren. The young woman was facing an often-frightening woıu, aıu
simply wanted the cooperation of others around her to keep it as safe
and navigable as possible. But, Peg reasoned, if she was successful in
that, what would happen when difficult things actually happened, as
they inevitably would?

"Bren, what would you prefer me to say? As I put the ashes on, I
mean?"

For the first time, Bren brightened. The momentary glow on her
face seemed to say, "Someone is hearing me!" She seemed surprised.
That made Peg feel a bit sad.

"I want you to say, 'Remember that you are light, and to light you
shall return!'" She smiled. Peg blinked. Bren Helvig was actually smiling. She didn't quite know what to do or say. She felt for Jesus' hand
again. Finding it, she steeled herself. She wanted to say, "That's
exactly the kind of spiritual bypass I was talking about!" but wisely
didn't. "Are you light, Bren?"

"Didn't Jesus say, 'You are the light of the world'?"

"Er...yes. But I don't think—" She stopped herself again. *Don't muff
this up, Pastor,* she reminded herself. She turned her attention to the
pressure of Jesus' hand. *Anytime now, Jesus. Something brilliant would be
perfect right about now.* But Jesus was silent. *Damn it,* Peg thought. *We're
gonna talk later, and you're not going to like it.*

It was not her habit to threaten the savior, but it was her habit to
be honest with him. And now it was her job to be honest with Bren.
"Bren, dear..." She cleared her throat. "Thank you for sharing this
concern with me. If it's alright with you, I'm going to carry this into
prayer and give it some careful discernment. I'm not promising I'll
change anything about the Ash Wednesday service, but I do promise
to bring it to Jesus and listen. Will that be okay?"

Bren's face seemed suddenly brighter. "Thank you, Pastor. Thank
you so much." Bren launched herself out of her chair and caught Peg
up in a hug, knocking her teacup to the floor. Peg's breath caught from
the shock of it, then grimaced at the sound of her shattering china,
but slowly gave Bren a squeeze until the young woman pulled back.

She didn't acknowledge the broken teacup, but instead simply gave the pastor a namaste-bow. Then she turned and marched to the door with an air of modest triumph.

Milala felt lost. It was an odd feeling for her. Usually, there was no place on Creator's good old earth that did not welcome her, did not kiss the bottom of her feet, was not delighted by her presence. But the concrete of this tiny town got between her and the earth in a way that irritated her. She knew that would not be the case if everything else had not gone wrong—if her drum had not been stolen, if she had a place to sleep.

A place to sleep... she breathed. If she could find a pretty *oje-ajnt* girl her own age to go home with tonight, she would have both bed and bath, and probably food and some fun as well. She decided to do a careful circuit of the town to see if she could find a gay bar.

She walked the streets like a grid, up one side and down the other. About two streets in, her mood began to sour even further. *This town is too small for a gay bar,* she thought. And in her bones, she knew this was true. And yet...she had found lovers in unusual places in the past. She remembered back to a feed barn she'd passed near Visalia a couple of years ago that had been converted into a drag bordello for the evening, one night only. What had been the odds that she would be passing by on that street, on that night? Astronomical. Sometimes, the wind blows just right, she knew. She hoped this would be one of those nights.

As she walked, she thought about Coyote. She knew he was being extraordinarily patient with her. She had been nothing but dismissive and disrespectful toward him—and among The People, there were few greater sins than disrespecting one's elders. But nor did she trust him. How did she know he was speaking for the Creator? What he asked of her made no sense, and for all she knew, he was just playing another one of his famous jokes.

She was getting nowhere looking for a gay bar. By the end of the fourth street, her shoulders slumped and she was dragging her feet. She had run out of town and had seen no evidence of other two-spirits. She thought of finding a regular bar and hoping to get lucky, but she knew she'd be more likely to get hit on by drunk men who found her "exotic" and assumed her easy. *Well, I am easy*, she thought, *just not for them.*

Finally, she screamed, aiming her voice at the moon, her fists shaking at the ends of her arms in rage. When her voice was ragged and spent, she began yelling, "What now, Creator? You wanted me to drum, but where's my fucking drum?! You wanted me to help these people, but they robbed me! Do you want me to sleep in the desert, without blankets? without fire?!"

Part of her hoped for a response—a flash of lightning or a peal of thunder or a minor earthquake. Instead, all she noticed was the breeze. She sighed. *Fire*, she thought. She could probably manage to make a fire. But the idea of sleeping on the ground near the end of winter, after it had just rained...no. The earth supported her and took care of her, but even The People needed shelter.

"Fuck these people," she said to the wind, to the sky, to Creator. She turned her face toward the 99 freeway and began walking.

Thom was almost at the Nyland farm when his radio crackled. "Adam One, this is Karlstadt."

Thom unhooked the mic from its clip and squeezed the button on its side. "Lind here, Karlstadt."

"Thom...you're not going to like this," Celia's voice began.

"Oh, Jesus. What now?" Thom said into the mic.

"Fifty minutes ago I got a code four from Adam Three. Barkley was following up on a lead in Coleman. She said if I didn't hear from her in forty-five minutes, I was to...sound the alarm, I suppose."

"Did she go there without backup?" Thom asked. Of course she had. There were only the three of them on the day shift, and he hadn't heard anything about it.

"Affirmative. In pursuit of a suspect, two outstanding warrants."

"Jesus, Barkley," Thom swore. "Have you called her?"

"No answer. It rings, but then goes to voicemail." Thom could tell that Celia's voice was high and tight, despite the radio noise.

Thom pulled over to the shoulder. He reached for the GPS unit sitting atop his dashboard in its bean-bag base. "Give me that Coleman address, Celia."

"4493 Sweetwater Circle."

"OnStar?"

"Shows her Jeep still at the address."

"All right. Looks like I can be there in forty minutes, give or take. Call Jake and tell him I can't spell him. Tell him to hang tight at the Nyland farm until I get back."

"He won't like i—"

"Fill him in and I doubt he'll complain."

"Yes, boss."

Thom swung the pickup around and kicked up a cloud of dust behind him as he gunned the engine. "Tell me everything you know," he said.

"I wish I had something for you," Celia said. "I know she was investigating the Nyland cubes. She'd been to Bakersfield, to a bookshop. She caught the Coleman lead there, I reckon."

"And that's it?"

"The address her Jeep is at—it belongs to one Otto Mercer."

"Can you give me some stats?"

"White, thirty-seven. In and out of county most of his adult life. Mostly drugs."

"Meth?"

"Yep. And some oxy."

Playing both sides, the up and the down, Thom thought. "Latest arrest?"

"Two years ago, got picked up in Bakersfield."

"Time?"

"Nope. Got off on a technicality."

"'Course he did. All right, Celia, you hear anything else—or remember anything else—you let me know. Radio Coleman PD and get me some backup. Register this as a code three with lights."

"Roger that, boss. Karlstadt out."

Thom flipped the strobes and the siren and pushed the accelerator to the floor.

"When is fucking dinner?" Paul yelled.

"Come and get it!" Becky sang. She set a can of beer by his plate and poured a glass of wine for herself. Paul thought nothing of drinking a full six-pack in an evening, but he guarded her drinking like a bulldog. He would never begrudge her just one glass. She held onto the table as she poured, to steady herself. This would be her third, but he didn't need to know that.

Sipping wine while she cooked was one of her favorite things. She got that from her mother; they imbibed openly when they were together. When she was alone, however, she sipped it from a coffee cup to disguise it. He rarely came close enough to smell her breath, and she kept a clove of garlic at hand in case he did.

She lit a candle and lowered the lights, hoping the romantic atmosphere would calm him or please him or both. He lumbered into the room and pulled out his chair with a lurch as it scraped on the linoleum. He sat in it heavily. He looked like a mountain poured into a teacup. She smiled at the thought of it.

"What?" he asked. "What's funny?"

Red alert, she thought. Paul was incredibly sensitive to being made fun of.

"Not a thing. I smiled because...well, I felt happy." She smiled at him as she lied.

He grunted. She felt momentarily awkward, as if they should say grace. She had grown up saying grace, and the impulse still triggered whenever she sat down to a formal meal. If she suggested it, Paul would laugh at her—or more likely, mock her—so she kept it to herself.

No one would know if you said a silent prayer, a voice in her head suggested. She supposed that was true. What was to stop her from saying grace herself? And what was more, what was to stop her from saying it when she ate alone? She felt a spaciousness open up within her that felt hopeful and free. She was sure the wine was amplifying this, but she reveled in the feeling nevertheless. She closed her eyes, and the voice in her head surprised her by saying, *Help me.*

Her eyes snapped open; she felt a moment of vertigo. She realized it was the first honest prayer she had ever uttered, and it almost undid her. Emotion rushed to her throat, momentarily choking her. She blinked back tears.

"What was that? Were you...*praying?*" Paul asked.

She swallowed and found her voice. "Just savoring the moment," she lied again.

Once more her husband grunted. She lifted the lid off the Pyrex pan keeping the meat warm and put three pork loin medallions on Paul's plate. She put two on her own. Then she added the peaches she'd cooked it in on the side. He would dish up his own potatoes. She offered them to him before taking some herself.

He didn't look at her as he dug in. Nor did he say anything. He was an unthinking eating machine. She had barely touched her own plate when he'd finished his. Once it was clean, he looked up at her with eyes that said, *Is that it?*

She sipped at her wine and smiled at him. "There's more pork, if you want it. And potatoes." There were always more potatoes. Paul liked them and they were cheap.

He pointed at the potatoes with his chin, and she moved to put down the wine glass in order to pass them. But she was tipsy. She misjudged and caught the glass on the side of her plate. It tumbled over, spilling white wine all over the table. "I'm so sorry," she said, springing up. She grabbed a kitchen towel from where it hung on the stove handle and began mopping up the spilled wine. "No harm done," she said soothingly.

"Are you drunk?" he asked.

"What?" she returned, her voice rising with panic. "Of course not."

"How much have you had?"

"Just the one, the one I spilled," she lied again.

"You're weaving back and forth," he noted. "And you never spill anything."

"A girl gets to make a mistake now and then," she said, channeling her mother's always-kind advice.

"You're drunk!" he said.

Something snapped in her. "And what if I am? How many have you had?"

"I will not be married to a lush!" he said. Ironically, he slurred his words as he said it.

"Oh, that's rich," she returned. "You won't be married to a lush, and I won't be married to a drunk. So where does that leave us?"

Quicker than she expected, he leaped up, grabbed her hair, and bashed her face into her plate. She heard the plate break, felt the ooze of food in her eyes and nose. She started to cry.

"Fucking lush!" he pronounced.

With all the dignity she could she raised her face from the plate, breathing heavily, trying with everything that was in her not to break into sobs. She felt under her apron for the revolver tucked into the waistband of her jeans, and her eyes widened. The gun was not there. *I forgot it,* she thought. The three words echoed in her head like doom.

She leaped up and ran into the hall. Paul had the disadvantage of the table between him and the hallway, but she knew it wouldn't slow him down much. She heard the crash of dishes, and she imagined him just pushing the table to the side, maybe turning it over. She felt the heavy footfalls of his steps just behind her. She burst into her bedroom and lunged under her side of the bed.

He grabbed her leg and hauled on it. With her left arm, she grabbed onto the bed frame and held it fast, while with her right arm she groped frantically at the storage tub where she put the pistol when she wasn't carrying it. But it wasn't there.

She yelped as Paul flipped her over onto her back. He'd done it by twisting her feet, and she felt her tendons and knees yelp with pain. He towered over her, a malicious grin on his face. He held up her pistol, dangling it by the trigger guard between his thumb and forefinger. "Looking for this, bitch?" he asked.

Her lips trembled, and she tried to scramble backwards, despite the pain in her knees, despite the fact that the bed was at her back. He raised his fist and brought it down. She heard the crunch of her nose before she felt it.

It took Thom thirty-seven minutes to get to Coleman. He pulled his SUV alongside Julia's Jeep and set the brake. Two Coleman black-and-whites were there, as well, their strobes still flashing. Not far away was a rusted-out AMC Gremlin, a model he had not seen in about twenty years. Thom stepped to the blacktop and surveyed the area. It was a subdivision with every house a variation on the same basic design. This was not a prosperous neighborhood though. The only landscaped yard was a halfhearted effort. It was mostly a wasteland of dirt, weeds, and the husks of rusty cars. A gaggle of preteen boys stood at a respectful distance, leaning on their bicycles and reveling in the novelty of the neighborhood drama.

Thom put his beat-up cowboy hat on his head and noticed there was still chocolate on his fingers. Looking around quickly, he sucked it off. Then he straightened his jacket and headed for the house, unclipping his holster guard.

Before he reached the landing a young uniformed officer met him. "You Sheriff Lind?" she asked him.

"I am," he held his hand out and she shook it.

"Sheila Ramos," she said.

Ramos was Latina, with one discolored eye. He wondered if she could see out of it, but then realized she wouldn't be in blues if she couldn't. He tried not to stare at it. "What do you have?"

She turned and walked toward the house alongside him. "House is clear—of people, that is. Looks like they left in a hurry."

"How do you figure?"

"There's a couple half-completed projects—they weren't expecting to leave when they did."

"How do you know there was a 'they' and not just a 'he'?"

"We *don't*, not for sure. But we'll have CSU through tonight and we'll know for sure how many people were living here, and maybe who they are."

"We know one of them," Thom said.

"Right. Otto Mercer. Meth legend. House is in his name. Also, his car is still here, out front."

"You've tangled with him before," Thom said. It wasn't a question. He'd seen the rap sheet.

"Many a time," she held the door open for him. "He's slippery as an eel, but we've nabbed him a couple of times."

"Any sign of Deputy Barkley?"

Ramos shook her head. "We found her cell phone in the house. And her car here. But other than that, no—oh, there *is* blood spatter."

Thom felt a chill shoot through his spine. Ramos seemed to notice. "But I don't think it's significant," she continued.

"Not significant?"

"It...looks old."

Thom swallowed, grateful for that news, at least.

Ramos continued, her tone a little softer. "What we didn't expect was the torture chamber."

"Torture chamber?" Thom asked.

"Relax. That's just what the boys are calling it. No evidence of actual torture, *per se*."

"*Per se?*" Thom asked. He realized he was just repeating what she said and resolved to stop it.

"You'll see."

They were in a foyer. A living room was to his right. It stank of sweat, cigarettes, cheap beer, and half-eaten pizza. A hallway led into darker depths. Ramos motioned him to follow her. He nodded and reminded himself not to look at her bottom as she plunged into the corridor. She turned left where the hallway ended in a T, the kitchen to the right. *This is a terrible layout,* he thought.

A moment later, he seemed to cross a threshold into a different world. One wall was lined with bookcases filled with books. "Mercer didn't strike me as the studious type," he mentioned.

"No, it took us by surprise too. But looking at the books...it makes sense."

Before Thom could get a look at the books, however, other features of the decor stood out to him. The place was dark even in daylight. A heavy shade was drawn over the room's small window. There were three lamps, but even with all three of them on, the place was still barely navigable. Books on the floor created an obstacle course. Cobwebs clung to the corners; one long string of web draped along a wall. On one side of the room, there was some kind of design laid out on the floor with yarn. Thom squatted near it and studied it. The yarn was tied to candle holders, forming a lopsided six-pointed star.

"What the Jesus-loving hell?" he asked. "I see what you mean about the torture chamber. Are we talking Satanic ritual abuse now?"

"We're not jumping to any conclusions," Ramos answered. "But there are plenty of books on Satanism here. All the others are on the occult too, one kind or another."

"Jesus," Thom swore, stretching again to his full height before his calves could start to complain.

"That's not the biggest find," Ramos said. "This way."

Reluctantly, Thom followed her. Part of him strongly suspected that the clues he needed to find Julie were in that room, if only he had the time to sort through that library...if only he knew what he was looking at. *If only I had Julie with me to explain it,* he thought. Her particular expertise in the occult troubled him, but it had come in handy on a couple of occasions.

They doubled back to the kitchen and then out a back door. Two short steps brought him to a cement porch floor. A small man was seated on a webbed folding picnic chair, his hands behind his back, probably cuffed. "We caught him sneaking around the backyard when we got here. We think he was trying to break in. Name's Benjamin Azor. Hasn't said a word since we cuffed him."

Azor locked eyes with Thom, his gaunt face betraying a mixture of anger, contempt, and uncertainty. And was there some regret there too? Thom wasn't sure.

"Armed?"

"Nope. The guy has some kind of disability. He can barely walk. Check out his special shoes."

Thom looked at the man's feet. He saw what Ramos meant—the sole of one shoe was thicker than the other and strangely shaped. Thom pulled at his jaw and thought. He reached for a folded picnic chair leaning against the back wall of the house and pulled it open. He placed it next to Azor's and sat in it. "Listen, son, I don't need you to talk. I just want you to listen."

Azor's eyes narrowed, but Thom sensed a shift in him. He was curious now. That was good. "We came here looking for a young deputy sheriff by the name of Julia Barkley. We call her Julie." He took his cowboy hat from his head and ran his fingers along its fraying rim as he talked. "She came here on an investigation. And now she's missing. Her car is still out front, and I'm..." He glanced up and waited until he caught Azor's eye. "Well, son, I'm not too proud to say I'm scared for her. I've lost people before,,." He looked back down. "I reckon we all have. But...I do not want to lose her. I...don't think I could live with myself. And to find her, I need your help."

Thom saw the defiance drain from Azor's eyes, some of the anger too. He just looked sad. Finally, he spoke. "I know Julie."

Thom jerked upright. "You do?"

"Yes. I—well, it's not an accident that we're both here, although...I didn't know anything would..." He looked away. "I should have told her to be careful."

"When did you last speak to her?" Thom asked.

"She came to the Lux—"

"Excuse me, son, the what?"

Azor blinked. "*Lux Revelare*—that's the bookstore I work at. She was there yesterday, asking about a book—the *Fenestram in Infernum*. The guy who bought it lives here."

"Mercer?" Thom asked.

"Yes," Azor said, nodding.

Thom looked at Ramos. She cocked her head, obviously not following. That was all right. She was there for muscle, not to be a detective —that was *his* job. "What can you tell me about this book, the *Fenester* —whatsit."

"*Fenestram in Infernum*. It's a grimoire. Julie was asking me about it. It's a very rare, very expensive volume. I sold it to Mercer."

"How much did it sell for?" Thom asked.

"Seven thousand."

Thom whistled. "That's a lot for a book."

"It's not just any book," Azor asserted.

"Right. It's a grim—thingy."

"Grimoire," Azor corrected him. "Think of it as a collection of written instructions for magickal rituals—scripts, or more accurately, liturgies complete with rubrics."

Thom nodded his head. He'd been in the seminary in high school. He was tracking. "Tell me more about it."

"It's rare, but it provided the source material for a very popular paperback, the *Necronomicon* by Simon."

"Why is that important?" Thom continued to play with the edge of his hat.

"People usually buy the *Necronomicon* for a lark. They don't usually actually perform the rituals…except when they do."

Thom waited.

Azor continued, "Real magickians don't usually give it the time of day. It's a workable grimoire, kind of. The problem is that the deities you're calling on are fictional."

Thom's brow creased. "Why would anyone call on fictional deities —I mean, on gods that they *knew* were fictional?"

"Fandom," Azor shrugged. It looked strange with his hands behind his back. "The Simon *Necronomicon* is a novelty item, produced specifically to appeal to fans of H.P. Lovecraft." He paused and looked from Thom to Ramos, then back again. He sighed. "Never read any Lovecraft?"

Thom shook his head. "Anything like Ray Bradbury?"

"That's like comparing Charles Manson to Mister Rodgers."

"Okay, okay." Thom began to bite at the inside of his lip. The clock was ticking, and he was no closer to finding Julie. His leg began to bounce. "You keep saying the *Simon* Necro—manny-thing—"

"*Necronomicon.*"

"Right. It's a strange way to phrase it. Are there other Necro… nom…icons?"

"Yes. Many."

Thom's eyebrows shot up.

"But they're all shit. None of them work. None but the Simon *Necronomicon.*"

"It works even though the gods in it aren't real?"

"Yes."

"How is that possible?"

"It works precisely because Simon lifted his text almost entirely from the *Fenestram in Infernum.* I told you."

He had, but Thom was just beginning to see how the pieces fit together. He felt a bit like he was back in his high school algebra class —about half a step behind his teacher and struggling to keep up. "Does the Fen—"

"*Fenestram in Infernum,*" Azor pronounced.

"Thanks. Does that book also contain rituals directed to fictional deities?"

"It's hard to say," Azor said. "They're *unknown* deities. Lovecraft… and Derleth after him—especially Derleth—amassed a vast pantheon of gods—"

"A fictional pantheon?" Thom clarified.

"Yes. As I was saying, it was vast. I don't know of many fans who can rattle off all of the deities found in the Cthulu cycle—"

"Backup. What is the Ka—"

Azor rolled his eyes. "Can I get my hands back, please? My arms are starting to tingle."

Thom looked at Ramos, then at the officer standing behind Azor.

"C'mon," Azor said. "What am I going to do, run?" He pointed to his feet with his chin.

Thom nodded. The officer leaned over and unlocked the cuffs. Azor blew out a deep breath and began to rub at his wrists. "Thank you. The Cthulu cycle is the collection of stories by Lovecraft dealing with the Great Old Ones. August Derleth was another writer, a friend of Lovecraft's. After Lovecraft's death, Derleth kept writing stories about the Great Old Ones, and introduced the Elder Gods into the mythos."

Thom nodded. He was tracking. "Tell me about the Great Old Ones."

A strange smile came over Azor's face. Thom had apparently hit upon an area of geeky pleasure. "Lovecraft's horror was based on the conceit that we live in a universe ruled by warring, amoral alien creatures so vast and powerful that we can only think of them as gods. The horror in his stories depended on the reader's feeling of vertigo when he realizes that the only reason the earth—and human beings— are still here is that the Great Old Ones simply haven't noticed us yet. But if they did...the illusion of our little bubble of safety would..." Instead of finishing his sentence, he made an explosion sound, separating his hands as if demonstrating the blast zone of a bomb.

"Why on earth would anyone want to invoke such a deity?" Thom asked.

Azor shrugged. It was a much more normal-looking shrug this time. "Because one could."

"Power?"

Azor nodded. "You get it."

He did. "But here's what I don't understand," Thom continued. "What good would it do to summon an alien being who doesn't exist?"

"Well, that's what I was trying to say. The beings in Lovecraft's stories are fictional. Most of the beings in the Simon *Necronomicon* are fictional. But the beings in the *Fenestram in Infernam* are just...unknown."

"And this Simon fellow just copied the rituals from this *Fenestram* book willy-nilly, including the names of the unknown...beings?"

"He sprinkled Lovecraftian and Derlethian deities throughout, but the names of the unknown beings...he left some of those in."

"Isn't that dangerous?" Thom asked. "I mean, if any of this is real, wouldn't that be...irresponsible?"

"Nobody ever accused magickians of being responsible," Azor said.

"So, this Mercer guy has a book of rituals—not the fake book, but the real deal," Thom said.

Azor nodded.

"And he has my deputy. What do you think he's up to?"

Azor locked eyes with Thom before answering. "Nothing good," he said.

Milala had no money for a bus ticket. She had no idea where she was headed. She only knew she needed to get out of this weirdly Swedish *oje-ajnt* town. It hadn't taken long to reach the 99 on foot. Getting a ride, however, was another thing.

Milala had heard of a time when hitchhiking had been easy. But she had never known that time. She only knew it as scattershot and dangerous. If she were lucky, she'd get a ride. If she were luckier, that ride would not turn out to be a sociopath.

She had found no luck thus far, so whenever there was a gap in cars, she walked north. Looking over her shoulder, Karlstadt was still visible, but it was receding, about to be swallowed up by the earth's beautiful brown skin.

Another car was coming, so she put out her thumb and forced a smile. A part of her knew that her smile looked forced and was probably more of a grimace. But when she tried to adjust her smile, she suspected she was only making it worse. She wished she had a mirror so that she could practice.

Bile rose in her throat over the need to appear "a certain way" to be acceptable to the *oje-ajnt*. How many years had The People contorted themselves in order to be less threatening, less Indian, less alien so as to make the *oje-ajnt* more comfortable? She wished she had a cigar so that she would have something to bite. For far too long her people had bitten their own tongues—she would not do that now.

Another car was coming, with a truck behind it. Truckers were sometimes a good bet, but the downside was they usually wanted something in return. It wasn't as if Milala hadn't done what was necessary at times, but she cringed at the thought of it now. She had suffered too much humiliation, too much disappointment, too much abuse—from the *oje-ajnt* and from her own people. She was not willing to suffer more, and she pitied the poor truck driver who tried to take advantage of her.

On the other hand, who knew what might happen? She might get picked up by a pole-thin young *oje-ajnt* woman her own age, maybe one who liked the taste of danger as much as she did. She would not mind sharing a car or a bed with someone like that. But it was a long shot, she knew.

But both the car and the truck whizzed by. She lowered her thumb and froze. Across the highway was an all-too familiar face. He grinned at her, showing her his teeth.

"Go away, Coyote," she yelled across the freeway. "I've had enough."

"You haven't drummed for the *oje-ajnt*." His voice was faint, like the breeze, but she heard it just fine.

"The *oje-ajnt* are just fine," she called back.

"No, they aren't. Their souls are sick. And they are getting sicker. They need medicine." Coyote was sitting up at full attention, yet Milala could see the tension ripple under his skin. He was ready to pounce.

She possessed nothing with which she might protect herself. She wondered how long she would hold out against him should he pounce on her and seek to tear the meat from her bones.

"I'm not afraid of you," she called to him. She shrank at the sound of her voice, as she did not sound convincing even to herself. Coyote's lips pulled back from his teeth again.

"If you don't turn around, someone will die," Coyote said.

"What do I care if the *oje-ajnt* die?" Milala called. "Let them die!"

"You must drum for them."

"They stole my drum."

"No, Daughter, they did not."

"Someone stole my drum!" She had forgotten her fear now. Now there was only anger. She planted her fists on her hips.

"Yes, *someone* stole your drum," Coyote conceded. "I did."

Milala's hands dropped. Her mouth opened. She blinked. "You— but why?"

"To see what you would do."

"But it was *my* drum!" Milala protested.

"No. It is Bear's drum. Bear said I could take it."

That was true. Bear had given her the drum. She had been one of the few female drummers among The People, and it had been that very gift that caused much of the tension between her and her tribe.

"Can you give it back to me?" Milala asked. "Or give me another?"

Coyote smiled again. This time it seemed less threatening. "Will you go back and drum for the *oje-ajnt*?"

She bit her lip. She turned and looked over her left shoulder at the town, the size of a postage stamp now. "If you give me my drum back —or give me a new drum—then okay, I will drum for them," she conceded.

"I will give you what you need to *make* a drum," Coyote said.

Milala nodded. She did not mind that. She didn't know how she would manage it, but perhaps that was part of what Coyote wished to show her. And she did not doubt that Bear would bless it. "All right."

"I am glad we have reached an agreement, Daughter." And with that, Coyote stepped out onto the road, striding toward her with confident, fluid movements—straight into the path of an oncoming car.

Peg pulled the sweater around her waist a little more tightly and then waved at Ted. The former priest pulled his car over and stopped. Peg got in at the passenger's side and shut the door with a firm pull.

"What's this surprise?" she asked.

"I'm not sure," he said. "I just know it's what all the cool kids are doing nowadays."

She raised one eyebrow as he pulled away from the curb.

"How are you holding up?" he asked.

"Are you asking about the cancer diagnosis? Or then there's the corollary problems, like Rachel Lindstrom's smear campaign and needing to have a heart-to-heart with a daughter who can barely stand to be in the same room with me. Or..." she was about to tell him about Imelda but decided against it at the last minute. Some things were just between a woman and her pastor, even if there wasn't an explicit agreement of confidentiality.

The truth was, she hadn't been able to shake the look on Imelda's face, and she'd thought about little else that day. She was relieved when Ted had phoned and suggested a surprise outing.

"Sure, all of that, and let's throw in the rumbly-tumbly on top of it." He smiled at her, his pencil-thin mustache perfectly groomed as usual.

She looked out the window. "I'm breathing," she said.

"You're doing a damn sight better than that," he said.

"I feel like I'm drowning," she confessed, "and it's all I can do to just keep my lips above the water line."

"That's more like it," Ted said, not uncompassionately.

"You know what you are?" Peg asked.

"Besides an aging queen?"

"You're addicted to confession."

"You wound me, madame."

"No, listen. You used to love hearing confessions and now that you've...retired...you manipulate everyone around you to make them confess to something, anything."

"No one expects the Spanish Inquisition," Ted quipped.

"Ha!" Peg laughed despite herself. She didn't feel like laughing, but there was something about being around Ted that always brought out the best in her. "I do have a confession," she said. "Or maybe it's just a bright spot on an otherwise bleak landscape."

"And what is that?"

"I've been asked on a date," she looked over until he met her eyes.

A smile curled on his lips. "Do tell," he said. "Anyone I know?"

"Maybe," she said in a sing-song voice. She waited a beat, then added, "Phil Prugh."

"Prugh?" Ted looked dubious. "He's hardly a catch."

"Speak for yourself. Have you looked at me lately?"

The smile had not yet left Ted's lips. "So when is the big night?"

"Friday. Dinner at the Hungry Sow."

"It doesn't get any classier around here," he quipped.

She punched his arm. Just then Peg noticed their surroundings. "Ted, I'm having déjà vu. Where are we going?"

"It's a secret until we get there," he said.

"No it isn't, not if you're going this way. I've already been on this road today. It leads to the Nyland farm."

"And what if it does?"

She turned in her seat and looked at him. "Ted, *why* are we going out to the Nyland farm?"

"Because it's what all the cool kids—"

"Right, it's what all the cool kids are doing. Who the *fuck* are you talking about, Ted?"

"Everyone." His eyebrows shot up.

"Everyone," she repeated.

Ted wasn't far off, she discovered. There were several other cars on the road, and when they arrived, Ted pulled in near a long line of parked cars and shut off the engine. A worried look fixed itself to Peg's face. "Ted, this is not my idea of a fun outing."

"It will take your mind off—"

"No, it won't," she said. "I've already been here once today. There is nothing to *enjoy* here."

He cocked his head. "You didn't tell me that."

"It's none of your...I was here with a parishioner earlier today. It's...Ted, it's horrible."

"Then be my pastor and accompany me and help me through it. Be my Virgil."

"I am not your pastor and I'm nobody's Virgil."

She felt Ted's hand on her wrist. "My dear, I'm sorry. I heard some gossip, and I thought it might be...diverting, or interesting, or...something...to see what all the fuss is about."

"Is there fuss?" she asked.

"There are at least fourteen cars worth of fuss," he confirmed.

"You're not going to think it's diverting when you see them," she said.

"The statues?"

"Yes. They're horrible."

"How many did you see?" He opened his car door and stepped out.

She did the same and answered the question. "Just the one."

"Then maybe it would be a good thing to see if the others are... similar. Who knows? Someone might need a pastor."

She shot him a black look, but fell into step alongside him as they walked toward the farm.

The sun was growing low in the sky and the clouds were shot through with the colors of orange and cream. She stumbled as they began to navigate the newly-planted rows, and he reached out to steady her. Once righted, he stuck his elbow out at her and she took his arm.

He steered her toward a small crowd, gathering around a cluster of four cubes.

"How very curious," he said aloud.

"They are that."

"The woman at the beauty parlor said they were statues."

"What were you doing at the beauty parlor?"

"My nails, of course."

"Your nails. You just wanted to flirt with that little Filipino boy, the manicurist."

"His name is Danny and he's eighteen if he's a day. An older man needs the touch of a younger man. And he's very gentle with my hands."

Peg rolled her eyes.

They slowed as they drew closer. Then they stopped. "Jesus on a bicycle," Ted breathed.

Peg didn't want to look—she had a good idea what she'd see. But she forced herself.

The cube was just like the one she'd seen earlier that day. It was the same size, the same color. And three sides of the thing were exactly the same as well. But the fourth wall was cut away, the pinkish material having been somehow scooped out to form a sculpture.

It was the sculpture of a man, a man she knew—Gary Schultz. It was unmistakably Gary—his thinning hair was just as he wore it, with a bit of a comb-over. And there was a scar on his chin, like someone had taken a ding out of him with a chisel.

Peg dropped Ted's arm and took a step closer, then another. The statue showed Gary clinging to a wall, staring straight at them, but something did not look right. Then Peg understood the perspective of the statue. It was as if the viewer were hovering in the air above him, looking down at him. Then she saw that Gary was actually depicted lying on the ground. There were dandelions cut into the stone on either side of his ears.

A knife lay near his right hand. A horizontal gash opened in his throat, stretching from ear to ear. The statue's eyes were immobile, of course—it was a statue—but they were wide with alarm. Peg took a step back and reminded herself that Gary's throat had not really been sliced open. It was just a statue.

Peeling her eyes away from the thing, she took in the people around her. Six or seven people were standing around Gary's statue, sometimes blocking her view of it. There was a look of excited wonder on their faces. One teenaged girl laughed and pointed at the cube. Her friend laughed in response to something she said, and her hand went swiftly to her mouth to stifle herself. She looked around at the others, as if to make sure no one else thought her inappropriate. No one glowered at her; she relaxed a bit, but more laughter followed.

She heard shouting and looked to her right. Another gaggle of the curious had gathered around another cube nearby. Several young men laughed uproariously, pointing at the cube. Peg was tempted to tug at Ted's sleeve and get a look at that cube too, but hesitated. Did she really want to see whatever horrors would be revealed? She did—and she didn't.

Instead, she hung back and looked at Ted. She'd wait to see what he did. If he moved to view another cube, they'd go. If not, they wouldn't. She mused on the fact that it had been a long time since she'd let a man make decisions for her. But she wasn't letting Ted lead because he was a man, she was letting him lead because he was her friend and she was overwhelmed. That felt okay enough.

And Ted did move. She followed him to the right, toward the new gaggle. Halfway there, they passed a cluster of teenagers heading toward Gary Schultz' cube. Peg's eyebrows raised when she realized that two of them had Halloween costumes on. She caught up to Ted and took his arm. "They're wearing costumes," she said. "I've heard of Christmas in July, but Halloween in March?"

"It's certainly...festive," Ted said.

"It's macabre," Peg countered.

As they drew near the new cube, Peg looked beyond, toward where she knew the Nyland barn must be—although it was too far away to see—and saw several other roving packs of people, picking their way over the sown fields. The sky was a brilliant orange now, and the image reminded her of the dead dancing across the hills in *The Seventh Seal*. She shook her head to clear it.

"Water!" a voice cried out, and Peg turned to see an enterprising young man with a canvas cooler hanging from his shoulder by a carry strap. In each hand, he held up frosty bottles of water. "Peanuts!" he called out next.

"This isn't right," Ted said.

"No," Peg breathed. "What do you want to do?"

Ted met her eye, and then looked away. "I...I suppose I want to look at the other cubes."

"And do you hate yourself for wanting that?" she asked.

"Yes. Yes, I do," he answered.

"Well, as long as we're clear about that," Peg said. She took his arm again. "All right, let's see the next one."

The car swerved and Milala heard the screech of tires, but it did no good. She closed her eyes at the moment of impact, and the sickening sound of Coyote's body tumbling under the car filled her ears.

"No!" she shouted, and tears gushed from her eyes. When she opened them again, the car was almost out of sight. Her belly shaking, she forced herself to look at what remained of Coyote. She cringed to see his twisted form—limbs broken into impossible angles, fur matted with blood. His snout pointed toward heaven, lifeless, lips pulled back in that same menacing grimace that passed for a smile.

Milala's hands clutched at her cheeks, her eyes wild and wet. She jumped when she realized more cars were on the way. "No no no no," she said, and rushed onto the freeway. She knew she didn't have much time before the next cars would pass, further grinding Coyote's body into the asphalt. She reached out to grab his body, to drag it out of the middle of the lane, but didn't know what to grab onto. His limbs were so twisted she feared they would twist off if she pulled on them. And she was afraid of his head.

Just then she felt a shadow block the red, setting sun. She glanced up and jumped again.

"Easy, Granddaughter," the mountain of an old man said to her. "We have little time." He was dressed in faded denims topped by a western-style shirt with pearl snap buttons and a bolo tie. A cracked and worn leather vest did not contain his bulging belly. His boots were pointed at the toe and scuffed. He wore a hat with a narrow brim and a large bowl, an eagle feather sticking out of its band. His hair was long and gray, pulled back in a ponytail, and he had a scar across a nose as gnarled as a cassava tuber. "He is heavy, so we must both pull."

Milala looked up at the oncoming cars and guessed that they might have a little over twelve seconds.

"Grab a handful of fur just behind his head," Creator said. He gathered a loose scrap of skin over one of Coyote's shoulders in his fist as

Milala did the same with the skin over his other shoulder. "That's it. And *pull*."

Milala's eyes were on the car, however, which she was panicked to see was not slowing down. But the tangled body moved as Milala strained against the flap of skin in her fist. Her ears were filled with the sound of dragging gravel, and a wet red stain stretched along the path of their dragging. They had just pulled him off the asphalt onto the gravel shoulder when the car zipped past. Milala exhaled and noticed that the shaking had migrated from her belly into her hands.

"Sit, Granddaughter," Creator said. He sat cross-legged near Coyote's snout. She sat near what was left of his tail. Her lower lip quivered and water blurred her vision. Creator stroked the fur along Coyote's nose, relaxing the god's lips so that they covered his teeth again.

"Why did he do it?" Milala asked. "Why did he kill himself?"

"Coyote draws straight with crooked lines," Creator answered.

"That...doesn't answer my question," Milala pointed out.

Creator smiled and nodded. "That is my Milala."

Milala wiped at her tears and realized she must have just smeared blood on her face.

"For thousands of years, people used sacrifice to get our attention. Coyote likes to turn things around. He has sacrificed himself to get *your* attention."

"He...but..." Milala began. She didn't know how to put her thoughts into words, but a thousand emotions battered at her from within. "I wish...I wish I had just *listened* to him."

"Wishes are fishes, they scit and they scatter—but never they mit and never they matter."

Milala narrowed her eyes at him. "I don't know that song."

"I know a lot of them." Creator smiled. His teeth were big and strong, yellowed but whole.

"You don't seem sad," Milala said.

"Coyote is a spirit of great power. Death is only a shadow. It will pass."

"Death will pass?"

"Death always passes."

"But when things die, they're dead."

Creator met her eyes and smiled at her. There was pity in that smile, and Milala did not think she liked that. "Now you sound like the *oje-ajnt*."

At that, Milala felt a flush of shame.

"It is good that you grieve Coyote," Creator continued. "It is good that you loved him."

"I didn't *love* him…" Milala began. She was about to say, *He annoyed the hell out of me,* but it seemed a rude thing to say to Creator. And she was confused by the rush of emotions coursing through her. She certainly respected Coyote. And she feared him. Could she have loved him too?

"I think you did. *I* love Coyote," Creator said. "He is my clown."

Milala frowned. The last thing she saw Coyote as was a clown. Creator was either messing with her, or was so different than her that she was not able to comprehend him. She knew in her bones it was the latter.

"Go ahead and cry, Granddaughter. Feed the earth with your tears. Grief is a poison that eats the soul. You must speak it and dance it and sing it and draw it out of you before it makes you sick." He pointed at her. "You can drum it out!"

"Girls don't drum," Milala said blackly.

"Don't they?" Creator said. There was a twinkle in his eye. He *was* messing with her.

"Coyote stole my drum," Milala complained.

"He did, eh?"

Milala glowered at him.

"Well, Coyote has just given you a gift. He has given you everything you need to make a new drum."

"What the hell are you talking about?" Milala asked.

Creator smiled and pointed to the wreck of a body before them. "He has given you his hide so that you can make a new drum. And this is a sacred drum, because it is made from the hide of a god." Creator reached into the pocket of his leather vest and pulled out a skinning knife. He tossed it to her. She caught it. "I will hold him in place. And I'll show you where to cut."

Malala pulled the knife from its leather sheath and stared at it. Its curved blade winked in the sun. "Grandfather, I don't understand why it is important to drum for the *oje-ajnt*."

"They need medicine. You are a medicine woman." He shrugged. "It is not difficult."

"Yes, but why should we care if they suffer?"

Creator cocked his head. "If any beings suffer, all beings suffer. This is not new to you."

"No, I just...I guess I just never thought 'all beings' included the *oje-ajnt*."

"They are beings." Creator shrugged again. "Their feet press upon your Mother, just as yours do. And their grief will poison the world unless it is healed. You should know this."

Milala shrank, still holding the knife. "Why me?"

"Because the medicine is not just for them."

Milala blinked. "I don't understand."

"I do not choose healthy people to be medicine people. I only choose sick people. When you get medicine for others, it heals you, too."

Milala felt the truth of this in her belly. She nodded.

"That is why Coyote would not leave you alone. He snapped at your heels because he loved you."

Milala wiped her eyes with her sleeve. She nodded some more.

Creator lifted the lifeless head of Coyote with one giant hand and pointed to a place just under the chin. "Cut."

Troy adjusted the squelch on his citizen's band radio. He didn't need to look at it, he had navigated it by touch for more than ten years. He reached for another handful of peanuts and was aware that he was eating because he was upset, not because he was hungry or needed to stay awake.

He'd caught a lift back to his rig after his unexpected detour to Nyland's farm, and now was pushing well past the speed limit trying to make up some time. They expected him in San Diego at midnight, and if he kept up like he was, he just might make it. He glanced at the LED readout on his dash and did the math in his head again. *Close to the wire, but possible,* he thought.

It wasn't the possibility of rolling into San Diego late that drove his snacking though. He couldn't stop thinking about the goddam cube. He hated the fact that someone had sculpted him without his permission. He scowled at the thought of it. The word "violated" flashed through his mind. He'd never been much for victims' rights— if he were honest, he tended to think that most people that got scammed or attacked or otherwise abused probably deserved it, at least a little bit. He was a card-carrying Libertarian, and his belief in personal responsibility and self-sufficiency ran deep. But now the shoe seemed to be on the wrong foot. *What did I do to deserve being mocked like that?* he wondered. He could not remember crossing anyone—at least not anyone capable of punking him on such a grand scale. The statue had to be expensive, unless it had been sculpted by...well, by whomever had it out for him. And that shortened his list of possible enemies to exactly zero. Most of the people he'd pissed off wouldn't know a chisel from a mozzarella stick. Grander conspiracies floated momentarily around his head until they collapsed under the weight of their own formidable improbability. Troy was no fool. He hated to think of himself as a victim of any kind, but he was certainly not delusional.

The image of his own face kissing glass made him shudder. It was, after all, his face—and most likely, it was depicting the very glass that protected him from the wind even now, not four feet ahead of him. It had not been a flattering depiction of him. The way his cheek was distorted as it smashed into the unseen glass was a haunting, startling detail that he could not shake. It made him look helpless, which was not a feeling Troy liked. The weightless quality to everything else in the statue only added to the surreality of it. Yet everything that seemed to float in the air around the "him" in the statue was familiar to him. That was his lighter that seemed to hover in midair, although he was sure that there was some supporting structure to the thing on the statue itself. The statue could not defy physics, after all, he reasoned. But that was the way of art, a voice in his head reminded him. It didn't need to be photorealistic to get the point across.

He reached for the peanuts again but couldn't find them. His right hand felt around everything on the console. Everything seemed to be in its place, all except for the peanuts. The jar had been there just minutes ago. But he had to admit that the cab was not as tidy as it should have been. Something shifted, and his thoughts were interrupted by the feeling of several hundred small objects pouring onto his legs. "Goddam it!" he swore, summoning a mental image of his entire jar of peanuts being emptied onto his leg, onto the floorboards. The last thing he needed was to grind peanuts underfoot into the carpet. He was hoping to sell the rig soon and did not need another detailing bill cutting into his profits.

Holding the steering wheel with his left hand, he ducked down to scoop up as many peanuts with his right as he could, swiping them away from his feet, toward the door where, he hoped, he'd be able to simply sweep them onto the pavement of the next truck stop he came to—a truck stop where he could also pick up some more peanuts.

But no sooner had his eyes left the road than one set of oncoming headlights separated itself from the others, forging its own optical burn trail from one side of the freeway to the other. Troy glanced back up a split second before the the collision ripped through the cab. In his last moments, he felt himself airborne, along with every other unattached item in the cab, including his lighter, including several hundred peanuts. His jaw smashing into the windshield was his last conscious sensation.

———————

When Julie awoke, she was staring straight into two gold, non-human eyes. The pupils were not round, but were horizontal slits. They radiated not fear, nor entreaty, but indifference.

Julie blinked. The eyes blinked back.

"Meh-heh-heh-heh," the goat bleated.

Julie felt confused. There was a dull ache at the back of her head. She tried to reach up to feel at it, but her hands were restrained.

Her hands. Now she was aware of the tingly ache in her wrists. Just a moment ago she was not conscious of it; now it almost consumed her in its intensity. She rocked forward and moved her arms as much as she could. Fire roared through her veins as achy feeling started to return to them.

It is early morning. It is still dark out. I am in a van without windows, she thought. *I am tied up. There is a goat.*

She wracked her brain, trying to remember how it was that she got there, but was not able to connect it to anything. Glancing down, she saw her khaki pant leg and her boots. She cocked her head. *That doesn't look like something I would wear,* she thought. Examining her clothes more closely, she saw the leather holster to her right, its clip awry, revealing only its empty cavity. *I carry a gun,* Julie thought. That connection now made, everything else rushed back in—her job, her life, her search for Clive, the cubes, the investigation that had led her to a run-down house in Coleman...

She broadened her gaze, taking in the other things in the van. There were shovels...which was ominous...there were boxes of rock salt. There was an open wooden box filled with what looked like very old, leather-bound books. And in the front, she saw the backs of two heads, one of them shaved bald, the other with long, stringy gray hair. Every now and then a light would race over those heads.

"Otto Mercer," Julie whispered, remembering the name of one of those heads. As if she had summoned him, the bald head turned at that very moment and looked back at her. It was Mercer in the passenger seat. He caught Julie's eye and a mirthless grin broke over his face.

"You're awake," he called over the din of the road and engine.

She said nothing, but she stared him down. Eventually, he turned and looked back at the road. Then she heard the click of a seatbelt. He was getting out of his seat. She frowned as she saw him climb over the engine console and shakily make his way into the back of the van.

There were no seats. It looked as if the van was intended to haul construction materials, but then Julie saw that there was PVC piping hanging from clips all along the far wall. Could it be a plumber's van? She'd look for more evidence of that, although she was not sure how it would help her. Still...the more information she had, the more ammunition she had.

Mercer stopped a few feet from her and sat down unsteadily as the van swerved. Once solidly on the floor, he quickly assumed a greater sense of confidence. "I'm glad you're awake. I was afraid Fritz had really hurt you," he said, with a look of faux concern.

Who is Fritz? Julie wondered. But she asked, "Where are we going?"

"To a place...a safe place."

"Safe from what...and safe for whom?" Julie asked.

Mercer cocked his head. For a moment, Julie thought he might actually try to answer her question. But instead he said, "When the sun comes up, it's going to be a very special day."

"Why so?" Julie asked.

"This will be a day the bards will sing about for millennia—"

"Who the fuck are 'the bards'?" Julie asked. "Is that even a job nowadays? Do you mean 'songwriters'?"

Mercer ignored her. "This will be a day that will live in infamy."

"You do know that 'infamy' is a bad thing, right?"

"This day will become a feast day—the highest of high holy days—in the new world."

"Which new world would that be?" Julie asked. She realized she was sounding snarky, but in truth she had no idea what Mercer was referring to. A part of her was honestly curious.

"The old systems are about to be swept away—the old gods, the old governments, the old system that rewarded rich fucks and left people like me to bleed in the gutter."

"What are you even talking about? You own a *house*—" Julie objected, but Mercer continued.

"This coming evening will be the Night of Holy Ingress. The Great Passing-Over. The Night of the Threshold."

"Those are all catchy," Julie noted, "but you should probably pick one and stick with it."

Mercer didn't lose a beat. "Tonight will be the night that everyone beaten down by the world will rejoice. Tonight will be the night our savior passes over from one world to another, from the eldritch caverns of deep space to the corrupt and crumbling pillars of the earth."

"Very poetic," Julie said. "But what the hell does that mean?"

"No more will the politicians lie to us and serve only themselves. No more will the military visit horrors upon the world. No more will cops bully and brutalize the poor."

"I've never—" Julie started to object, but Mercer was still ploughing ahead.

"No more will the rich get fat on the bellies of the poor—"

"That's not even a saying."

"No more will the little guys, the powerless, the downtrodden—"

"The pimply and unlucky in love?" Julie offered

"No more will genius go unrecognized or unrewarded. We take it and take it and take it, but no more."

"By 'take it,' do you mean suffer insult or injury, or do you mean you're the one who's taking? I'm a little lost," Julie asked.

"No more! No more!"

"I get it. Cue Twisted Sister, 'We're Not Going to Take It.'" She started singing the old song, pretending to head bash to the beat. Her hair metal phase in college was fun and nostalgic, but it had left its scars.

"Yeah, yeah, that's it. That's it exactly," Mercer said, acknowledging her contribution for the first time.

"And how are you going to effect this revolution?" Julie asked. "Let's see...you've got a service revolver, a vanload of plumbing equipment, and a goat. If you've got a ball of string and some chewing gum, I think we're in business."

Mercer narrowed one eye at her. "You did this."

"I did what, exactly?" Julie asked.

"I didn't ask for you to be here. You weren't part of the plan. We were going to effect the Night of Holy Ingress with no one the wiser. We didn't ask for fame. The world would just wake up tomorrow morning and would suddenly have new masters—masters with real power; masters who would inflict their own eldritch terrors upon any—"

"You really like that word, don't you—*eldritch*. Sounds like an old guy's name."

"—who opposed them...or us."

"Ah, there it is. You don't want any credit, oh no. But you do want *power*."

She flashed back to what Ben had said in the bookstore about magickians and power. She hadn't needed to think about it very long to see that he was right. And now, here was a case study worthy of the police academy oral exam.

"But you have...inserted yourself. So, whatever happens to you... it's your own damn fault."

"Why not just dump me along the road then? That way whatever you and your friend are about to do to this goat will just be between you and him and the goat and whatever eldritch entities you're about to invoke."

"No. You know too much," he said.

"I don't know shit—that's why I'm here. I'm trying to find something out. Maybe it has to do with you and maybe it doesn't. Maybe I could have asked my questions at the door, and maybe you could have just answered them. And if you had, maybe I'd have just hopped in my Jeep and gone back to Karlstadt. Did you ever think of that?"

"We're not cooking meth."

"I know that, you idiot. I don't care about the fucking meth."

"You showed up because of the book."

"If you mean the *Fenestram in Infernum*, yes."

"You came to stop us."

"That's ridiculous. I mean, if I'd known what you were up to, I'd —" She stopped. Was there a crime here? If they hadn't attacked and kidnapped her, was there anything to even question them about? She found herself staring straight into the eyes of the goat again. It bleated. "I was only interested in the book. I had no idea what you were planning, and I was *not* trying to stop you."

"I don't believe you."

Julie looked over at Mercer again. There was no idealistic passion in his eyes now. They looked dead. She shuddered. "What's the salt for?" she asked.

Mercer didn't answer. He kept staring. Julie looked away.

"You know, celebrating the Night of Holy Ingress with a goat just reeks of bestiality. I'm not saying you've got eyes for Fess Parker, here, but you know how people are. They talk. And it doesn't matter if you're innocent, because people are going to say what people are going to say. It doesn't look good, is what I'm getting at."

"You can laugh now," Mercer said, fixing her with one steely eye. "But when the Great Old Ones arrive, you will be their food."

CHAPTER EIGHT

J ulie stared out the back windows of the van at a field of unremitting black. The windows were tinted, and even the light of the stars was obscured. Except for the colored lights of the driver's console, Julie could see nothing.

She could feel the road beneath them as they hummed along the highway. And she felt it when they exited and slowed to a stop. She fantasized about making a break for it. Her hands were tightly tied in front of her, which gave her hope, but she could not see the inside door—was there a latch from the inside? She couldn't tell.

She paid attention to the driver's movements—rolling stop, a right turn, acceleration along an unpaved road. Julie rehearsed what she knew: They were somewhere in the Central Valley—perhaps the desert. They were less than a mile from a major freeway. They were in a van. There were two perps—that she knew of. There was a goat.

She wished she had her cell phone with her, but they'd taken that. She wracked her brain for some way—any way—to let Thom know where she was. She came up empty.

Suddenly, the van lurched to a halt, and both men got out. A moment later, the back doors opened, flooding Julie with cool, dry air. It felt wonderful. Not long after, it just felt cold.

"Get up," Mercer said.

Julie pushed with her boots and managed to scoot herself up against the wall of the van until she was almost standing. Then she pushed herself off the wall with her butt, ducked, and took the long step to the ground.

To her surprise, Mercer was chivalrous, grasping Julie's elbow and steadying her as she found her feet.

"Over there," Mercer pointed.

Julie looked in the direction he was pointing and began to take in her surroundings. She walked over to an open stretch of ground as Mercer coaxed the goat toward the door. Near her was a squat building with a flat roof. A large sign that ran the length of the building proclaimed, "Maranatha Car Pull," and a smaller sign said, "Praise Jesus and pay inside."

Looking up, Julie saw a half moon hanging low in the sky, and a cascade of brilliant stars above. Her eyes were pretty well adjusted after the ride in the dark van; the light from the heavens illuminated the place as if it were nothing more than a cloudy day. Julie saw an ocean of dead cars extending in every direction. In the distance she saw piles of cars, as if a giant child had been playing blocks with them, stacking them until they were precariously high. Julie saw no cranes and had no idea how the stacking could possibly have been accomplished. She decided that was a mystery for another time.

The driver exited the squat building and Julie got her first good look at him. Like Mercer, he was bone-thin, although he was shorter and older. His stringy gray hair hung down to his shoulders. He ignored her, making a beeline for the van. He got in and drove it into the labyrinth of cars and out of sight.

Julie heard the goat bleating and looked in that direction. Mercer had fitted the beast with a leash and was headed toward her. "This way," he said, indicating the direction with a twitch of his head. He waited, and she realized he intended for her to go first. She hesitated, as she had no idea what she'd be walking into, but there was no arguing with him. She stepped in front of him and began to walk in the direction he'd indicated.

They walked down a long row of cars, turned right hugging a wall of stacked cars, then walked between two stacks. After the length of a few buses, the space opened out into something of a courtyard. The area was circumscribed with dead cars on every side. A makeshift pavilion had been erected—really a tarp tied to the bumper of a car protruding from the stacked wall, its edges held out like bat's wings by some kind of rope, fixed to the ground with what must have been stakes. Folding chairs were stacked inside the pavilion, leaning against the wall of cars. It occurred to Julie that if she could just get away, the labyrinth of cars would give her good cover.

Mercer tied the goat to a side mirror. The goat bleated once but did not otherwise complain. Then he took a pair of handcuffs—Julie recognized them as her own—and fastened one to her wrist. This was hard to do, because her wrists were already bound up with rope. "What are you doing?" She asked, but then she got it. He was exchanging the rope for something more secure. He secured the other cuff to one of the chrome car handles. Then he unwound the rope.

"What's going on here?" Julie asked.

"We're setting up for a big ritual," Mercer said.

"Who is 'we,' exactly?"

"The faithful remnant," Mercer said.

"Is that the name of your 501(c)(3)?" Julie asked, "Or is it The Faithful Remnant, LLC?"

"We're actually the Fellowship of the Yellow Sign, but...the government doesn't need to know about what we're doing."

"No. That would be tragic. How many of you are there?"

"Around the world?" Mercer asked.

"Sure, let's start there. How many *are* the faithful remnant?"

"There's about six hundred of us."

"All over the world?"

"Sure." Mercer grabbed a folding chair and opened it up. "Here. Sit. It's going to be a long morning. We'll be waiting for the faithful to arrive. The ritual will be at sundown."

"Okay, great. So it'll be me and the goat hanging out under the tarp in the desert sun?"

"That's the plan. Stay in the shade—"

"I can't really move out of it."

"—and I'll bring you some water. Every now and then I'll take you to a rest room."

"That would be good right about now," Julie said.

"Not now," Mercer said. "Soon."

"Okay, I can hold it," Julie said, wondering how long she actually could. "And how many of the faithful will be in attendance this evening?"

"About a dozen."

"And you're all Cthulu worshippers?"

"No! We don't worship Cthulu," Mercer spat. "He's a low-level Old One. The fellowship serve Azathoth, the greatest of the Outer Gods. He speaks to us through his servant, Nyarlathotep."

"He speaks to you, does he?"

"He does."

"And how does he do this, being fictional and all?"

"If you don't believe, you can't understand," Mercer said, with a note of finality.

"Otto, I've read Lovecraft's stories. They're just that—*stories*. The Great Old Ones and the Elder Gods were all just things he made up. Praying to them won't do any more for you than, I don't know, praying to Jane Eyre or something."

"Who's Jane Air?"

Julie shook her head. "Never mind. I suppose you all met up over the internet."

Mercer jerked upright. "How did you know?"

"Lucky guess," she said. "So, Otto, am I going to survive this ritual?"

Mercer didn't even blink. "Not if everything goes right."

Julie nodded. She looked at the goat, and it seemed that for a brief moment, their eyes connected and they caught a glimpse of one another's souls. "Right, then. I suppose I'd better pray."

"You've got plenty of time," Mercer said. He pointed to the chair. Julie sat.

Thom stayed on until the last of the crime scene units finished their work. Sheila Ramos found him in what they were calling the torture chamber, staring at the spines of the books.

"Hey…" she said tentatively. She stepped up beside him. "We're… all done here. I'm sorry, but…we need to seal the place up."

He sighed and nodded. Prising his eyes away from the shelves, he looked at her. "'Course."

"You should go home and get some rest."

"I should."

"But you won't?" she asked.

Thom could tell she felt sorry for him. But pity wasn't any use to him. He needed a lead. Inside his head, Julie was screaming for help. *I'll be damned if I go home for a shower and a shave,* he thought. *Not while she's…out there.* Thom knew what it was like to lose people. He was *not* going to lose Julie.

Without answering, Thom put his hat on his head and turned to leave. But before he got out of the room, Ramos called after him. "Hey…"

He stopped and looked back at her.

She gave him an encouraging smile—more of a grimace, really. "We're going to find her," she said.

"Damn straight," he said. "What concerns me is…will we find her *in time?*" Without waiting for her reply, Thom left the house.

He went to his SUV and looked at the time display on the dash. 4:45am. He stood still and felt the breeze tug at his khakis as he thought. He watched Ramos climb into her black-n-white, wave at him, and drive away.

If Mercer's car was here…he couldn't be traced that way. But it meant Mercer and Julie left in another vehicle, so there had to be a third person involved—maybe more.

He looked for Mercer's car and found the lime-green AMC Gremlin. In the amber glow of the streetlamp, the gray of the Bondo just looked like another shade of green.

Thom looked around, then walked over to the Gremlin. Holding his breath, he tried the driver's side door. To his great surprise and relief, it clicked…and opened. Giving silent thanks to whatever powers might be, he ducked into the car, found the dome lamp, and turned it on. In its feeble glow, he rifled through the contents of the glove box, but other than the car's registration, there was nothing of interest there. Thom turned in the seat and looked behind him. The car reeked of week-old pizza, and sure enough, there was a box in the back. He gingerly lifted the lid, verified that there was indeed ancient pizza within, and let it fall closed again. He snatched at one of the many scraps of paper littering the floor—fast-food wrapping, much of it. He grabbed at another paper of a different shape. His eyes widened as he saw it was a receipt. He squinted to try to read the scrawled handwriting. "Goat?" he asked aloud. "$400."

But other than the word "receipt" stamped in blue ink along the top of the paper, there was no indication of where the receipt was from—no name of the farm or ranch or business. Thom cursed under his breath but resumed his search.

In the trunk, he found a box filled with things he didn't quite understand—a robe, a wand straight out of a Harry Potter movie, a long-handled knife, a crown, the smelly resin of some kind of incense rattling in the bottom of an old can like loose pebbles. Thom tested the blade of the knife and discovered, to his surprise, that it had no edge at all. Whatever its intended utility, it had not been designed to actually *cut* anything.

The first red rays of morning were leaking into the sky as Thom shut the car up again. His stomach was tight with anxiety, but he felt his energy flagging. "I need to canvass," he said out loud. He turned and looked up and down the street. *It's too early to start knocking on doors*, the reasonable voice in his head said. "But every minute we wait is another minute Julie might be…" He didn't finish his sentence.

He rubbed at his eyes. He needed coffee—and sugar. He dimly remembered passing a diner just this side of the freeway. "Food and coffee," he told himself, speaking out loud. "Not in that order." By the time he was done, it would still be too early to start knocking on doors. But it would be late enough that he wouldn't let it stop him.

Ted slid into the booth at Debbie's just as Phil was about to leave. "May I join you for a brief moment?" Ted asked.

Phil's eyes moved quickly back and forth, seemingly unsure what to make of this request. Ted smiled. They'd both lived in the small town for years—many years—they both knew who the other was, but they had never had a conversation.

"Oh. Good morning. What can I do for you, Father?" Phil asked, settling back in on the cushion. There was still some coffee in his cup, so he sipped at it.

"I'm here out of concern…for a friend," Ted said.

"Oh?" Phil asked. His face betrayed confusion and concern. "Does it have anything to do with…you know, up the farm?"

"Oh, no no no," Ted scowled. "Nasty business. Have you been?"

"No," Phil admitted. "But I've heard plenty."

Ted put his hand up and caught Tali's eye. "A coffee, if you please, Tali."

"Coming right up, Father."

"Thank you," Ted said. He turned his attention back to Phil. "I'm sorry to keep you, Phil. I know we've never really…gotten to know each other, but—" Ted watched Phil as he looked at his coffee cup, coughed, and squirmed in his seat. *Oh-oh, he's getting the wrong idea,* Ted thought. He cut to the chase. "I'm concerned about Peg."

Phil froze, then looked up and met Ted's eye. "What about Peg?"

"Well, she's…she's going through a lot right now."

"Yes?" Phil asked.

"And I know that…well, the two of you…have some plans." Ted smiled, but he wasn't sure what message his smile was sending. He took a deep breath. "I love her and I'm concerned about her. She's my dearest friend." He looked up and saw the honesty in Phil's eye. It encouraged him.

"I'm kind of fond of her too," Phil admitted. "You aren't…you know…are you…do you have designs yourself?"

"What? On Peg?" Ted reared back, an incredulous smile warping his mouth. "No, heavens. That would be like *schtupping* my sister. God would frown on that, I think."

"Then…?"

"I'm…I'm happy that you two are going on a date—truly I am. Peg needs and deserves some happiness in her life, God knows. She's shouldering more than her share of shit right now. Hell, I'll pay for dinner for the two of you—" Ted pulled his billfold out and selected a crisp $100 bill. He handed it to Phil.

"I don't need you to pay for dinner," Phil said, waving the bill away. "But thanks."

Ted saw that he'd offended Phil. He put the money away and waited as Tali spun in and placed a steaming cup of coffee in front of him. As soon as she spun away again, he cleared his throat. "Look, Phil, this isn't any more comfortable for me than it is for you."

"Father, whatever you want to say, just say it."

Ted looked at his coffee. He nodded without looking up. "Peg has cancer. Stage Four. She has a few months to live, no more. I'm sure she will tell you this herself…eventually. But I want you to know now because I don't want her nursing a broken heart while she's…declining. She needs to be supported by people who are on her side, 100% committed. I'm not saying you're not one of those people, but if you're not…I need to know. If you're on team Peg, then let's strategize. Instead of pulling for her separately, let's pull for her together. If you're going to be there until the end—as I will—let's exchange phone numbers and communicate with each other about how best to help her."

Ted focused on Phil's eyes and watched him closely. He watched the man's eyebrows rise at the mention of cancer, then watched him look away as he recommended their confederacy. Phil played with his cup, swirling the last bit of coffee in the bottom.

"I don't know whether I'm supposed to thank you or punch you," Phil said.

"Punch me?" Ted asked, feigning a start. "Whoever for?"

"For not minding your own goddam business and meddling in Peg's private affairs."

"Her private affairs? Let me tell you about her private affairs. I'm 99% sure she's going to refuse treatment. So in a couple of months, who do you think is going to be changing her sheets? Feeding her? Wiping her shit? It isn't going to be Julie. And unless you're volunteering for that duty right here and now, that means it's going to be me. Don't talk to me about her private affairs—I'm going to be neck deep in her most private affairs, the kind of private you don't think about when you're in the first flush of love."

"I might still punch you," Phil said, glowering.

"Oh, my dear, it won't be the first time." Ted sighed wearily.

"It would be the first time for me," Phil said.

"Then you've led far too sheltered a life," Ted said. He sipped at the coffee. It was only now becoming cool enough to do so. It was bitter.

"Do you think Peg would appreciate this little...pep talk?" Phil asked.

"Probably not," Ted conceded. "Definitely not. She would shit a calf."

"Then—"

"Because how she meets the next few months is more important to me than whether she's miffed at me for a day or two." Ted set the cup aside and stood up. "I'm sorry to bother you. I just...you have some decisions to make. I just wanted you to have the facts so that you can make good ones—good for you and good for Peg. I apologize for any presumption."

Phil didn't look at him, but he nodded. "I'll take this...under advisement."

"That is all I ask," Ted said. He put a five dollar bill on the table and set his own coffee cup on top of it. "I'll see you around."

"You definitely..." Phil trailed off, and it seemed to Ted that he was thinking through the novel ways his comment might be interpreted. If Ted were definitely going to see Phil around, that might imply that his commitment to Peg was total. If so, that would be good. Caring for her would be easier with two of them there. But Ted's heart sank a bit when Phil didn't finish that particular sentence.

After a plate of fried eggs, potatoes, and bacon, Thom felt like a new man. He also felt like a very, very sleepy man, and he resisted the urge to lie down on the restaurant's booth seats. *Just for a moment*, the voice in his head pleaded, *let me close my eyes for just a moment.*

Instead, he ordered a third cup of coffee—this one to go. Absentmindedly, he paid the bill. Stuffing his billfold into his pocket, he snagged five packets of sugar and put them in his shirt pocket. Then he stared at the little bowl containing the sugar packets. He put the rest of the packets in his other shirt pocket. Then he got up to go.

Outside, he put his hat on and climbed into Old Bill. It was almost 8:00am, almost an acceptable time to start knocking on doors. "It's close enough," he said out loud. Within five minutes he was pulling up across from Mercer's house again. He set the brake and started with the house directly across the street. No one answered.

Taking out his moleskin note pad, Thom wrote down the address and the result. Then he went to the next house. A woman near to Thom's own age answered the door. Her hair was in curlers and the crumbling remnants of yesterday's mascara highlighted her dark eyes. She took a drag on a cigarette and blew the smoke behind the door. "What do *you* want?" she asked.

Thom cocked his head, because she said it as if she knew him. Thom couldn't see how, so he set the observation aside. "Good morning, ma'am—sorry about the hour."

"Ain't nothin' wrong with the hour. I like morning best, don't you? It's the time of day when the greatest number of God's precious creatures are glad to be alive."

Thom opened his mouth to make a reply, but she stabbed her cigarette toward him and interrupted. "Do you know what 2pm is?"

"Uh...no ma'am."

"It's the time of greatest fatigue. It's the time the greatest number of God's precious creatures want to stab their own eyes out with push pins."

Thom was not a morning person, and felt none of this woman's violent antipathy for the early afternoon, but he decided not to take the bait. "Ma'am, we're in the middle of an ongoing investigation involving the house across the street—"

"Those meth-heads?"

"I can't discuss an ongoing investigation, ma'am. I just have a few questions."

"Oh, so you can ask questions, but I can't?" the woman asked. Then she picked her teeth for a stray strand of tobacco.

"Oh, you can ask them, ma'am, it's a free country. I just can't answer them. I'm sorry." He gave her his most sympathetic look. Unfortunately, he knew that particular look also made him look gassy. "Have you seen any suspicious vehicles near that house?"

"You mean more than usual?"

"Uh...yes. Actually, if you can describe any vehicle you've seen near that address, it would be helpful to us."

"There's people goin' in and out, in and out, all times of the day and night. Gives me the creeps. I get a cold chill in my bones just walking past the place. Don't you?"

This stopped Thom momentarily. In fact, he knew exactly what the woman was talking about. There was indeed something unsettling about the property. Thom did not mention the torture chamber.

"Ma'am, any vehicle descriptions?"

"Oh, I don't know cars."

"Well, you know what a car *is*—and I'm sure you know an SUV or a jeep when you see one. And you know trucks and vans. They're all different. And they all come in different colors. You don't need to be an expert in cars to notice those things."

"Are you *pay*-tro-nizing me, officer? Because I get the distinct feeling I'm being *pay*-tro-nized."

"Uh...no ma'am. I'm just trying to get some information for our case."

"Uh-huh. Well, there was a Jeep there yesterday. Still is." She pointed past Thom's shoulder at Julie's shop. "That's the same one as what was there yesterday."

"Yes. We haven't moved it yet," Thom said. "But that's good. Can you remember any others?" Thom sensed diminishing returns and was already itching to finish up with this woman and move on to the next house.

"A van. There was a van."

Thom stood instantly straighter, his eyebrows standing at attention. "A van? What color?"

"I don't know…tan, maybe? White? It was dark, and it's hard to tell with these lights here." She pointed toward the street. "They're yellow. Hurts my eyes to look at 'em."

Thom understood that she was talking about the amber streetlights. "What kind of van was it? Did it have windows for passengers? Or were the sides solid, like for a business?"

"No windows," the woman said. "There was writing on it."

"On the van?" Thom asked. He flipped open his moleskin and began jotting notes.

"Yeah."

"What did it say?"

"I don't remember."

Thom looked in the woman's eyes and tried to ascertain whether she was telling the truth. She took a drag of her cigarette and held his gaze.

"You really don't remember?" Thom asked. "Or perhaps you need something to…jog your memory?" He knew he was going out on a limb, but he was following his gut.

"Can't squeeze blood from a turnip," the woman said.

"I see," Thom said, closing his notebook.

"Hate for you to go to all this trouble for nothing," she said. "I wonder if you could come to the back room and maybe…help me with something?" She gestured with her head toward the back of the house.

Thom opened his mouth to respond, but hesitated. For the briefest second, he imagined what it would be like to have sex again. He imagined himself, five minutes in the future, heaving himself over the frail, tobacco-stained body of this woman, surrendering to his animal lusts. He imagined his legs shaking as he shot his seed into her; imagined how depressed and hollow he would feel immediately afterwards. "Thanks, ma'am, but I'm on...urgent business."

"I see. Well, you get tired, you wanna lie down, you come back here, you hear?"

"I do. Thank you kindly for your hospitality, and for your cooperation with law enforcement today."

She winked at him before she shut the door. He was embarrassed to discover his hands were shaking as he pocketed his moleskin and turned from the house. *Focus,* a voice in his head said. Mechanically, he turned at the sidewalk and headed toward another of the houses.

Thom forced himself to study the yard as he strode to the door. The owners had not made even the smallest effort at landscaping. Two cars were parked in the drive, and another was parked on the spot one might expect a front lawn to be. A lone pine tree swayed in the early morning wind, barely taller than Thom's belt buckle. He knocked.

The door swung open to reveal a teenage boy holding a piece of bread with jam on it. The kid seemed surprised to see a cop. "Wow. Yeah?"

Thom pointed to his badge. "County Sheriff, son. I'd like to ask you a few questions."

"Am I in trouble?" the kid asked.

"Did you do anything wrong?" Thom responded.

The kid looked instantly stricken. His quick eyes moved back and forth, as if scanning for an exit route.

"Relax," Thom said. "Whatever you're worried about, it's not that. I'm investigating a missing person. Have you noticed any suspicious vehicles lately? Maybe someone going in or out of your neighbor's house, there?" He pointed at Mercer's house.

The kid brightened. "Oh, lots happens there, all the time. That place is gangster."

"Uh-huh. And did you notice any cars out front that…maybe shouldn't have been there?"

The kid shrugged. Thom tried a different tack. "Tell me about a normal day for you. What do you do?"

"I dunno. Ride my bike—"

"Around here?"

"All over."

"What else?"

The kid shrugged again. "Take selfies, post them on Instagram."

"Show me some of the selfies."

"It's Instagram!" the kid complained.

Thom scowled at him. Grudgingly, the kid pulled his cell phone out of his pocket and navigated around. "Here. That's everything from yesterday." He handed the phone to Thom.

Thom began to scroll through the thumbnails—it just went on and on. "You took all of these pictures yesterday?" Thom asked, amazed at the sheer volume of photography.

"Yeah."

"Is that a pretty normal day?"

"Yeah."

The kid was photogenic, Thom had to admit it. He wore his hair short around the sides, but the hair on the top of his head was long, drooping over his eyes like a the tongue of a cow.

Thom paid special attention to the photos taken at night. He was surprised that the quality of the photos was as good as it was, given the light levels. He froze.

"What?" the kid asked.

"Do you mind if I…can you email this one and this one to me?"

"Sure. Let me set it up, and you can enter the email."

"Good."

A few seconds later, the kid handed the phone to Thom and he hastily punched his email address into it. He hit "send," and handed the phone back to the kid.

"Are we done?" the kid asked.

"Just a moment," Thom said. He pulled his own cell phone out and waited. The email appeared, photos intact. "Thank you so much for your cooperation."

"Don't I get anything?" the kid asked. "For helping with the investigation?"

"I've got a shiny 'junior deputy sheriff' badge in my SUV. Would you like that?"

"That's for kids. I was thinking about maybe a reward?"

"I'll make you a deal, kid. If these photos help, I'll come back and...well, I don't know what. But you'll be glad you helped me."

"Cool," the kid said. Then he slammed the door.

Thom blinked and wondered at the manners of kids nowadays. He pulled out his moleskin and made a note of the address, a description of the kid, and the result. He started walking back, but then jogged right to stand in the shadow of the garage. He pulled up the photos and studied them more carefully.

In the foreground of both photos, the kid was mugging it up for the camera—which he was holding, naturally. Thom did not believe that he had ever taken a picture that was as commercial and appealing as those this kid seemed to simply toss off on the fly. "Must be a gift," Thom said.

But it was the background that really interested him. Behind the kid, he could see the blurry bones of Mercer's house—it was a night shot and the picture was grainy. But in between was clearly a white van. Thom pinched at the picture, then spread his fingers, trying to make it bigger. The phone did not cooperate. He kept at it, and once was afraid he'd accidentally deleted the photo. He cursed and tried again. This time he was able to make the photo bigger. There was a name on the back of the van, but it was partially occluded by the kid on his bike.

Thom copied the letters into his moleskin. "M...A...R...A...N... A...T..." was all he got. "Maranatti?" Thom asked aloud. Sounded Italian. But was it a real Italian name? He didn't know. He forwarded the photos to Celia. He realized that she would just be getting into the office, so he called her.

"Boss? Where are you?"

"Still in Coleman—"

"What? Thom, were you there all night?"

"I was."

"But that's—" Celia began to splutter.

"It's all right. It's not like I slept on a park bench. I've been working the whole time."

"Any closer to finding Barkley?"

"Maybe. I just emailed you a couple of photos. You can see the Mercer house in the background. You can also see a white van—"

"Looks yellow to me," Celia said. That meant she was at her desk, with her email in front of her. *Good*, thought Thom. The woman was nothing if not efficient.

"That's because it was taken at night and the streetlights are that weird amber color."

"I hate those," Celia said.

"Thank you for your input. I'll let my superiors know," Thom deadpanned. There was something about Celia's calm under pressure that gave him permission to relax. A bit. "I think that might be the van they used in the abduction."

"Boy, did you get lucky," Celia whistled.

"Got that right. Take a look there...there's a name on the van. I copied it out—"

"Maranat..." Celia read. "That's probably '*maranatha.*'"

"Is that a name?"

"No...it's Greek...I think...or maybe it's Aramaic—what do I know? But it's a Jesus thing. It means, 'Lord, come.'"

"Lord, come," Thom repeated.

"Don't say it unless you mean it," Celia said. Thom knew she was a religious woman, but she wasn't usually very vocal about it.

"So, why is that on this van?"

"People love the word, for some reason. Lots of people use it to name things. Like churches—you heard of Maranatha Baptist Chapel over in Visalia?"

"Nope."

"Their pastor was busted on child porn a couple years ago."

"Ouch," Thom said. "Could this be a church van?"

"Does it have windows? Zooming in. Hm...no, it doesn't."

"So not a church van," Thom said. "What else could it be?"

He heard Celia's keyboard erupt into a tinny battery of clicks and clacks. "Well, there's a Maranatha Landscaping Company. Their motto is, 'When Jesus comes back, make sure you have a nice yard to greet him in.'"

"That's a terrible motto," Thom opined.

"Not pithy enough," Celia agreed. "Here's a Maranatha Bakery."

"It's too bad we don't have the plate," Thom said.

"Now, that would just be *too* easy," Celia said.

"Okay, run down all the Maranatha-themed businesses, and cross reference with DMV records. That van's a Ford E-series or I'll eat my hat. Let's see what we come up with."

"Will do, boss."

"How is it going over there?" Thom asked.

There were several seconds of silence. Finally, though, Celia said, "Nothing has burned down yet, but...I'll be glad when you're back."

Bill Arenson stared at the cube again. He bent in to study it, and suddenly there were scientists beside him, all around the cube, taking cuttings, dabbing it with chemicals, eyeing test tubes, dusting it for fingerprints. Their faces were obscured by something that looked like gas masks, and they didn't speak, but they didn't complain that he was in their way either, so he just continued his exploration.

Going around the other side of the cube, he noted that there were more pictures of him cut into the other sides. The physics of this seemed improbable, as each of them would have cut into the same interior, but he didn't wonder at this too much. He was too interested in the other scenes.

They all showed him dying—they just showed him dying in diverse ways. He'd started out looking at the scene where he was enveloped in flame, but then moving around the cube, he saw himself impaled by a massive spear, straight up through the anus, just like in those woodcuts he'd seen about Vlad the Impaler. That has to hurt, he thought. Moving on, he saw another scene, with him lying on the floor, a vial of something spilled out near him. Poison, now that's an elegant death, *he decided. It was also decidedly girly. He sneered at the poisoned corpse and inwardly cursed its cowardice.*

Moving on, he saw a shotgun blast that opened his chest up wide enough for an orange to pass through. That's more like it, *he thought, approving of the scene. Moving on to the fifth—wait, shouldn't this be the first again?—and final side, he saw a scene that he didn't understand.*

A child wearing a clown mask upside down was feeding bloody bits of dismembered fingers to a ravenous hound—Bill could see fingernails on some of them. The child was surrounded by a tiny chapel constructed entirely of meat— steaks stacked to form columns, and a chancel behind him molded from ground turkey breast. The child paused and looked at him. Bill could see his eyes through the mask—they were like tiny bb's, far smaller than a child's eyes should be, and there was no white to them. They were like insect eyes, he decided. "Got your nose," *the child said, holding up a severed thumb between two of his fingers.*

Bill started awake. For a brief moment, he didn't know where he was. Then he noted the light coming through the window and everything snapped into place. He had fallen asleep on his couch. The sun was up. His fingers detected wetness. A wave of shame rolled over him as he realized he'd wet himself in his sleep. He hadn't done that since he was a child. "Goddam it," he said, feeling at his pants.

He pulled the cushions off the couch and arranged them so they'd catch the most air and dry out quickly. He made a mental note to pick up some of that spray that pet owners usually have on hand for accidents. Then he headed to the shower.

As he stood under the stream of water, washing away both the dried urine and the wispy details of his dream, he held on to the image of the shotgun blast through his chest. *That is the way,* the voice in his head told him. *Not fire.* He knew there was no way he could self-inflict such a wound. He would need to be shot...by someone else. *I can manage that,* he thought. He would not let the cube's fiery prediction prevail. If he was going to go out, it was going to be on his own terms.

Dressing absentmindedly, he grabbed his keys and headed for Willington's Gun and Smoke Shop. Locals called it "The Smokin' Gun," and Bill half expected Dale Willington to change the name one day, since the nickname was so clever.

The bell above the door heralded his arrival. "Bill," a man said, not looking up from the newspaper spread out on the counter.

"Dale," Bill said.

"Whatcha in the mood for? Got some new glass bongs in, heavy motherfuckers. Won't tip over for nothin'."

"You know I'm a Jack Daniels guy."

"That stuff'll kill you," Dale said, still not looking up.

"I just came into some money," Bill lied, "and I thought I'd catch up on my wish list."

"Then you came to the right place," Dale brightened. He had a handlebar mustache that always seemed to be perfectly waxed. He folded the paper and set it aside so that Bill could see everything in the glass counter display.

"Don't need no handguns," Bill said.

"You looking for a shotgun?" Dale asked.

Bill flashed on the image of the fist-sized hole in his chest. "Sure."

"What gauge you looking for?"

Bill already had four 12-gauges. But a 12 gauge couldn't do what the picture in his head showed him. "You got an 8-gauge?"

Dale squinted. "I ain't never *seen* an 8-gauge. You need to take down a fucking elephant?"

"10-gauge, then."

Dale eyed him suspiciously, but nodded. "Sure. I got two of those. Hang on." Dale went into the back, and came out with two guns, one in each hand. He set both of them on the display counter, pointing in opposite directions.

Bill felt the same thrill he always felt when handling a new gun. His fingers felt electric as he picked up the first of the 10-gauges. It was covered with a camouflage pattern. "Didn't know you were a big game guy," Dale said.

"I'm not, normally," Bill said, fitting his eye to the sight. He set it down and picked up the other. This one was black with a maple stock.

"They're both Brownings. Essentially the same gun, except for the coloring."

"Sure. I like the maple," Bill said.

"She's a looker."

"Let me see a shell," Bill said.

"Shot or slug?" Dale asked.

"You got slugs for that thing?" Bill's eyes lit up.

"You really are going after elephant, aren't you?"

"Something like that."

Dale narrowed one eye at him but opened a drawer and pulled out two differently-colored shells. He set them on the counter.

"Those are massive," Bill breathed.

"They are that," Dale said. "A slug like that," he pointed to the red casing, "could put a hole in a moose the size of a softball."

"You say that from experience?"

"I do. Go huntin' up near Juneau every year with my old pastor."

Bill nodded. "I'll take it, and two boxes of the slugs."

Dale nodded. "You want that gift-wrapped?"

"You are a funny guy."

"Anything else?"

Bill cocked his head. "Yeah, you know, if I don't buy it now, I might never buy it."

"What'er we talking about?"

"I'm talking about that," he pointed at the wall, where there were about twenty rifles of differing models and makes. "The TNW Aoer Survival Rifle."

"Oh, now that's a thing of beauty." He waved at the shotguns. "Lemme get the ladder."

A moment later, Dale was lifting the TNW from its resting place and gingerly stepping down from the ladder. Instead of placing it on the counter, he put it into Bill's waiting hands. "That little siren has been singing to you for some time."

"It has."

It wasn't how he'd go out; Bill knew that much. But he also knew that he was not long for this earth. *A man gets to have nice things now and then,* the voice in his head counseled him. "A man does," he answered out loud.

"Huh?" Dale asked. "A man does what?"

"A man does...what he needs to do."

"And what do *you* need to do?"

Bill set the rifle down on the counter reverently. He fished for his wallet. "I need to give you my credit card."

Normally, Peg enjoyed working on her sermon. But today the words all seemed to be blurring together. She rubbed her eyes. "I'm not getting anywhere," she said to herself. Sermon preparation was rarely a linear process. It involved reading the scriptures assigned by the lectionary, reading them again, reading them again, and letting them stew as you went about your daily life. Somewhere in the mix, Peg discovered what the passages were saying to her personally. Once she knew that, she would know what her sermon was about. "Read until you find something that scares you," her homiletics professor had said, and it had never failed to work.

The phone rang. She fumbled for her cell and hit the red button. "Hello?"

"Hello, Pastor?"

Her phone had not recognized the number, but it was Jake's voice. "Jake! Lovely to hear from you."

"Uh...I'm not sure it is. I have...there's...I'm afraid I've got some bad news."

"Oh dear." Peg steeled herself. What else could go wrong. *Pile it on, Jesus, why don't you?* she thought at the Lord.

"Uh...there's a number of new cubes out at the Nyland place."

"I'm sorry to hear that." She wasn't surprised. But why was he calling *her?*

"And, uh...one of them is of you."

Peg felt her heart fall into her belly. "Oh."

"Just thought, you know, that you should know."

"Of course. Has...has Julie seen it."

"Uh...no. She's...indisposed."

Peg's brow furrowed. "Indisposed" was not a word that fit comfortably in Jake Hessup's mouth, and it didn't sit any easier in her ear.

"Should I come up there?"

"Uh...you can. But..."

"Jake, Ted and I are coming up tonight to companion people who... who come to look. I'll just...I'll look at it then."

"Yeah, okay. Uh...and your friend, Fr. Ted—"

"Don't tell me he has one, too."

"Uh...yeah."

Peg bit her lip and nodded. "Okay. Okay. Thank you, Jake." She hung up.

She felt numb along one side of her body. She glanced out the window and saw that the trees just outside were still dripping with dew. They reminded her of prophets of the eschaton, heralding the coming renewal of the earth, the greening power of God, the healing of everything wounded and broken. A desperate part of her hoped that included her.

A knock jolted her out of her eschatological reverie. "Oh dear. That snuck up on me." She got up and went to the door. The chair of her church council, Alec Marlowe, was there in a raincoat and a ridiculously broad-brimmed safari hat, even though it wasn't raining. It was almost an umbrella for his head—a thought that made her smile inside. "Alec, so good to see you," she said.

"Pastor," he said, pushing past her into the office. He was shorter than Peg, and even in his mid-fifties he still had a healthy shock of black hair.

She shut the door and pointed to a coatrack to one side of it. "Feel free to hang your things," she said. He nodded and hung up his coat and hat. "Tea?" she asked.

"No thanks. I'm in a bit of a hurry, I'm afraid."

"Oh. All right then." She waved him toward Ted's chair. He sat and scowled at her, his eyebrows bunching like storm clouds above the bridge of his nose.

"Pastor, the council had a meeting—"

"It wasn't a scheduled council meeting," Peg surmised.

"No."

"And you had it...without me?" Peg tilted her head. "That seems...ominous."

"Technically, you're not on the council."

"As pastor, I'm an *ex officio* member of the church council. I've never been excluded from a council meeting before."

He shifted in his seat and cleared his throat. "Yes, well, ahem...we didn't invite you because...well, we needed to discuss *you*, and it wasn't proper for you to be in the room."

"Asking someone to leave the room isn't the same as not being invited into the room at all," Peg countered. She wished she had tea. She wished she had something to do with her hands. She tucked them under her thighs to keep them from flittering. "It feels different, Alec. It would especially feel different if it had happened to you."

Alec blinked. "Let's not get off track here."

"I don't think we are."

"The council met," he said, a little too loudly. That meant, *Shut up, woman, the man is talking.* Peg understood him perfectly. "And there have been some...concerns."

Peg's eyebrows shot up. "Concerns? Plural?"

"Indeed. Uh...first, we've had a complaint from Ellen Wulfson."

"Oh, yes." Peg couldn't help smiling.

"Is something funny, Pastor?" Marlowe asked.

"Nothing at all. Proceed."

"Mrs. Wulfson said she came to you for pastoral counseling, and that you gave her shockingly inappropriate advice."

"Did I? I don't think I did."

Marlowe shifted in his seat. He was obviously uncomfortable. "I'd like to know the details of that conversation."

"That's too bad, Alec. My conversations with parishioners are confidential."

"Ellen Wulfson told me what you said."

"Ellen Wulfson is not professionally obliged to keep confidences. I am."

"She told me that you belittled her concern over her daughter's wanton behavior."

"She mentioned no 'wanton behavior' to me."

Marlowe leaned in toward her, his elbows on his knees. "Her daughter is shamefully trying to change her sex."

"Her daughter is a teenager trying to find herself...*himself*. If there's something shameful about that, then there's something shameful about being a teenager."

"You are supporting sexually licentious behavior."

"I did no such thing. Ellen didn't mention any sexual *behavior* at all."

"You're straining at gnats," Marlowe glowered at her.

"And you have me in a double bind. I can't defend myself without breaking confidences."

"It's part of a troubling pattern," Marlowe said.

"What pattern?" Peg shook her head incredulously.

"Which brings me to the next item of concern." Marlowe leaned back in the chair again. "The council questions whether you are making the best use of your time."

Peg frowned. "Best use of my time? That's a curious phrase. Whatever can it mean?"

"It means we hired you at three-quarter time and gave you a parsonage, and we just want to make sure that you're using your thirty hours a week as we—your parishioners—intend. We want to make sure you're not..."

"Not what?"

"We want to make sure we're getting our money's worth."

Peg blinked. Then she cocked her head. Then she blinked again.

Marlowe continued. "So, we'd like you to keep a full accounting of your time. And then we'd like you to make a weekly report to me, in writing, detailing your hours and activities."

"Oh, you would, would you?"

"We would."

"And why, all of the sudden, all this interest in my 'hours and activities'? Would it have something to do with Rachel Lindstrom?"

Marlowe looked away.

"Alec, Rachel isn't even a member of our church. She's a Methodist. And you know as well as I do that she ran the Methodist pastor off last year. They've been limping along without a pastor ever since, because the Methodist bishop doesn't have anyone to spare. And since she can't cause any more trouble for her own pastor, she's turned her sights on me. Alec, can't you see that she's one of those 'clergy killers'? You're supposed to protect me from people like that, not collude with them."

"She raised some…valid issues for concern."

"So you met with her personally?"

"Uh…yes—"

"Behind my back?"

"There were some…delicate issues."

"Name a few of those *delicate* issues."

In answer he pulled a folded piece of paper from his shirt pocket. Deliberately, he unfolded it. Then he looked at it. Then he looked up at Peg. Then he looked back at the paper.

"Oh, don't do that. Just spill it," Peg said. "Whatever you have to say to me, just fucking say it."

Marlowe reared back as far as the chair's headrest would allow. She saw him calculate internally whether to object to her language, and apparently decided to let it slide. He squirmed in his chair, then met her eyes and held them. "I was not chair of the church council when you were hired—"

"No, that was Evelyn White." Peg smiled. "I miss her."

"Yes, God rest her soul," Marlowe said. "But…nor was I on the search committee that found you and recommended you to the parish."

"No." Internally, Peg added, *Thank God for that.*

"Since Ms. Lindstrom's complaint—" he began. Peg rolled her eyes as he continued. "—I went and pulled your search and call files. And… there's a lot there that was not made public to the parish at large."

"Nothing was kept from the search committee, nor from the church council at the time," Peg said. "They decided what to communicate to the parish and what not to communicate—not me."

"Yes, well, be that as it may, the information was...enlightening to say the least," he said.

Peg wished she were anywhere but there. Then she remembered that one of those anywheres might be a hole in the ground. She reminded herself to stay present. Then she reminded herself that Jesus was present too. She reached for his hand. She couldn't find it. A part of her panicked. She hoped it didn't show.

"For instance," Marlowe said, studying the paper, "I did not know that you had worked as a prostitute in the 1980s in San Francisco."

She and Jesus would need to have a talk, she decided. It wasn't like him to abandon her at a time like this. She felt her chest tighten in anger. She just wasn't sure exactly who she was angry at. Then she realized she could be angry at more than one person. She could be angry at Ellen Wulfson, Rachel Lindstrom, Alec Marlow *and* the Lord all at once. And all at once she felt the rightness in her body. Yes, she could be angry at all of them, and she was.

Marlowe was looking at her, as if waiting for an explanation. Did she owe him one? She wasn't sure. "My father was...abusive," she explained. "I had to get out of the house. I figured I had a choice between the street and the grave. I chose to live."

"You could have gotten a job," Marlowe said.

"Burger King doesn't pay fifteen-year-olds a living wage," Peg said. "Or maybe you didn't know that. Have you ever had to work at Burger King, Alec?"

"I did not know you had had an abortion," Marlowe continued, ignoring her question.

"And no reason you should have. That's between me, God, and my doctor—and absolutely no one else."

"It reflects poorly on your character."

"It reflects poorly on the circumstances of my life at the time."

"Some people just make excuses for everything," Marlowe interjected.

"Some people ride their privilege all the way to the palace snacking on cake and the sweetmeats of their serfs."

Marlowe looked confused. He shifted in his chair. "You don't seem very penitent," he noted.

"Why should I be? It was thirty years ago. I've said all the apologies I need to say, and none of them needed to be said to you."

He looked back at the paper in his hand. "I did not know that you were divorced, not once but twice."

"You've got that wrong. I divorced Ned. William died."

"So you're only divorced once?"

"That's correct."

"That's not much better in the eyes of church folk," Marlowe noted.

"I hear Jesus has some very nice mud for that," Peg countered. "Works like a charm."

Marlowe cleared his throat. "I did not know that you had been fired from your previous church, Trinity UCC in Vallejo."

"It was very sad," Peg said. She did feel sad when she thought about it. It had been harrowing at the time. "Some congregations are just...deadly. They'd been through seven pastors in five years. I didn't stand a chance."

"It's disturbing to me how none of this is your fault." Marlowe narrowed one eye at her.

"Oh, on the contrary, I take complete responsibility for my life," Peg said. "I just don't see how I am accountable to *you* for any of it."

"Your lack of contrition is not going to be helpful, Pastor."

"I didn't realize I was on trial," Peg answered.

"You know, I'm curious," Marlowe said, a slight smile forming at the edge of his mouth, "with a...a *history* like this...what made you think, 'I should become a minister'?"

Peg did not hesitate. "For one thing, I figured Jesus was the only person who would have me. For another thing, I didn't choose it. Jesus called me to it. If you have an issue with that, I suggest you take it up with him."

"I find it disturbing the way you talk about Jesus as if he were a real person," Marlowe noted.

Peg felt a moment of vertigo at this assertion. "I find it disturbing that a person would show up Sunday after Sunday and sing praises to someone they consider fictional."

Marlowe folded the paper and returned it to his pocket. He stood up. Apparently, this little ambush was nearing its end. "Far be it for me to question the wisdom of the previous council chair or the search committee, but...we gave you a gift, Pastor, in taking a chance on you. It looks like we hired you when literally no one else would."

"It was truly an act of desperation," Peg agreed. She couldn't help taking a jab where she could.

"Well, we're not feeling so desperate now. We're going to keep a close eye on you, Pastor. You are officially on probation. We want a full accounting of your hours. And from now on we want your counseling to be...*appropriate*."

Without another word, he headed for the door. He took his coat and hat and left, shutting the door behind him a little too forcefully.

"Jesus, where were you when I needed you?" Peg asked.

———

Allison swung the trash bag out the back door of her shop into the alley. *Should have done this a couple days ago*, she thought. *It's going to break*. She heaved and dragged, and to her great surprise and relief, the bag held.

She paused when she got to the dumpster and straightened up to lift its large plastic lid. That's when she heard it. At first, she didn't know what it was. Her brows bunched together and she cocked her head, trying to figure out where the sound was coming from. Momentarily forgetting the trash, she followed the sound to the other side of the dumpster. There, hiding in the dumpster's shadow, curled almost into a ball, was a young man.

"Uh...are you all right?" Allison asked.

The figure froze, then lifted his face from his hands to look at her.

She gasped. His eyes were red and swollen—he had definitely been crying. A large square bandage hung off his cheek by a lone piece of surgical tape that still had purchase on his skin. About three inches square, the bandage dangled from his face, swinging back and forth with the boy's movements.

But it was his cheek that shocked her—there were four parallel cuts across it, no longer bleeding but inflamed and sore-looking. There were black splotches here and there that Allison guessed had scabbed over.

"Hey," she said, squatting near the teenager. She pointed at his cheek. "That looks painful."

The young man nodded. Allison turned her head and squinted—something about the young man was familiar. Her brain whirled as she searched it for some point of contact. Her shoulders relaxed as she found it. "Melinda?" The young man wasn't a young man at all, she realized. She was…but she caught herself. Melinda had done several summer courses with her in drawing and pottery several years ago. But her hair was shorn off into what almost looked like a military buzz cut, and the clothes were definitely masculine.

"Mel," the huddling figure corrected her.

"What?" Allison asked. She lowered herself so that her back was against the wall next to Melinda.

"Please…call me Mel, not Melinda. I'm…I'm a boy, not a girl."

"Oh," Allison said, taking this in. She made some internal adjustments. It wasn't hard. She gave Mel a compassionate smile. "That looks painful." She pointed at his cheek.

"It is," he confirmed.

"What are you doing back here?"

"Having a good cry." It was said with such an "isn't it obvious?" matter-of-factness that she almost laughed. But she didn't.

"I'm sorry I interrupted. Good cries are important to have."

Mel shrank into himself a bit and color bloomed in his cheeks.

"Hey, no need to be embarrassed," Allison said. "I have me a good cry every couple of days or so."

"You do?"

"Can I let you in on a secret?" Allison asked.

"Yes."

She leaned in so that their foreheads were almost touching and whispered, "Most people do."

Mel's eyes widened. "They do?"

"They do."

Mel's eyes flashed back and forth as he processed this new information. "I can't imagine my mom or dad crying."

"I'll bet they don't let you see it, because they don't want you to worry about them," Allison said.

"I don't know…" Mel did not seem convinced. That was okay.

"Hey, why don't you come into the shop and let me clean up your cheek?" Allison asked.

"I don't know…"

"C'mon. We'll stay in the back—no one will see you. Will that be okay?"

Mel looked uncertain for a moment, but then nodded. "Okay."

He stood, and for the first time Allison was able to take in the whole of the new Mel. She smiled. She reached out her hand to him. He took it and helped her stand. "Thanks for helping an old lady."

"You're not old," Mel said.

"Thank you for that," Allison said. She was in her mid-thirties, but she remembered how old that seemed when she was a teenager. She walked to the door and held it open for him. A bit sheepishly, he ducked into the doorway.

She let the door close behind her and indicated a stool near the utility sink. "Why don't you sit there, and I'll just grab some things?"

Mel nodded and climbed onto the stool. In a moment, Allison was back with a first-aid kit and a rough square of muslin cloth.

"I don't have a wash cloth, as such," Allison explained as she rinsed the muslin under the hot tap in the sink. "But this'll do."

Mel lifted his face to her and cringed. With a quick motion, Allison ripped the last bit of surgical tape off of the boy's skin and set the old bandage aside. Then she held the moist muslin about an inch from his cheek and paused. "Brave face," she said.

Mel relaxed a bit and met her eye. He nodded almost imperceptibly, and she lowered the warm cloth to his cheek. He flinched but did not move otherwise.

"We're just going to let that sit there for a moment, soften up those scabs and dried blood a bit," Allison said.

Mel said nothing, but kept his face frozen at an odd angle, looking straight at the corner where the wall met the ceiling.

"So you're a boy now," Allison said.

Mel nodded, not moving enough to threaten the cloth's purchase on his face, but enough to answer.

"I imagine that's been coming for some time?"

Mel nodded again.

"How did you hurt your cheek?"

"My mom."

"Your mom?"

"She did it. With a fork."

Allison caught the side of the utility sink to steady herself. "The shit," she breathed.

"Huh?" Mel's eyes widened. Allison realized he was not used to hearing adults swear.

"Sorry. That was unladylike," Allison said. She reached up and tenderly lifted the muslin from Mel's face. She began to dab at the dried blood, trying to remove what she could without irritating the wounds.

"And what did your dad do?" Allison asked.

"Nothing. He watched."

Allison's brows furrowed. "And she did that...why?"

"She doesn't like that I'm a boy. She has this idea in her head of who I'm supposed to be, and...well...I've never been that person. Ever. All I ever do is disappoint her."

"I'll bet that hurts a lot," Allison said. She saw tears well up in his eyes, but he said nothing. "No wonder you were having a good cry," she said. "I think you're allowed."

"Really?"

"Really." She set the muslin aside and inspected the wounds. They were infected, but not troublesome—not yet. "Okay, I'm going to dab some rubbing alcohol onto the cuts. It's going to sting a bit. Shit, I'm not going to lie to you, it's going to hurt like hell. Can you take it?"

"I can take it," Mel said, screwing up his face defiantly and presenting his cheek.

"Okay, here we go." She stuck a cotton wad into the mouth of a bottle of isopropyl alcohol. She smelled the sharp fumes and felt the cotton grow instantly cold in her fingers. Then, setting the bottle down next to the sink, she began to dab at the wounds.

"Ah..." Mel said, flinching again.

"That's the worst of it," Allison said. "It's all downhill from here." She pressed the cotton onto the wounds and waited before moving to an adjacent spot. After a few seconds, she moved it again until she had covered all the wounds.

She backed up a step and met his eye. "You okay?"

"Yeah," he said, although his eyes said differently.

"Okay, I'm going to rub some triple antibiotic ointment into it now. This won't hurt; it'll actually feel good. You ready?"

"Ready."

It occurred to Allison that the physical trauma was enough. Her curiosity wanted to know more about his home situation and his transition process, but wondered if that was piling on. She decided to change the subject. "Hey, how come I haven't seen you darken my door for a while?"

"Uh...it isn't summer...yet."

"I didn't see you *last* summer."

"No." He didn't explain further.

"Are you still doing art?" she asked. "Because you're very good."

"Oh, yeah! In fact, I've decided it's what I want to be." The thickness in his voice gave way to an eager weightlessness. "When I grow... when I get a job, you know?"

"You want to be an artist?"

"I want to be an architect," he said.

She put the cap back on the ointment and stepped back again. "Do you, now?" She gave him an encouraging smile.

"Yeah. I've been drawing up plans for buildings I like. Just to practice."

"You mean, instead of designing new buildings, you've been doing plans for existing buildings?"

"Yeah. I started with our house. Then I did the school—"

"The whole school?"

"Yeah, it was hard because there were some places I couldn't get in to measure. So there are some gaps…"

"Huh. What do your parents say about this ambition?"

"My mother says it's not ladylike, and I should draw something pretty instead."

"Ah. And what do you say to that?"

"I say, what's more beautiful than a building?"

Allison smiled then and shook her head. Just then the bell sounded —someone had entered the store. "Just a minute, my dear," she said, and strode into the shop. Nelly Gaiter waved at her, having already retrieved her project and tying on an apron.

"Oh hello, Nelly. Make yourself at home. I'll be in the back if you need me." Nelly nodded and Allison turned back. "Sorry about that," she said.

Mel shook his head. Allison was relieved to see that the wounds looked better already. She ripped one edge of the paper off a fresh 3 x 4 bandage. Carefully, she set it down on his cheek. He didn't flinch this time. "Hold that in place," she said.

Tentatively, he reached up and touched the bandage, pressing gently.

Snatching a pair of fingernail scissors from the first aid kit, Allison cut a length of surgical tape. "It's not easy being 'different,' but there are some advantages. I say this from years of experience."

"How are you 'different'?"

Allison's smile screwed into a confused scowl. "You can't tell?"

"Well…I guess you're pretty nerdy for a black girl."

Allison laughed out loud. "Uh, yeah. Here's another little secret. Lots of black folk are pretty nerdy, just between you and me. But people—especially white people, but sometimes black people, too—

they expect you to be one way, and when you don't fit into their ideas, they don't know what to do with you."

"I know *exactly* what that feels like," Mel said.

"Well, you can't know what it feels like to be a black nerd girl, but I get what you mean." Allison firmly applied the surgical tape and then cut another section.

"So what are the advantages?" Mel asked.

"What?" Allison bent over and bit her tongue as she placed the last piece of tape. She pressed it firmly onto his skin. "There!" she said. "How does that feel?"

"You said there are advantages to being different," Mel said. "What are the advantages?"

"Well, for one thing, you kind of have x-ray vision, like Superman. You can see things other people can't. And for an architect, I can't think of a better superpower."

The sun was high overhead when Thom finished canvassing the houses. He took refuge in his shop, settling into the driver's seat with an involuntary groan. He took off his cowboy hat and relished the cool air swirling around his crown. His radio crackled to life.

"Adam One, this is Karlstadt."

"Lind here, Karlstadt."

"Okay, Thom, I've got the definitive list—all the Maranatha-themed businesses within a fifty-mile radius of Coleman."

"I take it there's a lot?"

"More than you'd think, if you were not Maranatha-savvy."

"Jesus, come and get me," Thom said. "Okay, I'm beginning to understand the popularity of that weird word." His legs felt numb.

"Got a pen?" Celia asked.

"Jus' a sec," Thom said, and fished out his moleskin. "Okay, ready."

Celia began to rattle off the businesses, pausing at the end of each until Thom said, "Check," and then listing the next. When they were finished, Thom was looking at a list of thirteen businesses.

"That's a lot," Thom said.

"I gave all of them to you, for the sake of investigatory comprehension," Celia said, "But I think we can rule out a few."

"Such as?"

"Businesses that wouldn't likely have a van, for one. Like the Maranatha Nail Salon. I think you can strike that one."

"What's their motto? 'Come Lord, get your nails done?'" Thom asked.

Celia ignored him. "I think the three most likely are the caterer's—they really need a van—"

"Sure," Thom agreed.

"—the electrician, and the car pull."

Thom pursed his lips as he scanned the list. "I'm not connecting all the dots you are, Celia, but those three are as good a place as any, I suppose. Can you give me their addresses?"

Celia rattled off the street locations, which Thom entered into his moleskin with neat, all-capped letters. "Got it. Thanks. And er...dare I ask...how is Jake holding up?"

"He's uh...holding," Celia said.

"Do I want to know more than that?" Thom asked.

"Not if you want to find Barkley," Celia said.

"Then that's enough, I suppose. Lind out." He hung the mic on the clip near the radio and took a deep breath. "Stop one—the caterer's." He entered the address into the GPS and backed Old Bill into the street.

The Maranatha Catering Company was fifteen miles due west, heading toward the Nevada border. Thom didn't notice any of the landscape as it flew by. There was a slowly rotating knot in his gut, and he knew that every minute that passed made it more and more unlikely he'd find Julie—or find her in time. He pressed this out of consciousness as he focused on the task directly in front of him —driving.

The GPS led him to an industrial park—a collection of prefab boxes baking in the desert sun. There wasn't a tree in sight and precious few cacti. Thom checked the number and rolled the SUV around until he found something close. Then he parked, put his hat on his head, checked his gun, and stepped out.

A voice in his head advised caution. If Julie were here, he had every right to expect to be greeted with the smoking end of a rifle. *So be it,* he thought. He considered putting on his kevlars, but the stuff made him sweat profusely. *If the bullet didn't kill me, the vest would,* he thought.

He reached into his breast pocket and pulled out one of the sugar packets. He ripped it open and upended it into his mouth. As he chewed the sugar, he set his boots toward the caterer's pod and began walking. When he arrived at the right number, he stopped and listened. He imagined he might hear Julie struggling, maybe crying out for help, or moaning from a beating. But he heard nothing. He knocked.

For a moment, nothing happened. Then the door swung open, and a woman just a bit older than himself appeared in the doorframe. "What do—you!" The woman's brows bunched with offense. "What do *you* want?"

It seemed like an odd reaction to Thom. The woman acted as if she recognized him. He cocked his head as he looked at her. She did look familiar...

"Taking ten years of my life away from me wasn't enough—now you want another bite at the apple?" the woman spat out bitterly.

"What?" Thom asked.

"What do you want?" the woman repeated more forcefully.

Then Thom remembered. The woman he had arrested nearly twenty years ago had been much younger, much thinner, much prettier. "Agnes?" he asked.

"Ten years ago I never, ever wanted to see your face again," she said. "I still don't."

The details started flooding into Thom's head from somewhere. A voice in his head told him that if an ex-con was employed here, there was a much better chance of hitting pay dirt.

"I'm sorry to disturb you, Ms. Sulley. I'm not here to persecute you or check up on you or harass you in any way. I'm here investigating a completely unrelated case."

She narrowed one eye. She wasn't buying it. *That's a shame,* Thom thought, *because it's the truth.* He removed his hat and ran his right hand through his remaining hair. "Do you mind if I come in? The sun is really starting to warm up."

"I do mind. So unless you have a warrant, you'll need to stay right where you are."

"Do I need a warrant?" Thom asked. "Because that *can* be arranged."

"What. Do. You. Want?" The woman's face was dark with suspicion.

Thom pulled out his cell phone and scrolled to a picture of Julie. "Have you seen this officer?"

The woman barely glanced at the phone. "Nope."

"Look again," Thom said.

Agnes Sulley sighed, rolled her eyes, and then fastened them on the phone. Then she looked away. "Never seen her."

"Are you sure? Look again." Thom ordered.

She didn't. "You deaf? Never seen her."

Thom sniffed. "You cooking?"

"What are you talking about?"

There was the sound of a strangled shriek behind the woman, and Thom's spine jerked upward. He launched himself forward, drawing his service revolver with his right hand, and pushing Agnes aside with his left.

"Hey!" she protested.

He ignored her. Barely looking at her, he snatched up his cuffs from his belt with his left hand and secured Agnes to the horizontal interior door lever. "Stay put. Stay quiet," he said, for all the good it would do. She thrashed and yelled, but he did not hear her. The hair on the back of his neck and arms was at full attention. He held the stock of his revolver with both hands, rounding corners with jerky, sudden movements.

The place appeared to be what it was—a professional kitchen, tidy.

An office space, untidy. There was a line of racks on wheels against one wall. Against the other were ovens and stoves—all of them gleaming stainless steel, except for an ancient-looking cauldron that might have been ornamental. Set into the far wall was a door.

He ran to it, tried it, then threw it open.

Bright lights blinded him.

"Cut! Cut! What the fuck is this?" a voice from within the bright light complained.

Thom kept his gun raised in his right hand, his left shielding his eyes. Slowly, the light resolved into shadowy forms, then into recognizable shapes. Thom blinked, trying to take in what he was seeing. He was staring into the eyes of a goat.

"One goat, $400," Thom repeated, remembering the receipt.

The goat bleated. Then more goaty voices sounded in response. Thom realized that many of those voices belonged to sheep. There was even a cow in one corner. In another corner, an ostrich was chained to a duct by the neck. There was a crazed look in its eye, and it lashed out, trying to kick in his direction. Even though it was a good twelve feet away, Thom took an involuntary step to the side.

There were people there too, and Thom turned to focus on them. There were two cameras held by seedy-looking young men in their twenties. There was also a man with a handle-bar mustache, wearing a cowboy hat, chaps, and absolutely nothing else. Thom noticed the man had an erection that was failing fast.

In front of him were two women on their hands and knees, each of them naked, each one of them over three hundred pounds, and both in striking distance of the cowboy's wilting branding iron. "What the fuck?" the cowboy asked.

"What is this?" Thom asked.

"Should we get up?" one of the large women asked.

One of the men set his camera aside and tossed his long hair as if he were a model. "This is the set of *Fat Girls in a Barnyard VI*," he said.

"You're not fucking any of the livestock, are you?" Thom asked.

"You're thinking of another movie series," the kid answered.

"Have you got—" Thom began, but words failed him. Surely there was some kind of code violation going on here, what with livestock in a food preparation facility. But that was County Health's concern, not his.

"Who's in charge here?" he asked.

"I am!" Agnes Sulley called from the front door. Thom was amazed she could hear him.

"I, uh...huh." Thom put his revolver back in his holster and held up his phone. "Any of you seen this woman?" He showed each of them the picture of Julie, even getting down on one knee to address the kneeling ladies so they didn't have to expose themselves further by standing up.

All of them answered in the negative. Thom put his phone back in his pocket and tipped his hat. "Sorry to...to ruin your take. Uh... carry on." He shut the door behind him. He reminded himself to breathe.

"Goddam it," the woman cuffed to the door said.

"Shut up, Agnes," Thom said, uncuffing her. "You're lucky I'm not calling this in."

"You're not going to call County?"

"I'm not after you, no matter what you think. I'm only interested in..." He caught himself. He looked Agnes in the eye for a brief moment, then he looked away again. "Sorry to bother you."

Peg slid into the booth at Debbie's beside Allison. Ted was already there, in the middle of a story that Peg wasn't sure she wanted to hear —somehow it involved several young men, all of whom were "sassy," a flamethrower, and a flower-arranging contest. Ted nodded at her, but didn't slow down one bit, as he seemed to be at the climax of the story. Peg blocked him out by feigning interest in the specials card on the table. As she did so, she noted that Debbie's was not buzzing as it usually was. There seemed to be the same number of lunch diners, but it was quieter than it should be. *It's subdued*, Peg thought. *Why is it subdued?*

"Howdy Peg," Tali said, spinning in and placing a cup of coffee in front of her before spinning away again.

"Thank you, Tal," Peg shouted after her.

Across the room an argument exploded. Even Ted paused momentarily to take in the scene, but he only missed a beat. Peg watched out of the corner of her eye as Lucy Banning stormed from the restaurant and slammed the door. Peg's eyebrows shot up. She sipped at her coffee, but instantly put it down again. It was too hot.

"Oh, Ted, you're terrible," Allison said, which Peg took as her cue to start listening to her friends again.

"I *was* terrible. Now I just pine for my terrible days," Ted sighed. "They were *wonderful*."

"And that was in seminary?"

"Girlfriend, you have *nooo* idea," Ted shook his head.

Allison cocked her head. "Peg, what's up? You look down."

"Oh...no...just lost in thought. There's a lot going on."

"Would that 'a lot' involve a certain handsome-adjacent man named Phil?"

Peg blushed. "No, that's not part of 'a lot.' We have dinner plans. That is all. Now what's going on?"

"What do you mean?" Allison asked. "Going on with what?"

"This." Peg indicated the whole room with her eyes. Then she looked back at Allison.

"What?" asked Allison.

"Why is everyone quiet? And on edge? Lucy Bannon just—"

"I know, I know, shush," Allison put her hand on her arm. "Use your inside voice."

"I *was* using my inside voice," Peg said.

"You were using your Job-questions-God voice," Ted said. "It's louder than your inside voice."

"Fine," Peg said, almost in a whisper. "Now please tell me what's going on."

Ted and Allison shot each other a glance. *So there is something going on!* Peg thought. She was relieved that her reading of the room wasn't completely out-to-lunch.

"Word is getting around that Troy Swanson is dead," Allison said, dropping her own voice.

"What? You mean the trucker with the cube?" Peg asked, jerking upright.

"Inside voice!" Allison whispered.

Peg glared at her.

"That's the one," Ted said, sipping at his coffee. At his elbow were the containers for two creamers and the discarded husks of four sugar-in-the-raw packets.

"Dare I ask...how did he die?" Peg cocked her head.

"Head-on collision," Ted said.

Peg noticed how carefully Ted was watching her.

Allison added, "His seat belt didn't hold. He smashed like a bug against the inside of the windshield."

Peg blinked, her mouth open. "You mean, just like it was in the... in his cube."

"Exactly so," Ted said. Then he said it again, but slower. "Exactly...so."

"Oh, my God," Peg said. "O my God." She looked up at the diners again, but this time through an interpretive lens that made sense of their nervous restraint. "This is horrible."

"It's a rum day for Mr. Swanson," Ted said, taking another sip. "And a waste. He was a looker."

"I think you're missing the larger point, Ted," Peg said. Just then Tali spun in again, holding three steaming plates. Without a word, she set them in the proper places and once more spun away.

"I didn't even order," Peg said.

"What would you have ordered, if you had?" Allison asked.

"This," Peg conceded.

Allison shrugged. "So you're complaining about...?"

"That's just good service, there," Ted said, pointing at her plate.

"It's a little spooky," Peg said.

"Peg, dear, when you order the same thing two hundred and fifty days in a row, why should anyone expect the two-hundred-and-fifty-first day to be any different?"

"Well, that's precisely my point," Peg said.

"What point?" Allison asked.

"About Troy," Peg said.

"I don't follow," Ted admitted. He reached for a packet of jam.

"Have you been out there, Ally?" Peg said over her shoulder.

"Been out where?"

"To Nyland's farm," Peg clarified.

"Oh. Well, that's all anyone can talk about," Allison said. "But no, I haven't."

"I have. Twice. Ted and I were there last night."

"We were," Ted affirmed.

"And?" Allison asked.

"It was like the fucking county fair," Peg said.

"It was more like Hallowe'en," Ted offered. "There were even costumes."

"Well, it's a big, juicy mystery," Allison said. "And it's kind of a thrilling, spooky treat, isn't it? To glimpse how someone might die."

"But that's what's changed, now," Peg said. She moved some of her soup around with her spoon.

"What's changed, dear?" Ted asked.

"Up until now, when people went out to see these things, they thought, 'Oh, this is all a hoax. But what a lot of goofy, macabre fun!'"

"Are you making fun of my accent?" Ted asked. "Because it's a Boston accent, and you can't do it for shit."

Peg ignored him. "But now…now that Troy died *exactly as his cube predicted he would*…" she trailed off, looking Ted and Allison in the eye in turn.

"People are going to stop thinking it's a joke," Allison said. "They're going to…oh *my*…"

"Right," Peg said.

For several seconds, none of them spoke. Once more the mild volume level of Debbie's unsettled her. If ever there was a place that needed to be buzzy with chatter and activity, this was such a place. Something was deeply off.

"We have to do something," Peg said.

"We could make meat loaf," Ted suggested. "All three of us. We'll open a bottle of Grigio, and all get our fingers in there in the meat. We'll add crazy things, like sweet potatoes and raisins, and—"

"I mean," Peg interrupted him, "we need to do something for the townspeople. Something..." She looked away at some invisible object far beyond Debbie's bright yellow walls. Then she smiled.

"I don't like the look of *that*," Ted said.

"Yesterday, there was a steady stream of onlookers up at that farm," Peg said, her eyes shining. "Today...I think there are going to be more—a lot more. And I suspect, if I'm any judge of these things, that they won't be giggling at these cubes—not now."

"So what are you suggesting?" Allison asked.

"We need a pastoral presence out there," Peg said.

"Out where?" Ted asked, one eyebrow arching.

"At the cornfield. But there's no way just you and I, Ted, can handle all those people." Peg's eyes moved quickly back and forth as she thought. "We'll need to call all the clergy in driving distance—I can do that. Ted, dear, you're good with a spreadsheet. Let's get a schedule going. Let's try to have two of us out there, 24/7."

Ted frowned.

"We need to start immediately," Peg said. "First shift tonight, I think. I'll take it. Ted, maybe we should do this one together—feel it out, think it through, talk it through. What do you say?"

"You think...we should go out to the cornfield, to...stand there and...*be* clergy?"

"Yes."

"What are we going to do? Mass?"

"No, just...be there. Talk to people. Comfort them. Counsel them. Help them deal with their feelings."

"But I am no longer clergy," Ted sniffed.

"'Thou art a priest forever, after the order of Melchizedek,'" Peg quoted. "The men in funny hats revoked your ministry, Ted. Jesus didn't."

Ted looked like he was about to object, but before he could, Allison asked, "How about therapists, then? Or social workers?"

"I don't have those phone numbers," Peg asked.

"No, but I do," Allison said.

"How?" Peg asked.

"Art therapy," Allison said. "I know who comes to sling clay because their therapists prescribed it, and I know who those therapists are, too. And my sister is a social worker."

"That...that's good. Let's call a meeting then, get people ready."

"You're really serious about this, aren't you?" Allison asked.

"Serious as a cancer diagnosis, my dear," Peg said.

"That's not funny, Peg," Ted warned.

"I wasn't kidding," Peg countered.

Just then, Peg sensed a presence at her right elbow. She looked over and was surprised to find a young woman standing near their table. She was about Julie's age and unmistakably native. She stood several feet away, as if fearing that approaching would be impolite, yet obviously waiting to be noticed. Peg cocked her head and met the young woman's eyes. "Oh. Hello. And who are you?"

The young woman took exactly one step forward, and Peg saw in her face a mixture of ferocity and hesitancy. The young woman cleared her throat and said, "Coyote told me to talk to you."

"Who?" Peg asked.

"Who is 'coyote'?" Ted asked.

The young woman's eyes widened; she looked confounded. "Coyote told me you were spiritual leaders. How can you be spiritual leaders and not know Coyote? That would be like a mechanic unfamiliar with a carburetor."

Peg blinked. "I'm sorry, dear. I think your Coyote may have us mixed up with someone else."

"No. He says you are the ones." Her voice was resolute.

"What ones?" Allison leaned over the table a bit to talk past Peg in the booth.

"The ones who need my drum," the young woman said.

"Oh, she's not making any sense at all," Ted said.

Peg held her hand up at Ted.

"Would you like to have a seat?" Peg gestured to the seat next to Ted.

"Here now, we should vote on this," Ted said.

"I'm Peg," Peg held out her hand. Awkwardly, the young woman took it; she shook it as if she were trying to break the neck of a rodent. Peg was relieved when she let go.

"My name is Milala." She eyed Ted suspiciously but climbed into the booth beside him just the same.

"Milala," Peg repeated. "That's a very pretty name. This is my friend Allison. And this is Ted. He doesn't bite."

"Oh, but I *do*," Ted said, not looking at her.

"He won't bite *you*," Peg assured her. "Can we get you some coffee?"

"Thank you, but…I have no money. Co—someone stole my bag last night. In the park."

"Aaand there you have it. Give the urchin a five-spot and send her along her way," Ted huffed.

"Ted!" Peg warned. "The apostles were often without means and were supported by the people in whatever towns they went to."

Ted's eyebrows raised. "*She's* an apostle?"

"What is an 'apostle'?" Milala asked. "I don't know that word. Is it English?"

"It is now. It was Greek, originally. It means someone who has been sent, as in sent by God," Peg said kindly.

"Oh—then yes. I am an apostle," Milala nodded.

Peg and Ted locked eyes. He raised one eyebrow. Peg looked over at the young woman again. She truly did not know what to think. "Um… can I buy you lunch, Milala?"

Milala seemed to consider this. "I'm very hungry, and I have no money. It wouldn't make any sense to say 'no.' So I will say 'yes,' and I will say 'thank you.' But," Milala said, holding Peg's eye. "That is not why I am here." She looked over at Ted. "Many things can be true at once."

"Oh, look at the time," Ted said, pointing to his naked wrist.

"Ted," Peg objected.

"I really should be going," Ted insisted. "We all should, if we're going to get anywhere on Peg's mad project. I'm still not sold on it, mind, but I'll go along because I don't want anyone to say that I sucked the fun out of anything."

"No one says that, Ted," Allison informed him.

"Excuse me, please," Ted said.

Milala scooted down again and Ted got out. Peg rose. "I suppose you're right. We should be going. Milala, I'm going to talk to Talia over there—I'm going to tell her that you can order whatever you like, and I'll pay for it next time I'm in. Don't be bashful."

"By the looks of her, she isn't," Ted said, cracking his back as he rose.

"Don't mind him," Peg said. "And it was a pleasure to meet you." And with that, Peg headed for the cash register, and the others headed for the door.

The day crept by with all the haste of a drugged snail. As Julie sat, she watched the heat rise from the corpses of discarded cars in shimmering waves, distorting her focus on everything behind them. She counted the passage of time not in minutes, but in breaths, and it seemed to her that every now and then she slipped into a place of harmony with the desert around her. She noticed and gave thanks for the cooling breeze, just as she noticed the beetle carrying refuse with indefatigable industry. There was a timeless holiness to this silence, one that she rarely noticed, but which, once experienced, could not be denied.

"This is Mother," she said aloud to herself. And it struck her how very different the goddess, the Great Mother, was from her own mother. Great Mother was calm, impossibly calm, so unlike Peg's fluttering about. She hated the way her mother figured her life out by talking about it—loudly, incessantly, to anyone who would listen. Julie had stopped listening more than a decade ago. It hadn't seemed to her that Peg had gained anything worth talking about since then, so Julie saw no reason to reconsider her assessment. Some people wore their feelings on their sleeves, but her mother shouted them from a bull-horn, and Julie hated her for it. She was also determined to be as different from *that* as it was possible to be.

Mercer had come and gone, come and gone, his eyebrows bunched in concern over some dilemma he did not share with her. An hour ago, he had pulled up a folding chair of his own in the shade of the car wall and fallen asleep, leaning backward against the dented door of a Buick.

The goat bleated. Julie reached over and gave its neck a scratch. Leaning over, though, put pressure on her bladder, and pain shot through her guts. *Okay, I've been patient enough*, she thought. *A girl's gotta pee.* But just as she opened her mouth to wake Mercer and make her demands, the rope just fell away from the goat's collar.

Julie closed her mouth and cocked her head, looking at the end of the rope in her hand. She might not be able to get herself free, but might it be possible to frustrate Mercer's plan just the same? She looped the end of the rope through the goat's leather collar, but did not tie it. All the goat would need to do to get free was simply walk away. It seemed to her the goat was not happy with their situation, so there was a chance that if Julie and Mercer walked away, the goat would too.

"I need that restroom," she said, jumping a bit at the loudness of her own voice.

Mercer's arms were crossed and his chin drooped onto his chest. A cobweb of saliva stretched from his lip to his right boob.

"Hey! Mercer!" Julie shouted. She kicked the car next to her. Her bladder screamed.

Mercer's face screwed up into a scowl even before he opened his eyes. His mouth pursed up as if she'd just promised him an orange and had delivered a cut lime. Finally, he squeezed open one eye. "What?" he croaked.

"Gotta pee. Bad."

"So pee."

"You really think Azathoth is going to want me marinated in my own urine?"

Mercer shrugged.

"You promised me when we got here—" Julie said, her voice taking on a scolding tone.

"All right, fuck, back the fuck down," he said. He leaned forward until all four chair legs were on the ground again, and with a sigh of complaint heaved himself to his feet. He was shaky as he strode toward her. Julie figured the blood must be rushing to his head.

He pulled a pistol from his belt behind him and pointed it at her. Then with his other hand he threw her a set of keys. "Undo yourself," he said. He kept a cautious distance from her, and his gun hand did not waver. She unlocked the cuff around her wrist, and rubbed at it with her other hand.

"Now throw that back to me." She did. "That way, to your left," Mercer said, pointing with the pistol.

Julie turned and began walking. Every step was a new adventure in abdominal pain. She had never let her bladder get this full, this distended before. She vowed never to do so again. But she forced herself forward, thinking desperate and happy thoughts about the toilet bowl soon to come.

She could wait until she rounded a corner in the car labyrinth and make a break for it—but she realized there was no way she could run in her current condition. She could barely stagger. She could just empty her bladder and then run, and for a bit she considered this, but before she could work out a plan, the office building came into view, and all she could think about was the bathroom again.

She didn't remember crossing that final stretch of scorched earth to the office. The next thing she remembered was sitting down on the porcelain bowl, uttering a silent alleluia as her bladder shuddered in relief.

The toilet wasn't filthy, and it worked, which was more than she could say for the sink. But now that her bladder wasn't screaming, she found that her brain worked better as well. She spat on her hands and wiped them on her khakis as she looked around the tiny, grungy bathroom. There was a window up above the toilet, but she judged it was too small for her to squeeze through. She squatted and looked under the sink. And then she smiled.

There, on the wall just behind the U-shaped pipe leading from the drain, was an access panel. She duck-walked to it and felt at the edges of the panel. It was framed with molding, but the cheap plywood of the panel itself shifted when she probed at it. Intuitively, she lifted it up out of its groove, and pushed it backward, into...into what?

The panel disappeared into inky blackness, while at the same time the acrid odor of moldy earth wafted up. It smelled like many small creatures had died and rotted several years ago. It was also cool on her skin.

Without giving it another thought, she dove head first into the black space where the panel had been and surrendered to the tumble. She scraped her head on various pipes and the rusty ends of nails in her descent. In the end, she only fell about two and a half feet, spilling out into the crawlspace between the desert earth and the pre-fab floor of the building.

Ignoring the cobwebs and the rat skeletons, she scanned the perimeter, looking for a way out. Mercer helpfully aided her orientation by knocking on the door of the toilet and shouting. "Hurry up. Don't make me come in there."

She instantly began crawling away from the voice, toward what she now knew to be the far wall of the outbuilding. Her eye was drawn to a larger sliver of light than the many others along the wall, and she saw that the slits were actually the inadequate joins in a shingle skirt that ran the perimeter of the building. She jabbed her fingers into the largest of the openings and pushed, then pulled, then tested its movement to the sides. She felt some give. She pushed with everything she had.

She prized the shingle out and away from the building as the nail that held it bent, forming a makeshift hinge. Careful not to pop the nail out, she squeezed herself into the space the shingle had covered. It wasn't quite large enough, but she shimmied past the other shingles with minimal damage to herself or to the building. Swiftly, she swung the shingle back into its place, still held—however tenuously—by the bent nail.

Looking around, she saw that she was indeed behind the building. Mercer was shouting now, but her brain didn't register his words, only his commanding tone. Pivoting, she saw that there was a wall of ruined cars behind her. She was afraid she'd be seen running along it one way or the other, but she was relieved to see that one of the cars had an open window. The roof had been crushed in, but there was still daylight between the seats and the car's top. She threw herself into the window—which, she now saw, was busted out, not open. She scrambled on her elbows and knees across the bucket seat of an old Ford Falcon, feeling the stick shift press into her gut.

She heard Mercer yelling again, but this time it was closer. She turned and froze. The car's window wasn't tall, but it was as wide as a car window usually was, and framed within it was Mercer's blustering face. It was beet red—either from his blood pressure or from the sun, probably a bit of both. A vein the shape of a hookworm bulged on one side of his forehead.

Julie held her breath as Mercer swore. He then kicked the tire of the car just underneath the one she was hiding in. Then he kicked it again. For a moment, Julie was afraid that Mercer was looking directly at her, but then he looked away again and swore. As soon as he moved out of her sight again, she turned her attention to the other window, now near her head. Except that there was no window—the door had been torn off at some point. Peering into the dim space just beyond the edge of the bench seat, she saw that there was a very slim ribbon of space running between this wall of cars and another wall of cars just inches away. Grabbing the door handle of one of those cars, she lowered herself into the space between the two walls.

She could see that, at many points, these walls made of destroyed cars touched each other, that they were, in fact, leaning against each other. The cars were so irregularly shaped that the cavern she was standing in was actually navigable. There were many tight spots, and she found she had to climb up and over as much as from side to side, but she was relieved to find she could make progress. She followed the little streams of light pouring in between the cars until she found one large enough for her to fit through.

It opened out into another street, bounded on both sides by walls of stacked cars. Julie had no idea where that row led, and she was loath to leave a good hiding spot. But that was when she heard the dogs.

She couldn't tell which direction the sound of the dogs was coming from—only that it was growing louder. She had no doubt the dogs would be able to sniff her out without any difficulty at all, which left her with only one option—to run.

She launched herself into the corridor. Walls made of cars towered over her, twice and sometimes three times her own height, obscuring her vision on all sides. She picked a direction and ran as fast as she was able—and she prayed it was away from the snarling of the fast-approaching dogs.

CHAPTER NINE

Peg stood up and raised her voice above the hubbub. "I'd like to call things to order, please!"

The talking diminished to a low murmur as people scrambled to find their seats in the fellowship hall of the First Congregational Church. A few moments later, even the murmuring had subsided. Peg smiled at the fifteen or so people sitting in folding chairs arranged in a circle. She sat herself then, and folded her hands in her lap.

"Good afternoon, friends. I think most of us know most of us, but there are a few unfamiliar faces." She smiled as warmly as she could. "Why don't we just go around and introduce ourselves quickly?"

They did this. Peg counted four pastors including herself, two priests—one Roman, one Episcopal and female besides—two hospice chaplains, three psychotherapists, one retired rabbi, two spiritual directors, and one art therapy instructor. She might not have been so sure about the last, except that it was Allison, and even if Allison had never had any ministerial training, it was Allison, and she told herself that it would be okay. She was disappointed that Ted wasn't there. She had almost convinced herself to be furious at him, but she still hoped he'd show. *Ah, well,* she told herself. *You have a whole room full of people who did. Time to tend to them.*

"Welcome, everyone," Peg said after the introductions were finished. "I'm Peg Barkley, pastor here at First Congo. Thank you all for coming at such short notice. I'm sure you've all heard about the cubes."

She paused and looked around the circle. There were several nods. "How many of you have seen them?" she asked. Two hands went up. She nodded at Patrick Ney, one of the spiritual directors.

"One of my clients told me...*they*...had seen one, and it had upset *them*," Patrick said. Peg noted his use of the singular "they" in order to protect the gender identity of his client. She approved. "So I went to see for myself," Patrick continued.

Peg noted that his arms were crossed around his chest protectively, as if the man were cold. Yet the Fellowship Hall was plenty warm. She guessed he was hugging himself for another reason.

"It was horrible," Patrick said, staring straight ahead at nothing. "Just...horrible."

"It's the talk of the town," said May Björnson, talking out of turn.

"I've seen a couple of them," Peg said. "You're right. They're horrible. I don't want to endanger the confidentiality of your directee, Patrick, but...are *they* one of the people depicted in one of the cubes?" She winced at the awkwardness of the sentence, but Patrick seemed to track with her. He nodded. She nodded in return. "How are they handling it?" she asked.

"Not well," Patrick responded.

"That's why I've asked you here," Peg said, addressing the whole circle. "Every morning, it seems, there are more of these cubes. And I think the more people see them...especially as they see *themselves* in the cubes...the more of a pastoral crisis we're going to have on our hands."

There were general nods of agreement all around. "So here's what I'd like to propose. I propose we create a schedule, so that we have someone out in that field day and night, say, from 9am to 9pm."

"To do what?" the Roman priest, Fr. Eccles, asked.

Peg scowled at him, since to her mind it was obvious. "When people see those cubes, they're going to be...upset. I think we need to have someone on-site to counsel them, to comfort them, to help them process what they're seeing before..." She trailed off.

"Before what?" Fr. Eccles asked.

"Well, I don't know. Before people start freaking out, I suppose."

Tad Gandy, one of the psychotherapists, sat forward on his chair and interjected. "Yes, this is important. There's going to be a lot of fear, and anxiety, and grief—"

"That's it exactly," Peg said, pointing at him.

"—and the sooner we can help people process it, the less their emotions will...well, spill out in unhelpful ways."

"Yes," Peg nodded.

"Should we talk about some best practices?" the Episcopal priest, Sally Dodge, asked.

"Of course," Peg said. "That would be good."

Presbyterian pastor Randy George cleared his throat. "People are going to say, 'Why is this happening to me?'"

"Yes, they will," Peg agreed

"And the answer to that," Sally Dodge interjected, "is 'I don't know.'"

"It's the truth," Allison said.

There were nods of agreement all around. "We never have answers, anyway—" Randy said.

"Speak for yourself," Fr. Eccles interjected.

Randy continued, "What we have to offer is companionship."

"That's it," said Pastor Tremaine Clay from the National Baptist Church in Coleman.

"I pulled together a few reminders for us," Peg said, reaching under her chair. She passed around the xeroxed papers. "Perhaps we can take turns around the circle reading each one, and then we can discuss whether to amend or add to them."

There was a general murmur of approval, and Peg waited until everyone had a copy. "I'll start, and then we can go clockwise, all right? 'Be yourself and relate person-to-person.'" She nodded to Belle Murtz next to her, one of the spiritual directors.

"'Be ready to listen again and again.' Oh, excellent, I'm good at that."

"'Be respectful.'"

"'Be aware of feelings and non-verbal cues.'"

"'Be comfortable with silence.'"

"'Be genuine.'"

"'Most of all, be there.'"

Peg took a deep breath and savored the silence. Then she opened her eyes. "Would anyone like to add to this? Or tweak anything?" She looked around the circle. Everyone looked grave, but also determined. She was relieved to see it.

"All right, then, let's get that schedule filled out."

Thom let Old Bill roll to a stop within sight of Maranatha Electric. "Jesus," Thom breathed.

A billboard-sized sign announced the place, but there was no freeway for miles. *Protect yourself until Jesus comes*, it read. But it had begun to fade, and it seemed oddly lonely, proclaiming its message for no one to see. But just beneath the sign was the real attraction—a collection of shacks made from scrap lumber and corrugated metal. And surrounding the entire compound: an eight-foot-high chain-link fence with blooms of razor wire adorning its top. There were also large signs every third pole or so reading, "DANGER: ELECTRIC FENCE." There was no attempt at landscaping—just sandy desert within the compound and without.

Thom pulled the SUV further forward and parked parallel to the fence. He put his hat on and got out, wondering what the business owner was so afraid of that he needed an electric fence. What crime could there possibly be out here?

A chain-link gate operated on rollers, he saw, but it too seemed to be electrified. There was no keypad or doorbell. Thom wondered how the proprietor entertained his clientele, shut in like that. He cleared his throat and yelled. "Heyo! Anyone home?"

He waited, but heard nothing but the whining wind and the distant screeching of buzzards. He yelled again, this time more loudly. The desert was still. He reached for a packet of sugar and tore it open. He knocked its contents back quickly and chewed.

Then Thom saw some movement. A wall moved away from one of the corrugated roofs, and a man stepped out of the space he'd created. Without looking at Thom, he carefully pushed the wall back to where it had been. Only then did he straighten himself and look around.

At first Thom thought it was just a kid, but then realized it was a young man. The man waved at Thom. Hesitantly, Thom waved back. The young man smiled, and then looked away and trudged off across the yard. Thom watched as he disappeared into another shack.

Then Thom jumped as the gate lurched and began to roll away to his right. *Good thing I have a good heart,* Thom thought. The young man reappeared and began to walk toward the gate. "I'm Thom Lind, Inyo County Sheriff," Thom said as soon as the man was within earshot.

"I am the electrician," the young man said. The kid was wearing trousers, a long-sleeved shirt and a long black pea coat. His hair was thin, stringy, and almost unnaturally red. The skin around his eyes was dark, slightly discolored. The eyes themselves seemed a bit too small for his face. "But you can call me Nerf."

Thom blinked. "Is your name Nerf?"

"No. It's Albert. But my pa calls me Nerf. He liked them squishy balls. Guess I was squishy, once-upon-a-time."

"Do you have a last name, Nerf?"

"Castillo."

"I'll just call you Mr. Castillo then."

The man laughed and covered his mouth with his sleeve. "That's my pa."

"Uh...what's your pa?" Thom asked.

"Mr. Castillo. Nobody called me that before. That's my pa."

"Ah. Well, yeah, I remember that moment." Thom tried to smile sympathetically. "Is your pa home?"

"He's over there," the young man pointed to a silver trailer set off by itself. Thom could see a flower box full of dead daisies hanging just beneath its rear window. "But I'm the electrician now."

"Ah. Your dad taught you the trade, then?"

"He did."

"Tell me, Mr. Castillo, do you have a van?"

"Can't be an electrician without a van," the young man smiled at him. The smile seemed genuine.

"Can you show me the van?"

The young man looked both pleased and surprised. "Sure thing. This way."

Thom entered the compound and jumped a bit when the gate lurched to life behind him, rolling back into place. Being cut off from Old Bill made Thom feel a bit queasy, but he bit down on that feeling and fell into pace beside the young man.

He led Thom behind another of the many shacks and pointed. Thom looked up to see a white van, with "Maranatha Electric" printed in bright red on the side, alongside the image of a thunderbolt being thrown from heaven. Thom stared at the lettering and wondered if the red might have looked black under the amber streetlights in the kid's photograph. *Maybe,* he thought. "Uh...Mr. Castillo, can I take a look inside the vehicle?"

The young man's eyebrows shot up, but he didn't complain. Instead, he simply stepped forward and opened the sliding side door of the van.

"May I?" Thom asked, pointing at the van.

"Help yourself, Sheriff," the kid said.

Thom reached into his pocket and pulled out two latex gloves. Patiently, unhurriedly, he put them on, then approached the open door. Stooping slightly, even though he didn't need to, Thom looked inside the van.

It was what one might expect from an electrician's van. Cords hung from fasteners along the wall. Thom saw the dark green screen of an ancient oscilloscope. There were many boxes, some stacked neatly, and some looking like they'd just been tossed in. Thom moved a few of them to get a clear view of the floor. There was no blood, no hair, nothing that might indicate the van had been used for anything other than electrical jobs.

"Every now and then you need an electrician," the kid said behind him. "Everyone does."

Thom turned away from the van, pulling off the gloves and replacing them in his pocket. "That is, unfortunately, very true. Thank you, Mr. Castillo." He was about to say, "That will be all," but something stopped him. His gut told him something was off, and his gut was rarely wrong. "Before I go, I'd like to say hello to your father."

"Are you a friend of pa's?" the young man asked, his face opening up in a look of wonder.

Thom realized that the kid must worship his old man. "No, but... I'm an admirer."

"I get that. There's no one like my pa." The young man waved him away from the van. "He's set up over here."

Thom fell into step with the kid as they traversed the compound. Before they'd gone three strides, Albert said, "You've lost someone. I can tell."

Thom stopped and looked at him. There was nothing but compassion on the kid's face. He seemed sincere.

Warily, Thom continued walking. "You a religious man, Mr. Castillo?"

"No, not so's you'd notice. But my pa is. Thinks the world of Jesus. He's always talking about him coming to stay with us. We've got a whole shack set up for Mr. Jesus. Never been slept in. I'm beginning to think my pa likes Mr. Jesus more than Mr. Jesus likes my pa."

Thom stopped again and looked Albert Castillo in the eye. He tried to gauge whether the young man was fucking with him. He didn't know, and that troubled him. He could usually tell.

"Just through here," the kid pointed at the silver trailer with the flower boxes. "I'll wait here."

Thom nodded—the trailer wasn't big enough for two, let alone three. He ascended the two steps into the trailer.

His nostrils noticed it first—the sickly-sweet smell of rotten flesh, almost gone but not quite. The trailer was awash in candle light, accompanied by strings of Christmas lights draped over the concave ceiling of the trailer.

A bed filled up most of the space. And on that bed was a corpse. Thom had no doubts about that. The skin was ghostly white with a tinge of purple, and in some places it had begun to turn gray. There was still evidence of advanced seborrhea covering the man's forehead and the front of his scalp. He was dressed in a suit that might have been fashionable in the 1970s, brown with velvet lapels. His wizened hands were folded one atop another over his chest.

Thom's mind raced. Could the kid not know his father was dead? Then how to explain the baling wire? Just then, Thom wondered if perhaps Albert was of diminished capacity in some way. That made sense of a good number of things.

Thom's brows knit into a frown as he descended the steps.

"Did pa say anything to you?"

Thom looked sideways at the young man. "Does he talk to you, son?"

"Not anymore. I think he's...mad at me."

"I don't know how to say this to you, but...I think your father is deceased."

Albert looked confused. Thom tried again. "Son, I think your father has...passed on. I think he is...well, I think he's dead."

Albert looked at his feet. "I was afraid of that. But I didn't want to disturb him, just in case I was wrong. He has a temper."

Thom clapped a hand on Albert's shoulder. "It looks like Jesus *was* here, after all. And he took your pa to live somewhere else. He just... left that old husk of a body behind."

The kid looked distressed. Thom knew a call to social services was in order. He just wished it didn't have to be now.

"Albert, do you know someone else who can come stay with you? Like an aunt or a cousin or someone?"

Albert shook his head. "But I was just about to open a can of beans. Do you want some?" Thom opened his mouth to thank him and decline, but Albert continued. "I'm hungry. You must be hungry, because it's lunchtime. And you should stay for lunch because you look as lonely as I—" The kid's voice cracked and he looked away.

"It's going to be okay, Albert. I...some beans would be fine."

The kid's face brightened. He hurried away toward one of the shacks. Thom reached for the microphone attached to his epaulet. "Adam One to Karlstadt."

"Go, Adam One," came Celia's tired voice.

"Celia, I need social services to send someone out to Maranatha Electric, pronto. We're also going to need a coroner and a bus. But... make sure it's in that order. We need the social worker first."

"Copy that. You okay?"

"Weirded out, but okay."

"Any progress on Julie?"

"I wish I could say yes, but..."

"I'll get on the horn to social."

"Thanks."

Thom sighed and began looking around the yard. It was inconceivable that the kid lived there alone, surrounded by such squalor. He bit his lip and shook his head as he sized up the array of shacks before him. It looked like a stiff wind might just flatten the whole collection. Curious, Thom stepped into one of them. A naked bulb hung from the center of the room. The floor was dirt, and the walls and ceiling were corrugated metal. An abused selection of mis-matched cabinetry formed a makeshift workbench that ran the length of three of the four walls. Beside the door, along the fourth wall, was a row of contraptions Thom could not identify. At first, he thought they were yard equipment, because they were shaped more or less like weed-whackers. But there was no rotator at the end of them, just a ceramic knob wound with wire.

"I got beans," a voice at his elbow said. Thom jumped at the sound of it.

"Holy shit, Mr. Castillo. You scared the Jesus bugs out of me."

"I hate Jesus bugs. Itchy." He smiled. "I got your beans. They're hot, though, so you have to sing to them before you can eat them. Oh, and I got Cheez-its. I love Cheez-its."

"Oh...okay, then. Thanks for the tip."

"They're on the stump. And I brought you a spoon. It's *pretty* clean."

"Are you having some, too?"

"I thought it would be fun to watch you eat. I've never seen anyone but my pa chew before. I can eat later."

"Uh-huh." Thom nodded. "Albert, can you tell me what these are?" He pointed to the things that were clearly not weed-whackers.

"Oh, yeah. I made those!" His face brightened. He was obviously proud of his handiwork.

"They're...uh...what are they for?" Thom asked.

"Uh, well, I never thought of a name for them. And I don't rightly know what you might use them for. From now on, though, I think I'm going to use them to keep Mr. Jesus away before he takes me away from my body, too."

"How does that work, exactly?"

"Like this. You put on this glove—you want to be sure to put on the glove or...pissshhh!" He made a motion like an atom bomb exploding.

"Gloves, check," Thom said.

And then the kid did put on a glove. He swung one of the heavy contraptions into the cradle of his arm, and Thom saw how it balanced against his forearm. The thing was about four feet long, and about four inches around. "It's mostly battery," Albert said, pointing to the part closest to his body. "But here I've got a voltage regulator that steps it up—"

"How much?" Thom asked. "How much does it step it up?"

"Forty times."

Thom whistled.

"This here connects with anything metal. I've been calling it my lightning machine. See here." Albert stepped outside and Thom followed. Albert pointed the knobbed end of the device toward a pile of scrap metal near the fence. Thom jumped as a blast of blue electricity arced between the knob and the scrap. It only lasted a couple of seconds. Afterwards, Thom saw that smoke was rising from a tuft of grass near the scrap metal.

"That's...impressive," Thom said. "And dangerous."

"I was actually trying to solve a different problem, but this was too much fun."

Thom understood that kind of fun. Anyone who frequented a gun range knew it. "Mr. Castillo, what would happen if you pointed that at a person?"

Albert's eyes widened, and he shot a look over his shoulder at the silver trailer. Then he seemed to remember something. "Well, there's a couple rheostats here," Albert pointed at the midsection of his lightning machine. "At the highest setting...I suppose it could really hurt someone. But if you turned the amperage down, even if you kept the voltage up, it would make someone fall down and black out and maybe make their tongue bleed."

"That sounds like you speak from some experience," Thom said.

Albert gave him a sheepish grin.

"Just...don't point that at people, okay?" Thom said.

Albert nodded noncommittally. Thom sighed. "Okay, Mr. Castillo. I...I have to go. A nice lady from Social Services is going to be here soon. And the coroner is going to come and...take proper care of your pa."

Albert nodded. He looked momentarily sad. The end of his lightning machine drooped nearly to the ground.

Thom continued, "I've...one of my...a friend of mine is in trouble, and I have to find her."

"Her is a pronoun denoting the female gender," Albert said.

"That's...right," Thom said.

"I've never met a female gender-person before," Albert said.

"You..." Thom stopped. "Don't you...?"

"Pa drove the van out. I hold down the fort. It's my job."

"Ah. Well. Females. They...uh...it will be a whole new world for you, son. A whole...new...confusing...upside-down world."

Albert blinked. "Ain't you gonna eat your beans?"

"I think the beans were secretly your supper all along," Thom said. "Isn't that right?"

Albert nodded. "The Safeway delivery man doesn't come until Tuesday."

"And all you got is beans?"

Albert nodded.

Thom put his hand on the young man's shoulder. "Social Services is going to fix you right up."

"Is that good?" Albert asked.

Thom didn't answer that at first. He removed his hat and wiped the sweat from the top of his head. Then he put it back and said, "It's what has to happen."

Thom knew Albert didn't understand—how could he? But the kid seemed resigned to whatever fate had in store for him. It had to be better than the isolation of the yard. Perhaps, deep inside, the kid knew that. Thom hoped that was true.

"I can't wait for them to get here. My friend is in trouble. I need to leave now. Can you open the gate, please?"

"I'm sorry you have to go. We had fun, didn't we?" Albert asked.

Thom affirmed what he could. "It was very nice meeting you."

In silence, they walked toward the gate. Albert fished a remote from his pocket and soon the gate was rolling backward along its track. Thom tipped his hat.

"Oh, wait, Mr. Sheriff. Always give them your card." He fished a wrinkled business card from his breast pocket and handed it to Thom.

"Tom Castillo," Thom read. "Your pa and I have the same name."

Albert brightened at this information. "It must *mean* something."

"No. No, it doesn't mean anything. It just is."

Thom held his hand out, and was relieved that Albert knew what to do with it. The kid's grip was firm, solid. Thom walked out toward Old Bill. As he climbed into the cab, he watched Albert waving to him. He felt a twinge of sorrow, both for how the kid had been living, and for how wholly and completely his little world was about to be blown up. "You might as well shoot it with a lightning machine," Thom said to the confines of his cab.

Julie ran. She could hear the dogs, but they were dim and distant. She was grateful Mercer hadn't thought to take her boots, as she planted one in front of the other with military regularity. She adjusted her breathing for a marathon rather than a dash and followed the long line of cars as it slowly curved eastward.

She had no idea where she was relative to the opening, but it could be that the fences around the place had some porous sections here and there—if so, she was determined to find them. *Just one*, she reminded herself. *I only need one opening.*

And then the path through the cars ended. Julie stopped, staring at a solid wall of cars ahead of her. "Dead end," she breathed, and whipped around. She turned again, reminding herself to look for little spaces where she might slip through. She didn't find one.

She made a sign to alert the Goddess that she needed help. Then she began to jog back in the direction she had come. When she came to a place where she could make a turn, she took the path she had not already come down. She was grasping at straws, she knew, but she had no other ideas.

She knew why magickians did what they did. It was like any other heroic human endeavor. No one climbed Everest because it was fun, or useful, or because it made sense to do so. They climbed it because it was there, and they could. They did it for glory, for fame, to stir-fry their own tender ego. These magickians were no different, so far as she could tell. At least Mercer wasn't. She thought of his lazy eye and shuddered.

The dogs were closer now. She could hear not only their barks and whines, but their panting. Julie darted from one corridor of cars to the next, hoping beyond hope to catch a glimpse of the entrance. But at every turn she saw nothing but more cars. She began to wonder if the rows of cars really was patterned on a labyrinth. In a flash, her brain superimposed an 11-circuit *Chartes petit* labyrinth on the wrecking yard, but it was a fancy. The rows of cars did not correspond to the *Chartes* route so far as she could see. She shook her head to clear it and forced herself to think.

She froze when she saw the tail of a dog flash by in the distance. She darted to one wall and hugged the chrome bumper of the second car in a stack, looking for a hiding place. She found one—a narrow gap between a Cadillac and a much shorter compact. She darted for it, and disappeared into the wall of cars once more.

And just in time, it seemed. The barking was closer now, and more urgent. For the first time, she paused to wonder just how many dogs there were, and what they would do to her if they cornered her. It occurred to her that she was more worried about the dogs than she was Mercer. The dogs were a primal force of nature, they were dogs being dogs, doing what they were trained to do, what they had been bred to do for millennia. But Mercer was just an asshole meth-head. She wasn't afraid of him. Him, she could deal with.

She backed up as far as she could go but realized the space she'd entered was the metal equivalent of a cave, not a passage. There was no space here to move to the left or the right, there was no further back to go. There was only the small gap, filled now with her sweat, her heat, and the sound of her own breathing.

The dogs were sniffing at the Cadillac, now. They had caught her scent; they had treed their possum. Julie swore and as quietly as possible, felt at the space around her, hoping her fingers might find a passage where her eyes could not.

But she found none. Instead, she saw Mercer's face peering into the darkness that blanketed her. Somehow she was able to pivot in the small space, and aimed a kick at his face. He stumbled back and tripped over the dogs, barking now with frenzied urgency.

She raised her leg, ready for another shot at Mercer's face. This time he'd get the heel; she was positioned for maximum kick. But he did not put his face into harm's way again. Instead, she heard the report of a shotgun blast—and it was very near.

The dogs whined and their frenzy diminished in the wake of the explosion. Holding her breath, Julie heard a new voice—one that she did not recognize. "Death...is certain. We gonna kill you later, or we gon' kill you now. Makes no nevermind to me which. I still got this shotgun in there, I pull the trigger, you shot full of lead. Just is. Easy to do. An' I will, 'cause I don't care for shit. This one cares for shit—" Julie imagined that he must be referring to Mercer. "But me...not me. So you can stay in there or not. I shoot you or not. All up to you."

Julie held her breath, listening as she heard the man crack his 12-gauge and insert two fresh shells. She heard the solid snap of the stock moving back into place. "Fuck," she breathed. "Coming out!" she yelled.

She knew the dogs must be on leashes, or they would have already rushed in and begun to tear at her. She sniffed, swallowed, then raised her hands as high as her ears and began to move out of the metal cave.

She squinted at the sunlight as she passed into the corridor of cars. First, Julie saw Mercer, clutching at the leads of three snarling dogs, all of them mutts with boxy heads betraying pit bull somewhere in their lineages. They leaped at her, but were jerked shy by their leads. Mercer's eyes were wild with panic—even the lazy one—and a red welt lit up his cheek.

Julie heard the shotgun click again and looked over her shoulder. The driver had her directly in his sights.

"What do you want to do?" Mercer asked him.

"Open her up. Right here." The man was panting.

"The Old Ones don't want dead meat. They like their blood fresh."

"I don't give two fucks and an apron for your shitball cult. She's a *cop*. You brought her here, to *my* property. You fucked this up, but I gotta make this right. She *dies* here."

"Yes, okay, but...at the right time. Please!" She watched the older man waver. The end of the shotgun vibrated with his fear. She understood. He was right to be afraid. Cops frowned upon one of their own going down. It was the death penalty without any hope of clemency. Mercer was just stupid, but this man knew just how stupid the magickian was, and he wasn't taking any chances. Julie realized that Mercer was dangerous in the same way as a cat with its tail on fire was dangerous—running blind and mostly unconscious of the damage it was doing. But this man was more dangerous, because unlike the clueless magickian, this man *knew* what he was doing.

Just then, Julie heard the sound of bleating. She looked to her left and saw the goat, free of its lead, walking alone down the center of the corridor between the walls of cars. It walked with resolution, calm and unhurried, almost as if it were in a religious procession.

All three humans stood as though frozen, and watched it pass by, spectators at a very exclusive parade. The dogs barked incessantly, straining against their leashes. With another bleat, the goat ambled past them, continuing its languid advance until it disappeared around the curve of the corridor.

Julie felt a moment of pride as it passed. She half expected the old man to shoot it and was relieved when the goat disappeared from view, very much alive, at least for now.

"If'n you got cuffs, boy, now is the time to use them," the old man said, his shotgun still trained on Julie.

Mercer tied the dogs' leads to the sideview mirror of one of the cars, and flipped a pair of handcuffs out of his belt. "Turn around," he said. Julie did. She felt the cuffs bite into her wrists as he closed them.

"Those are too tight," she complained. But he didn't respond. Instead, he shoved her into the corridor. "Move," he said, waving in the direction the goat had come from.

Julie nodded and began to walk. Just then she heard the sound of a car's horn echoing through the corridor. "Shit," Mercer said. "I'm not ready for them. Thanks to you."

"Ready for who?"

"Looks like your party's here," the old man said. "You better keep 'em under control."

"Or?" Mercer asked, his defiance sounding pathetic.

"I got me dogs. I got me guns. I got me desert. You got shit."

"Guns? You got more than that one?"

"More? Son, who do you think you're dealing with? I got this gun here. I got one in my boot holster. I got another behind my back, tucked into my belt."

"That's a lot of—"

"I got four antique Maxim single-barrel recoil-activated machine guns in stationary tripods aimed at every entrance. They're running 7 x 57 mm Mauser shells and can shoot 600 rounds per minute at a muzzle velocity of 744 yards per second. They're all wired into a remote gadget I got in my pocket. Fill your friends so full of holes even their dental records will be useless. So let's not forget who is in charge, here, amigo. You rented the place for an evening, but I am the proprietor. Don't know what you're going to do with your goats and your cop-girls. Don't care. But you're not going to fucking cross me or you'll find yourself drooling in a nursing home, sucking Jell-o and picking buckshot out of your liver with chopsticks."

Julie nodded. This changed the lay of the land. "I'll go quietly. You won't have further trouble from me," she said. She watched the old man as one of his eyes narrowed.

"Hey!" She heard a voice call over the Grand Canyon of cars. "Where is everyone? Let's get the party *started*!"

———

Peg was feeling sleepy, and midafternoon sleepiness was the worst. She wondered if she should make a detour to Debbie's to get a cup of coffee. Then she decided she'd had more coffee than was good for her already. At the stoplight she paused and looked down. A single brown feather shuddered near her shoe. She reached down and picked it up. A smile broke out on her face as she studied it. The afterfeathers, she saw, were white, as were the downy barbs near the calamus. She suddenly wished she knew enough about birds to know what sort of feather it was. She raised it high over her head and released it, watching it drift on the breeze.

She crossed the street, then, feeling similarly lifted in spirit. The feather reminded her of the native girl—what was her name? *Milala*, the voice in her head said. *Milala*, she repeated silently. She was a strange one. She knew friends—and Ted was one—who would say all native people seemed strange, but Peg did not agree with this. She had made it a point to get to know some of the Yokuts in the area, and she found them to be warm and charming, if a bit insular. But Milala was cut from different cloth, she sensed, and she could not yet discern the young woman's stripes.

What haunted her was that Milala talked about Coyote the same way Peg talked about Jesus. Her heart sensed a kinship there that longed to be explored. *Lovers seek out other lovers, because only lovers understand,* she remembered hearing once. Was that something Rumi had written? She didn't remember. Was Milala a lover then? Peg wasn't sure, and warned herself that perhaps she was projecting what she wanted to see. *I'm lonely for other mystics,* she realized, and that thought almost made her stumble.

She saw a bench near the Feed & Tack and headed toward it. She sat, bent over, and rubbed at her ankle. *It's okay,* she told herself. She returned to the thought that had caught her up. "I'm lonely for other mystics," she said the words out loud, just to gauge the truth of them. She said it again and listened to her bones.

She decided it was true, but not the whole truth. "I'm lonely," she said, and left it at that. And as soon as she'd said the words, they rang true, just as they were. It wasn't about mysticism, she realized, it was about friendship, kinship, being touched, being loved.

She felt her throat swell up then. She had Ted, but Ted's intimacy was surrounded by barbs—trying to cozy up to Ted was like snuggling with a porcupine. It was possible, it just wasn't enjoyable or sustainable. She thought of her daughter; instantly, her heart ached. She wondered where Julie was, what she was doing, who she was loving... "Not me," she said out loud.

She had enjoyed meeting with the other clergy, but it had been professional, not social. Then she reminded herself that she was having dinner with Phil. She brightened at the thought of it, a little artificially. She dared not get her hopes up, and yet... Phil was bright. She thought him attractive, in a shabby way that appealed to her. He was kind, or at least he had always seemed so to her. He was also a Christian man—a Methodist. That was alright, so long as he didn't bring the episcopacy into their bedroom.

She gasped. "Too soon," she said out loud, scolding herself internally. It was far too early in the relationship to go there. *But oh, how I want to go there,* she thought. To feel a man's hands on her with tender desire, to feel his lips, his warmth beside her own. She closed her eyes and breathed in the image.

Her phone blared. "Jesus on a tortilla," she swore, and fished in her bag for it. Her heart skipped a beat when she saw the name on the touchscreen: Phil. What were the odds? She wondered then if her New Thought friends were right, and thoughts do actually create reality. What if thinking of Phil had summoned his call? Allison would never let her live it down if she voiced the possibility.

She passed a worried hand over her hair and then reminded herself that Phil couldn't see her on the telephone. She punched the green button. "Phil!" she said, instantly regretting that she sounded more thrilled than she ought.

"Peg, I'm so glad I caught you," he said, in a voice that betrayed… what? Depression? Sadness.

"Oh no, what's wrong?" Peg asked.

"I…Peg, I'm so sorry, but I think I need to cancel our date tonight."

Peg took a deep breath. "That's okay. Is everything all right?"

"It's…complicated."

"Oh. I'm sorry to hear that. Do you want to reschedule?"

There was a long pause. Her heart shrank with each passing second. "I, uh, I've just been thinking…that maybe now isn't a good time for me to…you know…start a relationship."

She felt her ire stir. "Phil, you asked *me* out."

"I know I did, and…jeez, Peg. I'm sorry. I really like you, but…it's just not a good time."

Peg counted to ten. She felt her throat swell, and she swallowed to soothe it. "What happened?"

"I…well, nothing *happened*. I just…I'm sorry, Peg." The line went dead.

Peg removed the phone from her ear and stared at its blank screen. She was tempted to throw it into the street, but mastered herself. She put the phone in her bag and sat staring at the quilting shop across the street. *What did I do?* the voice in her head wondered.

What did I say, or didn't say? In what way was I not what Phil was looking for?

Another voice countered, *Maybe it isn't about you. Maybe this is about Phil.*

She reminded the voice that this was the stupidest excuse in the world.

It might also be true. Or... And then she knew.

"Goddam it, Ted," she whispered.

––––––––––

Deena Knolls climbed the steps of the sheriff's office and opened the door. She was surprised to find the place unlocked and utterly empty. For a few minutes, she just turned around in place, looking for any sign of life. "Holy Christ, what happened to our police force?"

"Coming!" sang Celia's familiar voice. A moment later, she emerged from the break room holding a steaming pot of coffee.

"Thank God. I thought maybe you'd all been raptured," Deena said. "And since precious few of you are Bible-thumpers, it confused me."

"No, our heathen asses are still reliably earth-bound, I assure you, Mayor. We are, however, very very busy at the moment."

"Not too busy for coffee," Deena noted.

"All busy-ness recedes into diminishing returns without coffee."

"That sounds like a corollary to some bullshit law of thermodynamics," Deena said.

"If I had more than a high-school education, it might be." Celia dropped into her chair like a sack of rutabagas. "How can I help you, Mayor?"

"I've been hearing a lot about these...cubes."

"I thought Thom called you about that." Celia raised one eyebrow.

"Uh...he did. But in my head, I put it in the room marked, 'art oddities.' I hadn't put it in the room marked, 'civil unrest.'"

"Ah. Yeah, so did we, at first," Celia confessed.

"It's all anyone is talking about."

"Really? Well, I haven't been to Debbie's in a week, so—"

"Not just Debbie's. At the gas station, at the grocery store, at the tractor supply, at the beauty parlor, and although I can't say with authority, I imagine it's the same at the barber shop. I got people calling me morning, noon, and night."

"That does not surprise me," Celia said.

"Celia, is this something I need to worry about?"

Celia tapped the end of a pen against her desk blotter and considered. Finally, she leaned forward on her elbows and said. "Deena, honestly? I have no idea."

Deena nodded slowly. "Thank you for your candor. Well, I'd be grateful if you kept me...I don't know...closer in the loop."

"You want me to update you instead of Thom?"

"Is that allowed?"

"It is if you say it is. You're the mayor."

"But Thom is the sheriff, and I don't interfere with police business."

"I tell you what. Next time Thom checks in, I'll ask him about it. How's that?"

Deena nodded. "So, what are they?"

"What are what?"

"The cubes?"

Celia bit her lip. "I'll give it to you straight, Mayor. We haven't got a clue. But I think you'd do well to go up to the Nyland place and see 'em for yourself."

"But I...yes. I should do that. I—"

She suddenly heard shouting. She looked toward the street with a frown.

"What the holy hell is going on out there?" Celia asked.

"I don't know," Deena said. "I guess I'll find out."

The shouting continued as Deena opened the door and let herself out.

A small circle of people had gathered in the center of Main Street—about twenty, perhaps more. *Whatever this is, it happened fast*, Deena thought. She pushed through the onlookers until she found herself at the center of the crowd's interest. She stopped. She blinked. "Jesus Christ," she swore.

Before her were two Klansmen, complete with pointy hoods, sheets, and insignia. Their hoods concealed their faces, and even though it was broad daylight, they both held flaming torches. Directly blocking their way was Allison Williams, her face taut and her hands balled into fists.

The crowd had completely surrounded the Klansmen, blocking any escape. They couldn't go forward without contending with the town's most prominent African-American citizen, but neither could they retreat.

Deena laid a tentative hand on Allison's shoulder. "Allison, what's going on here?"

Allison's face was full of fury, but as soon as she broke her gaze away from the Klansmen and recognized Deena, her shoulders lowered and her hands relaxed. "Deena, I—"

"No need to explain yourself," Deena put her hand on Allison's back, more confidently now. "I get it. Tell me what happened."

"Just a peaceful demonstration," one of the Klansmen said. "It's my God-given right as an American."

"Terrorism is *not* a God-given right," Allison snapped, her ire reigniting.

Deena decided to let her be—if anyone had a right to her anger, it was Allison. But she did step into the space between the artist and the Klansmen. "Let me guess, one of you is Miles Pointer. Am I right?"

"He is." The Klansman on the right pointed to the one on his left.

"Jesus, Shredder, why not give her my driver's license, too?" the one on the left snapped.

"Hello, Miles," Deena smiled. It seemed like a quarter of the town was watching her. That was all right. "And your name is 'Shredder'? Did your mother give you that name?"

"Uh...no ma'am. I got it 'cause I was state skateboarding champion in '06."

"Ah. That will be easy to look up, then. Thank you for your cooperation."

"Who are you?" Miles Pointer asked.

"We've spoken before, Mr. Pointer," Deena said. "I denied your application for a march, as I recall. Yet here you are, in direct violation of my decision."

"We have a right to peacefully protest the systematic dismantling of White American culture," Miles raised his voice.

"Not in this town, you don't. Not like this, not if I say you don't."

"You can't trample on my constitutional rights as a white American."

"You have no constitutional rights as a *white* American, only as an American."

Pointer's voice was wet with poison as he leaned in and said, "What's the difference?"

Just then Deena noticed Celia at her elbow. In her left hand she held a flip-pad that she recognized from the last time she'd gotten a parking ticket. In her right hand was a pen. Celia gave her a wink and a nod.

A silent chuckle sent a shudder through her. She'd never thought of her and Celia as a dynamic duo, yet here they were. "Mr. Pointer," she said, raising her voice so that the whole crowd could hear her. "Mr...Shredder, for now." She waited until a hush came over the crowd in anticipation of her next words. *Oh yes, I can still work a room,* she thought, and smiled. "The first charge will be holding a demonstration in want of a permit—" she looked over to Celia, who dutifully entered the charge in the ticket book. Deena had no idea whether a ticket book was a lawful place to record such charges, but she was reasonably certain that neither Pointer nor Shredder knew that either. "The second is disturbing the peace. The third is criminal intimidation."

"Intimidation? How do you figure?" Pointer objected.

Deena turned to Allison, who was no longer brandishing her fists, she was relieved to see. "Ms. Williams, did you feel intimidated?"

"Damn straight," Allison said.

"Well, there you have it."

Celia cleared her throat. "I'm just gonna ask you gentlemen to step into the sheriff's office so we can get you properly processed and the charges duly recorded in anticipation of the sheriff's investigations. This way, please." With that, Celia turned on her heels and began to waddle toward the sheriff's office. A pathway opened up in the sea of people to allow her passage.

Deena looked to the two hooded men and waved them after her.

"I'm not going anywhere," Pointer said.

In answer, the crowd instinctively took a step forward, closing the circle around the two men menacingly. Shredder's head sagged, and he began to shuffle after Celia.

"And you," Deena said. She wished she could see Pointer's eyes.

"This ain't over, Mayor," he said.

"It is today, asshole," she answered.

"Goddam it, Jorge, we need to stand together."

"Not here," Jorge said. "She'll hear you."

"But—"

"The barn." Jorge said. Before Ellen could protest, he opened the bedroom door and clomped down the stairs.

Ellen cursed again and followed him. She ground her teeth all the way to the barn and realized that her head hurt. She was probably giving herself a headache.

Jorge held the barn door open for her. He looked around before he closed it again, as if to see if they had been followed.

"She's in her room, playing that...moody music."

He shut the barn door. "All right now, you were saying?"

Ellen put her hands on her hips. "I'm saying we need to present a united front."

Jorge leaned against his workbench and crossed his arms over his chest. "Because?"

"Because otherwise we'll just confuse her further—she's confused enough."

"Seems to me she knows her own mind."

Ellen's mouth opened, but at first she only spluttered. "Jorge Wulf-son, are you telling me you approve of this...this...this abomination?"

"I've seen abominations in my day, bumble-bee. This isn't one of them."

"Then what do you call it?"

"What it looks like to me is a teenager trying to figure out who she is." He shrugged. "I seem to remember you gelling your hair out into spikes and wearing a safety pin through your nose."

"For about five minutes!" Ellen clenched her fists.

"Well, that's just my point, bumble-bee," Jorge said in a voice that was maddeningly calm. "If we ignore this, then if it's just a fad, she moves on. If we fight her on it, she's going to dig her heels in because she won't want to admit she's wrong."

"She's a stubborn cuss." Ellen nearly spat.

"Uh-yup. Wonder where she gets that?"

Ellen scowled at him.

"What did the preacher say, when you talked to her?" Jorge asked.

Ellen shifted and avoided his eyes. "Pretty much the same thing you just did. But...dammit, Jorge, I felt like she was patronizing me. Really, she was on Melinda's side the whole time."

"Seems to me we should all be on Melinda's side."

"I—" Ellen spluttered some more. When she found her tongue again, she said, "I only want what's best for her!"

"For her...or for you?" Jorge asked.

"What are you implying?"

Jorge shrugged. For the first time, he uncrossed his arms, resting both palms on the workbench he leaned against. "I'm not implying anything, bumble-bee. I'm coming right out and saying it. If Melinda wants to be a boy, you'll be embarrassed in front of your friends."

"Of course I'll be embarrassed. It's a shameful thing, what she's doing!"

"Why?" Jorge asked. He cocked one eyebrow.

"I shouldn't have to explain it to you, Jorge. I shouldn't have to explain it to the preacher! This goes against God and nature! Why is this not as clear to everyone else as it is to me?"

Jorge nodded slowly. "It does go against the common sense you and I were raised with. But lots of things do. I listen to the radio. Heck, sometimes I even listen to National Public Radio. I know what the arguments are. And I'm afraid parsing gender is above my pay grade. And if I can't figure it out, how should I expect a fifteen-year-old to understand it?"

"It's simple, Jorge. It's black and white. It's right and wrong!" Ellen was nearly yelling now.

"You have a right to your opinion. Sure you do. And so do I. And my opinion is that it's more complex than that."

"So what are you going to do about our daughter's foolishness?"

Jorge blinked. "I'd like to start by stopping her mother from hurting her."

Ellen's mouth worked, but nothing came out. Jorge held his hand up. "She's wearing a 3-by-3 bandage on her cheek right now because you couldn't control your temper."

"But I—"

"I don't plan to encourage her. But I don't plan to discourage her either."

"And what are you going to do when she starts insisting that you refer to her as a 'he'?"

Jorge pursed his lips. "I don't know."

"Well, you'd better figure it out!"

Just then Jorge's pocket buzzed. He sighed and withdrew his cell phone. He frowned when he saw the number.

"What? Who is it?"

"It's the sheriff's office."

"Why? What has she done now?"

"Will you just stop?" Jorge said. He punched the green button and held the phone to his ear.

"Put it on speakerphone," Ellen commanded him. He did.

"—Wulfson?"

"This is Jorge. My wife Ellen is on the call, too."

"That's just fine."

"Sounds like Celia," Jorge said.

"It is. Sorry, Jorge, there's a lot going on here today."

"That's all right. How can I help you?"

"This is just a…well a courtesy call. We've…we don't want you to get blindsided…we want you to hear it from us first."

"Hear what?" Jorge's brows bunched in concern.

"There were several new cubes out at the Nyland's place this morning. I'm sure you've heard about—"

"I heard about 'em. New ones, you say?"

"Uh…yeah. And one of them is…well, of your daughter."

Abel Nyland felt at the tender green shoot, broken at the stem. He cursed and stood up, wiping the dirt from his fingers. Ginger Beer sniffed at the ground, "reading" the myriad scents left by the visitors. "Damn tourists," Abel spat. "They've trampled about six acres, as far as I can figure. Not all the plants, but they will soon, if we don't stop them." He scowled at Jake. Jake didn't know if that was because Nyland was angry at him, or just disappointed that he wasn't dealing with the sheriff.

Jake cleared his throat. "The way I see it, Mr. Nyland, we got two choices. We can let 'em come, or we can not let 'em come. We could block the road up by the juncture, just not let anyone through. The problem with that is access overland from other farms. It would be a hike, but some people would be up for that hike. It's going to take a lot to keep folks from coming to look at their…at themselves."

Nyland nodded and gave Jake an uncertain look, as if he were weighing not Jake's actual words, but whether the deputy was an idiot from the start. Jake knew he wasn't, but he didn't know if Nyland knew that. A part of him desperately needed to prove his mettle.

"The other option," Jake continued, "would be to let 'em come, but restrict their path. We could put up some parade poles, run some police tape between them, keep folks fenced into just the spaces we want. They'd still trample your plants, but not nearly so many."

"An' what do you suggest?" Nyland asked.

Jake removed his cowboy hat and ran his fingers through his sweaty hair. Ginger Beer ambled over to him and sniffed at his crotch. Jake put the hat back on. He desperately wished Thom was here. He considered calling his boss, but something stopped him. A voice in his head suggested that this was an opportunity to show he could handle an emergency by himself. He did not want to miss it. "To be honest, Mr. Nyland, I think there's public safety value in letting them come."

"Public safety value? What the hell does that mean?"

"It means people are upset. They're not likely to be terribly rational. Letting them come...it opens a pressure valve. We close it, and... well, people are likely to blow out in other ways, if you get my meaning."

"I get your meaning," Nyland said. He spat. "And I don't disagree with you. I just wish it wasn't here. Control the flow of traffic, you're saying?"

Jake nodded. "Yeah, if we let them come, we can direct them to park over there—" he pointed in the direction of a place just off the access road, but too far to actually see "—and over there, since those are where the two main clusters of cubes are. If we give folks some guidance on where we want them to walk and where we don't...well, some people are always going to color outside the lines, but most folks will oblige us, I think."

Nyland nodded. Ginger Beer sniffed at his hand, deliciously smelly from the loam that clung to it. He patted her head. "That doesn't sound like it's best for my fields, but it does sound like it's best for the townsfolk."

Jake's shoulders relaxed a bit. "Good. I'll ask Carmichael to bring out the parade gear."

"I can truck some hay bales out, if that will help," Abel offered.

"Absolutely. Maybe we can go over the best places for walkways?"

Nyland nodded again and started walking toward the first of the carparks Jake had suggested. Jake followed quickly, falling into step with the farmer. "I have another concern," he said.

"When will your boss be back?" Nyland asked, not looking at Jake.

"Um...I don't know. We've got an...well, we've got a situation."

"Well, if this ain't a situation, young man, what is it?"

"It's...*another* situation. It's worse."

"How could it possibly be worse?"

Jake knew he couldn't give the farmer details of an ongoing investigation, but he understood why it must seem unlikely that there were more important things for Thom to attend to. But Julie certainly counted as one of those things. "It just is."

"But you can't tell me anything about it?"

"Right."

Ginger Beer flashed past them, bounding over the plowed rows with canine glee.

"All right, then. What's your *other* concern?" Nyland asked.

"Over here," Jake said, inviting the farmer to change course slightly in order to intercept a couple of cubes along their way.

Nyland allowed for the change in direction and within a few minutes of silent walking they came across one of the many cubes littering the field. This one was unusual in that it showed two people —a woman and a man.

Jake sighed as he looked at the sculpture of the woman. It was Becky Travers, her eyes bulging and wild. Leaning in toward her was her husband Paul, his face frozen in a mask of rage. His hands were around her throat. Her mouth was open in a silent scream. The back of Paul's head was unfinished where it met the edge of the cube. The naked violence of it made him shudder.

"I can't imagine it," Jake said. "I know Paul Travers. We went to school together. I always thought Becky was too young for him, but... you know, you keep things like that to yourself. I'm wondering if maybe we ought to tent this one."

"Tent it?" Nyland asked, scowling

"Yeah. Just throw a tarp over it. I mean, these are all terrible, but this one..." he trailed off.

"Eeyup. I get it, deputy," Nyland said. "Don't that just mean people will try to peek through the tarp?"

"Could. Sure. I mean, of course. But..." His brain raced. He didn't need to think so hard about this, he knew, but he wanted—needed—

to come off as competent in the old man's eyes. "Most people will comply. Besides, this is a good spot to post someone. Maybe I'll just stand right here."

"All night?"

"If need be."

Nyland's nose was in the air—if he'd been wearing glasses, he'd be viewing Jake through the bottom lens of his bifocals. He looked the deputy up and down. "All right. That's your business, I suppose."

"What do you think about tenting this one?" Jake asked.

He was relieved to see Nyland nod.

"Good. I'll call in for the equipment we'll need."

"Just this one?" Nyland asked.

"Well...it's the worst."

"Shotgun kid is the worst," Nyland countered.

Jake instantly knew the cube he was referring to. A teenage boy? girl? It was hard to say. But the cube showed the back of the kid's head coming off, the business end of a shotgun in his? her? mouth. The impressionistic flair of the sculpture somehow made the brains seem more tolerable to look at, but it was terrible nevertheless. "You think we should tent that one, too?"

"If we're going to do one, let's do the other."

Jake nodded. "And what do we do if the people in those cubes want to see them?"

Nyland shrugged. "Arrange a private viewing? Something away from the crowd, away from the...spectacle."

Jake continued nodding. "Okay. We can do that."

They began walking back toward Abel's pickup, parked along the access road.

"How's Mia?" Jake asked.

Abel hesitated. "Still holed up."

"I'm sorry," Jake said.

"Been worse since she got news of Troy," he said. "Haven't seen her since breakfast. That's what I'm afraid of here. Troy...that changes things."

"It does. It means this is not a prank. It's a...hell, it's a prophesy."

Jake couldn't argue with that. As he climbed into the passenger side, he realized that this was not something he could just leave to the night crew. He had a long night ahead of him. And he did not feel up to the challenge.

———————

Thom punched up the Maranatha Car Pull on his GPS and waited for it to find the route. Within seconds, the screen had populated, and with little more than a glance, Thom knew where he was headed. He started the SUV, gave Albert Castillo a final wave, and started down the gravel drive toward the CA-178.

He worried about the young man—what would happen when social services arrived, when the coroner started to dismantle the trailer shrine to get the old man's corpse out? A feeling he wasn't terribly familiar with rose up and hovered just above his shoulders—he recognized it as pity, or perhaps its softer cousin, compassion, but he didn't know what to do with it. It felt like a stranger come to stay the night; he didn't quite know what to say to it or where to put it.

As he drove, it occurred to him why it was bothering him so much. *Me and that kid, Albert, we're not so different*, he thought. The kid was isolated by distance and the razor wire and the electric fence, but Thom realized he'd put up a fence of his own. It was emotional, rather than physical, but to anyone outside, it must have seemed just as impenetrable. But it was when he made the connection between the trailer shrine and the urn with Emma's ashes that he felt the cold chill. For a brief moment, he wondered what his co-workers thought of him. Did they pity him, just as he pitied Albert now? It wasn't a feeling he particularly liked. And he didn't like the idea of other people feeling it toward him.

Instinctively, Thom reached for another sugar packet, but then realized he'd need more to sustain him, and momentarily wondered if he'd been wrong to eschew the beans when offered. Spying a 7-11, he reasoned that the five minutes needed to buy and heat a bean burrito was not an indefensible indulgence. The burrito proved too hot to eat at first, but eventually Thom tore into it with an appetite he did not know he possessed. He chased it with a bag of Doritos and a Mountain Dew. For dessert, he sucked the nacho cheese powder from his fingers.

Thom was surprised to see the sign for the Maranatha Car Pull, and he realized he'd been so lost in thought that he hadn't noticed the time or distance passing. He turned right at the stop sign, and followed a dirt road to the front gate.

The front was made up to look like the entrance to a racetrack, but Thom suspected that most of it was a façade. As he got out of Old Bill, he sniffed at the wind. There was a light breeze, and the sun was beginning its descending arc. But other than those sidereal movements, the world seemed suspended in amber, frozen, as if holding its breath.

He sometimes wondered why he had chosen to make the desert his home. He had no affinity for it. He would have been equally at home in a pine forest in Washington State, he suspected. Being a farming community with water piped in from upstate, Karlstadt sometimes didn't seem to be desert country, but the green of the crops had always seemed ornamental, somehow—a shallow green toupee barely covering the bald dryness of the soil's natural state. And it occurred to him that it wasn't the land that called to him, but the people—the very people he held at bay.

He shook his head and reminded himself of the reason he was there. The paradox of his isolation on the one hand and his search for Julie on the other was not lost on him. It was a mystery to be pondered, *should* be pondered, and *would* be pondered. Just not now.

He hitched up his khakis and headed for the speedway façade. No one manned the ticket booth; perhaps the place was out of business. He walked through the opening in the façade near the ticket booth, and saw a long corridor made entirely of the crunched, stacked chassis of cars. He circumambulated the building until he found a sign that said "office." He knocked.

He nearly jumped out of his khakis when the door jerked open. The man inside looked just as surprised as Thom felt. And when he saw Thom's uniform, his eyes widened to undisguised fear. "What do you want?" the man barked.

That is the question of the day, Thom thought. He studied the man. He was older than Thom was, by about ten years or so, and a full head shorter. He had long, stringy, gray hair, and his eyes were quick and suspicious.

Thom held out his cell phone. "Have you seen this woman?" he asked.

When the man's eyes grew even larger, Thom had his answer. If there had been any weariness in him, any hunger, any despair regarding the futility of his efforts, it was all gone now. This man knew something, and Thom knew that he knew.

"Never seen her," the man lied.

"I think you have," Thom countered. The man looked at the ground, at Thom's belt buckle, at anything but Thom's face. "That there is my deputy. Her name is Deputy Sheriff Julia Barkley. I'd like permission to search your property."

The old man's face screwed up into a look of sour defiance. "Show me your warrant."

"Do I really need a warrant?"

"I think you do."

"Well, congratulations, then. You've just given me probable cause, in which case I don't need a warrant."

"Hey, I—" the man objected, but Thom doubted he'd followed his logic. That made little difference to him. In his own mind, based solely on the old man's reactions, Thom felt he had enough evidence for a walkabout. But before Thom could say anything else, he found himself staring into the barrel of a 12-gauge shotgun.

CHAPTER TEN

Mercer used a bicycle lock to fasten Julie's handcuffs to the door handle of the same car he'd tethered her to before. The makeshift pavilion rustled in the faint breeze as the noon sun started gathering its heat. As they'd marched past row after row of cars, it seemed that every step brought her closer to her doom, to the unsentimental severity of the desert, to the gaping maw of the Great Old Ones.

She'd hoped that the goat, at least, would have escaped, but after its brief flirtation with freedom, it had wandered back to the pavilion, and seemed quite content nibbling away at a bit of desert flora. Her heart sank. "Sorry, fella," she said. A part of her wanted to blame the goat for not making the most of its opportunity, but another part knew that was just silly.

Mercer didn't even bother tying the goat up again, she noticed. She kept expecting him to, but it seemed to her that he too realized the goat was in no hurry to flee. For some reason, she couldn't take her eyes off the beast, mentally wishing it to run, to escape, to save its life —to do what she could not.

Her wondering after the animal was interrupted by the arrival of guests. A wood-paneled station wagon edged its way through the narrow valley between the stacks of cars, the only sound being an irregular tic-tickering coming from the engine.

Mercer waved at the driver and directed him to a place to park. It was clear to Julie that Mercer wanted to make sure a large, flat stretch of ground was open and available. Julie had a grim notion of why.

Finally the tic-tickering stopped. The doors to the station wagon flew open, and people began to spill out. The first out was a lanky, skinny guy in a black t-shirt, black jeans, and Doc Martens, his hair hanging down to his shoulders. She couldn't see his eyes, as he wore a pair of mirrored sunglasses—absurdly large, round, and convex, like the eyes of a giant insect. He made a beeline for Mercer and high-fived him.

Following directly after him was a young woman about his same age, Julie guessed. She was in a flower-print dress that hung on her like a potato sack—several sizes too big. The collars were creased and the whole dress was wrinkled. Her hair had been braided and those braids wrapped around her head like a greasy golden tiara, with a few wildflowers poking out here and there. Julie noticed a large fly buzzing about her. Every few seconds, the fly would land on her head, then it would buzz around again.

Yup, they look just like magickians, Julie thought as she sized them up. Another couple emerged from the car, but while it was clear to her that there was a romantic connection between the first pair, she was not sure about these. The man was short, stocky, almost dwarf-like. He sported bright red hair and was gregarious. He was also older— maybe Thom's age. He wore filthy black chinos, a shirt with a ruffled front and long, frilly sleeves, and, improbably, a bright red vest adorned with a black paisley pattern. He was also vaguely familiar— where had she seen him before?

The woman with him defied the gravity of greeting, drifting off by herself as soon as she got clear of the station wagon. She did not squeal upon meeting the others; in fact she did not speak at all. She stared off into space and played with the zipper of her sweater—a sweater that she could not possibly wear for very much longer given the rising temperature. Her hair was a deep auburn, flashing red every now and then when the light caught it just right. She was painfully thin, her limbs perpetually sticking out at acute angles.

Julie could hear enough of the conversation to start piecing together some information about the new arrivals. The skinny goth kid was Perry, and the flower-child reject with him was Frazer; it must have been her surname. After more careful listening, she divined that the short, fat, flamboyant man was called, strangely, Lord Jay, although just what Jay was lord of was not clear to her. No one spoke to or about the young woman standing off by herself, so Julie named her The Loner.

Julie saw Mercer point to her and whisper something. A small cheer went up. Mercer also pointed out the goat, which resulted in another brief outburst of celebration. Perry sprinted over to the station wagon and pulled out a bright red cooler. Placing it in the shade of the makeshift pavilion, he threw a can of Coors Light to Mercer, then one to Frazer. He held one up to Lord Jay, but the short man shook his head. "Too damned early. I want to be alert and sharp when we meet our Lord. Got any water?" Hearing his voice, something clicked into place, and she realized where she knew him from—he had played the Master of the Temple at Dogstar Oasis' Rite of Saturn.

"Bubbles okay?" Perry asked.

"Bubbles preferred," Lord Jay said, brightening.

Perry tossed him a can of La Croix.

Frazer lit a cigarette and smiled as she blew out the smoke. She sauntered over to where Julie was tethered. She stopped a few feet shy and took another drag. It was obvious that she was trying to blow the smoke in Julie's face, but she wasn't standing close enough and the wind did not collude with her. The fly on the top of her hair took off and circled around her head a few times. It lit on her eyelid. She did not blink.

"So, you a cop, for reals?" Frazer asked.

"So, you a burnout magick whore, for reals?" Julie replied.

Frazer sucked at the end of her cigarette, betraying no emotion. "You think I'm just a hanger-on?"

"You don't look smart enough to be a full-on magickian yourself."

"Fuck that, bitch. I did the full Abramalin working last year, by myself."

"You didn't cut any corners?" Julie asked.

The young woman's eyes narrowed. "Define 'cut corners.'"

"That's what I thought," Julie said. "And did you make contact with your Holy Guardian Angel?"

"I felt all tingly inside."

"A buck-fifty will buy you a French Tickler. That's a whole lot cheaper, and a lot less effort to boot."

"For a cop, you seem to know a bit too much about this," Frazer said.

"I've been around the magickal block a time or two," Julie confessed.

"See there? We're going to be girlfriends," Frazer said. The fly on her eyelid took off and made a couple of quick passes. It landed again on the shoulder of the girl's yellow print dress.

"Why do you want to summon the Great Old Ones?" Julie asked.

Frazer's eyes widened and she giggled. "Because they're badass!" she squealed. She turned to Perry and said, "She knows! I didn't know she'd know."

Perry shook his head—apparently he hadn't known either. They'd assumed Julie was just being held in ignorant terror. Julie didn't know which would be better. She cleared her throat. "Um…did it ever occur to you that badass is…I don't know…maybe a bad thing?"

Frazer scowled and walked toward Julie, stopping just out of reach this time. She succeeded in blowing smoke into Julie's face, smiling as Julie grimaced. Perry walked up and stopped beside her. In a much more reasonable voice than Julie expected, he said, "We summon the Old Ones because the new gods suck. The whole system is fucked. Unsalvageable. It's time to wipe the slate clean."

"Wipe the slate clean?" Julie asked. For a moment she forgot that her hands were tied. She cocked her head. "Just what is this working going to accomplish, anyway?"

"And here I thought you knew stuff," Frazer said, a note of disappointment in her voice. The fly on her dress buzzed around, coming near enough for Julie to feel the wind of it.

"Why, my dear, can you not guess?" Lord Jay was walking toward her now. He held the can of sparkling water in one hand casually, as if he were at a tailgate party. "We plan to summon the Great Old Ones, the Ancients. We will clear the way for Azathoth—his name be praised —to seize the throne of earth."

"But Azathoth, and all the Old Ones...aren't they evil?" Julie asked, but was sorry as soon as she said it. She knew where that line of questioning would lead.

"Good, evil..." he shrugged. "As Chuang Tzu said in his fifth chapter, 'Life, death, preservation, loss, failure, success, poverty, riches, worthiness, unworthiness, slander, fame, hunger, thirst, cold, heat— these are the alternations of the world, the workings of fate. Day and night they change place before us and wisdom cannot spy out their source.'" He smiled, as if that settled everything.

Julie scowled, because the quote—which she did not recognize and half suspected Lord Jay of confecting on the spot—answered nothing. "Are you saying that it doesn't matter which gods are enthroned on the Earth?" she asked.

"I'm saying that it is high time for a change...what Chuang Tzu called an 'alternation.'"

"And what do you expect will happen when great Azathoth comes to claim the throne of Earth?" Julie asked, realizing that the flowery language of magickians was catching.

"I expect chaos and destruction. Oh, and death. Of course there must be death." Lord Jay smiled.

"Death for everyone?" Julie asked. "Or only for most?"

"The Great Old Ones will spare us, for we serve them," Lord Jay said, as if speaking to a small child. "Their gratitude will protect us."

"Good luck with that," Julie said.

Lord Jay blinked, and his head jerked as if he was about to turn away, but he changed his mind. He met Julie's eyes for a moment, then looked away, sighing and spreading his hands. "We cannot expect you to understand—"

"Because I'm stupid?" Julie asked, "Or because I'm a woman? Or because I don't know enough magick? Why can't you expect me to understand?"

Lord Jay did not answer her. Instead, he addressed his friends. "The sun has begun its descent. We have much to do. Let us waste no more time on the food."

"Now you just back away slowly," the old man said. His lip slid into a sneer as he registered Thom's reaction.

Thom put both hands up and said with as much calm as he could muster, "There's no need to escalate matters."

"Matters done escalated," the old man said. One long, greasy, gray lock hung off his head separate from the others, swinging crazily. "Now I want you to understand, Sheriff. I fill my own shells. This ain't birdshot in these shells. Hell, it ain't even buckshot. They's slugs, and hollow-bodied to boot. Ain't nothing that can stop 'em."

Thom knew that wasn't true, but he also knew that it might as well be, since he didn't have anything that could actually stop such a projectile with him. It would be deadly. His only chance was that the little guy was an inept armorer or a terrible shot. That wasn't a chance he wanted to take.

"Now you just take your service weapon and toss it into the room here."

Thom wondered if he were fast enough on the draw to disarm the old man. But he watched the man's eyes narrow as he said, "And don't try nothing funny. If you think I don't know how to use this, I am happy to disabuse you of such notions."

Thom believed him. Slowly, he undid the snap on his holster and slid the handgun out, holding it pinched between his finger and thumb as if it were a moldy fish. He tossed it past the old man, who smiled, revealing several missing and blackened teeth.

"Now you're going to turn around and march back to your car," the old man said. "And then you're going to throw whatever rifles you have onto the ground."

Thom nodded. He started backing away, navigating with quick glances over his shoulder. His brain began ticking through the weapons in his SUV. Hands still up, he called out, "Gotta get my keys."

"Get 'em," the old man said. He had followed Thom out, the shotgun leveled at his chest.

Thom reached into his pocket and slowly pulled out his fob. He pushed the button twice and heard his shop unlock all around. He went first to the passenger side and pulled his patrol rifle from its mount. He threw it several yards away, where it landed with a scattering of dust. Then, raising his hands again, he circled to the rear hatchback. The old man side-stepped around the circumference of an unseen circle, keeping proper distance from the sheriff, but making sure he had a clear shot.

"That's it," Thom said.

"I don't think it is."

"Look, I got pepper spray and a bean-bag launcher. Do you really want those?"

A look of distaste crossed the old man's features. "Nah..."

"All right then, that's it."

"Git in."

"All right." Thom slowly climbed into Old Bill's cab. His hands were touching the cloth of the ceiling.

The old man started to back away. Thom turned away from him a bit, enough to hide the actions of his right hand behind his head, and clicked the radio mic hanging from his epaulet. "Adam One, come in Karlstadt." But he heard nothing but static in return. He couldn't imagine that he was out of range—police radios were hardy beasts. But he had no other explanation. He started his engine. "Siri, call Celia."

"I'm sorry, Thom, but I can't get a signal," Siri's robotic American female voice replied.

"Damn," Thom swore.

And that was when Thom heard the first shotgun blast. His passenger window shattered, scattering glass shards into his right eye and punching an exit hole the size of a nickel in the roof of the cab.

"Holy shit," Thom swore, grimacing from the pain in his eye. He instantly leaned over to his right, trying to get as flat against the seat as he could. The next blast entered his engine block, shot straight through the radiator. Thom felt his whole shop lurch with the force of it.

Thom knew the old man was out of ammunition, as it had been a double-barreled shotgun. He'd need to reload, which meant Thom had a few precious seconds to act. He hit the "start" button. The engine should have roared to life, but instead he heard little more than a click and a whine.

Thom had served in the military. He knew just the place to cut someone to make them die, and just how to knock someone out so that they wouldn't. It occurred to him that the old man must know cars like Thom knew a soldier's anatomy. He probably knew just where to aim on any given make.

Involuntarily clutching his face with his left hand, Thom threw himself out of the cab and circled quickly, putting the bulk of the SUV between himself and the old man. Then he turned and ran as fast as he could into the desert.

It was only the early afternoon, so there was no cover of darkness. There was some scrub, but only enough to come up to his waist. He dove for it, duck-walking to stay low, moving as quickly as he could in the only direction that mattered—away. Thistles and thorns tore at his face, his skin, his clothing, claiming what was theirs as he ignored their purchases and pushed on, losing little bits of himself with every hook and snag. The pain kept him sharp, kept him alert, kept him moving.

He knew he didn't have long until both barrels were restocked—a matter of seconds, really. He hit an open patch just as he heard the shotgun's report and saw a billow of dust kick up a dozen feet ahead of him. He felt the second blast before he heard it, tearing at his back, at his shoulder, and pitching him face-first into the dust.

A strange quiet descended on the Maranatha Car Pull as the sun squatted on the horizon. The lower it got, the more the activity of the magickians increased.

Julie glanced at her cuffed wrist and despaired to see that, despite her best efforts, it was red and chafed. With growing dread she had watched the preparatory rituals. Mercer and Perry had spent most of the afternoon digging a shallow trench—more accurately, a series of trenches—that formed a hexagram, a six-sided star, about twenty feet from tip to tip. Once dug, Frazer had filled these with coarse salt—the kind Julie had seen spread on northern roads in winter. Sometime in the late afternoon, the goat had wandered through their project, carelessly scattering the salt. With a curse, Mercer punished the goat with the loss of its freedom. Once more, the goat had been tied to the wall of cars not far from Julie.

"You're an idiot," Julie had said to the goat after Mercer walked away. In response, the goat had nibbled at the chrome on a bumper.

But despite the goat's unconscious mischief, the star had been finished. Now candles were being set. To one side of the star, a large rectangle had also been dug—it, too, was set off from the dark desert earth with bright salt. The very notion of salt made Julie cringe. She was so thirsty that she tried not to think of it.

A party atmosphere had permeated most of the afternoon, but now that the light was failing a hushed reverence came over the car yard. The magickians continued their diligent work in relative silence— setting out ritual paraphernalia, checking angles with a protractor, arranging sigils that had been previously printed out on large sheets of paper. Mercer groaned as he lowered a large jar—eighteen inches high and at least twelve in diameter—to the ground near the star. It was filled with what looked like uncooked chicken gizzards, or perhaps the entrails of sheep or some other animal.

Mercer stood and wiped sweat from his brow. "Got any more of that beer?"

"Sure," Perry said.

"Not for you," Lord Jay interrupted. "Not for any of us. Not until the ritual is over. We need to be sharp." When Mercer scowled, Lord Jay pointed at him. "Our lives depend on it. We're about to open a window into the Great Old Ones' dimension—there can be no room for error."

Mercer grunted but did not protest.

Finally, it seemed, all was in place. Julie, despite her quickening pulse as her dread increased, marveled at the level of detail these magickians were tending to. Despite herself, she found she was impressed. *Maybe they do know what they're doing,* she thought, but it was not a notion she entertained for long.

Soon the stars were visible, and it became very dark indeed. Perry lit a string of tiki torches set into the hard desert earth, and the air became thick with the stench of kerosene. Frazer poured a leather bag of incense on a brazier, which did not completely mask the odor of the kerosene, but did alter it, folded it into itself, transforming it into something simultaneously more appealing and repellent.

Lord Jay rose from the webbed folding chair he had been holding court in, and drew forth a pocket watch. "Places, friends," he said. Turning back toward his chair, he lifted from its back a black robe, which he drew over his head. It settled over his lumpish frame only with effort, which he seemed to bear without discomfort or apology. The robe had a hood, which he pushed back from his head. He fastened the middle of the robe with a scarlet cincture.

So he's the real magickian, Julie thought, although she had suspected as much from the moment she had laid eyes on him. She did not doubt that the others fancied themselves adepts as well, but Lord Jay carried himself with an air of comfortable superiority that set him apart. The squat man situated himself in the southernmost triangle of the six-pointed star, stepping carefully over the salt trench so as not to scatter any of the precious, protective element.

Julie's heart began to beat loudly in her ears; she felt momentarily faint. She knew what would happen if she passed out—her wrist would certainly suffer, but she hesitated to even think about the rest of her. She gripped the handle of the car she was chained to and forced herself to stand straight and breathe deep and slow. As she'd hoped, the dizziness soon passed.

She watched as Lord Jay drew an athame—a ritual dagger—from the pocket of his ceremonial robe and pointed it at the heavens, directly above him. She could not see his face, only the back of his head, but she imagined what his face must look like—eyes closed, puffy lips pursed in concentration, a scowl upon his brow.

And then the little man began to sing. At another time, Julie might have found this ridiculous, but in the moment, she was both surprised and impressed by the loud, sonorous note emitted by the little man.

"Eeeeoooooooo-iiiiiii-aaaaahhhhhhh-tcht," the man sang. Then he sang it again. Then he began to sway as he sung it. After three repetitions, he added to it, "Leee-oooo-tellectanacht. Aiiiiiiiiii!"

At the final syllable, there were two small explosions. Julie jumped at their report, but then rolled her eyes as she saw they were nothing more than smoke bombs. Pink smoke began to fill the air, obscuring almost completely the cars on the other side of the small clearing.

"Holy crap," Julie muttered to herself. "Same old bullshit."

Lord Jay continued to sing, but soon his swaying turned to dancing. As the fat little man hopped from one foot to the other, Julie knew that she should find the sight humorous, but it wasn't. Instead, it was somehow ominous and ghastly. Lost amid the pink clouds, shimmering in the torchlight, the dancing little man became an avatar of chaos. There was no rhythm to his steps, there was no meaning that she could discern from his words, there was no sense in his wild gesticulations with the athame, as he thrust it up, then down, then cut from side to side.

At first, Julie thought perhaps Lord Jay was doing a variation on the Lesser Banishing Ritual, a staple of magickal ceremony. But she knew the ritual, and his actions did not correspond to it. Instead of the precision and grace of the time-honored movements she knew so well, these movements were violent, spastic, and seemingly random. It looked to Julie like the little man might have been fending off unseen attackers with his knife, enemies coming at him from all sides. Yet his face did not betray alarm, but calm.

She squinted to see him in the dim firelight, obscured by smoke, but for some time all she was able to discern was a shadowy silhouette against a billowy magenta backdrop. But when the smoke began to clear, she saw that something had indeed changed. She held her breath as she tried to make it out. The wall of cars beyond the hexagram seemed to have vanished, and in their place was a gaping black void.

With her hands tied in front of her, Julie had to twist to see what was happening, and her neck had begun to ache. She ignored it and willed her eyes to adjust, for…was there something within the void? She wasn't sure at first, but something was beginning to take shape.

She saw a shimmering, but as she moved her head back and forth for perspective, she realized that she was looking at stars—far distant stars, alien stars, constellations unknown to human eyes. And then, against the backdrop of those stars, she saw something move—something vast, something terrible, something ineffable. It moved like a centipede, turning its great and wormlike body to face the opening, as if noticing it for the first time, and not at all pleased at the discovery. It roared—and while Julie did not hear the sound of it with her ears, she heard it nevertheless in her soul, and its harrowing cry echoed with blind, unconscious, immeasurable rage.

Don't come this way, Julie thought desperately at the thing. *Don't come this way. Notice something else. Notice something else!*

To her great relief, it seemed the beast—whatever it was—could not be bothered. Instead, it roared again and turned away. And as it did, Julie felt like a spotlight had somehow been moved off of her, and she could breathe again. Her neck burned with pain. Instinctively, she tried to bring her right hand up to rub it, but it was arrested by the handcuff.

With the creature's gaze turned away, Julie forced herself to look more closely at the void and noted with alarm that the perspective was skewed. At first, it seemed to her like one of her college classmates' drawings—trying to imitate M.C. Escher but completely flubbing the perspective, so that none of the lines were in the proper place and the illusion was broken. But the scene before her now, distorted as the horizon lines might have been, did not break the illusion, but instead only seemed to make it more concrete, more baffling, more...wrong.

She noted that Lord Jay had stopped dancing. Instead, he was standing still, shoulders drooped, staring motionless into the maw of the void. Slowly, he turned toward the other magickians, huddled inside their rectangle of safety. "It is time," he said.

From far away, it seemed to Julie that she heard a single piper playing on a primitive flute—perhaps even an ocarina. The playing was not melodious, but dissonant, as if some idiot child were entertaining itself trying to make the most obnoxious noise possible for as long as he could.

Catching motion in the corner of her eye, Julie tried to turn her head even further, steeling herself against the pain of doing so. With despair she saw Perry leading the goat into the center of the hexagram and handing the lead to Lord Jay. Perry then dashed for the safety of the rectangle again, where he put his arm around Frazer as if they were cuddling on the Fourth of July, waiting for the fireworks to begin.

Julie's gaze whipped back to the goat. A cry of anguish escaped her lips as she watched Lord Jay draw a knife, positioning it just under the goat's jaw. And then, as Lord Jay moved the knife, a bright red gash looking for all the world like a macabre smile opened up in the goat's neck. It gurgled, thrashed, and then stumbled to the ground, its legs twitching with its futile efforts to regain its feet. In the torchlight, Julie could see the blood spreading out to form a black pool, a viscous pillow for the animal's head.

Raising the knife again, Lord Jay slashed down at the goat's body, opening up its belly, spilling its entrails upon the desert floor. Then the magickian took a step back and raised the knife above his head, along with his other hand. Under other conditions, he might have accompanied those actions with the words, "Don't shoot," but no guns were trained upon him.

Julie suspected that guns would have been pointless in this situation anyway. The beast to whom this sacrifice was being offered was light years away. Any bullet she might fire would lose its velocity and fall back to earth, nothing more than a useless husk of metal long before it left the atmosphere, let alone traversed however many million light years separated her from the Great Old One she now beheld.

Lord Jay backed away as far as he could shy of leaving his own circle of protection, etched in salt within the southernmost triangle of the hexagram. And then Julie saw why. Before her eyes, she saw that the spilled guts of the goat had become animated, rising up like the shuddering head of a cobra, perhaps dancing to the distant, heinous melody of the ocarina. But these intestinal snakes were not content with their alarming display, but slithered over and through one another in patterns Julie's eyes could not discern. Braiding themselves together, the entrails rose up to form a figure—vaguely human in shape, with a single leg like the trunk of a tree rooted in the carcass of the goat, but branching out higher up into spinning tendrils of rubbery flesh that vaguely resembled arms.

But it was the head of the thing Julie could not look away from. A bulbous assemblage of entrails, knotted together, wound tight like a turban, the flat expanse of the goat's rumen opened up into a face that sported neither eyes nor ears. There was, however, a terrible mouth in the center of what seemed its face—and when it opened, Julie saw nothing but a spinning circle of teeth, row upon row, extending far into the interior of the beast. Perspective failed her—the creature was far bigger inside than out. She shuddered at the sight of it, then a mad panic tore at her, causing her to thrash from one side to the other, the edges of the handcuffs cutting into her wrist until her hands was slick with gore.

She could not look away as the creature continued to grow. It hovered over the head of Lord Jay, its spinning teeth close enough to jab out and swallow his head entire. Yet it seemed the circles of salt somehow contained the creature. Its great and terrible mouth opened wide, and to Julie's surprise, a voice emerged—guttural and deep, yet cracking with every syllable, as if it were forcing its mouth to make sounds it was not designed to make and to which it was not accustomed. "Azathoth reigns," the creature bellowed, and a few seconds later Julie could feel the foul wind of it, reeking of rot and infection and the fetid carcasses of insects. "Let all who dwell in this world tremble. Humble yourselves and despair before him. His eye sees all. And no world can fill his belly."

Ted pulled up in his lightning blue Fiat convertible. Peg hated trying to squeeze herself into the little thing, but it was his only car and she resolved to refrain from complaining. But the worst thing about driving with Ted was never the car, it was the slapdash way he drove, with sudden turns and unnecessary roars from the car's engine. It was all a little ridiculous, but then again, so was Ted, and she loved Ted.

"You need to have a shoehorn handy for your passengers, Ted."

"You just couldn't help yourself, could you?"

"You try being a normal-sized middle-aged woman and squeeze your thighs into this. We'll see who's rolling her eyes then."

"Just get in."

She did. She had to exhale completely to get the door to close, but she did it.

"All right, first shift!" Peg announced. "Are you ready?"

Ted sniffed. "As ready as ever I can be to stand out in a cornfield."

"That's the spirit."

"I also got a call...about a cube," Ted said, his voice tinged with dread.

"So did I," Peg said.

"Oh dear. Here we are, going to minister to the grieving. Who will minister to us?"

Peg patted his arm. "We'll minister to each other, dear, like we always do."

"Who was it called you...about your cube?" Ted asked. "The sheriff?"

"No, Jake, the deputy—the other deputy, I mean," Peg answered.

"Skinny guy," Ted clarified.

"Look who's talking," Peg said. "And you know very well who Jake is. The last time you saw him, you said he made you want to get your daddy on, whatever that means."

"Oh, *him*. Yes...cuteness." Ted gave her a wicked sideways look. "He called me too."

She punched his arm. Just then Peg's cell phone sounded an alert. She snatched it up from her purse, but it was just a text message informing her that her prescription was ready to be picked up.

"Did you tell Julie yet?" Ted asked.

"No, I...I was hoping this was her. Damn." She put the phone down. "Jake says she was 'indisposed.' What the hell does that mean?"

"Usually, it means someone is in the loo."

Peg doubted that was what Jake had meant. But something else was nagging at her.

"Ted," she said, turning to him as well as she could in the cramped little car. "I need to talk to you about something...serious."

"Oh?" He raised one eyebrow.

"Phil called me last night."

Ted groaned and rolled his eyes.

"Knock that off. If I have to suffer through you ogling—and commenting on—every young virile male in the valley, you need to listen to me about my own love life. Deal?"

"Oh, all right."

"Phil called off our date."

"Oh. Ouch," Ted made a pained face. "Well, fish in the sea and all that rot."

Peg narrowed her eyes at him. "You know, I had a suspicion last night, but I wasn't sure about it. But now I am. *You* did this."

Ted's hand flew to his breast and he opened his mouth in protest.

"Don't even try to deny it. Phil was all hot to trot, and now he's... not. Something happened. Someone got to him."

"He might have simply had a change of heart, or a change in circumstances. Or—"

"Or a little bird pulled him aside and planted a worm in his ear."

"Would I do that?" Ted asked, feigning offense.

"*Would* you do that?" Peg asked.

Ted's eyes remained steadfastly fixed on the road.

"You *did* do that!" Peg said. "You know, at first, I didn't think you could. But now...You did it, didn't you, you jealous, cold-hearted little queen?"

"No need to get personal—"

"No need to get personal? Ted, how much more personal could this get? I had a date. With a man. And not just with Jesus, with a man who has an actual human body—"

"I don't suppose you want to debate the corporeality of the resurrection body of the Lord right—"

"He had skin and a little bit of hair and a penis and everything, and for some reason, he was interested in *me*. And you just couldn't stand it, could you?"

"My dear—"

"Don't you 'my dear' me, you asshole. You think my heart is a plaything you can just noodle around with to satisfy your twisted, fey sense of whimsy?"

Ted's visage darkened. "He needed to know, Peg. You aren't telling people about your cancer, and you need to."

"I was—"

"You haven't told Julie. You haven't told the man you have designs on. If you went on that date, it would be under false pretenses."

"But I—"

"It's bait-and-switch and you know it. It wasn't fair to him. And I couldn't stand by and—"

"Oh, because you care about Phil's feelings so much—"

"I care about my best friend leaving wreckage in her wake."

"Oh, so now I'm a tugboat? Always with the fat comments."

"What the hell are you talking about? You're not fat, you're just—"

"Don't talk to me. Just...don't."

Ted shrugged and gunned the motor.

"And no stunt driving! The life you save might be your own."

"I thought you weren't talking to me."

"I'm not."

"Could have fooled me."

"Just drive—safely. And kindly shut your festering pie-hole."

Ted's forehead scrunched together and he mouthed the words *festering pie-hole* silently, shaking his head.

The rest of the trip out to Nyland's farm passed in uneasy silence. When they arrived, Peg lost no time tugging at the tiny lever that opened the door. She spilled out onto the gravel. By the time she had regained her dignity, Ted was standing next to her. "What were you saying about someone being ridiculous?"

She ignored him and waved across the fields to Jake. Jake waved back and began to pick his way over the planted rows toward them. In a few moments he arrived, seemingly cheery and unwinded.

"Evenin' Pastor, Father," Jake said.

"Good evening, dear boy," Ted said, giving him the warmest smile the old priest was capable of.

"Where's Abel?" Peg asked.

"Haven't seen him in the past hour, but…" He shrugged. "He's expecting people. It's okay. We've got cones set up and stuff." He pointed out across the field at the hunter's-orange barriers and yellow police tape flapping in the breeze. "I reckon you'll want to see yours before anyone else gets here."

"Are we in the same cube?" Ted asked. "Because that would be awkward, since we're not talking right now."

Jake looked confused. Peg waved Ted away. "Don't listen to him, Jake, just…take us to the cubes, love."

Jake nodded and waved them toward the east. Peg struggled to keep up with the deputy, but she managed not to fall too far behind. Finally, however, they approached a set of cubes Peg had not seen before. She noticed that Jake was taking a circuitous path, and only when they arrived did she realize that he was intentionally bringing them to the back of the cubes. "These are of us," she whispered to Ted.

"Shh—you're not speaking to me, remember?"

"This one," Jake said, and pointed to the one nearest them.

Peg nodded gravely, and the two men stood in silence as she rounded the corner and looked.

Allison picked up one of the pots and frowned. It had cracked in the last firing. It pained Allison to see it, because she knew the little girl who made it would be crushed. She sighed. *I will need to explain why it happened and encourage her to try again.* That didn't sound so bad, but her heart felt heavy just thinking about it.

She picked up another piece and frowned, seeing that one of the children had etched a Confederate flag into a plate. *Why didn't I notice that one before?* she wondered. And why couldn't that have been the one to crack? Her mind flashed back to her confrontation with the two Klansmen on Main Street earlier that day. She'd been ready to punch one of them—the smart one—and if the mayor hadn't interrupted her, she might have. She knew that it was a good thing Deena had stepped in when she did, but she couldn't stop imagining what it would have been like to flatten the asshole's nose. Her lip curled into a smile imagining it, but her stomach soured at the same time. It was all right; she knew she was complicated.

The bell on the door tinkled and she looked up from her workspace. It was near to closing and she was surprised to have any customers so late. Her face brightened when she saw who it was. "Carey!" she said.

Carey was a bread delivery driver who had been stopping by to make the most beautiful woven clay breadbaskets for his favorite customers. Ordinarily, he was chipper, but today his eyes were wide and strange.

"What's wrong?" Allison asked.

"Uh...there's an Indian girl behind your shop playing with a dead animal."

"Really?" Allison asked. She set aside the Confederate plate and got up. "Maybe I should check that out."

"You want backup?" Carey asked. He was six-feet-five, she

guessed, but gentle as a lamb. His mouth said, "Can I help?" but his eyes were saying, "Please don't say yes."

"No, I got this. Four of your baskets came out fine. One of them cracked—"

"Damn."

"It's okay—that's why we do extra. But on another of them, the glaze came out uneven. I've put them in your cubby. Take a look. If you have a customer you don't like *quite* as much, you can give them that one."

"Thanks, Al."

Allison took off her apron and headed to the back. *Wow, it's really my day to play therapist, isn't it?* she thought. She passed the bathroom and the supply room with the kiln in it, then unlocked the door. She stepped out into the alley, and was surprised to see pretty much exactly what Carey had described.

At least, that was how it looked at first. Allison was surprised to see the young woman she had met at Debbie's. There were plenty of native people around, and from Carey's description, she had imagined a teenager up to some mischief.

"Milala?" she asked.

The young woman was squatting, her back against the brick of her building. Hanging out of the side of her mouth was the stub of a cigar. In front of her was a bloody tangle of skin. The young woman was likewise covered in blood. In one hand she held a glass shard, scraping the hide with long strokes away from herself.

Milala did not look up. "Oh. Hi," she said.

"I'm Allison. Williams."

"I remember you." Milala remained intent on the scraping.

"Um…what are you doing?"

"It should be obvious," Milala answered.

"The *what* is obvious, the *why* is not," Allison clarified.

"You wouldn't understand," Milala said.

"Try me."

Milala did not answer.

Allison squatted down next to her and studied the hide. "I see what you're doing. You're removing the viscera."

"It needs to be smooth."

"Listen, Milala, I'm going to tell you something about myself. I make things. And I help other people make things."

Milala still did not look at her. She set down the glass and, pulling a lighter from her pocket, tried to light what was left of her cigar. She puffed a few times and, apparently satisfied, picked up the glass again.

"You're making something, and I want to help," Allison concluded.

"I don't think you know how to do this," Milala said.

"No, but I'd love to learn," Allison said. "And I think I can help you with better tools and a better workspace. That's what I do—I give people space to work and tools to work with. I also encourage them. That's the secret sauce."

Milala looked at her for the first time. "Secret sauce?"

"Uh...it's a saying, from a commercial when I was a kid. I guess it means I'm getting old." Allison smiled then, broad and warm. She pointed at the glass. "You might hurt your hand with that—"

"I cut myself already," Milala confessed.

"But I've got a Bucker Plus Mosier that might be easier on your hand—that's a knife that's got a bit of a curve to it, and a good, solid, wooden handle."

"That would help a lot," Milala nodded. Allison saw her soften. "And...it's very kind of you."

Allison nodded. She pointed at the hide. "And we can clean up the skin a bit. We can also give it a pickling bath in the utility sink, to kill the bacteria."

"No, I've got Coyote's brain here. Creator told me to use his brain."

"Oh. Okay, then." Allison swallowed hard. "Let's definitely go with the brain."

Milala looked her in the eye, then. "Why are you being nice to me?"

Allison noticed the tiny black hairs on the young woman's arms rise with suspicion. "I told you. This is what I do. Let me do what I do best, and then you can do what you do best." Allison had no idea what that was, but she was thrilled by the notion of finding out. This young woman intrigued her. She was even starting to find her attractive.

Finally, Milala nodded.

"All right then," Allison said. "Do you need help with the skin?"

"No, it's in one piece."

"Okay, you can bring it right in here." Allison walked to the back door and held it open. She watched as Milala gingerly lifted the animal skin and carried it inside. Then Milala returned to the alley and carried in a plastic bag. Allison's hand went to her mouth as she realized that the bag contained the bloody parts of a dismembered animal.

"Um...you can put it there." She pointed to the double utility sink. "That way the...brains...won't go everywhere."

"Thank you," Milala said.

"Have you done this before?" Allison asked.

"No. Creator is telling me what to do."

"Oh. Creator. Right." Allison bit her tongue, realizing she might have sounded condescending.

"Do you have a large knife?" Milala asked.

"Of course." Allison went to her work table and came back with one, about nine inches long. She handed it to Milala, and then watched in fascinated horror as the young woman inserted it in the animal's eye socket and twisted, cracking the skull. With a deft flip of the wrist, she exposed the brains. She dropped the knife and began to scoop them onto the hide with her hand.

Allison excused herself—the excuse she gave was that she needed to check on the front of the shop, but in truth she needed to regain her composure. Carey was waiting patiently near the cash register. She apologized and rang him up. "Come back and do some more," she encouraged him. "You really got the knack of that weaving with the clay."

Once Carey was gone, she looked around the empty shop, and then walked back to check on Milala. The young woman was stooped over the utility sink, but something was different. Allison realized she was smiling. She hadn't seen her smile before. It was a lovely smile.

"You're pretty when you're not scowling," she said. That did it. The smile disappeared. Allison regretted opening her mouth, as she often did.

"You don't deserve my smiles."

"What? Me personally?" Allison asked.

"You, *oje-ajnt*."

"Ah, you plural, then. What does *oje-ajnt* mean?"

"It means anyone not of The People."

"Anyone not Indian?"

Milala nodded, not taking her eyes off the skin.

"Look, Milala, whatever someone did to you that hurt you so much, that made you so angry…it wasn't me."

Milala looked up and for a brief second met her eye. Allison noted that she seemed surprised by her words, perhaps even a bit shaken.

"I know," she said. "I'm not good at this. I'm…" She looked like she was about to cry. "I'm soaking the skin of my Father."

Allison frowned. The skin looked like it had come from a dog or something similar. "What do you mean?"

Milala shook her head sadly, but didn't explain. Allison came closer to her and placed a tentative hand on Milala's elbow. "I want to help."

"If you really wanted to help, you could stop buying and selling our land, make our people alive again, make the earth clean again."

Allison gave her a sad, compassionate smile. "Believe me, honey, if I had the power to make everything fair for everyone, I would. And I'm willing. My problem isn't unwillingness, it's usually cluelessness —same as most people. And, you know, I come from a people who also haven't had an easy time of it. I wish my people hadn't been kidnapped and forced to work as slaves for two hundred years."

Milala stopped stirring. "Oh. Yes. I'm sorry. I didn't…"

"Right. The thing about cluelessness is that there's usually plenty to go around. The point is, I think I might be able to get it—how you feel, about how your people feel—if you're willing to teach me."

Milala pointed to a macramé dreamcatcher hanging on the wall of the supply room. Allison had hung it there years ago, and had never given it another thought. Her heart rate shot up at the sight of it. It had never occurred to her before that it might be offensive. "You cannot become an honorary tribe member. You cannot put a feather in your hair and call yourself one of The People. You cannot hold New Age sweat lodges."

Allison felt like she'd been struck in the face. She hadn't been to a sweat lodge in ages, but she had certainly been to sweat lodge ceremonies presided over by a variety of New Age gurus and shamans with tenuous connections to native peoples.

"There is nothing New Age about our ways," Milala continued. "They are old ways, and they belong to us."

Allison nodded. She walked over to the dreamcatcher and took it down. Then she threw it in the trash. "Lesson number one, received."

"And our ways are not disposable."

Allison stared at the trash can. "You see? That's how clueless I really am." She pulled it out again, but then didn't know what to do with it. She set it on the countertop and patted it uncertainly.

Milala stood up straight and pointed at the sink. "This is ready."

"Okay, let's rinse it off, and you can get to work on it with a proper blade. But first, let me tend to the cuts on your hands."

Milala stared at her hands smeared with blood—some of it her own, and some of it clearly not. "Okay, I guess."

"First, wash your hands in the other sink. There's some granulated soap in the basin there."

Milala obeyed while Allison grabbed the first aid kit from the bathroom. Then she bade Milala sit on a stool by the workbench. Allison slipped on some latex gloves, sat on another stool next to Milala and began to daub her fingers with alcohol.

"You know what the problem is?" Milala asked.

"The problem with what?"

"With you. The *oje-ajnt*."

Allison tried not to laugh, but couldn't completely conceal her amusement at the young woman's bluntness. "No, please tell me the problem with me...*us*."

"You don't see that everything is living. You treat everything as if it is dead. And so it becomes dead to you. If you treated everything as if it were alive, it would become alive to you."

Allison stopped and blinked. She hadn't expected actual wisdom from this precocious young woman. But before she could reply, Milala continued. "You cover our Mother up with concrete and then you wonder why you can't feel her heartbeat. You buy her and sell her as if she belonged to you, instead of the other way around. You don't see that you are her eyes and ears. She rises up in our brains and sees how beautiful she is with our eyes."

Allison felt a catch in her throat. She swallowed against it and waited for her feelings to subside. Then she said, "I think you are right. I know you are right."

Milala shrugged. "It's obvious."

"It isn't obvious to everyone...but I agree that it should be." Allison applied some triple-antibiotic ointment to the cuts and waited to see if they would bleed anymore. Not much, she was glad to see. She ripped the paper sheath from a band-aid.

"Thank you," Milala said.

"You know, I hope you'll forgive me for saying this," Allison said. "But I get the feeling that your fingers aren't the only part of you that needs healing."

Milala scowled at her.

"You're...very angry," Allison said. She held her breath, waiting for the young woman to explode.

But instead, Milala looked away. And she nodded.

"Can I ask what happened?" Allison asked.

"When I was a girl," Milala said. "Some white men..." Her voice rose into a squeak and stopped.

Allison reached out and stroked her hair. "Oh. I think I understand. They took something that...wasn't theirs?"

Milala nodded, and then wiped her nose on her wrist.

"Oh, my dear," Allison said, handing her a tissue. "I am so, so sorry."

"And someone Also took my drum," Milala said.

Allison was disappointed in the change of subject, but she didn't press it. Milala had already given her an astounding gift in trusting her as much as she had. Allison place the band-aid and smoothed it down. "Maybe you should buy a new drum."

Milala scowled. "I think this is the cluelessness we've been talking about."

"Oh." Allison sat back. "Okay, I am totally open to owning that. Drums cost money."

"Drums aren't things you sell. They are things you make."

"Oh. I like that," Allison said, brightening a little. "You're going to make a drum?"

"I am," Milala said.

"Out of what?" Allison asked.

Milala pointed to the sink. "Out of the skin of my Father."

The goat herald loomed over Lord Jay, and for a few brief moments, it seemed to Julie that the monster would simply lean over, affix its circle of teeth to the top of his balding head and suck the brains right out of the magician. But instead, the beast wavered back and forth in the air, reminding Julie of the inflatable figures she'd seen at used car dealerships, the hot air forced into them making them billow and gyrate in the wind.

But while those figures were amusing, this was quite the opposite. This was the incarnation of pure malevolence, the mouthpiece of a voice she hoped, deep within her, never to hear—the voice of irredeemable chaos.

Lord Jay no longer danced. He lowered himself to the ground, his arms spread wide, and lay down, face to the dirt. At first, Julie could not figure out what he was doing, but then it struck her that the magickian was worshiping the beast. The other magickians quickly followed suit, putting their hands in the air and then lowering themselves slowly to the ground until they kissed the sand. Only Loner Girl did not offer her obeisance, but she did bow her head.

Throughout these ritual humiliations, the goat herald was not silent. Its booming voice continued to form words that seemed awkward and unnatural in its mouth. "Before him, all things are food," it was saying. "Before him, all beings are food."

"I. Am. Not. On the grocery list," Julie said aloud to herself. The blood pouring from her own wrist made the handcuffs slick.

"Get the fucking food," she heard Lord Jay's voice.

Julie didn't need to look to know that Mercer was coming for her. The magickian hovered over her for a minute, before jabbing a key into the remaining cuff. As soon as the cuff sprang open, Julie landed an elbow into Mercer's ribs. The magician had not seen it coming, and he doubled over from the blow. Julie had not paused even for an instant, but had swung away from her strike, allowing the momentum to carry her away from the wall of cars, away from Mercer. But Perry was right behind him, and before Julie could run three steps, the younger man had launched himself at her, landing heavily on the ground with his arms wrapped around her legs.

She went down hard, hitting her head on the cracked earth, which was softer than stone, although not by much. Julie wrestled with Perry, trying to twist out of his grasp. She lashed and writhed, but the younger magickian held her fast. Then he reached up and grabbed her hair. Julie had not expected that, and found that the young man's reach was longer than hers—long enough that he could hold her hair in his fist far enough away from himself that she could not land a blow. She flailed and kicked, but to no avail. The top of her head was on fire from where he had balled up his fist, pulling on her hair, and threatening to pull it out altogether.

Standing shakily, the young magician pulled her up and began to steer her toward the goat herald, toward the salt hexagram, toward the opening into chaos—into whatever fissure had opened up between the worlds.

Julie thrashed and began to scream for help—but it did no good. The goat herald continued to waver, its rubbery, intestinal limbs quivering in some sidereal breeze that Julie could not feel. It loomed and waved over her as Jamie threw her over his shoulder and sidestepped the lines made of salt so as not to disrupt the star cut into the earth.

In their struggle, she realized that they had only very nearly missed stepping on Lord Jay's head, which was still on the ground, his prostrate body hugging the earth.

It was an ironic show of affection for the planet he had just betrayed, but Julie had little time to wonder at it. Once they were on the inside of the hexagram, Perry threw her to the ground and dragged her toward the opening. Then he gave her a forceful shove, and she felt her feet fail to find purchase on the desert soil. They windmilled and kicked against empty air, and yet she did not have the sensation of falling. But she did have the sensation of crossing a threshold, from the safe, familiar firmness of the earth into...somewhere else.

Thom opened one eye, surprised that he could. *I'm awake...I'm alive...* he thought, and he wondered at it. He should be dead, he knew. He should be beginning the dirt nap, as he'd heard it called. But he wasn't. He looked around him without moving—he wasn't sure if he was capable of it yet. He thought he might see sand, some scrub, maybe starlight. But he did not see any of those things. Instead, he saw blurry colored lights and little else.

Then he noticed the fire along his back. He jerked, and pain shot through him—so intense he might have blacked out for a few seconds. But then he was back. "Hello?" he called. He marveled at the strangeness of his own voice. No one responded.

He steeled himself and pushed up with his hands, trying to sit up. The pain erupted along his back, but he pushed through it. He struggled into a sitting position and felt around. He found a lamp. He turned it on.

"Oh, shit," he said. The walls were strangely shaped and very close. Everything looked oddly familiar as well. Thom's brow furrowed as he tried to place himself. "Oh shit," he said again when the recognition hit.

He was in the tiny silver trailer; the one the electrician's old man had been lying in. *I'm the new old man,* a voice in Thom's head said. He shuddered. "That hurt," he said aloud, inwardly vowing not to shudder again.

Just then the door to the trailer opened with a jerk. The slack face of Albert Castillo rose into view. "There you are!" he said cheerily.

"Albert?" Thom squinted. Why was everything blurry?

"'Lo, Sheriff. Are you comfy?"

Thom ignored the question. "Uh...how did I get here?"

"I put a tracker on your SUV," Albert said, breaking out into a wide grin. It was obvious he was proud of this. "So I'd know where you was."

Thom wasn't sure how he should feel about that. He decided to worry about it later. "And?"

"And I followed you, straight to the shooting. It were loud."

"So how did I get here?"

"I drove the van to where you were crawling, and I loaded you up."

"All by yourself?" Thom asked.

"I'm a big boy," Albert said.

"I guess you are."

"I put you in here, since my daddy wasn't using it anymore. It's a place of honor."

"I...I'm grateful." Then Thom had a thought. "Uh, son, just out of curiosity, did you...you know, change the sheets after...after your father..."

"No sir. Was I supposed to?"

Thom flashed on just what it was he'd been lying on—was *touching*, even now. He jerked his hands off the sheets. "That's just...ghastly." He tried to hold them off the bed, but the pain was too great. He let them fall again.

"So...what happened to your father?" Thom asked.

"The men in the van came. They were very nice. I thought about killing them."

Thom swallowed. "Oh?" He held his breath.

"But they just did their work. In and out before I could really make a plan." Albert's fuzzy eyes widened in wonder. "I gotta say, I was surprised about their speed, like little lightning bugs."

"What about social services? Did they send someone?" Thom asked.

"The woman with the big hair?" Albert asked.

"Well, I don't know who they'd send," Thom confessed. "Was there a woman with big hair?"

"Piled on top of her head like a dancin' mushroom."

"Did she invite you to come live...somewhere else?"

Albert's eyes widened. "How did you know?"

"Big-haired women are all alike," Thom quipped. "So what did you tell her?"

"I didn't say anything. She was scary. So I just shot her. In the belly. She moaned and rolled around a lot."

Thom's mouth flopped open. "You...*what?*"

"I don't want to go live somewhere else. All my stuff is here."

"But why did you *shoot* her?"

Albert shrugged. "How does your back feel?"

"It feels like someone ripped hooks out of my flesh back there."

Albert grinned, laughed. He sat on the edge of the bed. "That was me. I picked the buckshot out of you. Had to really dig for some of it. I poured whiskey on you after." His grin widened. "You screamed."

Thom felt grateful not to remember this. "Albert...how long..."

"Only a few hours. I didn't expect you to wake up tonight."

Everything in Thom's body screamed, but he swung his feet off the bed. He tried to stand. Albert watched with bemused detachment. Thom clutched at the close walls and steadied himself as he put one foot on the step, then the other, and exited the trailer into the fresh desert air outside. The stars greeted him with an outrageous display of beauty.

"Where you going?" Albert asked.

"I'm just...I gotta..." Thom leaned against the side of the trailer, wincing as his back touched it. It was still warm from the afternoon sun. *That means there's time,* a voice in his head shouted. But how... He felt in his pockets, but his phone seemed to be missing. Thom flashed on a mental image of it lying in the sand outside the car pull, near a pool of his own blood. He had no idea if the image was a memory or just a vivid imagining. He shook his head to clear it. He pondered whether or not to ask Albert if he could use his phone. *I might end up with a belly full of lead,* he thought. *But I need backup.* Then he had an idea. It wasn't a very good idea, he knew, but his bandwidth had narrowed considerably. "Albert, I need to do some police work tonight. I need me a deputy. I wonder if you'll help me...some more."

"Will it be fun?" Albert asked.

"Do you mean will there be shooting and blood and mayhem?" Thom asked. "I have every reason to expect it."

"Let's go!" Albert said, sprinting out of the trailer with boyish energy.

"We need to go back to that car-pull," Thom said. "But we're going to need weapons...I lost mine, back in Old Bill...er, the SUV."

"I gots a shotgun," Albert said.

Thom knew that much. "We're going to need more than that. I'm thinking some of those lightning sticks you made might be just the thing."

"Yeah..." Albert's eyebrows shot up.

"Are they charged up?"

"I always keep 'em topped off."

"How many do you have?"

"Six, but some are newer and fancier. I keep making them better."

Thom nodded. "Bring all you got then. And bring a voltage regulator and generator too. And plenty of wire. And do you have a battery-powered soldering gun?"

"Oh, yeah. Daddy got me one."

"Well, bring that, too. Uh...did your Daddy have any pain medication?"

"Yeah."

"I'll take...whatever they gave him. Just bring me the bottle, please. Oh, and one more thing. Got any more of them Cheez-its?"

Peg started by looking at the statue's face. It was recognizably hers. Her shoulders fell as she took it in. If the Peg in the statue was any older than herself, she could not discern it. She was lying in bed, at home, her hair mussed and lopsided. Her head was drooping, chin resting on her collarbone, mouth slightly open. Her eyes were closed, however. She looked peaceful. She looked asleep. A part of her wanted to go and shake herself, but she knew it wouldn't rouse her alternative self, her statue.

If anyone else was present, the cube did not show it; its window was very limited. But it was enough.

"Oh, my dear," Peg said out loud. She stepped forward and touched the cheek of her face. It was hard, unpliable...stone. "Look at you, love." A swell of emotions stirred within her. Her first impulse was to berate the statue—to take her to task for all the myriad and profound ways she had fucked up her life. She wanted to rage at her for her choice of men, the depths to which she let herself sink, the things she had done to survive. She wanted to harangue her for the ways her unreliability had hurt Julie, for the rift between them, for the years of accumulated regret, stress, and worry. She wanted to kick in her teeth and pull out her stupid, lopsided hair.

But she didn't. Alongside all those feelings, others arose: compassion for what she had suffered, for the choices that were no choice, for the damage she would incur and cause. She had no impulse to cry or to panic or to wail. But nor could she deny the complex mixture of feelings that resisted being neatly sorted or settled. Instead, the statue confronted her with the truth. Staring at it, the whole sordid mess of her life unfolded in her memory. She did not run from any of it; she did not make excuses, even to herself; she did not reject its revelations. It was the truth, and she received the whole of it without objection or correction or complaint. It just was. She just was...or had been.

Leaning over, Peg placed one hand on the cube to support herself. Then she planted a kiss on her stone cheek. "I forgive you," she said. Then she straightened up and returned to where Ted and Jake were standing just a few feet away.

Ted's eyes were wide with concern. "Are you okay?" he asked.

She was still pissed at him, but strangely, seeing the statue had dissipated that somewhat. "I'm okay," she said.

Jake's brow furrowed and he scratched his head. "Pastor, excuse me for saying this, but...you didn't even flinch...when you looked at your cube. I have no idea what you were thinking."

Peg smiled and put a hand on his elbow. "When I was a little girl, the neighbors had a dog that scared the willies out of me. He stood just on the other side of the chain-link fence snarling and barking, and I was terrified that if he got through that fence, he'd tear my throat out." Peg's eyes were unfocused, as if looking at something far off that no one else could see. "My Dad saw how scared I was, and he went and had a word with the neighbor. I was shocked to see him go into the back yard with that vicious dog. But the dog wasn't vicious to him. His tail started wagging and he jumped up and barked, but in a playful way. My Dad rolled around in the grass with him, playing with him. And then he came home."

"Uh...okay," Jake said, shifting from one foot to the other. "But...I don't think I understand your point."

Peg chuckled and gave Ted a knowing look. "It means that a long time ago, Jesus looked death full in the face and made it his bitch." She patted his arm again. "He crossed the fence...and he came back. He revealed to the whole world that death wasn't the ferocious and scary bugaboo we thought it was."

Jake scowled in confusion. "But...that's just a story."

"Not to me it isn't, young man. To me it's history. To me it's more real than the morning paper. It's the reason I can look at that cube and not be afraid. Death loves to bare its teeth, and it has a fierce bark, sure. But in the end, I'm just going to rub its tummy."

Jake stared at her. She patted his back and moved toward where Ted was standing.

"Uh...well, do you want to see the other one?" Jake asked. "The other cube, I mean?"

"Want? *Want* may be the wrong word," Ted corrected him. "Ready, though? I am ready."

Jake nodded, accepting the correction without complaint. He turned and started walking toward another of the cubes. Along the way he handed his flashlight to Peg. "You might need this later," he suggested.

She patted the pocket of her coat. "Got one, thank you."

Jake nodded and continued toward another of the cubes. He stopped a few yards from it and pointed. Peg watched Ted's face as he rounded the corner. His features hardened until they looked like stone themselves. His eyes grew moist, but otherwise he was impenetrable. Peg searched him for some sign of what he was seeing, but Ted gave nothing away.

Finally, Peg stepped away from Jake and moved to stand next to her friend. She put her arm around his shoulder and only then looked at the statue. In it, Ted's head was on the ground. It also had a strange, oblong shape to it. A baseball bat impacted one side of it. The face was screwed up into a knot of pain. There were swollen patches around the eyes and many cuts. There was no question: this was a violent end.

"Oh honey," she said, drawing him into her.

Ted let himself be drawn, hugged, but he seemed as unresponsive as a Raggedy Andy doll. After a few minutes, he said, "That's about right."

"It's a hate crime," Peg said. "An anti-gay hate crime."

"Probably," Ted agreed.

"You don't know it's going to end like this," Peg said.

"Oh, I have a pretty good idea," Ted said, his voice dark with finality.

"It doesn't have to be a prophesy. It can be a warning," Peg said.

"You just keep telling yourself that, miss I-died-in-my-bed-and-my-pillows-are-fluffed."

"Ted," Peg warned.

"I'm sorry," Ted said.

They stood together for several minutes in silence.

"Are you still mad at me?" Ted asked. "I mean, are we even now?"

"Even? Oh, my love, why would I even be keeping score?" Peg whispered.

Ted buried his face in her neck and his shoulders began to shake. She pulled him in closer, hugging the birdlike bundle of sticks that was his body to her own. She held him until the shaking stopped. He pulled away from her at last, wiping his nose on the back of his hand. Then apparently remembering he had a handkerchief, he pulled one from his rear pocket and blew his nose into it.

"You need to make sure he doesn't die in vain," she said, pointing to the image of his busted head.

"Nothing to be afraid of now, I suppose," he agreed. He sniffed and wiped at his eye.

"It's okay to pity him, to let your heart go out to him, to...love him, you know," Peg said.

"No," Ted said. "That has *always* been me," Ted said. "From the very first time Father told me to pull my pants down in the sacristy so God could see if I was properly circumcised. Can't let uncircumcised boys be altar boys, after all." He spat. "And I always hated him. He let it happen. And I let this happen." He pointed at the cube. "Or I will, I suppose."

"You can't blame...the boy you were," Peg said. "And you can't blame *him*, either."

"I can and do. And will."

"Then I think that's very sad, and I feel sorry for you."

"Fuck off," Ted said.

"That's the spirit," Peg said. "Now, *now* we're even."

───────

There must have been something beneath Julie's feet, but she could not see it. She could stand, and she did. Whatever as beneath her was soft and yielding. She whipped around to see where she had come from, and there was indeed a spot—tiny, now, and limned with ghostly luminosity—through which she could see the tiki torches holding forth against the darkness.

But there were no tiki torches here. There were a billion stars, the brilliance of which astounded her. Confused her. She knew somehow that the light streaming from those myriad and distant stars was unfiltered by the earth's atmosphere—something she had never beheld before. A part of her mind wondered what she was breathing if there was no atmosphere, but it seemed a secondary concern.

Back on earth—for so it seemed to her—the hole that opened up seemed small. But here inside it was vast. Indeed, the distances were overwhelming. For many minutes, she simply stood there, mouth agape, staring upwards.

As her eyes adjusted, she began to make out more detail in the starlight. There were beings, she could see, adrift among the stars. No, not adrift, she realized, but making their way across the vast distances. They looked like insects—vaguely caterpillar-like, with enormous, bulbous heads, propelled, it seemed, by trailing tentacles that spun as they sped across the endless cold expanse.

There were hundreds of them...no, thousands...more. And she saw that some were greater. And then she saw that distance counted for little in this place—wherever she was. If she stared at something, it seemed to get closer, its details ever sharper, ever more magnified. She stared at the greatest confluence of the creatures, and as they grew larger and clearer in her vision, she saw that they ministered to an even larger being—and her hands and knees began to shake at the sight of it. It had a beak that broke at a cruel angle midway, surrounded by gaseous tentacles that swirled around its eyeless face. Its body was amorphous, bloated, black and covered with what looked like barnacles, or scabs where barnacles used to be. It shuddered, motion rippling through its vast gelatinous torso, causing the tendrils skirting all sides to spasm and twitch.

Julie watched transfixed as the beak tore into the oversized head of one of the caterpillar "ministers." Green-black ooze floated out into space as the caterpillar writhed and careened, but the beak held it fast. It was still jerking as the beak methodically shredded its body, occasionally spitting out vast jets of viscous fluids, which were set upon by the other caterpillars that circled it, tending to it...worshipping it.

"Azathoth," Julie whispered, although she had no idea if the dread beast she beheld was indeed the king of the Great Old Ones, or whether it was merely an underling of an even more terrible overlord. A quivering tendril, acting as an impossibly long tongue, lapped at the inside of the caterpillar's skull, sucking up every last bit of brain or sinew before withdrawing, spinning wet and wild, into its dread and eldritch mouth.

Julie forced herself to look away. And yet there was little to see but stars, and among those stars, everywhere she looked, both distant and near, were the dreadful insect ministers, large as planets, scurrying off to do the bidding of some cosmic tyrant she could not comprehend.

There was no part of the heavens she could see that was not filled with them or creatures like them. And as she stared, an idea pressed against her conscious mind—an idea she resisted, an idea she refused. Yet, she pushed it down out of consciousness in vain, for the effort itself caused it to erupt through the surface of her awareness.

This is how it really is, she thought. There was no benevolent deity behind the universe, no Jesus friend of sinners, no angels bending low to wipe away the tears of frightened children. There was no Goddess, no goodness, no light, no hope; no salvation awaiting anyone, no rescue coming, nor any savior to bring it. There was only this: A vast cold void filled with venomous monsters, intent on nothing but the ruthless domination of worlds, the wielding of mindless power, and the voracious slaughter of the innocent and the unholy alike.

Won't Mom be disappointed? Julie thought. Her lip trembled, and the meagre flicker of hope she had long held in her heart perished. Like a single candle holding at bay infinite and eternal darkness, it was snuffed out, swallowed up by hopelessness, despair, and triumphant, sovereign death.

She sniffed and wiped the wet from her eyes. *I should simply lay down,* she thought. *I should just lay my body down and die. Just lay down and wait for the beak.*

But she did not lie down. Instead, she lowered her gaze from the heavens to take in what was immediately around her. Yet there was not much to see. The space was infinite, but largely empty. No, not empty. The ground, she saw, was covered with crawling worms. She crushed them underfoot every time she moved. *That's why the ground feels soft,* she thought. And then another thought struck at her heart: *I am no different from Azathoth—I move and creatures die.* The universe was nothing more than a vast abattoir, she realized, a cosmic meat locker filled with remorseless slaughter and consumption.

She screamed.

CHAPTER ELEVEN

About five minutes shy of arriving at the car pull, Thom touched Albert's elbow. "That's good enough, son," he said. "They'll be expecting us to come by road."

Albert lifted his foot off the gas and allowed the van to slow naturally. "What do you want me to do?"

"As soon as you can safely pull off the road into the desert, head to the back of the place," he pointed diagonally, partly indicating forward but also toward the passenger-side window.

"Okay, boss." Albert squinted as he looked for ingress to the flat tabletop of the desert. He found one.

Hearing Albert call him "boss" sounded strange to Thom's ears. It was what Julie called him, and Jake. And here was his new deputy, doing the same. *My new* murderer *deputy*, he reminded himself, wondering how he was going to break it to the kid once all this was over and he had to take him in. He pushed the thought aside and forced himself to focus.

"Kill the lights," he said.

A split-second later, the headlights shut off, and the van was enveloped by darkness. But that was illusory. After a few minutes, Thom's eyes adjusted. The moon was almost full; the desert was subtly illumined by a steady blue light. It wasn't enough to read by, but it was enough to drive.

"We can't go in the front door," Thom thought out loud.

"Trash bins," Albert said.

"What?" Thom asked, only half paying attention to the driver.

"The trash bins. They're never by the front entrance—it's bad for business," Albert said, his voice electric with excitement and an eagerness to help.

"Where are they?" Thom asked, his attention now fully engaged.

"Somewhere the garbage truck can get to without too much fuss," Albert said. "Side entrance or rear."

"Find it," Thom said. It would have been easier in daylight, but the cover of night was an asset he was grateful for.

"Cars are made of metal," Albert said. "Metal conducts electricity."

"Uh…right," Thom answered, only half-listening again. He picked up Albert's 12-gauge and broke the action to check the rounds. Both shells were fresh. He flipped it closed again, felt the solid jolt of the mechanism as it slid into its accustomed place.

"You gonna use the big gun?" Albert asked.

"Yes. Is that all right?" Thom began to stuff shells into his pockets. He counted twenty-four of them, plus the two in the chambers. *Twenty-six*, he thought. *All I got is twenty-six shots, and no idea what I'm facing.*

"This here's it, pretty sure," Albert said. They had found a road of sorts—it was still made of dirt, but this dirt had been hard packed by years of fat, double-axle tires rolling over the same track. Once they were on it, the ride smoothed out considerably.

A shadow hid the moon, but Thom looked closer and saw that it wasn't a cloud that had occluded their light, but a wall. Squinting, Thom noted the extreme irregularities of the wall. "What's it—" he began, but Albert cut him off.

"S'cars," he said. "The wall is made of cars, all the way around."

"Well, I'll be," Thom said.

"You know, cars are made of metal," Albert reminded him again. "And metal conducts electricity."

"Uh-huh," Thom said, ruminating.

Albert coasted to a stop near a trio of trash bins, each of which loomed over the van. Just beyond them was a gate that ran on rails from left to right.

"Can you get us past that gate?" Thom asked. "Or will we need to climb?"

"I'll take a look," Albert said. He jumped out and ambled over to the gate. Then he came back to the van, a smile on his face. He didn't speak to Thom, but simply went to the back of the van, opened it, and removed a toolbox. Carrying it back to the gate, he set it down, opened it up, and began rummaging.

Thom sighed, wondering how long it would take the kid. He began to make a plan. But to his great amazement, he saw Albert walking back to the van, toolbox hanging from his arm. "That was quick," Thom said as soon as the door was open.

"Easy gate," Albert replied. When Thom looked over at it, he couldn't see it. It had retracted and Thom hadn't even noticed. He cursed himself. *That's how you wind up dead,* he reminded himself.

"Should we take it in?" Thom asked. "The van, I mean?"

"Nah, I think we should leave her right there."

"Because...?"

"Because we can walk in quieter. No one's gonna notice it here. Plus, this is the perfect spot for the generator."

"Generator? What are you thinking?"

"I'm thinking that cars are made of metal. And metal conducts—"

"Holy shit, okay," Thom said. "The penny just dropped. What are you thinking...exactly?"

"I'm thinking we set the generator up here—it's far enough away from the main entrance that no one will hear it."

"Good," Thom said, opening the van door, but not making a move to exit.

"I'm thinking we start up the generator, run it through the voltage regulator, step up the voltage, and electrify this whole wall of cars." His face was shining. "Then we just got to make sure the circuit is closed as we go along—a fender can bridge the current from one section of cars to the next."

"And we make sure-as-shit we don't touch any cars."

"Sizzzzzle!" Albert said, drawing out that "zzz" with apparent glee.

"Okay, set it up. Let's light this motherfucker up."

"Oh, there won't be any lights," Albert warned.

"No, it's just an...never mind. Electrify it, that will be good enough."

Julie winced with every step she took, feeling the tiny bodies of the worms pop and squish beneath her boots. Her eyes had adjusted now, and while it was still dim, the unfiltered light from a billion distant stars lent everything a cool, bluish glow.

The heavens were ghastly and glorious, all at once, but she forced herself to lower her gaze, to deal with her immediate surroundings. The fascination of the cosmos could wait, she decided firmly. She willed her police training to kick in. Steeling herself against the squishiness of the ground, she set out to explore her perimeter.

But there was no perimeter. She walked as far as she could before just losing sight of the luminous opening through which she had come. She had no sense of direction, she had simply headed to the left. But when she stopped, everything appeared much as it was, except that the opening had grown smaller.

But then she noticed something else that surprised her. It appeared to be a large pupa. It was a little longer than her, lying alone on the ground, surrounded by the crawling worms. It was roughly cigar-shaped, wrapped in tiny white translucent threads. "Silk," she said aloud.

She reminded herself not to get too close—who knew what horrors might erupt from it?

She backed up a few paces and looked around again. Her eyes widened as they noticed another glowing place—this one on whatever served as a floor in this place. "Another opening?" she asked herself.

Cutting a wide swath around the pupa—or cocoon, or whatever it was —she headed toward the glow.

Growing closer, she saw that it was indeed another opening. It was much like the one she had come through, only its edges were ragged. Nor was it as large as the other had been. It was much, much smaller, she saw, and not of a uniform shape—more a lopsided rectangle than an oval. Whatever or whomever had created this one had done it inexpertly, perhaps accidentally.

As she drew near it, she noticed the floor was beginning to swell. She stopped, hoping to understand what was happening to the floor before she stepped on it. Then she realized that the tiny worms were massing, squirming atop one another, clinging together to form a shape—not a recognizable shape, just an aggregate clump that roiled and grew as more and more of the tiny worms threw themselves upon the pile. As the clump accumulated mass, it began to move.

Thousands—hundreds of thousands of worms—crawled on its surface even as it crawled toward her. Appendages made entirely of the tiny worms separated themselves and reached toward her. A head formed, but no face—instead she was looking into nothing but a teeming surface of wormflesh. No legs separated themselves—instead it seemed to glide along the surface as if propelled by its fellows still covering every inch of ground.

And it glided straight toward her. Instinctively she backed up, until, catching movement out of the corner of her eye, she saw another aggregate worm-beast behind her—too close behind her. Without pausing to think, she darted to her right, around the first worm-beast, and dove for the awkward, luminescent opening and whatever mysteries lay within it.

Peg discerned the outline of Jake's cowboy hat and waved her flashlight as she and Ted picked their way through the cornfield.

"Pastor?" Jake asked as they grew closer. "I didn't expect to see you out here again today. Have you come to look at your cubes again?"

"No, no," Peg waved the notion away. She remembered not to shine the flashlight in Jake's face and lowered it so that its ambient light reflected up into their faces. "But we knew others would be coming out. We've come to...well, I haven't thought of a name for it. I suppose we're here to provide emergency spiritual care...for the people who do come."

"Cornfield chaplaincy," Ted quipped.

"That's...that's brilliant!" Jake said. The young man looked so relieved Peg was afraid he might cry. "I'm so glad you're here."

"Where's my daughter? And your boss?" Peg asked.

Jake's lips grew tight and a flicker of panic flashed in his eyes.

"Uh-oh," Peg said. "Is this one of those 'I-can't-tell-you-anything-but-don't-you-worry-your-pretty-little-head' situations?"

"Er...sort of," Jake confessed.

Peg harrumphed. "I've come to expect nothing more."

Jake looked confused and a little worried. Peg allowed herself to enjoy it for a moment. Then she took one of Jake's hands. "Not to worry, my boy. I'm used to it."

Jake grinned his relief.

Peg heard the distant roar of a motor. "Incoming," she said.

"What's going on with these?" Ted asked. He pointed his own flashlight at the two cubes with tarps over them.

Jake grimaced. "Those were...well, they're too...terrible, I guess. Mr. Nyland and I agreed that those shouldn't be, well, public."

Peg nodded, but Ted just looked more curious. "Mind if I peek?"

Peg looked at Jake. It was clear that the deputy did mind—that was the very reason for the tarps, after all.

"Ted, come away. The deputy did what he did for a reason. We should respect it."

Ted scowled at her but walked back over to her side just the same.

"Now you're going to pout about it," Peg said to him.

Ted sniffed. "'Tisn't true."

"'Tis."

"'Tisn't."

Jake looked confused.

"'Tis."

"'Tisn't."

Peg punched him, not hard. Ted feigned injury.

"You two *aren't* married?" Jake asked.

"Perish the thought," Ted said.

"Not if *I* want any action," Peg answered.

Jake blushed. Peg took his arm. "I don't know what my daughter and the sheriff are up to, but I'm glad *you're* here. We need a steady hand at a time like this."

Jake nodded, but she was surveying the fields. "Now Troy's dead, it isn't the same," Jake said. "Abel says it was a prank, but now it's a prophesy."

"That's exactly why we decided to come out here, my boy," Peg said, pulling his arm closer into her tummy as they walked together.

"But what we don't know is if these are predictive prophesies—as in, can this outcome be changed or avoided?" Ted added. "Or is it absolute—must the person absolutely die in the way shown in the cube?"

Jake nodded. It seemed the thought had occurred to him as well.

"Ordinarily, such a question would require an experiment," Ted continued.

"That seems a little callous," Peg noted.

"Quite," Ted agreed.

"How is Mia, dear, do you know?" Peg asked.

"Abel says she's been holed up since breakfast," Jake answered.

"Oh, dear," Peg said, shaking her head. "This is traumatizing." She indicated the whole of the cornfield. "Just seeing these is traumatizing."

"The problem is that we Americans don't acknowledge trauma," Ted commented. "We see it as weakness. Can't show weakness."

"Might conquers. Vulnerability heals," Peg said.

"That'll preach, Pastor," Ted said. For a brief moment, they shared a smile.

With her left hand, Peg patted Jake's hand, still clutched in her right. "We'll be a team tonight. You need us, you call. Hear?"

Jake nodded.

"All right, then." She let go his hand, and the young man looked like he was about to thank her. Instead, he rubbed at his wrist.

The headlights of a car bobbed into view, and the three of them watched as it pulled up and parked just off the access road.

"Working like a charm," Jake said. "So far."

"I see the cones and the tape," Peg said. "It's a good idea. We'll watch to make sure no one goes astray."

"What are we, then, Australian shepherds?" Ted asked.

"We're pastors."

"Ah! Well, then, we both drive sheep. Australian shepherds get more exercise though."

"Remember, Jake, we're here. And God is here." She reached for his hand and gave it another squeeze.

"Indeed, it seems we can hardly escape him," Ted said, watching people get out of the car.

The moonlight made the corridors between the cars seem even more surreal than they already were—Thom walked silently in a jagged canyon spiked by shadows. A voice in his head was berating him for involving Albert. He should have arrested him and waited for proper backup. *But no,* the voice insisted, *you now have the world's most undependable wing man. Congratulations.*

He shook his head to clear it and tried to focus. There was an intersection up ahead—Thom could see the wall of cars directly ahead of him, with one path snaking off to his left and another to his right. The conditions weren't right to flip a coin, so he just went with his gut. He turned left.

Almost immediately, he heard growling.

He had expected this, but he froze anyway. Moving between the shadows was a dark presence, and it was drooling and snarling.

"Hey, boy," Thom said soothingly. "I'm a friend, not an enemy." He took a couple of the Cheez-its from his breast pocket and positioned one in his hand for throwing. Then he waited.

The low, crouching figure stepped out of the shadows into the full moonlight. Thom thought it looked like a Rottweiler, probably black, but who could tell? It moved toward him cautiously, its motions reminding Thom more of a big cat than a dog. Thom waited for it to pause, then he tossed one of the Cheez-its, landing it about a foot shy of the dog. The Rottweiler sniffed at the snack, then snuffled it up.

A bit creakily, Thom sat down cross-legged. His back felt like raw hamburger, and every movement of his shirt was a new experience in pain. But instead of slowing him down, Thom used the pain for fuel. He held another Cheez-it up, waving it in the direction of the dog.

It sniffed at his hand, and Thom was relieved to see the stub of the dog's tail begin to tick-tock back and forth with the mechanical regularity of a windshield wiper. "What a good dog," Thom said, holding his hand still while the dog took another of the Cheez-its. Thom could feel the dog's drool run down his wrist. "Lovely," Thom said aloud. But he didn't mind, not really. He knew dogs. He loved them. They trusted him. An empty place in Thom's heart ached as he began to scratch the dog's ears.

This was not a dog that was starved or abused, he could see. It was healthy, strong, and stocky as a good Rottweiler ought to be. The dog was now sniffing at his shirt, having tracked the Cheez-its directly to their point of origin. He laughed and dug a couple more out, careful to keep a few in reserve in case this was not the only dog he'd need to win over.

Thom held the crackers out, but before the dog could snatch them up, a bolt of blue light blinded Thom and he felt the air directly around him crackle. The Rottweiler yelped and crumpled to the ground. The smell of ozone and burning fur filled Thom's nostrils. "What the fuck?" Thom breathed.

He leaped up, pain of his back be damned. Poised to fight or flee, Thom's eyes were wide with adrenaline. His right hand automatically went to his holster, but of course it was empty.

Albert walked out of the shadows, one of the lightning guns

hanging from his shoulder by a leather strap. He walked over to the still sizzling body of the dog and kicked at it. "I got him good," he whispered. Thom noted the pride in the young man's voice.

Thom felt sick. He opened his mouth to say, "There was no reason to kill that dog," but he didn't. The kid did not need to be cut down right now. Thom needed his confidence high. He shifted gears internally. "Uh…great…great shot, kid."

"I been practicing for years. S'little tricky 'til you get the hang of it."

"I believe you," Thom said.

"That dog just dropped!" Albert said, his voice raising a bit as he relived his moment of glory.

"Keep your voice down," Thom said.

"Sorry, boss," Albert said, looking down. The kid had four of the lightning guns slung across his back, plus the shotgun, which he'd placed on the ground momentarily. Thom picked it up and reflexively broke the action to check the chambers. He snapped the action back into place.

"C'mon," he said, and stepped out in front, heading down the left-hand path. He stepped over the body of the dog, trying not to think about it. *That was a good dog*, he thought. *A good, hardworking, loyal dog. He didn't deserve to die. And we had no right to kill it*. But however much that was true, he knew nothing would bring the dog back. The dog was gone, and he had to let go of it. He wrestled the tendrils of his brain away from the animal, willing every ounce of sensitivity to focus on the path ahead of him.

There was a turn in the corridor; Thom paused at the corner of it, resting his face against the fin of a '59 Edsel. Moving quickly but tentatively, he peeked around the corner, and then just as quickly pulled back. "Oh, shit," he said.

"What's that, boss?" Albert asked.

"I think I found them."

"Who?"

"Whoever took Julie, I hope."

"Did you see Julie?" Albert asked. The question sounded strange to Thom since Albert had never met Julie.

"No," he answered.

"Is that good or bad?" Albert asked.

"I...I don't know," Thom admitted.

"Well, whatcha gonna do?" Albert asked.

"I guess I'm going to crash this party," Thom said.

Julie dove into darkness and found herself falling. A thought flickered —*How far will I fall?*—*then* she hit something solid. The impact rattled her bones and knocked the wind from her. Her shoulder immediately began to blaze with pain, and she slid into something else solid, hitting her head hard enough that snow filled her vision despite the fact that there was no light at all.

Struggling to raise herself up on her elbows, she winced against the pain in her shoulder, and forced herself to breathe deep, even breaths. She glanced over her shoulder, back toward the place she must have fallen from, but she could see nothing. She felt at the floor and found it blessedly free of worms. "Thank God for small favors," she whispered, then kicked herself for making any sound. She had no idea where she was, or who or what might be lurking in the dark. She went back to focusing on her breath, and in the quiet that followed, realized what she had just said. She had thanked God instinctively— and it occurred to her how silly that was.

She had not believed in God in a very long time—not her mother's God anyway. Instead, she had found the Goddess in college, and had been an on-again-off-again solitary practitioner of Wicca for most of her life since then. But now... *There is no Goddess,* she thought to herself. *There is no Spirit of Gaia. There is no benevolent intelligence behind the universe. I have seen the only power behind the universe—I've seen it split the head of a monster the size of a planet and scrape its brains out with its fucking tongue. Hope is a lie.*

She shuddered, feeling more lost and alone and pointless than she ever had. The only appropriate response to such a malevolent universe was to find a razor and exit it with as little pain and as much efficient dispatch as she could muster. A single bullet to the brain would do the job handily, but her empty holster seemed to mock her. *Maybe I could find a knife?* she wondered. For a few short moments she thought about the cubes and realized she had completely misunderstood them. They weren't oracles of the end—they were signs of hope, monuments to the moment each of their subjects escaped the illusion of a benevolent universe and found salvation in oblivion.

It was the desire for exactly this blessed insensibility that forced her to rise to her knees, and then—one hand against what felt like a wall for support—to her feet. She felt along the wall with both hands until one hand touched a familiar feature—a light switch. The sound that escaped her throat was something in between a sob and a laugh. She hadn't expected something so normal, so mundane, so earthly.

She switched it on and squinted against the blazing light.

She was in Clive's apartment.

"Here goes nothin'," Thom said. He set his rifle on the ground and stepped around the corner into the firelight. Immediately, he breathed, "Holy crap." He blinked. He had no frame of reference for what he was seeing.

An enormous creature, twice the size of a man, twisted and wavered back and forth, looking for all the world like it was made of internal organs. It wasn't in the shape of a man, he saw, but some kind of beast, but it was too twisted and billowy to say what kind of beast. All Thom knew was that it was horrible, otherworldly, and sinister. There was one figure very near to it, a rotund fellow, Thom could see, but his head was on the ground and Thom couldn't tell if he was alive or not. But surrounding the beast were people—of normal size, he was relieved to see—and they seemed to be worshipping the creature. They were chanting, their voices grinding out some indecipherable language in a low drone. It was monotonous, it was ugly, and it made the hair on Thom's forearm prickle and stiffen.

Beyond the beast was something Thom could not fathom. He saw it, but didn't understand it. It was a door of some kind, a vertical shaft that ran from the ground to the heavens, about twenty feet wide, as near as he could estimate. It was dark all around it, and it was dark inside it, but they were different kinds of dark. There was a shimmering around the edges of the shaft. Thom couldn't see how high it went.

He wished to God he had his service revolver. But he didn't. All he had was Albert and several strategically placed lightning guns. His hands were empty as he stepped into the firelight. Somehow, he willed himself to move forward, toward the fire, toward the others, toward the beast.

He put his hands up to show he wasn't armed. There was no disguising the uniform, of course, so he couldn't expect anything from them but hostility. He hoped Albert was ready. He considered praying, but hadn't said a prayer since Emma had been sick and didn't get well. *No need to start now*, he thought.

"Hey!" one of the worshippers yelled, breaking the pattern of the chant, "who the fuck is that?" It was a young woman wearing a dirty dress that looked like it belonged on a much younger girl. Her face was hard, she was not at all pleased to see him.

The chanting stopped and all eyes turned to him. He saw, to his great horror, that the creature turned its eyeless head in his direction as well. Thom shuddered. It suddenly occurred to him to wonder if the beast had a mouth.

"It's the cops!" another of the worshippers yelled. This was a young man with jet black hair and a hip look. He had been on his knees, but slowly got to his feet.

"I am the Inyo County Sheriff, it's true," Thom yelled. "My name's Thom Lind. You can call me Thom or Sheriff, as you like." He held his hands up higher—his shoulder screamed in protest. "I'm not armed. See?" He turned so that his empty holster was facing them, although he didn't know if they could make it out in the firelight. He turned to face them again. "I'm...I'm sorry to interrupt...well, whatever this is. But...I'm looking for my deputy, Julie Barkley. I've tracked her this far, but...if you can take me to her, I'll be gone and out of your hair so that you can...well, sing to your monster, I guess."

He half expected the beast to react to that with some aggressive action, but it didn't. It just hovered over the fat man, looking strangely like the largest, slimiest, most malevolent balloon animal Thom had ever beheld.

"Ya'll get out of here!" the girl shouted. Thom did not know her, but he knew he didn't like her. He just didn't know why.

"I'm sorry. I know I'm interrupting, maybe something important. I don't mean to offend, especially something...I don't know, is this religious? Anyway, I'm just concerned about Julie. If you can show me to her, I'll be on my way." He was repeating himself, he knew. His plan was to simply keep doing that until they produced his deputy. His hands were shaking. He stuffed them into the pockets of his khakis.

He tried to take in the other worshippers. There was a skinny bald man just a little younger than himself. He recognized him, and it only took a moment to remember why. Otto Mercer, the prick Julie had been investigating. He'd keep an eye on him. There was a long, thin woman, also young, but with a detached, ethereal look to her. *Heroin*, Thom thought. He knew that look. She didn't appear to be worshipping, just observing.

The world seemed to freeze for a few precious moments, save for the waving, billowing motion of the beast. Then, to Thom's great surprise, the fat little man at the foot of the beast uncurled from the fetal position, like a pill bug opening its protective ball. Shakily, the little man got to his feet, his black robe falling to the desert floor. Thom was surprised to discover that underneath he was dressed like an old west saloon keeper, complete with vest.

That told Thom a lot about his character, though it wasn't particularly helpful at the moment. Thom was within spitting distance of the beast now. For the first time he noted markings on the ground and saw that they corresponded in some way to everyone's placement. He had been about to step over one of the lines. He didn't understand why, but instinct restrained him.

He looked up and gasped. Inside the shimmering shaft of darkness, he saw things, things that, once more, he did not understand. There were stars, but they were different stars than he was used to. And swimming among the stars were creatures. They were not like the creature that buffeted the air above his head—they looked much larger, much stronger, and somehow, much hungrier. He shuddered and resolved never to mock Julie's occult goofiness again. The girl had been right. She had always been right.

A part of him despaired. He had not listened to her, had not believed her, had thought her...strange. Yet he also loved her, in his own avuncular fashion. None of which mattered two half-damns if she—

He forced himself to focus. He was facing the little man now, and he turned his attention to him. "Good evening, sir. Are you...in charge here?"

Thom heard the click of a hammer being cocked. He was careful not to make any sudden movements. The beast waved over his head like a medieval battle standard. The little man in the vest ran his fingers through what was left of his hair and presented Thom an insincere smile.

"Your timing is for shit, sheriff," he said.

"Sorry about that," Thom said. "Story of my life."

"As you can see, we're in the middle of something...important."

"I can...it's dramatic, no doubt." Thom gave him a sad smile. He put his hands on his hips and waited. In his peripheral vision, he took note of the young man training a rifle on him. Thom had been in rifle sights before. A peace came over his body, a familiar feeling when he was under fire. He had always found that strange, but had taken it as confirmation that he was in the right job.

"I got a bead..." the young man said.

The little man held his hand up in the young man's direction. *Hold.* Thom saw the young man shift impatiently.

"Look, Mr.—"

"They call me Lord Jay," the little man said.

"Huh. Are you really a lord?" Thom asked. "Because we don't really have those here."

"It's an...affectionate nickname." Lord Jay cocked his head and smiled. The beast waved above his head. Thom had never considered the question of whether meat could *billow*. Now he knew.

"Would you be so kind as to let me in on what ya'll are doing, just now? It's...well, it seems strange and I'm curious."

"We're awakening the sleeping Great Old Ones. Or...actually, it's more like getting their attention. We are asking them to visit us with their terrible grace."

"That sounds very pretty and pious. It also doesn't ring terribly true," Thom said. "Why don't you try again, in less poetic terms?"

"You want the straight poop?" the young woman in the sack dress called over to him. He turned to look at her. She was standing outside the diagram drawn on the ground, close enough to the young man pointing a rifle to touch him. Thom put together that they must be a couple. In the firelight, he could see insects buzzing around her hair. Bees? Flies? He couldn't tell.

"Yes, please," he answered her.

"We're inviting ancient monsters to invade, take over the earth, and make us kings and queens over the dystopian hellscape they leave in their wake."

"Hmm...when you put it like that, it doesn't sound so bad," Thom noted.

"You see our problem, however," Lord Jay continued. "The portal to the other side of the universe is unstable, and we have work to do. The blesséd goat herald is here, the emissary," he pointed to the beast. "We must make the proper sacrifices while we can."

"It's a...delicate operation, is what you're saying," Thom summed it up.

"Exactly." Lord Jay gave precisely the kind of apologetic smile a waiter gives when he can't seat you for forty-five minutes. Thom hated that smile.

"Well, you're in luck, then," Thom said. "Because I'm eager to get out of your way. And I will. As soon as I find Julie."

"I'm afraid I don't know who you're talking about, Sheriff," Lord Jay said obsequiously.

Thom wanted to punch him, and might have if it weren't for the lines on the ground reminding him to stay exactly where he was. "Oh, I think you do. And you can either cooperate with me now, or you can come down to the sheriff's office and cool your heels in a cell until morning. Then we can try again. Which route do you prefer?"

It was the young man with the rifle who responded. "There's one of you, and six of us. We got weapons, and you don't. How you gonna make us—"

Thom jumped at the bone-crunching report of the shotgun. He jerked his head toward the young man, and saw the bloom of fresh blood erupt from the man's chest. The rifle clattered to the ground.

The girl with the bugs flying around her crouched as if ready to spring, her face contorting into a mask of rage. She howled and looked like she was ready to fling herself at Thom, but Lord Jay held his hand up. She stopped, panting, her eyes wild with rage.

"Did you think I wouldn't bring backup?" Thom asked. "Because, well I might be just a hick country sheriff, but honestly, I don't think I look *that* stupid."

"It's not much backup," Thom heard from behind him. He felt the blood drain from his face as he turned to face the voice. Otto Mercer stood just shy of the wall of cars, rifle fixed on a point lost in shadows —the spot where Thom knew Albert was hiding. "I can kill him right now, Lord Jay."

Thom looked back at the little man, whose face broke into a wicked grin. "Then *do*."

Just then there was the sizzling sound of electricity and a leap of sparks. Mercer collapsed to the dirt, his rifle rolling away from him. He'd touched the wall of cars, Thom knew, and had gotten the shock of his life.

He turned back to Lord Jay and put his hands once more on his hips. But this time, it was a gesture of victory. "Well, what'll it be?"

Thom caught movement out of the corner of his left eye and looked up. The thin, wan woman had set her face toward the shaft of alien space and had begun walking toward it. She walked right over the markings etched into the desert soil, heedless of their restrictions. The goat herald waved and buffeted, as if somehow cheering her on. She walked slowly, deliberately, as if she were alone and lost within the labyrinth of her thoughts. She walked right up to the shaft, and then entered into it. As soon as she passed the threshold, some strange optical effect wiped her from his sight. She was gone.

"Ah, Millie, bless you," Lord Jay shook his head, seemingly overcome with emotion. "She has completed the ritual. Even now, she is presenting herself to our lord to be his bride."

It was just after nine o'clock when the cars began to arrive in earnest. Peg was expecting more of what she'd seen the night before—Halloween costumes, a party atmosphere. But none of that happened. Instead, people emerged from their cars as if going to the morgue to identify the body of a loved one. There were a lot of people, but you wouldn't know it for the noise, for there was hardly any. Peg heard the crunching of gravel and the whisper of the wind, but little else. One by one, she saw people turn flashlights on, their beams strobing over the naked fields. People moved solemnly from cube to cube as if in a religious procession, as if stopping to pray at each gory station.

"Have you ever seen the like?" Peg asked.

"Yes, actually, in South America. Pick any of the Marian festivals."

"Noisier than this, though, I'd imagine."

Ted nodded. "More festive, yes."

"The festivity seems to have been drained like blood from a corpse," Peg said.

"I told you. Troy Swanson," Ted insisted.

"I never said you weren't right. I just didn't know how right you were," Peg admitted.

"There's a first time for everything, eh?"

She punched his arm. "Time to get to work."

She knew Ted wasn't going to lead, so she left his side and plunged into the crowd. Her radar was up and pinging as she scanned people's faces for tears. They weren't hard to find. She saw Bren Helvig standing by the cube depicting a young man lying face up on the ground, his eyes open and still as stones. She kept staring at the face, her chin quivering. Her cheeks glistened with moisture.

Peg remembered Bren's request that she change the ritual words at the Ash Wednesday service. Peg felt a prick of resentment at the memory, her hackles rising a bit at the entitlement of the request. She reminded herself that the art of pastoring was often loving people even when they are hard to love. She sidled up to Bren. "It's okay, my dear. Let the tears come," Peg said, placing a tentative hand on the young woman's back.

Bren jumped at the touch.

"I'm sorry. I didn't mean to frighten you," Peg said gently. "Do you know who this is, Bren?"

Bren nodded. "It's Greg Johannson. I..." she looked away. "We used to go out."

"I see," Peg said, replacing her hand on Bren's back. She did not jump this time. "Do you still have feelings for him?"

"I didn't think so. But now..." she trailed off. She looked back at the cube. "He's so young. He looks...just like Greg does now."

"Has Greg seen it?"

"How should—" the girl caught herself and visibly relaxed. "I'm sorry. I'm just..."

"It's okay, dear. You are allowed to have several strong feelings at once."

"He's going to die."

Peg stared at her. She was the kind of girl people normally thought of as plain, but Peg saw something deeper in her. The truth of her feelings was truly beautiful, and she wore that beauty without shame.

"We don't actually know that," Peg said.

"But Troy—"

"Showed us that the cubes could be telling us the truth, in some cases. But maybe not in others."

Bren looked over and met Peg's eyes. "But you don't know." It sounded like an accusation.

Peg shook her head. "No, that's true, I don't. No one knows. All we have are our best guesses. We have to be on guard against presenting our best guesses as if they were fact." She looked back at the cube, at the dead boy's eyes. "True in religion, as well, I suppose."

Bren did not respond to this.

"If you want to talk, Bren, you call me anytime, morning, noon, or night."

Bren nodded, then she looked back up at Peg with brimming eyes. "Thank you."

"Of course, my dear." She gave Bren's arm a squeeze and continued into the crowd. It seemed to her that Bren was struggling, but not in crisis. Her gut told her the young woman would be fine, but there were others who might not be. She often second-guessed herself, but she reminded herself to trust her instincts.

A moment later she stopped as if hitting an invisible wall. She instinctively raised her flashlight to be sure, but immediately lowered it again. There was no doubt. Straight ahead was Rachel Lindstrom.

Peg breathed deep and struggled to get a handle on her emotions. She heard the voice of Jesus in her head, *Love your enemies. Do good to those who hate you.* She gritted her teeth and whispered under her breath. "Easy for you to say." As soon as she'd said it, she knew it wasn't true. If there was anyone who knew how hard it was to love those who persecuted you, it was Jesus. "Okay, Lord," she said. "I hear you."

The hard work of active loving isn't easy, the voice went on.

"You're telling me," Peg said.

But it's what I've tasked you to do. Love one another, as I have loved you.

"You're right on the edge of rubbing it in," Peg warned.

The Jesus voice was silent then.

She stepped up beside Rachel. Rachel looked over her shoulder and when she saw who it was, her eyes flinched and her nostrils flared. But she didn't walk away or say anything. She looked back at the cube.

Peg's heart fell. The Rachel in the cube was not much older than the Rachel beside her. She was lying on what looked like the floor, one leg cocked, one straight, the way some people sleep. But she was not asleep. Her eyes were open, as was her mouth. A little pile of what looked like vomit peppered the ground. Near her was an open prescription bottle, with a few capsules strewn around.

So this is how my enemy meets her end, Peg thought. She expected to feel triumph, or perhaps the euphoria of satisfaction. But she didn't. She just felt impossibly sad. Instinctively, she put her arm around Rachel, resting her hand on her opposite shoulder, squeezing it. She felt Rachel waver, then collapse against her, folding in toward her, her opposite hand reaching for her own shoulder. Peg brought her into a hug, held her as the woman sobbed.

"Let it out, Rachel," Peg said. Was some, small mean part of her glorying in her enemy's vulnerability? Perhaps. But she did not focus on it. Instead, she heard the words of Jesus echo, *...the hard work of active loving...*

Doing it, she thought at him. *Back off. It's hard enough without the finger-wagging.*

Eventually Rachel's sobbing ceased, and she drew away. She seemed to cower, and Peg realized she was probably feeling shame—at displaying so much vulnerability, certainly, but probably even more so, from seeking solace from someone she had wronged.

Peg struggled to dismiss any thought of having the moral high ground. It was not the time, not the place. "Rachel, do you want to talk about it?"

"Not...with you," Rachel said, not looking at her, or at the cube, for that matter. Her face was limned in shadow and it was hard to read her.

"I understand," Peg said. "If you change your mind..." She slipped a card into Rachel's hand. "Call me anytime, day or night. I mean it." Peg gave the woman as sincere a smile as she could manage and turned away again.

She glanced over at Ted and saw him talking to a young couple. She recognized the woman. She fished for her name, and after a few moments of fumbling, found it—Olivia Harris. Olivia's eyes were red and wet, and the man was gesturing toward the cube. Ted's face was compassionate as he listened. Peg nodded and looked away. *I always knew there was a good pastor there underneath all that bitchy glamor*, she thought to herself.

She saw a small crowd of people gathered around one of the covered cubes. She froze when she saw Ellen Wulfson standing near it. Beside her was an androgynous teenager—formerly Melinda, now Mel. Peg picked up her pace, gliding into place alongside Ellen and Mel.

Ellen seemed surprised to see her, but didn't question her presence. "Good evening, Ellen," Peg said. "And it's so good to see you again, Mel. It's been a long time. I didn't realize what a handsome young man you'd grown into." She offered her hand to Mel, who shook it. The grip was firm, even though the young trans man looked like he was about to swoon from being addressed in such a way. His eyes shone and he rapidly blinked back tears.

"Can I ask about your interest in this cube?" Peg said tentatively.

"The deputy sent us a note," Ellen said. She looked nervous enough to leap out of her own sun-damaged skin. "Said we didn't have to come, but we could. Said if we did, he'd need to give us a… private viewing. We're supposed to wait for him."

"Oh, dear," Peg said. "May I wait with you?"

Ellen turned and really looked at her for the first time. Her eyes were moist as well, and Peg could see the strain on her face. "I'm supposed to be mad at you."

Peg cocked her head and willed herself to be calm. "And are you? Mad at me, I mean?"

"I was." She looked away, her face hardening. "Taking Melinda's side in this stupid trans phase of hers."

Mel's eyes fell to his shoes. Peg was sure that if he could burrow straight down into the earth, he would. She studied him, and saw that he'd done everything within his power to adjust his body to its proper gender. His hair was short, with a jagged cut that was just a little bit roguish. His clothes were lumberjack-chic—jeans, a black concert t-shirt with an unbuttoned red flannel shirt atop it, work boots. Everything about him said, "tough guy," so much so that Peg had to warn herself away from being amused at just how delicate and fragile he was. She wondered how he was faring at his high school—were the other students supportive? Cruel? She wanted to ask but didn't know quite how to frame the question.

Then she saw Jake walking toward them. The deputy looked more harried than Peg had ever seen him. He nodded at her but turned his attention to Ellen and Mel. "Thank you for waiting. I'm sorry about that, but—"

"There's a lot going on," Peg interjected.

Jake seemed grateful for the assist. He even laughed a bit—but it was a short, dry laugh that might have been a cough from all the dust kicked into the air by the crowd. "There is a *lot* going on," he agreed. "We've covered this one because it's...it isn't pretty. I will show it to you, because I feel like I should. But I don't think it's a good idea, and I...I guess I just wish you wouldn't."

Peg felt for the deputy. Jake had always been a good kid, possessed of keen instincts and a kind heart, even if his confidence always seemed to be playing catch-up.

"We don't *have* to look?" Ellen asked. There was a note of hope in her voice, mixed with pleading.

Jake shook his head.

"But we can," Mel said, "right?"

Jake met the kid's eyes and nodded gravely. "You can."

Ellen tugged at her son's flannel shirt. "Let's go."

"No," Mel said. "I want to see it." Peg's heart went out to the lad. She noted how he'd planted his work boots in a wide, fuck-you stance that dared anyone to mess with him. She wanted to catch him up in a hug, tell him he was fine, that he was lovable, that he would get through this. But she bit her lip and restrained herself.

Jake looked at Ellen for permission, but the woman just looked away. Peg knew that she should want to embrace and encourage her, too, but she found that even harder than extending grace to Rachel.

Gonna give that one to you, Jesus, she prayed silently. Intuitively, she felt the Lord accept the challenge.

"All right, then," Jake said. He raised his voice. "Please clear this area, just for a few minutes, please."

There were several people milling about, and now they all looked interested. But no one grumbled—at least not audibly. A minute or so later, the space around the covered cube was relatively clear, but Peg knew that would not last. *Nature abhors a vacuum,* the voice in her head reminded her. She ignored it.

Jake must have been thinking the same, for he lost no time in untying the rope from the grommets in the tarp. Then he grabbed one corner of the fabric and hesitated. "Are you sure?" he asked Mel directly.

Mel had squared off and was standing directly in front of the cube. He nodded. Jake nodded. Then he drew back the tarp.

Ellen screamed.

CHAPTER TWELVE

J ulie leaned back, allowing the wall to support her. "What the holy actual fuck?" she breathed. She looked around, as if seeing the place for the first time. There was Clive's couch, where they had spent countless hours together drinking cheap beer and watching monster movies. It had a rip in the left-side cushion, the padding stuffed back in lumpily. Clive had always taken the lumpy side. She smiled a sad smile at that.

"Clive?" she called out, but she knew it was pointless. She didn't need to look to know she was the only one there. But her training nagged at her, and she knew that she should search the place.

She began a visual surveillance, beginning with her far left, and working around to the right, to the kitchen. Then she walked into the bedroom. Empty, as she expected, and ripe with the smell of sweat. "Dude, how long has it been since you washed your sheets?" she asked the unmade bed. There were clothes on the floor, which she ignored.

Next she went to the bathroom. She switched on the light. She had intended to simply check for possible intruders—and here she finally beheld one. In the mirror, she saw herself, but it was a self she did not recognize. Her hair was a tangled mass. Her right wrist, forearms, and hands were a mottled smear of black and crimson. "You look like hell," she said to her reflection. Her reflection did not argue or object.

I should clean up, she thought.

A dissenting voice countered, *This is a crime scene. You can't disturb anything here.*

She answered it, *I don't know what this is. I don't know why I'm here. But I do know this is my best friend's house and I need a fucking shower.*

She took one.

She let the hot water pour over her head and shoulders. She finally turned it off before it ran cold. But in the meantime she had washed her hair, scrubbed the stink from her torso, and rinsed the blood off her arms. She had used a lot of soap on her arms, as she knew they needed disinfecting, and she doubted Clive had the proper first aid necessities. A nagging voice said she should go to the hospital. She answered the voice, saying, *There is no way in hell that is going to happen tonight.*

Drying off with a towel that was only beginning to turn sour, she studied her mangled wrist. She ransacked Clive's plywood bathroom vanity and was amazed to find an expired tube of triple antibiotic ointment and a two-inch roll of surgical gauze. She applied the salve to her wrist and then bound it in the gauze as best she could, using her teeth to tear it.

Then she went back into the bedroom and opened Clive's chest of drawers. There was nothing she could do about her underwear or trousers—Clive was too much larger than she to wear his pants—but she found a fresh t-shirt, orange with faded lettering that said, "Sour Diesel." She pulled it on and followed it up with a cleanish gray hoodie that covered her arms.

Feeling human again, she went back into the living room. "What now?" she asked herself.

Food.

There was no voice in her head that said the word. It was a word that simply appeared in her brain with neon urgency. But when she opened the refrigerator, she sighed and shook her head. "This is Clive we're talking about," she said aloud.

She found a half-full box of stale saltines and an unopened jar of peanut butter. She snatched up a butter knife and carried the lot to the table in the dining nook.

She ate ravenously, and as she did so, her eyes travelled over the things on the table. There was the usual stack of books—graphic novels and magick, normally. She removed a Sandman collection—#4, *A Season of Mists*—from the top of the stack and froze when she saw the black cover of Simon's *Necronomicon* beneath it.

It wasn't that she was surprised to see it—Clive was no stranger to grimoires, and more than familiar with the more popular side of occult literature. But it made her wonder, not for the first time, if and how her friend might be involved in...all this.

At the Rite of Saturn, he had said he was dabbling in Cthulu magic. He had admitted to his interest in the Simon *Necronomicon*. Could Clive be, somehow...?

As if seeing the yellowed paperback for the first time, she picked it up and felt the heft of it. It seemed insubstantial, which was apt, she knew. As a grimoire, it was a hack job, cobbled together with the sole intention of cashing in on the unexpected celebrity of Lovecraft's stories.

She had come through a rip in the universe into *Clive's* apartment. So why should she be surprised at the "coincidence" that he had the *Necronomicon*?

Still, she was both surprised and unsettled. This wasn't the flat of some nefarious, hip magickian in San Francisco, looking for all the world like Gaiman's Morpheus. This was Clive, who always seemed to look like he had just dented your car but couldn't bring himself to tell you about it. Clive was the kind of kid who seemed genetically predisposed to fail at everything he set his hand to. He wasn't exactly a fuckup, but he wasn't far distant from it either.

She licked peanut butter off her fingers and picked up a yellow legal pad. It was filled with sigils—sigils she did not recognize. Her brows knit into a worried knot as she flipped through page after page of the strange drawings. *Where is he getting these?* she wondered. She also wondered how she could decipher them. Another visit to *Lux*

Revelare might be in order. Flummoxed, she dropped the pad back onto the table.

Nearby was a Mead composition book with a faux leather cover announcing it was "wide ruled." Julie opened it.

It wasn't just one thing. It seemed to be a haphazard miscellany book, with diary entries, rough drawings of dinosaurs and electric guitars alternating with notable quotations that, it seemed, Clive did not want to forget. None of it seemed of any note—until she got to the sketch of herself.

She blinked and pushed the book away briefly. The image was strikingly close, and he had captured something about her eyes and the bridge of her nose that was spot-on. She was disturbed to see that the drawing showed her with a naked upper torso, her breasts prominent, round and full—nothing at all like Julie's actual breasts. "Ugh. I guess a guy can dream," she said, and turned the page with resigned disgust.

Then she stopped. The next page was filled with a long, unbroken string of text. She turned several pages, all of them filled with tight text—as tight as one could expect from Clive's pen, that is. There were no drawings of band names or cannabis leaves on these pages. She flipped back to the beginning of the dense section and began to read.

"Oh, shit," she breathed. She kept reading. It was a grimoire, or at least it had all the elements of a grimoire. There were words she didn't know, and she doubted that Clive knew them either. And yet this was definitely his hand. It was as if he were copying the text from another source, but from where?

She rifled through all the books on the table, and none of them corresponded with what she saw on the page. At first she had thought that perhaps he was copying a section from the Simon *Necronomicon*, perhaps as a mnemonic tool. But the text did not match anything in Simon's faux grimoire.

Then she realized the first line was a title. It was in Latin, which was why it took her a moment to notice. *Mors in Manibus Nostris*. She scowled and wished she had her phone. She was sure Clive must have a laptop around, but wasn't sure she'd figure out the password. Instead, she squinted at the words and tried to puzzle them out. "To touch death with our hands?" she guessed.

She blinked. And then she sat upright. "Oh, Clive, what have you done?"

She desperately wished her friend was there. She had so many questions, questions he could so handily answer if... "Why is there a hole in the universe that leads into Clive's apartment?" she asked herself.

As if in answer, she felt a breeze waft over her shoulder. Slowly she turned to look at where the breeze was coming from.

Abel picked up the coffee pot, swirled it, felt its lack of heft, and slammed it back on the stove. "Dammit, *gumman*." He looked up at the ceiling, as if he could use his x-ray vision to see right through it to the second-floor bedroom. A part of him wanted to go upstairs and pound on the bedroom door some more. Another part of him knew that was pointless, maybe even dangerous. For the first time, he felt like he really understood what acquaintances with children meant when they wrung their hands about how far to push with their teenagers. He didn't want to end up pushing Mia further away, further into whatever black hole she'd descended down. He wanted to lead her out, into the sunshine, into freedom, into— "Into making some goddam coffee! And supper!" he shouted out loud at the kitchen. He looked at the clock—supper was three hours late.

Ginger Beer looked up at him from where she was lying on the kitchen floor, eyes large. Abel saw the look in his dog's eyes and his heart went out to her. He sat down on one of the kitchen chairs and stroked her head. "I know it, girl. I feel the same way." *The universe has jumped its track and is now grinding its way toward oblivion,* he thought. At least that's how it felt. But it took a lot for the *offness* out there, outside his house, to challenge the *offness* of everything within the house. Without Mia at her appointed place, ruling the kitchen, managing the household, God himself must be on edge. Abel certainly was. Ginger Beer as well.

The phone rang. Abel nearly jumped out of his boots as its harsh clanging assaulted the quiet. He snatched the phone from its receiver, pulling the twisting cord along the floor. "Nyland."

"Abel, this is Mitch Wyock."

"Mitch." Abel tensed up. He locked eyes with Ginger Beer and watched her eyebrows jump, as if she were curious about who might be on the phone. Mitch Wyock owned the property to the north of Abel's farm, about twenty-seven acres between his cornfield and the freeway. The Wyocks kept to themselves, and while it wasn't unheard of to get a call from Mitch, it was pretty unusual. "Something up?"

"I keep waiting for one of them cubes to show up in one of *my* fields," Mitch Wyock said. "But they seem to like yours. Why is that?"

"I don't know, Mitch. How did I get so goddam lucky?" There was humor in Abel's voice, but there was an edge too.

"Well, I just thought you ought to know. I just saw a bus unload up here, right at the side of the highway. And there's about twenty cars just parked on the shoulder. People are...well, they're walking right across my field toward your place. And there's a lot of them. Maybe two hundred?"

"Two hundred people are walking across your property toward mine?" Abel asked, his voice rising with incredulity.

"E-yup."

"Why didn't you stop them?"

"I got two hands and one shotgun, Abel, same as most farms. But these folks? They are armed."

"There are two hundred *armed* people coming this way?" Abel asked. "Who the hell are they? What do they want?"

"Are you sitting down?"

"Do I need to sit down?" Abel asked.

"I don't know. Maybe. It's the Klan."

"The...the what??"

"Bakersfield chapter, looks like. Although there are some out-of-state plates on the cars. Arizona, Nevada. And some Neo-Nazis. Probably some Proud Boys mixed up in there too."

"What do they want?" Abel asked.

"How the hell should I know? I just know that some of them got their sheets on and they've got guns and they're coming your way."

"But...*why?*"

"Whatever is going on at your farm, Abel, it's news. It's a public event. You know how the Klan is around here with public events. They're always sticking their pointy little Aryan noses in wherever they can, wherever the attention is. I don't think they have any interest in what's happening at your farm, Abel. I think they just hate the idea of someone having a party if they can't bust some stuff up at it."

"This is...*not* a party." He did not know what it was, but whatever people were picking up on as "festive" completely eluded Abel. There was nothing remotely resembling fun at hand.

"Thanks for...for the heads up, Mitch."

"I strive to be neighborly."

Abel hung the phone back on its cradle. He strode from the room. He heard the click of Ginger Beer's nails on the hardwood floor as she followed him. He paused in the foyer. He swung open the cushion on the built-in cabinet seat set into the wall under the window. Thom had taken his best shotgun, but he had not taken his *only* shotgun. Abel filled his pockets with shells.

Thom found it hard to look away from the shaft that opened into the other universe. He'd seen the wan girl go in, but nothing of her since. Whenever he moved his head, however, he noticed that the perspective in the shaft was off—even given the massive distances, the angles didn't work the way his eyes were used to. It gave him a feeling of vertigo, and he almost lost his balance, so he focused on Lord Jay instead.

"Okay, let's wrap this up," Lord Jay said. "Kill him."

A half-second later, Thom heard the report of a pistol. He also felt like a bee had stung his ear. He reached up and touched it. Then he stared at his bloody fingers.

A shotgun erupted again, and suddenly the air was filled with explosions and lead.

Thom leaped for cover, but there was precious little of it in the open space where the ritual was. He rolled and found the cover of one wall of cars without further injury. He reminded himself not to touch the cars as he found his feet again. Bullets ricocheted and dust punched up in front of him, obscuring his view. He reached for one of the lightning guns they'd hidden and switched it on. He pointed it at the fly-girl, but his aim was uncertain. Squeezing the trigger, he jumped as blue lightning leaped out in a jagged, snaking pattern, completely missing the girl and hitting the station wagon beyond her. The wood panels roared to life, covering the car with surreal, short-lived rectangles of flame.

Another shotgun blast deafened him, but it was coming from a different direction. Peeking in-between the cars, but careful not to touch them, Thom saw Albert's head recoil as a slug entered his brain. He slumped to the ground, out of Thom's view. *Damn,* he thought. *He wasn't a good kid, but he was the only help I had out here.* Jerking his head back, Thom scanned what limited vision he had, but couldn't see who had shot Albert. Quickly, he counted on his fingers —there were only two of them left alive, if his count was correct—the girl with the flies and Lord Jay. But neither of them had a shotgun. That left...

And Thom knew. The noise had brought the proprietor out, and Thom had little doubt whose side the obstreperous old man would be on. Now that Albert was gone, it was three against one.

Thom heard the crunch of boots, and a blue moonshadow fell over him. Thom looked up, straight into the barrel of the 12-gauge. The old man's stringy gray hair seemed to defy gravity, standing out from the side of his head, one eye trained on him, and the other screwed shut. A string of drool looped between the old man's mouth and the stock of the shotgun.

"You come on out, sheriff, an' you do it real slow," he said. "An' leave the whatever-kind-of-weapon-that-is on the ground."

"Okay," Thom agreed. He stood up to his full height, more than a full head taller than the old man. He felt naked without a weapon, any weapon. A tiny voice in his brain said, *I am dead now.* But not just once; it wouldn't shut up. *I am so dead,* it chattered on. *I am going to die very soon...*

He forced himself to ignore the voice and focus. The old man gestured with the muzzle of the shotgun. Thom obeyed. He stepped out into the open.

"This is your mess," the old man called to Lord Jay. "How you wanna clean it up?"

But the sight of Thom in the open and vulnerable seemed to be too much for the girl with the flies—the girl, Thom knew, whose boyfriend Albert had just shot dead in the chest. Her throat opened in a howl of grief and rage and revenge as she launched herself toward him, running straight across the salt hexagram covering the empty space without regard for its limits or lines.

Thom flinched as he realized nothing and no one was going to stop her. He wondered whether the old man would react if he tried to defend himself, yet he seemed to have no choice. A split second before she collided with him he took a defensive posture, raising his dominant hand protectively and shifting his left leg behind him to absorb the blow.

And hit him she did, her fists flying and her face twisted into a mask of bloody vengeance. After the initial collision, Thom fended off her blows well enough, parrying and ducking and wondering if he should get in a blow himself. Yet he was enough of a gentleman to resist it. He wondered at the contradiction even as he fought her—he would have no problem shooting a woman, but punching her? He could not bring himself to do it.

With a forceful shove, he knocked her from her feet and won himself a few seconds of respite. He found it curious that the old man didn't object to the fight or try to stop it. He guessed that the old man was no friend of the girl with the flies, and didn't care if she lived or died—any more than he cared if Thom himself died. *There is nothing quite so dangerous as a man who doesn't care if he kills*, he thought, thinking he must have heard that somewhere but couldn't think of where.

But in the short space before the girl regrouped, everything changed. Thom heard an ear-splitting scream and whipped his head toward the sound. He blinked, not fully comprehending what he was seeing.

In her mad dash to end him, the girl with the flies had scattered the salt forming the hexagram, leaving trails and openings in the pattern. For some reason Thom could not fathom, that had seemed to change the situation considerably. The goat herald had stopped its apocalyptic vacillations and fastened its enormous, muscly mouth to the top half of Lord Jay's body. It appeared to be sucking the vital juices from him. As the fat man was lifted from the dirt, Thom watched his stubby legs thrash and kick at the air in a final dance that was all about helplessness and panic.

Other beings that Thom did not understand or even have mental categories for were now emerging from the shaft. It was clear that they were not human, nor were they any type of animal Thom could comprehend. The surface of their skins seemed to be crawling, and as they moved closer over the parched earth, it seemed to Thom that they were not so much creatures as aggregates of many smaller creatures.

"Worms," Thom breathed. And he saw that he was right—each of these creatures consisted entirely of worms, holding together in some way to form a larger corporate being. And then there were more of them, crawling out of the shaft like the worms they were, some not even bothering to stand up as the first had, but simply crawling, a great roiling mass of fetid peripatetic tissue.

And in the distance, Thom saw monsters the size of planets turn their snouts toward him, toward the shaft, and they started moving, they started...*coming.*

"Oh, shit," Thom breathed, not able to tear his eyes away from advent of the Great Old Ones.

The goat herald had nearly consumed Lord Jay in his entirety, and what little of his legs that was still visible had stopped thrashing. Thom saw the outline of Lord Jay's torso in the goat herald's distended esophagus, but the makeshift throat was still swallowing, making jerking motions with its head until the legs disappeared completely.

Thom had lost count of the number of worm-beasts that had escaped the shaft, knowing only that he was surrounded by them now, and they were closing in. They were terrifying enough from a distance, but up close, Thom's courage began to fail him. He watched as some of the worms that formed one of the beasts detached themselves and were absorbed by a nearby beast, as if one aggregate was as good as the next and the individual worms passed from one to the other indiscriminately.

They reached the girl with the flies first, and Thom heard a muffled scream as whatever had held the worms together released them, and the aggregate dissolved, spilling hundreds of thousands of tiny, crawling worms onto the girl, as though poured from a barrel. They covered her, crawling over every inch of her skin, seeking access to every orifice she possessed. Within seconds, she looked like nothing so much as an aggregate worm-being herself.

The old man and his shotgun forgotten, Thom willed his legs to obey him—to flee, to get the holy fuck out of there—but his legs did not move. Instead, he tripped and rolled and held up his arms defensively as the closest of the worm beings condescended to subsume him.

It was a loud scream, but it wasn't long. Ellen stood still for several seconds after the sound stopped, her hand frozen in front of her mouth, her eyes wide, her lower jaw trembling. The wind tugged at her hair in unflattering ways. People as far as they could see stopped what they were doing and looked back in her direction.

Peg tore her eyes away from Ellen and forced herself to look at the cube. Then she closed her eyes and tried to unsee it. "Sweet Jesus, help us," she prayed quietly.

The scene etched into the cube was simple. It showed Mel, lying on a bed, dressed as he was now. Both barrels of a double-barrel shotgun were in his mouth, and there was a length of what looked like clothesline wound around both feet, a section of which was pulled tight through the finger guard, touching both triggers. There was a craterous hole in the back of his head, which made his head look oddly misshapen. The headboard was stained with gore—or perhaps it was just shadow; the monochromatic nature of the sculpture made it hard to tell. One thing was clear: the boy's eyes were open but quite definitely dead.

Peg looked at Mel and fought against the maternal urge to rush to him, to catch him up in her arms, to comfort him. She had a hard time reading his face. At first there seemed to be a flicker of pride in his eyes, a feeling of accomplishment for a job well done. But then, like a cloud covering the sun, his face darkened.

Ellen collapsed to the dirt. Mel did not seem able to look away from the sculpture. Jake froze, and it seemed to Peg that he did not know the proper thing to do next. She waved at him to drop the tarp back into place. *Someone should comfort Ellen,* the voice in her head said, but she did not want that person to be her. Yet there was no one else…

Peg watched with amazement as Jake leaped toward Ellen, kneeling by her, reaching out for her tentatively. "Bless you, young man," Peg breathed. And she felt a wave of shame that Jake acted instinctively to do what Peg knew she *should* have done.

There was little propriety in Jake's actions, and that was probably for the best. Ellen had curled into a ball and was howling her grief without reservation or shame. Jake nearly covered her, with one hand on her shoulder, the other balancing himself on the soil. He lowered his head to touch hers, and after a few minutes, the howling eased into whimpers. Jake continued to hover over her, speaking gently and kindly, touching her shoulder, moving her hair out of her face, now offering her a clean handkerchief.

Eventually the crying stopped and Jake rose. Peg wanted to say, "Good job, son," but couldn't find a way to do it discreetly. She made a mental note to commend him later. She tapped Mel on the shoulder. The young man seemed surprised, but followed her until they were out of earshot of his mother and the deputy.

Peg laid her hands on the teen's shoulders and looked into his eyes. "You've seen...what you just saw was horrible. I'm sorry you chose to see it."

Mel looked back at the cube, its shame now covered by the tarp. "It's okay."

"No, it isn't," Peg insisted. "But it's what you fantasized, isn't it?"

Mel looked her in the eye again. He slowly nodded.

"So here's the good news," Peg said. "You don't need to actually do it now. You fantasized about how your death would affect your mother, how it would devastate her, how it would wound her, how it would teach her a lesson. People who commit suicide don't get to actually watch that moment when their loved one sees the damage they've done—but you did."

She watched him closely—watched his eyes widen, then look away again; watched his shoulders deflate. He opened his mouth, but nothing came out.

Peg continued, "You got to hurt her. You got to *see* her hurt. So... well, good for you, I guess. You got what you wanted. How did it feel?"

Mel swallowed. He started to shrink and back away.

"Hey," Peg said soothingly. "I'm not blaming you. I'm just asking you for the very thing you've hungered for, for years. I'm asking you to be honest about yourself. How did it *feel*?"

Mel didn't meet her eyes, but he didn't withdraw either. "It felt good. It felt better than anything I've ever, ever felt."

Peg nodded. "And what else?"

"I feel sick to my stomach. I feel like...like I do when I come home from trick-or-treating. Too much sugar..."

Peg stroked his hair and smiled compassionately. "That's the taste of revenge, sweetie. The cliché says that revenge is sweet, but they don't warn you that too much sweet goes sour. Always." She took his hand and slipped it through her arm. "Walk with me, Mel. An old lady needs a steady young man to keep her from twisting her ankle."

As if it were any other spring evening, they strolled in the direction of the service road. "I understand your desire for revenge," Peg said. "It's strong, and if you ask me, your mother had it coming."

Mel giggled, and it sounded for all the world like the carefree amusement of a teenage girl. Peg tightened her hand on his. "I understand why you would want to hurt her, because she hurt you. Bad. But...do you know what a better revenge would be?"

Mel stopped and looked her full in the face. He looked uncertain, as if he half expected her to either betray him or say something lame. She plowed ahead anyway. "The best revenge you could have would be to live a healthy, productive, happy life as a trans man, just to show your mother that you *can*. Show her she's wrong. Show her it's possible."

Mel looked away, his eyes moving back and forth, thinking. Peg tugged him onward again. "And besides, it isn't worth it—sticking it to her without getting yours."

"What do you mean?" Mel asked.

"I mean you have a life to live. You'll go away from here someday soon, go to school, become...someone else. You'll fall in love...probably numerous times. You'll break hearts, and you'll get yours broken, if life is fair. You'll find something you want to do that makes a difference to the world, and you'll do it. And this planet will be a better place because you had the courage to stand up to it and say, 'Fuck you, I'm going to do this my way.'"

Mel stopped again, his face aghast. "Pastor..."

"Now, don't tell your mother I swore. You know she has trouble with...well, she can be a bit of a prude, yes?"

Mel laughed then, and Peg could feel the tension draining out of him.

"But I'm not your mother. I won't judge you. I'm your pastor. You can talk to me anytime, about anything. Because you know what my job is?"

"Uh...to preach?"

"That's a very, very small part of my job, actually. People truly have no idea what we pastors do. But I'm telling you. The biggest part of my job? Loving people. Just as they are, wherever they are, no matter how they're feeling, or what they've done or haven't done. That's it. It's not my job to judge them or reprimand them or scold them. It's just to love them."

"That sounds like a great job."

"It is."

"It sounds hard though. Some people...like my mom...they're not..."

"Easy to love?" Peg finished his sentence. "No. That's the challenging part. You have to love everyone. Everyone. Everyone. It isn't easy, and I don't do it perfectly, God knows. But it does get easier with practice."

"Can you love her...my mom...*for me?*"

Peg narrowed her eyes at the young man. "Sure. For a short time, I can love her for you. But only until you can find your legs again. Then you've got to forgive her and find a way to love her yourself."

Mel walked slowly and silently. "And what if she can't...accept me?"

Peg considered the question. Finally, she said, "Well, you have two hands. Can you hold your love for her in one hand, and hold a new family who does accept you in the other?"

"I know I'll just...want to let her go."

"You'll want that, but that's a temptation. If you can resist it, you'll be happier, I think. I hope you can leave the door between your new world and your mom open. Who knows, she might surprise you. She might walk through it one day."

"I didn't know pastors could be cool."

Peg laughed. "*Cool* is not a word I have used to describe myself in a very long time, thank God. I suppose that you've just never gotten to know any pastors. Most people haven't. They'd think differently about us if they did. But do you want to know a secret? Most people don't know a trans person either. Just think how it would change them if they did? And every person you meet, you get a chance to give them that gift—a gift of 'the transformation of their minds,' as St. Paul puts it. You, my love, are going to change the world."

Peg felt the dirt clods melt beneath her feet as they walked.

"But what about…" Mel looked over his shoulder. "I mean, the cube. Aren't I…doesn't it…won't I—"

"How many shotguns do you have at home?" Peg asked.

"Just the one."

"Is it the one we saw in the cube, with the double-barrel thingy?"

"Yes."

Peg sighed. "Give it to me."

"What?"

"Give it to me. For safekeeping. If it's at my house, you won't have it. And if you don't have it, you won't use it. And if you can't use it, the cube…can't come true."

"Do you really believe that?"

"*Belief* is the wrong word, dear. I choose to trust it."

Mel nodded. "When can you come over?"

———

Julie felt the breeze, but when she looked over her shoulder, she saw nothing—just the four close walls of Clive's one-bedroom apartment. She saw scuff marks on the walls and movie posters where more mature people would hang pictures, but she did not see whatever rip in the universe she fell out of.

She looked away again, and when she did she noticed that she could sense it. In her mind's eye, a hole appeared just behind her, to her right, at the precise spot where the ceiling joined the wall. If she didn't look, she could point straight at it. But she did look, and saw nothing but the seam where the wall ended and the ceiling began. So she looked away and put her arm up and behind her. It occurred to her that to anyone observing it probably looked like she was about to begin a Spanish dance. She found some humor in the thought, but dismissed it, focusing on her hand.

She had a thought and quickly brought the hand to her mouth, moistening her fingers. Then she put her hand up and back again... and distinctly felt the breeze. Without looking, she walked backwards toward the coolness, toward the spot where the ceiling met the wall.

Julie was too short to reach that spot, but the draft was most pronounced when she stood just under it. She leaned against the wall and thrust her hand up as far as it would go. There was no question about the breeze.

Quickly, she got a chair, then a box to set on the chair, and then a few books. She looked at the rickety ladder she'd constructed warily. "Oh, well. If I fall, I fall. Won't be the worst thing that's happened to me tonight."

Intentionally not looking at the seam, she climbed up on the chair, holding onto the wall for support. Carefully, she put one boot on the box and pushed herself up. Then she stepped up on the books. She waved her free arm about when her balance threatened to fail her, but she caught it again.

She was as high as she could get, and indeed, the ceiling was pressing down on her shoulders, forcing her to push her head forward and down. Right hand still firmly planted on the wall, she reached back with her left, toward the joint between wall and ceiling, and felt...nothing. Breeze. That was it. She pushed her hand further into it, at every moment expecting to bash her fingernails against the wall or ceiling, but there was nothing but empty space and the gentle movement of air.

Then a thought struck her. Quickly, she dismounted the pile and snatched up a knife from the kitchen, the biggest she could find. She thrust it into her belt, where it pivoted awkwardly, its point against her leg. She moved it sideways so that it pivoted off her hip more. "Hmm..." she said aloud. She was not entirely happy with it, so she selected a smaller knife and tried that. It felt more secure in her belt and did not threaten to open any arteries in her leg.

Confident in its security, she once more ascended the stack until she had to stoop for the ceiling again. Then, reaching backwards, she found the hole. Carefully, she closed her eyes and turned around, reaching both hands forward toward the hole. She found it, feeling about inside it for a handhold. She found one, but of course it was crawling with worms. She bit her lip and closed her hand around it, squishing an untold number of the tiny beasts. Reaching one hand over the other, she dragged herself back into the void.

Once securely inside, she opened her eyes again. She was once more staring at the vision of the malevolent cosmos. Far in the distance, but somehow, impossibly, close enough to see in great detail, the Elder Gods shuddered and slew and ate in an endless orgy of violence and consumption. It occurred to her that many people spent their lives trying to grasp the All, the mysteries of the universe—from scientists to theologians to magickians. But Julie alone knew the truth now, it seemed. And that truth was nothing but an invitation to despair, depression, and dissolution.

She shook her head to clear it and waited for her eyes to adjust. The aggregate worm-creatures were gone—for the moment, at least. As soon as she could see well enough to place a step, she did. In all her time in the void, she had only found one other object of any size, save for the worms. It was that object she sought again.

She set out walking a grid, once more defaulting to her training. And within minutes, she found it: the cocoon.

It was bigger than she remembered. But then, she'd had no reference to its true size when she'd first encountered it. And nothing in the void seemed to scale. All proportions seemed "off" and untrustworthy. That was all right. It was a bit like being underwater—the refraction of light in the water distorted one's vision, but one managed. It was the same there.

As she hovered over the cocoon, thinking, she caught motion out of the corner of her right eye. Turning her head quickly, she saw that another of the worm-beasts was aggregating from the billions of slithering subjects covering the ground. Biting her lip, she squatted, and put both hands under the cocoon. Using her legs to lift, she put all her strength into it, and succeeded in rolling the cocoon one turn toward the opening.

She did it again and again. And then the worm-beast was upon her.

She snatched the knife out of her belt and whipped around to face it. She noted with horror that there was not one new aggregate creature, but four—each of them spreading out to approach her from a different side.

One was close, however—too close. She slashed at it with the knife, and it felt as if she were pushing it through slightly viscous water. But a section of the worms fell away where she had sliced them apart from their fellows. She slashed again and again before she learned to aim more strategically.

She could take out a leg in a second, but it took nearly a score of seconds for the beast to grow it back. Lunging at each of the beasts in turn, she succeeded in momentarily disabling them—long enough to manage one turn of the cocoon. She set into a pattern of disabling and turning, disabling and turning, until the giant silk cigar was teetering just at the edge of the rip.

She felt a slimy, crawling appendage close over her ankle and whipped about, slashing down, and scoring her own boot with the flashing blade. The appendage dissolved once separated from the main body. Julie lunged at each of the creatures in turn once more, before turning and kicking at the cocoon with every last ounce of strength within her. It rolled over, then paused, quivering, then rolled back. Julie uttered a stifled scream and kicked again. The cocoon toppled into the hole, and so far as Julie could see, simply winked out of existence.

Abel stuffed the flashlight in his pocket and gave a final glance up the stairs, where Mia was holed up. "Don't suppose you could stay here and keep an eye on her?" he said to Ginger Beer.

Ginger Beer's tail wagged and she pointed at the door with her nose.

"No, didn't think so." He opened the door and the dog rushed out. He closed the door behind him, cradled his 12-gauge over his arm, and clomped down the stairs. He looked first toward the barn and beyond it, to where god-knows-how-many townspeople were even now prowling over his cornfields, disturbing his seed, ruining his chances for a clean and consistent crop this year.

He wasn't really worried. The law of averages said that most of the seed would come up just fine, especially now that Jake had laid out some pathways with his police tape and cones. Abel knew that, but he also knew there was principle involved. He didn't like what had happened to his corn, to his farm, to his life...to Mia. His grip tightened on his gun and he grit his teeth.

Then he turned and started walking toward the opposite end of his property, toward the freeway, toward the Klan.

He knew something of the Klan's history in the Central Valley. Unlike in the south, the focus of the California Klan had historically been Mexican and Native American people. Abel had nothing against Mexicans—he hired many day-laborers during harvest, and he always paid them better than most, enough to catch some flak for it. He didn't care about that. He did care that people were adequately compensated for their labor, no matter what the color of their skin or hair. And the local native folk had always kept to themselves, and were right respectful when he had come across them. No, whatever the Bakersfield KKK were up to, he was not a supporter—especially when it involved walking over his newly-planted fields.

Ginger Beer ran point, which was fine with him. Ahead of him he could see nothing but the distant glow of Bakersfield reflected in the sky and the dark mounds of planted soil. Every now and then he caught sight of Ginger Beer's red coat in his flashlight's beam.

Abel stopped. Ginger Beer stopped too and looked back at him. Her sense of smell might have been a hundred times better than his, but he knew his eyesight was keener. Then she, too, detected movement ahead, and started barking. Cautiously, he moved forward again. A glow came into view, and gradually he realized what he was seeing.

A line of marchers walked toward him, stretching out a good distance on either side. They held torches, the flames mere pinpricks of moving light, but they were moving toward him. Abel realized that, aside from his flashlight, he was probably largely invisible. His clothes were dark, for one thing, unlike the brilliant white of the sheets that reflected the moonlight. So he waved his flashlight back and forth, like a strobe light. No one would miss him. Nor did he want them to.

He found a piece of level ground in the spot where he usually turned the tractor around. He planted his boots and double-checked his chambers. He felt at his pocket, bulging with shells. Then he moved one boot behind to absorb the shock and brought the shotgun to his shoulder. As soon as the nearest Klan member was within earshot, he called out, "That's far enough."

None of the men faltered or even slowed down. Ginger Beer barked furiously. "Hush!" Abel commanded. She continued to whine her complaint, but the barking stopped.

"Who are you?" one of the Klan members called to him.

"I'm the man who owns this property and farms it. You're walking all over my seed."

Strangely, they did slow down at this. They even paused.

The gun was starting to get heavy. Abel ignored the anaerobic ache in his muscles.

"You're not going to shoot anyone," one of the Klansmen called.

"I don't want to, it's true," Abel said. "But that doesn't mean I won't. I shot someone just yesterday."

"Uh-huh. Look, we're a philanthropic fraternity. All we want to do is promote our rich and venerable pan-European culture," the Klansman responded. "We don't want anyone to get hurt. There's something going on here, and we want to be a part of it."

"There's news trucks!" An unseen voice contributed, with obvious excitement.

"There are?" Abel looked back toward his house.

"Look, old man, we don't want any trouble. We just want to demonstrate peacefully, that's all."

Ginger Beer growled and whined, turning quick and impatient circles. "By walking all over my seed," Abel said, turning back around. "On my land...without my permission."

"We're just walking."

"In pointy hoods, holding fire and guns," Abel pointed out.

"That's how people know it's us," the Klansman said. "I mean, you take LeBron out of the uniform, and would people even know who he is?"

"The sheet's the shit," the unseen voice yelped. Others laughed their support.

"Not another step." Abel pulled the hammer back on both barrels. He was reasonably certain the sound of the click carried well enough.

For a moment, everything froze. The only movement Abel could detect was the shaking of his own hands, the slight weaving of his gun sight, and the leaping flames of the torches. For a brief moment, Abel wondered if perhaps they'd just turn around, get back in their buses and go back to Bakersfield.

But then Abel's heart fell. The Klansmen took a step forward. Then another one. Then another.

"Goddammit, I will shoot you where you stand!" Abel shouted.

They kept coming, and Ginger Beer resumed her barking. Abel squeezed the left trigger. The gun exploded and Abel braced himself against the kick to his shoulder.

The line stopped again. No one was hit, which was no surprise to Abel, as he had aimed over their heads. He trained the shotgun on his best guess as to which of the Klansmen had spoken to him. But they took another step, and then another. And then they walked past him.

Abel lowered the shotgun while Ginger Beer leaped with joy, running from man to man, sniffing at the sheets.

One of the Klansmen put a hand on Abel's shoulder. "It's all right, old man. We're just country boys. We're not here to hurt you or your farm. Walk with us. Those torches put out plenty of light."

Abel spun away from the man's hand. The Klansman shrugged and rejoined the line. "Ginger!" Abel shouted. The dog stopped what it was doing, looked at him, and then bounded toward him. He waited until the Klansmen were a good distance ahead before he followed them. He couldn't stand the idea of someone thinking that perhaps he *was* with them, or worse, had summoned them.

It occurred to him that none of the cubes—that he had seen,

anyway—depicted Klansmen. He hoped that was a good omen. He hoped it would mean that no one would die that night.

Jake heard his radio squelch. Then he heard Celia's voice. "Adam Three, this is Karlstadt."

Jake reached over to where the microphone dangled from his epaulet and gave it a squeeze. "Hessup here, Karlstadt."

"Jake, check in, please."

"Sorry, Celia. Time got away from me."

"That's all right, honey, that's why I'm here. How's it look up there?"

"There's a lot of people. And none of them are happy." Jake looked around as he said it. He saw people making eye contact with him. He resisted the urge to shrink, as it seemed that every glance was an accusation. He just wasn't sure what he had done.

"I hope you're not taking it personally." Celia's voice was full of static.

"I swear to God you're psychic, Celia. And it creeps me out."

"Not psychic, dear boy. I just know *you*."

"It's fucking creepy."

"Sounds peaceful so far," Celia said, but Jake took it for a question.

"I guess so. There's no violence, I suppose."

"Don't sound so disappointed."

"I'm not disappointed, I'm...I'm nervous."

"No one is dead yet, so you're doing fine," Celia said. "It's my rule of thumb."

"Gee, thanks. How, uh...any word from the boss?"

"None. He seems to have dropped off the face of the earth."

"Goddammit. I feel...stuck here."

"You *are* stuck there. Because that's where we need you most."

Jake clicked the mic, but decided not to say what was on the tip of his tongue.

"Check in again in a hour, you hear?" Celia's tinny voice demanded.

"Roger that, Karlstadt." He released the mic. It was good timing, as he saw a flock of bobbing flashlights wending toward him. Eventually he made out the shadowy forms of Becky and Paul Travers—but they weren't together. Becky was surrounded by a gaggle of women. Jake knew most of them—Becky's friends and a few of her old co-workers from the Sunkist plant in nearby Dorado. Traveling toward him on a parallel but separate path was Paul, his face stormy and unreadable. He didn't walk so much as stomp across the cornfield.

As they grew closer, Jake noticed that Becky didn't look like herself. Her face had purple and yellow patches he had not seen before. There were cuts under her eye. Jake had seen those kinds of markings before, and he knew what they meant. His heart sank in his chest and his stomach tightened into a hard knot. "Shit," he said to no one.

The approaching parties were within earshot now, so he said nothing else until they stopped in front of him. Becky came straight to him, surrounded by her people, but Paul hung back, glowering, his hands in his pockets.

Jake tipped his hat. "Becky. Mildred. Jane. Tuesday. Heather. Cheri. Dot. Maggie." He raised his voice to address Paul. "Hey, Paul."

Paul ignored him. Jake studied Becky's face. She must have realized what he was doing, because she pulled a hoodie up to conceal it somewhat. "Something you'd like to report, Becky?"

"Just here because we got Celia's call."

"Uh-huh." Jake had been to the Travers house on two occasions when neighbors had reported domestic abuse. Becky had always denied everything. Paul had, too, though that surprised Jake less.

Whatever had gone down had been recent, given Becky's bruising. It was also part of a pattern—the bruises that had turned yellow were evidence of that. And the fact that Becky had an entourage and was not walking with her husband told him the last fight, whatever it had been about, was fresh and still an open wound. He wished Becky would talk. He had been tempted to drag her down to the sheriff's office to see if she'd talk when alone, but there had never been a justifiable occasion for it.

"So...do I have to guess?" Becky put one hand on her hip. She was brave in the company of her friends. Cocky, even. Jake appreciated that.

"Guess what?" Jake asked.

"Which one of these damned...cubes...you called me down here to see."

"Uh...that's not...we didn't call you down here. We just...informed you about one of the statues. You didn't need to come."

"Yes I did," Becky said, her chin raised in defiance.

"Okay, then," Jake said, deflating a bit. He felt like an idiot. "Have you seen some of the others?"

"Hell yeah, I seen 'em," Becky said. "I was out here last night with Dot and Wanda."

Jake didn't remember seeing the three of them the night before, but he didn't question her. There had been a lot of people wandering around the cornfield.

"They're creepy," Becky added.

Jake did not disagree with that.

"And now you found mine," Becky said.

Jake didn't answer at first. But then he nodded. "I'm sorry."

"What are you sorry for?" Becky asked, sounding so much like Jake's grandmother it unsettled him. His grandmother's voice saying those very words rattled in his ears.

"I'm just...I'm sorry you have to see it." Jake realized what he had said, and hastened to add, "But of course, you don't *have* to see it. So I guess I'm really just sorry the cube appeared." A voice in Jake's head told him to *shut up now*.

"I know I don't," Becky said. She pulled the corner of the hoodie back a bit and made sideways eye contact with Jake. "I *want* to see it."

"Are you sure?" Jake asked.

"It's me, right?"

Jake nodded. "It's you."

"Then I want to see it. If I don't, I'll wonder about it for the rest of my life."

"You might regret seeing it for the rest of your life," Jake pointed out.

"That's not as bad as wondering what I should have seen."

Jake followed the logic, but wasn't sure he'd have come to the same conclusion. Still, it was her choice. He nodded. "Follow me, then."

He started walking across the cornfield. He wished that Pastor Peg were with them, and looked around for her as they traversed the field. He didn't see her—but then it was dark and there were a lot of cubes and a lot of people around. He didn't know what she could have done, but a part of him just felt better knowing she was there. He wasn't a religious man, so he wasn't sure it was about her being a pastor. He wondered if it was simply because she was Julie's mom, and it was the protective mom energy he was needful of.

He glanced over his shoulder and was surprised to see that the entourage had grown. For some reason, they seemed to be picking people up as they walked. Stragglers and couples and sometimes whole gaggles of friends joined the parade. Gooseflesh erupted on Jake's forearms. He shuddered and pushed the awareness away from him.

After what seemed like an eternity—but was probably only about five minutes—Jake halted in front of one of the cubes draped with a canvas tarp. He turned his flashlight around and waited for Becky to catch up to him. Paul continued to hover by himself just beyond normal speaking range. Becky's friends, however, flooded in, surrounding the cube.

Jake bit his lip. He had a bad feeling about this, but he didn't know why. He remembered back to a time when he'd said something he shouldn't have. The thought had been fully formed in his head, and an inner voice was screaming, *Don't say that*, but it had just tumbled out of his mouth anyway. The result had not been pleasant. Jake had the same feeling now, as if he were in the middle of the offending statement, knowing it was wrong, but incapable of stopping himself.

Becky nodded. "Do it," she said.

Jake fidgeted. "Maybe we should wait until one of the pastors—"

"Just fucking do it, Jake!" Becky shouted. There was anger in that voice, and it was righteous anger. Jake could feel it, and he knew it, deep in his deputy's marrow.

He blinked, swallowed, and then put his flashlight on the ground. He pulled at the knot and it came undone. With both hands he pulled the tarp back, throwing the end of it up and over the top, revealing the sculpture on the side that faced them.

The crowd gasped. Everyone froze. Every eye was riveted to the cube. The only sound Jake could hear was the rustling of the canvas and a tiny bit of wind. He didn't look. He didn't need to. He knew exactly what it looked like.

Taking one last swipe with her blade, Julie turned and dove through the rip. She steeled herself for the impact. She had left the lights on in Clive's apartment, so she was able to see the floor rushing toward her. She caught the brunt of it with her hands and rolled.

She banged up her shoulder, but otherwise seemed unharmed. She cast a quick glance toward where she knew the hole was, just at the seam of the wall and ceiling, but again saw nothing. If any beings were in pursuit, they were invisible.

"Can't worry about what I can't see," she said aloud. She rose stiffly to her feet and stumbled over to the cocoon. She checked her pockets, but it seemed she had lost the knife in her fall. "Probably for the best," she thought, realizing how dangerous falling on a knife might have been. She snatched up a pair of scissors from the table in the dining nook and knelt by the cocoon.

"Be alive. Please, goddess—" she began, but stopped. She knew the truth now: there was no one to hear her prayer, and whatever terrible gods there were would not be interested in helping her.

She attempted to tear into the silk with the scissors, but realized that they were left-handed. "Of course. Dammit," she said. Clive was left-handed, she knew, and it stood to reason that his scissors would be too.

She transferred the scissors to her left hand and attacked the silk again.

It was awkward, but not as hard as she feared. The silk was fine and cut easily. The layers of silk, however, were thicker than she'd anticipated. But as she cut with her left hand, she was able to tear the silk away with her right.

To her great relief, she uncovered Clive's face. Without bothering to uncover the rest of him, she dropped the scissors and pressed her hand against his neck.

It was faint, but there was a pulse. "Thank you, Jesus," Julie breathed, without realizing it. Julie cast about for a telephone, but found none. She did not think Clive had a landline, and a quick glance around the apartment confirmed this. She had lost her own cell phone long ago.

"Clive's cell," she said, and snatched up the scissors, cutting away the webbing as she neared his trousers. "Right or left?" she asked herself. A left-handed person would probably keep their phone in their left pocket, she mused, but it was not there. She cut toward his right pocket, creating a zig-zag pattern in the silk with no apparent rhyme or reason. She felt at the bulge in his pocket, and it was the right shape. She dug it out of his pocket, and almost wept with relief—it was indeed his phone.

She activated it, but realized she did not know his password. She knew she didn't need a password to dial 911, but she didn't want to speak to some faceless operator in Bakersfield—she wanted Celia. She blinked and looked around the room for a clue. She saw the band poster and tried "Metallica," but failed. She looked at the books and tried, "Therion," then "Lovecraft," but those did not work either.

"What does he *love*?" she asked herself.

And then she knew. She did not want to know, and at first she pushed it back out of consciousness, desperate to find another answer. But she knew that was pointless. She didn't have much time and she knew it. She closed her eyes to calm herself, and then typed with her thumbs, "Julie."

The phone sprang to life. "You sorry nutsack," she mumbled as she dialed Celia's direct line. Celia's voice answered, "Sheriff's office."

Julie shuddered with relief. "Celia, this is officer Barkley. I need a bus at 2752 Hawthorne."

"What, in Karlstadt?"

"Yes, in Karlstadt."

"You know Thom is looking for you out past Coleman somewhere."

"He—really?" Her eyes moved back and forth quickly, and she hesitated. But a moment later, she knew what she had to do. "I'm going back for him. But right now, we need a bus here."

"Okay, I don't understand it—"

"I don't either, really. At least...I can't explain it. Just...send the ambulance. Quick." She closed the call. Then she rose and unlocked the front door. Then she opened it wide.

There was only one more thing to do. She went into Clive's bedroom and switched on the light. Her nostrils flared at the reek of stale sweat and she forced herself to breathe through her mouth. She headed for one of the end tables and jerked open the drawer. Inside was a jumbo tube of Walgreen's brand hand lotion and a dozen wadded Kleenex. "Ew..." Julie said aloud, slamming the drawer. She crossed the room to where Clive kept a military-style trunk. Undoing the clasp, she threw it open and nearly gasped with relief. "There you are," she said, picking up a Glock in one hand and a Smith & Wesson revolver in the other. She checked the chambers, and discovered they were both fully stocked with rounds. She thrust them into the waistband of her jeans at the back, one ready to each hand. "Clive, I never thought I'd say this, but I'm so glad you've got guns."

She ran back out to where Clive's unconscious body still lay, wrapped in silk. "Just hang on, buddy," she said to it. Then she looked back at where she knew the hole was.

"Coming for you, Thom," she said.

The assembled crowd stood silent before the revealed cube. The wind tugged at the tarp, but otherwise there was little sound. Jake held his breath as he watched Becky's face.

He didn't know what he expected to see. Pain, rage, overwhelm. But Becky didn't reveal any of these. Instead, she just looked intensely sad, as if she were disappointed in a child. She drew closer to the statue and actually knelt down. She reached out a hand and touched herself. "I'm sorry," she said, but Jake didn't know to whom she spoke.

Agitation broke out among the crowd and people began to murmur and stir. Jake's right hand went instinctively to his service revolver, hovering over the holster catch. His eye went to Paul, and he saw the man staring at the cube, slack-jawed and pale, his hands hanging help-less at his sides.

"Murderer!" someone shouted. Another voice repeated it, and soon the crowd was teeming with the cry. Paul stepped forward, toward the cube, toward his wife. He looked stricken.

He put his hand on Becky's shoulder, and she whirled on him. "Don't touch me!" she screamed. "So that's how it's going to be, huh? Just like Samson?!"

Paul froze. He seemed to rock on his heels, then took a step back-ward, as if catching his balance. "Beck, I didn't mean—"

"Don't you *fucking* touch me," she repeated. Then, with a vicious-ness Jake had never witnessed in a woman, she lunged at him, tearing at Paul's eyes with her fingernails. Paul screamed and fell, but then Becky was on him, continuing to tear at his face.

"Becky, I need you to get off of Paul," Jake started, but no one was listening, and she probably could not have heard over the din of the crowd. He reached for Becky's arm, but the moment he touched her, the crowd reacted with howls of indignation. Jake felt several hands pummeling at his chest, his arms, pushing him backwards, away from where even now Becky was mangling her husband's face.

Jake struggled to find his feet, to escape the attacking crowd, to find a bit of open space. He watched helplessly as the mob pressed in on Becky, unseated her, and began a frenzy of slashing attacks aimed at Paul. Glintings of silver revealed that many of them were armed with knives. "Shit. Shit shit shit!" he yelled. Fumbling at his holster, he pulled out his service revolver and pointed it at the sky. He squeezed off one round.

The explosion wasn't as loud as it might have been—it was a corn-field, after all, and there was little to reflect the sound back—but it did the job. For a brief moment, the crowd went hush, until the vast majority had identified the noise. Eyes flashed to Jake, to his gun, back to Becky.

Jake stepped physically into the breach and positioned himself over the fallen body of Paul, one foot planted on either side of the man. "That's enough!" Jake warned. "You've done enough. My body cam is on, so if you've done anything to hurt this man, you're already in enough trouble."

The gaggle of women surrounding Becky began to scream again, but this time Jake aimed his pistol directly at them. Amazingly, his hand did not shake. He felt a strange calm descend on him. "I said *no more*." There was a note of command in his voice that he had never heard before.

He desperately wished one of the pastors would step up, although he wasn't sure what he hoped they would do. Quiet the crowd? Tell him what to do? Put the past five minutes into meaning-making context? Any of those would be helpful.

But Jake didn't see Peg or Ted. All he could see was the orgy of violence, the blood-smeared faces of the women in front of him, and the disco strobe of flashlights.

Then Becky moved. She nearly fell backwards, and the women around her reached out to keep her from falling. She kept her feet, but stumbled free of the crowd. She faltered, but moved away. Her face was streaked with blood, as if someone had squirted her in passing from a squeeze ketchup bottle. Her hair was a mad tangle, sticking up at odd angles. Her eyes were glassy and there was a gone look in them that make Jake shudder.

Some of the women followed Becky. Some turned back to him, their faces defiant, snarling with rage, eager for blood. For a moment, he wondered if, having been denied Paul, they would turn their murderous attention to someone else. Perhaps another man unlucky enough to be in the vicinity? Perhaps *him*?

Jake was not interested in becoming the metonymous stand-in for all malekind. Nor did he want to flee the scene. He did want to live. Every day he wondered if a cube bearing his own likeness would be revealed in Nyland's fields, but none had. And there was certainly not a scene of Jake himself being ripped limb-from-limb by a blood-crazed crowd.

"God help me," he breathed. It was a sincere prayer, but he was barely conscious of it. He didn't know how to handle the crowd, but he did know what had started it. Jake leaped for the cube and threw the tarp back over the statue portion of it.

As soon as it was covered, it was as if a spell had been broken. The women became quieter and began to back away. Some of the women turned their backs to him, and Jake hoped they would make their way back to their cars.

He saw Becky in the distance, halfway to where the cars were parked. A gaggle of girlfriends surrounded her. Someone had thrown a blanket over her shoulders. Jake saw one of the women lick her finger and try to wipe some of the blood from Becky's face, but there was so much of it that it was little more than a symbolic effort.

Jake knelt and felt at Paul's neck. The man was alive. He squeezed the mic on his epaulet and called for an ambulance. Jake's mind raced, outlining the next few minutes. He'd wait here with Paul until help arrived. Then he mentally rehearsed the steps he'd need to take to secure the scene. First, he'd need to run back to his shop and grab some cones and some police tape. Then—

Then he smelled the smoke.

CHAPTER THIRTEEN

Peg's thoughts were still with Mel and his mother when she heard the screaming. The piercing cry slashed at the bubble of her reverie. She emerged blinking, her vision a tangle of flashlight beams and shadow puppets. But the shadows resolved into people and no little bit of noise. Peg ran toward the sound, and soon found herself on the outskirts of a brawl.

A large circle of people surrounded two young women who were actively clawing at one another. This was no form of play, Peg could see—they were going for the eyes. Peg recognized both young women, but neither were parishioners and she didn't know either of their names. For a moment, both stood panting, catching their breaths, but then one, a lean blonde with a short, boyish hair style, lunged at the other, pummeling her face and scratching at her.

The other woman put her hands up defensively, frantically trying to ward off the blows. This one was a bit older, with shoulder-length dark hair and a tough look about her that would have made Peg suspect she was trouble at any time.

The dark-haired woman was on the defensive, but in a surprising move she punched the blonde woman in the stomach, stepping back as she doubled over, retching. The black-haired woman took advantage of her enemy's posture, and executed a perfect kick complete with follow-through, as if she were kicking a football. But the ball she connected to was the blonde woman's head. The blonde woman jerked up and over backwards, landing on her back.

She was stunned, Peg could see that, but before anyone could do anything to separate them, the black-haired woman was charging, ululating, leaping, and landing on the other woman, both feet making full contact with her chest, knocking her into the dirt with such force that Peg's own teeth hurt in sympathy.

The crowd was growing large now and was actively egging them on. These were adults, Peg could see—most of them anyway. Peg felt a wave of shame run through her. It was a collective shame; there was plenty to go around.

Then something shifted. A small gaggle of young women rushed in and surrounded the blonde woman protectively. Immediately, another throng surrounded the black-haired woman, taking up defensive postures.

"Oh my, this does not look good," Peg breathed to herself. She began to struggle through the crowd to the edge of the circle surrounding the combatants. She didn't have a plan other than to simply insert her own body between the two of them. Like an eager salmon, she swam upstream, and had no sooner gained the edge when shouts and conflict erupted. The girls' respective cliques had begun to argue. Their voices ratcheted up quickly, and in less than a few seconds, they came to blows.

Peg changed direction then, out of an instinct for self-preservation. She headed directly for the nearest edge in the circle of people. Before her very eyes the onlookers transformed into cheerleaders. Then a deeper alchemy in the darker regions of the human soul took over, and the cheerleaders transformed into combatants. The crowd had become a riot.

She smelled smoke. Looking around frantically, Peg's eyes widened at the brightness of the fire. Her brain searched, trying to figure out what she was looking at. Then she knew. The Nylands' barn was ablaze.

Over the course of the evening her eyes had adjusted, so that the barn appeared brighter than the sun at midday. It illuminated the whole of the cornfield with an angry, leaping yellow intensity that reflected the animal passions of the crowd. "Oh Jesus, help us!" Peg prayed, and began running toward the barn fire, though she did not know why. She only knew that, as a pastor, her job was always to run *toward* trouble.

And run she did—or as close to running as a middle-aged, modestly out-of-shape woman *could* run over the rifts and furrows of the fields. But she was soon out of breath, and found herself alone on the dark earth, her vision dominated by flame. Panting, her religious imagination kicked in, and she saw the scene before her in apocalyptic terms. It seemed to her that the dark of night had gathered and congealed to reveal the crouching form of the angel of death, hovering over the cornfield and reaching out a bony finger to claim his next victim.

She caught her breath and ran again toward the fire, but the heat repelled her long before she reached it. She was amazed by the reach of the heat, and circled the periphery of the barn, coming as close as she could bear. But as she circled the burning building, she saw the farmhouse beyond it. People were passing her, walking in the other direction—rather a lot of them. A part of her brain registered that they were wearing pointed hoods, and an even smaller part wondered at the strangeness of it, but the lion's share of her attention was on the house, and on the tiny figure of Abel running toward the house from the north, wildly yelling and gesticulating in a way that Swedish men simply don't do, unless—

Peg knew the man had reason to panic—this was his house, after all. But then she realized more was at stake. Mia had isolated herself; she wouldn't come out of the house.

The heat near the house was extreme. Ginger Beer was barking insistently, tail wagging anxiously, but the dog was keeping her distance from the fire. Peg made for the front door. Abel did not seem to register her presence as he blew past her. He half opened the door and half battered it with his shoulder. Even above the din, Peg heard the glass rattle when he hit it. She followed him in.

"Mia!" he shouted, and made for the stairs. Peg followed, taking the stairs two at a time, her sudden alacrity surprising even her. She gained the landing just a second or so later than Abel, and indeed, she almost plowed into him.

But she stopped herself in time and stood beside him, instantly realizing why he had frozen. Mia had opened the door of their bedroom and stood framed by the doorway. She had on a thin muslin gown, so thin that Peg could see the dark circles of her areolae. Her eyes were wet and glassy, and she seemed not to see them, but was somehow looking past them at some transcendent vision.

As if chasing a butterfly, Mia moved then from the doorway to the bathroom. Tatters of police tape fell away from the door like yellow crepe paper streamers. Mia opened the door, and Peg saw that she had drawn a bath, and had even lit candles.

"Mia, Mia what are you doing?" Abel called. "We've got to get out of here. We've got to—"

"No, you go," she said, not looking at him. "I have to get ready."

"Ready? *Gumman*, what are you talking about? Ready for what?"

Still not looking at him, she threw over her shoulder, "Why, ready to die, of course."

Thom closed his eyes just as the aggregate being dissolved and a cascade of worms fell toward him. He rolled to avoid the worst of them, but not before hearing the shots of fresh gunfire. He did not know who was firing, but the desire to find out propelled him. He rolled again, and then leaped up as quickly as his injured back would allow.

His mouth sprang open as he saw Julie step out of the void— disheveled, harried, and pissed as a hornet in hell. She had both arms raised, a pistol in each, muzzles erupting in twin blooms of flame as she moved onto the hexagram. She paused beneath the still-thrashing goat herald and shot straight up, through the bottom of its slimy, roiling maw. It shrieked its rage and surprise, but stopped when the fourth bullet ripped off the muscle serving as its jaw. Thom was terrified the beast would fall on her or whip her sideways—or worse, bat her back into the shaft connecting the worlds. But none of those things happened. The goat herald collapsed, rolling on the desert floor like the desperate and wounded beast it was. In moments, it looked like nothing quite so much as a pile of entrails.

But Julie wasn't waiting. She was still firing; she was still coming. As she came, she fired her pistols at the worm-creatures, but the bullets seemed to go right through them. Thom heard the old man cry out, and whipping his head to the right, saw him collapse, his shotgun clattering to the ground. Thom sprang for it, picked it up, but then had another idea.

Tossing the shotgun aside, he picked up one of the lightning guns and aimed it in the general direction of one of the aggregate worm-beings. He squeezed the trigger; a blue-white arc of light leaped from the node at the end of the gun to the nearest of the creatures. The being seemed to shimmer, to vibrate—then a fraction of a second later, it dissolved, as millions of stunned worms lost their cohesion and collapsed into a pile of quivering larvae.

"Deputy!" He tossed the lightning gun to Julie, who dropped one of her pistols and caught the contraption in one hand. She instantly seemed to know what to do with it. Thom grabbed another of the lightning sticks they'd hidden near the wall of cars and hastened to her side.

"I can't tell you how glad I am to see you," Thom said.

"I can't tell you how glad I am to be alive," Julie answered.

"Let's end this," Thom said.

And with that, white-blue arcs erupted from both of the lightning guns, sometimes catching one of the aggregate worm-beings, and sometimes not. One-by-one, however, they reduced each of the creatures to wriggling piles.

"The opening, it's—" Julie paused, glancing at the shaft between the worlds.

"Closing," Thom finished the sentence. "Can't say as I'm broken up about it."

It was closing slowly, but noticeably. The swimming monsters were still a good distance off, and Thom gauged with some relief that the portal would close long before the Great Old Ones were within striking distance.

"Thom, I—" Julie began, but her words were interrupted by a rifle report. Thom couldn't see where it had come from, but when he looked over at Julie, she stumbled. As he put his hand out to steady her, he saw the black bloom of blood in the moonlight. Her eyes met his, and they were filled with the disappointment of failure. She collapsed.

He leaped to catch her. He fumbled, but was able to keep her head from hitting the ground. He heard another shot, saw the dust near him punch up. Cursing, he rolled for the shotgun and emerged from the roll in a ready position, his finger trembling at the trigger.

Mercer lurched into the moonlight, rifle trained on Thom. The magickian was staggering. He looked unwell; one side of his face drooped. Thom cocked the hammers on the 12 gauge. He was ready.

"It's all over, Mercer. Put the rifle down and let's get you to a hospital."

"Looks like a draw to me, Sheriff."

"You got zero chance of hitting me, the way your arm is shaking," Thom said. "But I've got a shotgun pointed right at you, braced on my knee and still as a stone. There's no chance I'm going to miss you."

Mercer's eyes blazed. "They were almost here, damn you." Another bullet zinged past Thom's ear.

"Goddam it," Thom said, but before he could squeeze the trigger, two shots rang out in quick succession and Mercer froze, his face folding up in disbelief and outrage. Then he fell. Looking over at Julie, he saw her pistol hand drop to the dirt.

"You're a damn fine shot, deputy," Thom said, but Julie didn't answer.

Everyone saw the torches coming. Like fireflies skittering against the curtain of night, they came. Where moments before there had been a hubbub of talking, arguing, fighting, keening, now all was silent as every eye turned toward the open fields and the approaching lights of the torches. Several people looked at Jake, then looked back at the torches. Jake felt his palms start to sweat. He shrank into his uniform. Suddenly, it didn't seem to fit right. It felt huge, bulky, too big for him.

He breathed through his mouth and willed his stomach to stop flip-flopping. Everyone was throwing glances at him now, no doubt wondering what he was going to do. Jake wondered that himself. He knew that a good lawman would have a plan. Thom would have a plan. Julie would have a plan. But his head was empty. Inwardly, his brain screamed at itself, willing itself to be suddenly creative, but to no avail. No ideas were coming. His imagination was as fallow as Abel's fields in winter.

So he stood his ground and watched as the Klansmen came closer. He watched as they marched toward the Nyland house. Then more light flared. His jaw dropped as he realized what he was seeing. They had set fire to something—something large. The pinpricks of yellow light that were the torches were subsumed in a conflagration that could only be a building—either the barn or the house.

Jake's jaw dropped as he realized this had just become several orders of magnitude larger. There was trespassing and intimidation, and then there was arson. There were now people begging to be arrested, and he was the only one there empowered to do so. And his shoulders dropped as he considered how one of him was going to stop a hundred or more of *them*.

In his head, he heard Julie's voice saying, *Get the little stuff right. The big stuff will follow.* "The big stuff is *soooo* fucking here," Jake said out loud.

Apparently finished with whatever havoc they intended to wreak on the farm buildings, the torches began moving again...straight toward him. Jake swallowed and looked around. People met his eyes, and he knew what they were seeing—fear. He looked away. He looked at the dark ground. He took a deep breath. Then a voice in his head—Thom's voice—said, "Enough shilly-shallying, Hessup. Get to work."

He put his hands on his hips, on his belt, on his service weapon. He took a determined step toward the torches, then another. Then suddenly he was striding across the fields toward the Klan.

The torches closed in faster than he expected. Not only was he moving toward them, they were moving toward him. The flames grew from dots to fireballs. Soon he could see the hoods, and then the faces of those uncovered. He saw Nazi insignia on some, and others just looked like good old boys carrying their hunting rifles. Some had baseball bats resting on their shoulders.

Celia had briefed him on the recent conflict between the mayor and the Klan. Jake searched his brain for the name of their leader. For a moment, he panicked, not finding it. Then some neural tendril snatched at it—Pointer. Miles Pointer. He didn't know which of them was Pointer, but one of them had to be.

He stopped and spread his feet out into a solid stance. He undid the latch on his Glock and slid his right hand along the cool exterior of the holster, ready to draw it out. He cleared his throat and called out, "Miles Pointer!"

One of them stopped. His eyes latched onto that person. Others stopped now, seeing that their leader had. About twenty paces separated them, enough distance that Jake knew he would have to raise his voice. *Good*, he thought. *Maybe they won't hear it shaking*.

"Who wants to know?" the Klansman Jake assumed was Pointer asked. It was hard to tell who was actually speaking with the hoods on.

"Deputy Sheriff Jake Hessup," Jake called.

"Jake?" another voice called out. "Skinny-as-a-snake Jake?"

Jake felt the heat rise up his neck. The accumulated shame of high school rushed back to him. He knew that voice. Evan Jorgenson, his tormentor for most of his teenage years. *Shit, just what I need*, Jake thought. *Forget Evan. Focus on Pointer*. "I want to speak to Miles Pointer. Now."

The man who'd stopped stepped forward several paces. Then he removed his hood. His hair, charged with static electricity, stood up straight and hung on the air like the wisps of a phantom.

"I'm Miles Pointer," the man said. "What of it?"

Quick, what would Thom say? Jake's brain implored. Then he knew. "Mr. Pointer, I'd've thought you'd've had your fill of trouble by now. Do you really want to spend any more time at the sheriff's office? Or worse?"

"And who's gonna take me in? You?"

"If you take another step in this direction, then yes. Yes I am."

He saw a sneer come over Pointer's face. The man spat and took another step forward. "Then try it."

Pointer had called his bluff. Jake was grasping at straws and he had no leverage. He was tempted to give in, to admit defeat, to despair. *But that's not what Thom would do,* the voice in his head said. *Or Julie.*

He forced himself to stand up taller then. He cleared his throat again. "Mr. Pointer, I got half the townsfolk back there," he motioned with his chin over his shoulder. "You and your men are armed and primed for a fight. Anyone can see that."

None of the Klansmen or Neo-Nazis made a move to hide their weapons, although one good old boy did put the chain he was holding behind his back.

"I can't let you go any farther. I can't take the chance that you're going to hurt those people."

Pointer laughed and looked at the ground. Then, cocking his head, he looked back up at Jake. "Oh, yeah? Well, how do you suppose you're going to stop us?" He took another step toward Jake. Then another.

"Not another step, goddammit!" Jake said. He drew his Glock and aimed it straight at Pointer's head. He slid the safety off with his thumb. He expected to see his arm shaking, but it wasn't. Strangely, a sort of calm coursed through him. Time slowed down. He seemed to be watching himself from afar. He knew he should be afraid, but he wasn't. He was both in his body and out of it. He was both himself and not himself. He didn't understand what was happening to him, but whatever it was, it was helping him, not hurting him.

"If you shoot me, deputy, it will be in cold blood, and you will go to jail. I hear things in jail ain't too good for lawmen."

"That could be, Pointer," Jake heard himself say. "But you'll still be dead."

"They might even give you the death penalty," Pointer said.

"Could be," Jake agreed. "And you would *still* be dead."

Jake saw doubt flicker in Pointer's eyes. It gave him hope. He stood up taller. He felt a rush of euphoria and suddenly felt like he could lift a house with one arm.

"Deputy, if you shoot me, my boys will club you into the ground until your brains are nothing but hamburger sauce."

"That could be. And you. Would Still. Be dead."

"You wouldn't do it."

"Try me, motherfucker."

Jake was amazed by the sound of his own voice. He felt a rush of pride. *Yes, I might die tonight,* he thought. *Yes, this might be the last night I'm a cop. And if that's so, I'll go out like a fucking cop.* He was okay with that. He was fine with that. Even at peace.

His arm was rock-steady. He had Pointer's head lined up perfectly in his sight. Jake knew he was a good shot. He routinely bested Julie at the range. And this? This was close range. He knew he wouldn't miss.

Time was suspended. No one moved. No breeze blew. Were it not for his own breath coming in, going out, Jake wouldn't have had any evidence that time was passing at all.

And then, to his amazement, Miles Pointer turned to face his men. "We made our point, boys." And he walked away, back toward the burning building, back toward safety and their waiting cars.

———

Thom cradled Julie's head, listening for the sound of her breathing. It was there, but it was ragged and irregular. "Dammit," Thom swore. The bullet had entered her chest just below the collar bone and the exit out the other side was clean, but she was losing blood fast. He had to do something, or his deputy was going to die. He fished in his pocket for a handkerchief, wadded it and held it to the wound. Then he pressed his fingers against the wound on her back and put as much pressure on both sides as he could.

As he worked, his mind raced. He could pick her up and carry her to one of the cars—he'd have to fish in the pockets of dead people for keys, but so be it; he could do that. But would she make it?

He could also leave her here and run up to the office, where he hoped there would be a landline. An ambulance could be here in…half an hour? It seemed like a longer time than Julie had.

"Just hang on," he entreated her, and one of her eyes opened. Then the other. They weren't open wide, just a slit, just enough to see her pupils. Just enough to see *her*. "Hey," Thom said.

She must have read his dilemma on his face, because she said, "I'm not going to make it."

"Don't say that," Thom said.

"We need a shortcut," Julie said, her voice raspy and thin.

"That would be…" Thom couldn't finish the sentence. An over-whelming sadness came over him, rising up in his throat, thickening and threatening to choke him.

Julie's eyes opened wider, and she connected with him. For a brief moment, it seemed he could see more deeply into her soul than he ever had. And it was…precious.

"Do you…trust me?" she asked.

The question felt like a slap in the face. He hadn't trusted his deputies, and that fact had been gnawing at him ever since Celia had confronted him about it. "What? Julie, this is no time—"

"Thom, don't be a…don't be a dick. Do you…trust me?"

Thom took a deep breath, and swallowed. "Goddammit, Deputy, you know I trust you."

"Shortcut," she said, and raising one trembling arm, she let it fall so that it was pointing directly at the shaft between the worlds—which was closing fast.

"What?" Thom asked, his voice rising with incredulity.

"Trust…me," she said.

"You can't be serious," Thom said.

But Julie didn't answer. She just kept pointing. Thom knew that, in order to do anything, he'd have to carry her. Which meant he'd have to let go the pressure he was putting on her wounds.

"Julie, stay with me, honey," Thom said. "Stay awake."

Julie's eyelids fluttered.

"You need to put pressure on the wound, here." He guided her left hand to the handkerchief, now sodden with blood. He saw her hand grasp at the handkerchief, clutch it, press. It was good enough. It would need to be.

"Brace yourself," he said, and then with a groan he lifted her, cradling her in his arms. He turned to face the shaft and all that it contained—the vast unknown, the odd angles, the planet-sized monsters swimming full tilt in their direction. "You sure about this?" he asked.

She somehow found the strength to nod.

"All right then. If we die, I'll never speak to you again."

He started to move, then realized that the shaft was closing more quickly than he'd guessed. Holding Julie out before him, he began to run. He leaped over the bodies of dead magickians, over the quivering entrails that had once been the goat herald, over the salt lines that had kept everyone safe...for a time. He uttered a feral howl as he leaped into it, watched its blurry boundaries pass in his peripheral vision.

And then he was...inside. But he saw that he was not inside anything. The sky above him, churning with vast voyaging creatures, was just open space, an endless host of stars spreading out in every direction. He glanced below him and instantly wished he hadn't. The floor was crawling with worms, worms that were moving, collecting themselves together, aggregating into—

Julie's right arm moved again, pointing. "There, go there," she whispered.

Thom did, running with all the fury he could muster, crushing as many worms below as there were stars above.

"Stop," Julie said.

"What, here?" Thom asked.

"Look for the...glowing."

"The glowing? Look for the glow—" Thom had begun to panic, but then he saw it. A ragged rip in the fabric of whatever it was that formed the matter of this strange world. "Okay, yeah, I see it."

"Put me in," she breathed.

"What?"

"It leads to…town. Not head-first, please. There's a…bit of a drop." The last sentence had taken a lot out of her, he could see.

"Okay okay okay. This is crazy, you know." But she didn't answer. He let his left hand fall, lowering her legs. He clutched all the more tightly with his right hand, catching her up in a bear hug. Holding her securely, he leaned over and watched with awe as her feet dangled and then disappeared into the rip.

Swallowing hard, he lowered her further, finally holding only her wrists, and then letting even them go. And then she was gone—he could not see where. He was alone with the impossible perspective, the rapidly approaching monsters, and the crawling carpet of larvae.

"Here goes nothin'," he said, and jumped into the rip himself.

Mia turned and looked out the bathroom door. She smiled at her husband, then she seemed to notice Peg for the first time. She nodded politely, then her face fell, as if remembering something troubling. Then she shut the door.

"No! God—goddam it, woman, don't close the door!" Abel snatched at the handle. It wouldn't turn. "Dammit!" he shouted again. He turned back to Peg. "I'm going to kick it in."

"Don't you have a key?" Peg asked.

"Somewhere. But I don't have time to find it. Smell that?"

She did. It was smoke. It was close.

"I know fires. The barn is throwing off a lot of heat. The house is going to go up next. What we're smelling is the house."

"And if she won't come willingly?" Peg asked.

"Then she'll come unwillingly," Abel answered. "Look, if she wants to stay and burn, that's evidence that she's not in her right mind, isn't it?"

Peg didn't disagree with that. She nodded her assent.

He stepped back a few paces. Quicker than Peg would have thought possible for a man his age, he leveled a sidelong kick at the space just below the door handle. Peg heard the bang of the impact and the momentary splintering of wood. Then the door swung inward.

Abel entered, leaving Peg's sight. Peg heard splashing and bumping. Then she heard Mia shouting her complaint. But she also smelled smoke—much more than before. She brought her sleeve up to her mouth and tried to breathe through it. It was awkward and it didn't quite work. She coughed and realized it was time to follow Abel in or to flee.

Abel answered her questioning thoughts. He appeared in the door frame, wispy hair and glasses askew. There were gashes on his forehead and cheek and arm. "She won't budge. Scratches me if I try to come near." He glanced back at his wife and Peg saw the panic in his eyes.

"Let me try," Peg said.

"We don't have much time," Abel said.

"I get that," Peg said. Silently, she said a brief prayer, asking Jesus to go into the room ahead of her, to start working on the situation, on Mia.

Abel nodded. Peg stepped past him into the bathroom. There was Mia, naked now, resting in the tub. Her hair splayed out on the surface of the water. The candles framed her in flame, suggestive of the very pose revealed by her cube so many days before.

Peg closed the toilet seat and sat on it. She folded her hands and smiled at Mia. The smell of smoke was not as pronounced in the bathroom, but she knew it soon would be.

"Mia, it's me, Pastor Peg." In her head, though, she said, *You gotta show up, Jesus. You gotta do some of your magic shit right about now.*

"Hello, Pastor." Mia said, not looking directly at her.

"Mia, I'm going to say some things, and I want you to stop me when I get something wrong, okay? Just interrupt me and set me straight—about anything, any detail, no matter how small. Okay?"

To her great surprise, Mia looked at her. She nodded. "Okay."

Peg felt encouraged. She took a deep breath. "When you saw the cube—the one of you—you felt like the universe was spinning out of control. Am I right so far?"

Mia didn't say anything, so she plowed ahead. "And the only way you were able to assimilate it into some kind of order was to allow the cube to *define* the order, to become the new order."

Mia said nothing, but her eyes moved back and forth slightly. Peg could tell she was thinking. "But that new order was terrible, and… well, traumatizing. More people, more situations made you feel out of control again, so you retreated. You fiercely controlled your surroundings. Just four walls and a bed. That's manageable."

Mia was nodding. Peg noticed a tear slide down the side of her nose.

"But I'm going to tell you something true now, so I want you to listen very closely." Peg saw her cock her head. She was listening. Peg plunged ahead. "Sometimes the thing that feels the best is the most dangerous. It felt safe to hole up in your room—no Abel demanding things of you, no Ginger Beer barking and causing chaos. Just the quiet, predictable room."

Mia nodded again. Peg smelled smoke again, more strongly than before. Outside the window she heard the sound of popcorn popping. It took her brain a few seconds to realize that what she was hearing was the sound of the house burning.

"To retreat from the world feels good—it's like a safe little nest, a little hole. But the further you go into that hole, the harder it is to turn around and come back out. The further you go into that hole, the easier it is to just keep going, deeper and deeper, until there's no one and nothing but you. And that…depth of aloneness, we have a word for that in the religion biz." She waited for Mia's eyes to flick to hers. When they did, she said. "Hell. We call that Hell, Mia. And dying? Dying doesn't change anything. If you sow isolation on this side of the veil, you'll reap the same on that side. Likewise, if you sow community in this life, you'll be passed along into the other world by many hands, and you'll be received by many hands too—hands that care for you, hands that love you." She smiled. She prayed Mia was not so far gone that she could not hear her.

"Loving hands can carry you now, Mia. They can lift you out of your aloneness and carry you right back into the thick of us, into community, into salvation. These aren't just words, Mia. They never were. They're real things. You know they are because you are in the grip of the struggle right here. You're at the crossroads. Will you fumble and cry and make merry with us? Because we want you with us. Or will you cut us all off and go into the hole, to disappear forever?"

"We all go into the hole—"

"No, we don't." Peg smiled. She reached over and dipped her hand into the water. She closed her fingers around Mia's hand and pulled it out of the water. "No. We surround ourselves with people we love—people who love us—and we let them carry us when we can't stand any more. And they carry us over. It's messy. People are royal fuckups, just like I am, just like you are. We all need grace to get through the day. But in the end, messy and complicated as we are...it's people that save us. We can't save ourselves. We think we can, but we can't. Not ever. It's only when we give up doing it ourselves, when we allow ourselves to be helped, to lean on the people around us... That's what saves us."

She saw Mia nod.

"The cube doesn't have to win. It doesn't have to be the ordering principle any more. You can choose a new standard of order."

"Like what?"

"Like your wedding vows. To have and to hold, from this day forward, for better for worse, for richer or poorer, in sickness and in health—"

"Is this sickness?" Mia asked.

"You can let Abel carry you to health. You can let him carry you back to us. Will you let him?"

Before she heard Mia's answer, Abel rushed between the two of them and scooped Mia out of the water and slung her over his shoulder. "Stay close, Pastor," he said.

At least Mia wasn't screaming or thrashing. Instead, she seemed strangely peaceful. *Smoke inhalation?* Peg wondered, and then had a worried thought for herself. She followed Abel into the hall, only to find it ablaze. There was a small tunnel of blackness going down the stairs, surrounded by a roiling bloom of flame. Abel didn't hesitate, but plunged right into it. Peg followed as swiftly as she could, pressing her face to Abel's back, allowing him to go before her, to absorb the worst of the heat.

And then they were downstairs, heading toward the door, a great flaming archway. It seemed to Peg that there should have been a sign above the door, "Abandon hope, all ye who enter here," and it occurred to her how narrowly Mia had escaped—how narrowly she herself had.

And then suddenly they were in the open air. The night was brilliantly illuminated by the flaming barn, and Ginger Beer was leaping at them, scratching at their legs and tummies, whining her concern and relief. Helicopters buffeted the air above their heads like the winged beasts around the throne of God, chanting a buzzy "sanctus, sanctus, sanctus."

Peg got her bearings, then raced to where Abel was lowering Mia to the dirt a safe distance from the fire. He sat cross-legged and cradled her head in his lap.

"It feels chaotic right now, Mia," Peg said. "But just...just let yourself be held."

Thom tumbled in the dark, rolling to a stop. He thrashed about, grasping for bearings, but a voice in his head suggested calm. It was a familiar voice. It was usually right. Thom forced himself to relax. He slowed his breathing and paid attention to the air coming in...going out. That's when he noticed the lights—tiny green lights. "Electronics," Thom said aloud. That helped. He hadn't just transported to some alien prison or an incomprehensible dimension. He was somewhere terrestrial. It didn't matter where. They could be in Amsterdam or Mumbai or Tonga for all he cared. He was on earth. The little lights carried all the warmth of a cozy fireplace.

Instead of thrashing, he began to feel around methodically until he found a wall. Traveling up the flat surface with his fingers, he found a light switch. He turned it on. Light blazed.

He squeezed his eyes closed and turned toward the source of the light. He let his eyes adjust a bit before opening them a tiny slit, then a little more. Then, squinting, he looked around.

He was in a small apartment, probably a one-bedroom. The furniture was mismatched and tattered, the kind of stuff Goodwill would refuse. Then he saw Julie. He gasped and sprang to her side. She was splayed out on the floor like a rag doll, blood pooling near her shoulder. His hand instantly went to his right pocket for his cell phone, but it wasn't there. He swore, then remembered his radio. Perhaps, wherever they were, it would work?

He pushed the button on the mic dangling from his epaulet. "Adam One to Karlstadt. Karlstadt, do you copy?"

There was a choppy splash of white noise. Then Celia's voice responded. "Oh my God, Thom. I can't tell you how relieved I am to hear your voice."

"I need a bus—I need it now!"

"Where are you?"

That was a good question. "I-I don't know," Thom confessed.

"Did you get hit on the head?" Celia asked. The question seemed like a non sequitur at first, then he understood. "Worse...but I can't explain now," *and maybe not ever*. He cast around for some clue in the apartment. He sprang to the table. There was a laptop, a box of paperclips, a pair of scissors, several books on magick, and a stack of papers. He rifled through them. "Here—electric bill." He rattled off the address and the apartment number.

"Huh...popular place. Hang tight, boss." Celia's familiar voice sounded like heaven to him. "Help is on the way."

"Thanks, Cel." The radio crackled.

Thom raised up Julie's shoulder and got a hand underneath it. He felt the slickness of the blood and ballparked how quickly she was bleeding out. He applied pressure to the wound, pressing at it from both sides. Whether the bullet had hit her lung, he couldn't tell. "Hang on, deputy," he whispered.

The apartment seemed impossibly quiet. After all the terror and tumult and the free-fall into the utterly unknown, the silence threatened to swallow him. He concentrated on the sound of his own breathing, his own swallowing, the popping of his own vertebrae as he turned his head around to study the room. When the paramedics burst through the door, he nearly jumped from the explosion of sound.

"What do we got?" one of the EMTs shouted. He was a short, muscly fellow, about thirty-five with a buzz cut. With him was a slightly older woman, lean and tall. They fell on Julie, and Thom relinquished the pressure on Julie's wound as they took over.

"We need you to stand back, now, Sheriff," one of them said. Thom stood and retreated a step as a fireman wheeled a gurney into the room. Thom passed his fingers through his hair and panted as he watched the EMTs work. His fingers trembled. He snatched at his mic. "Karlstadt, this is Adam One. I need a pickup."

PART THREE
THE ASHES

No one is alone at the shrine. Every person pouring grief from their warehouse of sorrows is being attended by another. This is not a time to go it alone.

Attendants are there to witness and to provide whatever support is needed. Sometimes this means simply holding space for their deep work. Sometimes it means placing a hand on the person so he can feel that he is not alone. For others, the attendant becomes the lap into which the grieving person can crawl to weep her most bitter tears.

This display of compassion is an essential piece in our ability to truly lay down our sorrows.

—*Francis Weller, The Wild Edge of Sorrow*

CHAPTER FOURTEEN

Peg knew she shouldn't run in the hospital. She tried not to. Every couple steps she had to remind herself to slow down. *A second or two isn't going to help Julie*, she scolded herself silently, *and you don't want to do any more damage to anyone*. But she was not a young woman—her navigational skills were not what they used to be when she was younger and skinnier; she knew she was capable of harm.

She balled her hands into fists, trying to keep them from shaking as she spoke to the person at the information desk. "Julie Barkley, what room is she in, please?"

The woman nodded and checked her computer. Far too slowly she reached for a name tag and a large felt marker. "Full name, please?" she asked.

"Margaret Jean Barkley," Peg said. "You can just write 'Peg,' though. That's what people—"

"Peg. That's a lovely name."

"Yes," Peg said. "Uh…thank you." She realized she had not truly seen this person, and she felt the prick of guilt. She looked at her then, and discovered a woman about twenty years younger than she. Her gold, permanent name tag said, "Marie." Marie might have been

Mexican, or perhaps Colombian or Honduran. Her face was kind; she was far more patient than Peg felt.

"Here you go. Room 536 in the ICU." The woman flashed Peg a grim smile. She knew the score, and Peg suspected that Marie's compassion reserves had probably been depleted five years ago or more. Still, she was polite. She handed the name tag to Peg and pointed to the hall behind her. "Elevator's just down there to the left. Second floor."

Peg thanked her and once more tried not to run. She found the elevators and punched the square button that said "2." It lit up. The doors closed.

Peg bit at one painful fingernail. Then the doors opened again and she rushed into the corridor. Uncertain which way to go, she found a sign and discovered the ICU was straight ahead. Her reserve failed her at that point, and she began to jog. She ran straight to the closed, double ICU doors. She pushed on them. They didn't budge.

"Gotta hit the button there, and the nurses buzz you in," a familiar voice said. She spun in the direction of the voice.

"Thom!" she exclaimed. Her immediate impulse was to hug him, but his condition stopped her. "You look like hell."

He laughed, and she clasped at both of his hands, holding them tightly for a few seconds. "They're not letting us in just yet. Doctor is in there. They kicked me out, but said that as soon as the doctor is finished—"

"Is she all right?" Peg pleaded. Thom was always dispassionate, but his eyes were usually readable. She read them now. "Will she make it?"

"I...I don't know. They're doing their best. It's time we need now." Thom put a hand on her shoulder and squeezed it. "She was shot, Pastor."

Peg's hand went to her mouth. She emitted a squeak of distress as she fought for control of her emotions. "Where?"

"In the chest—bullet hit some lung tissue. She's out of surgery now, but...it was touch-and-go."

Peg nodded, trying to take it all in. She knew she should pray, but couldn't muster the presence of mind to do it. Instead, she folded into Thom's shoulder. He did not refuse her, but held her, tenderly and solidly.

"Thom, where in hell have you been?" she asked, pressing into his shoulder. "It's been..." She realized she had no words to describe the past day or so.

"I've been trying to rescue your daughter," Thom said.

"Well, you did. You did that. Thank God you did that."

"Too little, too late," Thom said.

Just then the door buzzed, and a woman's voice emitted from a crackling square speaker on the wall. "You can go in now, Sheriff."

Peg pulled away from Thom and he turned to the doors. He pressed on the horizontal bar on the right-hand door. It clicked and opened. Thom held it for her; Peg rushed through, biting her lip. She waited for him, since he'd know exactly where the room was.

She was correct. Thom walked right to it. He paused before going in and turned to Peg. "Don't...mention how bad she looks...not even if she's not conscious. Even if people can't hear...they know."

Peg understood what he was getting at. He was also giving her another, more subtle message, she realized. "Just...just a moment, Thom," she said. His hand was on the door, ready to push it open, but he paused and looked at her.

Peg closed her eyes. In her mind, she said, *Okay, Jesus. If I ever needed you, I need you now. Go in there ahead of me. Prepare the way. Make it...okay.* She waited until she felt the presence of the Holy surround her and buoy her. She waited until her heart was still. Then she opened her eyes and nodded at Thom.

Thom pushed open the door and held it for her. Peg stepped through.

And there was her daughter, looking completely unlike herself—frail and vulnerable. There was no sign here of Julie's fight, her indomitability, her ferocity, her attitude. There was just her little girl, hanging onto a thin thread of life.

She seemed to be sleeping. Peg was relieved to see that she was not intubated. A PICC line sprouted from her chest, sending plastic tendrils in myriad directions. A machine stood sentry near the bed, interpreting her vital signs as bright green sigils dancing on the face of a dark green monitor.

Peg rushed to her side and reached out to touch her hair. She pushed it away from her face. That was when she noticed the bruises and scratches. "My God, what happened to her?" Peg asked.

"That is a very long, very...weird story," Thom said. "And I'm pretty sure now is not the time for it. She was kidnapped, Pastor. All things considered, she's..." Peg saw him swallow, unable to finish the sentence. It was all right. He didn't need to.

Words having failed him, Thom turned to action. He found two chairs and brought them in close to the bed, one beside the other. They sat in them then, and spent many long minutes watching Julie breathe.

"I saw things tonight...last night, I mean," Thom began. Peg glanced at the window, at the dawn just beginning to seep into the world. "Things I can't...things I don't understand."

"What kind of things?" Peg asked.

"I...you wouldn't...you'll think I'm insane."

Peg looked sideways at Thom. Then she looked back at Julie. "And if I promise I *won't*...think you're insane?"

"I don't see how you wouldn't." Thom sighed. "Hell, *I* think I'm insane. Nothing has made any sense for a couple of days now."

"You can say that again," Peg agreed.

"But, no matter what I saw...and I don't really have words for what I saw—what *we* saw—the fact is that I failed her. It was my job to keep her safe, and I didn't."

"Funny, that's exactly how I feel," Peg admitted.

"We can't *both* feel responsible," Thom said.

"Oh no, you have that wrong. We may not both *be* responsible, but we can damn well *feel* any way we want—grounded in reality or no."

"I suppose," Thom grudgingly conceded. "I blame myself, is what I'm saying."

"As do I," Peg said.

"It wasn't your fault," Thom said. "You weren't even there."

"Yes. And that's the point. There was so much of her life that I simply…wasn't there for…until she gave up on me, and wouldn't *let* me be there, even when I wanted to. It's like our internal clocks were set to different times. When she needed me, I wasn't ready, and then when I was, she didn't need me."

"Except that she did…she does," Thom said. Peg didn't answer. "Celia kept telling me I needed to stop micromanaging her," Thom said. "Micromanaging. I hate that word. It drips of that new-corporate-speak that…" He trailed off.

"—that's not part of your world?" Peg suggested.

Thom grunted what might have been assent. "The point is, Celia was telling me to let go and trust her and Jake more…and the moment I did…*this* happened."

"And now you think Celia was wrong?" Peg asked.

"Of course she was wrong," Thom said.

"Or," Peg countered, "she was right, and then something unforeseen—and unforeseeable—happened."

"Maybe."

"You left Jake to face the whole cornfield fiasco alone."

"I had no choice," Thom said, through gritted teeth.

"He did splendidly," Peg said.

"I look forward to reading his report," Thom said. "But from what I've been able to gather since I got back, it was a complete shit-show."

"It was that," Peg agreed. "And he rose to that challenge."

"Did he?" Thom seemed incredulous.

"That kid has heart. And he has more sense than anyone gives him credit for…including you, I'll wager. He kept it together out there until—"

"Until the Nazis marched through and set the place on fire?"

Peg shrugged. "Nobody's perfect. He did get them to go home before they did any *more* damage. They didn't actually *hurt* anyone. That has to count for something."

"Mom?" said a thin, ragged voice.

Thom sat up on the edge of his seat and reached for Julie's hand. "You're awake."

"No thanks to you two," Julie managed. Her voice was a barely audible wheeze.

"Shhhh, dear," Peg said. She squeezed Julie's forearm, just above where Thom was already clasping it. "Don't strain yourself."

"Everything...strained," Julie said. With her free hand, she reached up and felt at the plastic nasal cannula. Content with that exploration, she let her hand fall.

"How are you feeling, love?" Peg asked.

Julie frowned.

"She feels like a truck ran her over, then stopped and backed over her, then ran over her again," Thom said. "Stop me when I get it wrong."

In answer Julie pointed her left index finger at him, cocking her thumb up and jerking back as if firing a gun.

Peg stood up and leaned over her, resting her cheek on the top of Julie's head.

"Mom...you were wrong."

Peg rose up and looked into her daughter's eyes. "Wrong? Yes, I've been wrong about pretty much everything up to now."

"No, I mean...about God."

Peg blinked. "How was I...how was I wrong about God?"

Julie's eyes were half-lidded, and Peg feared she'd drift off into sleep again without answering. But Julie did not fall asleep...not yet. With some difficulty, she swallowed. Then she fixed her eyes on her mother again. "There's no...embodiment of goodness out there, Mom. There's no one coming to save us. There's no kind old man in a beard on a cloud—"

"I never thought there was," Peg objected.

But Julie continued. "I was wrong too. There isn't any Goddess either...brooding over the world. There's nothing out there but... mindless hunger and...savagery. The only gods there are, are... vicious." She drew several deep breaths before adding, "I have seen them. I know."

"I've...seen them, too," Thom confessed. "Monsters. Cosmic,

world-eating...monsters." As best he could, Thom tried to describe what he had seen.

When he was finished, Peg nodded. "For we wrestle not against flesh and blood," she quoted, "but against principalities, against powers, against the rulers of the darkness of this world, against spiritual wickedness in high places."

Thom leaned back and stared at her.

"St. Paul," Peg explained, "kind of."

Thom looked confused, but Peg didn't explain further. Instead, she stroked Julie's hair. "I have no doubt that what you saw was...horrible, love. And big. But no matter what you saw, how big they were, how...terrible they were...I choose to trust that there is another power beyond them that is bigger than they are, stronger than they are, more...merciful than they are."

"But you didn't see—" Julie objected.

"No, love. But I didn't need to. That's why it's called *faith*. It's 'the substance of things hoped for and the evidence of things unseen.'"

"St. Paul again?" Thom asked.

"I don't believe that," Julie said "I didn't see it."

"I have a confession," Peg said. "I don't believe it either. Believing would be knowing, and I don't...nobody does. But...I choose to *trust* it. And that's enough."

"You...are an...idiot," Julie wheezed.

"It would not be the first time," Peg admitted.

"Clive?" Julie asked, her eyes flicking over to Thom.

"I'm sorry," Thom said. "Your friend...he didn't make it. Whatever happened to him, there was a toxicity level to whatever they did to him, the—"

"The worms." Julie finished.

"Yeah. The worms," Thom affirmed.

Julie's eyes focused on some faraway place not in the room. "Not surprised. He...died years ago, really. It just took a while...for it to catch up to him."

"I'm sorry, dear," Peg said, squeezing her shoulder.

A knock brought their attention to the door. A nurse stood in the doorframe, a somber look on her face. "Visiting hours are over," she said.

"But the sign says—" Thom began.

The nurse closed her eyes and shook her head. "Not for her." She opened her eyes. "This one needs to rest. You can wait out here."

Peg looked back at her daughter. The nurse was right. She was sleeping.

That evening Peg crossed the small, tidy yard between her parsonage and the sanctuary. Fitting her key into the lock, she opened the door and went in. She felt at the wall for the light switch. She found it. She crossed to the light panel that controlled the lights for the whole sanctuary and turned on the side lamps. Then she pushed through the doors separating the narthex from the nave and let them swing shut behind her. She found a pew and sat with a heavy "Oof."

The stained glass looked distinctly unmagical at night. With no light shining through the panes, they seemed lifeless and dull. In fact, the whole sanctuary seemed just a little shabby. There were streaks on one wall where she had tried to wash the crayon off after one young parishioner had decided to spontaneously create a mural during service. The little guy had made a great effort before someone had noticed and stopped him from defacing the wall further.

The pew pads had begun to fray. Whenever someone walked on the ancient teal carpet little tufts of dust shot into the air—it was as close to the smoke of incense as Congos got.

She realized that the sanctuary looked like she felt—worn and sad. But she was also grateful.

"Okay, Jesus," she said out loud. "If you were trying to get my attention, you have it."

Only the silence of the sanctuary responded.

Peg closed her eyes and imagined Jesus next to her on the pew. She leaned her head on his shoulder. He nuzzled her with his cheek.

"There you are," Peg said.

"Hey, my love," he answered.

"Thank you for...for sparing her life."

Jesus said nothing, but he stroked her arm. The silence didn't seem empty anymore, but was brimming with attention, with presence.

"I wasn't trying to get your attention," he said. "I haven't had a hard time getting your attention in a good long while."

"No, that's true. And you're the only man I can say that about."

He laughed. It wasn't a full-throated laugh, but a rumbling chuckle that she felt in his chest. She put her hand on his chest, then, and held the space right over his heart. He kissed her head. She relaxed, then, burying her face in his shoulder. Then she began to shake, and the tears came. He held her, making comforting shushing sounds. But she knew he wasn't telling her to be quiet, and so she did not try to be. And once the sobs had begun, they began to escalate in severity, until she was wailing. He did not let her go.

"Thank you for saving Julie. I just...I wish..." But she did not know what to ask for. "Please let her be okay. Give me another chance to..." She didn't finish. She leaned on his breast until she was empty of tears.

"I thought I'd find you here."

That was not Jesus' voice, but she knew whose it was. Peg sniffed and wiped her eyes. She lifted her head from Jesus' chest and turned. Allison was by the narthex doors. She smiled sadly. "I'm sorry to interrupt."

"No, I was...I was just praying."

"I thought maybe you were." She sat down in the pew next to her, on the other side of where Jesus had been just moments ago. "How is Julie?"

"She's going to make it...they think she will anyway. I've been with her all day. The doctor—and Thom, damn his eyes—finally made me go home. Doctor says she'll sleep through 'til tomorrow."

"Were you praying for her?"

Peg blinked. "I...I was just starting to."

"I don't understand how you pray," Allison admitted. "Don't you just tell God what you want?"

"I think you're confusing prayer with a to-do list," Peg said. She pulled a tissue from her pocket and blew her nose.

"So tell me," Allison touched her arm. "Tell me how you pray."

"I just...remind myself that Jesus is here, and I see him in my mind. And then we talk. Mostly, I just tell him about my feelings. And he listens."

"And then what?"

Peg shook her head. "That's...usually enough."

Allison sighed. "I wish I could find a man who listened to my feelings and didn't try to fix everything."

"Right?" Peg agreed. "That's it exactly."

They sat in silence for several long minutes. Finally, Allison said, "Something's happening down at the shop."

"What something?" Peg asked. She fished in her pocket for a Kleenex. The one she pulled out looked like a withered orchid. Allison handed her a sealed travel-pack. "Oh, bless you, dear." Peg cracked the plastic with her thumb and pulled out a fresh tissue. She blew her nose and then dabbed at her eyes.

"The place is full. I was wondering—"

"Full?" Peg asked. "It's past closing."

"The posted hours have gone out the window," Allison said, a little bit of mirth coloring her voice. "People need something."

"What do they need? And what people are we talking about?" Peg asked.

"Just...come see. Come down to the shop."

"When?"

"Now."

"Now?"

Allison nodded. "It's...important."

Peg felt torn. A part of her wanted to continue to cry on Jesus' shoulder. Another part of her wanted to empty a bottle of Chardonnay while stewing in a hot bath. The greatest part of her nagged that she should go back to the hospital and sit in the waiting room until Julie woke up the next morning. But being with her friend was weal to her heart. Just a walk with her to the studio would do her good. "All right, love. Let's go."

Allison squeezed her hand and rose. Peg flipped the switches off as she passed them and locked the doors. In moments, they were in the cool spring night, beneath the icy glow of the moon. Allison took her arm as they walked. Her friend didn't say anything else. She didn't need to.

They traversed the tiny downtown quickly, and in a few minutes, Peg saw the glow of Allison's art studio and crafts shop up ahead. It was ablaze with light and activity.

"How did you—?" Peg began. "Whatever gave you the idea—?"

"I didn't get any idea. People just started showing up."

"When?"

"Tonight."

"But...why?"

"I think because they need something," Allison said. She paused by the door.

"What do they need?" Peg asked.

"Just...look," Allison said. She opened the door.

Peg stepped in. The light was bright and she had to squint at first. A roar of greeting filled her ears, and several people waved. Allison was right. The place was packed. She recognized most of them—just people from the town, normal people, ordinary people. People she loved. She even saw a few of her parishioners. She smiled as they returned to their artwork.

Peg began to walk around. Some people were painting, but most were working with clay. Peg started when she saw one of them. "Oh, my," she said.

The artist looked up. It was Gary Schultz. "Hello, Pastor," he said. Peg nodded at him, at his combover, at the divot in his chin. But she couldn't take her eyes off his handiwork—it was a depiction of the cube showing his own death, scaled down to six inches by six inches. The figure of himself would not have been recognizable—Gary was not an artist, it was clear—but she recognized the cube. But it was not a replica—it was more like the sculpture was a suggestion of the original. Peg realized that his artistic talent was not the point. Whatever he was doing with the clay, the man was working something out—something psychological, perhaps even spiritual.

Gary smiled up at her, and she saw intention in that smile. She also saw anxiety and fear, as well as artistic passion, all of it bound up in the complexity that was Gary. She placed a calming hand on his shoulder and gave it a soft squeeze. He returned to his work, adding detail to the tiny figure of himself with a clay scalpel.

She moved to the next person and stopped short. "Mel," she said. The young trans man raised his eyes to her, and she saw that they were full of tears. He too was making a replica of his cube, about the same size as Gary's. He was a better artist, though, and his tiny corpus was recognizable. Peg shuddered. Mel bit his lip and wiped his nose on his flannel sleeve. Then he began to pinch at the corners of his cube, making the angles sharper.

"Oh, love," Peg said, placing a hand on each of the young man's shoulders.

"I don't want to go home," he said.

"What do you mean, dear?" Peg asked.

"Mom and I…we're not…I think she hates me."

"I'm sure that's not true," Peg said. "In fact, I *know* it's not true. Your mother came to see me. She was beside herself with worry. She cares about you very much." It was true, but there was also a lot she was not saying. "So where will you go?" Peg asked.

"I don't know. Here?" He threw a hopeful glance at Allison, but she was busy with someone else.

"Nonsense, you'll stay with me," Peg said. "I have a guest room at the parsonage."

"I don't know…" the young man said.

"I'm a pastor, I don't bite, and I'm not weird. Well, I'm a little weird, but in a good way, I hope." She hugged him from behind. "Look, love, no pressure. But if you want a warm bed and a bath tonight, you know where to find it. Just…make sure you let your folks know where you are. Alright?"

Mel sniffed and nodded and returned his focus to the cube. But he didn't do anything. Peg realized he had too many tears in his eyes, he couldn't even see his cube. Peg fished the travel pack of tissues from the pocket of her sweater and handed it to him.

"Thanks," he said. Gingerly, he placed the cube back on the work-table and took the pack. He tore a tissue from it and wiped at his eyes.

Peg patted his shoulder again and moved on. After a few minutes, she found Allison again. "They're making cubes—or painting them," she said.

"Yes," Allison said.

"But why?"

"Why don't you make one and see?" Allison said. She handed a lump of clay to Peg.

Peg took it. It felt heavier than she expected. "I don't know."

"You have a cube out there."

"I know that. I just..." She stared at the clay. "Perhaps I need to process it...another way."

"Art is the universal language of the soul," Allison said.

"Who said that?"

"I don't know...someone must have. And if not, I just did." She smiled at her friend.

"I guess I'm just not much of an artist."

"Neither is Gary," Allison pointed at him with her chin. "But that doesn't matter. It's about process, not product."

"You're just a flowing fount of aphorisms," Peg said.

"Go ahead, scoff—"

"I'm not scoffing, I'm...disturbed."

"In a good way or a bad way?" Allison asked.

"I'm...not sure yet," Peg said.

"The clay is perfect because the guys can punch it," Allison said. "It's therapeutic for them. You might want to punch it, too."

Peg blinked at the wad of clay in her hand. She set it on the countertop near her. "This is important, Allison, what's happening here."

"I know it. That's why I came to get you. I thought perhaps you needed to see it."

"It's not...enough," Peg said, although she wasn't entirely sure what she meant by it.

"It's a start," Allison agreed.

Just then a young native woman came through the door. Peg recognized her. It seemed like years ago, but Peg knew it had only been a day or so since she had spoken to her at Debbie's. Her hair was raven black, and her cheeks were fat and sun-weathered. She was short, even for a native person, and her hips were wide. Peg hated the weight she had put on in the past couple of years, but she did not hate it in this young woman. It suited her in a way that Peg could not explain.

The young woman—what was her name? Then Peg found it. *Milala.* Milala walked straight to Allison and spoke. "Is it ready?"

Allison smiled at her. "I don't know. Why don't we see? You remember Pastor Peg?"

The young woman looked at Peg, but with such dispassion that Peg could not read her. "Yes, I remember. Hello again." Then she turned away.

Peg wasn't sure how to feel about that, but Allison did not seem to notice. "Come on, let's check the kiln." Milala followed Allison to the back of the shop, and Peg brought up the rear. The small back room was blessedly empty of people, and Peg realized just how claustrophobic she'd been feeling. She loved people, but she didn't love small, crowded places, especially if she had to navigate them.

"I've had this set to 200 degrees Fahrenheit for about four hours, and I put in a bowl of water to raise the humidity level," Allison said as she clicked off the kiln's master switch. She reached for a pair of large black rubber gloves. "It's not the way I'd suggest drying animal skin, but it's the only way I know of to do it fast."

"Animal skin?" asked Peg.

"Coyote," Milala said.

Peg scowled her confusion, but bit her tongue. She watched Allison's maddeningly skinny waist as she leaned into the kiln. For a moment she wondered if her friend was going to fall in, but then Allison straightened up and pulled forth an object, holding it in front of her as if it were the holy grail. It was a drum.

"How's that?" Allison asked, beaming. She set it on a shelf. "Careful, don't burn your fingers," she said.

Peg saw that Milala was watching the drum intently, like a dog watching a treat in anticipation of getting it.

"What's the drum for?" Peg asked.

"It's for you," Milala said.

"For me?" Peg was confused.

"I mean, it's for all of you *oje-ajnt*," Milala clarified.

Peg opened her mouth to say that she still did not understand, but stopped when Milala extended her hand over the drum. She tapped it with one index finger. It responded with a resonant *thummm*. Milala nodded and blew on the drum.

For some reason that made Allison laugh. "It's not soup. Best to forget about it and come back in ten—"

But Milala had picked the drum up. It must have still been hot, but apparently not so much so that the young woman could not hold it. She fitted the fingers of her left hand to the leather cross behind the drum, then tentatively struck at the drumhead. The sound was booming this time, and the whole room seemed to vibrate. Milala smiled, and the expression of sheer joy took Peg aback. She had not seen Milala smile before, and it reminded her of the sun peeking out from behind dark clouds. She had not known what to make of the young native woman until that moment. Now Peg realized that she liked her.

"Will that do?" Allison asked.

"It will probably not last a long time, but it will do for now," Milala said. She looked Allison in the eyes and gave a shallow bow. "This...would have been much harder if you hadn't..." Peg saw emotion stir in the young woman's face. Finally, Milala just said, "Thank you."

"You're welcome, my dear," Allison said, catching Milala up in a hug. Peg was surprised to see that Milala returned the hug—a hug that lasted longer than most.

"Let's see how it goes," Milala said, breaking the embrace and turning toward the door.

Following Milala from the room, Allison whispered to Peg over her shoulder, "I don't know much more than you do."

"Did she say the drum was made from a dog?"

"A dead coyote, just outside of town. She kep calling it her 'Father,' which weirded me out a bit at first. She skinned it herself."

"I need to bone up on my Foxfire collection," Peg said.

"Your what?" Allison asked.

"Never mind—you need to be an old hippie to remember those. Used to be in every young back-to-the-land household, right next to the glass bong and the macramé dreamcatcher."

"Uh...yeah, the dreamcatcher," Allison looked momentarily worried. "I never took you for a hippie."

"No, I was a junkie," Peg clarified. "I was a little too late for the hippie thing, but I was hippie-adjacent."

Then they were in the main room again, the air electric with tension and grief and frenzied creative struggle. Peg noticed the knotted brows of the townspeople as they leaned over their clay masterpieces. And because she was one of them, her heart went out to them.

And then Milala struck the drum three times. It wasn't what Peg was expecting. Even over the din of activity, it boomed and resonated —so much so that she started a bit. Milala struck it three times again. People paused and looked up.

Then she began to play in earnest. It wasn't drumming like Peg was used to. It wasn't accompaniment. Nor was there any artistry that she could detect. There was no complex pattern. There was no melody, nothing that might suggest a song. Milala simply beat the drum at a steady rate, perhaps 120 beats-per-minute, Peg estimated. She did not waver, she did not add grace beats. It was just a steady rhythm, so loud that everyone in the shop heard it plainly.

As soon as people realized what it was, most smiled, and all went back to their artwork. But Peg's breath caught, because she did not anticipate what she saw next. Shoulders relaxed. The knots of tension in people's foreheads loosened. People began to smile more easily. Peg heard laughter.

Milala kept on drumming, seemingly without fatigue and without missing a beat. Peg pulled Allison aside. "Do you understand what's happening?"

"No," Allison said. "But it's good."

"Yes," Peg agreed. "It's very good. Very, very good."

Abel paused beside the open truck window. "Stay," he said.

Ginger Beer whined but settled down on the broad bench seat and put her chin on her front paws. Her eyes, large as billiard balls, never left him. She looked as sad as he felt.

He turned and walked toward the hospital. Dawn was breaking, and the sky above the emergency room was the same pink color as the cubes in his field. He shuddered and returned his gaze to the bright, warm, looming doors.

Once inside, he moved as if in a trance. He wasn't a man with much access to his emotions at the best of times, and in the worst, not at all. He felt numb.

The farmhouse was gone. The barn was gone. The fields were trampled. The only thing left to him was his truck, his dog, and his wife. *Everything that really matters*, a voice in his head reminded him. He did not answer the voice.

He stepped into the elevator and hit the button for the sixth floor. Just before the doors closed completely someone stuck a hand in. The doors opened again, and Thom Lind stepped in, his cowboy hat slightly askew and a courier bag slung over one shoulder.

Both men blinked. For a few minutes they stood together in awkward silence. "How's Mia?" Thom asked, finally.

"She'll live."

"I'm glad to hear it."

Abel saw Thom look down at the panel, selecting his floor with his thumb. "I'm sorry I wasn't there when all that shit came down," Thom apologized. "I'm sorry about your barn...and your house."

Abel nodded. "I'm not sure you could have stopped them."

"I sure as shit would have tried."

"I know you would. Is Julie...?"

"You heard," Thom said. "That's why I'm here. She'll live too."

Abel nodded. "I'm glad to hear it."

Thom asked, "Okay if I stop in and give Mia my best?"

"Sure. She'd like that."

Thom smiled. He punched the button on the elevator again. "I hope to see you then."

The doors opened, but Abel tugged on Thom's elbow. "He did fine, Thom," Abel said. "Jake, I mean. I misjudged him. I think maybe...I think maybe you did too. He stood up to them boys. Took a lot of courage to do that."

Thom looked at his boots. He looked back up. Then he put out his hand to stop the elevator doors closing. "Thanks for letting me know that, Abel."

Abel nodded, and Thom stepped out. Before the doors closed again, Thom said. "I'll see you soon."

And then Abel was alone with the stainless steel walls of the elevator. He had controlled his emotions well when talking to Thom, but in truth he wanted to punch something, or kick something, or smash something. But there was nothing here he could destroy with impunity. When the doors opened again he cursed inwardly and searched for Mia's room.

A nurse passed and smiled at him. "Visiting?" she asked.

"Yes. My wife," Abel said. "Room 645?"

"Down that-a way," she pointed behind her. "Where's your flowers?"

Abel froze. *Flowers?* he wondered. Of course. He should be bringing flowers, or at least some kind of gift. He wondered if perhaps he should go back downstairs, look for the gift shop, pick something out. Then he realized it was six in the morning, and doubted any gift shop would be open. He thought about going back out to the truck, finding a 7-11, finding...what? Did they have flowers at the 7-11? For the life of him, he couldn't remember.

"Damn," he said. Whatever anger he'd felt toward the sheriff had been forcefully redirected toward himself. New emotions were mixed in with it—shame for being such a clueless clod, and embarrassment. But the most crushing was the anticipation of her own disappointment.

He sighed. Then he found Mia's room. He knocked at the door but didn't wait for a reply. Mia looked like she was sleeping. Maybe he did have time to go find something for her. He almost turned around, but then he saw Mia stir. He found a chair and pulled it near to the bed. Her eyes opened. *"Gubben?"* she said.

"Hello, *gumman*," he answered.

"Where's Ginger?" she asked, her voice suddenly high with panic.

"She's in the truck. She's fine." He reached for her hand. He held it, squeezed it, caressed it. He felt an unidentifiable emotion swell in the back of his throat. He swallowed it down again. Whatever it was, it was big and he did not want to deal with it.

"How are you feeling?" he asked. He dreaded the answer. Bandages covered her face and head in a patchwork arrangement of white gauze. Somehow, he'd escaped with only minor cuts and bruises, but Mia had second-degree burns. He'd also somehow banged her head on the doorframe as he ran through it to get her out of the house. The concussion was deemed to be slight, but it bothered Abel even more than the burns.

"My head hurts," Mia answered. "Everything hurts."

"Do you need more pain medication?" Abel asked.

"Just got the shot," she said.

"You should have one of those things you can pump with your thumb," he said, mimicking the action with his free hand.

"Maybe I should...but I don't."

He wondered if he should complain. He couldn't stand to see her in pain.

"How are you feeling?" Mia asked. Abel jerked upright. He hadn't expected Mia to turn the question on him. And the truth was, he didn't know. He knew he was feeling a lot, but it was buried under decades of affective insulation and old hay. He'd felt angry at the sheriff, and that had felt good, if only because it was a feeling he could put a name to.

"I'm sorry, *gumman*," he said.

She winced. When she relaxed again, she said, "What do you have to be sorry about?"

Where should he start? "Uh…that I didn't do it differently, so that you wouldn't have…" He trailed off.

"Do what differently?" she asked.

"It…something…everything," he clarified.

"And what could you have done differently?"

He didn't know. He especially didn't know how he could have done anything differently given the facts he had when he had them. "I don't know, *gumman*. I'm just sorry, is all."

She smiled then. "Yes, but what else? How are you *feeling*?"

He squeezed her hand. He didn't know what she wanted from him. He rarely did.

"You know, I think that *you* think that the way to be a good husband is to do everything right."

He didn't answer that, but he did think about it. For several long minutes only silence passed between them.

She winced again. When her shoulders relaxed, she said, "I don't need you to do everything right. I just need *you*."

The emotion swelled again. He cleared the thickness from his throat. "*Gumman*, let me tell you…let me tell you how I *feel*…"

Her eyes opened more widely, and her lips turned up in a wan smile.

After the elevator door closed, Thom felt paralyzed. He hadn't expected to run into Abel; he wasn't sure he'd said the right things. He felt his gut tighten. "I need chocolate," he said out loud.

Just then his cell phone vibrated. He fished it out, transferring the weight of the courier bag to his other shoulder. He squinted at a text message from Celia. "Olivia Harris committed suicide. Jake on his way to the scene."

"Lord," Thom said. He desperately wished for a piece of chocolate. He set his face toward an alcove where he knew there was a bank of vending machines. He didn't know Olivia Harris well, but he knew who she was. She was one of those "lucky" enough to have a cube. Thom tried to remember the details of her cube, but they were all beginning to blur together for him.

Arriving at the vending machines, Thom selected a dark chocolate with bits of hazelnut and prune. It was a fancier bar than he normally bought, but the price was strangely low. He chose to think of it as a treat. He scooped it up from the long horizontal window and broke it open as he walked to Julie's room.

He had devoured half of it by the time he arrived. He put the rest in his breast pocket, knowing it would melt before he reached for it again. *It's just one of the hazards of chocolate,* he thought, patting the pocket. He paused by the door and knocked. He was surprised to hear an alert "Come in."

He took off his hat, leaned into the room, and saw Peg beside the sleeping Julie. He smiled politely at her, but the corners of his mouth dropped quickly. "How's she doing?"

"Still sleeping, but okay," Peg said.

"Mind if I come in?" Thom asked.

"Not at all," Peg said.

Thom entered and found another chair, placing it beside Peg's. He placed the courier bag on the floor and set his hat on top of it. Then he sat, issuing a long moan as he did so.

"That sounded like the groan of a tired man," Peg said. "Did you get any sleep?"

"Some," Thom answered. "I'm just...sore." *I've been shot,* Thom thought, but he didn't say that to Peg. She'd no doubt shoo him out and command him to go to the emergency room. She might even insist on accompanying him. He had more important things to think about.

"Maybe you should see a doctor," Peg offered, skirting dangerously close to exactly the territory Thom did not want to travel.

"Maybe I will, when this is all over," Thom said.

"It isn't over?" Peg asked.

"Olivia Harris committed suicide," Thom said. "This morning. That's...just between us professionals."

"Of course," Peg agreed. "How terrible."

"Did you know Olivia?"

"No, but I know who she is...was. She had a cube, right?"

"Yep."

"But...is this the way the cube said she'd die?" Peg asked.

"Nope."

"Well...thank God for small favors."

Thom nodded. Then he bolted upright.

"What?" Peg asked.

"She's awake," Thom said, pointing at Julie.

Peg looked. Julie opened one eye, then another. "You guys make a lot of fucking noise," she managed.

"I'm sorry we woke you," Peg said.

"What time is it?" Julie asked.

"6:15 AM," Peg answered.

"Ugh," Julie answered. "But time here...doesn't run on its regular tracks."

"No," Peg agreed. "You can sleep whenever you feel like it."

"Can I get you anything, Deputy?" Thom asked.

"Got any chocolate?" Julie asked.

The grin that broke out over Thom's face was genuine this time. He reached into his breast pocket and handed the rest of the bar to her.

"How did you know?" Peg asked her.

Julie didn't answer, but found the bed controls and raised the head up to more of a sitting position. Once settled, Julie broke off a square of the chocolate and put it in her mouth. She made a face. "What is that...raisins?"

"Prunes, with hazelnuts," Thom confessed. "And I think there's a little lavender oil in there too."

Julie made a face, but she didn't stop chewing. "I think I prefer blue-collar chocolate," she said, but she broke off another square just the same.

Thom lifted the courier bag from the floor and opened it. He pulled out a sheaf of papers and handed them to Julie. Cringing a bit from pain, she received them and rested them in her lap. Then she turned over the first page and began reading. She looked back up at Thom.

"This is from Clive's apartment," she said.

"It is," Thom confirmed. "I'm hoping you can decipher it for me."

"I'm not sure now is the time," Peg objected.

"No, it's...it's okay," Julie said, grimacing as she adjusted herself in her bed. "*Mors in Manibus Nostris*. That's Latin...'to touch death with our hands'?"

Peg frowned, but she added, "Or it could mean death is sensible... touchable...a real thing, as opposed to an idea."

Julie nodded. Thom looked from one to another. It was the first time he had ever seen mother and daughter cooperate on anything. He wondered if that was significant.

Then Julie's eyes went wide. "The Reification of Death," she said.

"The what?" Peg asked.

"You know Clive," Julie said.

"I *knew* Clive," Peg said. "I didn't think he was a good influence on you, but..."

Thom saw Julie bristle and saw that Peg saw it too. The pastor had abruptly stopped talking. Nevertheless, Julie continued. "He was experimenting with Cthulu magick. It was stupid, but...he was desperate."

"That boy always seemed desperate," Peg agreed.

Julie's eyes narrowed.

Thom interceded—he sensed they were getting at something important and didn't want to see it derailed by a mother-daughter spat. "I don't get the connection," he said.

Julie closed her eyes and took a deep breath. For a moment, Thom wondered if she was going to go back to sleep, but a moment later, she shifted in her bed and opened her eyes again. "It was the material of the cubes," she said, "the pink stuff, the unbreakable stuff—that led me to the *Fenestram in Infernum*, which is what led me to..." She sighed, then, apparently too tired to recount anything in detail.

It didn't matter. Thom was tracking with her. "Yeah, to all that."

Julie looked relieved. "I didn't imagine in a million years it would lead me back to Clive. I still don't understand how he...I don't think Clive ever got his hands on it—the *Fenestram* grimoire. Maybe he tried to get hold of it, I don't know. We found out...the hard way...that he wasn't the only one doing Cthulu magick...which is *insane*. But he didn't use the *Fenestram* grimoire, did he? He used this." She pointed to the manuscript in her lap.

"But where did that come from?" Thom asked.

Julie shook her head. "I'm wondering if there's some correspondence between this text and all those sigils he wrote."

"Sigils?" Thom asked.

"Symbols—usually corresponding to a supernatural force or..." Julie grimaced. "...entity."

"I wonder if this is automatic writing," Peg suggested.

Julie nodded, biting her lip in thought. "But automatic writing usually starts out as nonsense, and all of this text makes sense."

"Unless the English portion is a translation of the sigils."

"Sigils don't translate directly," Julie objected. "They're more like pictograms."

Peg shrugged. "But you can translate Chinese or Egyptian into English."

Julie's brows bunched together as she thought.

"What's automatic writing?" Thom asked, cocking his head.

"It's like channeling," Peg offered. "But the...entity...speaks through your pen rather than through your mouth."

Julie nodded, apparently grateful her mother was covering the explanations for now.

"It's a common phenomenon," Peg went on. "Several important books have been...brought through that way. Like...what was that one that was so big in the 1980s, thick as a doorstop—?"

"*A Course in Miracles*," Julie said.

"That's it!" Peg said.

"Or *Ohaspe*," Julie added wearily.

"And *The Urantia Book*," Peg said.

Thom had to stop himself from smiling. It was a rare thing to see these two in the same room. It warmed his heart. But there were important matters afoot. "So let me see if I've got this straight," Thom said. "This rare—grimoire—?"

Julie nodded.

"This rare grimoire can produce...result in...whatever...the material in the cubes. That's what led us into that whole wild goose chase in the desert. But your friend here didn't use that grimoire after all. He...what? Channeled? He channeled another book—"

"*Part* of another book," Julie corrected.

"—*part* of another book, and used the ritual that he...brought through...to do what? And what was the other book?"

"Probably the *Necronomicon*," Julie said.

"I thought you said that was a fictional book," Thom said.

"It is," Julie said. She closed her eyes. Thom realized they were taxing her, and they should let her rest.

"So...you're saying that your friend Clive channeled part of a fictional book in order to contact fictional...uh..." he grasped for the word.

"Deities," Julie supplied.

"Your friend Clive used a fictional book to contact fictional deities?"

Julie's eyes were still closed, but she nodded.

"But I saw them, goddammit. They weren't fictional," Thom said, a bit too loudly.

Peg touched him on the arm. He looked over to her and she jerked her head toward the door. Thom nodded and picked up his hat. He stood and quietly walked to the door. Peg was close behind him. Once in the hallway, Thom turned to her and said in a voice that was little more than a whisper, "How could I possibly see fictional deities that I don't even know anything about?"

"Thom, I think you have an impoverished sense of the imagination," Peg said.

"What the hell does that mean?" Thom bristled.

"It means that just because something is imaginal doesn't mean it isn't real. The imagination isn't a fantasy machine, it's an organ of perception. We don't perceive the world as it is—it would be too much information, it wouldn't make any sense to us. We would be assaulted by information with no capacity to process it. We would all be helplessly autistic. So we construct a shared universe, held together with story. I live in it, you live in it, everyone lives in it. It isn't real, it's just what we've...agreed upon...so that we aren't constantly tripping over the furniture like Dick Van Dyke."

Thom scowled. He was following her words, but the reality she was describing made no sense to him. "Stuff is stuff. People are people."

"I understood what you said only because we have a mutually agreed-upon symbol system to describe an essentially ineffable reality."

"I literally did not understand more than three words of that," Thom confessed. He was sweating and he could feel his pulse. He forced himself to be calm. His hand automatically went to his shirt pocket, but he had given the rest of his chocolate to Julie.

Good, a voice in his head said. *Because who the fuck puts prunes and lavender in chocolate? It isn't natural.* He forced his hand into his pocket. "The kind of universe you are describing is ridiculous."

"No...it's improbable, but it's not ridiculous. It's the *alma mundi,* the Soul of the World."

"Imagination is the Soul of the World?"

Peg looked at her feet. He could tell she was frustrated, too. "This is...very difficult to explain. Just..." She sighed and looked up at him again. "Plato, and Swedenborg, and Carl Jung...they were all onto something. There are archetypal forces at play in the universe—spiritual forces, symbolic forces. Some are beautiful and wise and good, and some...aren't. We all know about them intuitively because we all draw from the same pool of consciousness...Jung called it the 'collective unconscious.' But these...forces...they long to be made flesh, to incarnate."

"What, like...Jesus?"

Peg smiled. "In a way, yes. I suppose I worship one of those forces."

Thom felt dizzy. He reached for the wall. "So...you're saying *everyone* worships these...archetypes?"

"Everyone who worships," Peg said. "But you don't need to worship them to have intercourse with them."

Thom's eyebrows shot up. "Have *intercourse?*"

Peg closed her eyes and shook her head. "I meant that in the old sense. I'll try again. You don't need to worship them to *interact* with them...that's...that's what I mean."

"And we perceive these...forces...using the imagination?" Thom was taking baby steps, but he wanted to make sure he was getting it right.

"That's called 'faith,' by the way," Peg smiled. "It's how we 'see' the unseen. And 'prayer' is how we communicate with them—how we channel them and make them manifest in our lives."

"But...*why?*" Thom asked.

"Because we are dust and to dust we shall return. We are made of the very stuff of the earth—dirt and shit and growing things. We *are* the earth, and the earth is *us*. And our brains are what the earth uses to think with, to dream with, to experience itself through. And all of our brains are linked, like computers in a network—"

"They are?"

"—and so we are always downloading archetypes and living them out even as we are uploading our prayers and dreams and visions, and the two are constantly feeding one another and creating the world as we experience it, in real time. All the things up there," she pointed to the ceiling, "long to be down here, in the flesh, in the..." she chuckled. "*In Manibus Nostris*. In our hands."

Thom scratched his head. "Who believes this shit?"

Peg shrugged. "Well, we can start with the entire philosophical and theological edifice of Western culture. And, with a little translation, some Eastern philosophies as well, especially Hinduism. But...it doesn't matter who believes it. It's *true*. And you've got a whole corn-field full of cubes to prove it." She patted his arm. "It doesn't really matter how they got here, Thom. They're *here*. The real question is: What are we going to do about it?"

"Like...do a spell to get rid of the cubes?"

Peg closed her eyes. He imagined that she was counting to ten to keep from yelling at him. Or perhaps she was just tired. But when she opened her eyes, they were more compassionate than he had imagined they would be. "No, love. They've already done their damage. What I meant was: How are we going to help people heal?"

Hours later, Thom parked his rented Jeep as close to the Travers' home as he could. The sidewalk was thick with people spilling out onto the street. He climbed out and put his hat on. He pushed the button on the mic hanging from his epaulet. "Adam One to Karlstadt. I've arrived at the Travers' place."

Celia's voice crackled. "Copy that, Adam One. Ya'll be careful."

Thom nodded, but did not reply. Slowly he walked toward the house as the crowd began to part to let him through. Saucer-eyed, they watched him silently as he crossed the sidewalk and ducked under the police tape.

Rios bounded out of the house and made a beeline for him. "Rios," he said.

"Boss," Rios said.

"Get me up to speed so you can go home, get some shut-eye," Thom said.

"We got the call about 5am from the neighbors. They heard gunshots."

Rios fell into step with Thom, who had slowed down, but was still moving toward the house.

"How many?" Thom asked, pulling on latex gloves.

"One neighbor said five, another says six," Rios said. His short, jet-black hair stood straight up. It looked less like real hair than it did a hair-shaped helmet. He tried not to hold it against the kid, who was eager but solid in a way that Jake only aspired to be. Rios was the backbone of the night shift, and he had proved to be a reliable officer.

"And what do the shells say?" Thom asked.

"We found five…so far."

"Caliber?"

"9 millimeter."

"Figures."

Thom stopped and faced Rios. "How bad is it?"

Rios shrugged. "I've seen worse. So have you, I imagine."

"Don't…*imagine* anything. I'm having a complicated relationship with the imagination right now."

Rios blinked.

"Never mind," Thom said, waving the kid's confusion away. "Take me through it."

Rios climbed the stairs and Thom followed. Entering the door, Thom squinted, waiting for his eyes to adjust. His nose twitched. The air smelled strongly of stale patchouli and burned lasagna. His instincts told him that, where there was patchouli, something else was being burned as well—or more exactly, smoked. Not that that mattered these days. It was just a fact, an association.

Thom looked to his right and saw Becky Travers sitting on the couch. Her cuffed wrists were sitting quietly in her lap. When their eyes met, she seemed to shrink a bit. She looked away.

"Becky," Thom said. He waited for her to meet his eyes again. He gave her a pained smile that lasted only as long as it needed to. But she seemed to be heartened by it. She sat up a bit straighter and held her chin up a bit more.

"Don't take her in just yet," Thom said to Rios. "I want to talk to her first."

"You bet," Rios said.

"Where did it happen?"

"Kitchen."

"Take me."

Rios turned and headed deeper into the house. Thom followed, pausing at the threshold to the kitchen. The way was blocked by a quaint set of saloon doors. Thom guessed that Paul had insisted on hanging those, and Becky had hated having to push through them every time she moved from the kitchen to the dining table. But of course Paul had won that argument. Thom wondered how many arguments Paul had claimed victory over. *Not this one*, Thom thought.

He pushed through the doors and caught his breath. The corpse of Paul Travers lay by the stove, half propped up against it, half slid down on the floor. Two tributaries of blood coursed away from the underside of the body. Thom counted the bullet holes. There were two in the backsplash, coarse divots marring the cheery yellow tile. He scanned the cabinets downwards toward the body, but there were no other misses. "Her first two shots went wide, one to the left of him, one to the right. It took her a few tries to get the feel of the gun."

"She knew how to fire it," Rios agreed, "but she wasn't practiced."

Thom nodded. It wasn't unusual to see Paul at the firing range, but he had never seen Becky there. Thom knelt by the body. He snatched a ballpoint pen from the pocket he kept his moleskin in. "There's a cluster of bullets where his nose used to be," Thom said. The face was unrecognizable. A dripping mass of gore bloomed just below the man's eyes. Thom used the ballpoint to move a flap of skin from one position to another. "Two or three in the face?" Thom asked Rios.

"I can't tell, boss. I'm wondering the same."

"Coroner can tell us, I reckon," Thom said. There was one more bullet hole, in the chest, just above and to the left of mid-point. "I'm guessing three in the face, given how it looks like ground chuck. That means the other neighbor was right—there were six shots and we've got another shell floating around here."

"Either that, or one of the bullet holes in the wall was already there."

"That's a scary thought. We can ask Becky about that, I reckon."

"I...don't think she's a reliable witness, Boss," Rios objected.

"Well, unreliable or not, we still gotta talk to her. We know his side of the story—" He pointed at Paul with his pen. "—we need to listen to hers."

Thom straightened up. His back cracked audibly. His shoulder had begun to burn. He knew he should go to the emergency room, get himself cleaned up. *It's my next stop, I promise,* he thought, although whom he was promising wasn't clear.

"Do you have an ETA on CSU?"

"Bakersfield says they'll be here within the hour."

"Good. And, Rios...good job. This crime scene is neat as a whistle."

"I just do my job, sir."

"The weapon?"

"Bagged and tagged and in the safe in the Rover. I'll register it with Celia when I get back to the office."

Thom nodded. "I'll take it from here, son. I reckon you'll want a shower."

"Uh...yes, sir, that would be nice."

In his peripheral vision, Thom saw Rios leave the kitchen. Thom wasn't sure that what Rios wanted most was a shower, but it's what *he* always wanted after spending any amount of time at all at a crime scene, especially one with blood. "I warned you, Paul, you motherfucker. I warned you *twice.*" He sighed. Then he reminded himself that there was work to do.

He did a more thorough visual surveillance of the scene. He snapped a couple of pictures with his phone and replaced it in his pocket. Then he pushed through the saloon doors to the dining area.

Striding to the living room, he sat down on the couch next to Becky. "Oh, Beck," he said.

She said nothing, her head hanging.

"I always wondered when he was going to push you too far," Thom said.

"I beat it," she said.

"Beat...what?"

She looked him full in the eye now. "That cube. It showed me dying...Paul with his hands around my neck. He did that."

"He was strangling you?" Thom asked.

"Yes."

"Is that when you shot him?"

"Yes."

"Where?"

"In the chest."

Thom nodded. One shot accounted for. "Then what happened?"

"He backed away. He looked...like I had just betrayed him somehow. The look on his face, it was...he was surprised."

"I'll just bet he was."

"It was like he didn't believe it, like it couldn't possibly be happening to him. He said, 'You bitch.' And then he lunged for me."

"But you were still holding the gun," Thom added. It was a question, but he didn't phrase it that way.

She nodded. "I fired again. I missed. Twice. Then I didn't."

Thom nodded. "What are you feeling right now?"

Becky's face clouded. Thom could see that she wasn't sure. She was numb, in shock most likely. He reached for the back of the couch and lifted a sage-colored throw from where it had been draped. He put it around her shoulders. "I'm going to get you some water, and I want you to drink it."

Becky nodded again, not looking at him. She clutched the throw tightly around her shoulders. "Whiskey," she said.

"What?" Thom asked.

"Bring me a whiskey."

"Huh. Okay. I'll be right back."

Thom pushed through the saloon doors again and found a glass. Carefully stepping around the body, he filled it from the tap. Then he grabbed a smaller glass and began to look through the cupboards for the whiskey. He opened one and found himself staring at half a large bar of chocolate. He put it in his pocket. Then he put it back.

Peg stepped through the door of Allison's studio and relished the warmth. It was a cool morning, and she'd felt the chill as she traversed Karlstadt's tiny downtown. She'd looked at the window of Debbie's sorrowfully, as the warmth of that place would have been her first choice, but Allison had sounded insistent on the phone, so here she was. She was surprised to see that a tablecloth had been thrown over one of the working tables and a delightful breakfast spread had been set out. "This looks lovely, dear," Peg said.

"You didn't think I'd take away a Debbie's breakfast with one hand without providing something equally nummy with the other, did you?" Allison asked.

"Well, to my shame, I did doubt you," Peg confessed.

"Can I take your coat?" Allison asked, but Peg was already shedding it.

The door opened and Ted stepped through. His eyes were worried; he seemed subdued.

"Ted, good to...is there anything wrong?" Peg asked.

"I, uh...I just got a text," he said. "There've been two more suicides."

"*More* suicides?" Peg asked.

"There was one already. Now there are three," Ted said.

"And are these—"

"And it looks like the whole sheriff's department are all parked outside the Travers' place," Ted said. "I don't know what's going on there."

"The people who killed themselves..." Peg clarified, "...are they all...you know...people with cubes?"

"I think so," Ted said. "I didn't know one of them."

Just then there was a knock at the door. Ted scowled at Peg, but Allison brightened. "Milala!" she said, rushing to the door.

"Milala? That Indian girl?" Ted asked. "Why is she here?"

"I don't know," Peg confessed.

"She's here because I invited her here," Allison said in a loud whisper just before throwing open the door. "She just went out to pick up coffee. She's cute, don't you think?"

"Dear, you're blushing," Peg pointed out. "I didn't know African Americans did that."

Allison ignored this. "She's been sleeping in the back." She reached for the key, already in the door.

"Sleeping—" Ted started, but Peg shushed him as soon as the door was open.

Milala stepped through, balancing a cardboard tray of coffee drinks. She handed them to Allison. "They were out of oat milk, so they used almond milk instead," she said.

"That's just fine," Allison said.

"It's fine unless you have a nut allergy," Ted noted.

"Do you have a nut allergy?" Allison asked.

"I do not," Ted admitted.

"Then keep it to yourself please."

Ted harrumphed, but Peg smiled. "Good to see you again, Milala."

Milala did not look so sure, but she took a seat near the breakfast table and stared at it.

Everyone noticed. Allison smiled. "Uh...help yourselves, everyone. Peg, I've got a double caramel latte for you. Ted, an Americano, extra sour."

Ted received the cup without thanks, but sniffed at it. "Lovely."

"Milala, what did you get for yourself?" Peg asked.

"A large hot chocolate with a double pump of Irish Creme syrup and a dusting of cinnamon," she said.

"Oh, that's...very specific," Peg grinned.

Milala took out a cigar. "Can I smoke in here?"

"Oh, my," Ted brightened. "It seems I may have misjudged her."

"Uh...we have a strict no-smoking policy in the shop," Allison said, pointing to a sign and looking slightly rattled by the request. She cleared her throat and changed the subject. "Now, to order—"

"This is a business meeting?" Ted asked. "Shouldn't there be full disclosure about such things?"

Allison ignored him. "Ted says we've had three suicides since the... fiasco the other night."

"Three so far," Ted corrected.

"People don't know how to integrate this," Allison said.

"You're helping," Peg said. "The art is helping."

"Art always helps," Allison said. "My question is…what about the people who don't do art? Or *won't* do art?"

"Surely you aren't suggesting that people are ideologically ill-disposed to the arts," Ted objected.

"People are shy," Milala said. She had stacked two pastries on a small paper plate and was reaching for a third. "Art takes courage."

"That is so true." Allison nodded. Peg noted the shy glance exchanged by the two of them. She wasn't sure how she felt about it. She cleared her throat and said, "I agree with you. I felt it last night, while I was watching everyone making their sculptures. It feels like we need *more*, somehow."

"But what form should that *more* take?" Allison sipped at her coffee. Peg saw her eyeing a pastry. She also saw her friend resist the temptation. Peg picked up a pastry and threw it in Allison's lap. "For God's sake, skinny person, eat a fucking pastry."

Allison picked up the pastry, a bit sheepishly, and took a tiny nibble.

Milala spoke with her mouth full. "These *oje-ajnt* are suffering. If they suffer separately, they will die. They need to suffer together."

Ted's Americana froze halfway to his mouth. "Wait, we *want* people to suffer? What am I missing?"

Milala answered with a tone that indicated boredom, but Peg suspected she was not reading the young woman right just yet. "They're already suffering—that's why they're killing themselves."

"Heaven is community," Peg said. "Hell is isolation."

"What's that?" Allison asked.

"It's just a…Charles Williams. A mystic. He believed that Heaven is community and Hell is isolation."

"If you get cut off from The People, you die," Milala said, as if stating a self-evident truism. "If you want to live, you must be with The People."

Peg nodded. The young native woman was strange, but Peg could sense a deep wisdom in her. "If you want to live, you need to be with

The People," Peg repeated. "And if you are suffering, you should suffer...*with The People.*"

Milala nodded and took another bite of pastry. "Whenever someone is suffering, we all go to the *tcapu'ya*—the sweat lodge. That way everyone suffers together."

Ted scowled. "What is that? Some kind of group masochism?"

"This from the man who belongs to the tradition that used to whip themselves to pray," Allison said, her words directed specifically at Peg.

"Ask him to fill you in on the joys of a cilice sometime," Peg said.

"I have *never* used a cilice," Ted said. "At least...not on my leg."

"Too much information," Peg announced. She turned her attention back to Milala. "My dear, I think you are on to something."

Milala nodded matter-of-factly, as if there was no doubt of it. "When your people suffer, what ritual do you perform together?"

"We drink," Ted said.

It was Milala's turn to scowl.

"We don't do anything like...well, like what you do," Allison said. "It's not in our culture."

"No...but it used to be," Peg sat up straight, her eyes widening.

"What?" Allison asked.

"It used to be in our culture." Peg stood up and instantly began pacing, wheels turning in her head.

"What? You've got an idea," Allison prompted.

"I do, it's just...maybe five hairs too crazy," Peg said.

"Spill it, cupcake," Ted said, making a face at his coffee.

"The longhouse ritual," Peg said. She paused, as if waiting for a reaction.

She got none, but Allison did cock her head. "Say more."

"This is a Swedish town," Peg said.

"We're not *all* Swedish," Ted sniffed, pointing with his chin at Allison. "Obviously."

"No...but a lot of people are," Peg said. "The people who have lived here all their lives, they are."

"Okay, we've got a town full of third-generation Swedes. What of it?" Ted asked.

"In Swedish culture, they used to build these longhouses," Peg said.

"*You're* not a Swede," Ted objected.

"No, I'm not," Peg agreed. "The longhouses were constructed—"

"So where are you getting this stuff?" Ted raised his nose into the air.

"From the fucking Discovery channel, all right?" Peg snipped. "Who cares where it comes from, just…listen for a minute, dammit."

"All right, all right," Ted took a sip from his paper cup, pinky extended.

"I must've seen the same program," Allison said. "They used to live in them, everyone huddled in together."

"Yes, but sometimes they built them for special purposes too," Peg agreed. "They dug a trench down the middle of the longhouse and filled it with firewood or coal. Then they lit it."

"And then what?" Ted asked.

"And then   I guess they watched the fire," Peg said.

"So…how does that help us?" Ted raised one eyebrow.

"So your people have *tcapu'ya*, too," Milala nodded, and, it seemed to Peg, with approval. "It's a good plan. Your people can suffer together, and it'll heal their souls. It will restore their harmony."

"Didn't they burn down the longhouse after the ritual?" Allison asked.

"Sometimes, I think. But not always," Peg said. "I don't think that's an essential part of the ceremony."

"Were you there?" Ted asked.

Peg ignored him. "So…where do we get a longhouse?"

Milala blinked at them. "Well, you don't order them from the internet."

Allison opened her mouth, but nothing came out.

Milala continued, "You *make* it. It's part of the ritual." She shook her head. "Now I see why Creator told me to find you. You people have forgotten so many things—too many things. You need a teacher."

"You people?" Ted said, eyebrows rising so high Peg thought they might soar off his forehead. She tried not to smile.

"You need a clear patch of land," Milala said.

"There's an empty lot where they tore down the old drugstore," Allison noted.

Peg nodded. "It's easy walking distance from anywhere in town."

Milala looked pleased. "Then you need to build a frame. It's not hard. I'll draw it out for you." Milala looked around and almost instantly found what she was looking for. She brought a sheet of drawing paper to one of the tables and grabbed a charcoal pencil. She quickly sketched out a frame for the longhouse.

"That's very pretty. What are the measurements?" Ted asked.

"Long enough and high enough," Milala said.

"Ah," Ted said. "*That* will play in Poughkeepsie."

"I can call some young people from the church," Peg said.

"Do you know who you should call to organize this?" Allison asked, a smile breaking through her lips.

"No, who?" Peg asked.

"Oh, I don't know...young man, eager to prove himself..."

"I'm all for eager young men, but I have no idea of whom you speak." Ted shook his head.

"I'm talking about Mel," Allison said.

"Mel?" Peg breathed.

"Yes. He wants to be an architect," Allison continued. "Let's ask him to design *and* build our frame."

Peg nodded. She turned to Milala. "And once the frame is built?"

"You lay branches or leaves or scrap against it, and on the roof," Milala said. "It doesn't have to keep out rain. It's not forever. It's just for the ritual."

"How long will it take?" Ted asked, his brows furrowing.

Milala shrugged. "It should only take a couple hours to build."

"Branches..." Peg mused.

"I wonder," Allison looked as if she were studying something far in the distance. "What about hay?"

"Hay? Hay comes in bales," Ted said. "Or so I've heard tell."

"But it doesn't *have* to…" Peg said, nodding as her thoughts spun. "And it's the right time. Last season's hay is starting to go bad. It's been bound together, so you can actually pull it off in sheets—I've seen it, when they try to pull one of those old bales apart. You could just pull off a sheet of hay and…lay it on the roof or prop it against the walls."

"And then, when you're finished, you can light it on fire," Milala said.

"There's your burning longhouse," Ted said.

"Oh. But I really wasn't expecting us to do *that* part of it," Peg said. "Do we have to?"

"No," Milala said. "But it's easier than tearing it down."

"We'll have to see if it's far enough away from other structures, but…that *would* make it easy," Peg admitted.

"And cathartic," Allison added.

Peg nodded. She could see that. Burning the longhouse at the end of the ritual would provide a thrilling climax. It would provide a seal of the sacred on anything that happened within it.

"I can bless it," Milala said. She waved a cigar around, then put a cigar in her mouth. Peg was glad to see that it was still unlit.

"I beg your pardon. Blessing things is the pastor's job," Ted said, pointing at Peg with his chin.

At that, a reservoir of feeling that had been dammed up within Peg was released. Until that moment, she had not trusted Milala. She realized that she had not had an open heart toward her. She had considered her an outsider, and interloper, an intruder into her neat little world. *No*, she admitted to herself. *I thought of her as a nuisance.*

"Creator sent you to us," Peg said, and there was a note of wonder in her voice.

"Of course," Milala said with an edge of irritation. "I told you that."

"But I…" *I didn't believe you.* Peg's face softened. "I underestimated you, Milala. And I'm sorry."

Milala shrugged. "Eh. You get used to it. It doesn't surprise us or anything."

Peg shook her head. "No, but it hurts you. And I'm sorry."

Milala looked confused. "The *oje-ajnt* don't apologize. They don't really care about harmony."

"I think perhaps the underestimation is mutual," Ted noted, one eyebrow raised.

"Oh, but we *do* care for harmony," Peg said, reaching over to place her hand on Milala's arm. She gave it an affectionate squeeze. "We're just…clueless about it. We need teachers."

"I get it," Milala said. "Creator is wise."

"He certainly is, love," Peg agreed.

CHAPTER FIFTEEN

Thom was just about to reach for a piece of chocolate when he heard the knock at his office door. He looked up and saw Jake on the other side of the glass. Surreptitiously, he closed his desk drawer again. "Come in."

Jake looked a bit sheepish as he closed the door behind him. "You wanted to see me, Boss?"

Thom indicated a chair and the young man took it. "Jake, I've heard from a lot of people…about what happened out there, at the Nyland place."

Jake looked away and hung his head. "Yeah…"

"Some people say you muffed it up pretty bad. Others say you did everything just right. But do you want to know what I think?"

Jake's head was still turned away, but his eyes moved to meet Thom's. Thom smiled. "Son, I think you did about as well as anyone could have."

Thom watched his shoulders relax even as the kid sat up straighter. "You do?"

"I do. Good job. I'm thinking of giving you a promotion and a pay hike, but it would come with more responsibility."

"Sure—"

"Julie...it looks like she's going to make it, but...I don't know if she's coming back—" Thom watched Jake's face fall. He understood that. "I don't know if she'll be able to...physically, I mean. She's going to need months of physical therapy, and then..." He shrugged. "Well, who knows? I don't want to fill her place unless..."

"Unless you know for sure she won't...come back," Jake finished.

"Yeah."

"So you want me to take up the slack," Jake guessed.

"That's right. If you want it. I mean, I can move someone from the night shift. I'm sure Rios—"

"No," Jake said. "No, I can do it. I mean, between the two of us..."

Thom nodded. "Exactly what I was thinking. So...you're in?"

"I'm in. You can count on me, boss."

"Good. Because I need someone I can trust, Jake. And I think you've proven yourself."

"I hope that I have, sir," the young man said.

Thom saw that his eyes were shining. That was all right. He swallowed a lump of emotion himself and cleared his throat. "Okay, back to work then." He turned his attention to the papers on his desk.

"Thanks, Boss," Jake said. He stood and left the room.

Thom put the papers aside. They might have been written in Swahili, he wouldn't have known. He'd been hard on the kid, he knew that. But Jake had come through, more brilliantly than Thom could have imagined. He didn't want to give the kid a big head, but he knew it was time to give him a hand up.

Celia's voice came through his intercom, crackling with static. "Thom, Pastor Peg is here to see you."

Thom sighed. He wasn't getting much done, and it looked like he wouldn't. He wondered for a moment if it mattered. "Send her in."

A moment later, Peg poked her head in the door. "Gotta minute?"

"Always," Thom said, standing.

"Oh, pish, sit down," Peg said, closing the door behind her.

Thom sat. He opened his drawer. "I got chocolate and whiskey."

Peg sat and smiled, "Is that what passes for hospitality here?"

"I could also get you coffee, if you want. It's bitter as hell, black as midnight, and sour as a persimmon."

"I'd love to hear you tell a girl she's pretty sometime," Peg said.

Thom grinned, a little sadly.

"I'll take two fingers of whiskey and two squares of chocolate, if you've got it to spare," Peg said.

Thom opened his drawer and took out the large Trader Joe's chocolate bar he'd been working on. He peeled back the paper and foil and put it on the desk between them. Peg broke off one square while Thom grabbed a bottle and a mug from the shelf behind him and put them both on the desk. The mug looked stained, and Peg frowned.

"Don't worry. Nothing can survive this stuff," he poured two fingers into the cup, and another two in his own, cutting the remaining cold coffee.

Peg took the cup and looked at it uncertainly, but she sipped at it just the same.

"What can I do for you, Pastor?"

"You've noticed what's happening in the town?" Peg asked.

"You mean the suicides or the murder?"

"Yes, both, and...well, all the tension. They're not unrelated." She sipped again.

"I noticed," he said. In fact, he'd been brooding about that very thing before Jake stepped into his office.

"I...well, we've got a plan for that," Peg said.

"Uh...who's we? And a plan for what, exactly?" Thom asked.

"Me and Ted and Allison...and Milala—"

"Who the hell is Milala?" Thom narrowed his eyebrows.

"She's a native girl—Miwok, I think," Peg said. "She said the Creator...well, never mind about that. Anyway, we've been thinking... the cubes, they caused a lot of people to...well, to freak out."

"That they have."

"Have you wondered why?" Peg asked.

Thom blinked. "Uh...I don't think I have. I've been too busy dealing with the *results*. Besides, it seems academic."

"I can see why you think that, but...well, just as it's your job to worry about *what* people are doing, I think it's my job to ask *why* they're doing it. And…Thom, I think I know."

A few moments of silence passed. Finally, Thom could stand it no longer. "And?"

"And…I think it's all about grief."

"Grief?"

"Yes."

"I don't know anything about that."

Peg turned to look at the shelf bearing Emma's ashes, then she looked back at Thom. "Oh, I think you do."

Thom's jaw clenched. He meant to sip at his whiskey, but he was sloppy about it. Wet stains appeared on the front of his uniform.

Peg continued, "Grief twists people, if it doesn't get out somehow. Grief wants to be expressed. Hell, I think it wants to be howled."

Thom's eyebrows shot up. A chill ran through his spine, but he didn't let on. "Howled?"

Peg nodded. "Because if it doesn't get out…it eats you alive."

Thom opened his mouth, but nothing came out.

Peg placed her cup back on the desk. "Jesus said, 'If you bring forth what is within you, what you bring forth will save you. If you do not bring forth what is within you, what you fail to bring forth will condemn you."

"Jesus said that, eh?"

"Well, who knows what Jesus really said or didn't say—and the saying is not from a canonical source," Peg confessed. "But there's more than a little wisdom in it."

Thom did not disagree with that. He nodded slowly. "Pastor, I have no idea what you're driving at…but I wish you'd crash into it soon."

"We want to build a longhouse," Peg said.

Thom narrowed his eyes. "A longhouse?"

"Yes. It's an old Swedish—"

"I know what a longhouse is. The Indians have them too."

"Yes, that's kind of how we got the idea."

"From this…Milala?"

"Yes."

Thom nodded slowly. He wondered if it was going to take all morning to pry the point out of the pastor. He forced himself to relax. He owed her his attention. It occurred to him that perhaps whatever she was on about was how *she* was dealing with her grief.

"They dig a trench through the longhouse and build a fire in it."

"And then?"

"And then they sit in it..."

"In the fire?"

"In the longhouse... And... Well, they grieve. Together."

"And you expect the good people of Karlstadt to sit in your longhouse and...what? Grieve?"

"Yes. Yes, that's it exactly." Peg smiled at him. It was the most pathetic smile he'd seen all day.

"Um...I don't need to remind you that these are Swedes we're talking about," Thom said. "The only feelings we acknowledge are satisfaction for a hard day's work and disappointment in our offspring."

"I am painfully aware of that," Peg said. "That's...well, I'm hoping to change that."

"Two hundred years of exposure to American culture hasn't changed that, Peg," Thom said. "Tell me something. When people come to church potlucks, what do they bring?"

Peg blinked. She opened her mouth, but only stammered.

"I'll tell you what they bring," Thom continued. "They bring lutefisk and Jell-O molds. Do you know a single person who actually likes lutefisk?" She opened her mouth again, but Thom pressed ahead. "No. It's white fish soaked in lye. It's poisonous. It's a gelatinous mess. It's gross. But somehow, we have a never-ending supply of it around here."

"Maybe it's the same dish of lutefisk, and people just pass it around?" Peg suggested, the corners of her mouth turning up in a smile.

"People make that argument about fruitcake, but in the case of lutefisk it might actually be true," Thom conceded. "And Jell-O molds are also gross, but digestible, and generally nontoxic—at least, that is the prevailing opinion."

Peg looked at her hands in her lap. Thom sighed and softened. "Peg, the point is that our people here aren't your New Age touchy-feely type of Californian. They're from old world stock, and they hold to old world ways. Everyone has emotions, but it's not considered polite to let them leak out. You're not from here—" He saw Peg stiffen. If she were a dog, her hackles would be up. "I don't mean any offense," Thom was quick to add. "I'm just saying that what plays in Berkeley does not go over in Karlstadt. It's part of that rainbow of diversity crap you hear so much about. It's okay that we're different. It's a good thing. Just...don't try to change us."

"I'm not trying to change anyone," Peg protested, "I'm just...I'm trying to provide a way to relieve the pressure before the whole town blows up."

Thom nodded. He pointed at her. "Now that is a metaphor I understand."

"Then you'll help?"

"Help? What do you want help with?"

"Well, with everything. We're going to ask Mel to design the longhouse—"

"You mean the Wulfson girl?" Thom asked.

"The Wulfson *boy*, yes," Peg said. "He's...he wants to be an architect. We haven't asked him yet, so please keep your hat on about it."

"Huh."

"Anyway, we need a place to put it...and permission to do so. We need to clear this with the mayor, but I thought if you were on board..." She moved her head back and forth.

"If I were on board, it might grease the wheels a bit."

She met his eyes. They were soft and kind. They also made her feel a bit like a child who'd been caught sneaking a cookie. "Yes."

"So...what happens to this longhouse once the...grieving is over?"

"We burn it down."

"Oh, that's just great," Thom said before he was able to stop himself. He bit his lip. "Sorry. I didn't mean that to sound—"

"Yes, you did, and it's okay," Peg said. "That's why we need careful discernment. It needs to be away from other buildings, obviously."

Thom ran his fingers through his hair. "I don't know, Peg."

"Thom, were you ever a Boy Scout?"

"Uh...sure. Why?"

"Do you remember building a bonfire, sitting around it with the other scouts?"

"Yeah, of course—"

"How did it make you feel?"

Thom stopped to consider, but before he could answer, Peg stood. "Would you sleep on it? Maybe...pray about it?"

"Pray about it?" Thom's eyebrows rose.

"It can't hurt," Peg said, her tone faintly pleading.

"I'll *think* about it," Thom said.

"That's good enough." She nudged the chair back to the wall. "Thank you, Thom. Thank you for...everything. You've been a good friend."

Thom wanted to object that they weren't friends at all, but it seemed unnecessary and cruel. Instead, he said, "You're welcome." He stood and extended his hand. She shook it. It felt awkwardly formal. "See you at the hospital," he said.

"I hope so," she said.

Allison shut the door of Ted's tiny car and crossed to where he was standing. "You've been a good friend to Peg," she said.

Ted grunted. "I want a cigarette."

"How long has it been since you've had a cigarette?" Allison asked.

"Thirty-four years."

"And you still crave it?"

"Every minute of every damn day," he said, his tone black with bitterness.

"Huh," she said. "You bear it well."

"I bear it like a fucking hair shirt."

They were standing about a hundred feet from a yellow farmhouse that had begun to molt. Allison searched it for signs of life, but aside from an empty car and a pile of wood to be chopped, the place was deadly quiet.

"What I don't understand is *why* you and Peg are such good friends," Allison said. "I mean, you have very little in common. She's not gay, she's not a cynic, she's not snide—"

"Am I snide?" Ted asked.

"Ted, your brand of snide is so refined, it's artisanal."

"Ooh, I like that," he said. He offered her his arm and they began to walk toward the house. "But you're wrong. We have much in common. We both have a...an appreciation for a handsome man, for one thing. We both have a passion for Rodgers and Hart, and we share an equal loathing for Sondheim—the man couldn't find a melody with a divining rod. But the main thing, I think, is we're both pastors at heart—with a fierce antipathy for ecclesiastical nonsense."

Allison raised one eyebrow. "Isn't everything about the church nonsense?"

"Careful. Peg's Jesus is a real fellow. I don't recommend crossing him."

"And your Jesus?" Allison asked.

"Is missing in action," Ted said.

"For how long?" Allison asked.

"Are you sure this is it?" Ted asked.

Allison took a scrap of paper from her pocket and checked. "It is."

"Anyway, I have more respect for an absent Jesus than your pixie dust and channeled Ascended Masters."

"Have you ever read any channeled writings?" Allison asked.

"I have, you might be surprised to know."

"Really? Who?"

"I read the Seth books back in the 70s, when I was a fierce young wisp of a thing with raven-black hair and a jaw sharper than a shard of glass."

"Uh-huh. Haven't heard that name in a while."

"Then I tried to read your precious *Course in Miracles*."

"And what did you think?"

"I thought it was a kitschy repackaging of Valentinian Gnosticism."

"I don't know what that is," Allison said.

"It's the fucking *Course in Miracles*," Ted said. "And of course I was endlessly entertained by Ramtha."

"J.Z. Knight is a charlatan," Allison admitted.

"Why her and not the others?" Ted asked.

"She's an entitled horse person," Allison said.

"Oooo, I wasn't aware of your hidden antipathy for horse people. Or do you mean she's a centaur?"

Allison slapped his arm. "Let's just do this."

"You're afraid?" Ted asked, disentangling himself from her arm and turning to face her.

"I...I think his parents are unpredictable."

"All humans are unpredictable. It's the chief reason I loathe them in general. At least with cats, the disdain is consistent."

"*Your* disdain is consistent," Allison pointed out.

"I chalk that up to the influence of cats."

"Who's going to do the talking?" Allison asked

"Now you're overthinking it," Ted said, and he headed up the walk to the door. Allison jogged a few yards to catch up to him.

Ted knocked and stepped back. Allison listened and heard movement within. A moment later, the door opened to reveal Ellen Wulfson in a dressing gown and curlers. Her mascara was smudged. Her eyes widened and her brow furrowed as she glared at them through the screen door mesh. "What do you two want?"

"Greetings, Mrs. Wulfson," Ted said, his pencil-thin mustache turning up in a wan smile. "We'd like to speak to Mel, if we may."

"What business do you have with my daughter?" the woman asked.

Allison winced. "We have a commission for him."

The woman blinked. "A commission?"

"Yes," Ted answered. "He wants to be an architect, does he not?"

"He—I mean, she does?" Mrs. Wulfson's mouth twisted into a pucker.

"Do you *talk* to your son, Ellen?" Ted asked.

"He's not my son, he—*she's* a messed-up whore. In the head."

Ted's eyebrows knit in a scowl. "Do you mean she's—he's a whore in the head—and I don't even know what that means, although..."

"I think she means he's messed up in the head," Allison offered. "Or, more accurately, she *thinks* he's messed up in the head."

"Ah. Probably so." He smiled again. "Please bear with me. When talking with some, it's good to have a translator."

Ellen frowned, clearly uncertain whether she was being insulted or mocked or both.

"Anyway, our business is not with you, but with your son, regardless of your opinion of him," Ted said. "Would you be so kind as to summon him?"

"No, I won't—"

"Who is it, Ellen?" came a masculine voice from within.

She ignored the voice, but a moment later Jorge Wulfson came up behind her. "Oh, Father. Good to see you. And Miss Allison." He was a full head taller than his wife. His face was pockmarked by the ghost of acne past, and he looked uncertain. "How can we help?"

"We've come to ask Mel if he'd like to do a job for us." Ted's face brightened as if he were delivering good news.

"Oh, yeah. She'd love that. She's a hard worker, you know." He frowned slightly. "But it's too early in the year for lawn-mowing."

"It's an architectural commission," Allison interjected.

"Well, then," Jorge stood up straight and grinned. "I'll get her straightaway." He turned from the door and raised his voice so to be heard at a distance. "Hey there, Mel! Someone's at the door for you."

Ted and Allison exchanged a quizzical look. Ellen fumed. She turned on her heel and stormed off into the bowels of the house.

"I am beginning to understand many things," Ted said.

"Yeah," Allison said. "This is better clay than I thought. We can work with this."

Ted pulled a handkerchief from his breast pocket and dabbed at his nose. He had just replaced the cloth when Mel came to the door.

There was a look of wonder on his young face as he pushed open the screen door. "Oh, hullo."

"Hello, Mel," Allison said. "How are you?"

Mel swallowed and lowered his eyes, seeming to be taking stock and uncertain where to start.

"You can give us a list later," Ted interjected. "We're here to offer you a job."

"A job?" Mel's head cocked slightly to the left.

"A rush job, actually," Ted said. "You'd need to drop everything and have at it immediately, and then we'll need to build it tonight. Time is of the essence."

"And we'll pay you for your services," Allison said.

"Wh...what is it? The job?" Mel asked. He looked slightly disoriented, as if he'd just awoken from a dream.

"We want you to design a building for us," Ted said.

"And you're going to build it...tonight?" Mel asked.

"We are. Gods willing," Ted affirmed.

"But...why me?" Mel asked, his eyes beginning to shine.

"Because we trust you," Allison said. "And besides, when it comes to buildings, neither of us has a clue."

"What is it?" Mel asked. "The building, I mean."

"A Swedish longhouse," Ted said. "With a fire trench."

And with that, Mel turned on his heel and ran back into the house. The screen door slammed after him.

"That was odd," Ted said.

"No it wasn't," Allison said. "Artists never walk to their brushes. They run."

When Peg opened the door, it triggered a bell just above her head. She jumped a bit, and then felt foolish. It happened every time she entered this particular building, and she knew she should have expected it.

Sy Knolls grinned at her. "I'm thinking of installing an electronic thingy that roars at you like a tiger when you open the door."

"I prefer the bell, Sy," Peg said. She wound her way through the hunting and fishing supplies to the front counter.

"Bass are biting up at Owens Lake," he said. "I recommend the nightcrawlers. We've got some extra fat ones from a farm near Bakersfield. Purple motherfuckers."

"Sy, have you ever known me to fish?" Peg asked

"No, but it would do you a world of good. Natural stress-reliever."

"Hmm...you may have a point. But that's not why I'm here—"

"Hunting license?"

Peg narrowed one eye at him. "I am here to see the mayor."

"Oh. Well, why didn't you say so?" Sy lifted a section in the front counter to allow her through.

"Because you were too busy trying to upsell me on worms." Peg's hip brushed the counter as she squeezed through.

"You won't find better."

"You'd make more money selling cars."

"Except I wouldn't be doing what I love."

Peg couldn't argue with that, so she didn't. "What's her mood?"

Sy wiggled his hand back and forth.

"Anything I should know?"

"Are you going to ask her for something?"

"Uh...probably."

"Is it going to cost money?"

"Probably...not."

"Oh." He looked surprised. "In that case, your regular cheery demeanor should stand you in good stead."

"Thanks."

"Go on through."

Peg knew her way. She ascended three steps to the short hallway. The bathroom to her right reeked of urine. She stepped down again into the back part of the store. The mayor's door was half shut, so she paused just shy of the frame and knocked.

"Come in," came a familiar voice.

"Hey, Deena," Peg said.

"Oh...Peg." Deena looked surprised. She brushed her gray hair back over one ear and stood as straight as her five-feet-and-four frame would allow.

"Am I interrupting anything?"

"Well, I've got the lawyer for the Nylands on one line, and the lawyer for the KKK on the other. I'm thinking of ordering the two of them into a room and locking it until only one emerges alive."

"Yes, but will you sell tickets?"

"We could put them in an operating theater." Deena snapped her fingers.

"A hospital is perfect; they can deal with injuries and they already know how to handle blood."

"I'm not sharing profits with you." Deena narrowed one eye.

"Not asking for any." Peg sat in a tattered chair, its stuffing hanging out in drabs.

"Will you be here long enough for coffee?"

"I don't know. It depends upon how much patience you have in reserve."

"My tank is about half full."

"Two sugars, then, and milk."

"Trust me, you don't want milk that's been in the same fridge as the insects. It always smells...off."

"I will trust you on that and forgo the milk. I've been falling behind on my ascetical practices anyway."

"Sy!" Deena shouted, so loudly that Peg winced. "Two coffees, bring the sugar!" She turned her attention back to Peg and gave her a professional smile. "What can I do for you?"

"Don't you have lawyers on the line?"

"Has a lawyer ever kept you waiting?" Deena asked.

"Every damn time," Peg said.

"Taste of their own medicine then," Deena sat down behind her desk. She folded her hands. "What can I do for you, Pastor?"

"I don't know if you've noticed, but...emotions are running pretty high," Peg began.

"What was the giveaway?" Deena asked. "The goddam cubes? The unauthorized KKK march? The Nyland farm burning to the ground?

The suicides? The brawls? The fact that 911 calls have tripled in the past three days? Or maybe you're referring to the fact that Becky Travers just shot Paul in the face?"

"Uh...all of the above, really."

"Yes, I've noticed."

"Well, I'm here representing a loose coalition of...helping professionals. We have an idea."

"An idea for what?"

"To defuse the current situation...a bit...perhaps."

"Your confidence is infectious. What's the idea?"

"Well, in traditional Swedish style, we'd like to construct a temporary longhouse—maybe on an empty lot?—and then we'd like to hold a ritual to help people release their emotions, their stress. Then we'd...well, burn the longhouse down."

Deena blinked. Peg shrank in her chair. The plan never sounded quite so ridiculous as it did just then. "So...you're here about a permit for public assembly? Or a building permit? 'Cause that's a county thing, and you'll have to drive into Independence to get that. Or do you need a waiver for a one-time refuse burn? You'll need the fire chief to sign off on that." She locked her eyes on Peg's and waited.

"Um...I guess I'd like to ask you to waive all of that."

"With my magic wand, perhaps?"

"I think the mental health of our citizens is more important than bureaucratic red tape." Peg tried to keep the edge out of her voice. She wasn't sure if she'd succeeded. But she knew that Deena knew that she could give as good as she got.

Deena shook her head. "Peg, this is nuts. I don't have time for this."

"It's not nuts, it's what people need—"

"What people need is for things to go back to normal around here."

"I agree, but even if we snapped our fingers and everything was the way it was last month, we still have to deal with the trauma that's happened since. Because if you don't...it doesn't go away. It just leaks out someplace else—like Becky shooting Paul."

Deena's face fell. Peg sat up straighter, feeling a momentary thrill of hope. Deena seemed to hear her. The mayor looked down at her desk. She sighed. "I can't do that. I just...don't have the authority. There are regulations and procedures for a reason, and if I tried to circumvent them I would...the legal exposure—"

"Oh, fuck the legal exposure," Peg said. She instantly regretted it.

Deena leaned back, her face becoming impassive. "I'm sorry, Peg. I can't help you."

Peg nodded. "I understand. Thank you for your time, Deena."

"My door is always open."

Peg opened her mouth to dispute this—Deena was notorious for taking off unannounced for spontaneous hunting and fishing trips, but pointing that out would avail her nothing. "Thank you for your time."

"Thank you for your crazy idea." Deena didn't look at her as Peg rose and headed for the exit.

Bill Arenson nodded at the volunteer at the information desk. The Southern Inyo Hospital was bustling, and the halls were filled with people. He pulled the ball cap lower down on his head and loosened his fingers so that the duffel he carried hovered as close to the ground as possible without dragging. He walked quickly, but without any sign of panic. His eyes, hidden behind dark sunglasses, were fixed straight ahead of him.

No one seemed to recognize him. No one stopped him. No one even seemed to notice him. But he was sure that, if anyone cared to look, he might look suspicious, nervous even. He willed his shoulders to relax. He consciously took deep breaths and let them out slowly.

He had done his research. He knew exactly where he was going. He was headed to the one room in the hospital that was usually empty. He passed the cafeteria, and the odor of Salisbury steak with mushroom gravy was so strong that he began to involuntarily salivate. For a brief moment, he considered making a detour. After all, don't the condemned get one last meal? But he was a disciplined man. He tightened his grip on the handles of the duffel and kept walking.

He paused by the door of the chapel and looked around. There were lots of people—nurses, doctors, civilians—but no one was paying any attention to him whatsoever. Satisfied, he pushed the door open and stepped through.

But someone was there. He froze, his shoulder muscles cramping. The room was small, but there were a few rows of chairs facing a non-religion-specific altar area. A stained glass window of a sunrise hung just behind a maple table, with a lectern to one side. There were flowers in a vase on the table, their genus a little too obviously plastic. In the second row, an older woman sat facing the table. Her hair was an unnatural auburn, and she was hunched over, perhaps in prayer. She wiped her nose on a wadded tissue. She did not turn to look at him.

Bill hesitated. Should he leave? Should he make a different plan? Should he strangle the old woman and lay her out on the bench for others to find later? She looked sweet and reminded him of his own grandmother, now long gone.

He sat in the back row. He bowed his head. He looked at his watch. What did it matter whether he did what he was there to do now, or in a half hour? It didn't. His leg bounced with nervous energy, creating a clacking sound as the chair protested the rapid movement. He forced his leg to be still. It could not. He shifted its position until it no longer made any noise.

Bill studied the room. At first it had seemed quiet, peaceful, a welcoming place to grieve or commune. But now that he had a chance to see it more closely, what impressed him was its gratuitous shabbiness. There was a water stain on one wall. Two of the ceiling panels were cracked and one was missing—he could see ducts and wires in the dim recesses beyond. Ancient hymnals and prayer books were stacked willy-nilly on and around the table and the lectern, with one particularly large stack on the floor against the wall. The stained glass window hung slightly askew, and as there was no window behind it, it depicted an unexpectedly dark and foreboding sky. The yellow-glass sun seemed to suck in the light from around it, instead of showing it forth in glory as the artist seemed to have intended. It occurred to Bill that he was looking at an artistic representation of his soul.

He realized he was grinding his teeth, and he willed his jaw to relax. It hurt. He worked it, as if he were chewing gum. He looked at the chairs next to him. He wondered if he might stretch out on them. But no, there was no reason for it. He knew he could not sleep. But he needed a way to pass the time.

He noticed a hook extended down through a hole in one of the ceiling panels, where a plant had probably once hung. In his head, he imagined fixing a meat hook to it, and hanging the old lady's corpse on it. Her head would hang at an odd angle, her shoulders sloped, her ancient breasts dangling like bags of rice. Her legs would be thick with cellulite, ballooning out wider than her hips. He would make the first incision at the femoral artery to drain the blood. He imagined it pouring out into a copper spittoon for some reason. He smiled at the thought. It was not what he would use at the butcher shop, but it seemed fitting for the shoddy decor here. He began by removing the arms. He'd then clean out her abdominal cavity—

Sudden movement startled him, and he saw that the old woman had stood up. She genuflected in the direction of the altar to no-god-in-particular, and turned toward the door—toward him. He slunk down in his seat and shut his eyes, pretending to be praying. He waited until he heard the door shut behind him before opening his eyes and breathing a deep sigh of relief.

He stood and picked up his duffel bag, moving it to the front row where there was room to move around between the chairs and the altar area. He unzipped it and glanced once more toward the door. There was no movement. He pulled the stock of the TNW Aeor Survival Rifle from the bag and set it across the chair cushions. Then he pulled the barrel out and quickly screwed it into the receiver. He pulled an Allen wrench from a pocket and adjusted the ratchet tension. Then he fished out the first of seven 10mm clips and inserted it into the magazine well. It settled into place with a satisfying click.

He tested the safety with his thumb, applying just a bit of pressure, feeling its resistance. He closed his eyes and inhaled deeply. He wasn't a religious man. He had no need for prayer. But he felt a need to commune with some sense of larger purpose. He found it. He punched at the safety with the side of his thumb, and this time it shifted into the "off" position.

He lowered the rifle until it was parallel with his leg. It was a light-weight weapon, designed for backpacking, and of such an unusual profile that many people might not immediately register it as a weapon at all. It also had a mottled blue paint scheme, which might lead some to dismiss it as a toy. All of these factors were assets to him. Keeping the barrel close to his leg he strode toward the door of the chapel, toward the hallway, toward all those sons-of-bitches who would soon know what it felt like to stare into the face of their own deaths, just as he had.

Thom paused outside the jail cell. "Hey. How you doing?"

Becky sat with her back to him, hugging her knees, staring at the wall.

Thom sighed. "Okay, you don't have to talk to me. You just need to listen. I want to tell you what's going to happen to you, is all." He waited. She did not turn around. "In about an hour the transport van from the county jail will be here. They're going to take you to Independence, where you'll go through the whole processing procedure. If you want to know more about that, I'll be glad to tell you. At that point, you'll be arraigned and, unless I miss my guess, you'll be eligible for bail. I'm going to make a statement in favor of that. If you want to call a lawyer, you can do that now—and I recommend it. There will be a full investigation, but that's usually handled by the county detectives. They'll have some questions for you later. Your attorney can be present for those interviews, and I want you to know that, because they might try to trick you into talking to them alone. Don't do it. Don't say a word without your attorney. Do you hear me?"

Becky turned and met his eye over her shoulder. "Why are you being so nice to me?"

"I'm not being nice to you, B—" Thom stopped. "It's true I don't give advice like this to everyone we pick up, so...I guess I am being nice; I just wouldn't put it that way. I just...I want you to know, Beck, I don't blame you for what you did. Paul was a mean-assed bastard, and I don't mind saying that out loud. And I know you loved him, and I know it's...complicated. But I believe the system is going to work for you. I know it's hard to trust that right now. And it's going to be a rough ride. But I want you to know that you have a lot of people in your corner, including me. And in my professional opinion, I think you're going to be okay."

Becky's eyes betrayed fear, and tears, and for a brief moment, hope. She nodded and sniffed, but said nothing.

"I thought you might like some chocolate," Thom said. He reached through the bars and handed the rest of the tattered wrapper to her. "Sorry. It isn't pretty. But the chocolate is clean."

Incredibly, she uncurled herself and turned around. Silently she moved across the concrete floor and took the wrapper from him. She didn't immediately tear it open, though. She cast her eyes down to her feet. "Thanks."

"You're welcome. You let Celia know if you want some coffee too. Just yell. She's busy, but she'll hear you. I warn you, though, this chocolate is radioactive and could probably be classified as hazardous waste."

The tiniest hint of a smile flashed on her face, but it didn't last more than a second. She fumbled with the candy wrapper, then she sat down on the bed again, the rusty springs protesting with a fierce squeak.

Just then Celia appeared in the hallway. "Thom, you gotta come now. We got an active shooter situation."

"We do? Where?"

"The hospital."

"Holy—" He turned to Becky. "I gotta go."

She nodded, and he followed Celia into the main squad room. "Single shooter, from the report we got."

"Do we know who?" Thom asked, jogging toward the door.

"Bill Arenson," Celia called to him.

But he was already out the door. "Awww shit," he said as he ran full out toward a rented Range Rover. "Holy Christ, that's all we need." He swung himself into the cab, but suddenly Celia was banging on his window. He rolled it down.

"It's the South hospital," Celia said.

"Figured that," Thom said.

"Do you have the firearms you want?" Celia asked.

"Shit," Thom swore, internally berating himself for wasting time.

Celia pointed to a bag hanging from the end of her right arm, too heavy for her to lift up to the window. "I've got the AR-15 here, with six full clips."

Thom felt a wave of relief roll over him. "God bless you, Celia."

"God has nothing to do with it, Thom." It occurred to Thom that Pastor Peg may have a different opinion on that matter, but he didn't say so. Instead, he leaned through the window and planted a kiss on Celia's cheek.

Unfazed, she opened the back door of his shop and swung the bag onto the seat. She slammed the door and stepped back. He gunned it, leaving her in a cloud of spraying dust.

Too many of his own townsfolk were in that hospital. Mia Nyland was there. Julie was there. He switched on the siren, then the strobe just as he hit the main street. Cars pulled over to allow him passage. Even though it was cool in Range Rover, sweat beaded up on his forehead. He grasped the wheel with a grip worthy of strangulation and pressed the accelerator to the floor.

CHAPTER SIXTEEN

Peg sighed and hung her head over her coffee cup. It did not have coffee in it. She had decided to throw caution to the wind and get a hot chocolate. It was a guilty indulgence in comfort food. She looked out the large picture window of Debble's Cafe into the street.

Two young men were blocking traffic, arguing out in the street. Then one punched the other in the stomach. The second man doubled over, clutching at his gut. Peg sat up straight, surprised at the spectacle, her own dark obsessive thoughts momentarily forgotten. Peg thought the second man was about to go down, but to her great surprise he kept his feet. Then he launched himself at the first man, driving his shoulder into the other man's chest. The second man was briefly airborne, then both collapsed on top of the other, fists flying.

Peg had to look away. It had gotten ugly so fast. A small crowd gathered, and no cars were able to pass in either direction. In the corner of her eye, Peg saw Ted and Allison forcing their way through the onlookers toward the Cafe. The bell rang as they entered.

Everyone in the place was facing the window now. Peg allowed herself to look back at the combatants for a moment. She was instantly sorry, as one of the young men had open gashes on his face and was streaming blood onto a bird's-egg blue windbreaker.

Ted sat across from her, and Allison squeezed in beside. "It's hard to look, and it's hard to look away," Peg confessed.

"My money is on David," Ted said. "He looks like he's losing now, but you wait. Even money he's going to snap and then it's all over for Ben."

"You know those guys?" Allison asked.

"I baptized both of them," Ted said. "Of course they were smaller then, and there was less blood."

"It's the cubes," Peg said. "It's the stress."

"Either that or they're shooting *Spring Break—Central Valley Edition*," Ted said, not taking his eyes off of the fight. "Do you see any cameras?"

"Just cell phones," Allison said. "I don't think this is one of those times when your fantasies come true in front of your eyes. Sorry, Ted."

"We should stop them," Peg said.

"We should stay out of harm's way," Ted countered.

"I need to do something," Peg said.

"There's twenty people out there. No one is going to let any real damage be done," Ted said. He picked up a menu.

"How can you be so callous?" Peg asked.

"Fifty years as a diocesan insider," Ted said, as if that explained everything.

Peg started for the door, but Ted turned out to be right. Ernie Calzone, built like a tank with a bleached buzz cut, had wrapped his arms around Ben's waist and dragged him backwards, and the Miller twins grabbed hold of David's wrists. Peg was horrified to see large, jagged pieces of a broken bottle in both of his hands. Blood ran down his forearms, covering the hands of the Miller twins as well.

"See?" Ted said. "All is well."

"All is *not* well," Peg countered.

"No, but it will be, if Lady Julian is to be believed. 'All shall be well, and all shall be well, and every manner of thing shall be well.'"

"I'm not sure an eschatological prediction is relevant in the here and now," Peg's brow furrowed.

"If not now, when?" Ted asked. He waved at Tali to get the waitress' attention. "Did you see what I just did? I commented on Dame Julian using the Talmud."

"I have *no* idea what you two are talking about," Allison confessed.

Ted sniffed. "That's because you're theologically illiterate. No offense, my dear, just stating a fact."

Allison glowered at him, but then apparently chose the better part of valor. "How is Julie?"

Peg took a deep breath. "She's in bad shape. But she's talking. She's still...Julie, for better or worse." Peg wiped at her eye.

"It's going to be okay. She's going to be okay," Allison put a hand on her friend's elbow.

"Yeah." Peg patted her hand and gave her an unconvincing, complicated smile.

Tali rushed to the table. "Who won? Fucki—sorry—*stupid* Mr. Tillman wanted to contest something on his check and I missed it."

"What is this, high school?" Allison asked

"What'll it be? Ya'll aren't usually in here so late," Tali said, snapping her gum.

Peg noticed a section of Tali's arm was inflamed and red. Then she realized she was looking at a new tattoo. Then she realized the tattoo was a picture of a cube. She reared back as a wave of vertigo rolled through her.

When she rejoined the conversation, everyone was staring at her. Ted and Allison had already ordered, it seemed, and they were waiting on her. She usually took her cues from what others were ordering, but she had missed what her friends had just said, and she was too embarrassed to ask them to repeat themselves. So she simply said, "I'll take the special, please, Tali," and prayed it was something edible.

Tali spun away. Peg noticed that Ted's eyebrows were high on his head. "Hungry, are we?"

"I don't...maybe."

"I guess cancer gives you an appetite," Ted said. "It usually works the other way."

"It's *chemo* that makes you want to avoid food, you idiot, not cancer," Allison slapped his forearm.

"My only information comes from Lifetime original dramas," Ted admitted.

"I think I'm going crazy," Peg said.

"Well, we have good news that might just bring you back from the brink," Allison brightened.

"Oh?" Peg asked, her voice tentative.

"You know the corner where the Tully Pharmacy used to be?"

"Yes," Peg said, "next to the dry cleaner. It's a vacant lot now."

"Yes, at the corner of 7th and Bjorn Street. Allison and I went to meet with the owner, and he's given us permission to build our long-house in the lot."

"But...the buildings—"

"Are only on one side. We'll build it close to the street." Ted smiled, a little too smugly.

"But I wasn't able to get the permit—"

"Permit schmermit." Ted waved her objection away. "It's easier to get forgiveness than permission."

An uncertain smile broke out on Peg's face. "It's...we're going to do this?"

"Who's going to stop us?" Ted asked.

"What's our next step?" Peg asked.

"Meeting with our architect," Allison said. "Mel has plans to show us."

"So soon?" Peg saw that Tali was on her way with coffee on her tray. She paused as the young woman deposited cups in front of her friends. She couldn't not look at the woman's new tattoo. She felt her guts tighten at the sight of it. As soon as Tali spun away, she said, "Well, that's good, then. There's no time to lose."

"We told Mel tonight, but I'm just not sure we can get it all together by tonight. Do you think we should do it tomorrow?" Allison said.

"No. Fuck tomorrow," Peg said, pointing to the window. "I don't think the town will survive until tomorrow. I think we need to do it tonight."

"Mel should be here any minute," Ted said.

"I texted him," Allison added. "I got an emoji of an armadillo giving a thumbs-up in return. I'm not exactly sure what that means, but I expect we'll see him any minute."

"It's really going to happen," Peg said.

"Inshallah," Ted said, blowing on his coffee.

"How do we get the word out?" Peg asked.

Julie stared at the lunch tray before her. A warm bologna sandwich on white bread lay on a pink institutional plate. Next to it was a mound of warm coleslaw and an unopened Jell-O cup, also warm. Julie picked up the sandwich and inspected underneath the bread—a thin layer of mayonnaise mocked her. "Would it kill you to spice it up with a bit of mustard?" Julie asked the room.

The room did not answer. She sighed and put the unappealing sandwich back on the plate. She looked at the window. She didn't know why she looked at the window. She was on the second floor, and there was nothing to see but the overcast sky—a relentless wall of gray. "Why have a window at all?" she wondered aloud. Once again, no one responded.

She glanced around the room. There were flowers from Jake—that had been sweet. Julie felt herself soften as she looked at them. She liked Jake. She even missed him, she realized. She also knew that Thom was working him overtime trying to make up for the fact that she was not at work. A stab of guilt pierced her, and she suddenly felt more restless than ever. "This sucks," she said to the room.

She wanted to get up, to stretch her legs. What she really wanted was to go home. Julie wasn't much of a homebody, and her apartment was nothing special—but it was hers, and at that moment it seemed a hundred times more comfortable and inviting than the hospital room could ever be. She thought about her own bed—which had never once been made in two years—and missed it. She thought about the half dozen or so girls she had made love to there...and missed it even more. She sighed.

Her eyes lit upon the picture her mother had brought her. The faded guardian angel escorting two little children over a bridge had never looked so menacing. The angel held a flaming sword, which was not immediately obvious unless you looked closely at it, because the angel was not wielding it overhead, but holding it low, parallel with its diaphanous leg. The children looked like clueless shits, ripe for the demonic picking. *Did I ever identify with one of those children?* she wondered. She knew she had, but that seemed like a hundred years ago. How might she re-vision a picture like that, using the Wiccan theology she had come to embrace?

Her mind went blank. Her shoulders slumped as she realized the task was futile. She had seen too much. There was no Goddess surrounding her with loving, maternal arms. There were only monsters in space prowling about seeking someone—anyone—to devour. She shuddered at the memory of it; an emptiness of cosmic proportions expanded within her. It was horrible.

She glanced at the picture again and a voice in her head reminded her that her mother had given it to her to comfort her. It wasn't comforting at all, but she knew Peg meant well. She felt the knot in her stomach loosen, and she felt regret for how she had treated her mother. Yes, she could make a long list of all the ways Peg had failed her, but she could make an equally long list of the ways she herself had been a complete brat. Julie sighed.

She knew she should talk to her mother, but it seemed impossibly hard. *I could write her a note,* Julie thought. *I don't even have to give it to her. I could just write it and see how it feels.* Picking up a notepad the candy striper had brought her and the little pencil she had only seen at miniature golf courses, she wrote a brief note. She felt herself relax as she did so. It felt good to think those words, to write them. Maybe, just maybe, she would be able to say them one day.

Her head felt suddenly heavy. She thought about trying to sleep again, and knew it was what the doctor wanted most. But inwardly she chafed at the idea. "I have to get out of here," she said to the room. The room did not try to talk her out of it. She tried standing. The pain in her chest raged as she contracted the stomach muscles necessary to sit up, and then to move her legs. She grit her teeth and bore it. Careful not to rip the IV out of the back of her hand, she reached for the IV pole to steady herself with one hand, the other firmly on the bed. She cringed as she swung one foot off the bed and let it hang. She did the same to the other, then she paused to catch her breath. She marveled at the effort it took. Grimacing, she pushed off the bed, and dropped the last three inches to the floor. She landed uncertainly and almost fell—but for her grip on the IV pole, she would have.

"Goddam," she swore at the unexpected difficulty. She knew how quickly limbs atrophied when people did not use them, but it had always been an intellectual knowing—feeling it was a whole different kind of disturbing.

She took one tentative step and stumbled. She renewed her grip on the IV pole and let go of the bed, dragging the pole along with her. She took one, two, three steps. Then she noticed she was perspiring. She glanced over her shoulder at the bed and wondered if she should return to it. *Just where am I going?* she wondered. But when she turned her face forward again, she knew: the bathroom. She was going to the bathroom.

She stood up a little straighter. It was a good goal, a noble goal, a goal none could fault her for—not even the nurses who insisted she use the awkward urinal pan beside her bed. *Fuck bedpans,* she thought, and launched herself toward the waiting toilet.

She made it, and was able to situate herself on the toilet seat with a minimum of pain. As she peed, she lifted the neck of her gown and inspected her wound. A mass of gauze was held to her chest with white surgical tape. Tiny blooms of red seeped through the gauze. With unconscious movements, she reached for the toilet paper, wiped herself, and stood.

She felt a moment of dizziness but held fast to the diagonal rails near the toilet until the feeling passed. Then she began to shuffle back to the door—and, she realized, probably back to bed.

The sound of an explosion stopped her. "What the fuck—" she said to the bathroom, when another explosion sounded. Her mind raced, searching for the sound. She found it.

"10 millimeter Glock rounds," she said, even as her brain registered that it was not being fired from a handgun. *That's a rifle.* Several more explosions erupted in quick succession. *Make that a semi-automatic rifle,* she thought. *In a hospital...*

The horror of it slapped her to attention. She instantly forgot about the bed, about her wound, about her frailty. Adrenaline cleared out the fogginess in her head in mere seconds, her brain operating now with crystalline clarity. Without even stopping to consider it, she tore the tape from her IV and drew the needle out, upwards toward her arm. She felt no pain. She tossed the dangling cords to one side and lumbered to the bathroom door. Briefly, she held the handle, then propelled herself beyond the door, across the open threshold of her room, into the hallway. She didn't know where she was going, or why. She only knew one thing: The shooter needed to be found and stopped. And unless or until she knew that there was someone else to do it, the job fell to her.

Peg paused and wiped the sweat from her brow. Her breathing was heavy, and her throat was parched. "I'll be right back," she said. She walked over to Allison's picnic basket and poured herself a paper cup full of lemonade. She sat down cross-legged and drained half the cup in one gulp. She took a bit more time with the rest of it.

As she sipped at it, she surveyed their progress. Mel had mapped out a fifteen-by-forty-foot structure indicating where the support beams would go, as well as interstitial beams to rest the sheets of hay on. He had also devised a clever "clamp" system for holding the bales in place, using rope and three-tined hand forks. A call to a couple of parishioners had secured the materials from the lumber yard and hardware store. Mel had called the one person on his high school foot-ball team who spoke to him, and to his amazement, most of the team had showed. All were busy at work separating sheets from the sour hay bales and fixing them to the structure's frame. The sun had almost completed its descent, and Peg bit her lip, wondering if they'd finish in time.

Allison walked toward her, removing her gloves. Peg poured her a cup of lemonade and handed it to her as she arrived. She plopped down next to her and received the cup with thanks. She wiped a stray strand of wavy hair from her eyes. "Are you okay?" she asked.

"Yes. I just needed a bit of a rest," Peg answered.

"You take more than that if you need it," Allison said.

"I'm fine."

"You're fighting stage-four cancer," Allison said. "You're not *fine*."

"I'm fine enough," Peg said. "I just get tired more quickly."

Allison pointed at the structure. "It's amazing how fast it's coming together."

Peg nodded. "I'm a bit in awe." She watched Ted peeling off the sheets of hay. Milala was instructing newly arrived high school students in how to attach the sheets. Others were bustling up and down the walls of the longhouse, climbing ladders, putting everything in its place. "Do you think it will be done before dark?"

Allison shrugged. "Done enough."

Peg nodded. "I suppose. I've always been a fan of the good-enough. You know, it's okay to be the good-enough pastor."

Allison laughed. "Or the good-enough artist."

Peg nodded. "Or in Ted's case, the good-enough aesthete."

"What about the good-enough mother?"

Peg's face fell and she looked down. "I don't think I ever achieved that."

Allison reached out and touched her friend's knee. "Hey, sorry I said that. I didn't mean to..."

"No, it's all right. It's something I think about a lot, really."

"Julie is going to forgive you, you'll see. Just as soon as she has kids of her own."

"That'll be the day," Peg said. She watched Joel Tarnack digging the trench with a pickaxe at the near end of the longhouse, the thick muscles of his shoulders cording incongruously with his thick, black-framed glasses.

"Stop looking longingly at young men," Allison said. "It's creepy."

Peg looked away. "Is it creepy to admire beauty?"

"You've been hanging with Ted way too much."

"That certainly could be," Peg agreed. "Did you get the word out?"

"I posted on neighborhood-dot-com, so everyone who's on that will know. I also sent out an email to everyone on the shop's mailing list, and I asked them to tell their friends. I posted on the town's Facebook page. You?"

Peg sighed. "You know me, I'm old school. I activated the church's phone tree. It's supposed to be for prayer, but—"

"It *is* for prayer," Allison countered.

"I suppose," Peg agreed reluctantly.

"Have you thought about the ritual?" Allison asked.

"Oh?" Peg blinked.

"Let's say people actually come tonight—in, what? Two hours? They'll sit in the folding chairs from your church's fellowship hall, and...what?"

"I hadn't thought about it," Peg said.

"Well, you're the priest...pastor, whatever," Allison said. "So maybe instead of tiring yourself out physically, you ought to do the kind of mental work you do best, figure out the structure of the ritual, what you're going to say. You are going to be leading this, right?"

"I suppose so," Peg said.

"Then you better get to work."

"That's...a very good idea," Peg conceded. She watched Joel some more, although this time dispassionately. "Do you think anyone will come?"

"I don't know. Some will," Allison answered. "Would you come? If someone else had had the idea, I mean?"

"That's a very good question," Peg said. "And one that I don't know the answer to."

"You have a cube, after all. Isn't there stuff you need to process?" Allison asked.

"I suppose there is. But I'm used to dealing with that stuff in prayer, and with my spiritual director."

"Most people don't know how to pray on their own," Allison said. "They think they do, but they don't."

Peg turned and looked at her friend. "How would you know that?"

"I'm an art therapist. People tell me things."

"People ask you how to pray?" Peg asked.

"Yes, of course. All the time."

Peg's face gathered into a troubled look. "But...well, what do you tell them?"

"I tell them to go ask you. Do they?"

"Not to my knowledge," Peg said. "I wonder why?"

"People are afraid of you," Allison said.

"Whyever for?" Peg asked. "I'm just a fuckup and a sinner, like everyone else."

"See that, right there? That's why. People don't like to be reminded that they're sinners."

"The truth hurts," Peg said. "But it's also liberating."

"What's liberating about being a sinner?"

"Well, since you'll never *not* be a sinner, once you admit it you don't have to pretend you're anything else."

"Christians are fucking weird," Allison said.

"That's the bumper sticker I want for my car—Christians: Fucking Weird Since 33AD," Peg said.

"It's like wearing the scarlet letter or something, proclaiming to the world, 'I'm bad,'" Allison said.

"No, not at all. To admit I'm a sinner isn't to say, 'I'm bad,' it's to say, 'I'm sick.' Sin isn't something bad that I've done. It's a sickness that I've caught. It isn't my fault. God isn't mad at us because we're sinners. God's heart breaks for us, because we're suffering from a chronic illness. God's response to human sin isn't anger, it's compassion."

"Well, if that's true, I've never met any other preacher who got the memo," Allison said.

"It's part of the earliest teaching of the church, going back to St. Ireneaus in the second century," Peg said.

"So what happened to it?" Allison asked.

"St. Augustine happened," Peg sighed. "And ever since we've been telling people the Bad News: you suffer because you're evil; instead of good news: you suffer because you're sick, and there's a way to manage that sickness."

"Not cure it?" Allison asked.

Peg smiled sadly. "Not on this side of the grave."

Allison stood up and put her gloves on. "Well, on that happy note, 'Once more unto the breach, dear friends,'" Allison quoted. "And you, get thee to thy study, talk to Jesus, or whatever. Because once we're finished here, you're on."

Julie lurched across the linoleum with all the grace of a zombie from an afternoon matinee. Her feet were bare and so unaccustomed to walking that the ground beneath her felt like alien. The muscles in her calves ached. It seemed incredible that her muscles could have atrophied so much in just a few days, but the struggle was real. She gritted her teeth and pressed on.

She made a half-hearted attempt to keep her gown closed at the back, and for a moment wondered if she should try to find another one to put on backwards. But with every fresh burst of shots, such worries receded further and further away. The only thing front and center in her brain was the gun and the shooter.

She passed people in general alarm, but most were confused about what to do or which way to flee. People rushed in all directions; she struggled to stay upright as one nurse practitioner bumped into her, causing the pain in her wound to flare unbearably. She grabbed the handrail lining the hallway and held on until she regained her equilibrium. Then she set out again, always moving toward the sound of the shots.

She came to an elevator and paused. The shooter was probably not on this floor—it was a small hospital, and its orientation was more vertical than horizontal. But which way, up or down? She wouldn't be able to tell in an elevator. *But I might be able to tell with stairs,* she thought. The idea of climbing stairs in her current condition made a part of her recoil, but she overrode the objection.

Finding the stairwell door, she entered and let the door close behind her. She gripped the handrail and waited. There was another burst of shots. The sound was coming from below her. Bracing herself, she took the steps as quickly as she could.

At the bottom, she peered out the small window in the stairwell door. She saw a couple of people running past her, but no shooter. She pushed it open and lurched into the hall.

Coming to a corner, she hugged it and pressed her eye to the wall. The wall felt solid, and she welcomed the support. She moved her eye to the corner, and then just beyond it. The hallway was clear. She moved back to a safe position to think. *That hallway is never clear,* she thought. *You've got the cafe to the left and the gift shop and information desk to the right. It's the busiest hub in the hospital.*

So she knew the shooter must be close. If she were going to plan a rampage like this one, that's where she'd do it—in the very spot where she was likely to see the most people. She put her eye to the corner again, but this time looked at the floor. "Shit," she breathed. The linoleum was littered with bodies. White lab coats were scattered among the dark clothing of civilians, like new snow on asphalt.

She moved her head back to safety again and listened. She heard the click of a magazine nesting into place. Whoever it was, he was close—the sound of the click reverberated in her ears. She put her eye to the corner again, but this time leaned out farther, exposing more of herself. And then she saw him.

"Bill?" she breathed. He hadn't seen her yet. He was facing away. She desperately wished she had a gun.

"Security guards have guns," she whispered to herself. She put her eye to the corner again and looked down, hoping to see a blue uniform among the patchy snow of lab coats. She did. He had fallen face down. His ass was in the air, as if he had been listening to something in the floor or perhaps had been performing Muslim prayers without a rug. She could see his gun, where it had fallen from his hand, about two inches from his still fingers. She judged the distance to be about twelve feet from her.

She glanced up at Bill. He was looking at the people he'd shot—perhaps checking to make sure none were still moving? Or perhaps admiring his handiwork? Julie couldn't tell. She moved back to safety and involuntarily began counting her breaths. At twenty, she looked again. He was coming her way.

She threw a panicked look around her, looking for a place to hide. A restroom door beckoned. She shuffled toward it with all the speed she could muster. She opened the door just enough to slip through, then held it slightly ajar, peering out at what she could see of the hallway.

Bill passed her position. She could see his head turning, first to the left, then to the right, looking for movement. She waited until he'd gone about fifteen feet, then she slipped out of the restroom. Moving as quietly as she could, she went back to the corner. She didn't bother to check to make sure there wasn't a second shooter, and instantly cursed herself for her own carelessness. But there was not another shooter, and the cafeteria was empty of live bodies. She hobbled to the security guard, squatted, couldn't hold her position, fell to the floor, trying not to grunt in pain. She looked up and was relieved to see that Bill had turned right, and was out of sight. She snatched up the security guard's pistol. She felt around at his pockets, and found his security card, a ring of keys, and a lighter. Any of those things might be useful, would be useful, but she had no pockets.

Nearby, she saw a woman's body—a tan windbreaker covered her torso. She lurched to the woman and peeled off the jacket, cringing as the woman's head struck the floor again, sounding for all the world like a ripe melon. Quickly she pulled on the jacket and instantly felt less exposed. The woman was larger than Julie, and the jacket felt like a drab dress once it was on. She stuffed the items she'd found into the pockets and turned once more in Bill's direction.

She gripped the pistol in her right hand; it was shaking. She cursed herself under her breath and steadied her grip with her left hand. Her hand wasn't shaking out of fear—her brain was clear of fog now, operating with a crystal clarity she rarely experienced. No, her hand was shaking because her body was frail.

Her feet still dragging, she shuffled in the direction Bill had gone, as quickly and silently as she could. She realized he was headed toward Imaging. Thank the Goddess—there wouldn't be any helpless people lying in beds in there, unable to move.

She was startled out of her thoughts by the sharp report of Bill's rifle. She cursed herself and focused. She realized she was staying far enough away to avoid detection, but not close enough to prevent him from doing any harm. As she rounded a corner, she saw a little girl lying on the ground, and wondered if the last blast had been aimed at her. As she drew nearer, she saw that the girl was about twelve. She also saw that she was still moving. She glanced ahead and saw Bill turn a corner to the left.

She knelt by the girl and held her finger to her lips. The girl had been hit twice—once in the shoulder, and once just above her hip. Julie touched the girl's face and made soft shushing sounds. "You have to be quiet or he'll hear you, and then he'll come back to finish the job. You hear me? Lie still. Play dead."

The girl's lips were trembling and her eyes were huge with fear. She put her hand over the girl's eyes and said, "Close them. Don't look at anything. Count your breaths. Count them as high as you can go." When she removed her hand, the girl's eyes were closed and her breathing was slower. "That's it. Just like that. Whatever you do, don't panic, don't make any noise."

She could barely struggle to her feet, but she rose and continued to follow Bill. *If only I could move faster,* she thought. In her old body, her hale body, her cooperative body, she could have run from corner to corner. But now...

Suddenly it occurred to her how very much she had lost—she had lost her best friend, she had lost her health, she had lost whatever hope she had ever had in the universe, in the Goddess, in goodness itself. She knew she could have survived any one of them singly, but all together...

She stumbled and dropped the pistol. The sound of it clattering to the ground reverberated throughout the hallway. She cursed herself and snatched it up. She moved as quickly as she could to the nearest corner and peered around it.

Bill was heading her way. He had heard it. Of course he had. It was loud. She swallowed and her legs felt liquid and heavy. She withdrew from the corner and frantically cast around for a place to hide. She saw a door nearby, its gray surface adorned with bright yellow stickers warning that there were oxygen tanks within. She lurched for the door, but when she pushed on it, she heard a click—it was locked. Then she heard another click. She turned and faced Bill, his TNW Aeor Survival Rifle pointed directly at her, his eyes wild with the lust for blood, his breath coming in ragged gasps.

CHAPTER SEVENTEEN

In a haze, Peg walked back to her office. Halfway across Durban Street she realized she was hugging herself, and she didn't know why. She forced her arms to let go, to hang by her sides, to swing in long, breezy arcs. "I look like an aging orangutan," she said to herself. It occurred to her how difficult it was to walk normally if you were paying attention to it.

Stepping up on the other side of the curb, she saw old Mrs. Spenser. She waved, but then stopped. Smeared onto Mrs. Spenser's forehead was an ashen cross. Mrs. Spenser nodded politely—she had never been friendly with Protestants. Peg nodded back, offering a pained smile as the realization hit.

She stopped. "It's Ash Wednesday," she said. Peg looked around her, feeling like she was noticing her surroundings for the first time. "It's Ash Wednesday. How did I miss the fact that it is Ash Wednesday?"

Her brain supplied multiple explanations: She hadn't looked at her calendar in days; there was a *lot* going on; she was a bad pastor. She could hear Ted's voice in her head, *Fucking Congos. No respect for the liturgical calendar.* Yet Ted had said nothing about it either. With all that was going on, it had slipped *his* mind, as well?

One part of her brain registered that the oversight was a dereliction of pastoral duty—and one of some magnitude. Another part of her brain cautioned her to go easy on herself. An image flashed through her mind of her arms pinwheeling as she nearly toppled from the peak of a mountain. She was just barely clinging to solid ground. A momentary feeling of vertigo rushed through her. She felt dizzy and faint. She sat down on the sidewalk, cross-legged, holding onto the concrete with both hands until the dizziness passed.

"Pastor, are you all right?" She glanced up to see Alec Marlowe, the chair of her board, glaring down at her.

"No, Alec. No, I'm not."

He looked uncomfortable; it was clearly not the answer he wanted to hear. His eyes were shooting daggers of alarm, not comprehending her undignified state. "Is...is there anything I can help you with?" he asked.

He was being polite, which was almost worse than his unspoken but evident fear. "I don't know, Alec. Can you help with the fact that my daughter can't stand the sight of me? Can you help with the fact that I have stage-four pancreatic cancer and have about six months to live? Can you help with the fact that my livelihood is being threatened by petty gossip hounds and vindictive board members? Or perhaps you can help me with the emotional volatility of this entire town, and the fact that it's about to explode. Which one of those things are you capable or willing to help me with, Alec?"

And then she began to cry. She drew up her knees and hugged them, her shoulders shaking as the sobs burst forth from whatever interior reservoir she had been storing them in. Hot tears formed a pattern on the concrete beneath her. She felt a loving presence descend on her, surrounding her, holding her, gently rocking her back and forth. She smelled the spiciness of his skin and knew who it was. "Oh, Jesus," she cried, "Oh, Jesus. Oh, Jesus." The Lord made shushing sounds near her ear, and she felt the heat of his cheek on hers.

Eventually, her tears stopped. She opened her eyes and the Lord was gone. Not gone, just...invisible again. She wished she had a

Kleenex. She wiped her nose on the back of her sleeve and panted. Looking around, she saw that she was alone. Wherever Alec Marlowe had gone, he was not here now. Maybe he had gone to get help? Probably he was just uncomfortable with such unseemly displays of emotion. Shakily, she got to her feet and, with tottering steps at first, continued her journey.

After a couple of blocks, she was walking normally again. Then she was at the church. She fumbled for the key in her pocket and let herself into her office. Quickly, she grabbed a sheet of paper out of the printer and a magic marker from the cup on her desk. With quick block letters, she wrote out, "The Ash Wednesday Service Tonight will be at the corner of 7th and Bjorn St." She glanced at the clock. She had less than an hour.

She had been grasping at straws trying to come up with a ritual worthy of the moment, but with the realization that it was Ash Wednesday, everything had fallen into place. She wondered if she had enough ashes on hand and felt a spike of panic. "Silly, we'll have a fire trench," she heard her own voice say. "There'll be more than enough ashes." She relaxed. She forced herself to think through the Ash Wednesday ritual in her head. She walked quickly to her bookshelf and pulled out her beat-up, pocket-sized copy of the UCC *Book of Worship*.

Then she went to the sacristy cabinet, opened it, and rummaged around for her oil stock. She found it, a small thing about the size of a quarter across and about half an inch high, a Celtic cross design etched on its lid. She unscrewed it and peered uncertainly at the yellowed wad of cotton within. She remembered replacing the rancid oil with fresh chrism just a couple of weeks before when she'd taken the oil stock to the hospital to anoint old Mrs. Hutchinson for healing. It would be fine. She dabbed at the cotton with her thumb, then smeared it on the back of her hand. It was slick with oil. Satisfied, she screwed the lid on it again and put the stock in her pocket.

She then lifted the small clay pot containing ashes made from last year's Palm crosses. She taped the lid in place and prayed that she might keep it upright and not spill ashes all over everything. She then reached for her purple stole, a busy but beautiful thing woven with Guatemalan patterns. She folded it and tucked it under her arm. Turning off the light, she snatched up a sweater from the hook by the door, closed her office door behind her, and set out again toward the longhouse at a brisk pace.

"Give it here," Bill said to her, pointing to the pistol she gripped in her right hand. It was still shaking. Fleetingly, she wondered if it might be possible to raise it and fire before he got off a round. But she knew the answer to that. Before she even aimed she'd have at least twelve slugs in her.

She dropped the pistol to the floor, and then attempted to kick it to him, but her leg would not obey her with enough fidelity to accomplish the task—her foot waved past the gun in one direction, then the other. "Sorry," she said. Frustrated, she turned her torso and tried again. This time the pistol slid, but not in Bill's direction.

He intercepted the weapon and picked it up with his left hand, fitting it into his belt at the small of his back. Then he turned to face Julie again. He stopped. He blinked. Confusion washed over his face. Then he looked pained. "Julie?"

"Hi, Bill."

"Oh, shit. Motherfucking—" He stopped mid-curse, looking away, and then looked back at her. "Oh my god."

"Are you going to shoot me?"

"You're a deputy sheriff," he said, his face still working through a range of emotions.

"That's right. I was shot a few days ago. I'm here...recovering."

"I'm sorry, Julie, I—"

"I'll take three pounds of lean ground chuck, and two chicken breasts. No bones, please."

A smile lit at the corner of his mouth. Then he laughed. "That'll be seventeen dollars, twenty-three cents, please."

"Can you put it on my tab? I'm a little short until payday."

"Sure, but you're up to fifty-four dollars and sixteen cents, just so you know."

"No problem, Bill. I'm good for it."

Julie looked up at Bill's face again. His eyes were red and his mouth was working but no sound escaped. Then he said, "Shit, Julie, I'm so..."

"It's going to be okay, Bill." She heard herself say the words, but she didn't for a moment believe them. Did she sound sincere enough though? She didn't know. Bill seemed too caught up in a barrage of emotions to read any specific reaction. What she wanted to say was, "I have seen the gods, and they are no less murderous. As above, so below," but she didn't. It might have been true, but it wouldn't have helped.

To be eaten by the Great Old Ones or to be shot by Bill Arenson—what was the difference? Indeed, did not all flesh fall to Time the Devourer? What did it matter how it happened, or when? To have a few more years of subjective experience before falling to the dust, what difference would it make? Her consciousness would dissipate like the morning fog on the fields as the sun burned through it. To have twenty-four years of consciousness or fifty-five years like her mother, what did it matter? The book would be closed, never to be read again.

A great heaviness descended upon her. She might have collapsed to the floor in despair, but instead she laughed.

"What's funny?" Bill asked, the point of his rifle lowering.

"I don't know," Julie confessed. "Nothing. I'm just..." She didn't finish. There was so much unfinished. "Are you going to shoot me, Bill?"

She looked at his eyes and saw her answer. He had no choice. He knew it and she knew it, but neither of them wanted to say it. Julie said, "You need to go down. You *want* to go down. That's what this is all about."

"Yes, but I have to go down *different*."

"Different than in your cube?"

"Yes."

Julie nodded. "If you're shot, you prove them wrong." Julie didn't need to specify who "they" were—"they" were whoever had sent the cubes. But she knew there was no "they." Clive had performed a stupid, angry, adolescent ritual and there had been unintended consequences, magickal collateral damage. Mistakes were made. But now Clive was dead. There was no one to hold accountable. There was no one to prove wrong.

But it made no sense to say that to Bill. He needed to lash out. He needed to blame someone. He needed revenge more than he needed life. Julie thought about her mother and felt a burst of regret. It was time to stop blaming her, she knew. But by this time it was a reflex, muscle memory. It would feel awkward and uncomfortable to do it differently. But she knew it was time.

"Do you remember old Arnie Kettleston?" Julie asked.

"Yeah, I remember Arnie," Bill said, his face showing confusion at her question.

"He told me about a horse he really loved. Studebaker. The horse was really sick, and the vet said it was time to put him down. He was going to give him a series of shots."

Bill nodded.

Julie continued, "But Arnie said no. He loved that horse, and if he had to go, Arnie was going to be the one to do it. So he went and got his shotgun."

Bill nodded some more, his eyes still searching for comprehension.

Julie sighed. "Bill, this only ends one way. You know it and I know it. Just...don't let it be a stranger."

There. His eyes widened and the muzzle of the rifle lowered completely. Tears wet his cheeks. He nodded. He kicked the pistol back toward her, but before she could reach for it, a familiar voice rang out.

"Don't nobody move!"

She looked beyond Bill, down the hallway behind him, directly at Thom. His pistol was out, trained directly on Bill. Instinctively, she knew she was in the line of fire. If Thom missed, it was just as likely that the bullet would hit her instead. Forgetting the pistol at her feet, she edged to her right, out of Thom's sightline. She saw Thom nod, saw Bill's rifle arc up defensively.

"Bill, it's okay. It's Thom," Julie said, her voice as soothing as she could make it. She watched Bill turn slowly to face him. "You know Thom," she continued. "He's been a good friend to you. What does it matter if it's me or him that does—"

But before she could finish, Thom took his shot. The first bullet took Bill full in the chest. He lurched backwards. The second and third shots were affected by the kick of the first. They went wide, striking the door behind her.

Then the world was engulfed in flame.

When Thom opened his eyes, he saw nothing but a field of white littered with tiny dots at irregular intervals. *Ceiling panels,* he registered. He blinked and turned his head. War zone? For a few moments, he had no sense of himself. He was a detached observer, viewing the sad events of earth from a safe distance. But then his back screamed, and an awareness of his physicality rushed into him. He blinked again and suddenly everything hurt. *Where am I?* he wondered. There was a ringing in his ears, and his face hurt as if he had been out in the sun far too long the day before. *Do I have my limbs?* the voice in his head asked. It seemed an odd question, but he resolved to answer it nevertheless. He tried to move his right hand and heard tinkling glass and sharp pain. He stopped moving his hand. He focused his awareness on his left hand and tried to make a fist. He could, but without looking at it, he didn't know if the fist was real. A hundred obscure philosophical questions flooded into his brain, which did not help him situate himself in whatever reality this was.

A face floated into view, covered with blood and screaming. The ringing in his ears was too loud for him to make out the words. He was vaguely aware of people running past him. He turned his head and saw their feet pass in a blur. The bloody face hovering over him grabbed his cheeks in one hand and moved his face so that he was staring at the ceiling again. Then there was an index finger in front of his eyes. He watched as the finger moved to the left, then to the right, then to the left again. The bloody face was shouting again, but this time the voice was clearer. The face looked at him again, and he distinctly heard the words, "What is your name?"

Thom blinked. What *was* his name? It seemed like such an irrelevant, academic question that he bristled inside with irritation. But the fact that he did not immediately know the answer troubled him. Then he found it. "Thom," he said, but for some reason his tongue felt huge inside his mouth. *Is it always like that?* he wondered. He didn't remember.

Then there were other people scattered around him, and many hands reached beneath him. He felt immodest and exposed, but then they surprised him by lifting him into the air. It seemed so surreal that the thought that he was dreaming floated through his brain. *I hurt too much to be dreaming,* he thought. The hands were lowering him now, and there was something solid beneath him again, but the solid thing was moving. *I'm on a gurney,* he thought. *Am I dead? No, I hurt too much to be dead.*

Other thoughts began to crowd in as the ceiling panels moved overhead with increasing speed. *What happened to me? Why am I here? And where—?*

A hospital. He was in a hospital. But had he been *brought* to the hospital? Why had he woken up on a hospital floor? What city was he in? What state? More questions fought for his attention, but as he couldn't find the answer to any of them, they rushed past like an irritating breeze that smelled of livestock manure.

"Sheriff, what year is it?" The original bloody face had asked him. *Why is the doctor covered in blood?* he wondered.

"Uh…" He didn't know.

"Sheriff, who is the president of the United States?"

"Uh…" He didn't know that either. They had called him "sheriff." *I am Thom, the sheriff,* his brain said to him. It was like tipping a ball over the top of a hill. Suddenly images and facts and faces came flooding back into his head. He sat bolt upright. "Julie!" he shouted.

"Sheriff, we need you to—"

"Fuck that, where is Julie?" He looked down at his body. He saw his boots, and they seemed blessed because they were his. He had his legs. He tried to move them. They moved. A third of his pant leg was missing; the skin of his leg looked blistered and angry. In moments it began to hurt. He raised his hands in front of his eyes and flexed his fingers. Not all of them were there. He was missing a finger on his left hand, the pinky. His hand looked misshapen, like an odd thing that did not belong on his body. *Well, if you have to lose a finger, that's the one to lose.* He noticed no emotions at this realization, it was just a fact, like the weather or a mathematical sum.

The gurney had stopped moving. Others were gathering around him, pushing him back down on the gurney. He resisted their efforts and tried to swing his legs off the side of the gurney.

"Sheriff, you need to lie down," the bloody face said to him, in a tone used to being obeyed.

Thom was also used to being obeyed, however, and he was the law.

"You're going to step back, Doctor, and I'm going to get up. And if you don't, I'm going to crack your nose with my fist, and that's a promise." His voice sounded so calm and reasonable that it surprised him.

To his great relief, the man stepped back. Thom groaned as he sat upright. He pushed off the gurney and felt ground beneath his feet. His knees buckled at first, but he caught himself on the gurney and held on until he felt steady. Looking around him, he saw that he was in an emergency room examination cubicle, with curtains drawn on all sides. Medical personnel surrounded him, some of them wearing masks and gloves, and others looking nearly as bad as he felt. The bloody face seemed to be in charge, so he turned to it. "I assume you're a doctor."

"I am. But Sheriff—"

"There was a shooter. And my deputy, she was a patient. And she—"

And then he saw the whole scene play out in his mind again. Bill Arenson with his rifle. Julie wearing a tan windbreaker and little else. He had taken a shot at Bill. Then the world caught fire. That was it.

"Is she dead?" he asked.

"There were two people near the explosion," the doctor confirmed. "They are both dead."

Thom blinked and reached out to support himself once more. *No no no not Julie too,* he thought. His adrenaline spiked and the voice in his head began to keen. With a sudden jerk, he started walking. He felt a sting in his neck, and he lashed out with his arm, punching a young man holding a needle. He grabbed the needle out of his neck on the backstroke and looked at it. He had no idea what it was or how much the nurse had injected him with, only that there was plenty left in the syringe. He threw it to the floor with a look of disgust and tottered to the curtain. He batted it out of his way and made for the door.

Thom's eyes were wild as he lurched into the hall. Fortunately, few would notice, since pandemonium seemed to reign throughout the hospital. EMTs and firemen jogged past him, along with security guards going the other way. Tears streamed from his eyes, but he did not blink. As he walked, the kinks in his stride subsided. With every step his gait became more like his own. After a few lengths of hallway, he was jogging.

He felt lost—every hallway looked the same. Then he noticed a couple of landmarks, and with only a few wrong turns, managed to find his way to the scene of the explosion. A nagging suspicion had begun to tickle his brain. *What if I did it? What if it was my bullet that caused the explosion?* But he repressed the thought because, if it were true, it would simply be too horrible to bear.

He approached the very place he had been standing and stood there. A chasm split the wall behind where Julie had been standing. His gaze travelled down to the ground, steeling himself against what he expected to see.

He was surprised he did not see bodies. Had the explosion been so great that there were no bodies? He pondered the possibility. *But surely there would be body parts,* he reasoned. And as soon as he began to search for those, he found them. A glint of silver caught his eye. "No," he breathed as he bent down. He recognized the pentagram ring—now dented and twisted, but still recognizable. His face screwed up into a mask of grief; he did not try to stop the tears, nor did he even seem to notice them. He rose without knowing it and bit his lip, turning the ring over and over. "I'm so sorry," he said. He put the ring in his breast pocket and buttoned it. Then he held his hand over it as he tried to collect himself.

He scoured the ground for more evidence of Julie, but could not be sure what belonged to her and what belonged to Bill. Then his eyes lit upon a bright yellow sign, blackened and twisted but still legible: "Danger: Oxygen." He *had* done it, he realized. It had been his bullet that set off the explosion.

His knees buckled then. He fell. His head found the cool linoleum; he rolled it back and forth, his still bleeding left hand pooling into the thickening blood on the floor. *You lost another one, you lost another one, you lost another… That's all you do—sign 'em up and take 'em down.*

"Stop," he said to the voice in his head. "Stop it."

The voice did not obey. And another, even louder voice asserted itself: *You still have a duty to her. You need to inform her mother.*

That stopped him. His head jerked up; he suddenly became conscious of the people rushing past him in all directions. Wiping his nose on his sleeve, he pushed himself up and then stood. He needed to tell Peg.

He started walking again, stiffly at first, but then with more fluidity. His tears had stopped and his haggard face settled into a grim look of determination. No one questioned him, no one stopped him, no one even spoke to him as he passed through the large sliding doors into the cool evening air.

When Peg arrived back at the longhouse, it was finished. Twilight gave its last amber gasps as she approached it; she stopped just shy of the corner to admire it. It looked very much like one of the Native American longhouses she had seen so many times in books. Only the nylon rope draped over its dome connecting the triforks that held its hay thatching in place betrayed its chronological provenance. Ted, Allison, and Mel stood together in front of the entrance, talking. Ted noticed her and waved. She waved back, smiled, and crossed the street.

"Oh, Mel, it's beautiful," she said, catching the young man up in a hug. Mel returned it with something approaching desperation, and it occurred to her how very hungry he was for approval, for validation. She held him by the shoulders and looked into his eyes. "Thank you for helping us. We couldn't have done it without you."

"Yes, but the question is, will it all be for naught?" Ted asked.

"Are the chairs here?" Peg asked.

"Those high school chaps were *not* quiet," Ted sniffed. "You didn't hear them banging away in the fellowship hall?"

"I didn't," Peg confessed. "But...I was praying."

"Gee, you pray hard," Mel said with what might have been wonder in his voice.

"I suppose I do," Peg agreed.

"Peg doesn't do much halfway," Allison took her arm and led her toward the longhouse door.

It was dark as midnight inside. But as her eyes adjusted, Peg felt as if she were going back in time. She nearly tripped over the fire trench, but Allison held her steady. The trench ran the full length of the long-house, and Peg saw that there was already kindling, firewood, and charcoal briquettes scattered within it. Her nostrils twitched at the sharp scent of lighter fluid. As her eyes adjusted, she saw that mirroring the trench was a slit open at the top of the longhouse, to let out the smoke.

"All you need to do is light a match and the whole thing will go up," Ted's voice came from behind her.

"He means the fire trench, not the longhouse," Allison clarified.

"One hopes," Ted added.

Peg nodded and glanced at her watch. It was too dark to see it. "What time is it?"

"Almost seven," Mel said.

"Did you remember that it's Ash Wednesday?" Ted asked.

"I've got my oil stock right here," Peg confirmed.

"Well then, perhaps you're not hopeless after all."

There was a flare of sudden flame. Peg jerked her head toward it and saw Allison lighting a candle. The light seemed impossibly bright in the dark longhouse. Peg felt the rightness of it settle into her bones. Allison smiled at her as she lit another candle.

Peg saw that they were Mexican candles, the kind you used to be able to buy three-for-a-dollar, their tall glass enclosures sporting sentimental portraits of saints. She watched as Allison set them at various points around the longhouse. As she lit more of them, the interior began to glow with a primeval luminescence.

"This is good," came a voice from the door. Peg turned to see Milala stepping into the longhouse. She was holding her drum and nodding at her surroundings.

"I'm so glad you approve," Peg said, and she moved to catch the young woman up in a hug.

Milala seemed to endure it more than she enjoyed it. When Peg released her, the young woman set her drum down on one of the chairs. There was another flare of light, and Peg saw that she was holding a lighter beneath a parcel of sage bound up with string. She blew on the sage, pulled a feather from a pocket in her skirt, and began to fan the smoke in one direction, then another, until she had turned completely around.

All eyes were on her now. Peg saw her lips moving in some kind of silent prayer. Peg noticed Allison's breath just over her shoulder. "She's inviting the spirits," she said.

"Which spirits?" Peg asked.

"The spirits of her ancestors—and ours, I imagine. All the animals, the spirits of the land. Good spirits."

"How do you know?" Peg asked.

"She told me earlier," Allison said, her voice tinged with mock hurt.

"Oh."

Peg watched as Milala began to circumambulate the room, blowing sage smoke into every corner until she had completed her circle. She smudged out the sage bundle and threw what was left of it into the fire trench.

"It is ready now," she said to no one in particular.

Peg expected a snide retort from Ted, but his face was sober and he was nodding. It seemed he approved as well. She was glad of it.

"The sun set today at 7:02pm," Allison said. "I checked. I told people to arrive by seven o'clock."

"So where are they?" Peg asked.

No one answered. Peg felt a knot in her stomach tighten. She opened her mouth to worry aloud, but decided against it. But the questions hurled themselves at her brain, anyway. *What if we've gone to all this trouble, and no one else comes? What if people just think it's a stupid idea? What if it is a stupid idea?*

She headed for the door. Once outside, she began to pace. She'd expected Thom to come, at least. She'd texted him hours ago, just to be sure he got Allison's email, but had heard nothing. She checked her phone again. Nothing. And it was thirty-five after the hour. She sighed and began to pace back and forth in front of the entrance.

"Why are you walking that way?" Milala's voice came out of the darkness. She turned to face it and saw the young woman approach. "You walk like you're angry at the earth."

"No, I..." She stopped. *Was* she angry at the earth? Was she angry at someone else? Perhaps she was angry at herself. She didn't know. A familiar feeling rose within her, a feeling that was not her friend. It was a feeling that threatened to undo her whenever she was about to do something significant, something important to her, something in which the well-being of others was on the line. She had had the very same feeling at her ordination. She'd had it at the first service in her first parish. She'd had it the first time she held someone's hand as they slipped from this world into the next. "I'm just nervous, is all."

"Why?"

"Because..." Peg stopped. It was a good question; she didn't immediately know the answer to it. Was she nervous because the spiritual and psychological health of the community was at stake? That sounded grand, but it didn't land in her gut. It wasn't untrue, but it wasn't true either. She dug deeper. Was she nervous because she was afraid that no one would show? Yes, but that was not the whole of it. Then she realized what it was. She didn't need to say it, but she did. "I am afraid of looking foolish."

Milala moved to stand beside her; together they stared out into the empty street. "I know that feeling," the young woman said, so softly that Peg could barely hear. "You think about things. You and Creator are...acquainted."

"I believe we are," Peg agreed.

"I was wrong about you."

Peg looked down at the young native woman. She put her hand on her shoulder and squeezed it. "I was wrong about you too."

"I gotta get my drum before somebody steals it," Milala said. "*This* drum can't be replaced. This drum was made from Coyote's own hide." Then she walked away.

Peg frowned as she watched her walk back to the longhouse. There was something intriguing about Milala that Peg could not quite put her finger on. Something oddly sacred. She respected her, she realized. She looked at her watch again but had to turn to catch the streetlight just right in order to read it. Six-forty-five. She sighed.

And then she heard the music. It rode the wispy wind from several blocks away, but she heard it. It sounded like old-time jazz, and it was coming closer. A banjo provided a steady beat, while a clarinet floated above it, skirling and dancing, carrying the melody. Then she recognized the tune, an old African American spiritual. As she listened, the words came back to her too.

> *We shall walk through the streets of the city*
> *Where our loved ones have gone on before*
> *We will sit on the banks of the river*
> *Where we'll meet to part no more...*

It was a funeral song, played in typical exuberant New Orleans style. "God bless you, Martin," she said. At least Martin Olofson was coming. The band was marching toward them from the center of town, and as Peg gained her first glimpse of them beneath the street-lamp, her heart skipped a beat.

Ted was suddenly beside her, reaching for her hand. He squeezed it and she squeezed back. Together they watched the band grow closer. Behind the musicians a small parade of people followed, trailing off into darkness.

"That's got to be half the town," Ted breathed.

"Or more," Peg agreed.

"They're really coming," he said.

"You were worried too?" she asked.

"Well, I didn't want to let on, but..." He didn't finish.

Allison came up on her other side. "Do you think we'll have enough chairs?"

"If we don't, they'll stand," Ted answered.

Peg began to recognize faces now as they passed beneath the streetlights. She saw several people who had cubes—Janet Ring-weather, Clem Odinswood, Matt Cooper, Greg Johannson, Olivia Harris, and many others. She blew a kiss to Imelda Johansen, who took off her big floppy hat and waved it at her.

Martin led the jazz band directly to the longhouse, and then to one side of the entrance, and continued to play. Ted leaped to the door and began to wave people in, looking for all the world like one of the models on a game show, gesturing with long, looping movements.

"We should go in," Allison said, "before we're swamped."

Peg agreed and walked quickly to the entrance just ahead of the first of the marchers. She realized Martin must have started on the other end of town, where he and the band normally rehearsed at the Methodist church. They must have played their way along the main street, picking up people as they went. Others who were already walking to the longhouse no doubt joined them. There was a feeling of somber festivity in the air, much different from that first night out in the cornfield surrounded by the cubes. Martin's music brought release to the moment, a touch of the sacred. It was an invitation to mourn. *That's why his music irritated me so.* New Orleans jazz held the mournful and the joyful in edgy juxtaposition, and she had been resisting the mourning. But now she didn't; now she was grateful for it. The very music she had despised transformed from an irritant to a balm.

Peg turned and went back into the longhouse. She put her stole on over her blouse and sat in the first chair. The chairs were not arranged facing the front as they might be in church. Instead, they all faced the fire trench running down the middle of the longhouse, half on one side and half on the other, so that people would face each other across the trench. There were four rows of chairs on either side; every five chairs or so there were aisles created by removing a column of chairs. As Peg settled herself, she watched people take their places.

Without thinking about it, she began to search faces for Julie's. *Julie's not here,* she reminded herself. *She's in the hospital. She'll be there for a while.* The rational part of her knew that, even as the maternal part of her wished her daughter were with her. Julie had never seen her preside; she had always boycotted her mother's religious services. Peg felt impossibly sad just thinking about it. The irrational part of her hoped that this time might be different. But Julie was hurt, and that was just the way it was. Peg forced herself to relax.

Gazing at the crowd taking their places, she noted that the faces were uncertain—curious, but excited. She felt a fleeting spirit of uncertainty herself, and she hoped she would not disappoint them. After all, she had very little planned. All she really needed to do was call things to order, to offer an invitation. Then she would stand back, watch, and wait. Either the Spirit of God would move in and do something, or She wouldn't. Peg felt curious and a bit excited.

The band was still playing outside. She hadn't planned it, and yet it was undeniably perfect. For all the times Martin and his raggedy band had annoyed her, she felt nothing but gratitude now.

Most people had found their seats; the hubbub began to die down. Ted hovered in the doorway and nodded at her. Apparently everyone was inside that was coming inside. Even the band members had set down their instruments or were cradling them in their laps. Peg glanced at Milala, who had taken the seat directly across the trench from her. The young native woman's features were unreadable. For comfort, then, Peg looked to Allison, sitting next to Milala. They were holding hands. Allison smiled encouragingly at Peg and raised her chin. It was time.

With a feeling of surreal detachment, Peg rose. It was as if she were looking at herself from a great height. She had to imagine herself back in her fleshy bones. With an air of dignity, she walked to the midpoint between the two choirs of chairs. The trench started just in front of her, about two feet from her own shoes, and with her eyes she followed it to the back of the longhouse, where it disappeared into darkness. She clutched at her UCC *Book of Worship,* and cleared her throat.

"My dear friends," she began stiffly. Then her shoulders relaxed. "And you *are* my friends. This...this community has become family to me, and I know you feel the same. We don't have the luxuries of the big city out here, but we choose to live here because we've found something better—a connection to the past, a connection to the soil, and a deep connection with each other. And for myself, all of that adds up to a pretty solid connection to God as well. And God is here now, because *we* are here now. Let's just take a moment to breathe that in, to feel connected to the Spirit within us and around us."

She paused then, closing her eyes and taking a deep breath. In her imagination, she saw the Holy Spirit filling up every inch of space in the longhouse, surrounding and permeating everything and everyone. A shudder ran through her and she knew it was so.

Opening her eyes again, she said, "We don't know why bad things happen to good people—hell, we don't even know why they happen to *bad* people. Things just *happen*...some things are good, and some aren't. It's one of those mysteries that I hope we'll get to ask God about some day. But we do know that most of the time, when it's people causing the hurt, it's usually because they've been hurt themselves. Hurt begets hurt, in a never-ending cycle—unless that cycle is interrupted somehow.

"These cubes...everyone has a theory about them. I've heard some doozies, and you have too. And if my daughter is right, the truth is even weirder than the doozies. She thinks they happened because someone was hurt. Bad. So bad that he transmitted that hurt to the whole community. He didn't mean to, but...it happened. This is more common than anyone would like to suppose; it's not as dramatic in most cases, but it turns out the same in the end.

"The cubes...well, they've brought out the worst in us. I think it's because...they scared us. And fear...it's a sure-fire way to bring out the worst in anyone, even in a whole town."

Peg heard a murmur of protest stirring in the gathered assembly. She held her empty hand up. "I'm not blaming anyone. I'm not saying it's anyone's fault. I'm saying it's human, and we're acting pretty much like humans *do*. The cubes didn't just shake us up, they didn't just scare us, they reminded us—forcefully—of something we don't like to be reminded of: We are going to die. And...it's true. We *are* going to die. Intellectually we know this, but the cubes touched something deeper in us than simple head knowledge. They made it real. *Mors in Manibus Nostris*. They made death...touchable. They brought home to us the fragility of our lives, the brevity of our lives, and the preciousness of the time we have left. They reminded us of the fundamental sadness at the heart of the world—that nothing is permanent, that we are dust and to dust we shall return.

"There's only one appropriate human response to this: grief. The problem is, we don't *do* grief. In fact, we kind of suck at it."

There was a murmur of recognition and even a few cackles of levity at her choice of words. Encouraged, Peg continued. "Swedes are *especially* bad at it—you know it's true. But Americans, in general, are not much better. We feel things, but it's bad form to let on what we're feeling, especially if the feelings are...well, not *good* feelings. We don't want to burden others with them, which is laudable. But at the same time, we don't want to look weak either. So we hide them, we stuff them down, we ignore them. But grief, like so many of the other 'negative emotions' we feel—like anger or resentment or hate—if it doesn't come out in a healthy way, it grows bigger within us, it festers, and it leaps out in unhealthy ways. You all know what I'm talking about, because every time we've turned around this week, we've crashed into it."

She saw nods of agreement and tears of recognition. "This is a mystery. It's a deeply human mystery. Grief is a mystery. Mysteries can't be ignored forever. They must be faced. They must be honored. They must be *passed through*. It's why we've invited you here tonight, so that we can pass through this mystery together—not unconsciously, but consciously; not unhealthily, but with integrity. This is our work tonight. I invite you to actually feel what you're feeling—don't push it down. I invite you to express what you're feeling without shame or embarrassment. I invite you to hold your grief in your hands, and to make an offering of it—to God, to Life, to whatever it is you hold sacred. I invite you to summon it from your depths, to acknowledge it, and if you can, to give thanks for it. And then I invite you to stop holding on to it, to let it pass through you, to release its energy, its force into the fire."

Peg saw that many of the eyes shone. She shook her head. "Fire purges. It transforms decay into beauty. There aren't any rules for this. There's no liturgy or method or process. I'm asking you to find whatever feels out-of-true within you, whatever feels painful or confusing or overwhelming, and to bring it forth. I'm asking you to sit with the fire, to trust it. Because, if you can, it will heal you."

And with that, Peg returned to her seat and lowered herself to it with as much dignity as she could muster. She glanced over at Ted. He nodded his approval and encouragement. She looked at Allison, who gave her a thumbs-up with her free hand. She took it in and closed her eyes.

She didn't know how long she sat in the peace that followed. But she heard movement, and when she opened her eyes again, she saw Mel standing. He strode to the front of the longhouse and stood in the place she had been standing. Without a word, he opened a box of matches and took one out. He struck it, knelt, and touched it to the trench. There was a sound of rushing air, and then a tongue of flame leapt up. The young man jerked up as the flame expanded more quickly than he'd been expecting. A gasp of surprise erupted from the assembly as the flame raced down the trench to its end. The air was filled with the sound of snapping as the kerosene caught the kindling. Orange light cast a multitude of shadows on the ceiling of the longhouse, dancing over their heads like the communion of saints.

Every eye was on the trench, beholding the fire, reverencing it. Peg felt someone squeeze her shoulder. She looked up and saw Ted hovering over her, nodding. She reached up and put her hand over his, interlocking their fingers.

After several minutes, people began to look around. Peg knew that look. It was the "what's next?" look. The problem was that there *was* nothing next—nothing planned, anyway. What was next was people bringing their own feelings, expressing them. Peg knew that was going to be a hard sell. *I hate improvisation*, she thought. *It's just not safe.*

People shifted in their seats; more than a few people looked worried...or bored. Peg's lips drew back in a grim frown as she considered what to do. She recognized the feeling. It was one she had often when a parishioner came for counseling or spiritual direction. She didn't have any answers for them. She didn't have advice. She often had no idea what to say. But she knew what to do. She closed her eyes and did that now. *Okay, Jesus*, she prayed, *this is your time. I have no idea what to do or say. Whatever you have in your back pocket, bring it out now.*

In her imagination she reached out her hand for his. The Lord always seemed to be just within reach of her left hand, often sitting cross-legged on the floor. She reached out now, and felt his hand meet hers. She felt him gently squeeze. But he didn't say anything. She took a deep breath and trusted the silence. This too was familiar. And as usual, it was a hard thing to trust.

And then, just as the silence was about to become unbearable, a booming sound filled her ears. Her eyes snapped open and she jerked her head toward the sound. It was Milala, still seated, her eyes closed. She held her new frame drum loosely in one hand. In her other hand she now held a stick with a wad of padding tied to its end, secured in place with a strip of hide. The sound was louder than Peg would have expected, its resonance filling the space in the longhouse with a rhythm that seemed older than humankind. The beat was fast—three, maybe even four beats per second. It was not at all what she was expecting, but in the moment, it seemed somehow perfect. She felt each beat like a strike to her heart, felt it go into her, through her, and out the back again. Each beat pierced her, thrilled her, soothed her— all at the same time. She drew in a deep breath and felt a euphoria wash over her. When she exhaled, it was as if every anxiety she had been clutching to her fearful breast was melting like a handful of ice cubes, water running down her fingers, then sucked up wherever it struck the soil. She felt her shoulders relax, felt her breathing slow.

Jesus had come through. He always did. But this time, he had sent Milala. She heard the echo of the young woman's voice saying, *Creator told me to drum for you.* She hadn't believed it before, not really. She had rarely been so happy to be wrong. She felt Jesus squeeze her fingers. "Well, aren't you just the shit?" she asked him out loud. In her head she heard him laugh and felt another squeeze. A shudder passed through her body, and she welcomed and savored it. It felt like the Spirit.

She opened her eyes, then, and looked around the room. The worried expressions were gone. Many still stared at the fire, but the glow of novelty had faded into something more like contemplation. They beheld the fire, but they did not see it. Instead, they were looking deeper. Many cheeks were wet with tears.

And then there was movement. Peg watched as Gary Shultz rose from his chair, holding a small square object. Peg recognized it imme- diately. It was the replica of his own cube, sculpted at Allison's shop. He held it before him and walked slowly, deliberately, as if he were leading a religious procession. At the fire trench he stopped. He looked upwards, perhaps at the gap in the ceiling, at the stars. But Peg's deeper wisdom intuited that he was praying. Then Gary knelt and placed the cube in the flames. He watched as it was engulfed. He stood, tears streaming, and bowed to the fire. Peg searched his face. Whatever stress or strain Gary had been carrying, he had released it there. There was only one word for what she saw on his face: peace. Peg felt the tension remaining in her own body release. Her belly shook, but it was not from cold. She watched Gary turn, then, and return to his seat—unburdened in hand and spirit. "Thank you, Jesus," Peg said out loud. She felt a squeeze in her fingers.

Others rose then. One after another. More cubes were put in the fire. Some burned artwork—pictures they had drawn, photographs they had taken—others burned poetry and other writing. In every case, the fire in the trench flared a bit, as if acknowledging each sacrifice. Peg tried to take it all in. Then her eyes widened.

A shadow moved behind the last row of people facing her, and as it grew closer, Peg saw what was casting it. A coyote moved silently along the wall of the longhouse, larger than any she had ever seen, its mottled brown-gray coat bathed in oranges and reds from the fire. Its muscles rippled along its withers; it almost seemed to be moving in slow motion. Peg looked around to see if anyone else had noticed, expecting panic and pandemonium to erupt, but it seemed that no one else saw it. Her pulse increased as the coyote reached the end of the longhouse, and turned to its left, heading toward the fire trench, toward Peg herself.

Peg felt sweat gathering in her palms as the coyote moved closer. Looking up into its approaching face, her eyes locked onto its own. It rounded the end of the fire trench, and in a few quick strides came up directly beside her, turned, and then sat in exactly the spot she imagined Jesus had been sitting. Peg looked over at Milala, perhaps for help, perhaps for some clue what was happening, but the young woman's eyes were closed, concentrating on her drumming. She looked to Allison, but her friend's eyes were closed as well.

Warily, Peg turned her head back toward the beast. It did not look directly at her, but gazed into the fire. Then it spoke. "You have helped Milala come into her power. Her own people have shut her out. She has bitten too many fingers. But you trusted her. Creator sends his thanks." Then he turned and pressed his muzzle so that it was almost touching her cheek. Then she felt his hot breath on her skin, bathing her in a Presence so profound that she thought she might faint. It smelled like Spirit.

Just as quickly as he had arrived, he left, rising from his haunches and sauntering past the seated townsfolk until he disappeared into the shadows once more.

Peg blinked. Her fingers were suddenly cold. Had she just had a hallucination? or was it an epiphany? or a theophany? Did it matter? Real or imagined, revelation or no, the message had been delivered, and it had been one of gratitude. For her. Peg's breath caught, and she closed her eyes. She pressed her hand to her bosom and breathed deep, trying to take it in, trying to snatch at the wisps of memory to recall exactly how the beast's breath had smelled. And she wondered if Jesus' breath smelled the same way in the upper room all those many years ago when he had breathed on his pack.

Milala's hand kept steady time on the drum. Her eyes were closed, and she swayed slightly back and forth as the waves of energy poured forth from her drum. She did not drum her own heartbeat—her own heartbeat was too slow, too small. Instead, she drummed the heartbeat of the earth—quick with life, bursting with green, groaning for its restoration.

Her hands were moving, but they did not seem like her hands. She was the instrument of the earth. It was the earth herself who drummed, it was the earth moving her hands, catching her up in her verdant, healing, yearning rhythm. She had surrendered to that rhythm. She had opened her mind to receive the alma mundi, the Soul of the World, and she reveled in its presence, gave thanks to Creator for the privilege of being its vessel.

Of their own accord, her eyes opened, and she saw something she had never expected to see in the white man's world—a grieving people gathered around the fire and drum, crying out to Creator for healing, for peace, for the mending of everything broken. It was not different from how her own people prayed. The moment that thought impressed itself upon her she felt her shoulders relax, felt her lungs open up, felt the knot in her stomach unwind.

I have been a foolish, wicked child, she thought. Creator knew what he was doing. Of course he did. And Coyote... Her heart sank at the thought of him. She had been terrible to him. So terrible that he had to die for her to do the very simple thing Creator had asked her to do.

And then, as if her thought had summoned him, she saw him—Coyote. She blinked, her face grew suddenly slack and pale, her hand faltered for a beat upon the drum. She recovered quickly, and looking up again, saw that Coyote was looking straight at her.

He was sitting next to Peg. Why was he sitting next to the pastor? She could not guess. Something in her heart bloomed, and she wondered if she was imagining it; or was it perhaps a vision? or could it be that her father was alive again, presiding over the ceremony he had sent her to drum for?

Tears streamed over her cheeks, and her vision swam. It became so blurry that she could not see. She blinked rapidly as she drummed, trying to clear her eyes. When she could see again, Coyote had moved —she could not find him. But it did not matter. She beat upon his hide, and his music filled the longhouse. Was there any place Coyote was not? No, she knew that there was not. He would appear, or not appear, as he pleased. It was his way. He was the trickster. But now she knew—and not in the way that children learn from books, but knew it in the marrow of her bones—that his tricks were always in the service of the earth, the whole, the All. Never again would she doubt him, no matter how inscrutable or wily he appeared. She loved him. It was a new thought. It was a good thought. And it was true.

Peg sensed that someone was standing before her. She opened her eyes, saw the expensive loafers and creased trousers and realized it was Ted.

"Ashes, please," he said.

Peg smiled at him, snatched a wadded tissue from the pocket of her sweater, and dabbed at her eyes. She reached up for his hand, and he gently pulled her from her seat. Once on her feet, she moved a few steps to the front of the longhouse, just to one side of the fire trench. Unhurried, she pulled the top from the pot of ashes. Then she pulled the oil stock from her pocket and unscrewed its lid. Balancing both the pot and the oil stock in her left hand, she dipped her right thumb into the chrism, then pressed it into the ashes and gave it a twist.

Ted had followed her to her new spot and now stood before her, his bald head bowed in prayer. She touched her thumb to his forehead and smeared the ashes to make the sign of the cross. "Remember, O man, that you are dust, and to dust you must return," she said. He nodded, opened his eyes, and winked at her. Then he moved away, and to Peg's great surprise, she discovered there were two people lined up behind him.

As Milala continued to drum, Peg repeated the ritual, giving a little bow after every imposition of ashes to signal the ritual's end. She was amazed that more people were coming, people who were not even her parishioners. Her heart stirred within her and she blinked back tears.

"Pastor," a voice said.

Peg looked up into the eyes of Bren Helvig. Bren had wanted her to say different words to her on Ash Wednesday, and it had irritated Peg. For a moment, Peg flailed inwardly. *What were those new words?* she wondered. Then she found them. She breathed deep and forced herself to relax. She offered Bren a kind smile and moved to mark her forehead with the chrism. But Bren stopped her.

"I'm sorry, Pastor, but...could you do the traditional words?"

Peg cocked her head. "Of course, dear, but—"

"No," Bren said. "I get it now. I...I didn't...there wasn't a cube for me, but my friend...I understand the words in a way that I didn't before. They aren't harsh or negative, they're just...well, they're kind because they're honest. I guess I'm hungry for that honesty, you know?"

Peg nodded. "I sure do, love. I really do." Peg gave her a compassionate smile, then moved her hand to her forehead again. "Remember, O woman, that you are dust, and to dust you must return."

Bren bit her lip and nodded, her eyes shining as she moved to return to her seat.

Peg felt faint. She waved at Ted, who rose quickly and leaned in, his ear at her lips. "Dear, can you take over for a few? I need a minute."

"Of course," Ted said. He removed the stole from her neck and settled it on his own. She handed him the pot of ashes and the oil stock and then moved away, walking between the last row of chairs and the wall of the longhouse. She kept expecting—perhaps hoping?—to see the coyote again, but she didn't.

When she reached the entrance, the cold of the air met her like a slap in the face. She was amazed how warm the longhouse had grown. In the doorway she turned and beheld the whole of it from a new perspective. There was a long line before Ted now. And many others were laying objects in the trench. One woman was openly wailing. It took a moment for Peg to realize who it was—Janet Ringweather. She'd had a cube as well.

Peg wondered if there was anything she herself needed to lay in the fire. She put her hand on her breast and closed her eyes. She quickly had her answer. No. There was nothing she needed to release there. She felt full, grateful, complete.

"Peg?" a voice came from behind her.

She spun about toward the voice, instantly recognizing the familiar growl. "Thom?" She rushed from the longhouse toward the sound of his voice. "I'm so glad you came. I didn't—" She stopped then, as she noticed his clothes. Much of his pant leg was missing. One hand was bound in gauze, and it did not look like it had been professionally done, but simply wound around haphazardly, its end tucked in place. Red stains seeped through it.

She looked at his face then, and saw the cuts, the dirt, the bruises that had begun to form. But what arrested her was his eyes. They began as sorrowful pools, but almost instantly they filled with water. He blinked and tears wet his cheeks.

"Oh no," Peg said. "No no no no…"

Thom said nothing, but simply moved toward her. He caught her up in a hug, holding her close, holding her tight. A pained sound escaped her. He held her tighter.

"There was a shooter," he said. "Your daughter got out of her bed to stop him. And...and she almost did."

"No no no," Peg repeated. Her knees gave way, but Thom caught her. Gently he lowered her to the ground.

"It was my fault," Thom said. "I did it. I was trying to stop the shooter, but..."

She opened her mouth and filled the air with a wail well known to the earth, the sound of a mother bereft of her child. Guided by some primal impulse she did not understand, she crawled out of Thom's arms, away from the news she did not want to hear, could not fully take in. Stomping on the earth with hands and knees, she moved back into the longhouse, back to the fire. She fell on her face before it and howled.

EPILOGUE

"How are you feeling, *gumman?*" Abel asked.

Mia looked up from the counter where she was placing the newly fried bacon onto folded paper towels. The air in the tiny kitchen was thick with the smells of coffee, grease, and maple syrup. It smelled like heaven. Before answering, Mia flipped a piece of bacon onto the floor, where Ginger Beer greedily scarfed it up.

"*Gumman*," Abel said disapprovingly.

"It was burned anyway," Mia explained.

He scowled at her, but a smile tugged at one side of his mouth. "Feeling?" he asked again. He looked back to his newspaper.

"Cramped," she said, but before he could open his mouth to object, she added, "but happy."

Abel lowered the paper again and looked around. They had rented a mobile home and moved it onto their land until the new house was built, but it was a tight fit. If there had been an upside to the fire, it was the fact that they had precious little to clutter up the tiny place. It was just the three of them, and what necessities they had picked up at the Walmart in Bakersfield.

There was barely room to turn around in the kitchen. Abel found the booth that served as kitchen table was not hospitable to an old man's belly. But he bore it without complaint. It was enough that Mia was alive, and that she was well, more-or-less. She'd been on the new medicine for two weeks, and Abel was starting to see a difference. She didn't smile more, but she cried less. She lacked passion, but she didn't squirrel herself away. He tried to make her laugh on occasion, but this usually had the effect of her rubbing his arm with affection. He would take that and call it a win.

"I thought the cranes were supposed to be here already," Mia said.

"Oh, sorry. I should have told you. Jeff said he had a holdup on his last job. They'll be here tomorrow, or so he says. I'm not going to hold my breath, but I'm not going to look for another company just yet, either."

Mia slid into the booth across from him, putting a large plate in front of him—two eggs, yolks runny, bacon and toast. The lingonberry jam had a permanent place on the table.

Abel grunted his approval and breathed in the intoxicating aroma. Then he looked up at the table in front of his wife. "Not eating anything?" he asked.

"I want to finish my coffee," she said, raising her mug three inches from the table. "Then...I'll make myself eat something."

"You'd better," he warned.

She gave him a grim smile and sipped from her mug. "Once all the cubes are in the same field," she began, "what kind of budget will I have? I'd like to start mapping out the garden."

"Oh, I don't know. I hadn't thought that far ahead," Abel said.

"We're bringing in about $300 dollars a day," she said. "Yesterday was $350."

"Was it?" Abel's eyebrows rose. "Well, that's more than I expected." He spread some jam on a piece of toast and sampled it. "How much do you figure you'll need?"

"I imagine we could start small—just plant enough to surround the immediate area around the cubes, and then later—next year, maybe, or the year after that—expand the garden to the edge of the field."

Abel nodded. "Do you think $10,000 would be enough?"

Mia blinked. "Where in the world are you going to get $10,000?"

"If you keep bringing in $350 a day, you'll make that 10,000 back in a month."

"Really? That seems…incredible."

"It's just math, honey-pot."

"I never was good at math," she confessed.

"I can take it out of the insurance money we got for the house—"

"But we'll need all of that for the new house."

"Yeah, but not this month we won't. Gonna take three months or more before the house is done. Jeff's got a lot of other projects going, you know."

"Have you seen them?" Mia asked.

Abel cocked his head and put his toast down. "Seen what?"

"The cubes."

Ginger Beer barked by the back door. Mia rose and let her out.

"I try to avoid them." Those cubes were the cause of all their trouble, after all. If he never laid eyes on them again, he would consider himself a lucky man. "Besides, we still have two hundred other acres to farm."

Mia returned to her place at the table. "People are putting flowers in them, like it was a cemetery or something. They're laying them inside the sculptures. Complete strangers are bringing them."

"I don't understand," Abel said.

"I don't either," Mia admitted. "I asked this girl about it. She had a ring through her nose, like we've seen on TV—"

"Yeah. What did she say?"

"She said it just seemed like the respectful thing to do. And she's not the only one. I wouldn't say that *most* people are bringing them… but some are. Enough that there always seem to be some in every cube."

Abel picked up his mug but didn't drink from it. "*Gumman,* does it bother you to…be around them?"

"I thought it would," she said. "But it doesn't. It…it's kind of like we *own* a cemetery, you know? You get used to it. I can even look at mine now."

"You shouldn't do that," Abel said. "We should cover that one."

"No. I...I confess I don't like looking at it, but only because I'm naked and I look fat. And my breasts are saggy."

"Your breasts are just fine," Abel objected.

"You're sweet."

"And you're far from fat. You need to put more meat on those bones. The doctor said so."

"You're not hearing me, Abel."

He put down his coffee cup and took a deep breath. "I'm sorry, *Gumman*. What were you trying to say?" He knew he wasn't very good at this sensitive-husband-thing, but he was determined to get better.

"I was saying that...yes, it's hard to look at my own cube, but not for the reasons you think. I don't like the way I look, but I don't like looking in the mirror, either."

"I think you're as pretty as the day—"

"What I'm trying to say, if you'd let me," she interrupted, "is it doesn't make me feel scared anymore. I beat it. *We* beat it. I know I'll die someday. That doesn't bother me...not much, anyway. That's... natural. But I know I won't be going out like *that*."

Abel was about to object that even a mobile home could catch fire, but he thought it the better part of valor to take a bite of eggs instead.

"And there won't be a bathtub in the new house," she said. She seemed to almost melt with relief.

Abel nodded. The architect had argued with them, but Abel had been firm. If there ever came a time they needed to sell, the new owners could just put in their own damn bathtub if they wanted it so bad. Its very absence would be a negative symbol of triumph.

"Can I order some plants then?" she asked.

"Absolutely. Use the Wells Fargo card. I'll settle it up after I go to the bank," Abel said.

"Thank you, *Gubben*," Mia said.

"You know how you can thank me?" Abel asked.

Mia raised one eyebrow at him.

"Not that," he said, blushing. "Just...eat something. Please."

Dust swirled around Milala, doing a kind of hula dance in the sunset. When the dust cleared, she saw what had caused it. A Greyhound bus had pulled up—far too fast, she thought. The door swung open and she was surprised to see Coyote in the driver's seat. He drew his lips back and showed her his teeth. That was always unsettling, but she chose to receive it as a smile. "Got your drum?" he asked her.

Milala's eyes snapped open and she found herself staring at a ceiling. It took a moment to realize where she was. Then she remembered. She looked over to her right and saw the sleeping face of Allison, a silver strand of drool hanging from her lip.

Milala smiled. She stretched and sat up. The bedclothes were a tangle from when they had thrown them off during the night. Milala realized she was cold and tugged on them, throwing part of a comforter over Allison as well.

Allison stirred then. "Hnnn?" she said, opening one sleepy eye and wiping her lip on the bottom sheet.

"Good morning, lovely," Milala said. She leaned over and planted a kiss on Allison's nose.

Allison scrunched her nose up playfully. Then she scooted over and pressed her body close to Milala's own. Milala snuggled into her.

"Whose turn is it to make breakfast?" Allison asked.

"I think it's yours," Milala said.

"Mmmm...what do you want?"

"I'm always fine with oatmeal..." Milala began.

"Bleh..." Allison reacted.

"...especially with a bit of honey and bourbon," Milala continued.

"Oh...well now you're talking," Allison said.

"I think the question may be: What do you want to fix?"

"A good question. A frittata, perhaps."

"We have lots of leftovers from dinner to throw in," Milala offered.

"That was my evil plan," Allison admitted.

Milala kissed her, and Allison kissed her back. She reveled in the taste of Allison, even in the morning.

Allison pushed her away. "You gonna make me want more than breakfast."

"Would that be bad?" Milala asked.

"That would be *anything* but bad," Allison said. "But I have a full day. Later?"

"It may have to be a lot later," Milala said.

A worried look crossed Allison's face. "What? Why?"

"Coyote needs my drum."

"Oh." Allison propped herself up on one elbow. "How do you know?"

Milala sighed. "A dream."

"Maybe it was just a dream," Allison said.

Milala gave her a sad smile. "There's no such thing as 'just a dream.'"

"Oh. I guess I agree with that," Allison confessed.

"Besides, it was very clear. Coyote showed me his teeth."

"That sounds threatening."

"He pretends he's smiling, but he's really saying, 'don't fuck with me,'" Milala said.

"Better not fuck with him then," Allison said.

"No. It's time to pack up."

Allison reached out and pulled her closer. "I don't want you to go."

"This is my *tawhany*, my work."

"Peg would say it's your ministry," Allison offered.

"I don't like that word...but it fits."

A long silence passed between them as Milala listened to her lover's breathing. Finally, Allison asked in a tentative voice, "Will you come back?"

Milala thought about how to answer. Should she say what she was thinking, or should she play it safe? She didn't know. She decided to test Allison. "I think I would like to know...if I did come back...would I be a visitor or not?"

A confused look passed over Allison's face. "I'm not sure how you want me to answer that."

"Don't worry about what I want. Just...tell me the truth."

"All right. I wish you'd think of it as coming home."

A knot of tension Milala had been feeling released. She sighed. "It's been a long time since I had a place to call home."

"No pressure," Allison said. "Why don't you try it on for size, making this your home base. I won't tie you down. I know you have important work to do. You go do it. And when you're done…"

"I'll come here," Milala said.

"You come here," Allison said. She moved on top of Milala and kissed her again, more deeply this time, and longer.

Jorge Wulfson rose quietly before his alarm. He had carefully laid out his clothes the night before so that he could slip into them without disturbing Ellen. He was especially careful this morning, as she had been sleeping fitfully, and sometimes not at all.

She was distressed about Melinda, and he understood that. She was a woman with a strict sense of order in the world. The Way of Heaven dictated the proper ordering of society, household, and family, and she was profoundly uncomfortable when any of those things was out of order. Melinda was upsetting that order, and it threatened to undermine the foundation Ellen's life was built upon. He had compassion for her—she was a nervous woman at the best of times—and she was suffering. But he had compassion for his child too. She was undergoing an underworld journey unlike anything that had ever confronted Jorge or his wife. He was impressed by her courage and her willingness to face it, even if that meant facing it alone.

Jorge sighed. In a little over an hour, he would be free of all this domestic drama. In a little over an hour, he would be watching the sun come up over the Rake River. He would cast his fly, feel the gentle ripple of water passing by his waders, feel the cool gentle breeze on his neck. He would feel at one with nature, and for a few precious hours, it would restore peace to his soul. He took a deep breath. Just imagining it made him feel better.

He leaned over and planted a light kiss on his wife's forehead. She made a sleepy snort and turned over, gathering the blankets into a ball at her neck. He smiled at her form in the shadows, and then headed to the hallway. He padded down the stairs in his stocking feet and turned toward the kitchen.

He was surprised to see the light on. Already, the delicious aroma of coffee filled his nostrils. "What's this?" he asked. Just then Melinda stepped out of the walk-in pantry. Except that it wasn't Melinda. *Melinda is dead,* a voice in his head reminded him. This was Mel, dressed similarly to Jorge himself—thermal trousers, several layers of shirts topped by red flannel. The gashes in his face had scabbed over, he was relieved to see. But Jorge was still unnerved by the new haircut. Indeed, his offspring's whole presentation unnerved him. He reminded himself that anyone might need a bit of adjustment if they'd had a daughter for fifteen years, and then woke up one day to discover they had a son instead.

"Good morning, Daddy. I got breakfast almost ready."

"Well...that's fine. What a...what a great surprise." Jorge looked at the stove. Bacon was already fried and sitting in the pan, staying warm. Piles of fried, cubed potatoes sat on two plates, steaming. "Can I help?"

"Almost done," Mel said. He held up a can of black beans. "Just need to heat these up, and we're ready to go."

"Alright then," Jorge said. He grabbed a cup and poured himself some of the coffee from the machine. He sat at the table and stared at his new son. Emotion welled up in his throat, but he didn't understand it. He blew on his coffee and willed it to cool so he could use it to soothe his esophageal reaction. "You're dressed like you're going fishing," he noted.

"I didn't want to ask in front of Mom," Mel said. There was no skulking to his tone, only a statement of fact. "She wouldn't get it."

"No," Jorge agreed.

"It's a boy thing," he added.

"Right," Jorge agreed.

"She'd make a fuss about it, and it would get ugly."

"She probably would," Jorge said.

Mel set the plates on the table and Jorge sniffed at the delightful aromas. "This is fine, Mel."

When he looked up, he saw his son's eyes shining.

"Thank you," Mel said. "For calling me Mel."

Jorge picked up his fork and went first for the bacon. "Seems to me a man gets to be called what he wants to be called."

When he looked up again, Mel was wiping a tear from his eye. "I'm sorry," Mel said. "Boys don't cry."

Jorge reached over and put a hand on his son's arm. "Like hell they don't. You go on and have your feelings. It doesn't make you any less a man. And whoever tells you different is a liar and a scoundrel." He saw hope come into Mel's eyes, as well as more tears. He wished someone had told him those very words when he was fifteen. It would have saved him a lot of heartache.

As he lifted a forkful of potatoes to his mouth, Jorge reflected on how difficult it had been to connect to Melinda, his daughter. He didn't know how to relate to girls or girl things. Something had shifted now. He realized he could tell Mel, his son, things that he himself needed to hear. He felt a warmth pass through him that he didn't understand "I always wanted a son," he said out loud.

Mel only nodded. Perhaps he'd always known that, perhaps he'd sensed it, perhaps... Jorge put the fork down. *Is this my fault?* he wondered. *Did Mel become a boy so that I would love him?*

It was too terrible a thought to contemplate. He pushed it out of his awareness and gave his son a sad smile. "I figure we'll go up to the Rake and do some fly fishing. I'll put my old rod in the truck once we get outside. I'll need to teach you a trick or two."

"I'd love that," Mel said.

"It's going to be messy, and you might think it's uncomfortable. It's cold out."

Mel only grinned. Jorge nodded and tucked into his potatoes with renewed vigor.

"We'll need to leave Mom a note," Mel said. "She's going to be mad."

"You leave that to me," Jorge said, picking up a pen from a pile of kitchen detritus in the middle of the table, next to the salt and pepper shakers. "I'll write it right now. I'll just tell her...*Going fishing with my son. See you at supper.*"

Peg pressed the green button on her cell phone. "Hello?"

"Peg? Peg, this is Thom."

"Oh. Hi, Thom."

"Um...how are y—...uh...hey, I...uh...I got to do something today, and I thought...well, I thought maybe we could do it together."

Peg stared at the stained glass panels in the windows of her study. Normally she loved them. Today, though, they seemed to only get in the way of the light. So many things did.

"I was planning on doing a hospital visit this morning, but...I suppose there's no reason I couldn't do it this afternoon."

"Uh...good. That's just fine then. Uh...pick you up in a half hour?"

"Sure. Where are we going?"

"Someplace...beautiful."

"I won't say no to that. Will I need any special shoes or clothes?"

"Some solid walking shoes maybe. And a sweater."

"That describes my typical apparel. See you soon." Peg pushed the red button on her phone and slipped it into the pocket of her sweater. She sighed and groaned a bit as she rose. She moved to the bathroom and checked her hair. She hadn't worn makeup in twenty years, so all there was to do was her ritual regret of the bags under her eyes. "You look fine, dear," she said to her reflection with just a little bit more than half a heart. She shook off her slippers and put on her walking shoes.

It had been a few weeks since Julie had died, since the night of the longhouse ritual, since she had debased herself rolling on the floor screaming like a banshee. But however much she still suffered twinges of shame at her complete and utter collapse of decorum, no one had said "boo" to her about it. In fact, everyone had been extraordinarily kind. Even Alec Marlowe had shown up at her door along with the entire board, who had embraced her, cried with her and given her flowers. They had offered their condolences, and suggesting that she take a couple of weeks off to grieve. She had done that, and gratefully. She had spent nearly every night of that short sabbatical with her head on Ted's shoulder, bursting into the occasional sob. The sobbing had subsided, but the tears still leaked out at what seemed like completely random intervals.

When Thom arrived, she had already locked up and was waiting outside. She climbed into the passenger seat of his 4x4 before he could get out to help her. She closed the door beside her with a loud and satisfying clutching sound.

"Thank you," Thom said.

"Beats another day bursting into tears." Peg forced a smile.

Thom nodded and pulled onto the road. They travelled in silence for what seemed like half an hour, although it might have been slightly more or slightly less. They were heading away from the desert, Peg noted, toward the mountains and the trees. Eventually, Thom let Old Bill roll to a stop and pulled on the emergency break, which responded with a percussive series of clacks.

Thom looked over at her, and she saw a reflection of her own sorrow in his eyes. He nodded and opened his door. He stepped down and snatched a small backpack from behind the seat. He slung it over his shoulder and began to walk. She quickly climbed down from her seat, shut the door, and then followed him as he wound his way onto a trail and into the woods.

Sun dappled everything around her in yellows and the tender greens of spring. The rocks and dirt beneath her feet felt solid, even buoyant. Her nose was assaulted by a complex bouquet of pine, decay, and the hint of wood smoke somewhere in the far distance. Following a bend in the path to the left, Peg gasped as the trees parted before her to reveal a valley exploding with color. "Thom, this is...this is beautiful."

Thom sat on a long-felled log that served very well as a bench. She sat near him, unable to look away from the verdant spectacle. He seemed content to simply stare at it too. As they sat together, the silence between them took on a luminous quality. Between the beauty before her and the deliciousness of the silence, Peg felt a deep peace enter her bones. It bade her muscles relax, and they did. In the sacred emptiness of that moment, her grief became her companion rather than her oppressor. Instead of pressing down upon her, it sat beside her, Thom on one side, her sorrow on the other. The relief of it sent a chill through her that had little to do with the breeze.

She felt a little bit disappointed when Thom cleared his throat. She wanted to reach over and touch her finger to his lips, to shake her head slowly, to warn him away from defiling the sacredness of the moment. But then the moment passed, and she realized any effort toward extending it would be artificial. Like every other thing she loved, every other thing that had any meaning or value, it was ephemeral.

"I, uh, I asked you here because I was hoping you might serve as a witness."

Peg blinked at him. She forced the corners of her lips to edge upwards into the analog of an encouraging smile. It occurred to Peg how very much of her job entailed pretending to be someone who might be of use to people. Usually, the pretense itself was enough. She wondered, though, if her charism for deceit would fail her at this particular moment, would fail Thom.

With slow movements that suggested reverence, Thom pulled the drawstring at the top of his small backpack and widened the opening. Reaching in, he pulled out a wooden box. Gingerly, he placed it on the log between them. Peg noticed his fingers were shaking as he released the box. He must have noticed too, because he stuffed his hands into the pockets of his jacket.

Thom looked out at the valley again. "No matter how hard I try, I just keep messing up."

"I know just what you mean," she answered. "But I think the problem isn't our intentions. I mean, I always mean well. I think you do, too." She offered him a sad smile. He glanced over and nodded at it.

"So what's the problem?" he asked.

"I think it's finitude."

It was Thom's turn to blink. "What do you mean?"

Peg looked down at the valley again and paused to gather her thoughts. "We want to control everything...but we can't. We want to control what happens around us...but we can't."

"That's for damn sure," Thom agreed.

"I mean, look at this whole cube mess," Peg continued. "Julie's friend was just trying to gain some control of his life, and without meaning to he just threw everything into chaos."

Thom nodded, rocking back and forth on the log slowly. "I tried to protect Jake, and I ended up holding him back, stunting his growth, you know?"

Peg wanted to say, *I could have told you that a long time ago,* but she didn't. Thom couldn't have heard it then.

Thom continued, "I tried to protect Julie, and I just...I ended up getting her..."

Water gathered in Peg's eyes and she reached over and pulled Thom's hand from his pocket. She held it. He let her. When she looked up at him, she saw him blinking back tears of his own. Peg swallowed thickly and said, "The fact that we have control of anything is an illusion, I think. If we think we have it, we're living in a lie. It's... delusional. It's an ever-receding goal. We keep chasing it, but..."

"But we never catch it," Thom finished.

"No," Peg agreed.

"That's...terrifying," Thom said.

"As terrifying as those monsters you and Julie saw, out there in the universe?"

Thom was silent for several long moments, and it seemed to her that he was thinking. Finally, he said, "I'm beginning to think those monsters *are* that chaos you're talking about. The embodiment of it somehow."

Peg nodded. "You think you know how the universe works, and then..."

"Yeah," Thom said. "Thing is, I don't know how to fight them...or it...the chaos."

Peg squeezed his hand. "I think maybe the trick is learning to be okay with the fact that we *can't* control everything...or much of anything."

"I'll never be okay with that," Thom said. He looked over at her. "Are *you* okay with that?"

Peg shook her head. "Oh no. But I think I'm learning to be okay with not being okay with that, if you can follow what I mean."

"Is that the best we can hope for?" Thom asked.

"Maybe it is, on this side of the grave, anyway," Peg answered.

For some time they sat in silence. Thom moved his arm so he could intertwine his fingers with hers. A calm passed between them.

"I have a couple things for you," Thom said.

"Oh?"

"I...this was on the notepad next to Julie's hospital bed." Thom let go of her hand and pulled a folded, 4-inch by 6-inch piece of notepaper from his shirt pocket.

Peg took it but didn't unfold it. "Thom...do I want to read this?"

Thom nodded. "I think you do."

Fingers trembling, Peg unfolded the paper. She recognized Julie's scrawl, just barely decipherable. At the top "Peg" was written, then crossed out. Underneath, Julie had written "Mom." Peg took a deep breath and read on.

Mom, you were a real shit to me when I was young. And I've been a real shit to you ever since. I guess I feel sad about both things. Can we call it even and maybe start over?

It wasn't signed, but it didn't need to be. Tears flowed over Peg's cheeks, and she let them come. A sob burst out from her bosom and her shoulders shook. A few moments later, she was leaning into Thom, his arm around her shoulder, his neck wet from her crying. "You know, I tried so hard to get Julie to love me. I'd almost given up hope. Now I wonder, if we'd had the chance, if we'd had the time... maybe we could have gotten there."

Thom rocked her slowly. A few minutes later he said. "Maybe you still can."

"What do you mean?" Peg asked.

"Well, I don't know about anyone else, but those I've loved...who have died, I mean...they don't seem to go away. Not really. I mean, I know they're gone, but it doesn't sever..."

He seemed to be fumbling for words, but Peg understood. "Your relationship with them goes on," she said.

"Yeah. It does. Somehow."

She sniffed and sat up straight again. "Maybe that's enough for God to work with. But I wonder...when I pass, will Jesus let me into the Goddess' territory for a visit?"

Thom blinked.

"Sorry," Peg said, barking out a nervous laugh. "Theological ponderings. It's an occupational hazard."

"You're definitely asking the wrong guy about that."

"It's all right." She held the note up. "This means a lot to me, Thom. Thank you." She refolded the paper and put it in her pocket. It felt warm. From her other pocket she pulled a tissue and blew her nose.

"You had Julie cremated?" Thom asked.

Peg nodded. "I remember Julie saying once that she preferred it."

"You got the ashes back yet?" Thom asked.

"No, not yet."

Thom grunted and let go of her fingers. He reached over and opened the lid of the wooden box between them. Inside was a plastic bag filled with ashes. On top of the plastic bag was a red collar, with three metal tags attached to its ring. They tinkled when he lifted it out.

"Emma?" Peg asked, a sad smile breaking out over her face.

"Yeah," Thom said.

"Emma was a dog?" Peg asked, not bothering to hide the surprise or delight in her voice.

"Yeah."

"Well, I...why didn't anyone tell me that?"

He shrugged. "She wasn't an ordinary dog."

"My dear, there are no *ordinary* dogs."

"She's the dog I got when my wife died," Thom confessed.

"Ah...that hurt is deep," Peg said, although she felt stupid once the words were out. But Thom didn't deny it. "I always thought it was your wife's ashes in that box."

"No, she...wanted to be buried...with her family. It was okay with me. In some ways, I still miss Emma more than I do Allie."

"Allie was your wife," Peg said, not really a question.

"She was. Emma and I used to come to this spot a lot, after Allie died. It...I was able to feel her presence here, more than in the cemetery."

"Yes," Peg said.

"Emma always got so excited when she realized we were coming up here. I always intended to scatter her ashes, but...I was never able to part with them."

Peg nodded. Then Thom stood up, undid the twist tie, and opened the bag of ashes. Holding it in one hand, he licked the index finger of his other hand and held it up. *Checking the wind,* Peg realized. *That was smart. I wouldn't have thought of that until it was too late.*

Turning so that the bag was downwind, he opened it and began to pour its contents into the air.

At just that moment, the wind whipped up and carried the ashes further than Peg could have predicted. They swirled like a tiny gray tornado. *How fitting,* Peg thought. *Dogs turn in a circle when they lie down to sleep.*

In a few moments, the bag was empty. Thom shook the last of it onto the ground. When he turned back to her, his cheeks were wet and his eyes were red.

"Remember that you are dust, and to dust you shall return," she quoted. She held her hand out to him and guided him back to his seat.

He didn't look at her, but only stared out at the valley. He sniffed several times and finally reached into his back pocket for a handkerchief. Peg looked away to give him his privacy.

"Oh, there's something else. Julie...when she died, she was

wearing this." With his left hand, he pulled a pentagram ring from his pocket and gave it to her. "If you want it...it belongs to you."

Peg would cherish it, and she opened her mouth to thank him, but something stopped her. She teased the idea out until she became convinced of it. Then she said, "I'll be going through her apartment next week. I have lots of her things to choose a keepsake from. Why don't you keep that?"

She saw the gratitude in his eyes, saw him nod. Gingerly, he placed the ring in the box. Then, drawing what looked like newspaper clippings from his left pocket, he placed those on top of it. Then he closed the lid.

"Are you going to keep that in your office?"

"I am."

"People might still think it's Emma."

Thom shrugged. "I can't control what people think, can I?"

"Are you okay with that?"

He looked over and caught her eye. "I'm learning to be okay with not being okay with that."

"Then we're in this together," Peg said.

"I guess we are."

AUTHOR'S NOTE

This novel was begun in the second week of March, 2020, almost exactly at the same time that the coronavirus hit and we all went into lockdown in California. It was a fascinating kind of synchronicity, writing a book about grief while experiencing numerous cumulative losses myself. The book became a kind of therapy for me as I explored how grief manifests itself in ways both subtle and dramatic. Other losses, more personal and even more significant, hit just as I was finishing the first draft. I don't think that any kind of meta-narrative developed—I was never writing about the coronavirus or other losses or their effects directly, but I do think reality and fantasy performed an unusual kind of tango in the writing of this book.

When I first had the idea for this story, I knew I wanted it to revolve around a character inspired by my friend, the Reverend Nancy McKay, to whom this book is dedicated. Before I began writing, I asked Nancy for her permission to base a character on her. She wasn't too sure about the idea at first, but after some hesitation, agreed. I am so glad she did.

As I wrote, Pastor Peg went through a lot of changes. She and Nancy don't look alike, nor are their histories or life circumstances similar in any way. In fact, I think it's fair to say that the only thing that remains of Nancy in Peg's character is her sense of calm, her lovingkindness, and her deep wisdom. Endowed with those qualities, Peg became the north star around which the rest of the story unfolded. I hope that I have given Nancy a character she can be proud to have inspired.

A big thank-you to Yulu Ewis, a Miwok novelist and editor who served as my sensitivity reader. She graciously poured over this manuscript to help me bring the character of Milala into true. I was nervous about depicting a Native American character and wanted to make sure that I could depict her with accuracy and integrity. Yulu's insights and suggestions have been invaluable to me in realizing her character.

I also want to thank Daniel Harms and John Wisdom Grace for their great book *The Necronomicon Files*, which I have read more than once, and which first alerted me to the fact that there are people who actually do magickal workings that address the fictional deities depicted in Lovecraft's Cthulu mythos. Their research gave me lots of ideas which found their way into this book.

I feel the need to apologize to my friends in the occult community for, once more, choosing magickians as my villains in this novel. I want to assure them (and other readers) that I believe—and know!— that there are plenty of good-hearted people in the occult community, and that includes practitioners of ceremonial magick. But there is something dangerously Promethean about magick, which I think most thoughtful magickians would acknowledge. Magick addresses forces that we don't really understand, and all magickal workings are playing with fire. It is my personal opinion that, like explosives and bullfighting, you can minimize the risk through expertise, but it is near to impossible to actually do it safely.

Lord Tim's quotation from Chuang Tzu in Chapter Ten was taken from Burton Watson's translation, which has always been my favorite. When Milala says, "She rises up in our brains and sees how beautiful she is with our eyes" in that same chapter, I want to credit Nikos Kazantzakis' *The Saviors of God* as the inspiration for this paraphrase.

Fauré's Requiem was the soundtrack to the book's writing. It played constantly as I wrote, and its melancholy pierced with hope definitely influenced the tone of the book. If you really want to feel what I was feeling as you read, I recommend that you put it on. I was listening to the Decca release featuring the Choir of St. John's College, Cambridge, conducted by George Guest.

I want to thank my wife, Lisa Fullam, for her unflagging support of my writing. Pretty much every morning she'd greet me by asking, "Got a scene?" I usually did. Sometimes, when the writing got hard, it was wanting to have a new scene for Lisa that kept me going.

I also want to thank my writing support group. Bob Lutz, Calvin Giroulx, and Clay Dutcher—you're all ripe bastards who can't tell an Oxford comma from your bungholes. I love you guys. Thanks for checking in with me every week and threatening that, if I kill any characters you like, you'll come after my dog. My dog now has a bodyguard who has orders to shoot on sight. Eat that, bitches.

J.R. Mabry

Made in the USA
Middletown, DE
23 December 2022

17022238R00352